The Daughters of Lancaster County

The STOREKEEPER'S DAUGHTER

The QUILTER'S DAUGHTER

The BISHOP'S DAUGHTER

BARBOUR
PUBLISHING

The Storekeeper's Daugher © 2005 by Wanda E. Brunstetter
The Quilter's Daugher © 2005 by Wanda E. Brunstetter
The Bishop's Daugher © 2006 by Wanda E. Brunstetter

ISBN 978-1-59789-839-3

Scripture quotations are taken from the King James Version of the Bible.

Scripture quotations are also taken from the HOLY BIBLE, NEW INTERNATIONAL VERSION®. NIV®. Copyright © 1973, 1978, 1984 by International Bible Society. Used by permission of Zondervan. All rights reserved.

For more information about Wanda E. Brunstetter, please access the author's Web site at the following Internet address:
www.wandabrunstetter.com

Cover art by Müllerhaus Publishing Arts, Inc.
Cover photography by Gloria Roundtree

Published by Barbour Publishing, Inc., P.O. Box 719, Uhrichsville, Ohio 44683, www.barbourbooks.com

Our mission is to publish and distribute inspirational products offering exceptional value and biblical encouragement to the masses.

Member of the
Evangelical Christian
Publishers Association

Printed in the United States of America.

The STOREKEEPER'S DAUGHTER

WANDA E. BRUNSTETTER

BARBOUR
PUBLISHING

To Leeann and Birdie, my dear friends and critique partners.
To Audrey, Marijane, Monk, and Melissa, who willingly
shared their knowledge with me. Thank you all!

Trust ye in the LORD for ever:
for in the LORD JEHOVAH is everlasting strength.
ISAIAH 26:4

PROLOGUE

"Naomi, come! *Schnell*—quickly!"

Naomi hurriedly finished the job of diapering her two-month-old brother, pulled the crib rail up, and turned to face her younger sister. "What is it, Nancy? You look upset."

Nancy stood just inside the bedroom door, her green eyes wide and her lower lip trembling. "It's our *mamm*, Naomi. She's been hit by a car."

Naomi stood there a few seconds, staring at an odd-shaped crack in the wall and trying to let Nancy's words sink into her brain. Mama hit by a car? How could it be? Their mother couldn't have been in the road. Only moments ago, she had announced that she was going out to get the mail, and Naomi said she would change Zach's diaper. When they were done, they planned to meet in the garden to pick peas. The mailbox was at the end of the driveway, several feet off the main road. There was no way a car could hit Mama. Unless. . .

"Don't just stand there, Naomi!" Nancy shouted. "Mama needs you. We have to get her some help."

A chill crept up Naomi's spine, and she trembled. Mama had to be all right. She just had to be.

"Stay with the *boppli*!" Naomi ordered.

"No, Mary Ann's in the house, and he'll be okay. I'm comin' with you."

With her heart pounding so hard she feared it might burst, Naomi dashed down the stairs and bolted out the front door.

As soon as she started down the graveled driveway, Naomi could see a red car parked along the shoulder of the road. An English man knelt on the ground next to a woman's body.

"Mama!" The single word tore from Naomi's throat as she dropped to her knees beside her dear mamm. Mama's eyes were shut, and her skin was as pale as goat's milk. There was a deep gash on the side of her head, and blood oozed from the open wound.

"I used my cell phone to call 9-1-1," the man announced. "An ambulance should be here soon."

Naomi looked up at the middle-aged man. Sympathy filled his dark eyes, and deep wrinkles etched his forehead. "What happened?" she rasped.

"I—was driving down the road, minding my own business, when I noticed an Amish woman at her mailbox. Never thought much of it until she dropped a letter to the ground. Then the wind picked up and blew the envelope into the road." He shook his head slowly as his eyes clouded with tears. "Sure didn't expect her to jump out after it. Not with my car coming."

Just then, Naomi noticed the letters strewn every which way along the roadside. Mama must have dropped the mail she had been holding when she was struck by the man's car.

"I'm so sorry." The man's voice shook with emotion. "I slammed on my brakes, but I couldn't get stopped in time."

Naomi squeezed her eyes shut and tried to think. How bad was Mama hurt? Should they try to move her up to the house? No, that wouldn't be a good idea. What if she had something broken? What if there were internal injuries?

"Is Mama gonna be all right?"

Naomi had forgotten her younger sister had followed her out the door. She glanced up at Nancy and swallowed hard. "I hope so. *Jah,* I surely do."

Sirens could be heard in the distance, and Naomi breathed a prayer of thanks. Once a doctor saw her, Mama would be okay. She had to be. Baby Zach needed her. They all needed Mama.

"Naomi?" Mama's eyes opened, and Naomi could see the depth of her mother's pain. "I need you to—" Her words faltered.

"Be still, Mama," Naomi instructed. "An ambulance is comin'. You're gonna be okay. Just rest for now."

Tears slipped out of Mama's eyes and trickled down her cheeks. "I—I need—to ask you a favor—just in case," she murmured.

"What is it, Mama? I'll do anything to help." Naomi took hold of her mother's hand, so cold and limp.

"If I don't make it—"

"Please, don't even say the words." Naomi's voice came out in a squeak. She couldn't bear to hear her mother acknowledge that she might not survive.

"That's right, Mama. You shouldn't try to talk right now," Nancy added tearfully.

"I must." Mama's imploring look made Naomi's heart beat even faster.

"If I should die, promise you'll take care of the *kinner*—especially the boppli."

"You're gonna be fine, Mama. See here, the ambulance has arrived now, and soon you'll be at the hospital." Panic edged Naomi's voice, and when she swallowed, the metallic taste of fear sprang into her mouth.

More tears splashed onto Mama's pale cheeks. "This is important, Daughter. Do I have your word?"

Naomi hardly knew what to say. She could continue to insist her mother was going to be all right, or she could tell Mama what she wanted to hear. Naomi decided the latter would be better. No use upsetting poor Mamm more than she already was. She would agree to her mother's request, only to make her feel better. However, Naomi felt certain she would never have to keep the promise. Her dear mama was going to be all right.

Naomi gently squeezed her mother's hand. "Jah, Mama, I promise."

CHAPTER 1

Naomi Fisher tiptoed out of the back room and headed to the front of her father's general store. She'd finally gotten Zach down for a nap and felt ready for a break.

"Since there aren't any customers at the moment, would it be all right if I ate my lunch now?" Naomi asked Papa, who was going over his ledger behind the counter near the front of the store.

"Jah, okay. Just don't be too long." He raked his fingers through the long, full beard covering his chin. "That new order of candles still needs to be put on the shelves."

Naomi's hand brushed against her father's arm as she reached under the counter for her lunch pail. "I know."

"Your mamm would've had those candles out already," he mumbled. "She'd never allow the shelves to get dusty, either."

Naomi flinched as though she'd been slapped. She enjoyed working at the store, but it was getting harder to help run the place. There was no way she could keep up with the chores she was responsible for at home and do everything Mama used to do, too. It wasn't fair for Papa to compare her with Mama, and she wished he would consider hiring a maid to help out. She squeezed the handle on her lunchbox. If only Mama hadn't stepped into the road and been hit by a car. The bishop said it was God's will—"Sarah Fisher's time to die," he'd announced at her funeral.

Naomi wasn't so sure about that. How could Mama's death be God's will?

"I—I think I'll take my lunch outside if you've got no objections," she said, forcing her troubling thoughts aside.

Papa shook his head. "Schnell—quickly then, and eat your lunch before the baby wakes."

"I'm goin'." Naomi's sneakers padded across the hardwood floor. When she reached the front door, she turned around. "Papa, I'm not Mama, but I'm doin' the best I can."

His only response was a brief nod.

"I'll tend to the dusting and those candles as soon as I'm done eating."

"Jah, okay."

She hurried outside. Some fresh air and time alone would be ever so nice.

Naomi leaned against the porch railing and drew in a deep breath. Spring was her favorite time of the year, especially after it rained the way it had this morning. The air was invigorating and clean—like newly laundered clothes hung on the line to dry. Today the temperature was warm but mild, the grass was as green as fresh broccoli, and a chorus of birds sang a blissful tune from the maple tree nearby.

"It looks like you're takin' a little break. Is your *daed* inside?"

Naomi hadn't even noticed Rhoda Lapp heading her way. "I'm eating my lunch, and Papa's inside going over his books," she replied.

"I guess keepin' good records is part of running a store." Rhoda chuckled, and her pudgy cheeks turned slightly pink. "Them that works hard eats hearty, don't ya know?"

Naomi nodded and stepped aside so the middle-aged Amish woman could pass.

"You have a *gut* lunch now, ya hear?" Rhoda said before entering the store.

Naomi lowered herself to the top step and snapped open the lid of her metal lunch pail. Even a few minutes of solitude would be a welcome relief after her busy morning. She'd gotten up before dawn to start breakfast, milk the goats, feed the chickens, and then, with her ten-year-old sister Nancy's assistance, made lunches for everyone in the family.

This morning, when breakfast was over, the three older boys headed for the fields. Naomi saw the younger children off to school, and then she'd washed a load of clothes, bathed little Zach, and baked a couple loaves of bread. By the time Papa had the horse hitched to their buggy, Naomi and the baby were ready to accompany him to their store near the small town of Paradise. She'd spent the next several hours waiting on customers, stocking shelves, and trying to keep one-year-old Zach occupied and out of mischief.

Tears clogged Naomi's throat, and she nearly choked on the piece of bread she had put in her mouth. Mama would have done many of those duties if she hadn't died on the way to the hospital. Mama would be holding Zach in her arms every night, humming softly and rocking him to sleep.

Naomi and her mother had always been close, and Naomi missed those times when they'd worked side by side, laughing, visiting, and enjoying the pleasure of just being together. Some days she still pined for Mama so much it hurt clear down to her toes.

A vision of her dear mamm popped into Naomi's mind, and she found comfort in memories of days gone by—a time when life seemed less complicated and happy. . . .

"Sit yourself down and rest awhile. You've been workin' hard all morning and need to take a break."

"In a minute, Mama. I want to put away these last few dishes." Naomi grabbed another plate from the stack on the cupboard.

"Let's have a cup of tea together," Mama said. "I'll pour while you finish up."

A few minutes later, Naomi took a seat at the kitchen table beside her mother. Mama looked more tired than Naomi felt, and the dark circles under her eyes were proof of that.

"Here you go." Mama handed Naomi a cup of tea. "It's mint. . .the kind I mostly drink these days. Hope you're okay with it."

"Sure, Mama. Mint's fine by me."

Naomi knew her mother had been plagued with morning sickness ever since she'd become pregnant. She was in her fifth month but still fought waves of nausea. Mint tea helped some, although there were still times when Mama was forced to give up the meal she'd eaten.

Mama leaned over and brushed a strand of hair away from Naomi's face, where it had come loose from her bun. "I'm awful sorry you have to work hard and have so many extra chores now. If I were feelin' better, I'd do more myself, but this awful tiredness and stomach rollin' has really got me down."

Naomi touched her mother's hand. "It's okay."

"You sure?"

She nodded in reply.

"But a girl your age should be goin' to singings and other young people's functions, not doing double chores and waitin' on her old mamm."

Naomi fought to keep her emotions under control. She did wish there was time to do more fun things, but this was only temporary. Once Mama had the baby and regained her strength, everything would be as it once was. She'd be able to attend social functions with others her age, someday she would be courted, and then marriage would follow. Naomi could wait awhile. It wouldn't be so long.

The unmistakable *clip-clop, clip-clop* of a horse and buggy pulling into the store's parking lot brought Naomi back to the present. Caleb Hoffmeir, the young buggy maker, stepped down from his open carriage and waved. She lifted her hand in response.

As Caleb sauntered up the porch steps, his blue eyes twinkled; and when he smiled, the deep dimple in his right cheek was more pronounced. He flopped onto the step beside her. "It's a *wunderbaar* fine day, wouldn't you say?"

His face was inches from hers, and she could feel his warm breath against her cheek. Naomi shivered, despite the warmth of the sun's rays. "Jah, it is a wonderful day."

"Did ya hear there's gonna be a singin' out at Daniel Troyer's place this Sunday evening?"

Her heart clenched, but she merely shrugged in response. She was eighteen years old the last time she attended a singing.

Caleb lifted his straw hat, raked his fingers through his thick blond hair, and cleared his throat a couple times. "You—uh—think ya might be goin' to the singing, Naomi?"

She shook her head, feeling as though a heavy weight rested on her chest.

"Was is letz do?" he questioned.

Naomi sniffed deeply. "Nothin's wrong here, except I won't be goin' to no singing. Not this Sunday—and probably never."

Caleb raised his eyebrows. "Why not? You haven't been to one since long before your mamm died. Don't ya think it's about time?"

"Somebody's gotta feed the kinner and see that they're put to bed."

He grunted. "Can't your daed do that?"

"Papa's got other chores to do." Naomi squeezed her eyes shut and thought about the way her father used to be. He wasn't always cranky and out of sorts. He didn't shout orders or come across as overly critical. He used to be more easygoing and congenial. Everything had changed since Mama died—including Papa.

"Abraham could surely let you go to one little singing," Caleb persisted.

Naomi looked up at him, and Caleb leveled her with a look that went straight to her heart. Did he feel her pain? Did Caleb Hoffmeir have any idea how tired she was? She placed the lunch pail on the step and wrapped her hands around her knees, clutching the folds of the long green dress that touched her ankles.

Caleb gently touched her arm, and the tiny lines around his eyes deepened. "I was hopin' if you went to the singing, I could take you home afterwards."

Naomi's eyes filled with unwanted tears. She longed to go to singings and young people's gatherings. She yearned to have fun with others her age or take leisurely rides in someone's courting buggy. "Papa would never allow me to go."

Caleb stood. "I'll ask him."

"Nee—no! That's not a good idea."

"Why not?"

"Because it might make him mad. Papa's awful protective, and he believes my place is at home with him and the children."

"We'll see about that. If Abraham gives his permission for you to go to the singing, you'd better plan on a ride home in my courtin' buggy."

Courtin' buggy? Did Caleb actually believe they could start courting? It wasn't likely to happen because Naomi had so many responsibilities. Truth be told, Naomi felt confused whenever she was around Caleb. His good looks and caring attitude appealed to her. But if she couldn't go to singings and other young people's functions, it wasn't likely she'd ever be able to court.

"Maybe I should talk to Papa about this myself," she murmured.

Caleb shook his head. "I'd like to try if ya don't mind."

Naomi's heartbeat quickened. Did she dare hope her daed might give his consent? "Jah, okay. I'll be prayin'."

Caleb glanced over his shoulder. Naomi sat with her head bowed and her hands folded in her lap. She looked so beautiful there with the sun beating down on the white *kapp* perched on her head. The image of her oval face, golden brown hair, ebony eyes, and that cute upturned nose brought a smile to his face. He'd taken a liking to Naomi when they were kinner, but during their teen years, he'd been too shy to let her know. Now that he'd finally worked up the nerve, Caleb didn't know if they'd ever have the chance to court, what with Naomi being so busy with her family and all. He wasn't sure if Naomi returned his feelings, either, but he'd never know if they couldn't find a way to spend time alone.

He pulled the door open with a renewed sense of determination.

When Caleb stepped into the room, he spotted the tall, brawny storekeeper stocking shelves with bottles of kerosene. *"Gude mariye."*

Abraham nodded. "I'd say 'good morning' back, but it's nearly noontime."

Caleb felt a penetrating heat creep up the back of his neck and spread quickly to his face. "Guess you're right about that."

"How's your daed?" Abraham asked.

"He's gut."

"And your mamm?"

"Doin' well." Caleb rubbed his sweaty palms along the sides of his trousers.

"What can I do for you?" the storekeeper asked, moving toward the wooden counter near the front of his store.

Caleb prayed he would have the courage to ask the question upper-most on his mind. "I was wonderin'—"

"I just got in a shipment of straw hats," Abraham blurted out. "Looks like the one you're wearin' has seen better days."

Caleb touched the brim of the item in question. It was getting kind of ragged around the edges, but there were no large holes. He could probably get another year's wear out of the old hat if he had a mind to. "I—uh—am not lookin' to buy a new hat today." Caleb hoped his voice sounded more confident than he felt, because his initial pre-sentation had dissolved like a block of ice on a hot summer day.

Abraham raised his bushy dark eyebrows and gave his brown beard a couple of tugs. "What are ya needin' then?"

"There's to be a singin' this Sunday night in Daniel Troyer's barn."

"What's that got to do with me?" Abraham yawned and leaned his elbows on the counter.

"It doesn't. I mean, it does in one way." Caleb shuffled his boots against the hardwood planks. He was botching things up and felt powerless to stop himself from acting like a self-conscious schoolboy. After all, he was a twenty-two-year-old man who built and repaired buggies for a living. Abraham Fisher probably thought he was *letz in der belskapp*; and truth be told, at this moment, Caleb felt like he was a little off in the head.

"Which is it, son?" the older man asked. "Does your bein' here have something to do with me or doesn't it?"

Caleb steadied himself against the front of the counter and leveled Abraham with a look he hoped would let the man know he meant business. "I'm wonderin' if Naomi can go to that singing."

Abraham's frown carved deep lines in his forehead. "Naomi's mamm died nearly a year ago, ya know."

Caleb nodded.

"Ever since the accident, it's been Naomi's job to look after the kinner."

"I understand that, but—"

Abraham brushed his hand across the wooden counter, sending several pieces of paper sailing to the floor. "It ain't polite to interrupt a man when he's speakin'."

"I—I'm sorry," Caleb stammered. Things weren't going nearly as well as he'd hoped.

"As I was saying. . .Naomi's job is to take care of her brothers and sisters, and she also helps here at the store."

Caleb nodded once more.

"There's only so many hours in a day, and there ain't time enough for Naomi to be socializin'." Abraham's stern look set Caleb's teeth on edge. "You might have plans to court my daughter, but the truth is, she ain't right for you, even if she did have time for courtin'."

"Don't ya think that ought to be Naomi's decision?" Caleb clenched his fists, hoping the action would give him added courage.

"Anything that concerns one of my kinner is my business." Abraham leaned across the counter until his face was a few inches from Caleb's.

If Caleb hadn't known Amish were not supposed to engage in fighting, he would have feared Naomi's father was getting ready to punch him in the nose. But that was about as unlikely as a sow giving birth to a calf. If Abraham was capable of anything, it would probably involve talking with Caleb's father, which, in turn, could end up being a thorough tongue-lashing. Pop had plenty of rules for Caleb and his brothers to follow. He often said as long as his children lived under his roof, he expected them to obey him and be well mannered.

Caleb figured he would have to watch his tongue with Abraham Fisher, but maybe it was time to take a stand. How could he expect Naomi to respect him if he wasn't willing to try for the right to court her?

"If Naomi started attending singings again, first thing ya know, she'd be wantin' to court," Abraham continued. "Then gettin' married would be her next goal. I'd be left with a passel of youngsters to raise by myself if I let that happen." Abraham made a sweeping gesture with his hand. "Who would mind the store if I was at home cookin', cleanin', and all?"

"Have you thought about getting married again or even hiring a *maad*?"

"Don't need no maid when I've got Naomi. And as far as me marryin' again, there ain't no one available in our community right now, except for a couple of women young enough to be my daughter." The man grunted. "Some men my age think nothin' of takin' a child bride, but not Abraham Fisher. I've got more dignity than that!"

Caleb opened his mouth to comment, but Naomi's father cut him off. "Enough's been said. Naomi's not goin' to that singing on Sunday." Abraham pointed to the door. "Now if you didn't come here to buy anything, you'd best be on your way."

All sorts of comebacks flitted through Caleb's mind, but he remained silent. No use getting the man more riled. He would bide his time, and when the opportunity afforded itself, Caleb hoped to have the last word where the storekeeper's daughter was concerned.

CHAPTER 2

Naomi had just taken a bite from her apple when the screen door creaked open. She looked over her shoulder and saw Caleb exit the store. The scowl on his face told Naomi things probably hadn't gone well with Papa, and a sense of disappointment crept into her soul.

"He said no, didn't he?" Naomi whispered when Caleb slumped to the step beside her.

"Your daed is the most stubborn man I've ever met." He shrugged. "Of course, my pop's runnin' him a close second."

"Matthew says Papa's overprotective 'cause he cares." She blinked against the tears flooding her eyes. Truth be told, Naomi wasn't sure her father cared about her at all. If he did, then why had he been keeping it to himself? Not once in the last year had he said he loved her or appreciated all the work she did.

"I'm thinkin' your daed saying no to my request has more to do with his own selfish needs than it does with him carin'. Tell that to your oldest brother."

Naomi tossed what was left of her apple into the lunch pail and slammed the lid shut. "Papa's not bein' selfish. He's hurting because Mama died."

Caleb crossed his arms. "That was a whole year ago, Naomi. Don't ya think it's time your daed got on with his life?"

"When Mama was alive, Papa used to be fun-loving and carefree. He'd joke around with the brothers and tease me and the sisters sometimes, too." Remembering how happy she used to be, Naomi fought to control her emotions. Things were all mixed up now that she was trying to fill her mother's shoes. Life had been much better before Naomi's mother got pregnant with Zach. It had come as a surprise to everyone in the family because Mama was forty-two years old and hadn't had any children since Mary Ann was born six years ago. All during her mother's pregnancy, she'd been sickly. Naomi's only consolation was her confidence that the dear woman was in heaven with Jesus, happy and healthy, no more cares of the world—cares Naomi now shouldered.

"Ain't ya got nothin' to say about all this?"

Caleb's question drew Naomi's thoughts aside, and she turned to look at him. "What's to be said? My daed won't let me go to the singin', I've gotta take care of my family, and I have a store to help run." She grabbed her lunch pail and stood. "I'd best be getting back to work before Papa comes lookin' for me."

Caleb scrambled to his feet and positioned himself between Naomi and the door. "There has to be some way we can make your daed listen to reason. I want to court you, Naomi."

She hung her head. "Maybe you should find someone else to court, 'cause it doesn't look like I'll ever be free. Leastways, not 'til all the kinner are old enough to fend for themselves."

Caleb lifted her chin with his thumb. "I care for you."

Naomi's throat constricted. She cared for Caleb, too, but what was the point in saying so when they couldn't court? Too many problems plagued her mind already. She didn't need one more. "You'd better find someone else." She pushed past him and hurried into the store.

Naomi found Papa kneeling on the floor, holding a sheet of paper, with several more lying next to his knee. He looked up, and a deep frown etched his forehead. "I'm glad you're back. I think I heard the baby fussin'."

She glanced at the door to the back room and tipped her head. She didn't hear anything. Not even a peep out of Zach. Naomi was tempted to mention that to Papa but thought better of it. "I'll go check on the boppli."

A few seconds later, Naomi stepped into the room used for storage. The baby's playpen, a rocking chair, and a small couch were also kept there. Sometimes, when there weren't many customers, Papa liked to lie down and take a nap, which was usually whenever Zach was sleeping.

Naomi liked those moments when she could be by herself. It gave her a chance to daydream about how she wished her life could be. If an English customer came into the store, she worried about her father scrutinizing everything she said or did. Naomi often wondered if Papa was afraid something an Englisher might say would cause her to become dissatisfied with their way of life and turn worldly.

She remembered the last time Virginia Meyers dropped by. Papa hovered around, acting like a mother hen protecting her young. Virginia, who liked to be called "Ginny," came into the store at least once a week, sometimes to buy rubber stamps, other times just to look around. Naomi and Ginny were about the same age and had struck up a friendship, although Naomi was careful not to let Papa know.

She stared at the playpen where her little brother lay sleeping. He looked so peaceful, lying on his side, curled into a fetal position. One hand rested against his rosy cheek, a lock of russet-colored hair lay across his forehead, and the tiny little birthmark behind his right ear seemed to be winking at Naomi. "Sleep well, little one, and enjoy your days of untroubled babyhood," Naomi whispered. "Soon you'll grow up and see life for what it really is—all work and no play."

Tears clouded Naomi's vision. *Oh, Lord, You know I love my family and want to keep my promise to Mama, but sometimes it's ever so hard.*

If there were someone to help on a regular basis, Naomi's burdens might be a bit lighter. Her maternal grandparents were both dead, and Papa's folks had moved to an Amish settlement in Indiana several years ago to be near their daughter Carolyn. They were both ailing now, so even if they had lived close, Grandma Fisher wouldn't be much help to Naomi. Many of the women in their community offered assistance after

Mama died, but they had their own families to care for, and Naomi knew she couldn't continually rely on others. Looking after the family was her job, and even though she was exhausted, she would do it for as long as necessary.

Naomi swiped at the moisture on her cheeks. *Nobody understands how I feel.*

Naomi was twenty years old. She should be married and starting a family of her own by now. Her friends Grace and Phoebe had gotten married last fall. Naomi had been asked to be one of Phoebe's attendants, and it was a painful reminder that her chance at love and marriage might never come.

Drawing in a deep breath and forcing her pain aside, Naomi slipped quietly out of the room. Zach was obviously not ready to wake from his nap, and she had plenty of work to do. There was no more time for reflections.

Abraham Fisher glanced at his daughter when she entered the room. It was clear by her solemn expression that Naomi was unhappy. No doubt Caleb had told her what had been said in regard to the singing. He grabbed the broom and gave the floor a few brisk sweeps. Naomi didn't understand. No one did. Life held little joy for Abraham since Sarah died. Even though Zach's first birthday last Saturday had been a happy occasion, it was also a painful reminder that ten months ago the baby's mother had gone to heaven, leaving Abraham with a broken heart and eight kinner in his charge. He couldn't care for them alone, and he relied on Naomi's help.

Naomi strolled past him without a word. She reached under the counter, grabbed a dust rag, and started working on the shelves near the front of the store.

"Where's Zach?" he called to her.

"Still sleeping."

"Oh. I thought I heard him cryin'."

"Nope."

"Guess maybe I'm hearin' things in my old age."

"You're not old, Papa."

Abraham pushed the broom back and forth. "Forty-four's old enough. Don't get nearly as much done as I used to."

"Mama was a big help, wasn't she?" Naomi asked.

"Jah, she was. Your mamm loved workin' at the store. Since this place used to belong to her folks, she grew up helpin' here."

"Do you ever wish you were doing something other than working at the store six days a week?"

Naomi's question startled Abraham. Did she know what was on his mind? Had she guessed he wasn't happy running the store? Truth of the matter, he'd much prefer to be at home farming with his boys than stocking shelves all day or dealing with the curious English who often visited the store.

"Papa, did ya hear what I asked?"

He nodded and grabbed the dustpan he had leaned against the front of the counter. "Jah, I heard. Just thinkin'; that's all."

"Mind if I ask what you were thinking about?"

Abraham did mind. He didn't want to talk about an impossible dream. He was committed to running the store. It was the least he could do to preserve his late wife's memory. "Just remembering how things were when your mamm was alive."

Naomi didn't say anything. He figured she probably missed her mother as much as he missed his wife of twenty-five years. Their marriage had been good, and God had blessed their union with eight beautiful children. Things had gone fairly well until Sarah's life had been snuffed out like a candle in the breeze.

Wish it had been me God had taken, Abraham thought painfully. Truth was, he'd blamed himself for Sarah's death. If he hadn't closed the store that day last June and gone fishing with his friend, Jacob Weaver, his precious wife might still be alive. If he hadn't suggested Naomi stay home from the store and help her mamm in the garden, Sarah probably wouldn't have gone to the mailbox.

During the two months of Sarah's recuperation from Zach's birth, she hadn't worked at the store. Abraham had insisted she stay home and take it easy. Up until the fateful day of her death, someone else had always gotten the mail. Sarah probably felt since Naomi was there to watch the baby and the younger ones, it would be fine for her to take a walk to the mailbox.

He thought about the way Jacob had helped him work through his grief as well as the guilt he felt. Yet, there were still moments when Abraham berated himself for going fishing, and he'd not gone again since Sarah died.

Didn't God care how much I loved that woman?

Abraham thought about Caleb Hoffmeir's suggestion that he find another wife. The young man hadn't been the first person to recommend he remarry. Several of his friends, including Jacob Weaver, had also made such a remark.

"There will always be a place in your heart for Sarah," Jacob said the other day, "but takin' another wife would be good for you as well as the children."

Abraham squeezed the broom handle. *No, I can't bring myself to marry a woman merely to look after my children. There has to be love, and I doubt I could ever care for anyone the way I cared for Sarah.* He swept the dirt into the dustpan and dumped it in the wastepaper basket. *As I told Caleb earlier, there ain't no available widows in the area right now, and I'm not about to court some young, single woman, the way I've seen others do.*

Feeling a sudden need for some fresh air, Abraham leaned the broom against the wall and grabbed his straw hat from the wooden peg by the front door. "I'm goin' out to run a couple errands," he announced.

"Can ya manage okay by yourself for a while?"

Naomi nodded. "Sure, Papa. I'll be fine."

"See you soon then."

Caleb was halfway home before he remembered that he'd planned to stop by the bookstore in Paradise to see if the book he'd ordered on antique buggies had come in. Besides working on Amish buggies, Caleb had recently expanded his business to include building and restoring old carriages. It hadn't taken long for word to get out, and he'd already built some finely crafted buggies for folks as far away as the state of Oregon. Caleb made a fairly good living, and he'd even hired two of his younger brothers to help when things got busy. He knew he could easily support a wife and a family, and he wanted that wife to be Naomi Fisher.

"Maybe I should set my feelings for the storekeeper's daughter aside and find someone else to court like Naomi suggested," Caleb muttered. It made sense, but it wasn't what he wanted. He had been interested in Naomi for a long time. He remembered the exact moment he'd known she was the one he wanted to marry. . . .

"Somebody, come quick! There's a kitten stuck up there." Ten-year-old Naomi Fisher pointed to the maple tree in their schoolyard. Sure enough, there was a scraggly white cat perched on one of the branches, meowing for all it was worth.

"Ah, it's just a dumb cat, and if it climbed up there, it can sure enough find its way back down," Aaron Landis said with a smirk.

Caleb was tempted to climb the tree and rescue the kitten, but recess was nearly over, and their teacher would be ringing the bell any second. Besides, Aaron was probably right about the kitten being able to come down on its own.

Naomi thrust out her chin. "If no one will help, then I'll do it myself." With that, she promptly climbed the tree, paying no heed to her long skirt.

Caleb stood mesmerized. She was as agile as any boy and not one bit afraid.

Across the branch Naomi scooted, until she had the kitten in her arms.

How's she gonna get back down? Caleb wondered.

Naomi slipped the cat inside her roomy apron pocket and shimmied to the ground. The girls all cheered when she landed safely with the animal in tow, but Caleb stared at Naomi with a feeling he couldn't explain.

When I'm old enough to get married, she's the one I'm gonna ask. Any man in his right mind would want a girl as brave as Naomi Fisher.

Steering his thoughts back to the present, Caleb had half a mind to turn his buggy around and return to Paradise. He could go to Byer's Bookstore and see if his book was there, and afterward he'd stop back at Fisher's General Store and try once more to reason with Abraham.

He glanced at the darkening sky. It looked like rain was heading their way, and his open buggy would offer little protection if there was a downpour. Besides, Caleb needed to get home. He had work waiting at the buggy shop, and Pop would no doubt have several chores he wanted done. It was probably for the best. Caleb was pretty sure Abraham Fisher wasn't going to change his mind, so if there were any chance for him and Naomi, he would have to be the one to make it happen.

Naomi was at the back of the store when she heard the bell above the front door jingle. Could Papa have returned so soon? She hurried up front and was greeted with an enthusiastic "Hi, there! What's new?" Ginny Meyers's green eyes shimmered as she gave her blond ponytail a flip with her fingers.

"I'm okay. And you?"

"Great, now that I'm away from our crowded restaurant for a while, but you look kind of down. Is everything all right?"

Naomi shrugged. "As all right as it's ever gonna be, I guess."

Ginny looked around the store. "Is your dad here?"

"No, he's out runnin' errands." Naomi motioned with her hand. "There's no one else in the store right now, either. Except me and Zach, who's asleep in his playpen in the back room."

"Sorry to hear the little fellow's taking a nap. He's such a cutie, and I love to watch him play."

Naomi nodded. "He is a sweetheart, even though he does get into things when I let him crawl around during the times there are no customers in the store."

"Is he walking yet?" Ginny asked.

"Nope. He turned one last Saturday, and we were all hopin' that would be the big day."

"Wish I could have been at his birthday party. Zach is always so friendly toward me." Ginny snickered. "I think the little guy would go with a total stranger if given the chance."

Naomi opened her mouth to reply, but Ginny cut her off. "Since nobody's here except you and me, you can bare your soul." The young English woman took hold of Naomi's arm and led her to the wooden stool behind the counter. "Take a load off your feet and tell Dr. Meyers your troubles."

Ginny moved to the other side of the counter and leaned her

elbows on the wooden top. She always seemed so enthusiastic and sure of herself, completely opposite of Naomi. Ginny attended college in Lancaster part-time, and when she wasn't in school, she worked at her parents' restaurant. Even so, she seemed to find time for fun and recreation. Last week, she'd come by the store and invited Naomi to go to the movies. Of course, Naomi refused. She knew her people viewed going to shows as worldly and not something parents wanted their children to do. Still, many young people like Naomi who hadn't joined the church yet often went to shows. Naomi wished she were brave enough and had the time to sneak off with Ginny, even for a little while.

"Don't sit there staring into thin air," Ginny said, snapping her fingers in front of Naomi's face. "Spill it!"

Naomi chewed on her lower lip. How much should she tell Ginny? Would the young woman understand the way she felt, her being English and all? "Well," she began hesitantly, "Caleb Hoffmeir was here earlier, and he wanted me to go to a singing this Sunday night."

"What'd you tell him?"

"I said I was sure my daed wouldn't allow it, but Caleb thought otherwise, so he was foolish enough to ask Papa outright."

"What'd your dad say?"

"He said no, as I figured he would."

Ginny clicked her tongue. "Why is it that parents think they can control their grown kids?" She drew in a deep breath, and when she released it, her bangs fluttered above her pale brows. "My mom and dad are bound and determined for me to take over their restaurant someday. That's why they insisted I go to college and take some business classes."

That made no sense to Naomi. She'd been helping at the store ever since she was a young girl, and she'd never had more than an eighth-grade education.

"I've got other plans, though," Ginny continued. "As soon as I get my degree, I'd like to buy my own health club. Instead of serving a bunch of tourists plates full of artery-clogging food, I'll be helping people stay fit and trim."

Naomi studied her English friend a few seconds. Not only was Ginny blessed with a pretty face but also a healthy, robust body. Ginny had told her that she worked out several times a week, and it showed.

Of course, Naomi reasoned, *I'm in good shape from all the chores I have to do here and at home. I don't need any fancy health club to make me strong.*

Ginny leaned across the counter. "You want to know what I think?"

Naomi shrugged her shoulders.

"I think you should stand up to your father and tell him you've got a life to live, which doesn't include baby-sitting his kids seven days a week or cooking and cleaning from sunup to sunset."

Naomi's cheeks burned hot as she considered that option. Papa would have a conniption fit if she ever talked to him that way. She'd been raised to be respectful of her elders, and even though she might not agree with everything her father said, she'd never speak to him in such a disrespectful tone. Besides, she had an obligation to fulfill.

"You won't get what you want out of life if you remain silent and keep doing what everyone else thinks you should." Ginny shook her finger. "Determine to stand up for yourself, and then just do it."

"I've a family to care for," Naomi mumbled. "So even if I could stand up to Papa, I wouldn't be able to get away."

Ginny reached over and patted Naomi's hand. "Don't you think you deserve to do something fun for a change?"

Naomi blinked. Of course she deserved it, but it wasn't meant to be.

"I'm planning a camping trip sometime this summer with a couple of friends. I'd like it if you could figure out some way to go along," Ginny announced.

Going camping did sound like fun, and there was something about being with Ginny that intrigued Naomi. Maybe it was her friend's perky attitude and determined spirit. Or it could be just the idea of spending time with a worldly English woman that held so much appeal.

Naomi thought about how she and her siblings used to camp out by the creek behind their home when they were younger, but they hadn't done that in some time. Maybe when the weather turned warmer, she could talk Papa into letting them pitch their tent and sleep outside one Friday night. It wouldn't be as exciting as going camping with a bunch of English women, but at least it would be a reprieve from their normal, busy lives.

The bell above the door rang again, and two Amish women walked in. Ginny turned to go. "I've gotta run, but think about what I said. I'll get back to you when the camping trip is planned, and if there's any way you can go, let me know."

Naomi nodded as a ray of sunlight burst through the window she still needed to wash. "Jah, okay, I'll think on it."

CHAPTER 3

Jim Scott leaned over to kiss his wife. "I should be home by six, so if you have dinner ready by then, we can go shopping for baby things after we eat."

Linda looked up at him and frowned. "What for? We already bought a crib and set up a nursery in the spare bedroom, but we still have no baby."

"Not yet, but our lawyer's working on it."

With a look of defeat, she folded her arms. "We've heard that before. Max Brenner had a baby lined up for us twice, and both adoptions fell through."

Linda's blue eyes filled with tears, and with a feeling of compassion, Jim stroked her soft cheek. "We need to be patient, honey. You believe in fate, don't you?"

She lifted her chin. "What's that got to do with anything?"

"When the time's right, we'll have our baby. Just wait and see."

Linda's gaze dropped to the kitchen floor.

Jim bent his head, entwined his fingers through the back of her soft, golden curls, and kissed her on the mouth. "See you after work."

She offered him a weak smile and reached up to tousle his hair. "You'd better stop and get a haircut on the way home. You're beginning to look like a shaggy bear."

He shrugged. "Aw, it doesn't look so bad yet."

"Have you looked in the mirror lately?"

He wiggled his eyebrows. "Yep, whenever I brush my teeth. And the other day, I noticed a couple of gray hairs poking through my dark tresses."

She studied him intently, until he broke out laughing. "I had you worried there, didn't I?"

Linda playfully squeezed his arm. "I wouldn't care if you turned prematurely gray—just don't lose these hunky biceps."

He kissed her again. "Don't worry; as long as I keep on painting, I'll have muscular arms."

Jim stepped out into the garage and opened the door of his work van. He knew Linda wanted him to stay, but if he didn't leave now, he'd be running late. Jim had owned Scott's Painting and Decorating for the past six years, and they'd been living in Puyallup, Washington, a year longer than that. Jim's business provided them with a good living, and he'd recently hired three new employees, which gave him a crew of six. He and Linda had everything now—a successful business, a nice home. The only thing they lacked was a child, and Linda wanted that more than anything.

With each passing day, Jim had watched her sink slowly into depression. They'd been married eight years, and she hadn't been able to conceive. At first, Linda believed there was something wrong with her; but after she and Jim both went to the doctor, it was determined he was the reason she couldn't get pregnant. He tried not to feel guilty about it, but Linda wanted a baby, and Jim couldn't give her one. Two years ago, they decided to adopt. They'd hired a lawyer who specialized in adoption cases, but so far everything had fallen through. Now they were in limbo again, waiting and wondering if it would ever happen.

As Jim backed out of the garage, he waved at Linda and mouthed the words, "I love you."

She lifted her hand in response and stepped into the house.

If only I could make her smile again. Suddenly, an idea popped into Jim's head. *Maybe I'll call Mom in Ohio this morning and see if she can find Linda an Amish quilt. She's wanted one for a long time, and it might make her feel a little better.*

Jim snapped on the radio. *On second thought, maybe I'll see about taking some vacation time so the two of us can go to Ohio for a visit. I'll take Linda on a tour of Amish country, and she can buy that quilt herself.* He smiled. *Besides, it'll be nice to see Mom and Dad again.*

Naomi scrubbed at the spot on the bathroom floor where Mary Ann had recently vomited. "Ick! I'd rather slop hogs than clean *kotze*."

She didn't see how her life could get any busier, but for the last several days, things had been even more hectic than usual. Her two younger sisters were both sick with the flu and had to stay home from school. Since Naomi needed to care for them, she couldn't go to the store, which she knew did not set well with Papa.

Naomi didn't enjoy home chores nearly as well as the tasks she did at the store, but there was little she could do about it. Her brothers Matthew, Norman, and Jake had to work in the fields; and Samuel, the youngest boy, complained how unfair it was for his sisters to stay home when he had to go to school. To make things worse, Zach was cutting another tooth and fussed continually.

"I'm sorry I'm sick and my kotze didn't make it to the toilet."

"It's not your fault you got sick."

"But I should have been faster to the bathroom."

Naomi washed her hands at the sink, then turned to face her six-year-old sister. "Come here." She opened her arms.

Mary Ann snuggled into her embrace. "You aren't mad at me?"

She shook her head. "How could I be mad at someone as sweet as you?"

The little girl leaned her head against Naomi and sobbed. "I hate bein' *grank*. I'd rather be in school."

"It's never fun being sick, but soon it will go better." Naomi felt the child's forehead. "Your fever seems to be gone. That's a gut sign."

Mary Ann's dark eyes looked hopeful. "Sure hope so."

"Jah." Naomi gently tapped the little girl's shoulder. "Now, back to bed with you."

"Okay." Mary Ann scampered out of the room.

Naomi sighed. *Maybe in another day or so, things will be back to normal.*

By Friday, Naomi felt frazzled and wondered if she, too, might be coming down with the flu. Every bone in her body ached, and she had a splitting headache. Of course, the headache might have been caused from listening to her younger sisters whine or from hearing the baby's incessant howling. Naomi's achy body could have been the result of doing so many extra chores. She'd had to change her sisters' sheets every morning since they'd taken sick, as the girls left them drenched in sweat after each night of feverish sleep. Then there were dishes to be done, cooking that included several batches of chicken soup, and the chores Nancy and Mary Ann normally did. When the children took their naps, Naomi longed to do the same, but she had to keep working. If she didn't, everything would pile up, and she'd have even more of a workload.

Since Naomi was home all day, her brothers decided they could come to the house whenever they felt like taking a break from their work in the fields. Those breaks always included a snack, which they thought Naomi should furnish.

Naomi popped two willow-bark capsules into her mouth and swallowed them with a gulp of cold water, hoping they might take care of her headache. "Air is what I need. Fresh, clean air to clear my head and calm my nerves."

The girls and baby Zach were sleeping, so if she hurried and cleaned up the kitchen, there might be time to take a walk to the creek, where she could rest and spend a few moments alone. The sound of gurgling water and the pleasure of sitting under the trees growing along the water's edge had always helped Naomi relax. She hadn't made a trip to the creek in many weeks, and she'd missed it.

Ten minutes later, with the kitchen cleaned and straightened, Naomi stepped out the back door. Free at last, if only for a short time.

Abraham wiped the sweat from his brow as he finished stocking another shelf with the kerosene lamps that had been delivered on Tuesday. It had been a long week, working at the store by himself. He'd had a steady stream of customers from the time he opened this morning, with barely a break so he could eat the lunch Naomi had fixed for him at dawn.

"Sure wish the girls hadn't come down with the flu," he grumbled. "I really could have used Naomi's help this week." Abraham knew his oldest daughter was needed more at home than at the store right now, but that didn't make his load any lighter. He hadn't been able to take a single nap these past few days. How could he, when he had to attend to business and there was no one to take over when he became tired? He'd been sleeping a lot since Sarah's passing. Maybe it was because he felt so down and depressed.

He glanced at the clock on the wall across the room. It was two in the afternoon, and for the first time all day, he had no customers. This was the only chance he'd had to restock, which was why the lamps had been sitting in the back room for the last two days.

Abraham reached into the box for another lantern when the bell above the door jangled and in walked Virginia Meyers. She was not one of his favorite customers, as the sassy young woman seemed to have a bad attitude. She had a way of hanging around Naomi, bombarding her

with a bunch of silly questions, and insinuating she should explore some of the things found in her English world. Virginia probably thought she was being discreet, but Abraham had overheard her speaking to his oldest daughter on more than one occasion.

"Is Naomi here?" Virginia asked as she sashayed across the room.

He shook his head. "She's been home most of the week, takin' care of her sisters. They're down with the flu."

Virginia pursed her lips. "That's too bad. Sure hope Naomi doesn't get the bug. She's got enough problems without taking sick."

Abraham reached around to rub the kinks in his lower back. "If you've got something to say, Virginia, please say it."

"Ginny. I prefer to be called Ginny."

"What kind of problems do ya think my daughter has?"

She shrugged her slim shoulders. "Naomi works hard. Seems to me you ought to cut her some slack."

Abraham frowned. "Some what?"

"Some slack. You know, give her a bit of space."

He raised his eyebrows.

"Let her do some fun things once in a while. Nobody should have to spend all their time doing chores and baby-sitting. Especially not a twenty-year-old woman who's never even been on a date."

He squinted. "How would ya know that? Has my daughter been whining about how unfair her daed is by makin' her work so hard?"

Virginia shook her head. "Naomi's too sweet to whine."

Abraham was tempted to tell the English woman she didn't know anything about his daughter, but he decided to change the subject instead. "What brings you to my store this afternoon? Shouldn't you be at school today? Naomi's mentioned you attend some fancy college in Lancaster."

"I'm done for the day, and I came by to see if you have any new rubber stamps. I'm doing a scrapbook of my Christmas vacation to Florida."

"Haven't had anything new since the last time you came askin' for stamps."

"I see."

"If there's nothin' else I can help ya with, I need to get back to settin' these lamps in place." He gestured to the shelf where he'd already put four kerosene lanterns.

A ripple of strange-sounding music floated through the air, and Virginia reached into her pocket and retrieved a cell phone. She wrinkled her nose when she looked at the screen. "That's my dad calling. Guess I'd better head over to the restaurant and see what horrible things await me there. Tell Naomi I dropped by." Virginia marched out the door, not even bothering to answer the phone.

Abraham bent down and grabbed another lamp. "If that girl was mine, I'd wash her mouth out with a bar of soap!"

Naomi gathered the edge of her dress so it wouldn't get tangled in the tall grass and sprinted toward the creek. By the time she arrived, she was panting for breath but feeling more exhilarated than she had in a long time. She flopped onto the grass under a weeping willow tree, leaned her head against the trunk, and lifted her face to the warm sunshine. So many days Naomi used to spend here when she was a girl and life had been uncomplicated. She wished she could step back in time or make herself an only child so she wouldn't have any siblings to care for.

"No point wishin' for the impossible," Naomi mumbled as she slipped her shoes off and curled her bare toes, digging them into the dirt. "I'm supposed to be satisfied, no matter what my circumstances might be."

At their last preaching service, the bishop had quoted a verse of scripture from the book of Philippians, and it reminded Naomi she should learn to be content. The apostle Paul had gone through great trials and persecutions, and he'd been able to say in chapter 4, verse 11: "For I have learned, in whatsoever state I am, therewith to be content."

Naomi sighed deeply and closed her eyes. *Heavenly Father, please give me rest for my weary soul and help me learn to be content.*

Naomi awoke with a start. She'd been dreaming about camping with Ginny and her English friends when a strange noise woke her. She tipped her head and listened, knowing she shouldn't have allowed herself the pleasure of drifting off. No telling how long she'd been down here at the creek. What if the kinner were awake and needed her? What if Papa had come home and discovered she wasn't in the house taking care of his sick children?

She clambered to her feet as the noise drew closer and louder. What was that strange sound?

She looked up. "Oh no! Bees!"

Naomi ducked, but it was too late. It seemed as if her head were encased in a dark cloud. One that moved and buzzed and stung like fire. She swatted at the enemy invaders as they pelted her body with their evil stingers, and she shrieked and rolled in the grass.

It seemed like an eternity before the swarm was gone. When she was sure they had disappeared, Naomi crawled to the edge of the creek. She grabbed a handful of dirt, scooped some water into her hands, mixed it thoroughly, and patted mud all over the stingers. Her face felt like it was twice its normal size, and her arms ached where the buzzing insects had made their mark. *If Caleb could see the way I look now, he would surely change his mind about wanting to court me.*

"I need to get back to the house and fix a real poultice," Naomi muttered. She'd never had an allergic reaction to a bee sting, but then she'd never had so many all at once. Even if she wasn't allergic, she had a homeopathic remedy that should help the swelling go down and take away some of the pain.

Naomi took off on a run. Beside the fact that the stingers hurt something awful, it had begun to rain. By the time she reached the back porch, raindrops pelted her body, while streaks of lightning and thunderous roars converged on the afternoon sky.

Naomi flung the door open and bounded into the kitchen. She screeched to a halt and stared at the floor. *"Was in der welt*—what in the world?" she gasped.

Mary Ann knelt in the middle of the room and looked up at Naomi with tears in her eyes. "Me and Nancy woke up and were hungry. We're feelin' better and wanted to make ginger cookies."

Streaks of flour dotted the little girl's face and pinned-up hair, which made the otherwise mahogany tresses look as though they were splattered with gray. The floor was littered with broken brown eggshells mixed with runny yellow yolks, and a sack of flour had been dumped in the middle of the mess.

Naomi's gaze traveled across the room where Nancy stood at the sink with a sponge in her hand. "What happened here?"

"Everything was goin' okay 'til Mary Ann dropped the carton of eggs," Nancy huffed. "I was haulin' the flour over to the cupboard and slipped." She lifted her chin. "The flour spilled and landed on Mary Ann's head, and it's all her fault."

Naomi groaned. Nancy was four years older than Mary Ann and usually managed fairly well in the kitchen. She also tended to be a bit bossy where the younger ones were concerned. *Why did I allow myself the luxury of falling asleep at the creek? For that matter, why did I go there in the first place? Now I'm paying the price for my desire to spend a little time alone.*

A piercing wail shattered the air, and she whirled around. It was Zach hollering from his playpen in the adjoining room.

"The boppli's awake," Mary Ann announced.

"Jah, I know the baby's awake, but I can't go to him now." Naomi lifted her arms, covered in mud. "I've been stung by a swarm of bees."

"Oh, Sister, you look so *elendich*!" Nancy cried. It was obvious she hadn't even noticed Naomi's condition until now.

Naomi nodded. "I'm sure I do look pitiful, but I feel even worse than I appear."

"Are you gonna help us bake ginger cookies?" Mary Ann asked, scooping up a handful of eggshells.

"No." Naomi tried to keep her voice steady and calm. There was no point getting upset and yelling at her sisters. It wasn't as if they'd made the mess on purpose. "I need to tend these bee stings."

Naomi opened the cabinet door above the sink, grabbed a box of baking soda and her bottle of medicine. "I'm going upstairs to the bathroom. While I'm gone, one of you needs to clean this mess, and the other can get the baby before he tries to climb out of his playpen." She pointed toward the living room where Zach still screamed. "When I get back, I'll see about gettin' the little guy diapered and fed." Naomi hurried out of the kitchen.

Ten minutes later, she reentered the room, only this time her face and arms were covered with baking soda instead of mud. She stopped inside the door. The mess had been cleaned, and Zach was in his highchair eating a cracker; but her brothers Matthew, Norman, and Jake sat at the table, dripping wet.

"*Ach*, my! You're gettin' water everywhere!" Naomi shouted. "What are you three doin' in here anyways?"

"It's rainin' cats and dogs outside, and we sure couldn't keep on plowing the fields in this kind of weather," Matthew answered. His dark brown hair was plastered against his head like a soggy leaf, and his cheeks were as red as a raspberry. At the moment, he looked like a little boy rather than a twenty-two-year-old man.

"That's right; it's a real downpour out there," Norman agreed. "If it keeps up for long, we'll have us a flood, and that's for certain sure." He raked his fingers through his hair, almost the same color as Matthew's and just as wet. A spray of water splattered onto the table, and Norman grinned at Naomi, kind of sheepishlike.

"What happened to you, Sister? You look awful," Jake commented. The seventeen-year-old had recently celebrated his birthday; but soaked to the skin and with his hair in his face, he, too, looked like an overgrown child.

"I had a run-in with some bees." Naomi glanced at the clock above the refrigerator. It was half past four. Samuel should have been home from school by now. She ran to the back door and flung it open. No sign of her little brother—just pouring rain and jagged lightning.

She spun around to face her brothers. "One of you needs to go after Samuel. He'll catch his death of pneumonia if he walks home in this terrible weather. Besides, he could be hit by lightning."

"It wonders me so that you're such a worrywart. Why, a little rain won't kill the boy, and he's sure smart enough to stay out from under a tree if lightning were to strike." Matthew reached for a wad of napkins and swiped them across his forehead.

"Yeah, that's right." Jake's blond head bobbed up and down. "I can't begin to tell ya how many times I walked home from school in the rain when I was a boy."

Zach let out another ear-piercing yelp, and Naomi thought she was going to scream. Wasn't there a single person in her family who cared about anyone but himself?

She clapped her hands together and stomped one foot. "Now listen to me! One of you had better go after Samuel—now!"

Matthew blinked, then turned to face Norman. "Guess the boss means business, Brother. Get the buggy hitched, schnell!"

"Okay, I'm goin'." Norman pushed his chair away from the table. He sauntered past Naomi but halted when he got to the back door. "You'd better have supper started before Papa gets home. He won't like it if he shows up expectin' to eat and nothin's ready."

Naomi had taken as much as she could stand. She grabbed a wet sponge from the sink, took aim, and pitched it at her brother. It hit its mark, landing in the center of Norman's back.

He didn't seem the least bit affected but merely chuckled and marched out the door.

"Brothers!" Naomi hollered. She hurried over to Zach, scooped him into her arms, and headed upstairs.

Caleb couldn't believe how hard it was raining. When he left for town to get supplies a few hours ago, the weather had been warm and sunny. By the time he left Zook's Tool Shop, a noisy thunderstorm churned across the sky, dropping buckets of rain. He'd planned to stop by Fisher's General Store and see if he could catch Naomi alone, but now he thought it would be best to go straight home. Besides, judging from the time on his pocket watch, Abraham's store was probably closed.

Speaking softly to his four-year-old gelding, Caleb stood near the front of the buggy and stroked the horse's ear. "I don't like storms any better than you, but we need to be gettin' home."

The horse snorted and nuzzled Caleb's arm. He patted the animal's head and hopped into his open carriage.

"Sure wish I'd driven one of Pop's closed-in buggies today," Caleb mumbled. "By the time we get home, we'll both be near drowned." He pulled the brim of his straw hat down and leaned into the wind. From the way the rain pelted the ground, there might be some flash flooding in the area.

Caleb drove the horse and buggy as fast as he could. He'd only gone a short ways, when he came upon a gusher of muddy water running over the road and into a nearby field. Several cars had pulled onto the shoulder, obviously stalled.

"Guess there's some good in us Amish usin' *real* horsepower. At least my buggy's got no engine to peter out on me."

By the time Caleb reached the halfway point between the town of Paradise and his folks' farm, the floodwaters had become a hazard. He noticed a herd of horses owned by one of the English farmers who lived in the area. They stood up to their flanks in a lake of murky, brown water.

Caleb wondered if the pond at the back of his folks' farm might be flooded, too. If it was, Pop would need Caleb and his brothers to put the animals in the barn.

Moving on down the highway, Caleb spotted a closed-in buggy sitting on the shoulder of the road. He swiped his hand across his rain-drenched face and squinted. It looked like Abraham Fisher's horse and buggy. Was something wrong? Were the Fishers stranded? Maybe they'd had an accident.

Caleb guided his horse to the edge of the road and stopped behind the rig. He jumped down and sprinted around to the right side, where he knew the driver would be sitting. When he peered through the window, his heart lurched. Abraham Fisher was hunched over, his head leaning against the front of the buggy, but there was no sign of Naomi or her baby brother.

Caleb grasped the handle and opened the door. Abraham didn't budge, although he could see by the rise and fall of the man's shoulders that he was still breathing.

"Abraham, can ya hear me?" Caleb touched the storekeeper's shoulder. There was no response, so he shook the man's arm.

Naomi's father jerked upright. "Ach, my! What are ya doin', boy?"

"I thought you might be hurt or had broken down."

Abraham yawned. "I ain't hurt—just pulled over to take a little nap. With the rain comin' down so hard, it was gettin' difficult to see, and since I've been minding the store by myself most of the week, I was feelin' kind of tired."

"You've been at the store by yourself?" Caleb's mouth dropped open like a broken hinge. "But I came by on *Mondaag,* and Naomi was helping you."

Abraham grunted. "Jah, well, Monday was the only day I had my daughter's help. She's been home the rest of the week, takin' care of her sick sisters."

"Everything's okay with you then?"

The storekeeper frowned. "Why wouldn't it be?"

"Like I was sayin'. . .I saw your buggy pulled to the side of the road and figured I'd better stop and see if you were hurt or anything."

"Except for bein' tired, I'm right as rain." Abraham shook his head. "Sure hope this storm lets up soon. It's gonna cause a passel of trouble if the creeks and ponds should flood."

Caleb didn't bother to tell Abraham about the swamped farm he'd already seen. He figured it would be best if they both headed for home. He tapped the side of Abraham's door. "Guess I'll be on my way then. Glad you're not hurt." The only response was a muffled murmur.

When the door shut, Abraham took up the reins.

Caleb hurried to his own buggy, shaking his head. The storekeeper hadn't even said thanks.

CHAPTER 4

Naomi stood at the kitchen sink with a sponge in her hand. She needed to hurry. They'd soon be leaving for Sunday church at the Beechys' house.

At least the swelling from my bee stings has gone down, she mused. *I no longer look like a bumpy old horny toad. The floodwaters have gone down, too, and it's not raining. That's something to be thankful for on this Lord's Day.*

Naomi washed each dish in one container, then rinsed it in another. As she finished, the dishes were placed in the draining rack for Nancy to dry and put away. Every step was done with attention, adding up to a simple, unspoken task performed after each and every meal. Strangely enough, Naomi found this ritual comforting. It gave her time to think and sometimes pray.

"Baby Zach's hollerin'. Want me to get him out of the playpen?"

Nancy's question drew Naomi's thoughts aside, and she whirled around. There stood Zach, gripping the playpen rails with slobbery hands while tears streamed down his chubby cheeks.

"I'll tend the baby," Naomi told her sister. "All but two cups and three plates have been washed, so you can finish those and get them dried and put away. Hopefully, we'll all be ready to go by the time Papa gets the horse and buggy hitched."

"Why can't I take care of the boppli while you finish the dishes?" Nancy asked with a lift of her chin.

Nibbling on the inside of her cheek, Naomi contemplated her sister's suggestion. Finishing the dishes would be much easier than trying to calm Zach, who probably had a dirty diaper. Even though she wasn't looking forward to changing it, she knew she could get the job done quicker than Nancy.

"I appreciate the offer," she said, "but I think it would be best if I get the baby."

A look of disappointment flashed across Nancy's face, but she slid over to the sink and grabbed the sponge without a word.

Naomi hated to be in charge of her younger siblings, always telling them what to do and sometimes handing out discipline when it became necessary. That was supposed to be a mother's job.

Naomi dried her hands on a terry cloth towel and went to get her baby brother. Zach quit crying the minute she picked him up, and after a quick check of his diaper, she was relieved to see there was no need for a change. How glad she would be when the boppli was potty trained and no longer needed to wear *windels*.

Zach squealed and kicked his hefty legs as she carried him across the room. Apparently, all the little guy wanted was to be out of his playpen.

Naomi hugged her little brother. "You're gettin' mighty spoiled, ya know that?"

"Guess that's because he's so *lieblich*," Nancy put in.

"Jah, he's adorable all right." Naomi nuzzled the boy's cheek with her nose. "Adorable and spoiled rotten."

She took a seat in the rocking chair near the fireplace and rocked Zach as she sang a silly song she had made up. "Spoiled little baby, you're awfully cute. You're sure to grow up happy and loved to boot."

Zach giggled as she tugged gently on his soft earlobe.

Nancy placed another dish in the cupboard when the back door swung open. Papa entered the kitchen, followed by Samuel.

"A sly old fox was in the chicken coop last night," Samuel announced.

"How do ya know that?" Nancy asked.

"We found evidence of it. . . .several dead chickens," their father said with a frown.

"Papa's gonna set a trap for the scoundrel," Samuel added excitedly.

"I hope you're plannin' to set it someplace where the kinner won't get hurt," Naomi said.

Papa moved toward the rocker, and his blue eyes narrowed. "Don't ya think I've got brains enough to know how to set a trap without taking the chance of one of my youngsters gettin' injured?"

Tears stung the back of Naomi's eyes, and she blinked to keep them from spilling over. "I—I meant no disrespect, Papa."

He fingered the tip of his beard. "Jah, well, your mamm never questioned my decisions when she was alive."

There he goes again—comparing me to Mama.

"Is everyone ready for church?" Papa asked, changing the subject.

"I think so," Naomi replied.

Papa studied Nancy. "Where's your head covering?"

She pointed to the back of a chair.

"Put it on now. Mary Ann's already in the buggy, and the older boys left a few minutes ago in Matthew's rig."

Nancy shut the cupboard door, grabbed her kapp off the chair, and scampered outside.

Papa glanced at Samuel, who had taken a seat at the kitchen table. "Get your lazy bones up and hightail it out to the buggy. If we don't hurry, we'll be late."

Samuel jumped up, grabbed his hat from a wall peg, and made a beeline for the door.

Papa turned to Naomi again. "If your mamm were here, the kinner would be ready for church on time—with their head coverings in place."

Naomi stood, positioning Zach against her hip. "Papa, why do you always compare me to Mama?"

He blinked as though surprised by her question. "I ain't comparin' you, and I don't appreciate your tone."

Feeling the need for comfort, Naomi hugged the baby. "I'm sorry, Papa."

He cleared his throat but said nothing in return. For a minute, Naomi thought she saw a look of tenderness cross her father's face, but it disappeared as fast as it had come.

Oh, please, Papa. Can't you just say, "I love you, Naomi, and I appreciate all you do?"

"You got the boppli ready to go?"

She nodded.

"Then let's be off."

Caleb paced back and forth along the side of Beechy's barn, where twenty buggies were already parked. He'd seen Mathew, Norman, and Jake Fisher arrive awhile ago, so he figured Naomi and the rest of the family wouldn't be far behind.

Caleb hadn't seen Naomi since he stopped by Fisher's General Store on Monday, so he'd had nearly a week to come up with a plan. He hoped to speak with Naomi about it today. If he could get her alone for a few minutes, that is.

"Hey, Caleb, how's it going?"

At the sound of Aaron Landis's deep voice, Caleb turned around. Aaron tipped his head and grinned.

"It's goin' okay. How 'bout with you?"

"Things are great with me and Katie." Aaron slapped Caleb on the back. "We just found out she's gonna have a baby in late November."

Caleb clasped his friend's hand. "Congratulations. I know you'll make a gut daed."

Aaron's smile widened, and his dark eyes twinkled in the sunlight. "Sure hope so. Katie and me want a whole houseful of kinner."

Caleb only nodded in reply.

"Well, I should go see how Katie's feelin' before we go inside for church. She's had the morning sickness real bad."

"Tell her I'm happy to hear your news," Caleb said, forcing a smile.

"Sure will." Aaron ambled off in the direction of the women gathered on the Beechys' front porch. No doubt about it—Aaron was one happy man.

I wonder if I'll ever have a wife or a boppli.

Naomi took a seat on a backless bench near the kitchen door. She wanted to be close to an exit in case Zach started to fuss. At the moment, the child was sitting quietly on her lap, but Naomi had a box of baby crackers tucked inside a wicker basket in case he got hungry. The basket also contained a stack of diapers, a change of clothes for the baby, and a bag of dried fruit for Nancy or Mary Ann if they became restless. Naomi knew the worship service would last a good three hours, and it was hard for the younger ones to sit so long.

She glanced across the room and noticed Caleb sitting on the men's side between his younger brothers, Andy and Marvin. He smiled, but she looked away. No use giving him hope she might care for him. If they couldn't court, Caleb should find someone else. Naomi didn't expect him to wait until she was free of her responsibilities to the family. Matthew was Caleb's age, so if he ever got over his shyness around women, he might find a suitable wife soon. Norman was nineteen and not far behind; but Jake, Nancy, Samuel, and Mary Ann still had several years before they could marry.

Naomi jerked her hand when Zach bit down on her thumb. *And then there's the boppli, who won't be ready for marriage for another eighteen years or so.*

Tears stung the backs of her eyes. *By then I'll be so old nobody will want to marry me.*

She reached into the basket and withdrew a cracker. At least Zach wouldn't be chomping on her thumb anymore.

Such a week this has been, she mused. First, her sisters had gotten sick and she'd stayed home from the store to care for them. Next, that horrible encounter with the bees. Then, Mary Ann and Nancy's egg and flour mess, followed by the brothers coming into the kitchen, dripping wet. *I don't know how Mama managed so well.*

Naomi's thoughts went to Papa. *Why must he always compare me to Mama? I try my hardest to please him, but nothin' ever seems to be good enough.*

A familiar lump lodged in her throat, and she swallowed against the constriction.

" 'I have learned, in whatsoever state I am, therewith to be content,' " Bishop Swartley quoted from the book of Philippians. Crippled with arthritis and in his eighties, the man could still preach and lead the people, even if he did often repeat the same verse of scripture.

Naomi closed her eyes. *Help me, Lord, for I'm still havin' trouble learning to be content.*

When church was over, Naomi stepped outside. As she stood on the front porch, Zach clung to her neck while he wrapped his legs around her waist. Naomi held him tightly and inhaled. The trees and grass were such a deep green, and everything smelled clean and new after the rain they'd had a few days ago. A group of children gathered to play in the yard, including her three younger siblings.

Naomi had only a few minutes to savor the peaceful scene, for it was time to help with the meal. She sighed and turned toward the door.

"Why don't you let me hold the little one awhile?" Anna Beechy spoke up from her rocking chair on the front porch.

With a grateful heart, Naomi handed Zach to the elderly woman. Anna smiled as she snuggled the boy. She had a special way with the kinner. After all, she'd raised ten of her own and now had twenty-five grandchildren. Naomi knew she was leaving her baby brother in capable hands, so she headed into the house and busied herself with pouring coffee and serving bowls of bean soup to the menfolk.

When the meal was over, the men meandered into the yard, breaking into groups so they could visit, play horseshoes, or relax under the shady maple trees.

Naomi shook her head when she noticed her dad already nodding off. He'd been doing that a lot since Mama's passing, and it worried her some. Was Papa dealing with his depression by napping so much, or was he simply tired from not sleeping well at night?

Directing her focus back to the meal, she ushered her sisters to a table and took a seat on the bench between them. She'd just finished her bowl of soup when she looked out the window and noticed Emma Lapp across the yard, standing near one of the open buggies.

Naomi squinted. Was that Caleb Hoffmeir Emma was talking to? She squeezed her napkin into a tight ball and clenched her teeth. Was Caleb asking Emma to tonight's singing? Would he be taking her home in his courting buggy? A pang of jealousy stabbed Naomi's heart as she imagined the couple beginning to court.

Caleb's only doing what I told him to do, she reminded herself. *I really can't fault him for that.*

"Naomi, did ya hear what I said?"

"Huh?" Naomi forced her gaze away from Caleb and Emma, turning her attention to Mary Ann.

"I'm full now. Can I go play?" The child pointed to her empty plate.

Naomi nodded. "Jah, you ate well. Run along, but don't be gettin' into any trouble, ya hear?"

"I won't." Mary Ann scrambled off the bench and hurried outside.

Naomi glanced at Nancy. "You about done, too?"

Nancy crammed another piece of bread in her mouth and mumbled, "Am now."

"Okay, you can go."

Nancy bounded away, and Naomi scanned the yard once more. Caleb and Emma were gone.

Probably snuck off somewhere to be alone. She squeezed her eyes shut, hoping she wouldn't give in to the threatening tears.

When Naomi felt someone touch her shoulder, her eyes snapped open. Emma smiled and dropped to the bench beside her. "I've got a message for you. It's from Caleb," she whispered.

Naomi's mouth went dry, and she quickly reached for her glass of water.

Emma leaned closer. "He wants you to meet him at the pond behind the house."

"Is that what the two of you were talkin' about out there by Caleb's buggy?"

Emma's pale eyebrows furrowed. "Of course. What'd ya think we were talkin' about?"

"I—uh—never mind."

Emma adjusted her wire-rimmed glasses and stared at Naomi. "You didn't actually think—" She giggled. "I'm not romantically interested in Caleb, if that's what you were thinkin'."

"Well. . ."

"Go to him, Naomi."

Naomi shook her head. "I can't."

"Why not?"

"I've got to keep an eye on Mary Ann, Nancy, and Samuel, not to mention little Zach."

"The last time I saw your baby brother, he was asleep on the Beechys' couch." Emma nodded toward the yard. "As far as the other kinner are concerned, I'll watch out for them while you're gone."

"You mean it?"

"Of course. Now be off with you."

Caleb hunkered near the edge of the water, watching a pair of mallard ducks float past. *Will Naomi show up? Did Emma deliver my message?*

A twig snapped, and Caleb turned his head. "You came."

Naomi smiled and he stood. "I can't stay long," she said breathlessly. "My daed might come lookin' for me if I'm gone too long."

Caleb motioned to a grassy spot beneath a white birch tree. "Should we have a seat?"

She shook her head. "The grass is still damp from that awful storm we had on Friday."

He shrugged. "Guess we'll have to stand then."

"What'd you want to talk to me about?"

"I'd sure like to court you, Naomi."

"You said that the other day, but you know it's not possible."

"Because your daed says no, or because you have too much work to do at home?"

"Both."

Caleb's stomach clenched, and he lifted Naomi's chin with his thumb. Her brown eyes were still as large and inviting as he remembered. A man could lose himself in them. "If Abraham had his way, you'd never have any fun. Probably never get married, either."

Naomi's eyes filled with tears, and her chin quivered. "That may be true, but I made a promise to Mama before she died, and I aim to keep it."

"I understand that, but I think we can still be together." He smiled. "I've come up with a plan, and I hope you'll give some consideration to it."

"What kind of plan?"

"You can still take care of your family while we see each other in secret."

"I can't. Papa might find out, and he'd be furious."

Caleb shrugged. "I'm not worried about that. We can meet at night, after your family has gone to bed."

Naomi shook her head. "I'm needed at home, Caleb. I thought I made that clear the other day."

"You won't even think about meetin' me in secret?"

Tears rolled down Naomi's cheeks, and she swiped them away. "I can't."

"But you would if your daed said it was all right?"

Her eyes widened. "Papa would never allow it. And even if he did, I'd still be too busy."

"Is that your final word?"

"It has to be."

He grunted. "Fine then. Don't blame me if you end up an old maid."

CHAPTER 5

The next few weeks seemed to drag by, even though Naomi had been plenty busy. Maybe that was the problem. There were too many chores to do. Last Friday had been the kinner's last day of school, which meant she would be taking the three youngest ones with her to the store until the end of August, when they returned to the one-room schoolhouse. Matthew said he'd be in charge of Samuel, who would be put to work in the fields. It was hard for a boy of eight to labor in the fields all day, but Naomi knew he would work well under Matthew's supervision.

As Naomi bent to grab another towel from the basket by her feet, she made a mental note to be sure and pack plenty of cookies to give her brothers in case Samuel or the others got hungry between breakfast and lunch. She planned to take some cookies to the store as well so the girls and Zach could have a snack. Even though having Nancy and Mary Ann along meant two more children Naomi had to watch, it was nice to know when the baby got fussy or needed to be fed, Nancy could help out. Also, both girls would have jobs to do at the store, like dusting, stocking lower shelves, and sweeping the floor.

Naomi's thoughts drifted to Caleb and the discussion they'd had when they met at Beechy's pond. Oh, how she wished they could court. She wouldn't blame Caleb if he found someone else and married straight away. "I sure can't expect him to wait for me," she mumbled.

"Help! Help!"

Naomi whirled around. Mary Ann clutched a basket of eggs as she circled the yard with Hildy the goose in hot pursuit.

"She's after the eggs!" the child shouted. "Get her away from me, please!"

"Calm down and stop running. She'll only keep chasin' if you don't."

Mary Ann's eyes were wide, and several strands of blond hair had come loose from the back of her head. Naomi could see her sister was struggling with the need to keep running, but the child screeched to a halt in front of Naomi's basket of clean clothes.

"Hand me the basket," Naomi instructed. "Then get behind my back and stand very still."

Mary Ann complied, crouching low and whimpering as she clung to the edge of Naomi's long dress.

Naomi bent down. She grabbed a wet towel, snapped it open, and smacked Hildy on the head. The goose let out a blaring squawk, spun around, and honked her way to the barn.

"That was close!" Mary Ann exclaimed. "I thought that old bird was gonna peck me to death."

Naomi knelt in front of her sister. "She didn't draw blood, did she?"

"I don't think so. Just scared me silly—that's all."

Naomi hugged Mary Ann and stood. "I'm going to ask Matthew or Norman to put that nasty critter down."

Mary Ann's eyes filled with tears. "You mean to kill Hildy?"

"That's the only way to keep her from chasin' folks, and it's become an everyday occurrence here of late."

"Please don't let her be killed. She don't mean to be bad."

"I know. We'll see what Papa has to say." Naomi handed her sister the basket of eggs. "Now hurry into the house and tell Nancy she needs to have Zach fed and diapered by the time I come inside."

Mary Ann grabbed the basket of eggs and scampered off.

At least one problem has been solved. Naomi hung the last towel on the line and turned when she heard a horse trot out of the barn. Norman led the gelding into the yard and proceeded to hitch him to the waiting buggy.

"What do you think you're doing?" she called.

"What's it look like? Papa asked me to hitch up a horse so he could leave for the store, and that's what I'm doin'."

She frowned. "You'd better think about choosing a different horse. This one's barely green broke."

Norman waved his hand. "Aw, Midnight will be fine. All he needs is the chance to prove himself."

Naomi shook her head, wondering if it was the horse that needed to prove himself or her nineteen-year-old brother. She gathered the empty laundry basket and started across the yard. Without warning, the horse whinnied, reared up, and kicked his back hooves against the front of the buggy.

"I refuse to ride to the store with that horse!" she shouted.

"Whoa there! Steady, boy." Norman stepped in front of the gelding and reached for his harness.

"Look out! You might be the next thing he kicks."

"He'll settle down soon." Norman's face was cherry red, yet he continued to struggle with the boisterous animal. Midnight alternated between rearing up and kicking out his back feet. The buggy rocked back and forth.

Naomi covered her mouth to keep from screaming, which would rile the horse more. Things were getting out of control, and if Norman didn't do something soon, she feared the buggy would overturn.

"Let that horse loose!" Papa's voice shattered the air like a gunshot, and Norman quickly did as he was told.

He led the panicked horse back to the barn and returned a few minutes later with one of their gentle mares. "Guess Midnight wasn't quite ready yet," he mumbled.

"You think?" Papa shook his finger. "If you were a few years younger, I'd take you to the woodshed for a sound *bletsching*."

Norman hung his head. "Sorry, Papa. I didn't expect Midnight to act that way."

"Jah, well, use your brain next time." Papa turned to face Naomi. "You and the kinner 'bout ready to go?"

She nodded. "I'll run inside and see if Nancy's got Zach ready." She figured now probably wasn't the best time to tell Papa about Hildy.

Jim Scott heard his cell phone ringing in the distance, and he glanced around to see where it was. He usually kept it clipped to his belt, but he'd been on a ten-foot ladder and didn't want to take the chance of the phone coming loose and falling to the ground. That had happened several months ago, and since he hadn't been smart enough to buy insurance on the phone, it had cost him plenty to buy a new one. Today, he'd put the phone in a safe place. He just couldn't remember where.

"Your phone's on the lid of that paint bucket, and it's ringing like crazy," Ed called from across the yard. "Want me to get it for you?"

"Sure, if you don't mind."

Jim climbed down the ladder, and his feet had just touched the ground when his employee handed him the phone. "The guy says he's your lawyer."

"Thanks."

When Ed kept standing there with his hands in the pockets of his painter's overalls, Jim nodded and said, "You can finish up with the trim on those windows now."

"Oh, sure. Right." Ed sauntered off, and Jim turned his attention to the phone.

"Hello, Max. How are you?"

"I'm fine, and I have some news that I think will make your day."

"Really? What's up?"

"My friend, Carl Stevens, is a lawyer in Bel Air, Maryland. He called this morning and said a young woman came to his office the other day. She's a single mother and can no longer care for her one-year-old boy, so she's decided to put him up for adoption."

Jim's heart skipped a beat. Did he dare believe this baby might be theirs? Should he risk telling Linda and getting her hopes up, too?

"Jim, are you still there?"

"Yeah, Max. Just trying to digest this bit of news."

"Carl said he'd be meeting with the woman again in a few weeks and should be able to tie things up then. My question is, would you and Linda be interested in a child that old? I know you had wanted a newborn."

Jim blew out his breath and sank to the grass. "Whew! This is so sudden, and I'm not sure Linda would want an older child."

"One isn't that old," Max said with a chuckle. "He's still pretty much a baby in my book; and at his young age, it shouldn't be that difficult for the little guy to adjust to his new surroundings."

"What about a father? Is there one in the picture?" Jim asked.

"No. Carl said the woman severed ties with the baby's father, and he's married to someone else and living in another state. He's signed away all parental rights to the child."

"Hmm. . ."

"Talk it over with your wife tonight, and then give me a call with your decision."

Jim frowned. "I hate to get Linda all fired up about something that might not even happen. It's not a done deal with the mother yet, right?"

"Not quite."

"And you'll know something definite in two weeks?"

"I believe so."

"Then I think it would be best if I wait to tell Linda until we know for sure that the woman is actually going to give up her son."

"Sounds fair to me," Max said. "I'll get back to you as soon as I hear from Carl again."

"That'd be great. Thanks." As Jim hung up the phone, his mind swirled with mixed emotions. If the woman in Maryland decided to give them her child, they would have two reasons for making a trip to the East Coast—one to pick up their son and the other to visit his folks. He was sure it would be a vacation they would never forget.

Naomi grabbed a stack of invoices Papa had asked her to go over. She had to take this time to get caught up on paperwork. Summer was not far off. Then there would be carloads and busloads of tourists flocking to their place of business. Some would be coming in merely to gawk at the curious Plain folks who ran the general store. Others would drop in to purchase something made by one of the locals. Papa didn't care much for English tourists, but he said it was a free country, and it did help their business.

When the front door opened, Naomi looked up from her work, and her heart skipped a beat.

Caleb removed his straw hat and offered her a dimpled grin. "Gude mariye."

She slipped from behind the counter and moved toward him. "Good morning. What can I help ya with?"

He glanced around the room. "Are we alone?"

Naomi nodded. "For the moment. Papa's out back with the kinner. He could come inside at any moment, though."

Caleb shrugged. "I'll take my chances."

"What are you needing?" she asked, feeling a bit impatient.

"I'm sorry about last Sunday and sayin' I thought you were gonna end up an old maid. I didn't mean it, Naomi. I just spoke out of frustration."

She sniffed. "It's okay. I understand."

Caleb smiled. "Since this Sunday comin' is an off-week and there won't be any church, I'm plannin' to go fishing at Miller's pond. Want to join me there?"

Naomi released an exasperated groan and moved back to her wooden stool. "I can't. You know that."

Caleb leaned on the edge of the counter and studied her intently. "It's not fair, Naomi. A woman your age should be having fun, not babysittin' her brothers and sisters and be expected to slave away here as well as at home."

Naomi felt her defenses rise, and she stiffened. "For your information, Caleb Hoffmeir, I like workin' in this store."

"That may be, but you should still have a little fun now and then."

The back door creaked open, and Naomi jumped. "That's Papa and the kinner. Look as if you're buyin' something," she whispered.

Caleb grabbed a straw hat off the rack nearby and plunked it on the counter. "I'll take this one," he announced in a voice loud enough so Papa could hear. "My old hat's seen better days."

Naomi had just put Caleb's money inside the cash register when her father came sauntering up front. He held Zach in his arms and was followed by Naomi's younger sisters. He spotted Caleb right away and gave him a nod.

Caleb smiled in return and pointed to his new hat. "Last time I was here, you said I should buy a new one. Finally decided to take your advice."

"I'd say it's high time, too." Papa set the baby on the floor, and Zach crawled off toward a shelf full of wooden toys. "Watch your brother now," he said to Nancy.

Nancy and Mary Ann both knelt next to Zach, and Caleb turned his attention back to Naomi, giving her a quick wink.

She shook her head, hoping he would take the hint and leave. He just stood there gazing at her, however. "Want me to dispose of your old hat?" she asked.

"Naw. Think I'll hang onto it awhile. I might decide to wear it for everyday and keep the new one just for good."

"Makes sense to me," Papa said.

Caleb grabbed the new hat off the counter, gave Naomi another wink, then headed out the front door. "See you around, Abraham," he called over his shoulder.

Papa's only response was a muffled grunt, and Naomi almost laughed out loud. Sometimes it amazed her the way a twenty-two-year-old man could act so big and smart one minute, and the next minute he was carrying on like a little boy.

As soon as Caleb pulled into his yard, he realized something was amiss. Timmy, one of their goats, had gotten out of his pen and was running around the yard, *baa*-ing like crazy.

"Get back in your pen, you stupid animal, and leave my buggy alone!"

Caleb jumped down from his rig as his dad whizzed past, brandishing a buggy whip and hollering like the barn was on fire.

"What's goin' on?" Caleb called.

"That stupid goat was in my buggy, and he chewed up the front seat." Pop jumped to one side as the goat whizzed past him and leaped onto a tree stump. He raised the buggy whip, but the critter took off before he could take aim. Timmy jumped onto the front porch, toppling a chair in the process. He raced back and forth two times, then ran down the other side and headed straight for Pop's buggy.

"Oh no, you don't!" he railed.

When Pop climbed in after him, Timmy hopped into the front seat and made a beeline for the back. Out the back side the goat went, tearing the canvas cover in the process.

Deciding to join the chase, Caleb sprinted after Timmy, with his dad right behind him. They cornered the goat near the barn, but when Caleb reached for him, the animal skirted away and took off again. Pop was on his heels, with the buggy whip swishing this way and that.

Caleb ducked to avoid being hit, but it was too late.

Snap! The whip caught Caleb's left shoulder, and he winced. "Hey, it's Timmy you should be after, Pop, not me!"

His dad halted. "I hit you?"

Caleb nodded and reached up to rub the welt that had already formed on his shoulder.

"I'm sorry, Son. Sure didn't mean that to happen."

"I know you didn't do it on purpose," Caleb said, forcing a smile. He'd never admit it, but the welt stung like crazy.

Timmy made another pass, this time right between Caleb's legs. He leaned over and grabbed the goat's back legs, and the animal hollered like a stuck pig.

"It's off to the goat corral for you." Caleb lifted the squirming animal into his arms and trudged toward the pen. If this were any indication of how the rest of his day was going to be, he might as well take the afternoon off. Only trouble was, he had tons of work to do. Now, thanks to Timmy the goat, he'd have his daed's buggy to fix, as well.

"You'd better let your mamm take a look at that shoulder. Don't want to chance infection," Pop called as Caleb headed to his buggy shop.

Caleb shook his head and kept walking. "I'll be okay. It can't be any worse than the bletschings I used to get when I was a boy."

CHAPTER 6

As Caleb rolled out of bed the next morning, a stinging pain sliced through his left shoulder. He winced as he lifted one arm to slip on his cotton shirt. "Should have asked Mom to put some salve on it last night," he muttered as he stepped into his trousers.

A short time later, he found his mother in the kitchen, slicing an apple crumb pie. His younger sisters, Irma and Lettie, were busy setting the table for breakfast.

"How ya feelin' this morning?" Mom questioned. "Your daed never said a thing about the goat gettin' out and him hitting you with the buggy whip 'til we went to bed last night."

Caleb shrugged. "I'll live, and Pop didn't do it on purpose."

"Of course not." Mom pushed a wayward strand of grayish blond hair back into place and pulled out a chair. "Have yourself a seat, and I'll put some peroxide on that welt. No doubt it's hurtin' this morning."

Caleb's manly pride called for denial, but he knew he'd be miserable all day if he didn't get the pain to subside. Besides, as Pop had said yesterday, it could become infected if left untreated.

He undid his shirt and slipped it over his shoulder.

Irma, who was nine, let out a low whistle. "Ach, my! That sure looks elendich."

"Never mind how pitiful it looks," their mother scolded. "Run over to the cupboard and get some peroxide and salve."

Irma and Lettie both stood near Caleb, each of them peering at his wound as though they'd never seen anything like it before.

"Hurry and get the salve," Mom persisted as she gently washed the welt with a damp piece of cloth.

Irma trotted across the room and returned a few seconds later with both salve and peroxide.

The cold, stinging contact of the cleansing liquid caused Caleb to let out a little yelp.

"Sorry, but it's really red, and this should keep it from getting infected." Mom allowed it to dry a few minutes, then she slathered some healing salve on the area. "We should probably cover it with a bandage, but I don't think we've got one large enough."

Caleb slipped his shirt back in place. "That's okay. It'll be fine now. *Danki*, Mom."

Her dark eyes held a note of sympathy. "Haven't had to tend a wound on my oldest boy in ever so long. Still hurts me as much as it does you, ya know."

"That's what Pop always says when he gives me a bletsching," Lettie said, wrinkling her freckled nose.

Mom patted the young girl's arm. "It's true. Neither your daed nor I take any pleasure in doling out punishment."

"You punish us 'cause you love us—that's what Pop has told me many times," Irma interjected.

"And don't you ever forget it," Caleb said, giving his little sister a tickle under her chin.

She giggled and scampered away from the table.

Caleb had just poured himself a cup of coffee when his two younger brothers, Andy and Marvin, entered the room, each carrying an armload of firewood for the cookstove. Mom hadn't begun using the gas stove yet, as she said she much preferred wood and wouldn't use propane until the summer days became too warm.

"Say, Caleb, Bishop Swartley's outside waitin' to see you," Andy announced.

"Why didn't you invite the man in for a cup of coffee or to join us for breakfast?" Mom asked.

Marvin gave Mom a look that resembled a young boy rather than a nineteen-year-old man. "I did ask, but he says he's in a hurry and needs to speak to the buggy maker."

Caleb pushed his chair away from the table. Even though Andy and Marvin worked part-time in his shop, many of their customers wished to speak with Caleb instead of his brothers who didn't know a lot about the business yet. "Keep a plate of breakfast warm for me, Mom," he said on his way out the door.

Caleb found Andrew Swartley standing beside his buggy with one eye squinted, his nose crinkled, and lips set in a thin line. The straw hat on the man's gray head sat at an odd angle, nearly covering his other eye.

"What can I do for you, Bishop Swartley?" Caleb asked as he strode alongside the elderly man.

"Got a little problem with my buggy wheel." The bishop motioned to the left side of his rig. "It wobbles something fierce."

Caleb squatted down beside the wheel. "Looks like you're missing a couple spokes, and the wheel is bent besides. What happened?"

The bishop cleared his throat a few times and dragged the toe of his black boot in the dirt, much like a young boy might do when he was caught doing something wrong. "Well, it's like this. . . . Me and Mose Kauffman were havin' ourselves a little race the other day, and I kinda ran off the road and hit a tree."

Caleb nearly choked on the laughter bubbling in his throat. He knew a lot of the younger Amish men raced their buggies against one another, but the bishop was eighty-two years old, for goodness sake. He ought to have better sense.

Fighting for control so as not to appear disrespectful, Caleb clenched his teeth.

"Think you might be able to fix it while's I wait?" the bishop asked.

"I suppose I could. Since Pop and my brothers finished most of the planting yesterday, I'll have Andy and Marvin's help today." He motioned toward the house. "Why don't you come inside and have some breakfast with the family? After we eat, me and the boys will get right to work on your buggy wheel. You can sit on the front porch and visit with Pop, if he don't have too many other things to do, that is."

Bishop Swartley smiled, revealing a gold crown on one tooth that sparkled in the sunlight. "That sounds right gut to me."

Caleb grinned and followed the bishop inside. On days like today and despite the pain in his shoulder, he felt really good about the occupation he'd chosen. Truth was, he didn't think he'd be happy doing anything else.

"Hand me that packet of peas, would you?" Naomi said to Mary Ann.

"I'll get it." Nancy grabbed for the package, which had been left on the grass, while Naomi made furrows in the dirt to plant the peas. It should have been done weeks ago, but there hadn't been time.

"Hey, Naomi asked me to get those!" Mary Ann grappled for the peas, and in so doing, spilled the whole packet.

"Now look what you've gone and done," Nancy said, shaking her finger at her younger sister.

Naomi stood and arched her aching back. She was in no mood to referee a quarrel between the girls. "Please, pick up those peas, and be quick about it—both of you."

"But it was Mary Ann who spilled them," Nancy protested.

"It wouldn't have happened if you hadn't grabbed for 'em first," Mary Ann countered.

"Enough!" Naomi shouted. "I've had about as much as I can stand."

The girls became silent, but Naomi could see by the frowns on their faces that neither was happy with the other. They were probably miffed at her, too.

Papa had closed the store today so he could help the brothers get some of the plowing and planting done in the fields. Naomi thought at first he would expect her to take the kinner to the store and manage things on her own, but he'd suggested she stay home and get caught up on things needing to be done. She'd been hard at work since breakfast, and nothing had gone right. She'd dropped a shoofly pie on her clean kitchen floor, Zach had been difficult to get down for a nap, and ever since she and her sisters came to the garden, all they'd done was bicker.

I wish I'd been an only child, Naomi fumed. She was tempted to haul both girls into the kitchen and give them a bletsching but figured that wouldn't help things any. Maybe it would be best to separate them awhile.

"I'll tell you what," Naomi said as she knelt next to Mary Ann and helped rescue the peas. "Why don't you and I finish this job, and Nancy can go inside and start lunch?"

Nancy thrust out her lower lip. "By myself?"

Naomi nodded. "You're ten years old now and gettin' quite capable in the kitchen. I think you'll do a gut job making lunch for everyone."

Her sister's eyes brightened. "You really think so?"

"Sure do."

"I'll ring the dinner bell when the meal's ready." Nancy hopped up, brushed the dirt from her apron, and sprinted for the house.

Naomi released a weary sigh. At least that problem had been solved.

"I don't see why we can't use Midnight in the fields," Norman complained to his father as they walked toward the house for their noon meal.

Abraham gave an exasperated moan. "If I've told you once, I've told ya a hundred times. That horse is not yet broke. Have you forgotten the way he acted up the other day when you tried to hitch him to the buggy?"

"How's he ever gonna learn if we don't put him to work?"

"He'll be put to work when he's broke."

"Papa's right," Matthew put in. "I've been workin' with Midnight whenever I have free time, but it'll be awhile before he's ready to pull a buggy."

"All good things take time," Jake put in.

"I'll be glad when I'm on my own," Norman grumbled. "Then I can do whatever I want."

Abraham grabbed Norman by the shirttail. "What was that?"

The boy shook his head. "Nothin', Papa."

"Seems here of late, all you do is gripe and complain. If you're not careful, I'll be sendin' you to the store with Naomi every day, and I'll stay here to help Matthew and Jake." The thought of farming appealed to Abraham more than he cared to admit, but he'd made a commitment to run the store, and for Sarah's sake, he'd see it through. She'd loved the place, and he was committed to keeping the business going in memory of his precious wife.

If only life weren't so full of disappointments. Norman might think he'll be able to do whatever he wants when he's a grown man, but he's in for a big surprise.

Naomi and Mary Ann had just finished planting the last of the peas when Papa and the brothers walked into the yard. Papa, Norman, and Jake headed straight for the house, but Matthew stopped at the garden patch. "How's it goin'?" he asked. "Any trouble with Hildy today?"

Naomi shook her head. "If I had my way, she'd be gone." She wiped the perspiration from her forehead and grimaced.

"I begged Papa not to kill the goose, so he made me promise to stay out of her way and try not to act scared whenever she comes around," Mary Ann put in.

Matthew nodded at Mary Ann, then turned back to Naomi, offering her a sympathetic smile. "Wish I could help you in the garden, but there's a lot to be done in the fields yet."

"I know." Naomi turned to her little sister. "Run up to the house and get washed. If Nancy doesn't have everything ready, see what you can do to help."

The child skittered away, and Naomi faced Matthew again. "Sure wish I didn't have so much to do. Between workin' at the store most every day and all the chores to do here, I'm plumb tuckered out."

Matthew shuffled his feet, and a wisp of dust curled around his boots. "I'm sorry you're so miserable, Sister. Things have been kind of hard since Mama died. Sorry to say, but you've had to shoulder more than your share of the work." He patted her arm with his solid, calloused hand.

Naomi smiled through her tears. "It means a lot to know someone cares."

"Of course I care. Papa cares, too—he just has a funny way of showin' it."

She sniffed. "You really think he cares?"

"Jah."

"Then how come he never says so? If Papa cares, why does he yell so much and expect me to do everything like Mama used to?"

Matthew shrugged. "Don't know. Why don't you ask him?"

"I did, and he said he wasn't tryin' to compare me to Mama."

"Maybe he's not then."

"He is so. All the time he's saying, 'Your mamm didn't do it this way or that.'" Naomi looked away. There was no point saying anything more. If she broke down in front of Matthew, he'd probably think she was a big boppli.

"Things between you and Papa will work out, Naomi. You'll see."

She stared at the toes of her sneakers. "I hope so. I surely do."

CHAPTER 7

By the first week of May, Naomi wondered how she would make it through the summer. The store had been bombarded with customers, many of them curious tourists, and the garden was growing weeds faster than she could keep up. Every evening after they returned home from the store, Naomi and her sisters tackled the weeds. It was backbreaking, especially when Naomi was already tired from doing her regular chores and helping out at the store.

Tonight, as she prepared for bed, tension pulled the muscles in her neck and upper back. *Will things ever get easier? It's been a year since Mama died, yet I still struggle to get everything done. How did you do it all, Mama?*

Naomi took a seat on the edge of her bed, pulled the pins from her hair, and brushed the golden brown waves cascading across her shoulders. Tomorrow was an off-Sunday, and there would be no church. Maybe she could get caught up on her rest, since they had no company coming and no plans to go calling.

Zach stirred from his crib across the room, and Naomi went to check on him. He'd kicked off the covers, exposing his bare feet.

"Sleep well, little one, and may your days ahead be trouble free," Naomi murmured as she pulled the boy's quilt over his body. *The quilt Mama made before Zach was born. It's all my little brother has of our mamm now.* Naomi's nose burned with unshed tears. *I won't cry. There's been enough tears already.* She leaned over and kissed the baby's forehead, then tiptoed across the room.

Letting the weight of exhaustion settle over her body like a heavy blanket, she flopped onto her bed. As soon as her eyes closed, a vision of Caleb came to mind. What would it be like if they could marry and start a family? Would she be happier raising her own children than taking care of her siblings?

"Guess I'll never know," she murmured before drifting off to sleep.

Holding a single red rose in one hand and his lunch pail in the other, Jim stepped into the kitchen. "Honey, I'm home!"

When there was no response, he decided Linda might be upstairs taking a nap. She'd been doing that a lot lately, and he suspected it had something to do with her depression over not having a baby.

"That's about to change." He dropped his lunch pail on the counter, opened the door under the sink, retrieved a small glass vase, and inserted the rose. Eager to share his good news, he headed upstairs.

As Jim expected, he found his wife on the bed. She wasn't sleeping, though—just lying there staring at the ceiling.

He bent over and kissed Linda's forehead, then held up the rose.

"What's that for?"

"We're celebrating."

"Celebrating what?"

"Our lawyer, Max, called this afternoon, saying a young woman in Bel Air, Maryland, has agreed to give us her son. If you're agreeable, we can head east by the end of next week. That'll give me time to get some jobs lined out and be sure my foreman knows what to do in my absence."

Linda sat up, her eyes wide and her mouth open. "A baby? We're finally going to get a baby?"

"Not exactly a baby. He's a year old, but—"

"A year isn't that old, Jim. He's almost a baby," she said excitedly.

Jim smiled. "I was hoping you'd see it that way."

She clambered off the bed. "The end of next week, you said?"

"I think we can be ready by then, don't you?"

She nodded and wrapped her arms around him, almost crushing the rose. "Will we fly or drive?"

"I thought it would be best if we drove. It's been several years since we've had a real vacation, and we can see a few things on our way to and from."

Linda rushed over to their closet and pulled out a suitcase. "There's so much to do between now and then. I'll need to pack, make motel reservations in Maryland, buy some baby things, get the nursery ready—"

"Whoa! Slow down, sweetie. I'll take care of the motel reservations, we can go shopping together, and you can pack. How's that sound?"

She grinned, reminding him of the carefree young woman he'd married eight years ago. "This is going to be the best vacation ever!"

"Yeah, I think so, too."

❧

Naomi stood at the stove, stirring a pan full of scrambled eggs. Papa, Matthew, Norman, and Jake were still outside doing chores. Samuel and Mary Ann had gone to the henhouse to gather eggs. Zach sat in his high chair across the room, while Nancy spoon-fed him cereal.

"Is breakfast ready yet?" Nancy asked. "I'm so hungry I might start eating the boppli's mush."

Naomi chuckled. "The eggs will be done soon. I think you can wait."

"Since there's no preaching today, can we do somethin' fun?"

Naomi considered her sister's question. She'd planned to rest most of the day, but doing something fun might be a better way to relax.

"What would you like to do?" she asked.

"How about if we go over to the Beechys' place? I hear they have a batch of new piglets and a couple of baby goats."

The idea of spending time in the company of Anna Beechy did

have some appeal. The woman was old enough to be Naomi's grand-mother, and since Naomi had no grandparents living nearby, Anna was the next best thing. Always cheerful and bursting with good advice, Anna was a joy to be around.

Naomi sprinkled salt over the eggs. "If Papa says it's okay, then I'll take you, Mary Ann, Samuel, and Zach over to the Beechys' after our noon meal."

"Then I hope he says yes, 'cause I'm ready for some fun." There was a pause before Nancy added, "I'm sick of workin' so hard, aren't you?"

"We've all been working hard, and with summer upon us, it's not likely to get much better," Naomi replied. "The garden will soon be producing, and then there will be canning to do."

Nancy groaned. "I don't like to can. It gets too hot in the kitchen."

"I know, but it has to be done. We can always cool our insides with some of Papa's homemade root beer, you know."

"That's true. Do ya suppose he'll be askin' us to sell some to neighbors and English folks who see our sign at the end of the driveway?"

Naomi added a bit of pepper to the scrambled eggs. "No doubt he will be wantin' us to do just that."

"Hey! Cut that out, you little rascal!"

Naomi turned in time to see a blob of cereal fly out of Zach's grubby little hands and hit Nancy in the middle of her nose. She chuckled. "At least it's not me feeding the stinker this time."

Naomi had no sooner pulled their buggy into the Beechys' yard, when Samuel, Nancy, and Mary Ann scrambled down and hurried to the barn.

She smiled as she hoisted Zach into her arms and stepped out of the buggy. Even though it had been a long time since she'd felt the exuberance her younger siblings obviously felt, she could still remember how wonderful it was to see newly born critters on a farm.

75

As she strolled across the Beechys' lawn, Naomi couldn't help but notice the weed-free garden bordering the house. Colorful flowers danced in the breeze, making Naomi mindful of her own flowerbeds choked with weeds. It wasn't the way of the Amish to allow their gardens to be neglected. But then, most families had many helpers, not just three younger siblings who pulled more pranks on each other than they did weeds.

"It's gut to see you," Anna called from her rocking chair on the front porch. She waved and beckoned Naomi to join her. "Did you come for a little visit, or were you needing something?"

"I brought the younger ones to see your baby animals." Naomi stepped onto the porch, holding Zach against her hip. "They've already headed to the barn, so I hope that's okay."

"Oh, sure. Abner's out there, and he'll be glad to show off his new piglets and the twin goats born last week." Anna's wire-rimmed glasses had slipped to the end of her nose, and the strings of her white head covering draped over her shoulder. "Have a seat, won't ya?"

Naomi sat in the wicker chair beside Anna's rocker and placed Zach on her lap. He squirmed restlessly, but she held on tight. "You're not gettin' down, ya hear?"

"Is the boy walkin' yet?" Anna asked.

"No, but he crawls plenty fast, and I'm afraid if I put him down, he might try to follow the others out to the barn."

"You can take him there now if you'd like. We can always talk later." Anna leaned over and chucked Zach under his chubby chin. "You're sure growin', ya know that?"

"I think we can stay here awhile," Naomi said. "It won't hurt him to learn how to sit still."

"Would ya mind if I hold him?" Anna asked with an eager expression.

Naomi handed Zach over and smiled as he nestled against the older woman's chest. "You're sure good with kinner. I can tell he likes you."

Anna chuckled. "I'd better be good with 'em, for I've had plenty of practice over the years, what with raisin' my own young'uns and now havin' *kinskinner*."

Naomi couldn't imagine having grandchildren. Since it wasn't likely she'd ever marry, she would probably never have any children, much less grandchildren.

"Your flowers are sure beautiful. Not a weed in sight," she said, changing the subject.

"My daughter Lydia helps some, but mostly the flowerbeds are my job." When Anna smiled, her wrinkles seemed to disappear. "I love the feel of dirt beneath my fingers, not to mention the wonderful gut aroma of the flowers as they come into bloom."

"Who takes care of the vegetable garden?"

"It's a joint effort, with me, Lydia, and my older granddaughters, Peggy and Rebecca, taking turns at weed pullin' and the like." Anna chuckled. "Leona doesn't help yet 'cause she's too little and would just be in the way."

Naomi thought about three-year-old Leona and how she often came with her father, Jacob Weaver, to the store. Jacob had been Papa's friend for as long as she remembered. His oldest boy helped in his painting business, his two older daughters assisted their mother at home, and Leona, the youngest, was a real cutie.

"Our vegetable patch doesn't look nearly so good," Naomi admitted, bringing her musings to a standstill.

Anna pushed the rocker back and forth, and Zach giggled. "Have you got much celery planted this year?" she asked.

"Not much a'tall. Why do you ask?"

"Thought maybe somebody at your house might be gettin' married come November."

Naomi shook her head. "Not unless one of my brothers decides to find himself a wife, and then it would be her family who'd need to supply the celery for the wedding supper."

Anna clucked her tongue. "I figured a young woman your age would have a serious beau by now and be thinkin' of marriage."

Naomi's voice lowered to a whisper. "That's about as likely as a cat makin' friends with a dog."

"I've known that to happen a time or two."

Naomi smiled. Anna Beechy always looked on the bright side of things.

"There's no special man in your life then?"

"Not really." An image of Caleb Hoffmeir popped into Naomi's head. "Even if there were, I'd never have enough time to court."

Anna shook her head. "Such a shame your daed hasn't found himself another wife by now. If Abraham were to get married, you wouldn't have so many responsibilities and would be free to court."

Naomi opened her mouth to reply, but Zach's high-pitched scream cut her off.

"I think the little guy's hungry," Anna said. "Why don't I take him inside and see if I can find something he might like while you walk out to the barn and check on the others?"

"You wouldn't mind?"

"Not a'tall." Anna stood. "Now run along and have a little fun. Me and the boppli will be just fine."

"All right then. I'll be back soon." Naomi jumped up, took the stairs two at a time, and sprinted toward the barn, determined to make the most of her unexpected free time.

A few minutes later, she found her sisters and brother kneeling in the hay beside the twin goats.

"Look, Naomi," Samuel announced. "They like us already."

"Well, sure they do," Abner Beechy agreed. He sat on a bale of hay nearby, his straw hat tipped at an odd angle, a wide smile on his weathered face.

Mary Ann looked up at Naomi and grinned from ear to ear. "We seen the new piglets, too."

"Come, pet Floppy. She won't bite." Nancy motioned for Naomi to join them.

She knelt between her sisters. "You've already named the twins?"

"Yep. This here's Floppy 'cause his tail flops around," Samuel said, pointing to the smaller of the two goats. "And this one we've decided to call Taffy, since her skin's the color of taffy candy."

Naomi stroked each of the goats behind the ears and touched the tips of their wet noses. They were soft and silky and awfully cute. She laughed when one of the kids made a *baa*-ing sound and licked her finger. Maybe there was some joy in life, after all. Maybe she just needed to look for it more often.

"I still don't understand why we couldn't have flown to the East Coast. It would have been much quicker than driving."

Jim glanced at his wife, sitting in the passenger seat of their minivan. "I told you before—this will give us a chance to see some beautiful country between here and there."

She frowned. "I just want to bring our little boy home. Didn't you say you'd set up an appointment for us to meet with the woman and her lawyer on Saturday morning?"

He nodded. "This is only Monday, Linda. That gives us five whole days to get there."

"And we can stop in Lancaster to see the Amish?"

"Bel Air's only a few hours from Lancaster," he said, feeling his patience begin to wane. Wasn't Linda listening the first time he'd explained all the details, or was she becoming forgetful like her mother? "I told you we can stop in Lancaster before we head to our hotel in Bel Air."

"Okay."

"I called my folks the other day and told them we'd be coming to Ohio soon after we picked up the boy. They're eager to meet their new grandson." Jim flicked on the blinker and headed up the ramp taking them to the freeway. "Think how much fun it will be to see the Amish. And you can finally buy that handmade quilt you've been wanting, Linda."

"Amish quilts are expensive, you know."

He shrugged. "You're worth it."

They rode in silence for a while, then Linda spoke again. "What if he doesn't like us, Jim?"

"Who?"

"The baby."

"You worry too much. What's not to like? You've got enough love in your heart for ten babies, and I'm. . ." Jim chuckled. "Well, what can I say? I'm gonna be the world's best dad."

She reached over and touched his arm. "I know you will."

"You're not disappointed because he isn't a newborn?"

She shook her head. "I can't wait to hold our son and tell him how much I love him."

CHAPTER 8

Naomi pushed an errant strand of hair away from her face as she washed a new picking of peas. Today had been busier than usual at the store, and she was so tired this evening she could barely stand at the sink, much less prepare supper.

"The family's counting on me, and it won't get done unless I do it," she mumbled with renewed determination.

"You talkin' to yourself, Sister?"

Naomi turned her head. She'd thought she was alone in the kitchen.

Nancy stood near the back door with another basket of peas in her hand. This was the third one she'd brought in for Naomi to wash.

"Guess I was talking to myself," Naomi admitted. She nodded toward the counter. "Just put 'em over there, and then you need to get washed and start setting the table. Papa and the brothers will be in soon, and they'll expect the meal to be ready and waiting."

"Why can't Mary Ann set the table?"

"She's in the living room with Zach at the moment—hopefully keepin' him out of trouble."

"I'll be glad when Saturday comes and we can stay home. I'd rather be sellin' root beer at home than workin' at the store all day."

"There'll be plenty of work to do here, as well," Naomi reminded. She poured the clean peas into a kettle and placed it on the stove. "Remember, we won't just be sellin' root beer on Saturday."

Nancy set the basket on the counter. "Jah, I know."

"If things go well, maybe we can take time out to have a little picnic."

"Can we have it down at the creek?"

"I don't think so. We've gotta stay close to the house in case we get any root beer customers."

Nancy scowled. "Then how are we gonna have a picnic?"

"We can eat it at the picnic table on the lawn. That way we can watch for customers, and if there's time, maybe we can play a game of croquet."

"Sounds gut to me." Nancy started for the stairs. "I'm goin' upstairs to wash, but I'll be back to set the table."

Naomi blew out her breath. She didn't have the heart to tell Nancy they might not have time for a picnic lunch if they had a lot of customers or didn't get all their chores done on time. She figured the child needed something to look forward to. All work and no play was bad for any soul, especially the kinner.

Jim stood at the window, looking down at the hotel parking lot. They had arrived in Lancaster, Pennsylvania, that morning; but after only a few hours of shopping and sightseeing, Linda developed one of her sick headaches and begged Jim to stop. He'd been fortunate enough to find a hotel with a vacancy and had canceled their reservation in Bel Air. They would leave the hotel in Lancaster at eight in the morning and be in Bel Air by ten. By this time tomorrow evening, they'd be a family of three.

Jim's cell phone rang, and he pulled it from the clip on his belt. His conversation lasted only a few minutes, and during that time he kept glancing at the bathroom door, where Linda had gone to take something for her headache and to try to relax in a warm bath.

A few seconds after he hung up the phone, she returned to the room with a questioning look on her face. "I thought I heard your cell phone ring."

He nodded.

"Who was it?"

"Carl Stevens. The lawyer representing the baby's mother."

Linda's face paled. "Please tell me there's nothing wrong. She didn't back out or anything, did she, Jim?"

"Mr. Stevens called to let me know our meeting tomorrow is still on schedule."

Linda frowned. "I wish it had been today."

"The way you're feeling, you wouldn't have been up to it today, Linda. You'll feel better by tomorrow." Jim took Linda's hand and led her over to the bed. "Please, lie down and try to relax. You look all done in."

She flopped down on the bed, pulling her legs underneath her and leaning against the pillows. "I am kind of tired, and this headache doesn't seem to be going away. It's been a long five days on the road."

"I know, honey, but it'll be worth it when we get the baby. You'll be so excited you'll forget you were ever tired or had a migraine."

"I hope so." Linda rubbed her forehead.

Jim massaged her shoulders and neck. "Lie down now and rest awhile. You hardly slept last night, and I'm afraid you're going to feel worse if you don't get some sleep."

She yawned. "You're right. I haven't slept well since we left home. A nap might really help."

"That's my girl. You'll feel better after this is all behind us and we're heading to Ohio with our boy."

She nodded and scooted farther down on the bed. "We've waited so long for a baby. I just want to hold him."

He pulled the cotton bedspread over her. "Soon, Linda. Just one more day and we'll have our son."

As Caleb headed for home, he felt a renewed sense of determination. He'd been in town on errands today and had gone by the Fishers' store in hopes of seeing Naomi. Just like the other times he'd dropped by lately, she was busy. Too busy to talk, she'd informed him. Even if she hadn't been busy, Caleb knew Naomi's father was there, watching Naomi's every move and listening to whatever she and Caleb said.

Caleb clucked to the horse to get him moving faster. "Probably shouldn't have left Andy alone at the buggy shop while I went to town, but I wanted the chance to see Naomi again."

The only good thing that had happened during his visit to the store was the minute he'd spent talking to Nancy Fisher, when she'd given him the news that Naomi and the younger ones would be staying home on Saturday to sell root beer from their front yard. Abraham would probably be working at the store all day, which meant Caleb could drop by the Fishers' place for some root beer and the chance to speak to Naomi without fear of her dad eavesdropping. He hadn't given up on their relationship yet and was determined to find a way for them to be together.

"Maybe I'll see if Mom has a nice plant I could take Naomi," he mumbled. "That oughta make her take notice of the way I feel."

Caleb talked to his horse the rest of the way home, and by the time he pulled up to the mailbox beside the driveway, he was feeling pretty confident. He opened the box and withdrew the day's mail. Smiling, he noticed a letter from his cousin, Henry, who owned a buggy shop in Holmes County, Ohio. He tore it open and read the letter out loud.

Dear Caleb:

I've been to an auction and have acquired some antique buggy parts—wheels, axles, springs, moldings, a couple of old seats, and a surrey top. If you're interested in buying some, hop a bus and come take a look. Don't be too long, though, 'cause a couple of other people are interested. Wanted to give you first pick.

Your cousin,
Henry Stutzman

Caleb grinned. He would leave Andy and Marvin in charge of his shop for a few days, and come Saturday, he'd be on a bus bound for Berlin, Ohio. He would have to see Naomi some other time.

Whistling a happy tune, Caleb entered the buggy shop a short time later, but he stopped inside the door, shocked by the sight that greeted him. Andy was sitting on the floor, moaning and grasping the palm of his left hand.

"What's wrong?" Caleb dashed over to his brother and dropped to his knees.

Andy's face contorted. "It's my thumb! Shot a nail straight into it."

"How'd ya do somethin' like that, and where was Marvin when it happened?" Caleb reached for Andy's hand, and his stomach churned at the sight. A three-inch nail was partially embedded in his brother's thumb.

"I was usin' that new air gun you bought awhile back—and guess my aim was off." Andy's lower lip jutted out, making him look much younger than his eighteen years. "Marvin's still out in the fields helpin' Pop, John, and David." He grimaced. "This sure does hurt like crazy."

"I can only imagine." Caleb put his arm around Andy's waist. "Here, let me help you up. Then we'd better get one of our neighbors to drive us to the emergency room."

Andy's dark eyes widened as he shook his head. "The hospital?"

Caleb nodded. "You need to get this taken care of right away. Can't go around with a nail stickin' out of your thumb for the rest of your life."

"But I hate hospitals. They use big needles and do things to folks that hurt somethin' awful."

"Nothing they do to you at the hospital could be much worse than what you've done to yourself. Now let's go."

Andy allowed Caleb to lead him out of the shop and into Caleb's open buggy. As soon as he had his brother settled in the passenger seat, Caleb ran into the house to tell Mom what had happened and let her know they'd be driving to the Petersons' to see about getting a ride to the hospital. So much for doing any more today. At the rate things were going, Caleb wondered if he'd be able to go to Ohio on Saturday.

Abraham took a seat on a bale of straw and leaned his head against the wooden planks of the barn. The sweet smell of hay tantalized his senses, and he drew in a deep breath. *Too bad I can't enjoy my farm all the time. If only I weren't so tired after workin' at the store all day.*

"*I have learned, in whatsoever state I am, therewith to be content.*" Abraham thought about the verse of scripture Bishop Swartley had recently quoted from Philippians 4:11. Just this afternoon, his friend Jacob Weaver had reminded him that Hebrews 13:5 said, "Let your conversation be without covetousness; and be content with such things as ye have: for he hath said, I will never leave thee, nor forsake thee."

Of course, Jacob was talking about the need for Abraham to be content with his family and learn to enjoy them more. He said it was time for Abraham to quit grieving over Sarah's death and realize God hadn't left him and would never forsake him.

Abraham closed his eyes, and a vision of his sweet wife burst into his mind. He blinked and tried to dispel the image, but it only became stronger.

It was the day of their wedding, and he could hear Sarah's voice and feel her soft touch. Sarah's dark eyes revealed the depth of her love for him, and they had promised to cherish one another until death parted them.

"Papa, are you sleepin'? The supper bell's chimin', and it's time to eat."

Abraham forced his eyes open, reluctantly letting go of Sarah's image. Little had he known on their wedding day that she would be the first to pass on.

When he looked up at his oldest son, he noticed a worried frown on Matthew's face.

"You okay, Papa?"

"Fine. Just restin' my eyes." He stood and arched his back.

Matthew started for the barn door. "You comin' then?"

"Right behind you." Abraham took one more look around the barn. He'd been grieving for Sarah long enough. It was time to move on. Jacob was right. He needed to be content with what he had. Maybe tomorrow, after he got home from the store, he'd set up the tent in their backyard, and they'd have themselves a little campout. He figured the younger ones would like it, and truth be told, he was looking forward to it, as well.

CHAPTER 9

"Linda, are you awake? It's time to get up. Our appointment is in three hours."

Linda's only response was a deep moan.

Jim touched his wife's forehead. She wasn't running a fever; that was good. "What's wrong, honey? Are you still feeling sick this morning?"

She nodded but kept her eyes closed.

"Maybe you'll feel better once you've had some breakfast."

Linda rolled onto her side. "My head is pounding, and my stomach's so upset, I don't think I could keep anything down."

Jim climbed out of bed. "I'll go take my shower and check on you when I get out."

"Okay."

Ten minutes later, when Jim returned to the bedroom, he discovered that Linda was no better.

"Honey, I think you're gonna have to stay here while I go to Maryland to pick up the baby."

"I have to go with you." She lifted her head but let it fall back on the pillow.

"You don't have to go, Linda. It will be better if you sleep off that migraine."

"What about the papers? Won't I be expected to sign something?"

"We both signed the necessary papers in Max's office several weeks ago. He faxed them to the woman's lawyer, remember?"

"Oh, that's right." She opened her eyes, and when she looked up, Jim noticed there were tears ready to spill over.

Linda's face looked pale and drawn, and he knew she would never make the two-hour trip to Bel Air without throwing up. He bent over and kissed her forehead. "Close your eyes and get some sleep. By the time you wake up, you'll be feeling better, and I'll be here with our boy."

She nodded, and a tear trickled down her cheek. "Don't stop anywhere on the way back. Bring him straight to the hotel, okay?"

"I will, honey."

Before Papa and Samuel left for the store in the morning, he'd nailed a sign to the fence at the end of their driveway, and Naomi placed several jugs of root beer on the picnic table. By nine o'clock, they'd had a few English customers who said they'd driven by the farm and seen the sign. A couple of their Amish neighbors also dropped by. Naomi wondered how she would get any chores done when she had to race back and forth from the house to the yard to wait on customers. Nancy wasn't good at making change, so Naomi put her and Mary Ann to work inside while she handled the root beer sales. During the slack times, she rushed into the house, tended to Zach, did some cleaning, and instructed her sisters on what they should be doing. At the moment, they were supposed to be cleaning their bedroom while she mopped the kitchen floor. Instead, they were arguing, and Naomi was afraid they would wake Zach, who was taking his morning nap.

She set the mop and bucket aside and trudged up the stairs.

"What's the problem?" Naomi asked when she entered the girls' room.

Mary Ann sat on the hardwood floor with a stack of papers in her lap, and Nancy stood off to one side, her hands on her hips and a scowl on her face.

"Mary Ann won't help me clean," Nancy tattled. "She's been sittin' there goin' through old school papers for the last ten minutes."

"Mary Ann, please get up and help your sister clean this room," Naomi instructed.

The child pointed to the garbage can a few inches away. "I am cleanin'. I'm throwin' out all the papers I don't want."

"You can do that later, after the room is clean." Naomi grabbed the broom, which had been leaning against the wall, and handed it to Nancy. "You sweep, and Mary Ann can hold the dustpan. After that, the windows need to be washed, and your throw rugs should be shaken."

A horn honked in the yard, signaling another root beer customer.

Naomi turned and started for the door. "I'll be back soon to check on your progress." She left the room, praying she'd have enough patience to get through the day without losing her temper or having to spank someone.

Jim was glad traffic was light that morning, and he had no trouble finding his way to Carl Stevens's office in Bel Air. He parked the minivan in the parking lot, and a few minutes later he entered the building and introduced himself to the receptionist. The middle-aged woman invited him to take a seat, asked if he'd like a cup of coffee, and said Mr. Stevens would be with him in a few minutes.

As Jim sat in a straight-backed chair, holding a mug of coffee in his hands, he wished Linda were with him. Would the lawyer be reluctant to hand the boy over to Jim without meeting his wife first? Would the child willingly go with Jim, or would he make a fuss?

I sure am glad I bought that car seat for the baby before we left Washington. I'm so nervous, I'd probably have forgotten to get one if we'd waited to buy it until we got here.

Jim was more than a little anxious about becoming a father. After eight years of marriage, he and Linda had developed a pleasant routine.

Their whole life was about to change, and he hoped it would be for the better and that he wouldn't regret his decision to adopt this little one-year-old boy.

"Mr. Scott?"

Jim's thoughts came to a halt, and he looked up. A tall man with thinning gray hair and rimless glasses offered him a halfhearted smile.

Jim stood and extended his hand. "You must be Carl Stevens."

"That's right." The man glanced around. "Where's your wife? Linda, isn't that her name?"

"She's at the hotel with a bad headache."

The lawyer raised his eyebrows, but before he could ask any questions, Jim quickly added, "It's just a tension headache. She'll be fine in a couple hours."

"I see. Well, please come into my office." The older man led the way, and Jim followed.

When they entered his office, Mr. Stevens nodded toward a chair. "Please, have a seat."

As he sat down, Jim scanned the room. He and Carl Stevens seemed to be alone. He cleared his throat. "Excuse me, sir, but where's our baby? Will I be meeting the child's mother?"

The lawyer took a seat in the leather chair behind his desk and leaned forward, his hands tightly clasped. "There's been a change in plans."

"Change in plans? What do you mean?" Jim's heartbeat picked up momentum, and a trickle of sweat rolled down his forehead. He didn't like the fact that there was no mother or baby waiting to greet him, and Mr. Stevens's grim look gave no comfort, either.

"Shelby, the boy's mother, phoned me this morning."

"And?"

"I'm sorry to say she's changed her mind."

"About the adoption?" Jim's face heated, and it was all he could do to remain seated.

The lawyer nodded solemnly. "I'm afraid so, and as you already know, she has the right to do that."

Jim jumped up. "But she can't back out now! Linda and I were counting on this adoption. We've come a long way to get the boy."

"I'm aware of that, but you knew there was a chance this could happen. I'm sure your lawyer advised you of the birth mother's rights."

"Yes, he did, but we hadn't heard anything to the contrary since we signed the papers on our end, so we assumed—"

"I'm sorry, Mr. Scott. I'm sure once you explain the details to your lawyer, he will try to find you another child."

Jim trembled as he fought for control. "What details? Why did the birth mother change her mind at the last minute? I need to have something to tell my wife when I show up without the baby."

Mr. Stevens nodded toward the vacant chair. "Please be seated, and I'll explain."

Jim remained firmly planted in front of the desk with his arms folded.

The lawyer shrugged and took a sip of his coffee. "Shelby said after thinking it over, she's not able to part with her son. She's had him a whole year and has grown quite attached."

"Then why in thunder was she planning to give him up for adoption?"

"If you wish to hear the rest of the story, then I insist you calm down."

Jim drew in a deep breath and sank to the chair. "I'm listening."

"The birth mother and the baby have already bonded, and she feels her son will be better off with her."

"That's ridiculous! What can an unwed mother give a child that my wife and I can't?"

"In a material way, probably nothing, but she does have a mother's love to offer her son."

"We would have loved him." Jim clenched his fingers until they were digging into the palms of his hands. "I own a successful painting business. We could give the boy a good upbringing, and he would lack nothing in the way of material things."

"I'm sure that's true, which is exactly why your lawyer should have no trouble finding you another child."

"So that's it then? There's nothing more to be said?"

"No. I'm sorry."

As Jim stood, a sense of defeat crept into his soul and wrapped itself tightly around his heart. How could he face Linda and tell her they had no son? There would be no grandbaby to show off to his folks in Ohio. The truth was, there might never be.

Without another word, Jim stormed out of the lawyer's office, slamming the door behind him. When he climbed into his van and drove away, it felt like a fifty-five-gallon drum of paint rested on his shoulders. He headed out of Bel Air, up Interstate 1, and onto Highway 222 toward Pennsylvania, wondering what he could tell Linda that might soften the blow.

He gripped the steering wheel and clenched his teeth. "If there's a God in heaven, why would He have allowed this to happen?"

Two hours later, when Jim drove into Lancaster County, he was still fuming. "I need to get myself calmed down before I go back to the hotel." He rolled down his window, but a blast of hot, humid air hit him full in the face.

Snapping on the air conditioner, he turned off the main road and drove aimlessly along the backcountry roads. Over a covered bridge, past several Amish farms, he went farther and farther. A sign nailed to a fence at the end of a driveway caught his attention: HOMEMADE ROOT BEER—$3.00 A GALLON.

He turned in. "Root beer won't solve my problems, but it might take care of my thirst."

Since Zach was happily crawling around on the clean floor, Naomi decided to tackle the kitchen cupboards. The girls had finished cleaning their bedroom and were downstairs in the cellar gathering canning jars, which would be put to use next week.

Naomi pulled out a step stool and was carrying it to the cupboard when she heard a horn honk.

"Ach! Why now?" She turned toward the door and was about to open it, when Zach let out a howl. Her first thought was to ignore him, but then she remembered her sisters weren't able to watch the little guy while she waited on the customer.

Scooping Zach and his small quilt into her arms, Naomi grabbed a tissue from her apron pocket and swiped it across his nose. The horn blared again, and she hurried outside.

An English man stood near the picnic table.

"Can I help ya?" she asked, balancing Zach on her hip.

"I was wondering if you have any cold root beer."

Naomi nodded. "There's some in the house."

"Do you sell it by the glass or only in gallon jugs?"

"Just in jugs, but I'd be happy to give you a paper cup if you're wantin' to drink some now."

The man looked awfully tense, but he did return her smile. "Cute baby you've got there. Is it a boy or girl?"

"He's my youngest brother. Just turned one in April." She plopped Zach in the center of the picnic table, wrapping the quilt around his bare legs. "He weighs a ton, and I'll sure be glad when he starts walkin'."

"Do your folks have many children?" the man asked.

"My mother was hit by a car and died when this little guy was only two months old. That left eight kinner—I mean, kids—for my dad to raise."

He raised his eyebrows. "That's too bad about your mother."

Naomi was about to comment, but a loud shriek caught her attention. "That must be one of my sisters. I'm guessing our crazy goose is chasing one of them again. As soon as I see what's up, I'll be right back with your cold root beer." She dashed off, leaving Zach on the picnic table.

Jim waited patiently for the young woman to return with the root beer, the whole time keeping an eye on the diaper-clad boy sitting in the center of the picnic table. At first the child never moved, but after a few minutes, he began to squirm.

"Sit still, little guy, or you might fall," Jim said.

When the baby grabbed hold of his blanket, scooted to the edge of the table, and tried to climb down, Jim's heart slammed into his chest. "No, no, little boy. You'd better stay put until your sister gets back."

The child's legs dangled precariously over the edge of the table, and Jim knew if he didn't do something, the kid would fall. He grabbed the boy around the waist and lifted him into his arms.

The baby giggled and kicked his chubby feet as a blob of drool rolled down his chin.

Jim grabbed the edge of the colorful quilt and blotted the boy's face with it. "There, that's better, isn't it?" He looked back at the house. *Where is that girl, and what could be taking her so long? Does she think I came here to buy root beer or baby-sit her brother?*

When the child burrowed his downy head into Jim's chest, his heart welled with an emotion he'd never felt before. *So this is what it feels like for a father to hold his son.*

Jim cast another quick glance at the house. All was quiet, and not a soul was in sight. With no thought of the consequences, Jim made an impulsive decision. He whirled around and dashed for the car.

Jerking open the back door, Jim slipped the child into the car seat and buckled him in. He glanced at the house again, and seeing that the coast was clear, he hopped into the driver's side. He slammed the door, turned on the ignition, then sped out of the yard.

CHAPTER 10

Inside the kitchen, Naomi found her sisters standing in the middle of a big mess. Broken glass and some of last year's peaches were splattered on the floor. Nancy swept at it with a broom, while Mary Ann sat at the table, sobbing.

"What happened here? I cleaned this floor once already." Naomi pointed to the sticky linoleum. "I thought you two were supposed to be bringing up jars from the cellar for canning."

"We were, but Mary Ann wanted some peaches, and even though I said no, she took a jar anyway," Nancy said.

Naomi turned to face her youngest sister. "How come?"

"I—I—was hungry, and seein' all those jars of fruit made my stomach want food." Mary Ann hiccupped. "I cut my hand on the glass when I tried to pick up the pieces."

It was then that Naomi noticed Mary Ann's hand was wrapped in a napkin and there was blood seeping through. Naomi hurried to her younger sister and gently took her hand. "You'd better let me take a look at that."

"Don't make it hurt more." Mary Ann's lower lip quivered.

"I'll be careful." When Naomi pulled the napkin aside, the child winced. "This needs some antiseptic and a bandage." She clicked her tongue. "Don't think it's gonna need any stitches, though."

Mary Ann sniffed. "I'm glad. I don't wanna go to the hospital; that's for sure."

Naomi nodded at Nancy. "As soon as you get the glass picked up, would you mind gettin' a jug of cold root beer from the refrigerator?

I've got a customer outside waiting."

"Jah, okay."

As Nancy finished her job, Naomi led Mary Ann upstairs to the bathroom, where the first-aid supplies were kept.

When they returned to the kitchen a short time later, the floor was still a mess and Nancy was gone.

Probably took the root beer out like I told her. Naomi grabbed a mop from the utility closet and tackled the sticky floor. "Is there no end to my work today?" she muttered.

The back door opened, and Nancy sauntered in, holding a jug of root beer and looking kind of miffed. "You sent me outside for nothing. There was no customer waitin'."

"Sure there was. He asked for cold root beer, and I told him there was some in the house. Maybe he's in his car." Naomi grabbed the jug of root beer from Nancy and handed her the mop. "Finish this up while I go check."

When Naomi turned, she stubbed her bare toe on the rung of a chair. "Ach!" She limped out the back door and around the side of the house.

When she reached the front yard, Naomi came to a halt. The man was gone, and there was no car in the driveway. "Guess he got tired of waitin'." Her gaze swung back to the picnic table, and she felt the blood drain from her face. Zach was gone, and so was his quilt.

Naomi's stomach clenched as a wisp of fear curled around her heart. She set the jug on the picnic table, willing herself to breathe. *It's okay. Zach's here someplace. He just climbed down from the picnic table and crawled off.*

"Zach! Where are you, baby?" She scanned the yard and strained to hear anything that might give some indication that her little brother was nearby. "He has to be here—just has to be." The only living thing in sight was a chicken wandering up the driveway.

Naomi's knees, decidedly unsteady, threatened to buckle beneath her. She clutched her midsection and held herself in order to keep from collapsing. *Why was I so stupid? I should never have left Zach sitting on the picnic table with a stranger. What am I gonna tell Papa if I can't find him?*

Ignoring the pain in her foot from her stubbed toe, Naomi rushed back to the house, calling her sisters to come quickly.

Nancy ran out the front door. "Was is letz, Naomi? You look upset."

"Zach's missing, that's what's wrong," Naomi panted.

Mary Ann followed Nancy onto the porch, her dark eyes huge as saucers. "What do you mean, he's missin'?"

Naomi swallowed hard as a raw ache settled in her stomach. "I left him on the picnic table when I came inside to get cold root beer for the man and to see which of you was screaming." She pointed to the table. "But he's gone now. I don't see him anywhere."

Nancy glanced around the yard. "Who was the customer, Naomi? Was it someone we know?"

Naomi shook her head. "It was an English man."

"How come you didn't bring Zach along when you came to the house? What made you leave him all alone?"

Nancy's question was nearly Naomi's undoing. Guilt clung to her like a fly trapped in a spider's web, and tears she'd been fighting to keep under control rimmed her eyes. "I wasn't thinkin' straight. When I heard the scream, all I could think of was getting to the house to see what happened." She shook her head. "I never dreamed Zach would try and climb down or crawl off somewhere while I was gone. Besides, he wasn't alone. I figured the English man would see that Zach stayed put."

Nancy tipped her head and gave Naomi a look that sent shivers up her spine. "How do ya know the boppli crawled away?"

"He sure enough didn't walk, unless he's learned something new without us knowing." Naomi was in no mood for these silly questions. They needed to find Zach, and she knew it had better be before Papa got home.

Naomi's shoulders were tense, and a jolt of pain shot up her neck. "I need you two to help me look for him. He couldn't have gone far."

For the next half hour, the girls searched in the garden, the woodshed, the chicken coop, and all through the house, even though Naomi didn't see how Zach could have crawled there without her or one of the sisters seeing him.

With a sigh of resignation, she finally sent Nancy out to the fields to get the brothers. They needed more help looking.

After Naomi explained to Matthew how she'd left Zach on the picnic table, everyone spread out, searching a second time in every nook and cranny and calling Zach's name.

"I'm hitching up the buggy," Matthew announced. "I'll look for Zach along the road."

"Come now," Naomi said with irritation. "There's no way he would have crawled up the driveway. Not with the sharp rocks and all."

"Did you ever think maybe that English man took him?" Norman said, squinting and looking at Naomi like she didn't have half a brain.

Reality settled over Naomi like a dreary fog. She didn't want to acknowledge the possibility that her little brother had been kidnapped. "The man seemed so nice, and—"

"Did you get a good look at the car he was driving?" Jake asked.

The thought that Zach could have been taken by the English man pierced Naomi to the core of her soul, and her head began to spin. She grabbed hold of the porch railing. "I—uh—think it was a van, but I can't be sure. It could have been a station wagon or even a truck."

"Didn't you see it parked in the driveway? Think, Naomi. Surely you must have noticed."

Matthew's words weighed on Naomi like a sack of grain. "I—I did see it but barely took notice. I'm not sure if it was a van or not, and I don't even know the color of the vehicle."

"Then I suppose you didn't pay attention to the license plate, either?" This question came from Norman.

Naomi's only response was a slow shake of her head.

"Well, did ya see what direction the car was headed when it left?" Matthew asked.

She blew out her breath. "Now how could I have noticed when I was inside the house when it left? I already told you, Matthew."

"I'm goin' out to search the roads just the same." Matthew turned to Norman. "You'd better come along, and Jake can stay here and keep looking."

As she headed for the barn to look one more time, a sense of dread weighed heavily on Naomi's shoulders. How she wished she could erase what had happened and start her day over again. She would have done everything differently if she'd only known the way things would turn out.

"Oh, Lord," she prayed, "please keep my little brother safe, and help us find him real soon."

Jim glanced in the rearview mirror. No police cars. No Amish buggies in pursuit.

If I get caught, I'll be arrested for kidnapping. If I go back to the hotel empty-handed, Linda will be devastated. He gripped the steering wheel with determination. *Just keep on driving, and don't think about what you've done.*

The child in the backseat gurgled, and Jim turned his head for a brief look. "You okay, little guy?" Could it have been fate that took him to the Amish farm for root beer? After all, he needed a baby, and that family had plenty of kids to go around. The little boy was just one more mouth to feed, and he didn't even have a mother. *Maybe I did them a favor by taking the baby off their hands.*

When he caught another glimpse of the boy, his thoughts turned to more expedient matters. "Clothes. The kid's gonna need to be wearing more than a diaper before I take him to see Linda. Otherwise, she'll ask a bunch of questions."

A short time later, Jim pulled into the parking lot of a Wal-Mart store. As soon as he turned off the engine, he hopped out of the car and went around to open the back door. The baby giggled when Jim lifted him out of the car seat. "Sure are a trusting little fellow, aren't you?" Not once since Jim grabbed the boy off the picnic table had the baby cried or even fussed. In fact, the baby seemed perfectly at ease with Jim, which only confirmed in his mind that he'd done the right thing by taking the child.

"Out you go," Jim said as he hoisted the baby into his arms. "We're off to do some shopping, then you're going to meet your new mom."

It had been a long day, and Abraham was eager to get home. A few minutes ago, he'd sent Samuel out back where they kept the horse, telling him to give the animal a couple of apples. Abraham would close the store at five, then go out to hitch the horse to the buggy. They'd be home in half an hour or so, then he would tell the family about the campout he'd planned for tonight.

At two minutes to five, Abraham turned down the kerosene lamps he used to light his place of business. He'd just gotten to the last one when someone entered the store. It was Virginia Meyers, his least favorite customer.

"Hello, Mr. Fisher," she called with a wave of her hand. "Is Naomi here?"

He shook his head. "She and the girls stayed home today to sell root beer and do some cleanin' and such."

She pursed her pink lips and gave her ponytail a flip. "That's too bad. I was hoping to speak with her."

Abraham moved toward the young English woman. "Mind if ask what about?"

"Just girl stuff. You know—stamps and things."

Abraham wasn't sure why, but he didn't believe her. He had a feeling Virginia wanted to talk to Naomi about more than just rubber stamps. He'd heard the two of them a time or two and gotten the gist of the conversation on more than one occasion. Virginia wanted to show Naomi the world—her modern, English world. As far as he knew, Naomi had declined the invitations to do something fun, and he prayed she always would.

"Is there something I can help ya with?" he asked, feeling more impatient by the minute. "I'm about to close, so if you're needin' something, then you'd best hurry and get it."

She glanced around the store. "No new stamps yet, I take it."

"Nope."

"Okay then. Tell Naomi I dropped by."

"Right, Virginia."

"It's Ginny. Remember?"

He shrugged his shoulders. "Ginny then."

"Guess I'd better get back to the restaurant. The supper crowd will probably be filing in by now. See you later, Mr. Fisher." Ginny bounded out the door, and Abraham heaved a sigh of relief.

He grabbed his hat from the wall peg, locked the front door, and headed for the back of the store.

Thirty minutes later, Abraham pulled the buggy into his yard, and Samuel jumped down. "Run inside and tell Naomi she can put supper on," he told the boy. "I'll get the horse unhitched and be right in."

"Sure, Papa." Samuel scampered toward the house, and Abraham went around to the front of the horse. He'd only begun to take the harness off when Naomi came running toward him with the older boys, Mary Ann, and Nancy right behind her.

"Hey, there!" he said with a smile. "Guess what I've got planned for tonight?"

"Papa, I think you'd better hear what I have to say before you share any plans," Naomi said with a catch in her voice. She looked downright flustered, and Abraham wondered if she'd had a rough day with the kinner.

"Is everything okay here? Did the girls do their work as you asked?"

Tears splashed onto Naomi's cheeks, and she grasped his arm.

"Daughter, what is it? Tell me what's wrong."

"It's Zach, Papa." There was a note of panic in her voice, and Abraham steeled himself for the worst.

"What about the boy? Is he sick?"

"Please, take a seat at the picnic table, and I'll tell you everything."

He shook his head. "Tell me now."

"Papa, I think it might be best if you sit down," Matthew interjected.

Abraham looked at Naomi, then back at Matthew. They both had awfully grave looks on their faces. He was sure something terrible had happened in his absence, and he dreaded hearing the news.

Stumbling over to the picnic table, he dropped to the bench. "Tell me now, and be quick about it."

Naomi rattled off a story about how she'd been asked by an English man to get some cold root beer and said she'd heard one of the girls scream and how, fearing Hildy the goose might have been chasing them, she had left Zach sitting on the picnic table while she rushed off to see about things.

"When I discovered Mary Ann's hand was cut, I sent Nancy outside with the cold root beer while I tended the wound. When Nancy came back in, she said the man was gone." Naomi took a deep breath and rushed on. "Then I went out to have a look-see, and sure enough the man wasn't there." She gulped. "The worst part of all was when I realized Zach was missing, too."

Abraham's eyes darted back and forth. "Is this true?"

Matthew nodded. "I'm afraid so. Naomi thought Zach might have climbed down from the picnic table and crawled off, so she sent Nancy to the fields to get me, Norman, and Jake." He swallowed hard, and his

Adam's apple bobbed up and down. "We searched and searched but couldn't find Zach anywhere."

"Yeah, we even drove out on the road a piece," Norman added.

Abraham sat there several seconds, feeling as though he were in a daze. This couldn't be happening. It had to be a dream—a horrible nightmare. Soon he'd wake up and find everything as it had been that morning.

He shook his head as though it might help him think straight. "That man took our boppli, didn't he?"

No one said anything, but everyone nodded.

Abraham stood on trembling legs. "Matthew, you'd better go to our English neighbors and ask them to phone the police."

CHAPTER 11

As Jim pulled into the hotel parking lot, his head swirled with confusion. He'd been told a few hours ago that the son they planned to adopt was no longer available—the mother had changed her mind. Then, in a moment of desperation, he'd stolen an Amish baby right off the picnic table where his older sister had left him sitting. Since she hadn't returned right away, it had been so easy. It almost seemed as if she had no intention of returning. This only confirmed in Jim's mind that his going there had been predestined. He and Linda were meant to have the boy, and he would be better off living with them than he would be growing up Amish. The young woman had told Jim her mother died and there were eight children in the family. As far as Jim was concerned, that was too many for one man to raise alone.

He climbed out of the van and went around back to retrieve his new son. "Your mommy and I can give you so much," he said as he unbuckled the boy's seat belt and started to take him out of the car seat. The Amish baby quilt was tucked around the child's legs, and Jim removed it. "Can't leave this bit of evidence for Linda to see. She'd ask a ton of questions for sure."

For some reason, when Jim had dumped the boy's cloth diaper into the garbage at Wal-Mart, he couldn't throw the quilt out. He'd been tempted to, but it didn't seem right to pitch the child's only link with his past life.

I'll hide the quilt for now and decide what to do with it later. Jim set the baby back in the car seat, grabbed the blanket, and stuffed it inside his toolbox behind the backseat.

The child started to wail.

"Okay, okay, I'm coming." Jim lifted the baby into his arms and grabbed the bag of diapers he'd purchased. A few minutes later, he inserted his key card into their hotel room door and let himself in. *I wonder if Linda's awake and feeling better.*

He was pleased to see that she was up, sitting on the small couch in front of the television. She jumped up when she saw Jim and ran to greet him.

"You're back—with our baby!" Linda reached for the child, and Jim felt relief when the boy went willingly to her.

Her eyes filled with tears. "He's even more beautiful than I'd imagined." She returned to the couch, muted the TV, and hugged the boy. "I take it everything went well?"

Jim sat beside her. "Without a hitch."

"Did you get all the paperwork? His birth certificate and the adoption papers?"

Jim froze. In his haste to pull off this little charade, he hadn't given any thought to the legal papers they might need. If the baby didn't have a birth certificate, how could they enroll him in school?

Linda can homeschool. Yes, she should do that anyway. She's home all day, and it will be better for the boy to learn from her. Still, when the child grows up and wants to get a driver's license, passport, or marriage license, he'll need some proof of his identity.

Jim clenched his teeth. Why hadn't he thought about all this before?

"Jim, you didn't answer my question about the papers."

He gently squeezed Linda's arm. "Not to worry. It's all taken care of. The adoption papers and new birth certificate for our boy will be mailed to my paint shop address."

"Why there and not our home?"

"Because that's where our safe is kept, Linda."

"Oh, right."

I'll have to see my friend Hank when we get home. He has connections, and I'm sure he'll be able to get exactly what I need. We can apply for the baby's Social Security number as soon as I get a phony birth certificate.

"Let's call him Jimmy," Linda said, breaking into Jim's thoughts.

"Sure, honey. Whatever you want."

"Are you ready to go shopping now?"

He blinked. "Huh?"

"Shopping. You said we came to Lancaster County so I could look for a quilt and tour Amish country. My headache is gone, and I'm ready to do some sightseeing." Linda kissed the top of the baby's head. "Besides, he's sucking on my hand, which probably means he's hungry. We'll need to get him some food, Jim."

Jim groped for the right words. Shopping and sightseeing was not a good idea—at least not here, where the baby might be recognized. What if the boy's sister had gotten a good look at his van? The police could be out looking for him.

"We can stop somewhere for some food for Jimmy, but I think we should head for Ohio today. Right away, in fact."

Linda looked at him like he'd lost his mind. "You're kidding."

He shook his head and stood. "I'm anxious to show Mom and Dad our new son."

"What about the Amish quilt you promised me?"

"You can get one in Holmes County. I'm sure Mom will know the best places to look."

"You think so?"

"Yep. Now let's pack our things and get going."

As Linda stood, she held Jimmy against her chest. "You make it sound critical that we leave. Is there something wrong, Jim? Something you're not telling me?"

Each lie Jim told seemed to roll right off his tongue, yet each seemed to complicate things that much more. He leaned over and kissed her cheek. "Of course not, honey. I'm just excited to see my folks and have them meet Jimmy."

She gazed lovingly at the baby. "He's so cute, but I wonder why his hair is cut so funny. It almost looks like a bowl was set on his head and someone cut around it."

Jim gulped. "Uh—it's—probably the boy's birth mother couldn't afford a real haircut."

"That makes sense." Linda touched the back of Jimmy's ear. "Look at the cute little heart-shaped birthmark."

Jim only glanced at the red blotch. "Uh-huh. Interesting." He hurried to the closet and retrieved their suitcase.

"My parents will want to see him soon, too. Can we go to Idaho after we get home?" Linda asked.

"Sure, but not right away. I've got a business to run, you know. After taking this much time off work, there'll be lots for me to do."

Linda nodded. "Okay, but let's try to make a trip there as soon as we can."

"Right. I promise we'll do that." Jim plunked the suitcase on the end of the bed. "I'll pack our clothes, and you can get the cosmetic bag ready."

"What about the baby? Who's going to hold him if we're both packing?"

"Why don't you put him on the bed?"

"But he might fall off."

Jim's mind flashed to the moment the baby had been left sitting in the middle of the picnic table. He'd tried to climb down and would have probably fallen if Jim hadn't been there to catch him. "Put him on the floor then. He can do a little exploring while we get ready to go."

"I wonder if he can walk. He's a year old, and many children walk by their first birthday. Did the mother say whether he's walking yet or not?"

"Uh—no, she didn't say." *The boy's sister mentioned that he's not walking yet, but I sure can't tell Linda that.* "If you put him on the floor, we'll find out if he can walk."

She did as he suggested, and the boy crawled off to investigate Jim's slippers, sitting on the floor near the bed. "I guess he either can't walk or doesn't want to right now."

He shrugged. "Guess so."

Linda gave Jim a lingering kiss. "Thank you for coming all this way so we could adopt our precious child."

He swallowed around the lump in his throat. What he'd done was illegal in the eyes of the law, but as far as he was concerned, it had been the right thing. Jim had never seen Linda so happy. She was fairly glowing.

Naomi took a seat in the rocker next to Zach's playpen and tried to pray. The police had come awhile ago, followed by reporters from the local newspaper. With no information about the vehicle the man had been driving, the police said it would be difficult to track him down. Not only that, but the Fishers had no pictures of Zach, since it went against their beliefs to own a camera or have their picture taken. Naomi knew a few Amish teenagers who owned cameras and kept them in secret, but Papa would have punished anyone in his family who tried something like that.

"Zach ain't never comin' back, is he?"

Naomi jerked her head. Nancy stood by the back door with tears coursing down her cheeks. Mary Ann stood beside her, looking like she'd lost her best friend.

"Things aren't lookin' so good, but we have to pray believing." Even as she said the words, Naomi knew she didn't believe them. She'd been praying all afternoon and into the evening, and it hadn't brought Zach home.

The tension Naomi felt in her neck earlier mounted with each passing moment. She was scared. Even more so than when her mother was hit by a car and she worried Mama might not live. If God had done nothing to prevent her mamm from stepping into the road to retrieve some mail, what made Naomi think He would bring her little brother home?

"Papa's still outside talking with the police and those newspaper reporters," Nancy said, moving across the room. She dropped into a chair and leaned her elbows on the table. Mary Ann followed and did the same. "They want to take pictures of the family, but he won't let 'em."

"That's right. Papa said, 'Absolutely no,' " Mary Ann put in.

Naomi shook her head. "I wouldn't think he'd agree to anyone takin' pictures." Tears clouded her vision. She was the cause of all this. *How can I go on living, knowing it was because of my carelessness Zach was taken? What if I never see my little brother again? What if something awful has happened to him?*

Naomi remembered reading an article awhile back in the Amish newspaper, *The Budget*. It told about two little Mennonite girls who'd become trapped inside a cedar chest. Three days later, they were found smothered to death.

She feared the worst for her baby brother, and visions of Zach being mistreated threatened to suffocate her. What if the English man planned to hurt the boy? She knew that many children who'd been kidnapped were either killed or physically abused. She'd read accounts of such things in the newspaper. There were many evil people in the world, and for all she knew, that English man who'd asked for root beer could be one of the worst.

Naomi spotted Zach's bib draped over his high chair. It looked the same as always, as though Zach would be sitting in the chair at supper, wearing the bib tied behind his chubby little neck. She could almost taste the sweetness of her little brother, but he wouldn't be here tonight. Truth was, he might never sit in that high chair again.

A renewed sense of loss rocked Naomi, and she doubled over, letting her head fall onto her knees. Her world was spinning out of control, and she was powerless to stop it. *Oh, Zach, my sweet little brother, what I have done to you? What have I done to this family?*

Someone touched her head, and she looked up.

"Don't cry, Naomi. Please, don't." The sorrowful look on Mary Ann's face only made Naomi feel worse.

"Ball wollt's besser geh—soon it will go better," Nancy said as she left the table.

Naomi wanted to be brave in front of her younger sisters. She wanted to believe things would go better. She wished she could offer words of comfort and be strong for the others. It was her job to look after the family. She'd promised Mama she would, and now it seemed she was incapable of caring for anyone. She had proven that by leaving Zach on the picnic table.

Oh, Mama, I've let you down. I'm so sorry.

The back door squeaked open, and Papa marched into the room. She could see the pain behind his dark eyes and knew she was the cause.

"Are the reporters and policemen gone?" Naomi asked.

He nodded curtly and stalked across the room, stopping a few feet from where she sat in the rocker. "Matthew and Norman are out on the road looking again, but I'm sure it's no use. Zach's gone. They won't find him."

The look of defeat on Papa's face was nearly Naomi's undoing.

"Where are Jake and Samuel?" Nancy asked. "I thought they'd be asking for something to eat by now."

"Yeah, I'm gettin' hungry, too." Mary Ann glanced at Naomi. "When are ya plannin' to start supper?"

Papa shot the girl a look that sent shivers up Naomi's spine. "How can you think about food at a time like this? Don't ya care that your baby brother's been kidnapped?"

Naomi stood. "Mary Ann's only a child, Papa. She doesn't fully understand what's happened today, and I'm sure she didn't mean she doesn't care."

She cringed when her father shook his fist and hollered, "This is all your fault, Naomi! You were supposed to be in charge of the kinner, and leavin' Zach outside with a stranger was downright *schlappich*."

"I know I was careless, Papa, but I—"

He shook his head. "You weren't just careless. What you did was *narrisch*."

"Naomi ain't crazy, Papa," Mary Ann defended.

He whirled around, and for a moment, Naomi was afraid he would strike the child. "When I want your opinion, I'll ask for it! I didn't say Naomi was narrisch. I said what she *did* was crazy."

Nancy grabbed hold of his shirtsleeve. "What are we gonna do now, Papa? How can we make things right?"

He released a deep moan. "The newspaper is plannin' to run a story about our missing boy, so all we can do is pray and hope the English man brings Zach home or that somebody saw him drive away from our place and can identify the vehicle." He shook his head. "I fear the worst. If I ever see my baby again, it'll be a miracle."

The room began to spin, and Naomi grabbed for the chair to steady herself. *"Der Herr, bilf mir*—the Lord help me. Please, help us all."

CHAPTER 1 2

Naomi sat in the rocking chair long after Papa went upstairs. He'd said some hurtful things earlier, yet she felt she deserved every cutting word. It was her fault Zach was missing, and if they didn't get the baby back, she would never forgive herself. As much as it hurt, she couldn't blame her daed or anyone else in the family if they chose not to forgive her.

"Naomi, I'm gettin' awful hungry," Mary Ann complained. "Can't we please have some supper?"

Naomi stood as though in a daze and moved slowly to the kitchen cupboard. "Jah, okay. Maybe some sandwiches then." She would feed the younger ones, but she doubted Papa would want anything to eat. Truth was, she had no appetite for food, either, and wondered if she would ever feel like eating again. Her body felt paralyzed with grief. She didn't want to eat, talk, or even move, yet she knew she must do all three.

If Zach comes home, everything will be all right, she told herself. *I need another chance to prove I'm responsible. That's all I want. Just one more chance; is it too much to ask?*

Naomi's heart pounded when she heard a horse and buggy trot into the yard. Were her brothers back so soon? Had they found Zach? Oh, she hoped it was so.

She lifted the shade and strained to see who was outside. It was getting dark, and the yard, lit only by the moon, was full of shadows.

A knock sounded at the back door, and Naomi realized it wasn't Matthew or Norman. They would never have knocked.

"Want me to get it?" asked Nancy, who had begun setting the table.

"If you wish."

A few seconds later, the door opened, and Marvin Hoffmeir stepped into the room.

Naomi squeezed her eyes shut as she leaned heavily against the cupboard. *What's he doing here, especially at a time like this when our world's been turned upside down? We don't need company now; that's for certain sure.*

"Naomi, are you okay?" Marvin asked.

She forced her eyes open and turned to face him. "Something terrible happened here today."

He nodded, and she noticed his blond hair was sweat-soaked around the edges where it met his straw hat. Marvin was two years younger than Caleb and had the same color hair, but his eyes were dark brown, not clear blue like his brother's.

"I know about Zach," Marvin said. "I ran into Matthew and Norman on the road when I was returning from the bus station."

"What were you doin' at the bus station?" Nancy asked.

Marvin removed his hat. "Took Caleb there so's he could go to Berlin, Ohio. Our cousin Henry has a buggy shop there, and he wrote a letter saying he got in some old parts he thought Caleb might like to have." He took a step toward Naomi. "Sure sorry to hear about Zach, and I wanted to drop by and say so."

"Danki. It's appreciated," Naomi murmured.

"Wish there was something I could say to make your family's pain a bit less."

"You can pray," Mary Ann piped up. "It's what we're all doin'; ain't that right, Naomi?"

Naomi opened her mouth to respond, but her dad's booming voice cut her off before she could speak. "What are you doin' here, Marvin?" Papa asked as he marched into the room. "This isn't a good time to come calling."

Marvin explained about running into Matthew and Norman on

the road. "Matthew mentioned how upset everyone was, and I thought maybe I could offer some words of comfort or maybe help in some way."

"Who went and made you the new bishop?" Papa asked mockingly.

Naomi flinched. She could hardly believe her father had said such a thing. "There's no call to be rude, Papa."

"It's okay. I understand," Marvin said. "You've had a terrible shock today."

"You know nothin' about what we've been through!" Papa shouted. "My boppli's been snatched by a stranger. Can you understand the pain of losin' your son? Well, can ya, boy?"

Marvin shook his head. "No, but my brother Andy ran a nail through his thumb the other day, and—"

"A hurt hand is nothin' compared to our loss. I think you'd better head home. We don't need your sympathy." Papa drew in a deep breath and clenched his fists at his sides. He was visibly shaking, and Naomi knew he was taking out his frustrations on Caleb's brother.

She took a few steps toward her father. "Papa, Marvin only wanted to offer his support. He knows we're upset and feels our pain, just as the others will when they hear what's happened."

Papa pulled out a chair at the table and lowered himself into it with a groan. "Jah, well, it ain't you I'm mad at, Marvin. Sorry for speakin' thataway."

Naomi swallowed around the lump in her throat. She knew *she* was the one her papa was angry with. He'd already made that clear enough. *Well, he can't be any angrier with me than I am with myself.* The pain of losing Zach was like having a sliver in her thumb. She'd felt its presence ever since she discovered her little brother was missing.

Marvin shuffled his feet a few times. "I—uh—guess I should get goin'."

"Wanna stay and have supper with us?" This came from Mary

Ann, who had taken a chunk of ham out of the refrigerator. "Naomi's gonna make sandwiches."

Naomi frowned at her youngest sister. "I never said that."

"Did, too."

"I did not. I only agreed to fix you something to eat. I never said what it would be." Naomi couldn't believe she was arguing with Mary Ann—and over something so petty. *What's wrong with me? I'm not thinking straight right now. I'm not myself at all. Maybe I did agree to make sandwiches and just don't remember.*

Naomi took the ham from her sister. "All right. I'll fix a plate of sandwiches." She glanced at the back door. "Matthew and Norman will probably be hungry when they get home, too."

Papa's fist pounded the table, clattering the silverware and almost toppling over the glasses. "This talk about food is ridiculous! Our Zach has been stolen, and all anyone can think about is eatin'? What's wrong with the lot of you?"

Mary Ann's lower lip quivered, and Nancy cringed. The children weren't accustomed to seeing their father so agitated. They weren't used to losing their brother, either, yet it had happened, and they would have to deal with it. Starving the children sure wasn't the way. Naomi knew that much.

Marvin cleared his throat, and Naomi swung her gaze back to him. She'd almost forgotten he was still here, what with all the fuss about sandwiches and Papa's angry outburst. "I—uh—appreciate the offer to stay for supper, but I need to get home. Mom will be expectin' me," Marvin mumbled.

"I'll see you to the door," Naomi said, moving in that direction.

He shook his head. "That's okay. I know my way out." Marvin took two steps, then looked back. It was as though he wanted to say something more but was afraid to say it. Maybe it was for the best. Everyone had said enough already.

"Good night, Marvin. It was kind of you to stop by," Nancy said, surprising Naomi and causing Papa to glare at her.

"Night," he mumbled. "I'll be prayin' for you. Please keep me and the family posted." With that said, Caleb's brother walked out the door, closing it quietly behind him.

Naomi turned to her father. "Papa, is it all right if I fix something for the girls to eat?"

He stood and headed for the back door. "Do whatever you like."

"Where ya goin'?" Mary Ann called.

He never replied, only slammed the door behind him.

Naomi's hands trembled as she reached inside the cupboard and retrieved a loaf of bread. This didn't make sense, her fixing supper as though it were any other night of the week, the brothers out combing the roads in hopes of finding Zach, and Papa outside probably ruing the day Naomi was born.

"I—I—don't know if I can do this," she whimpered.

"Here, let me help." Nancy took the bread from Naomi and buttered several slices. "Why don't you fix yourself a cup of herb tea? Might help to calm you down. Mama always said tea was like a soothing balm whenever she was tired or had a bad day."

Naomi didn't feel like drinking a cup of tea any more than she did eating a ham sandwich. All she wanted to do was reach into Zach's playpen, lift him into her arms, and drink in the sweetness of her little brother until she felt dizzy from the joy of holding him. She glanced at the playpen, filled only with a couple of Zach's homemade toys. The reality that they might never see him again hit her one more time. She stifled a sob and stumbled out of the room.

Caleb would be glad to get off the bus and stretch his legs. He had called Henry from the bus station in Lancaster to let him know what time he'd arrive in Dover and ask if he could arrange for him to get a ride to Berlin. It was nice Henry had a phone in his buggy shop. It was much easier to make contact that way.

"Too bad Pop's against the idea of me having one," he muttered.

"Were you talking to me?" the elderly woman who sat beside Caleb asked.

He'd thought she was asleep. Her eyes had been closed, so he figured. . . "I—um—sorry to disturb you. I've got a habit of talkin' to myself."

"That's all right," she said, pushing a wayward strand of silver gray hair back into place. "My husband, rest his soul, used to talk to himself all the time."

Caleb leaned his head against the seat back and closed his eyes. He didn't mean to be rude, but he wasn't in the mood to talk to anyone right now.

"You're one of those Plain people, aren't you?"

He opened his eyes. "Yes, ma'am. I'm Amish."

"Are you from Holmes County?"

"No, Lancaster County, Pennsylvania."

"But you're heading to Ohio?"

"Jah. My cousin has a buggy shop there."

"Isn't that interesting? Arnold, my late husband, used to own an old Student Buggy, made by G. & D. Cook & Co. Carriage Makers."

Caleb's ears perked up. "Is that so? I'm a buggy maker, too, and I also repair antique carriages."

"Really?"

Caleb nodded. "I bought a book on antique buggies the other day, and there was a picture of an antique Student Buggy in it. Looked a little like the open carriages we Amish sometimes drive."

"Do you make a good living selling buggies?" she asked.

"Fair to middlin'. Make enough so's I could support a wife and family." Caleb thought about Naomi. He sure wished she were free to court. He wished she didn't have to work so hard, either. Maybe when he got back to Pennsylvania, he'd finally get over to see her, like he'd planned on doing today. *Of course, I'd better wait 'til her daed isn't at home.*

Jim knew he was pushing hard, stopping less often than he usually did, but he was in a hurry to leave Pennsylvania and get to Ohio. They had stopped to get something for Jimmy to eat as soon as they left Lancaster County. Linda stocked up on formula and bought two baby bottles, not knowing if the boy had been weaned. She'd also purchased several jars of baby food, as well as some teething biscuits, juice, and a few outfits. She made a comment about how odd it seemed that the baby's real mother hadn't sent more than a package of diapers and one outfit with him.

I can hardly tell her the truth about that, Jim thought as he glanced in the rearview mirror. He hadn't seen any cops, or at least none had paid him any mind. That was good. Must mean no one had identified him or the van. Hopefully, he was in the clear.

As he took another look in the mirror, Jim caught a glimpse of Linda. She hummed while she stroked the baby's golden brown hair. She had insisted on riding in the back with the boy. "I can care for his needs better this way," she'd said when they left the hotel in Lancaster.

That was fine with Jim. It gave him a chance to think; and since Linda was preoccupied with the baby, she wouldn't be likely to pester him with a bunch of questions he didn't feel like answering.

Jim glanced at his watch. It was almost four o'clock. Pittsburgh was four hours from Lancaster, and they'd been traveling two hours, so they were halfway there. *Maybe we should stop for the night and get a hotel in Pittsburgh. We can have some dinner, get a good night's rest, and arrive at Mom and Dad's in Millersburg a few hours after breakfast.*

He smiled and turned on the radio. Everything was going to be fine. By this time tomorrow, they'd be sitting in his folks' living room, watching TV, and playing with their son.

CHAPTER 13

Naomi spent a fretful night. It didn't seem right trying to sleep when her baby brother wasn't in his crib across the room.

She awoke with a headache and wished she could stay in bed—wished, in fact, she could stay there forever and never have to deal with anything again. But she couldn't. Nancy was pounding on the door, telling her it was time to start breakfast. She rolled over and punched the pillow around her head.

"Naomi, are you awake?" Nancy knocked again. "Naomi?"

"I'm comin'. Just give me a few minutes to get dressed."

"Jah, okay. I'll go downstairs and get things started."

"Danki."

Naomi sat up and glanced at the baby's crib. It was empty. Same as it had been last night when she'd crawled into bed. "What have I done?" she moaned. "Life will never be the same without Zach."

Ten minutes later, Naomi entered the kitchen. Nancy was mixing pancake batter, and Mary Ann was setting the table. Zach was gone. His empty playpen was a constant reminder.

"I take it Papa and the brothers are still outside chorin'?" Naomi asked, grabbing a jug of milk from the refrigerator and forcing her mind off her missing brother.

"As far as I know," Nancy answered. "Haven't seen any of 'em this morning."

Naomi glanced at Mary Ann. She'd finished setting the table and stood beside Zach's empty high chair, staring at it as though he were sitting right there.

"You won't bring the boppli home by starin' at his chair." Naomi's voice sounded harsh, even to her own ears, but she seemed powerless to stop the cutting words.

Mary Ann hung her head. "It's my fault Zach's gone, and I'm afraid God's gonna punish me for it."

"It ain't your fault," Nancy hollered from across the room.

"That's right; it's not," Naomi agreed. "What would make you say such a thing, Mary Ann?"

The little girl kept her eyes downcast as she slid her bare toes back and forth across the linoleum. "If I hadn't dropped the jar of peaches and screamed 'cause I cut my hand, you might not have rushed into the house without Zach." She looked at Naomi with tears in her eyes. "And if you'd gone outside sooner, Zach might not have been kidnapped."

Before Naomi could voice her thoughts on the matter, Mary Ann spoke again. "I'm afraid, Naomi. Are you gonna let some Englisher take me, too?"

Naomi's mouth fell open. "What are you talking about?"

Mary Ann closed her eyes and drew in a shaky breath. "If you think I did a bad thing, you might want me to go away, same as Zach."

Her little sister's comment was nearly Naomi's undoing. She took hold of Mary Ann's arm, flopped into a chair, and lifted the child onto her lap. Rocking back and forth, Naomi let her tears flow. "It wasn't your fault, Mary Ann. I'm the one to blame, and I'll never let anyone take you away."

After a sleepless night, Abraham had gone to the barn before daylight, thinking he might get the animals fed and do a few other chores. How could he go to bed and rest when his youngest son was in the hands of a stranger? What did the Englisher want with Zach? Did he plan to hurt him? It happened to other children who were kidnapped; he'd read terrible things in the newspaper about little ones who'd been taken from their families and were abused by the abductor. Many had been found dead, with their little bodies mutilated beyond recognition.

Abraham trembled as he sank to his knees in front of a bale of hay. He bent into the pain that threatened to squeeze the life out of him. "Father in heaven, please keep my boy safe. Even if Zach never comes home, I pray You'll protect him from harm."

Tears coursed down Abraham's cheeks, and he swiped at them with the back of his hand. Yesterday afternoon he had hoped to start over with his family by having a surprise campout in the backyard. A few days ago, while praying and reflecting on God's Word, he'd come to the point of accepting Sarah's death and thought he could do better by his children. That had all changed now. He couldn't deal with the second tragedy that had befallen them. God could have prevented it from happening, same as He could have saved Sarah.

"This is your fault, Naomi," he wailed. "You were supposed to be watching the boy. I trusted you to care for my kinner, and look what happened." He sniffed deeply and nearly choked on his saliva. Naomi was in the house and couldn't hear his tirade, but he didn't care. His heart was full of bitterness, and she was the cause. "I'll bet you were thinking about Caleb Hoffmeir or that English girl, Virginia Meyers, instead of watchin' out for Zach. You probably don't care a mite for this family—thinkin' about yourself, that's all."

As the angry words spewed out of his mouth, Abraham grew even more tense. He clenched his teeth and fought for control. Deep in his soul, he knew Naomi did care for the family, yet he couldn't find it in his heart to forgive her carelessness. If Zach wasn't returned, Abraham didn't know if he could ever look at his oldest daughter again without feeling she was to blame for his misery.

"Sorry to disturb you, Papa, but I was wonderin' if you're about ready for breakfast? The bell rang a few minutes ago."

Abraham jerked upright at the sound of Jake's voice. "You go ahead, Son. I ain't hungry."

Jake moved closer to the spot where Abraham knelt. "You okay? Ya haven't hurt your back again, have you?"

Abraham remembered the last time his back had gone into spasm, and he'd been forced to crawl from the barn to the house. That had been painful, but nothing compared to the way he felt right now.

He made a fist and touched his chest. "Hurtin' here but no place else."

Jake's brown eyes revealed obvious concern. "I'll leave you to your prayin' then. That's all we can do, isn't it, Papa? Pray and ask God to bring Zach home."

Abraham nodded. "And to keep our little boy safe."

"Oh, look, Jim. There's a quilt shop across the street. Let's stop." Linda, still in the backseat with Jimmy, leaned forward and tapped Jim on the shoulder.

"I thought we'd go straight to Mom and Dad's. Besides, it's Sunday, and most of the shops are closed," Jim said as he kept driving. "You and Mom can go shopping tomorrow."

"I really want to stop now. It would feel good to stretch my legs, and I'd like your opinion on which quilt to get."

"Wouldn't you rather have Mom's opinion? She knows more about that kind of thing than I do."

"She wouldn't know how much money you're willing to let me spend."

Linda had a point. Mom would probably tell his wife to get whatever she wanted—that money was no object. It would be easy for her to say; it wasn't her money she'd be spending. Still, he thought it would be better if the women went shopping while he and Dad stayed home and visited over a cup of coffee or watched TV. They could keep an eye on the baby, too. Surely Linda didn't want to shop for a quilt while holding a fidgety child.

"Please, Jim," she pleaded. "Won't you turn around and head back to Fannie's Quilt Shop so I can see what they have in the window?"

"What about Jimmy?"

"What about him?"

"Wouldn't you rather shop tomorrow, without him?"

"No. I don't want to leave him alone."

"He wouldn't be alone. He'll be with me and Dad while you and Mom come to town."

They had entered the town of Berlin, and Jim had to stop for an Amish buggy that had pulled away from the curb. Seeing the buggy made Jim think of the Amish farm where he'd gone for root beer. Root beer he'd never gotten. He'd left with a child, instead.

"Jim, are you going to go back to that quilt shop or not?"

Linda's pleading voice pulled his thoughts aside, and he was grateful. No point dwelling on the past. Especially one he wasn't free to talk about.

"Okay, okay. Just let me look for a good place to turn around."

"It looks like there are a lot of tourists, doesn't it? Even for a Sunday," she remarked.

"Yeah, plenty of people like us who want to find something made by the Amish to take home." Linda would not only be taking an Amish quilt home after this trip, but an Amish baby, as well. She just didn't know it.

"I'll meet you at the Subway place on West Main Street," Caleb called to his cousin.

"Okay, but don't be late. Cleon, my driver, will be pickin' us up later this afternoon, and then we'll drive over to Dover so you can catch the bus."

Caleb waved at Henry and strolled up the sidewalk. He'd decided to take a walk before they ate and check out some of the shops in the area. He would have to sit for a long time on the bus, so stretching his legs beforehand would be good.

Caleb had arrived at Henry's last night, and they'd spent the evening getting caught up on one another's lives. Since today was an off-Sunday and there'd be no church, first thing this morning, they'd gone to the buggy shop to look at the antique parts Henry had recently acquired. Caleb chose to buy a set of wheels, some spokes and hubs, a couple of shaft bars, and one old seat that was sturdy but would need to be reupholstered. He'd have them shipped to his place; and if he decided to stay in Holmes County a couple more days, the parts would probably be waiting for him when he got home.

However, Henry said he had a lot of work to do this week, and Caleb was eager to get home, so he decided to catch the evening bus back to Pennsylvania. He should arrive in Lancaster early Monday morning.

As Caleb neared a store called "Fannie's Quilt Shop," he saw a young couple with a baby looking in the window.

He squinted against the glaring sun. *That little guy looks kind of like Zach Fisher. He's dressed in English clothes, but his hair is cut like an Amish baby's would be. Don't rightly see how it could be, though. Zach's at home with his family, whereas this baby has English parents.*

"Yes, honey, I promise to bring you back sometime tomorrow so you can buy a quilt," he overheard the man say to the woman.

Caleb stared at the baby a few more minutes, then finally moved on. *I'd better find myself somethin' cold to drink, 'cause this hot, humid weather must be gettin' to me. Naomi's baby brother dressed in English clothes, bein' held by English folks outside a shop in Ohio? No, it couldn't be. I'm just missing Naomi, that's all.*

CHAPTER 14

Naomi stood at the kitchen sink, washing dishes. It was hard to think about working at the store today, but she knew it would be expected of her. They had to make a living, and that wouldn't happen if they all stayed home worrying about Zach and blaming themselves for his disappearance. Of course, Naomi knew she was the only one to blame. She'd let everyone down—Mama most of all, since she hadn't kept her promise to care for the family. Naomi had failed miserably, and now she feared nothing would ever be the same.

As she placed the clean dishes into the drainer, Naomi's thoughts continued to spiral. Where was Zach now? Was he safe and being cared for, or had he been abandoned somewhere? Worse yet, could her baby brother have been murdered?

She shuddered. *Oh, Lord, give me a sense of peace about this. Some word—anything—that will let me know Zach is okay.*

The roar of a car's engine drove Naomi's thoughts to the back of her mind. She dried her hands on a towel and went to see who had driven into their yard.

Outside, Naomi spotted a police car, and Papa came running from the barn. Did the police have information about Zach? If so, she hoped it was good news.

Naomi stepped off the porch and hurried toward the car. "I'm sorry, Mr. Fisher," she heard one of the men say. "I'd like to say we're hot on the suspect's trail, but the truth is, there is no trail. We don't have a single lead on your son."

"Nothing a'tall?" Papa asked with a catch in his voice.

The policeman shook his head. "We spoke with all your neighbors, and no one saw anything out of the ordinary on Saturday. Some said they'd seen cars going in and out of your place, but nobody noticed an English man with a baby."

Papa's forehead wrinkled, and he stared down at his boots. "Guess it's hopeless then."

"It's not hopeless, Mr. Fisher. The local newspaper and TV station have run a story on the kidnapping, so we're hoping someone will come forward with helpful information."

"Without any pictures of your son or a good description of the man and his vehicle, it's going to be difficult to solve this case," the other police officer said.

Naomi felt as if her heart had plunged clear to her toes. She breathed in and out slowly, trying to calm her fears. So it *was* hopeless. Zach was gone for good. The days ahead looked bleak and frightening. Without Zach, nothing would ever be the same.

Papa nudged Naomi's arm. "Now that you've had more time to think on it, can you remember anything else?"

She shook her head and blinked against the tears that sprang to her eyes. "Sorry."

"Was the man old or young?" the first officer asked.

"I told you Saturday night, he wasn't old. I'm sure of that much."

"But you have no idea if he was in his twenties, thirties, or forties?"

"And what color was the man's hair?" the other policeman asked.

Naomi wanted to scream. She'd been through these questions the other night and told them all she knew. Why did they keep on asking?

"Answer the man, Naomi," Papa instructed.

She swallowed hard. "I—I'm not sure. I think it was brown, but it could have been black. The man was younger than Papa, but to tell ya the truth, I didn't pay close attention to much of anything. I'd had a busy morning, and—"

"That's just an excuse. You should've been payin' more attention,"

Papa barked. "You wouldn't have left Zach on the picnic table if you had been."

Will I ever hear the end of this? Does he have to keep reminding me of what I've done?

"I'm sorry. Sorry for everything." Naomi whirled around and dashed for the house.

Caleb entered his house, ever so glad to be home. Leaving Marvin and Andy in charge of the buggy shop was okay for a day or two, but much longer and things might not go well. He knew Andy's hand was still bandaged after getting that nail stuck in his thumb, so he couldn't do much to help if they got busy. Marvin sure wasn't able to do all the work by himself.

When Caleb first arrived in Lancaster, he'd called Ken Peterson for a ride home; and from the smell that greeted him as he entered the kitchen, Caleb figured he'd arrived in time for breakfast.

"I'm home," he called.

Mom, who stood in front of the stove with her back to him, whirled around. "Caleb! We didn't expect you for another couple of days."

He grinned and hung his straw hat on a wall peg. "Couldn't stay away from my mom's great cookin'."

She smiled. "You would say something like that."

"Caleb always did like to eat," Levi, his eleven-year-old brother, put in from his place at the table.

Caleb crossed the room and ruffled the boy's blond hair. "What would you know about it, huh?"

Levi chuckled and reached for his glass of milk.

Caleb glanced around. "Where's everyone else?"

"Your daed's in the fields with John and David," Mom replied. "Andy and Marvin went out to the buggy shop a few minutes ago."

"They've had breakfast already?"

"Jah."

"And the sisters? Where are they?"

"Irma and Lettie are down in the cellar gettin' canning jars. We've got a bunch of peas to put up later today."

"Thought the peas were done," Caleb said, taking a seat across from Levi.

"This is the last picking."

"So am I too late for breakfast?"

"Not a'tall. Haven't eaten myself yet, and as you can see, Levi's waitin' for seconds."

Levi patted his stomach. "I'm a growin' boy."

Caleb laughed. "How's things around here? Everything okay in the buggy shop?"

Mom set a plate of scrambled eggs in front of Caleb and frowned. "Things are okay at our place, but it's really bad over at the Fishers' right now."

"How so?"

"Baby Zach's missing."

"What do you mean, Mom? How can the little guy be missin'?"

"Seems he was kidnapped right out of their yard early Saturday afternoon. Some English man came askin' for root beer, and they're sure he's the one who took him."

Caleb's thoughts flashed to the quilt shop outside of Berlin, Ohio. He'd seen an English couple there with a baby who looked like Zach. Was it possible? Could it be? If there was even a chance. . .

Caleb pushed his chair away from the table and stood. "I've gotta go, Mom."

"What about breakfast?"

"I can eat something later."

"But where are ya off to?"

"I'll be back as soon as I can, and I'll explain everything then." He grabbed his hat and raced out the door before his mother could say another word.

Abraham didn't know how he was going to go about business as usual today, but somehow he must. Staying home and moping around or railing at God for His unfairness wouldn't bring in any money. It wouldn't bring Zach home, either.

He lit the gas lanterns near the front of the store, placed the OPEN sign in the window, and went to the back room to fetch the box of children's books that needed to be set out. Naomi could tend to any customers coming in, and he would enlist the help of his two youngest daughters with the books. He'd left Samuel home today to work in the fields with the older boys.

As soon as he and the girls entered the storage room, Abraham spotted Zach's empty playpen. A sting of pain sliced through his body, and he winced, feeling like he'd been stabbed with a pitchfork. *Zach. Zach. Oh, my sweet little boy, how my soul pines for you.*

Nancy and Mary Ann must have noticed the place where Zach had taken so many naps, for they both stood like statues, staring at it.

"I miss my little brother." Mary Ann touched the railing of the playpen and whimpered.

"You think we'll ever see Zach again, Papa?" Nancy questioned.

Abraham wished he could offer his daughters some comfort or hope that Zach would be returned. He couldn't. Not when he knew, short of a miracle, they would never see their precious boppli again.

"Papa, will Zach come home?"

Abraham clenched his teeth to keep from snapping at Nancy. Since Saturday night, he'd said too many unkind words and knew his attitude was wrong.

"I'll carry this box of books into the next room for you," he mumbled, "and while you two are settin' them on the shelf, I'll come back here and do some rearranging."

Nancy and Mary Ann looked at each other, then back at him. *Are they expecting me to say more? Maybe offer some reassurance that Zach will be coming home?*

He bent down and lifted the cardboard box into his arms. "Go on now."

The girls followed him to the other room, and as soon as they started on the books, he returned to the storage area and shut the door.

Abraham grabbed the playpen and folded it up. *No use leavin' this out as a reminder of what can't be undone.* With the toe of his boot, he kicked one of the wooden blocks that had fallen out of the playpen along with several other toys. "Besides, it's only in the way."

He shoved the playpen behind some containers against the wall, then grabbed an empty box and tossed all of Zach's toys inside. As he was finishing that chore, someone knocked.

"Come in."

The door squeaked open, and his friend Jacob Weaver entered the storage room. "The girls said I'd find you in here. What are ya up to?"

"Cleanin'. Organizin'. Tryin' to forget." Abraham flopped onto the cot where he sometimes took a nap, as a feeling of despair washed over him like a drenching rain.

Jacob's hazel-colored eyes showed compassion. He took a seat beside Abraham, and in quiet solitude they sat there.

After several minutes, Jacob cleared his throat. " 'O Lord of hosts, blessed is the man that trusteth in thee.' Psalm eighty-four, verse twelve."

Abraham grunted. "Jah, well, the Bible also says, 'The Lord giveth and the Lord taketh away.' " He clasped his hands tightly together. "He's taken my youngest son, Jacob, and I don't think Zach's ever comin' back."

"It wasn't God who took your boy. It was an English man who was probably desperate and didn't know right from wrong."

"Humph! Everyone knows right from wrong."

"Maybe here," Jacob said as he touched his head, "but not necessarily here." He laid his hand against his chest.

Abraham swallowed around the lump in his throat. "I'm thinkin' you oughta be our next bishop. You always seem to know what to say."

Jacob gave a small laugh. "We have a bishop, remember?"

"Andrew Swartley won't be around forever. He's in his eighties now and gettin' pretty forgetful at times."

"Don't matter how forgetful the man is; as long as he's alive, he'll be our bishop."

Abraham knew a bishop was chosen by lot and remained the head leader until his death. Still, no one lived forever, and when Andrew Swartley passed on, there would be a need for a new bishop.

"Never know what the future holds," Abraham said, elbowing his friend in the ribs.

"That's true enough."

"If I had known my boy was gonna be kidnapped, I sure would have done things differently."

"No one can foresee the future, only God," Jacob said. "And He can take something bad like Zach's disappearance and turn it into something good."

Abraham groaned. "The only good that'll ever come outta this would be if Zach is returned to us."

Naomi sat on the wooden stool behind the counter near the front of the store, trying to insert figures from receipts into the ledger. It was hard to concentrate. Hard to think about anything other than Zach. Over the last couple of days, a sense of sadness had pervaded every step she took, every thought that popped into her head. Her heart felt as dark as the night sky.

She was glad when Jacob Weaver showed up, asking to see her dad. He and Papa had been close friends for a good many years, and if anyone could help Papa through his grief, it would be Jacob. *Sure wish someone could help me with mine.*

She glanced at the clock on the wall across the room. Jacob had been in the storage room with Papa for half an hour already. *Wonder what they could be talking about? Jacob must be takin' a break from his painting business. I'm sure he knows Papa is hurting real bad right now.*

Mary Ann and Nancy had finished unloading the books from the box Papa had brought out, and they'd wanted to ask him what they should do next. Naomi caught them before they knocked on the door, telling the girls they could go outside for a while, as long as they stayed on the front porch. From her spot behind the counter, she could see the entire porch through the window, so if anyone bothered her sisters, she would know about it.

The front door suddenly swung open, and Caleb rushed in.

"Naomi, I came as soon as I heard the news."

She fought against the urge to dash around the counter and throw herself into Caleb's arms. His gentle expression gave evidence of his concern, and she felt sure he wouldn't judge her the way Papa had done.

Naomi held herself in check and managed a brave smile. "It's been rough since Zach was kidnapped."

"I'm awful sorry it happened, but I think I might have some information that could be helpful." Caleb stepped closer. "I don't want to give anyone false hope, but I may have seen Zach."

"What? Where?" Naomi's mouth fell open, and her heart thumped so hard she feared it might burst.

"Just outside of Berlin, Ohio," he said. "I went there to look at some buggy parts my cousin was selling."

"And?"

"On Sunday I went for a walk in town before my driver took me to the bus station in Dover."

Naomi jumped off the wooden stool and skirted around the counter. "And you saw Zach there? Is that what you're sayin', Caleb?"

He gave his earlobe a couple of tugs. "I can't rightly say it was Zach, but it sure enough looked like him."

"Was there an English man with him?"

Caleb nodded. "A woman, too. She was holding the baby, but the little guy was wearin' English clothes, so I told myself it couldn't be Zach." He shrugged. "Besides, I thought he was home with you. I had no idea he'd been snatched right off your farm. When I got home this morning, Mom told me what happened."

"Stay here while I get Papa. He's in the back room with Jacob Weaver."

Naomi bolted for the rear of the store and pounded on the storage room door. "Papa, it's me! Caleb Hoffmeir's here with some news about Zach."

The door swung open, and Papa and Jacob emerged.

"Where's he at? What'd he say?" Papa's eyes were wide, and he looked downright befuddled. It was the first time he'd spoken to Naomi since that morning, when the police stopped by their house.

"He's up front by the counter. He thinks he may have seen Zach in Berlin, Ohio."

Papa rushed past her, with Jacob Weaver following. Naomi was right on his heels.

"What's all this about you seein' Zach in Ohio?" Papa asked Caleb, who stood with his back against the counter.

"Not sure it was him," Caleb answered, "but he had the same dark brown eyes and light brown hair cut in a Dutch bob. If I hadn't thought he was home with his family, I probably could have convinced myself it was him."

"Who was he with? Where exactly did you see him? Was he okay?"

Caleb held up one hand. "Slow down, Abraham, and I'll try to answer your questions one at a time."

135

Papa gripped the edge of the counter with both hands. "Okay, I'm listening."

"I went to Berlin to see about some buggy parts, and—"

"Forget the buggy parts! Just tell me about my son!"

Jacob stepped forward and laid his hand on Papa's shoulder. "Calm down once, and let the boy talk."

Papa sucked in a deep breath, and Naomi could tell he was fighting hard for control. "Go on," he mumbled.

"On Sunday, before I headed home, I decided to take a walk." Caleb paused a moment. "I was goin' past this quilt shop, when I noticed an English couple looking in the window. The woman was holding a little boy who looked sort of like Zach."

"Did you say anything to 'em?"

"No. Didn't see a need."

"Did you get a look at the vehicle they were driving?" This question came from Jacob, but Caleb shook his head.

"I kept on walking, so I didn't even see if they had a car."

"But you're sure it was a quilt shop they were in front of?" Papa asked.

Caleb nodded. "The sign out front said FANNIE'S QUILT SHOP. I'm sure of that much. Also heard the man say they'd be goin' back on Monday to buy a quilt."

Papa paced back and forth, making sounds like "*Hmm. . . Well now. . . I wonder. . .*" Finally he halted, turned to face Naomi, and announced, "You're gonna have to mind the store a few days 'cause I'm goin' on a trip."

"Where are you going, Papa?"

"To Ohio. To Fannie's Quilt Shop."

CHAPTER 15

Naomi couldn't believe her dad planned to leave her in charge of the store, much less the children while he went to Ohio. She wanted to believe he trusted her again but figured more than likely he was just desperate for any news of his missing son. It could be a trip made in vain, however, and what if something bad happened while Papa was gone?

"Do you have to leave right away?" Naomi asked, touching her father's arm.

He pulled away. "Don't be tryin' to tell me what to do."

She blinked. "I—I wasn't. I just thought—"

"I need to go to Berlin," Papa said. "Don't have a moment to lose."

"Would you like me to give you a ride home so you can pack and find a way to the bus station?" Caleb asked.

Naomi had almost forgotten he was still there, standing on the other side of the wooden counter. He offered her a brief smile, but she looked away, afraid she would break down in front of him.

Papa hesitated and gave his beard a couple of tugs. "Well, I suppose I would need to leave my horse and buggy here so Naomi and the girls have a way home."

"I can call my cousin Henry who runs a buggy shop near Berlin and see if he'd be willing to put you up for a couple of nights."

"I'd be much obliged," Papa said with a nod.

"Want me to see about gettin' you a bus ticket and a ride to the station?" Jacob Weaver asked.

Papa nodded. "Jah, sure. That would be a big help."

"Richard, one of the English fellows who works for me, was gonna drive me into Lancaster today, so we can drop you off at the bus station first, if you like."

"I appreciate the offer, Jacob. Danki.

"I'd better get a move on then," Papa said. He glanced over at Naomi. "Don't know how long I'll be gone but probably won't be more than a few days at the most."

She opened her mouth to respond, but he turned his back on her. "Ready, Caleb?"

Caleb nodded.

"Can you and your driver pick me up in an hour at my place?" Papa asked Jacob.

"Sure, no problem."

Papa opened the screen door, and the three men stepped onto the porch. Naomi heard her father say something to Mary Ann and Nancy, and when she glanced out the window, she saw him hug them.

She sniffed and fought for control. *Papa never gave me a good-bye hug. He's still angry with me, and I fear unless Zach is found, he always will be.*

On a sudden impulse, Naomi darted for the front door. Papa was already in the parking lot, heading for Caleb's open buggy. She hurried after him, a surge of guilt giving power to her legs. She had asked God for a sign that Zach was all right. Maybe Caleb's news was that sign. "Papa, wait!"

He stopped and whirled around. "What's wrong?"

"Take me with you. I want to be there when you find out if the quilt shop owner has any information about Zach."

Papa's forehead wrinkled, and his eyebrows disappeared into the creases. "Who would watch the kinner if you came along?"

She gulped back the sob threatening to explode from her lips. "I don't know. I'm sure the older boys could manage on their own, and maybe we can ask Anna Beechy to care for the younger ones."

"What about the store, Naomi?"

"Couldn't we close it for a few days?"

"No. This is something I need to do alone." Papa turned away as though the matter was settled.

With a heavy heart, Naomi watched him climb into Caleb's buggy. She knew he couldn't be persuaded to change his mind. When Papa said no, that was it, plain and simple.

Caleb waved as he pulled out of the parking lot, but she didn't respond. He was being so nice, yet she couldn't even find the words to thank him.

"What's wrong with me?" she moaned. "I'm not acting right anymore." Hunching her shoulders, Naomi trudged back to the store. Maybe, just maybe, Papa would return from Ohio with good news.

"Papa said he's goin' to Ohio to see someone about Zach," Nancy said when Naomi stepped onto the porch.

Naomi nodded. "That's right. Caleb was there on Sunday, and he saw a little boy who looked like Zach."

"Will Papa be bringin' the boppli home with him?" Mary Ann questioned, her expression hopeful.

"I don't know what Papa will discover in Ohio," Naomi answered as honestly as she knew how. Truth was, she didn't hold out much hope that the person who ran the quilt shop would know anything helpful.

"Can me and Mary Ann stay out here awhile?" Nancy asked, changing the subject. "It's hot inside, and we like watchin' the people go by."

Naomi nodded. "If we get lots of customers, you'll have to come back in the store. I can't watch you and wait on people at the same time."

"You don't hafta watch us," Mary Ann said with a huff. "We're big girls, and we can look out for ourselves." She thumped her older sister on the arm. "Ain't that right, Nancy?"

"Yep. We'll be just fine."

"I'll keep the door open so you can call if you need anything."

Naomi pushed on the screen door and entered the store. She figured she might as well get to work unloading the shipment of rubber stamps that the UPS man had delivered first thing this morning. Maybe Ginny Meyers would drop by later today, and she could show her what came in. She needed something to take her mind off Zach—and Papa heading to Ohio for what could very well be a complete waste of time.

Half an hour later, Naomi gathered up the garbage and headed outside with the idea of giving the plastic sack to Nancy to deposit in the trash bin. She was surprised to see her sisters leaning against the porch railing holding red lollipops in their hands.

"Where'd you get those?"

Flash!

Naomi jumped.

Flash! Flash!

She pivoted to the right. A middle-aged English man stood on the far end of the porch with a camera in his hands. He nodded and grinned at Naomi. "They said I could take their pictures, and I offered them candy as payment."

A jolt of heat shot up Naomi's neck, and her stomach rolled. She dropped the sack of garbage and yanked the candy from her sisters' hands. "You two know better than to accept anything from a stranger." She shook her finger in Nancy's face. "You also know how we stand on picture takin'. What were you thinking?"

"Didn't figure there'd be any harm. Sarah Graber said she let someone take her picture a few days ago."

"If Sarah jumps off the barn roof, are you gonna follow?" Naomi's voice was shrill, and her hands shook as she clenched the candy she held at her sides. Didn't her sisters have any idea how dangerous talking to a stranger could be? And allowing the man to take their pictures. . . She was sorely disappointed in them.

"Get inside, both of you," she hollered. "The shelves need dusting, and the windows could use a good washing, too. Now get to it!"

The girls stomped off, slamming the screen door as they went inside.

Naomi dropped the lollipops into the garbage sack she'd left on the porch and turned to face the photographer, ready to give him a piece of her mind. Before she could get a word out, he lifted his camera and snapped a picture of her. She gasped. "How dare you!"

He slipped the camera into a canvas satchel and slung it over his shoulder. "Looks like somebody got up on the wrong side of the bed this morning."

Naomi whirled around and stomped into the store, leaving the garbage sack where it lay. She found Nancy washing windows, but Mary Ann was crouched behind the counter, crying.

Naomi dropped to her knees in front of her youngest sister. "I didn't mean to make you cry, Mary Ann, but you should know better than to do what you did out there."

The child wiped her eyes with the back of her hand. "I only wanted a piece of candy."

"Then you should have come inside and asked for one."

Mary Ann looked up, her brown eyes reminding Naomi of a wounded animal. "I figured you'd say no."

Naomi pulled the little girl into her arms. "When you're done with the dusting, you can help yourself to a lollipop from the candy counter."

Mary Ann sniffed. "Nancy, too?"

"Jah." Naomi grabbed the broom and started sweeping the floor. *What was Papa thinking, leaving me alone to care for his children? I can barely function, much less take charge of things 'til he gets back home.*

"Mom, if you don't need me for a while, I think I'll take my lunch and go out back to the picnic table," Abby said.

Fannie nodded. "Sure, Daughter, go right ahead. Since it's almost noon, there probably won't be too many customers."

Abby smiled, her dark eyes gleaming. She was such a sweet girl, always helpful and ever so pleasant. And Abby was mighty good with a needle and thread. She'd done her first piece of quilting when she was ten years old and had been making beautiful quilts ever since. Fannie didn't know what she would have done without Abby's help after her husband, Ezra, had a massive heart attack two years ago, leaving her a widow. Fannie's son, Harold, had married Lena Graber two years ago, and they lived next door to her, so Fannie knew she could rely on them, as well. Fannie hoped she'd have her only daughter around awhile. Abby was only eighteen and didn't even have a serious boyfriend yet.

"I'll trade off with you when I'm done eating," Abby said, breaking into Fannie's musings. "You've worked hard all morning and could use some time in the fresh air."

Fannie grunted. "Hot and sticky air, that's more like it."

"It's much cooler under the shade of the old maple tree."

"That's true, and I'll probably take your suggestion." Fannie pointed to the back door. "Now go eat your lunch. Time's a-wastin'."

When Abby hurried away, Fannie returned to her job at the cutting table. She had a Log Cabin quilt she was planning to work on, and it sure wouldn't get done by thinking about it.

She'd only taken a few snips when the bell on the front door jangled. She looked up and saw an English couple enter the store. The woman held a little boy in her arms. *Probably not much more than a year old,* Fannie figured. The baby had light brown hair and eyes so dark it made her think of chocolate syrup.

Fannie fought the urge to ask if she could hold the baby. It had been too long since her kinner were little. She'd always wished for more children, but the Lord must have thought two were enough. After Abby was born, Fannie never conceived again. Since she had no husband now, it wasn't likely she'd ever have any more children, either.

"May I help ya with somethin'?" she asked, moving toward the

English couple, who glanced around the store with confused expressions.

The man fidgeted and glanced out the front window. "We—uh—need a quilt," he mumbled.

"What size are you needin'?"

He looked at the woman. "Queen?"

She nodded. "That's the size of our bed, so that's what we want."

"All the quilts are hung on racks, according to their dimensions," Fannie said, pointing across the room. "Do you have any particular style or color in mind?"

The woman shook her head. "No, not really. I guess maybe something with blues would be nice. Our bedroom is blue and white."

"There are several quilts with blue in them. Would ya like to browse, or do you want me to show them to you?"

"You'd better show us, or we'll be here all day," the man said. Fannie figured his edginess was probably because he'd rather be doing something other than looking at quilts. Most men didn't like shopping. Leastways, Ezra never had.

"Right this way." Fannie led, and they followed.

The woman handed the baby over to the man while she looked at quilts.

"Sure is a cute baby," Fannie said. "How old is he?"

"He's—uh—one."

"What's the name of this pattern?" the woman asked, pulling Fannie's attention back to the job at hand.

"That one's called Lone Star. My daughter, Abby, made it."

"Do you make every quilt here in the shop?"

"Oh no. We'd never have time to make 'em all." Fannie waved her hand. "There are several Amish and Mennonite women in the area who sew for us."

"They're all lovely," the woman said, "but I think I'll take this one." She glanced at her husband and pointed to the price sticker. "It's six hundred dollars, Jim. Can we afford that much?"

He grimaced but nodded. "I think we can swing it."

"Will you take a credit card?" the woman asked.

"We'll be paying cash," her husband said, reaching into his pants' pocket and retrieving a brown wallet.

"But, Jim, that's a lot of money and—"

"It's fine. I've got enough cash left to get us home."

"Where you folks from?" Fannie asked as she lifted the quilt off the rack.

"We're here visiting family," the man answered before the woman could open her mouth.

Fannie figured that was all the information he cared to give, so she dropped the subject. Some English folks were sure odd. So close-mouthed about things.

She took the quilt to her work counter and carefully wrapped it in tissue paper, then placed it inside a lightweight cardboard box.

Obviously pleased with her purchase, the woman fairly beamed. She took the baby from her husband, and he picked up the box.

Fannie followed them to the front door. "I hope you'll get many years of enjoyment from the quilt you bought. Have a good day now."

"Yes, thank you," the man muttered. "You, too."

For the next few hours, Naomi and her sisters cleaned and stocked more shelves. When that was done, she sent Nancy and Mary Ann to the back room so they could play while she inserted more figures into the ledger.

She had just seated herself behind the counter when Ginny Meyers entered the store. Naomi looked up and feigned a smile. "We got a new shipment of rubber stamps in this morning. You'd probably like to have a look-see."

Ginny raced over to Naomi. "I can't even think about stamps right now. I read about Zach's kidnapping in the newspaper this morning and came by to offer my support."

Naomi nodded. "It happened on Saturday."

"That's what the paper said." Ginny reached across the counter and took hold of Naomi's hand. "I'm sorry, Naomi. It must be awful for you."

Naomi blinked back the tears threatening to spill over. Having someone's sympathy was awful nice, but for some reason, seeing Ginny and hearing her kind words made Naomi feel worse.

Ginny released Naomi's hand and clicked her tongue. "You've got dark circles under your eyes. I'll bet you haven't slept hardly at all since Zach was taken, have you?"

"No," Naomi admitted. "Truth is, I haven't been able to do much of anything since then."

"What I want to know is, what kind of maniac would drive onto an Amish farm and snatch a baby right out from under his family's nose?"

Naomi drew in a deep breath and almost choked on her words. "I don't know, but it's my fault Zach was taken, and Papa is furious with me."

"Why's it your fault?"

"The man who stopped by for root beer asked if I had any that was cold." She gulped. "I was going to get him some from the refrigerator when I heard one of the girls scream. So I raced to the house, leaving Zach on the picnic table. When I returned, the man was gone, and so was Zach."

Ginny's mouth dropped open. "You're kidding?"

Naomi shook her head. "If Zach isn't found, I don't think I'll ever forgive myself, and Papa sure won't."

"He's upset right now, but I'm sure in time he'll realize something like that could have happened to anyone."

"I didn't leave the boppli there on purpose; surely Papa must know that."

Ginny's clear blue eyes seemed full of understanding. "Of course you didn't."

"I'd had such a busy morning, and I just wasn't thinking."

Ginny nodded. "I understand. You're overloaded with too many responsibilities and can't do them all. If your dad would hire a maid and give you some time to yourself, you could probably function a whole lot better."

Naomi sniffed and blew her nose on a tissue she'd pulled from under the counter.

"You know what I think you need?"

"Uh-uh."

"You need to get away for a while and do something fun." Ginny smiled. "Why don't you make up some excuse to leave the store for a couple hours and sneak away with me to see a movie? It might help take your mind off your troubles."

"I can't. Papa's headed to Ohio today, and that leaves me fully in charge."

Ginny's pale eyebrows lifted. "Ohio? Why'd he go there?"

Naomi explained about Caleb's recent trip and what he'd seen outside the quilt shop near Berlin. "Papa thinks if he talks to the shop owner, he might learn something about the couple with the baby who looked like Zach."

Ginny tapped her pink, perfectly manicured fingernails along the edge of the counter. "Maybe the man who stole your little brother lives in Ohio. If your dad gets a lead on him and calls the cops, you could have Zach home real soon."

Naomi managed a weak smile. "I hope so, Ginny. Jah, I truly do."

CHAPTER 16

Fannie opened the front door of her shop and held it for Abby, whose arms were full of quilting material.

Abby stepped inside. "Thank you, Mom. I'll put these on the shelves in the back."

Fannie was about to reply when she heard footsteps on the stairs behind her. She turned around quickly and nearly bumped into a tall, middle-aged Amish man with the bluest eyes she had ever seen. She didn't recognize him and figured he was probably from another district.

"Can I help you?" she asked.

"I'm lookin' for the owner of this quilt shop."

She smiled. "That would be me. I'm Fannie Miller."

He cleared his throat. "I've got some questions."

"About quilting? Are ya lookin' to buy a quilt?"

He glanced around, kind of nervouslike. "Don't need no quilts. Would it be all right if I came inside?"

"Yes, yes, of course." Fannie stepped into the shop, and she knew he was right behind her, for she could hear the *clomp clomp* of his boots against the wooden floor.

"I was here yesterday evening, but you were closed for the day," the man said.

"Must have been after six."

"Jah. My bus didn't get in 'til seven, then it took me some time to get a driver and make my way over here." He removed his straw hat, and Fannie was amazed at how thick and shiny his brown hair appeared to be. Not a sign of gray, either, although his full beard had a sprinkling in it.

She moved toward the counter where they waited on customers, and he followed. "If you're not here about a quilt, what can I help you with?"

He gave his beard a couple of pulls. "I heard there was an English couple outside your store on Sunday. Since your shop was closed that day, they said they'd be back Monday morning to buy a quilt."

"Who'd they say it to?"

"The man told the woman, and Caleb Hoffmeir, the young buggy maker from my district in Lancaster County, was walking by and heard their conversation."

"I see."

"So, I'm wonderin' if they did come to your store on Monday."

Fannie smiled. "Lots of English come here, Mr.—"

"Abraham. Abraham Fisher." He shifted his weight from one foot to the other. "The English couple had a little boy. Would have been about a year old."

"Hmm. . .let me think." Fannie tried to picture some of the customers she'd had yesterday. It had been a busy day, full of tourists, as well as several of her regular customers.

"Please, try to remember. This is awful important."

Fannie took a seat on the wooden stool and tried to concentrate. "Do you know this English couple?"

He shook his head. "No, but when Caleb told me he'd seen them, I bought a bus ticket and came right here."

"Could you explain things better, Abraham? Why would you be so interested in an English couple with a baby, who you don't even know?"

Abraham clasped his hands tightly together. "I live near Paradise, Pennsylvania, and my baby was kidnapped out of my yard on Saturday afternoon."

Fannie's heart clenched. She could hardly fathom such a horrible thing. "I'm so sorry. You and your wife must be frantic with worry."

"My Sarah died a little over a year ago when she was hit by a car. Our baby, Zach, was only two months old at the time."

Fannie could almost feel the man's grief. "I lost my husband when he had a heart attack two years ago, so I sympathize with your loss."

He paced back and forth in front of the counter. "Losin' Sarah was hard enough, but now that I've lost my boppli, too, the pain's nearly unbearable."

"I can imagine."

"Caleb Hoffmeir said the boy with the English couple looked like my Zach." He grimaced. "I'm thinkin' maybe they could be the ones who kidnapped him."

Fannie clasped her hands. "You must be beside yourself with worry."

He nodded. "If you could help me on this, I'd be much obliged."

She drew in a deep breath and tried to focus her thoughts. "Let's see now. . . Mary Zook and her sister Catherine came in first thing Monday morning. They bought some material for a new quilt they wanted to start. And then a young English mother and her daughter stopped by." Fannie smiled. "They live in the area and are regular customers."

Abraham's eyebrows furrowed deep into the folds of his forehead. She could tell he was growing impatient and wanted some answers.

Fannie licked her lips. "After Carol and her daughter left, about ten women arrived. I think they were with a tour bus."

When Abraham made no comment, she continued. "Then later, around lunchtime, an English couple came in, asking to buy a queen-sized quilt." She snapped her fingers. "Say, they did have a little boy. Fact is, I couldn't get over how sweet he was. Cute as could be and seemed to be quite even tempered. Never fussed a bit the whole time they were here."

Abraham leaned across the counter until she could actually feel his warm breath on her face. "What'd the boy look like? How old would you say he was? Did he have a Dutch bob?"

Fannie sat up straight and moved away from Abraham. It made her nervous to have him breathing on her that way. "I'd guess he was around a year or so, and he had such pretty hair—golden brown, I'd say it was. Don't know if it was Dutch bobbed or not, though. It was slicked back away from his face."

"And his eyes? What color were the boppli's eyes?"

"Brown. Dark brown, like chocolate."

Abraham's breathing intensified. "Did ya get a look behind his right ear?"

She shook her head. "Can't say that I did. Why do you ask?"

"Zach has a small heart-shaped birthmark there."

Fannie rubbed her forehead and tried to get a better picture of the little boy in her mind. "I'm sorry to say, but I didn't notice behind his ear. Fact of the matter is, I was more concerned with showin' the woman the right color quilts than anything else."

"Did they buy a quilt?" he asked.

"Jah. Got a nice Lone Star pattern with shades of blue."

"Did you happen to get their names?"

"No, but I heard the woman call the man 'Jim' a couple of times."

"No last name?"

She shook her head.

"If they bought a quilt, you must have made out a receipt."

"I did, but they paid cash, so I had no reason to get their name and address." Fannie frowned. "Funny thing, though, I did ask 'em once where they were from, and the man only said they were here visiting family."

"Did you get a look at the car they were drivin'? Maybe the color or license plate?"

"Sorry, but another customer came in as they were leaving, so my attention was turned to her. Truth is, I never saw the Englishers' car."

Abraham groaned. "And that's all you know?"

"Afraid so." Fannie skirted around the counter. "Sure wish there was more I could do to help. I know this must be awful frustrating for you."

Abraham rubbed the bridge of his nose. "Don't know how I'm gonna return home and tell the family I came all this way for nothin'."

"I'll be praying for you, Abraham." She paused. "You said you live near Paradise, right?"

He nodded.

"I've got a cousin who lives near that area, and she's been after me to spend some time with her this summer."

"You should do it. Lancaster County is a right nice place to visit."

"Jah, I've been there before, but not in many years."

"If you do get over our way, feel free to stop by my store and say hello. It's called Fisher's General Store and is located just outside the town of Paradise."

"I might do that. I'd like to see how things are, and I pray by then you'll have found your boy."

He smiled, but she could tell it was forced. The creases in Abraham's forehead gave indication that he was deeply troubled. "I'm prayin' for the same thing," he said, turning toward the front door. "Thanks for being willing to speak with me, and I'm sorry for takin' up so much of your time."

She followed him to the door. "It was no trouble. I only wish I had more information to give."

"You told me what you knew, and I appreciate it." Abraham pulled the door open and stepped onto the porch. "Good day to you, Fannie Miller."

"Da Herr sei mit du—the Lord be with you," she said in return.

"Who was that man?" Abby asked when Fannie shut the door. "I stayed at the back of the store because I could see you two were in deep conversation."

Fannie nodded. "He was askin' about an English couple who bought a quilt yesterday."

Abby tipped her head. "Mind if I ask why?"

"The man and woman had a little boy, and someone who knows Abraham Fisher saw them outside our store on Sunday." She pursed her lips. "Seems Abraham's boppli was kidnapped off his farm Saturday afternoon, and the young fellow who noticed the English couple window-shoppin' thought their child looked like Abraham's boy."

Abby's dark eyes revealed her usual compassion. "That's awful. I can't imagine such a thing."

"Me neither." Fannie sighed. "Sure wish there was something I could have said to make Abraham feel better. He seemed so distraught over the disappearance of his son."

"You can pray for him, Mom. Pray the people who took his baby will come to their senses and return the boy home."

Fannie gently squeezed her daughter's arm. "You're sure a smart one; ya know that?"

Abby smiled. "Well, what can I say? I'm only followin' in my dear mamm's footsteps."

Abraham figured there was probably no use in him hanging around Berlin. If he had a lick of sense, he'd catch the next bus home and be done with it. Still, he had a strong feeling the English couple who visited Fannie's Quilt Shop yesterday were the ones who took Zach. At least the man. Naomi never mentioned anything about a woman being involved. Of course, she'd been so befuddled that day she didn't seem to remember much of anything.

He meandered down the sidewalk, heading for the other side of town. *Might as well take a look around, just in case those people are still in town.*

For the next couple of hours, Abraham wandered up and down the streets of Berlin, looking inside stores, checking out every English person he saw. He scrutinized each car parked along the street, as well as those passing by. He saw lots of English people, many with children. None looked like Zach, however.

"It's hopeless," he mumbled. "Might as well head back to Henry's Buggy Shop and ask him to call someone to take me to the bus station in Dover."

Abraham turned and started down the street in the direction of Henry's place, which was about a mile out of town. Henry had dropped him off this morning, saying he'd be happy to come back for Abraham if he knew what time and where he wanted to be picked up. Abraham declined the offer, telling Caleb's cousin the walk would do him good.

As he plodded along, Abraham noticed he was coming to Fannie's Quilt Shop again. He fought the urge to go inside and ask a few more questions. *That would be dumb,* he decided. *Fannie said she didn't know anything more.*

Feeling a muscle in his back begin to cramp, Abraham took a seat on the wooden bench outside the quilt shop. He'd rest awhile before continuing his journey to the buggy shop. While he sat, he would watch every car going past and check each person who walked by.

Maybe if he begged God hard enough, his prayer would be answered. He leaned forward and rested his chin in his hands. *Please, Lord, let it be so.*

Time passed, and Abraham continued to watch and pray. He didn't know how long he'd been sitting there, but the touch of someone's hand on his shoulder jolted him upright.

"Abraham, are you all right?"

He turned his head. Fannie Miller stood behind him, her hazel-colored eyes looking so sincere. Two little wisps of dark brown hair had escaped her white covering. He ignored the sudden urge to push them back in place.

"I–I'm okay," he sputtered. "Just sat down for a spell to rest my back. Guess I lost track of time, 'cause from the way that sun feels, I'd have to say it's past noon."

Fannie nodded. "My daughter just finished her lunch break, and I was lookin' to take mine. Took a quick glance out front before I did and saw you sitting here." She moved around to stand beside the bench. "I was worried about you."

"It's nice of you to be concerned," he replied. "I've been walkin' up and down the streets of Berlin all morning with the hope of spotting the English couple I told you about."

She stared down at him, compassion evident on her round face. "I take it you saw no one with a child who looked like your son?"

He shook his head.

"Have you had lunch?" she asked suddenly.

"Naw, I wasn't in the mood to eat."

"How would you like to share my lunch? There's a picnic table under a maple tree behind the store, and I'd be glad to have you join me."

"I couldn't ask you to do that."

"It's no bother." She chuckled and patted her stomach. "I packed way too much food this mornin', and you might save me a few added inches if you share it with me."

He smiled in spite of his dismal mood. "Jah, okay. I'd be happy to then."

"Let's go into the store first," Fannie said. "My lunch basket's there, and we can go out the back door." She led, and he followed.

There was a young woman with dark brown hair cutting a piece of material at one of the tables near the back of the store. She was younger than Fannie and several pounds lighter, but he could tell they were related.

"This is my daughter, Abby," Fannie said as they approached the young woman. "Abby, this is Abraham Fisher from Lancaster County, Pennsylvania."

Abby looked up from her work and smiled. She had a dimple in her right cheek, just like her mother's. "It's nice to meet you, Abraham. Mom told me you were here earlier, asking about an English couple with a little boy who looked like your son."

A renewed sense of hope welled up in his chest. "Do you remember them? Did you get any information about who they were or where they were goin'?"

She shook her head. "Sorry, no. I was outside havin' lunch when the couple came in. Mom told me about it later."

He released a heavy sigh. "Sure wish someone knew something."

"God knows, Abraham," Fannie said sincerely. "I'm sure He feels your pain."

She held up a wicker basket. "I've got our food right here. You ready?"

He nodded. "Ready and feelin' hungrier by the minute."

For the next half hour, Abraham and Fannie got better acquainted as he told her about his family and the way it had been since Sarah's death. He was amazed at how understanding and sweet she was, offering words of encouragement and saying she would keep him and his family in her prayers.

Fannie shared a bit about her life, too: how she'd only been able to have two children—a boy, now married, and Abby, who helped at the quilt shop.

Abraham studied Fannie as she sat on the other side of the picnic table smiling at him. *Too bad there aren't any widows like you in my area,* he mused. *If so, I might change my mind about gettin' married again.*

CHAPTER 17

Naomi glanced out the kitchen window. Half an hour ago, she'd sent Nancy and Mary Ann to the garden to pick strawberries, and they still hadn't returned. Didn't they realize she was in a hurry?

She placed two pie pans on the counter and slipped the flattened dough inside each one. After another long day at the store, she didn't feel like baking, but the girls had been begging for strawberry pie, and the garden was overflowing with ripe berries. "Sure hope Papa gets here soon," Naomi muttered. He'd been gone two full days, and she had no idea when to expect him. Had he found the English couple with the baby who looked like Zach? If so, had the police been called? How she hoped Papa would return with her little brother. "Everything will be all right if Zach comes home."

"You talkin' to yourself again?"

Naomi whirled around. Norman stood inside the kitchen door, his face and arms covered with dust.

"You shouldn't be sneaking up on me like that."

He sauntered across the room and opened the refrigerator door. "Wasn't sneakin'. Just came in to get a glass of lemonade."

"You're dirty as a pig," she scolded. "Should have washed up outside before you came into the house."

He grunted. "Don't tell me what to do, Naomi. Just because Papa's gone don't mean you can boss everyone around."

She balled her hands into fists and planted them on her hips. "I'm not."

Norman set the pitcher of lemonade on the table and went to get a glass from the cupboard. "Jah, you are. Ever since Mama died, you've been kinda bossy, and now that Papa's gone to Ohio, you think you can tell everyone what to do."

Heat crept up the back of Naomi's neck, and she struggled to keep her tears at bay. She didn't understand why her brother was being so mean, but she had to keep control of her emotions, especially in front of her siblings.

"Norman, do this," he taunted. "Nancy, do that. All you ever do is order folks around."

"I'm only doing what I was asked to do," she countered. "Papa said I should look after things, and that means—"

"Ha! Look after things? Were ya lookin' after Zach when he was snatched off the picnic table last Saturday?"

She winced. The pain of her brother's words sliced through Naomi like a knife. She opened her mouth to defend herself, but she couldn't. Norman was right. She hadn't done a good job of looking out for Zach that day, but she didn't need to be reminded of her error. Naomi had berated herself aplenty these last few days, but to be told she was negligent by one of her family members was like a slap in the face.

She turned back to the pie shells. What was keeping those girls? Tears slipped from her eyes and landed on the counter with a splash.

"Don't see how you can expect anyone to do what you say anymore," Norman went on. "You'd better quit bossin' and start being more responsible."

Naomi choked on a sob, pushed the pie pans aside, and rushed out the back door. She stopped long enough to blow her nose and gulp in a deep breath, and then hurried to the garden.

The sound of children's laughter drifted on the wind, and she halted at the edge of the grass. Nancy and Mary Ann ran back and forth between the rows of strawberries, laughing, hollering, and throwing berries at one another.

Naomi cupped her trembling hands around her mouth and hollered, "Stop that!"

When the girls ignored her and kept on running, she marched into the garden, picked up one of the half-empty plastic containers, and shoved it at Nancy. *"Des is mer gen greitz*—this is annoying to me."

Mary Ann screeched to a halt and hung her head. "Aw, Naomi, we was only havin' a little fun."

"I sent you out here to pick strawberries, not have fun! I've got pies to bake, and there aren't nearly enough berries in this container for even one pie."

Nancy scrunched her nose. "How come you're always yellin' at us?"

"I wouldn't have to yell if you did as you were told."

"Norman said we don't hafta mind you anymore," Mary Ann said.

Naomi clenched her teeth. "Oh, he did, did he?"

Her little sister nodded soberly.

"You should know better than to listen to Norman. He's only trying to make trouble."

Nancy's lower lip quivered. "Why can't we ever please you, Sister? Ever since Zach was taken, you've been cranky and shootin' orders all the time."

Overcome with remorse, Naomi bent down and grabbed both girls in a hug. "I love you so much, and I'm sorry for takin' my frustrations out on you," she said tearfully. "It's just that I'm feeling awful about Zach being kidnapped, and I want to take good care of you girls—see that you do things right and are kept safe."

Mary Ann buried her face in Naomi's neck. "It ain't your fault Zach was taken."

"That's right," Nancy agreed, "and Papa's gonna bring him back home; you'll see."

"I hope so. I truly do." Naomi sniffed. "Forgive me, girls—for being such a grump?"

"Jah," they said in unison.

"All right then. Please get busy and fill these containers with berries. I want to get the pies started before we have supper."

Nancy and Mary Ann grabbed their plastic tubs and started picking right away. Naomi turned and headed back to the house. She hoped Norman had returned to the fields. She was not in the mood to listen to more of his unkind remarks.

She had only taken a few steps when she heard a horse and buggy pull into the yard. It was Caleb.

He waved and stepped down from his buggy. She noticed right away that he held a book in his hands. "This is for you," he said as he approached her.

She tipped her head. "What for? It's not my birthday or anything."

"It's my way of letting you know I've been thinkin' about you. I wanted to come by yesterday and see how you were doing, but I had so much work in the shop I couldn't get away." He handed the book to Naomi. "This is about all the sights out west. I remember once when we were kinner, you said you'd like to see Mount Rainier and what's left of Mount St. Helens."

Naomi blinked against threatening tears. "That was kind of you."

"How are things going? Heard anything from your daed yet?"

She shook her head and moved toward the house. "Would you like a glass of lemonade or something?"

"That'd be nice."

"Have a seat on the front porch. I'll take the book inside and be right out with the lemonade."

Caleb plunked himself down on the top step, and Naomi went into the house. When she entered the kitchen, she was relieved to see that Norman was no longer there. She placed the travelogue on one end of the counter and went to the refrigerator. A few minutes later, she returned to the porch with two glasses of lemonade and handed one to Caleb. "Here you go."

"Danki." He smiled when she took a seat beside him. "So ya don't have any idea when Abraham might be home?"

"Nope. I'm hoping his bein' gone these three days means he might have discovered something about Zach."

"I could go to one of the English neighbors and call my cousin in Berlin."

Naomi sucked in her bottom lip. "I suppose you could, but Papa might not like it if he thought we were checkin' up on him. Besides, he's not too keen on makin' phone calls that aren't absolutely necessary."

Caleb shrugged. "Guess he'd call one of your neighbors and ask them to get you a message if there was anything important to tell."

She sighed and set her glass down on the step. "Jah, which probably means he hasn't found Zach."

"If he does find your little brother, maybe he'll come home and surprise everyone."

"That would be wonderful—the answer to my prayers."

Caleb took hold of Naomi's hand, and the contact of his skin made her flesh tingle. "I know there are some in our district who feel you were negligent by leavin' Zach on that picnic table." He gazed into Naomi's eyes, and she could see the depth of his understanding. "Some, like me, know it was just an accident. Could have happened to any one of us if we'd been distracted."

Her eyes filled with tears, and she nodded. "That's what happened all right. I'd been awful busy that morning, which probably didn't help things any, but when I heard Mary Ann's scream, I lost track of what I should be doin'." She pulled her hand from his and reached up to wipe the tears on her cheeks. "Even so, I can't quit blamin' myself for what happened, and the worst of it is, Papa blames me, too."

Caleb frowned. "Wish there was some way I could get him to let you start goin' to singings and the like. Maybe then we could begin courtin'."

Naomi opened her mouth to respond, but a car pulled into the yard, and she and Caleb both stood.

"Looks like Mr. Peterson, the man we often call for rides when we can't take the horse and buggy," Naomi said.

The door of the passenger side opened, and Naomi's father stepped out, holding his suitcase. A chorus of cheers went up from the garden patch as Naomi's sisters rushed out to greet him. Naomi and Caleb followed.

Naomi's heart sank when she realized Papa was alone. No precious little brother to hold and welcome home.

"How was your trip?" she asked Papa after he told Mr. Peterson good-bye and shut the car door.

He looked tired, and his face was drawn. "Long. It's gut to be home."

"Any news about Zach?" She had to ask, even though it was obvious he'd returned empty-handed.

He shook his head. "Fannie didn't have much information to give me."

"Who's Fannie, Papa?" Nancy asked.

"She's the woman who owns the quilt shop on the outskirts of Berlin, Ohio."

"Did she say whether an English couple had come to her store with a baby who looked like Zach?" Caleb questioned.

Papa frowned. "Caleb, what are you doin' here?"

"I dropped by to see if the family had received any news from you yet."

Naomi was glad Caleb made no mention of the book he'd brought. That probably wouldn't set well with her daed.

"I see," Papa said. "That's nice of you, but there is no news. None that's good anyways."

"So the woman at the quilt shop didn't know a thing?" Caleb asked.

"The description of the baby she saw seemed to fit Zach. Same as what you said, Caleb."

"Did she know who the English people were or where they were going?" Naomi asked.

"I just said she didn't have any real information," Papa snapped.

She stared down at her bare feet. "Sorry. I thought maybe—"

Papa started moving toward the house. "Where's the rest of the family?"

"The boys are still out in the fields," Nancy replied. "Want me to ring the dinner bell so they'll come up to the house?"

He shook his head. "Naw, let 'em keep workin' awhile longer. Since I have no good news to share, there's not much point to callin' them in 'til suppertime."

Naomi was surprised at Papa's attitude. Despite his abruptness with her a few minutes ago, he didn't seem near as edgy as before he left for Ohio. After making the long trip and not finding Zach, she thought he'd be cranky as all get out.

"Let's go inside. I'm bushed," Papa said.

The girls started to follow, but Naomi stopped them before they got to the porch. "What about the berries? Have you got both containers filled?"

"Just about," Nancy answered.

"Please get it done. I've still got those pies to bake."

"Ah, do we have to?" Mary Ann whined. "I wanna go inside with Papa."

"Do as your sister says," he scolded. "We can talk when you're done pickin' berries."

The girls walked away with their shoulders hunched, and Papa stepped onto the porch. He stopped before he got to the door and turned around. "Caleb, would ya like to join us for supper?"

Naomi was even more surprised by her father's question than she was by his easygoing attitude. What in the world would make Papa invite Caleb to supper? As far as she knew, he didn't want the buggy maker hanging around.

Caleb shuffled his feet. "That's a real nice offer, and I'd sure like to, but Mom's expectin' me back right away. Maybe some other time."

Papa lifted his hand. "Just want to say thanks for tellin' me about those English people you saw in Ohio and also for settin' things up so I could stay with Henry while I was there."

"You're welcome." Caleb turned to Naomi and gave her a quick wink. She was glad Papa's back was to them. He wouldn't have liked Caleb flirting with her, even if he were in a better mood than she'd seen him in some time.

"Thanks for the book," she whispered to Caleb.

He smiled, waved, and headed for his buggy.

Naomi followed her father into the house. Things might be looking up. Leastways, she felt as if they were somewhat better now that Papa was back home. She didn't know why he seemed less agitated than before, but she might as well enjoy the change for as long as it lasted. Come tomorrow, like as not, they might all sink into depression again.

CHAPTER 18

Naomi climbed the stairs to her bedroom, feeling the burden of weariness with each step she took. It was nearly midnight, and as usual, she was the last one to bed.

The past two weeks had gone by quickly as the garden brought forth an abundance of produce that needed to be either canned or frozen. Each evening after they returned from the store and every Saturday, Naomi and her sisters tended the garden. Samuel had been put to work helping with the picking, but he flatly refused to do anything in the kitchen. "Canning is women's work," he'd boldly announced.

Naomi sighed deeply as she entered her room. She was still having trouble getting the children to mind, even the youngest like Samuel and Mary Ann. Ever since Zach's disappearance, they had been hard to deal with.

Maybe it's me who's hard to deal with, she considered. *Maybe I expect too much. I'm not their mother, after all. If I were, Zach would have been better cared for.*

Naomi glanced at her little brother's empty crib. It was a constant reminder of her loss and the remorse she felt for being so incompetent. At Papa's insistence, the high chair and playpen had been dismantled. Yet Naomi couldn't seem to part with the crib in her room. If she kept it there, it would remind her to pray for Zach. And if God took pity on them and returned her baby brother, his bed would be ready and waiting.

Naomi removed her kapp and placed it on the dresser. She pulled the pins out of her bun, and soft brown waves cascaded down her back and around her shoulders. She picked up the hairbrush and sank to the bed as a vision of her mother came to mind.

"Always brush your hair one hundred strokes every night, and it will stay healthy and shiny for years to come," Mama often said. Even when Naomi was so weary she could barely find the strength to lift her arms, she had followed her mother's suggestion. It made her feel closer to Mama, thinking about how she used to watch the dear woman brush her own silky tresses until they shone like a new penny.

Tears welled up in Naomi's eyes and clouded her vision. "Oh, Mama, I miss you so much."

Plink.

Naomi tipped her head and listened. What was that strange noise? It appeared as if something had hit her bedroom window.

Plink. Plink. There it was again. It sounded like pebbles being thrown against the glass.

She hurried to the window and lifted the dark shade. A man stood in the yard below her room. When he stepped out of the shadows, she realized it was Caleb.

He waved at her, and Naomi's breath caught in her throat. *What's he doing here? Doesn't Caleb know Papa could hear the noise and go outside to investigate?* Of course, her father had been the first to go to bed that night, saying he was tired and his back hurt. More than likely, he was sound asleep, and since Naomi had been the last person to head for bed, she was probably the only one still awake.

She tiptoed out of her room and down the stairs, listening for any sounds coming from the other bedrooms. There was nothing but quiet and the subtle creaking of the stairs as she slowly descended them.

With her heart pounding, Naomi slipped out the back door and into the night. Caleb stood beside a shrub, still gazing upward.

"What are you doing here?"

He whirled around. "Don't scare me like that."

"Were you throwin' pebbles at my window?"

He nodded. "Came to see you, and when I saw the light, I figured that was the best way to get your attention."

She stifled a yawn. "Jah, and it could have caught Papa's attention, too. Caleb Hoffmeir, what were you thinking?"

He took hold of her hand and led her across the yard. "I was thinkin' about you and how I wished I'd accepted your daed's invitation to supper a couple weeks ago."

They stood under the old maple tree now, and Caleb nodded at the swing hanging from its branches. "Have a seat, and I'll give you a few pushes."

She glanced around, half expecting to see Papa or one of the brothers come charging out of the house, but all was quiet.

Naomi sat on the wooden seat and grasped the rope handles. This was crazy, her sitting here in the middle of the night, allowing Caleb to push her on the swing as though they were a courting couple.

"I've waited so long for this chance to be alone with you," Caleb murmured against her ear.

Naomi filled her lungs with fresh air and tried not to shiver.

"You're tremblin'," Caleb whispered. "Are ya cold? Want me to get a buggy robe out of my rig?"

She shook her head. "I'm okay. Just a little nervous is all."

"Afraid your daed might catch us?"

"Jah."

"He's been much friendlier to me lately, so maybe he wouldn't mind if he did find us together."

"Something must have happened in Ohio. When Papa returned, he seemed softer," Naomi said. "I'm sure he hasn't forgiven me for leavin' Zach on that picnic table, but he's not been quite so harsh when he speaks to me, either."

"Have you tried talking to him about things? Explain the way you feel and all?"

"No. I doubt it would do much good. Papa's always been pretty closemouthed about his feelings, and this thing with Zach has put a barrier between us that might never come down." She released a heavy sigh. "Truth is, it's affected the whole family. None of the kinner acts the same toward me anymore."

"Sorry to hear that, Naomi. Wish there was somethin' I could do to make your life more pleasant."

"I'm afraid there isn't much anyone can do. What we need is a miracle—to have Zach come home."

Caleb continued to push the swing back and forth. The musical rhythm of singing crickets filled the night air, and for a few moments, Naomi felt a sense of peace, as though it had permeated the air she breathed.

"Naomi, will you continue to see me like this—after it's dark and everyone's asleep?" Caleb asked.

She moistened her lips with the tip of her tongue. How she wanted to say yes, but what would be the point in leading Caleb on? If they began to secretly court, soon he'd be talking of marriage, and she knew that was impossible. Papa would never give his consent. She had a responsibility to the family, a promise to Mama that must be fulfilled. Naomi had already messed up by allowing her busyness to cloud her thinking. She sure couldn't allow thoughts of love and romance to lead her astray.

"Naomi?"

She jerked her head. "Jah?"

"What have you got to say about me comin' by like this again?"

Naomi opened her mouth to respond, but her words were cut off. *"Net*—never!"

Naomi swiveled around. There stood Papa, his arms crossed and his face a mask of anger. He'd looked at her the same way the day Zach was kidnapped.

Papa turned to face Caleb. "I give you a foot, and you take three yards! What's the meaning of all this huggin' and kissin' going on behind my back?"

"Papa, we weren't. Caleb just came by so we could talk."

"*Humph!* I know all about the thoughts on a young man's mind, and the buggy maker didn't come here in the middle of the night to talk!"

"That's not true, Abraham. I only wanted to speak with Naomi about her and me courtin'."

Papa smacked his hands together, and Naomi jumped right off the swing. "I thought I made myself clear on that subject awhile back. Naomi's not courtin' you or anyone else. She's needed here. Plain and simple." He pointed at the house while he glared at Naomi. "Get on to your room. We'll discuss this more in the morning."

He turned to face Caleb. "And you'd better get back in your buggy and head for home!"

A sob caught in Naomi's throat, but she did as her father commanded. Was there never to be any peace in this family? Would she ever be free from her guilt or experience the joys others her age felt when they were courted by some special fellow?

"Have you got the baby's car seat? I don't want to leave it in the car, where someone might steal it," Linda called as Jim was about to close the garage door.

He clenched his teeth. The whole time they'd been in Ohio visiting his folks, Linda had been overprotective of Jimmy, barely allowing Mom and Dad to hold the baby. On their trip home, she'd insisted on sitting in the backseat with him. Now she was acting paranoid over the boy's car seat. *What next?*

"Linda, it's not likely someone's going to break into our garage, get into the locked car, and steal a kid's car seat, for pity's sake."

She stood at the door leading to the house and frowned. It was that "I want my way, and I'll cry if I don't get it" kind of scowl she had learned so well.

They had been driving all day, it was almost nine o'clock, and Jim was too tired to argue. "Fine. Whatever."

Jim opened the back door of the van and unhooked the car seat. He lifted it out, set it on the concrete floor, and went around to open the hatch in order to get their luggage. In the process, he spotted a piece of the baby quilt sticking out of his toolbox. He glanced at the house. Linda had already gone inside with Jimmy.

"Whew! I've gotta ditch this thing." He opened the toolbox, withdrew the quilt, and headed into the room adjoining the garage, where he kept some of his painting supplies.

"Don't know why I didn't throw this silly quilt out when we were in Pennsylvania." Yet even now, Jim had no inclination to permanently dispose of the small blanket. It was weird, the way he felt when he looked at the little quilt. Jim knew if he threw it away, he'd be getting rid of the last shred of evidence to link him with the kidnapping of an Amish baby. Yet, he couldn't bring himself to throw the colorful blanket away.

Maybe later, he decided. *After Jimmy's older and I feel more like he actually belongs to Linda and me.*

Jim grabbed the canvas bag where he kept his paint rags and stuffed the quilt deep inside. Linda never went into his shop, so there was no danger of her discovering the quilt there.

A short time later, he was inside the house. He'd brought in their luggage, as well as the car seat. "Where do you want this thing?" he called to Linda, who had gone into the living room with the baby.

"How about the hall closet?"

"Sure, okay."

When Jim stepped into the room, he saw Linda sitting on the floor in front of the couch, and Jimmy stood by the coffee table, holding onto the edge. The child pivoted toward Linda, let go, and took two steps forward.

"He's walking!" Linda shouted. "Jim, our little boy took his first steps!"

Jim smiled at his wife's exuberance. She was going to make a great mother, and he'd done a good thing by providing her with the chance.

I sure wish there were some way I could notify the baby's family that he's safe and in good hands. If my child disappeared, I'd be worried and wondering if he was okay. That was another part of this whole thing that bothered Jim. How was the boy's family taking his disappearance? Jim had made an impulsive decision when he'd grabbed Jimmy off that picnic table. At the time, he hadn't felt much remorse. Truth was, when the adoption fell through, taking the baby seemed like an answer to his problem. He also convinced himself that he'd done the Amish family a favor. There were eight kids, the young woman had said. *That's too many for anyone to raise, let alone a man with no wife.*

"He's doing it again!" Linda's excited voice drove Jim's thoughts to the back of his mind.

He smiled as the baby took two more steps, flopped onto the floor, and giggled.

Jim leaned over and helped Jimmy to his feet. "There you go, little guy. Let's see if you can take a couple more steps before we call it a night." He held the boy's chubby hands and walked him a few feet from where Linda sat. "Trot on over to your mommy. Come on, I know you can do it."

He let go, and the baby toddled toward Linda's extended arms. She grabbed him in a hug. "Good job, Jimmy! That's my big boy.

"He's certainly adjusted well, don't you think?" she said, looking up at Jim. "It's as though he's always been ours."

He nodded and took a seat on the couch.

"When did you say the papers should arrive?"

"What papers?"

"His birth certificate and the final adoption papers."

"I told you before, they're being sent to my paint shop, where I plan to put them in our safe."

"I trust you to take care of everything, just like you always have," she said sweetly.

"I do my best." Jim pinched the bridge of his nose, feeling a headache coming on. *Thanks for the reminder, Linda. I'd better see about getting some phony papers drawn up—and soon.*

"I think I'm going to take this little fellow to his new room. It's been another long day of travel, and he's probably ready for bed." Linda yawned. "For that matter, I'm ready to call it a night, too."

"I'll put the suitcases in our rooms, and then I'm gonna give my foreman a call and see what he's got lined up for tomorrow."

"Oh, Jim, I hope you're not planning to go back to work right away."

"I've got to, Linda. My business won't run itself."

"But I thought you'd want to rest a few days and spend some quality time with me and Jimmy."

"We'll do something fun over the weekend. I don't have the luxury of taking any more time off to rest."

She sighed. "All you ever do is work. Sometimes I think you care more about your painting business than you do me."

His face heated. "What do you mean? I just spent three weeks with you, didn't I?"

"Yes, but—"

"And I made sure you got the Amish quilt you've always wanted. Doesn't that count for anything?"

"Of course it does, but *things* don't make up for time spent with those you love." Linda kissed the top of Jimmy's head. "I can't believe how much love I feel for this little guy already."

Jim stood and went to her side. "I love you more than you'll ever know, Linda." He bent to kiss her cheek. *Enough to steal an Amish baby so you could be a mother.*

"I know, and I love you, too. Guess I'm just tired and not quite ready to let go of our vacation."

"I understand." He took hold of the baby's chubby hand. "Let's get Jimmy settled in, then we can take a dip in the hot tub and head for our room."

Her eyes widened. "You want me to leave him alone on his first night?"

"Well, I thought—"

"Jim, he might be frightened sleeping in his new crib. And what if he wakes up during the night and needs me?"

Jim massaged his forehead. "You're not planning to sleep in the kid's room, I hope."

She nodded. "I thought maybe I'd sleep on an air mattress. Just for tonight, of course."

"Yeah, okay. Whatever you want to do." He grabbed the suitcases and trudged up the hall behind her.

CHAPTER 19

By the middle of August, Naomi felt defeated. The days were longer, the work was harder, the children became more difficult, and Papa seemed crankier than ever. Naomi was irritable, too; and no matter how many times she said, "I love you" or "I'm sorry for snapping," her siblings still acted as though she shouldn't be the person in charge.

Except for Sunday services, Naomi hadn't seen or spoken to Caleb since the night her daed caught them under the maple tree. Papa had made it clear when he spoke to her the next morning that she could not be courted by Caleb or anyone else.

Naomi leaned against the wooden counter and groaned. A little boy and his mother had just left the store. Every time Naomi saw a child about Zach's age, she thought of him. It had been two months since her little brother had been kidnapped, and in all that time, the police hadn't had any leads. Since there was nothing to go on, Naomi was sure they had quit looking.

She clutched the notebook lying in front of her. *After this much time, we may as well give up on the idea of Zach ever coming home. If that English man was gonna bring our boppli back, he would have done so by now. All we can do is hope and pray Zach's okay.*

The bell above the front door jingled, and in walked Ginny Meyers. Naomi's gaze darted to the back of the store, where Papa and the girls were stocking shelves. The last thing she needed was for him to see her talking with Ginny. He'd made it clear he didn't care much for the young English woman, and he didn't like Naomi talking to her.

"Hey, how are you?" Ginny asked, leaning across the counter.

"Haven't been able to get away from the restaurant much lately, and I've missed our little visits."

Naomi sighed. "Things are pretty much the same around here."

"No news on Zach?"

"Not a word."

"Sorry to hear that." Ginny leaned closer. "Can you meet me for lunch today? We can talk better if we're away from here."

Naomi turned her head toward the back of the store. She could only see Mary Ann and Nancy. Papa must have gone to the storage room for more boxes. "I—I don't see how I could get away."

"Tell your dad you want to go for a walk or something. Say you're bringing your lunch and will eat it somewhere along the way." Ginny smiled, her blue eyes twinkling with mischief. "I'll meet you in the park at noon."

Naomi's hands grew sweaty. She hadn't done anything so bold since she crept out of the house to see what Caleb wanted. What if someone saw her with Ginny and told her father? And what about the girls? Would Papa mind her leaving them at the store with him while she went off by herself for a while?

"I can't make any promises, but I'll see if I can get away," she whispered. "If I'm not there by twelve fifteen, you'll know I'm not coming."

Ginny winked. "Fair enough. See you soon." Her long, blond hair hung down her back this morning, and it swished back and forth as she swaggered toward the front door. Naomi couldn't help but wonder how she would feel if she could let her hair down in public. She'd been thinking about the English world a lot lately. The worse things got at home, the more appeal the modern world had for her. If she were English and not Amish, she'd be allowed to do more—probably wouldn't have so many brothers and sisters to look after, either.

The door closed behind Ginny, and Naomi took up her work again. She had to make a list of things they needed to order. Papa would be expecting it to be ready by the time he was done at the back of the store.

Half an hour later, Naomi was finished, and just in time.

"Have ya got that list done yet?" Papa asked as he stepped behind the counter and peered over her shoulder.

She lifted the tablet and without turning around handed it to him. "Say, Papa, I was wonderin' if it would be all right if I take my lunch pail and go for a walk. I sure could use some fresh air."

"*Humph!* The thermometer in the window shows it's almost ninety outside. Most likely the humidity's at ninety percent, too. Nothin' refreshing 'bout that."

She nodded. "I know, but it seems even hotter inside the store."

"Jah, well, I don't mind if ya eat your lunch outside, but you'll have to take the girls along."

Naomi swiveled on the stool. "Why can't they stay here with you? Won't you be needing their help if a bunch of customers shows up?"

Papa gave his beard a quick tug and stared over the top of her head, refusing to make eye contact. "Guess you've got a point."

"I can go then?"

He nodded curtly. "Don't be gone long. I've got some errands to run later, and I can't leave Nancy and Mary Ann in charge of the store while I'm gone."

"I won't be late. I promise."

Jim entered the house through the garage door. He and his crew had started painting an apartment complex nearby, and Jim thought he'd swing by the house and get a couple jugs of iced tea. They were having unusually warm weather here in the Northwest, even for the middle of August. The last thing he needed was for any of the guys to keel over with heat exhaustion.

"Linda, I'm home for a few minutes!" he called.

When there was no response, he headed down the hall to their room. He discovered Linda asleep on the bed with Jimmy curled up next to her. At the foot of the bed was a stack of things they'd picked up on their trip to the East Coast in June.

He tiptoed out of the room. No point in waking Linda or the baby. Besides, he needed to get some aspirin from the medicine cabinet. He had another headache and wondered if it was from the heat. The guy on the radio said the temperature had reached almost eighty degrees. It was only eight o'clock in the morning, so Jim figured it might be in the high nineties later in the day.

When he emerged from the bathroom a short time later, Linda and Jimmy were still asleep. Jim scooped up the brochures and headed for the kitchen. He was surprised after all this time that Linda hadn't thrown the stuff away.

Jim grabbed two jugs of iced tea from the refrigerator and decided to take the time to pour himself a glass. His painting crew was already hard at work, and he figured he could take a few minutes before heading back to the job site.

Dropping into a chair at the table, he flipped through the stack of magazines and other papers. A newspaper called *The Budget* was at the bottom of the pile. It was published in Sugarcreek, Ohio, for the Amish and Mennonites. Jim discovered there were numerous articles written by Plain people all over the nation. There was even a want-ad section. *Hmm. . .this might be a way I could let Jimmy's family know he's okay.*

Jim jotted down the address and information needed to place an ad and stuck it inside his shirt pocket. He'd get something drafted soon and send it off. *Better not mail it from here, though. Don't want to take the chance of anyone tracing its origin.*

Jim decided he would write up the announcement tomorrow, and when they went to Boise next weekend to see Linda's folks, he'd take the ad and mail it from there, along with cash. *I'm not dumb enough to send a check, that's for sure.*

"What are you doing home, Jim? I thought you were at work."

Jim jumped up, dropping *The Budget* to the floor. "Don't scare me like that, Linda."

"Sorry. I thought you heard us come into the room."

She held the baby, and Jimmy smiled and said, "Da-Da-Da."

"Yep, that's me. I'm your daddy, little guy." Jim extended his arms, and the child went willingly to him.

"What are you doing with all our vacation stuff?" Linda asked.

"I—uh—found the brochures at the foot of our bed and thought I'd take a look." He sat down at the table, balancing Jimmy on one knee. "I was surprised to see all this stuff. Figured by now you'd have thrown out the junk you brought home from our trip."

She wrinkled her nose and took the seat across from him. "It's not junk, Jim. There's a lot of interesting things about the Amish in those brochures." She bent over and picked up *The Budget*. "Look, there's even an Amish newspaper."

"Yeah, I noticed."

"Earlier today, I was reading some of the articles written by Amish and Mennonite people," she said. "They sure live a different lifestyle from the rest of America."

He nodded and kissed the top of Jimmy's head.

"I'd like to visit Pennsylvania Dutch country again sometime. Maybe try to learn a little more about the Amish people's unusual culture. When do you think we might make another trip to Pennsylvania?"

Jim nearly choked. The last thing he needed was to bring his wife and boy back to Lancaster County so he could be snagged for kidnapping. "I—uh—think Mom and Dad are planning to make a trip out here next summer, so there's not much point in us making plans to go to the East Coast for a few more years."

Linda's lower lip protruded, but it wasn't going to work this time. Her whining, pouting, or cajoling would not get her a trip to Pennsylvania or even Ohio—not if Jim had anything to say about it.

"Naomi, I'm glad you could make it."

Naomi looked over at Ginny, who had flopped onto the picnic bench. "I was surprised Papa had no objections to me leavin' the store."

Ginny smiled. "That is one for the books."

"Maybe he's sick of seeing me." Naomi stared down at her clasped hands. "Ever since Zach was taken, he's had trouble lookin' me in the eye."

Ginny clicked her tongue. "Well, shame on him. Doesn't your dad realize you didn't leave Zach sitting on that picnic table on purpose? It's not like you were hoping he'd be kidnapped or anything."

Naomi swallowed the bile rising in her throat. "I've never admitted this to anyone, but the truth is, I've often wished I could be free of caring for my family—even daydreamed about how it would be if I were an only child."

Ginny elbowed Naomi in the ribs. "Get real, girl! Anyone with brothers and sisters has wished that more than once. I can't tell you how many times I've wondered how much better my life would be if my brother, Tim, had never been born."

Tears welled up in Naomi's eyes, and she sniffed in an effort to hold them back. It seemed like all she did anymore was cry. Cry and feel sorry for herself.

"I'm here to tell you that just because you wished you had no siblings to care for doesn't mean you were the cause of your brother being abducted."

"But I'm the one who left him in the yard with a complete stranger." She gulped on a sob. "If Zach never comes home, I don't think I'll be able to forgive myself."

"If your family was more supportive, you could probably deal with this a lot better." Ginny squeezed Naomi's hand. "Want to know what I think?"

Naomi shrugged, knowing Ginny would probably give her opinion no matter how she replied.

"I think you need to get away from this place."

"What place? The park?"

Ginny snickered. "No, silly. Lancaster County and your accusing family."

Naomi's mouth fell open. "What are you saying?"

"I'm saying you and I should hit the road—jump in my sports car and head for parts unknown." Ginny frowned. "I'm getting sick of helping out at my folks' restaurant. If I don't strike out on my own pretty soon, they'll have me tied to that place."

Naomi trembled. Just the thought of leaving home sent shivers up her back. She had never been any farther north than East Earl and no farther south than Strasburg. Truth was, the Fishers were a stay-at-home kind of family. They didn't hire English drivers to take them on vacation trips like some in their community were fond of doing.

"Promise me you'll think about what I said. Your family doesn't appreciate you, and my advice is to get away. Put as many miles between you and them as you can."

"What about the promise I made to Mama before she died? I told her I'd look after the family, and if I leave, I'll be breakin' that vow."

"Get real, Naomi. Nobody in your family listens to what you say anymore. You've told me that several times. You wouldn't be reneging on your promise; you'd be setting your family free."

Naomi swiped her hand across her damp cheeks. "You think they'd see it that way?"

Ginny nodded.

Naomi filled her lungs with the humid air clinging to her clothes like flypaper. Would she be dishonoring her mother's wishes if she left? Could she do it? She grabbed hold of her lunch pail and squeezed the handles. "I'll think about it. That's all I can promise."

CHAPTER 20

Naomi awoke in a cold sweat. She'd been dreaming about Zach again. She'd done that several times since his disappearance, but this dream was the worst. In the nightmare, Zach sat on the picnic table, his arms outstretched, tears coursing down his rosy cheeks. She stood in the doorway, wanting to go to him but unable to move her legs. She'd tried calling Zach's name but couldn't find her voice. A thick fog settled over the baby, and when it lifted, he was gone.

Naomi closed her eyes and drew in a deep breath. She was glad it had only been a dream. The vision of Zach with his arms extended still disturbed her. "Be with him, Lord," she prayed. "Be with my baby brother wherever he is."

Naomi sat up and swung her legs over the side of the bed. Maybe it was time to take down the crib. Seeing it sitting there empty was a painful reminder that her baby brother was gone. Maybe this was the reason he haunted her dreams so often. She'd left the crib up at first, hoping Zach would be returned. Then she justified it by telling herself that leaving it there was a reminder to pray for him.

"I'll remember to pray for Zach even without seeing his crib," she murmured.

Naomi tasted salty tears as she dismantled her little brother's bed. "I'm such a failure," she moaned. "Maybe Ginny's right. My family would be better off without me."

She hauled the crib across the hall and positioned it behind several boxes in the storage closet. *Guess Ginny didn't actually say they'd be better off if I was gone. She just said I'd be setting them free. But that adds up to the same thing in my estimation.*

Naomi tiptoed back to her room. It was only five in the morning, and she didn't want to wake the younger ones, who were still asleep in their beds. *I need to have a heart-to-heart talk with Papa before I make any decisions that could affect the rest of my life. I have to find out how he really feels about me. If there's even a chance he thinks we can iron things out, I'll keep trying to make it work.*

Naomi slipped a dark green dress over her head, quickly did up her hair, and put her white head covering in place. She padded across the room in her bare feet and grabbed the doorknob. Papa would probably be doing his morning chores in the barn by now. If her brothers weren't working near him, she'd go there and talk to Papa before starting breakfast.

Several minutes later, Naomi stepped into the barn. It was dark and quiet, with only the occasional nicker of the horses to break the peaceful silence. She made her way toward the goat pen, knowing Papa usually started milking the goats first thing.

Soon she heard his muffled voice, and the steady *ping, ping, ping* of milk spurting into the bucket confirmed that Papa was there. She halted at the door when she perceived his first words.

"Oh, Lord God, You know how hard I've been tryin'," he wailed. "I want to forgive the man who stole Zach from us. I want to forgive Naomi for her part in Zach's disappearance, too, but it's ever so hard." He sniffed, and Naomi could tell from her dad's quavering voice that he was close to tears.

"I thought if I kept praying and trusting, You'd bring Zach home to us, but that hasn't happened. Where is Your goodness, Lord?" There was a pause, followed by a deep moan. "Naomi hasn't been happy since Sarah died and she was left to care for the kinner. Truth is, I think all my oldest daughter wants is to be free of us. . .to marry the buggy maker and forget about her responsibilities here. I have to wonder if she didn't leave Zach outside with that English fellow on purpose, hopin' he might take him. Then she would be shed of one little brother." He grunted. "Maybe she'd like to get rid of the rest of her brothers and sisters, too."

Naomi covered her mouth with the palm of her hand and steadied herself against the wall in order to keep from toppling over. Papa was baring his soul to God, and she was witness to it. For the first time since Zach's kidnapping, she'd heard her daed say what had been buried deep in his soul. Papa not only blamed her for the kidnapping, but he thought she'd done it on purpose.

"Truth is, Lord, I can barely look at Naomi anymore," Papa continued. "Sometimes I wish—"

Naomi couldn't stand to hear another word. She choked on a sob, spun around, and rushed out of the barn.

Abraham felt washed out as he trudged toward the house. He'd been up since before dawn, done all his chores, and had spent more than an hour in the barn, praying and telling God everything on his heart. It hadn't helped. He felt as miserable now as when he'd begun praying. If only there was a way to relieve his pain. If he could just make things right again.

When Abraham entered the kitchen, he thought it was strange that none of the gas lanterns were lit. Naomi was usually up by now, scurrying around the kitchen and yelling at Nancy and Mary Ann to get the table set for breakfast. There was no sign of her, and none of the children were around.

Maybe she overslept. If Naomi isn't up yet, there's a good chance the others are still in bed, too. His three youngest children relied on their older sister to rouse them each morning. They'd probably sleep 'til noon if she didn't make them get up.

Abraham ambled across the room and set the pail of goat's milk on the kitchen table. When he lit the lantern overhead, a piece of paper came into view. It was lying on the table, right where he sat for every meal. *Looks like some kind of a letter.*

He sank into a chair and began to read.

Dear Papa:

I came to the barn earlier, hoping we might talk. We never got that chance because I overheard you speaking to God. I've known for many weeks, ever since Zach was taken, that you blame me for everything. I understand. I blame myself, too.

After hearing the rest of your conversation with the Lord, I was hit with the cold, hard fact that you believe I wanted Zach to be taken. It's not so, Papa. I would never want harm to come to any of the kinner, and I sure didn't wish for that English fellow to take my baby brother.

I've come to the conclusion that it would be best for the family if I left home. I'm no good to anyone, and none of the children want to mind me anymore. I'm heading out with Ginny Meyers into the English world. Don't know where we're going, but it'll be far from here.

Please know that I love you and the rest of the family, and I pray someday you'll find it in your heart to forgive me. I'll never stop praying for Zach and his safe return, but if God doesn't answer that prayer, then I'm askin' Him to give Zach a good life with the one who took him.

Your oldest daughter,
Naomi

Abraham let the paper slip from his fingers and fall to the floor. He sat there for several minutes as though in a daze. This couldn't be happening. It had to be a horrible dream. Naomi always looked out for the kinner. Surely she wouldn't set out with that spoiled English girl and leave her brothers and sisters to fend for themselves. And what about the store? Who would help him run the place now?

Abraham fell forward, his head resting on the table. *First, I lost my dear wife in death, then my baby boy was snatched away, and now my oldest daughter has run off.* He lifted his head as hot tears streamed down his face and dripped onto his beard. *Dear Lord in heaven, I've lost them all. Oh, God, help me! What have I done?*

Naomi stood trembling at the back door of Meyers' Family Restaurant. It was still early, but she knew someone was inside because there were lights on. *Probably getting ready for the Saturday morning breakfast crowd.*

She drew in a deep breath, trying to steady her nerves. She should be at home, getting breakfast on and lining out the chores she and the children needed to do for the day. Instead, she was about to embark on a journey that would likely change the rest of her life. Her family's life would be different now, too. *Will Samuel, Nancy, and Mary Ann be better off without their big sister telling them what to do? And what of Matthew, Jake, and Norman? Will they be relieved to hear I've run off?*

She gulped in another breath and sank to the concrete porch. Her legs were still wobbly from running most of the way to town. *What will Papa think when he reads my note? Will he be glad I'm gone? Will he hire a maid to help out now, or will he try to do everything alone?*

After hearing the hurtful words her daed said to God in the barn, Naomi had made a beeline for the house, where she scrawled a note to Papa and hurriedly packed a few clothes and personal things. Then she'd headed out on foot, not wanting to take the time to hitch up the horse and buggy and knowing Papa might have heard if she had. Besides, taking the buggy would have complicated things. She would have had to leave it somewhere in town for Papa or one of the brothers to pick up later on. No, it was better that she'd come on her own.

Naomi stared across the empty parking lot. No customers yet, so it must be too early. Would Ginny be working today? What if she wasn't? How would Naomi let her friend know she was ready to leave Lancaster County behind? She knew Ginny lived somewhere in the nearby town of Soudersburg, but she didn't know the address.

Maybe I could ask her folks or someone else who works at the restaurant. Naomi got to her feet, and the back door suddenly opened. Relief flooded her soul when Ginny stepped onto the porch carrying a sack of garbage. She wore a pair of blue jeans and a yellow T-shirt with a white apron tied around her waist.

"Naomi! What are you doing here at this time of the day?"

Naomi's knees threatened to buckle. She sat back down with a moan.

Ginny tossed the plastic sack into the dumpster beside the porch and took a seat on the step. "What's wrong? I can tell by your swollen eyes and red cheeks that you've been crying."

"I—I—came to see you."

Ginny pointed at the suitcase sitting on the other side of Naomi. "You've run away from home?"

Naomi nodded as tears streamed down her cheeks. "I can't go back, Ginny."

"Why? What happened?"

Naomi quickly related the story of how she'd overheard her father praying in the barn. "He believes I left Zach on the picnic table on purpose. He thinks our family would be better off without me."

Ginny draped her arm over Naomi's shoulder. "You did the right thing by leaving. I've told you many times that your family doesn't appreciate you." She sighed. "Truthfully, I don't think my parents appreciate me, either. They've got me doing kitchen duty this morning, and Mom knows how much I hate it."

Naomi swiped her hand across her face and sniffed. "If you're still wantin' the two of us to run away together, I'm more than ready to go."

"Now?" Ginny looked over her shoulder as though someone might come out of the restaurant and catch the two of them making plans.

"Jah, if you can get away."

Ginny chewed on her bottom lip. "Let's see. . . . I drove my own car to work this morning, so transportation's not a problem. However, I would need to go home and get some clothes and my bankbook. Can't very well leave town without any money."

"But today's Saturday, and the bank's not open," Naomi reminded. "I have a little money with me—took it from my dresser drawer where I'd been savin' up to buy a present for Jake. His birthday is two weeks from today."

Ginny scrambled to her feet. "That's going to be one birthday you'll have to miss."

Naomi didn't need the reminder. The pain of not being there to help celebrate any of her family's birthdays smarted like a bee sting.

"I doubt you have enough money to take us very far, but I've managed to save up a pretty good sum." Ginny smiled. "And for your information, the bank we use in Lancaster is open 'til one today, and even if it weren't, there's always an ATM machine."

"After you get some money, then what?"

"First off, I'm going into the restaurant to get my purse. It's got my car keys and driver's license, which are both vital items. Then I'll leave a note for my folks. When I'm sure nobody's looking, I'll come back outside; we'll jump in my sports car, head for the house, grab a few things, and be off to the bank." She grinned as though she was finding great joy in all of this. "From there, it's hit the road and never look back!"

Abraham sat up. He didn't know how long he'd been leaning over the table with his head resting on his arms. Rays of light streamed through the kitchen windows, bouncing off the walls and sending swirls of tiny dust particles through the air.

The older boys must be outside doing their chores yet, but he was sure the younger ones were still in bed. If there was ever a day when Abraham felt like closing the store and staying home, this was that day. Not since Zach's kidnapping had he felt such anguish. How could he go about business as usual when Naomi had run off? How could he have let such a terrible thing happen? All Abraham wanted to do was climb the stairs to his room, crawl into bed, and pull the covers over his head.

But I have a family to support, he reminded himself. *Besides, closing the store won't bring Naomi home. Only God can do that, same as with Zach.* He grimaced. Would God answer his prayers where his two children were concerned? He'd obviously failed them—probably failed God, too. If only he'd hired someone to help out after Sarah died. If he hadn't been so stubborn and tightfisted, Naomi wouldn't have had to work so hard. If she'd had more free time—time to do some fun things with others her age—maybe she wouldn't have been preoccupied and left Zach alone in the yard.

"I've been too hard on her," he moaned. "Now it's too late."

"Who ya talkin' to, Papa, and what's it too late for?"

Abraham turned in his chair. Samuel stood inside the kitchen door, a lock of blond hair in his eyes, his cheeks still rosy from sleep.

"Where are your sisters?" Abraham asked. "Are they up yet?"

Samuel shrugged. "Don't rightly know. I woke up and didn't smell anything cookin', so I thought I'd come down here and have a look-see."

Abraham pushed his chair away from the table. "You'd better wake 'em. Nancy and Mary Ann are gonna have to fix breakfast."

Samuel's blue eyes reflected his obvious confusion. "What about Naomi? Why ain't she in here cookin'?"

Abraham grabbed the pail of goat's milk he'd set on the table earlier and lumbered across the room. He jerked open the refrigerator door, placed it inside, and withdrew a bottle of cold milk. "Naomi's gone."

"Gone? What do you mean, Papa? Where'd she go?"

Abraham opened his mouth to respond, but Nancy's shrill voice cut him off. "Papa, when I woke up, I looked in Naomi's room 'cause she didn't wake us like she usually does. The door was open, and most of her clothes were lyin' on the bed." She wrinkled her forehead. "Zach's crib wasn't there no more, and I'm thinkin' it's all kind of strange."

Mary Ann, who stood beside her older sister, nodded. "Where is Naomi, Papa? How come she don't have breakfast started yet?"

Abraham set the bottle of milk on the table and pulled out a chair. He motioned his children to do the same. "I'm afraid I've got some bad news concerning your older sister."

"What's wrong? Is Naomi sick?" The question came from Mary Ann, and she looked mighty worried.

Abraham drew in a deep breath as he prayed for the right words. He bent down and retrieved Naomi's note, which had fallen to the floor after he'd read it. "Naomi left me this," he said, waving it in the air. "Says here she's leavin' home because she feels guilty about Zach being taken." Truth was, there was a lot more to it than that, but Abraham didn't have the courage to admit to his children that he was the primary cause of Naomi going.

"She's run away? Is that what you're sayin', Papa?" Nancy's eyes were wide, and her mouth hung slightly open.

He nodded as a lump formed in his throat.

"Why would she do such a thing? Don't Naomi love us no more?" Samuel's chin quivered as he spoke.

"I'm sure she loves us," Abraham said, "but she blames herself for Zach's kidnapping, and she thinks we'd be better off without her."

"That ain't true!" Nancy hollered. "I love my sister, and since Zach left, we've needed her more'n ever."

It was a fact. They did need Naomi, but no one in the family had shown her that—least of all Abraham. He placed the note facedown on the table. "We're gonna have to find a way to deal with this, ya know."

"Let's go after her!" Samuel yelled. He jumped up from the table and grabbed his straw hat from the wall peg where he'd hung it last night.

Abraham shook his head. "Slow down once, Son. We can't go runnin' all over the place hunting for Naomi when we don't have a clue where she's gone."

"But she must've said somethin' in that note," Samuel argued. "Sure as anything, she'd want us to know where she was goin'."

"All she said was that she was taking off with Virginia Meyers, the flighty English gal who hangs around the store always askin' for rubber stamps."

"Ginny?" Nancy's eyebrows lifted.

He nodded. "Jah. Said the two of 'em were headin' into the English world and didn't know where they were goin'."

Mary Ann dropped her head to the table and sobbed. Nancy whimpered and patted her sister's shoulder. Samuel stood at the door with his arms folded.

"All we can do is pray for Naomi, same as we've been doin' for Zach," Abraham said with a catch in his voice. He hated to see how miserable the children were. More than that, he couldn't understand how he had let such a shocking thing happen.

CHAPTER 21

"I'm glad we're about the same size and you could wear some of my clothes," Ginny said, reaching over to tap Naomi's jeans-clad knees. "It would have looked like you'd hired me as your driver and were going on vacation if you'd kept wearing your plain, long dresses and head covering." She glanced over at Naomi and smiled.

Naomi sat in the passenger's seat of Ginny's fancy red sports car, uncomfortable with the speed they were going and unaccustomed to the cold air blasting her in the face from the air-conditioning. She stared down at the faded blue jeans and pink T-shirt Ginny had loaned her. The items of clothes were one more thing that felt foreign. "I'm not so sure about this. It feels odd wearin' men's trousers and havin' my hair hanging down my back with no kapp."

"You'll soon get used to it."

Naomi wasn't sure she would ever become accustomed to the English world. She and Ginny had only been on the road a few hours, and already she felt out of place and missed home.

"Anytime you're ready to stop for lunch, just say the word." Ginny tapped the steering wheel with her long fingernails. "Since we left in such a hurry this morning, I didn't get breakfast."

"Me neither." Truth be told, Naomi had no appetite for food. Things were so mixed up, and her brain felt muddled. She doubted she could eat a bite of food, much less keep it down.

"Do you know where we're heading?" Naomi asked.

Ginny nodded. "West."

"How far west?"

"All the way."

"You mean clear to the Pacific Ocean?"

"Yep. I've always wanted to stick my feet in the frigid waters along the Washington or Oregon coast. I've got a friend living in Portland, and we can probably stay with her awhile."

Naomi shivered. Just thinking about being that far from home and staying with strangers gave her the chills. Had she done the right thing by leaving? Would she be able to adjust to life in the modern world? Going English seemed like the best thing to do, since she had no other place to go. Ginny was her only friend right now, and Naomi knew she couldn't make it on her own.

"You'll be fine once we get out of Pennsylvania. This will be such an adventure that soon you'll forget about your unappreciative family and the nasty way they've treated you."

Naomi stared at the passing scenery, forcing her tears back. She'd left home feeling it was the thing to do, but she would never forget her family. How had Papa and the rest of them taken the news of her leaving? Did they feel sad, or were they glad she wouldn't be around to tell them what to do?

"You think you'll miss your folks?" she asked her friend.

Ginny wrinkled her nose. "I think they'll miss me more than I do them. After all, they won't have my help at the restaurant anymore. To tell you the truth, I believe that's all they think I'm good for."

Naomi could relate to that feeling. Ever since Mama died, she'd felt unappreciated.

"I've got enough money to take us to Oregon, but we'll have to get jobs after we get there," Ginny said. "My friend Carla used to live in Pennsylvania, but she works at a fitness center in Portland now. I'm hoping she can get me a position there."

"But what can I do? I only know how to work at the store and around home."

"Guess you could get a job at a restaurant, waiting tables or doing dishes in the kitchen."

Naomi grimaced. The last thing she wanted to do was wash dishes.

"Mom, the mail's here, and there's a letter addressed to you from your cousin Edna in Pennsylvania." Abby waved the stack of letters and placed them on the kitchen table. Fannie rinsed the last dish in the sink full of clean water, grabbed a towel, and quickly dried her hands. "Guess I'd better take a peek. I haven't heard from Edna in several weeks."

Abby pulled out a chair for her mother. "Have a seat, and I'll pour you a cup of mint tea."

Fannie smiled appreciatively. "That'd be nice." She ripped open her cousin's letter and withdrew a note card with a hand-drawn picture of a chocolate cake on the front. Inside was written: "Count your age by friends, not years. Count your blessings, not your tears. Hope you'll help me celebrate my fiftieth birthday on Saturday, September sixth, with a picnic by the pond."

Fannie smiled. "Leave it to Cousin Edna to plan her own party. She always was one to do things a bit differently than others."

Abby chuckled and handed her mother a cup of hot tea. "You thinkin' about going?"

Fannie took a sip, enjoying the unique flavor of her homegrown lemon mint tea. "Sure would be nice, but who would mind the store while we were gone?"

"Not *we*, Mom," Abby corrected. "Edna invited you, and I can look after the store for the few days you'd be gone."

"Hmm. . ." Fannie pursed her lips. "What if things got really busy? Sometimes it's hard for both of us to wait on customers when the tourists come by."

Abby shrugged. "I could always call on Lena to help. I'm sure she wouldn't mind bringing her quilting to the store to work on. That way, she'd be available to help whenever I might need her."

Fannie stared into her cup, watching the steam curl, lift, and disappear into the air. It would be nice to see Edna again, and since she'd be in the area, she might even be so bold as to drop by Abraham Fisher's store and see how he was doing. Ever since his visit to the quilt shop, she'd been praying for him and his kidnapped boy. She'd never admit it to anyone, but truth was, she'd thought of Abraham quite often. She could tell he was hurting bad. Even though he'd seemed kind of terse when they first started talking, underneath it all, she sensed he was a man with a tender heart.

"Mom, what do you think?" Abby's sweet voice broke into Fannie's thoughts.

"Think about what?"

"Me mindin' the quilt shop while you go to Pennsylvania?"

Fannie drank the rest of her tea and set the cup aside. "I'll pray about it. How's that sound?"

Abby smiled. "I'll be prayin', too. Prayin' you'll realize how badly you need to get away." She patted her mother's hand. "You work too hard, ya know that?"

Fannie pushed her chair away from the table. "I like to work. Keeps my hands busy and my mind off things I'd rather not be thinkin' about."

"Like Dad? Are ya still missin' him, Mom?"

Fannie stood. "I'll always miss your daed, but as time goes by, the pain gets less, and only the pleasant memories of the past remain. Besides, as my mamm used to say, 'There's no sense advertising your troubles, 'cause there's no market for 'em anywhere.'"

"Guess that's true enough." Abby sobered. "I miss Dad, too. I can't imagine what it must be like for you, Mom. Losin' the man you'd loved so much must have felt like someone put a hole in your heart."

Fannie nodded. "That's the way it was at first. I couldn't understand why God would allow your daed to die of a heart attack. After searching the scriptures, I came to realize God could use my grief for good if I let Him."

Abby placed the cups and saucers in the sink and quickly washed them. "Guess we'd better hurry if we're gonna get to the store on time."

Fannie glanced at the clock on the far wall. "Yep. We've spent more time blabberin' than we usually do in the morning, but it's been good, don't ya think?"

Abby dried her hands and grabbed her head covering from the back of the chair. "I always enjoy our time together." She leaned over and kissed her mother's cheek. "And I thank the Lord every day that He gave me a special mamm like you."

Tears welled up in Fannie's eyes, but she blinked them away. "Go on with you now. Let's get the buggy hitched."

Caleb climbed out of the open carriage and headed for the Fishers' store. Mary Ann and Nancy sat on the front porch, eating their lunches. "Got anything good in those pails?" he called.

"Just a sandwich and a few cookies," Nancy answered. "Everything was so confusing at our place this mornin', we didn't have a chance to put much together."

"Jah, Papa seemed pretty upset, and so was we."

Caleb leaned against the porch railing. "What's the problem? No one's sick, I hope."

"Naomi left."

He squinted at Nancy. "Left?"

"She's run off with that English girl, Ginny."

Caleb could hardly believe his ears. "Would you repeat that?"

"She's run off with Ginny Meyers. Left a note on the kitchen table this mornin'." Nancy shook her head. "I still can't believe she'd do something like that. I think it's a sin and a shame the way she ran out on us."

Caleb was sure there was more to the story. Naomi wouldn't just run off and leave her responsibilities for no good reason. Her obligation to care for the family was why she couldn't go to young people's functions or court. She'd told him so several times. "What exactly did her note say?"

"Said she feels guilty about Zach bein' kidnapped and that she was takin' off with Ginny Meyers out into the English world."

Caleb thought this was the worst possible news. Naomi didn't know how to function in the fancy, English world. She was in for a rude awakening, and leaving her family didn't make a lick of sense. If Naomi didn't come home, all his plans and dreams for them getting married would vanish like vapor from a boiling pot.

Caleb had come to the Fishers' store in hopes of trying to talk Naomi into seeing him in secret again. That wasn't going to happen. Not today and maybe not ever.

I'd go after her if I knew where she was goin', but I don't. He turned and clomped down the steps, his boots echoing against the wooden planks.

"Where ya headed, Caleb?" Mary Ann called. "I thought you was goin' into the store."

He shook his head but kept on walking toward his buggy. "No need to now."

Abraham sank onto the wooden stool behind the counter in his store. He didn't know how he had made it through the morning. As soon as he'd come to town, he had gone to Meyers' Family Restaurant, hoping Virginia's parents knew where the girls had run off to. Their daughter had left them a note, same as Naomi had, but it said nothing about where they planned to go, how long they would be gone, or how they would survive. Abraham knew the words Naomi had heard him speaking to God had been the cause of her outlandish decision.

He glanced at the clock on the opposite wall and tried to concentrate on the invoices in front of him. It was a little past noon, and the girls had taken their lunches outside to eat on the front porch. Normally, he'd be ravenous by now, but not today. Abraham had no interest in food. All he wanted to do was find his missing children. If he could have Zach and Naomi back home, he'd be happy and would change. No more pushing Naomi to get things done. No comparing her to his wife. No expecting his oldest daughter to take charge of the kinner without any outside help.

Abraham leaned over and massaged his aching head. *I'd love on my boy lots, too. Should have spent more time with him when he was here.* He closed his eyes and tried to focus on the work he needed to do today. It was no use. All he could think about was how badly he'd messed up.

"You don't look like you're gettin' much work done. What's the matter; have you got a headache?"

Abraham looked up. Jacob Weaver stood on the other side of the counter, holding his straw hat in one hand and a fishing pole in the other. "Jacob, I didn't hear ya come in."

"No, I guess not. Been standing here for several seconds. I'm taking the day off, and I was hoping the two of us could go fishin'."

"Sorry, but I can't."

"Isn't it time to put aside your memories of the day Sarah was killed and quit blaming yourself because you went fishing? I thought you were giving things over to God."

Abraham shook his head. "This isn't about that. Things are really bad for me and the family right now."

Jacob leaned the pole against the counter and hung his hat on the nearest wall peg. "What's the trouble, my friend? Have you heard something about Zach that's not good news?"

Abraham shook his head. "Haven't heard a word about the boppli, but now Naomi's gone, too."

Jacob's dark eyebrows lifted. "What do you mean? Where is she?"

"I don't know. She left a note on the kitchen table sayin' she was leaving—running off with that English friend of hers, Virginia Meyers."

"Did she say why?" Jacob's question pierced Abraham clean to his soul.

He hung his head, unable to look his friend in the eye. "It's because of me. She overheard me talkin' to God this morning out in the barn."

"Mind if I ask what you were saying?"

"I told the Lord I haven't been able to forgive the man who took my boppli or Naomi, either, for leavin' Zach out in the yard with that English man. Said I thought she might have done it on purpose and that she wanted to be free of us in order to marry the buggy maker."

Jacob's sharp intake of breath was enough to let Abraham know what his good friend thought about that kind of prayer. More than likely, the man thought he was not only a bad father but also a way-ward Christian, talking to God that way.

"I didn't mean all those things," Abraham was quick to say. "Just got confused about the way I was feelin' and all." He drew in a shaky breath. "I thought maybe if I had a little heart-to-heart talk with my Maker, I'd feel better."

"Naomi heard your prayers, left a note on the table, and has run away?"

"That's about the size of it, and I feel like I've been kicked in the stomach."

"I imagine you do."

"Isn't it bad enough that God took my little boy? Does He have to punish me further by taking my oldest daughter?" Abraham felt a burn-ing at the back of his eyes, and he squeezed them shut as he fought for control.

Jacob stepped around the counter and placed his hand on Abraham's trembling shoulder. "Give it to God, Abraham. He's not the cause of all this, ya know."

Abraham shook his head. "No, I don't know. He could have stopped it from happening. He could have—"

"God don't work that way, and we must remember His ways are not our ways." Jacob squeezed Abraham's shoulder. "God loves you. Focus on His person and His goodness. Wait for Him to act. Allow Him to heal your heart and help you forgive those who have trespassed against you."

"I—I don't know if I can do that."

"You can, and you must. Release the anger. Pray for the man who took your boy. Give Zach and Naomi over to the Lord and rest in Him." Jacob paused. "First Corinthians ten, verse thirteen reminds us that He will never suffer us to be tested above what we are able to bear. God told Paul, 'My grace is sufficient for thee.'"

"I feel more like Job than Paul," Abraham said. "Everything I dearly loved has been snatched away from me. Sarah—Zach—and now Naomi."

"That's not true, Abraham. You still have six other kinner who love you and need your support."

Abraham cleared his throat, trying to dislodge the lump. "Wish I knew for sure that Zach and Naomi are all right. I could rest a lot easier if I had the assurance they're both safe."

Jacob's eyes were watery as though he, too, were fighting tears. "Maybe God has plans for your boy—and Naomi, too. Might could be one or both of 'em has a job to do out there in the English world."

"A job? What kind of job?"

"Maybe the man who took Zach will find his way to God because of something Zach says or does."

"But how could that be? Zach's only a year old. What does he know about God?"

Jacob shrugged. "Probably nothin' yet, but in the days ahead, a lot could happen."

"And Naomi? How do you think God will use her running away to bring about something good?"

"Can't rightly say, but I do know if you turn them both over to the heavenly Father, trust Him in all things, and picture the two of them livin' healthy, happy lives, you'll have a lot more peace." Jacob smiled. "Isaiah forty, verse thirty-one: 'But they that wait upon the Lord shall renew their strength.' "

" 'They shall mount up with wings as eagles; they shall run, and not be weary; and they shall walk, and not faint.' " Abraham finished the verse of scripture with tears rolling down his cheeks. "I'll wait, Jacob. Wait on the Lord and ask Him to protect my kinner and use them in a mighty way. It won't be easy, though."

CHAPTER 22

Before boarding the bus, Fannie hugged her daughter one last time as a knot rose in her throat. She and Abby hadn't been apart more than a few hours since Abby was a young girl and used to spend the night with her friend Rachel. Ever since Abby's dad passed away, she had preferred to be with her mother. Fannie hoped Abby would be okay during the few days she would be gone.

"It's all right, Mom," Abby said, as though sensing her mother's concerns. "I'll be fine, and so will the quilt shop."

"I'm sure you're right, and I've asked your brother to check in on you, so if you need anything, be sure to let either Harold or Lena know."

"I will, Mom." Abby handed her mother a newspaper. "Here's the newest issue of *The Budget.* I thought you'd like to take it along so you'll have something to read on the bus."

"Danki." Fannie forced her tears to stay put. "See you in a few days. Be well, and don't work too hard."

Abby smiled. "I won't. Have a good time, and tell Cousin Edna I said hello and to have a right nice birthday."

"I'll tell her." Fannie turned and stepped onto the bus. She was sure she would feel better once she was on the road. She found a seat near the back and was glad when no one sat beside her. Though normally quite talkative, this morning she wasn't in the mood to engage in conversation. All she wanted to do was read *The Budget* and relax.

As the bus pulled away from the station in Dover, she settled herself in the seat and opened the newspaper. Usually she read it from front to back, but today Fannie felt inclined to check out the classified ad section first. One never knew when they might find a good deal on quilting material or notions, and sometimes there were auctions advertised, asking for quilts.

She scanned the want ads first, and sure enough, there was an ad telling about a quilt auction to be held in Indiana next month. When she got back home, she'd have to see if she had anything she might want to send.

From there, Fannie's gaze went to the notice section. One notice in particular caught her attention. It was titled, "To the Amish Boy's Family." Her interest piqued, Fannie read on. "This is to notify the family of the Amish baby taken from a farm in Lancaster County in June of this year—the boy is fine. He's healthy, happy, and well cared for."

Fannie let the paper fall to her lap. *This could be Abraham Fisher's boy. Sure sounds like it's so. After all, how many Amish babies could have been kidnapped in Lancaster County during the month of June?* Goosebumps erupted all over her arms, and she shivered. *Has Abraham read this? Does he subscribe to* The Budget? She knew immediately where her first stop in Lancaster County had to be. She should arrive at the bus station in Lancaster sometime this afternoon. A friend had given her the number of a woman who lived in the area and drove for the Amish, so the first thing she planned to do was phone the English woman. She would ask to be driven to Fisher's General Store outside the town of Paradise. If Abraham hadn't read this ad, he certainly needed to. If this was his boy, he had to know the child was safe.

"Don't get me wrong. Our trip has been a blast, and I loved seeing all the sights with you in Chicago and along the way as we came out west, but I'm ready to get off the road now and settle in. I bet you are, too. I think we should be in Portland in about three hours." Ginny turned up the volume on the radio, and a country-western song blared through the speakers. "I sure do like this type of music, don't you?"

Naomi frowned. "It's kind of loud, don't ya think?"

"I prefer it that way. Helps me stay awake."

"Maybe we should stop awhile and stretch our legs."

Ginny glanced at Naomi. "Are you needing a rest stop?"

Naomi didn't really have the need, but it would feel good to walk around and get away from the annoying music for a while. It might also help Ginny to wake up, which was important since she was their only driver. "Jah, I'm thinkin' it would be nice to stop."

"I'll pull into a rest stop then. The sign I saw back a ways said the next one was ten miles. Should be seeing it soon, I imagine."

Naomi pushed the button to make her window roll down and tried to relax. Did her family miss her as much as she missed them? What were they doing in her absence? It was September already, and toward the end of August, the younger children had no doubt gone back to school. Were they managing all right? Night and day, so many unanswered questions plagued her, but she kept reminding herself that leaving home had been for the best. She'd mailed Papa a postcard last week to let him know she was okay. She had made no mention of where she and Ginny were or where they were heading. He probably wouldn't care anyway.

Naomi leaned over and pulled a notebook and a pen from the small canvas bag at her feet. The day after they'd left Lancaster County, she began keeping a journal. At first she'd only written about places they'd seen along the way, but then she started writing down her private thoughts. It helped some, yet there was still a deep ache in her soul that no amount of note taking could dispel. If only she could change the past—go back and make things right. But that was impossible. All Naomi could do was make a new life for herself. She was convinced her family didn't want her anymore.

"We're almost to Oregon," she wrote. *"Clear across the country we've*

come. Everything looks different on this end of the United States. Lots of tall mountains, like beautiful Mount Rainier. Even though it's warm right now, there's no humidity. Ginny says we'll be in Portland in a few hours. Guess she's lined things up with her friend, Carla, for us to stay at her place until we both get jobs."

Naomi sighed. Would she even be able to find a job in the big city? It seemed like Ginny might be working at the fitness center Carla had told her about, but Naomi had no prospects at all.

"I used to envy Ginny and think I might want to be part of the English world," she wrote in her journal. *"Now I'm not so sure. Truth is, I feel like a chicken tryin' to build a nest on top of a hot stove. It's like I don't belong anywhere now. I'm not Amish 'cause I left that behind, yet I'm not really English, either."* She glanced down at her faded blue jeans, which used to be Ginny's. *"I'm dressed in English clothes, wearin' my hair down, and have started to use some makeup, but inside I still feel Plain."*

"We're here. You ready to use the rest room?"

Ginny's question drove Naomi's thoughts to the back of her mind, and she quickly returned her notebook to the canvas bag.

Naomi got out of the car and followed Ginny up the path toward the women's rest room. She glanced over her shoulder and caught a glimpse of a man heading to the men's side of the building. She halted and stood there, her heart pounding like a hammer. Was that him—the Englisher who took Zach? But how could she be thinking such a thing when she'd told the police she barely took notice of the man who'd come to ask for root beer? Had she seen and remembered more than she realized, not recalling it until now, or was her mind merely playing tricks on her?

"Naomi, are you coming or not?"

Naomi jerked her head. Ginny glared at her as though she'd done something wrong.

"What are you standing there for? I thought you had to use the rest room."

"I—I—do, but—" Naomi turned to take another look at the man, but he was gone.

Ginny furrowed her brows. "What's the matter with you, girl? You look like you've eaten a bunch of sour grapes."

"Nothin's wrong. I'm fine." Naomi started walking again. The stress of leaving home and trying to make her way in a foreign world must be getting to her. Jah, that's all it was.

Abraham was glad the kinner were back in school. He didn't have to worry about watching out for them at the store during the day. Only trouble was, he had no one's assistance now. Even though his younger girls weren't nearly as much help as Naomi had been, Nancy and Mary Ann could stock shelves and do some cleanup around the place. Now he was faced with doing everything himself, and there was certainly no time for naps.

Today was one of those days when he really needed a rest. He'd been stocking shelves all morning when there were no customers, and he barely had enough time to choke down a sandwich at noon. It would be nice if he could head for the back room and lie down on the cot. Just a few minutes to close his eyes and let the weariness drain from his body.

"Maybe I should close the store for a day or two. Then I could stay home and get caught up on my sleep." He grabbed a dust rag from under the counter and attacked the accumulated grime on the shelves behind him. "That wouldn't make much sense. If I closed the store, then I'd be losin' money. Besides, there's as much work at home, and unless I decide to hire a maid, it'll just keep piling up."

"I see you're talkin' to yourself again."

Abraham whirled around. Jacob Weaver stood inside the door with a smile on his face. "I admit it. I was talkin' to myself." Before Jacob could comment, he added, "How's the painting business, and what brings you to my store in the middle of the day?"

"We're paintin' the outside of the bank in Paradise," Jacob replied. "I've got the crew all set up, so I thought I'd stop by and see how you're doing." He glanced around the store. "Guess there's no customers at the moment, huh?"

"Nope, but it was sure busy this morning. Can't hardly handle things by myself—here or at home."

Jacob leaned on the counter. "I'm sure some of the women in our community would help out if you weren't too stubborn to ask."

Abraham put the dust rag away and sank to the wooden stool on his side of the counter. "What's the point in askin' when it would only be temporary? Sooner or later they'd have to stop helping and take care of their own families."

"I've told you before that you should hire a maad."

"I know, and I've been thinkin' on it." Abraham sighed. "Trouble is, I don't know who's available or who would work out good with the kinner. They can be a handful. Been worse since Naomi up and ran off."

"Have you heard anything from her?" Jacob asked.

"Just a postcard, and that didn't tell much."

"She never said where she and Virginia Meyers were heading or how she was doing?"

Abraham shook his head. "Just that she was fine and didn't want me to worry. I checked with Virginia's folks again, and they haven't heard a word from their daughter."

"At least Naomi had the decency to let you know she's all right."

"Jah, but that don't tell me if she's ever comin' back."

"Do you want her to?"

Abraham's defenses rose, and he clenched his teeth. "Of course I do. Been prayin' every day that she'll come back and we can make amends."

"You're not casting blame on her now?"

Abraham shrugged.

"Jesus commanded us to forgive others the same way He forgave us. Until you forgive Naomi and the man who took Zach, it will be like someone tied a stone around your neck and is pulling you down."

"Are you tryin' to goad me into an argument this afternoon, Jacob Weaver?"

"Why would you think that?"

"You keep sayin' things that make me believe you're against me now."

Jacob shook his head. "You know better than that, Abraham. You're my gut friend, and I want you to find peace within your soul."

"I doubt that'll ever happen. Not unless Naomi and Zach come home again."

Jacob groaned. "We've had this discussion before, and I thought you were gonna turn things over to God. You need to work on your faith, my friend. Allow yourself to forgive, trust the Lord to do His will in your children's lives, and wait on Him."

Abraham slapped his hand down on the counter, causing several pieces of paper to fall to the floor. "That's easy for you to say! All your kinner are safely at home. If young Leona or one of the others was snatched away, I'll bet you'd be singin' another tune."

Jacob shrugged his shoulders. "Maybe so, maybe not. I'd like to think I'd be praying every day, studyin' God's Word, and having the faith to believe He would bring something good out of the mess I was in."

Abraham massaged his forehead. He was sure the escalating pain would burst his head wide open. He knew all the things Jacob said were true, but he was tired and discouraged and couldn't muster enough strength or faith to believe in miracles anymore.

"I can see I've upset you," Jacob said, leaning over the counter and touching Abraham's arm.

Abraham was about to comment when the front door opened and an Amish woman walked in. He blinked. She looked familiar, but he couldn't quite place her.

"Can I help ya with somethin'?" he asked.

She smiled and nodded. "Remember me. . .from the quilt shop on the outskirts of Berlin?"

"Well, sure enough, I do remember you." He skirted around the counter and nearly bumped into Jacob. "Never thought I'd see you again, though."

"My cousin, Edna Yoder, who lives near Strasburg, invited me to come for her fiftieth birthday. I just arrived in the area, but I wanted to drop by your store and see you before I headed out to Edna's place."

Abraham grinned. She wanted to see him, even before her cousin. Now that was a fine howdy-do. He turned to Jacob then. "This is Fannie Miller. I met her when I went to Ohio awhile back."

Jacob shook Fannie's hand, then he cleared his throat and gave Abraham a silly-looking grin. "Well, I'd best be goin'. It was nice meeting you, Fannie."

"You, too."

He waved and hurried out the door.

Abraham smiled at Fannie. "Would ya like a cup of cider? I have some in the back room, in the small cooler I usually bring to work."

She shook her head. "Thanks anyway, but I don't have much time. My driver is waitin' outside, but I have something I need to show you before I go."

"What is it?"

Fannie pulled a newspaper out of the canvas bag she held in one hand. "Have you seen the most recent issue of *The Budget*?"

"Can't say that I have. Don't have much time for readin' anymore." He frowned. "Things have really gotten bad around here since Naomi took off."

"Who's Naomi?"

"She's my oldest daughter—the one who left Zach sittin' on the picnic table back in June."

"Oh, yes, I believe you mentioned her. Just couldn't remember the name."

"She overheard me prayin' out in the barn one morning, tellin' God I blamed her for Zach's disappearance." Abraham swallowed hard. Just talking about it brought back all the pain. "The worst part is, I told God I thought she may have done it on purpose."

"Why, Abraham? Why would Naomi have left her little brother alone on purpose?" Fannie questioned.

"I thought she wanted to marry the buggy maker so bad she'd do most anything to get out of her responsibilities at home." He stared at the toes of his boots, feeling too ashamed to look at Fannie. "I was only speakin' out of anger and frustration. Didn't mean all that, not really."

She patted his arm tenderly, the way his wife used to do. It felt warm and comforting, and he looked into her eyes. "Sorry for dumpin' all my troubles on you. I know you didn't come here for that."

"No, I didn't, but I'm glad you felt free to share with me." Fannie smiled. "I think my visit might give you a ray of hope about your missing boy, too."

"Oh, how's that?"

Fannie snapped the newspaper open and laid it on the counter. "See here, in the classified ad section?"

Abraham stared at the part where she'd placed her finger, and he read each word out loud. "To the Amish Boy's Family. . .This is to notify the family of the Amish baby taken from a farm in Lancaster County in June of this year—the boy is fine. He's healthy, happy, and well cared for." Abraham's knees almost buckled, and he had to grab hold of the counter to keep from toppling over. "Zach. This has to be about my missing son."

CHAPTER 23

Abraham couldn't believe he hadn't been able to track down the origin of the ad in *The Budget*. Thanks to Fannie showing him the paper, he felt closer to finding Zach than ever before. Yet the lead took him nowhere. He and Fannie had walked down the street to use a payphone, but when he called *The Budget* and asked about the ad, he'd been told the person placing the notice had mailed it and paid cash. There was no return address, and the postmark had been smudged beyond recognition.

"It's hopeless," Abraham said to Fannie as they headed back to his store.

She shook her head. "Nothing is hopeless. All things are possible with God."

"My friend Jacob says I should accept this tragedy and move on with my life. He thinks God will use Zach's and Naomi's disappearances for His good."

"Jacob could well be right." Fannie stopped in front of Abraham's store. "I should go now. My driver's quite patient, but I've kept her waitin' long enough."

"Sure wish you didn't have to run off. How long will you be in the area?" He felt a sudden need to be with this woman in whose presence he felt remarkably relaxed.

"Edna's birthday is tomorrow evening, and I had planned on catching the bus home the next day since it's an off-Sunday and there won't be any preaching."

Disappointment flooded Abraham's soul. "So soon? I'd kinda

hoped we could see each other again. Maybe visit over a nice meal, the way we did at the picnic table out behind your shop."

Fannie's face lit up. "Say, I have an idea. Why don't you bring your family and come over to Edna's party tomorrow night? We're gonna eat outside on picnic tables, and I'm sure there will be plenty of food, so you needn't worry about bringing anything."

"But I don't even know your cousin. Wouldn't she think it a bit odd if a bunch of strangers showed up at her party?"

Fannie shook her head. "Edna's turning fifty this year and has planned her own party. She's always done things differently than others and loves surprises." Fannie chuckled. "I'm sure she'd be happy if my surprise was a few unexpected guests."

Abraham wasn't sure about all this, although he had to admit it did sound like fun. "That's awful nice, but—"

Fannie held up her hand. "Now I won't take no for an answer. I'd like to meet your family, so please say you'll come."

"Well, I—"

Fannie reached into her black handbag and pulled out a small notebook and pen. "I'm gonna jot down the directions to her place, and I'll expect to see you there. It begins at six o'clock."

Abraham took the piece of paper and said he and his family would try to make it. He didn't know why, but for the first time in many weeks, he was actually looking forward to something. It probably wasn't the party nearly as much as it was thinking about seeing Fannie again.

Fannie waved and headed for the English woman's car, still parked in the graveled lot next to the Fishers' store. "See you tomorrow night, Abraham," she called over her shoulder.

Abraham strolled up the steps to his store, surprised at how much energy he felt. He'd been tired earlier in the day, but now he could probably clean the whole store and not feel the least bit winded. "Sure hope the rest of the family will be eager to go to Edna Yoder's party, for I don't want to miss another chance to spend time with Fannie."

Jim had just finished lining out a job his crew would be doing tomorrow. It involved painting the trim on a three-story office building, which meant they'd have to use scaffolding. It wasn't something he used that often, but lately he'd been getting more jobs like this one in Tacoma, so he was glad he'd recently bought the necessary equipment.

"Guess we've got everything pretty well ready," he told Hank, his foreman. "Make sure the guys know to be on the job by seven tomorrow morning. I want to get an early start because Saturday's supposed to be another warm day."

"I'll see to it." Hank sauntered off as Jim's cell phone rang.

"Scott's Painting and Decorating," he said into the mouthpiece.

"Jim, where are you? I thought you'd be here by now. You said you were coming home for lunch today, remember?" Linda's tone was high-pitched and whiny.

"We worked a little later than usual this morning, and I'm just now ready to take a break," he said patiently. "I had to get a job lined out for tomorrow."

"You're working on Saturday again?" He could hear the disappointment in her voice.

"It's the only way I could fit the paint job in Tacoma into my busy schedule, and we have to take advantage of this good weather when we're doing an outside job. Never know when it will turn rainy again."

"I guess Jimmy and I will have to go to the park by ourselves."

"I'll be home soon, honey," Jim said, making no further comment on either of their Saturday plans.

"I was wondering if you could stop by the store and pick up a couple of things on your way here," Linda said.

"Sure, what do you need?"

"Jimmy's cutting another tooth and could use some of that numbing gel to rub on his gums."

"No problem."

"Also, we're almost out of disposable diapers."

"Got it."

"And could you buy a new thermometer? I believe Jimmy's got a fever, but our old one reads normal, so I think it must be broken."

Jim groaned. "If it says the baby's temperature is normal, then it probably is, Linda." She was too protective and had been since they got Jimmy. Jim thought things would settle down after a few weeks, but they'd had the boy for three months now, and still she acted paranoid about anything concerning the child. Jim had even installed one of those baby intercoms so Linda could keep tabs on Jimmy when he was sleeping. If he hadn't, she probably would have insisted on sleeping in the baby's room, the way she had the first night after they returned from Pennsylvania.

"Get a new thermometer anyway, just in case," she pleaded.

"Okay. Tell my boy his daddy will be home soon, and we'll eat our lunch together." Jim turned off the phone.

"She'll probably be holding our son's hand until he's old enough to leave home," he mumbled as he headed for his van. Jimmy was a special kid, and Jim loved him as if he were his own, but he didn't think it was good for Linda to smother the boy. *He'll either grow up to be a mama's boy, or he might end up rebelling. Neither would be good. I guess I'm going to have to do something to prevent that from happening.*

Jim opened the door and climbed into the driver's seat. He had been feeling much better about taking Jimmy since he'd gotten some phony papers drawn up and tucked safely in his deposit box. Also, placing an ad in the Amish newspaper when they'd gone to Boise to see Linda's folks had given him a sense of peace.

"Sure hope the little guy's Amish family sees that notice. If they know he's okay, maybe they won't miss him so much."

Jim rubbed his temples, feeling as though a headache might be forthcoming. "Who am I kidding? A notice in the paper wouldn't make me feel much better if someone took my baby."

He slipped the key into the ignition and started the van. "I can't admit to Linda what I've done or take Jimmy back to his rightful home. Linda's become too attached to him, and so have I. Just need to put it out of my mind, that's all. The longer he lives with us, the more it will seem like he's always been ours." Jim pulled out into traffic. "Besides, I took him to make my wife happy, and she is. That's all that counts, and I'm sure Jimmy's better off with us than he would be living among the Amish."

Naomi sat on the couch in Carla Griffin's apartment, looking through the want ads and feeling completely out of place. Truth be told, she wasn't sure she would ever feel comfortable again. Since they'd arrived in Portland, she'd felt like a fifth wheel. Until they came here, Ginny had acted like she was her friend. Now Ginny seemed more interested in Carla than she did Naomi. The two young women had gone off to the fitness center this morning, leaving Naomi alone.

"Naomi, you need to find a job," Ginny had said before they walked out the door. "There's a newspaper in the living room. Why don't you browse the want ads and see what you can find?"

Before Naomi could reply, Ginny added, "We should be back by noon, and it would be nice if you had some lunch waiting for us."

Naomi sniffed and reached for a tissue from the little square box on the table by the couch. Despite having access to fancy clothes, TV, and modern appliances, she felt alone and misunderstood. Not only was she lonely and discontent, but as she scanned the paper, she soon discovered there didn't seem to be any jobs she was qualified to do. Nothing except waitress work, and she wasn't sure she would even be good at that. Waiting on customers in a crowded restaurant was not the same as serving her family back home.

She circled a couple of restaurant jobs and tore them out of the paper. Would Ginny or Carla have time to drive her there later today? Would anyone want to hire a Plain girl from Pennsylvania who knew so little about the modern way of doing things? She wondered if she could find her way around the large town of Portland. No doubt she'd have to take a bus to and from work, as she didn't have a car or know how to drive.

Doubts mingled with her misery as she shed one tear after another. What if she couldn't make it in the English world? What if she felt forced to return home, knowing she was the object of her father's anger?

Naomi stood, forcing her tears to stop. "I won't know if I can make it here until I try to get a job, so in the meantime, I'll head for the kitchen and see what there is to eat. Might as well find something to do while they're gone, even if I don't appreciate Ginny's attitude and her bein' so bold as to ask me to have lunch ready when they get back."

When she entered the small kitchen, Naomi went straight to the refrigerator. One side was full of canned soft drinks and a few bottles of beer. She wrinkled her nose. "Hope Ginny's not gonna drink that awful stuff, and I won't be tryin' any, that's for certain sure."

By the time Ginny and Carla returned, Naomi had lunch ready to serve. She'd made ham and cheese sandwiches and fixed a tossed green salad. She would have liked some pickled beets, but of course, there were none. Once more, she found herself wishing for the things she'd had at home.

"How'd the job interview go?" she asked Ginny as the girls took a seat at the table.

"Great. They said I could start on Monday."

"That's gut. I mean, good," Naomi replied. If she was going to live among the English and try to become one of them, she knew she'd have to quit saying Pennsylvania Dutch words. Nobody would want to hire someone who used to be Amish; she felt sure of it. She would try hard to keep that part of her life a secret and do all the things expected of her in the fancy, English world.

"Did you find anything in the paper you can apply for?" Carla asked. She combed her fingers through the ends of her shoulder-length auburn hair.

"Yeah, did you?" Ginny chimed in.

Naomi felt their scrutiny piercing her bones. She grabbed the newspaper off the table and pointed to one ad. "I believe this one's not far from here. Maybe I'll see about it first."

Carla nodded. "Good idea. Everyone pulls her weight here, so you are going to need a job."

When Abraham arrived home from the store that evening, he was aggravated by the sight that greeted him. Not only was supper not ready, but the girls hadn't even started cooking. He found them both sitting at the kitchen table, drawing pictures of colored leaves.

Mary Ann looked up when he cleared his throat. "Oh, hi, Papa. Did ya have a good day?"

"It was all right 'til now," he grumbled.

"How come? What's wrong?" Nancy asked, never looking up from her work.

"I come home after a long day at the store and find you two sittin' at the table drawing, and there's no supper ready. That's what's wrong."

Nancy pushed her chair away and stood. "Sorry, but we got busy and lost track of time. Is it okay if we just have cold sandwiches?"

"I guess if I don't want to wait all night for something to eat, then sandwiches will have to do." Abraham trudged across the room and set his lunch pail on the cupboard. "Naomi would have had supper goin' by now, ya know. She always fixed something hot to eat for the evening meal."

"But Naomi ain't here," Mary Ann said.

"Don't get smart with me, girl! I know perfectly well where Naomi is."

Nancy rushed to his side. "Really, Papa? Have you had word from her?"

Abraham frowned. "No, haven't had nothin' but that one postcard. I only meant—oh, never mind. Just get busy fixin' us something to eat, and be quick about it!" He grabbed a glass from the closest cabinet and turned on the cold water at the sink. "Where are the brothers? Shouldn't they be inside by now?"

"I think the older ones are still out in the fields," Nancy said as she pulled a loaf of bread from the breadbox. "Samuel said he was gonna play in the barn awhile."

"I see. Well, let me know when supper's ready, and I'll ring the dinner bell." He gulped down the glass of water and was about to head for the living room when the back door swung open, and all four of his sons sauntered into the room.

"Is supper ready yet? I'm hungry as a bull," Matthew announced.

"Don't smell nothin' cookin'," Jake added. "That's not a good sign."

"Supper ain't ready?" Norman asked with a scowl.

"I'm workin' on it," Nancy said sharply. "For your information, I'm making cheese sandwiches."

"Is that all we're havin'?" This question came from Samuel, who had a chunk of straw stuck to his hair.

Abraham reached down and plucked it out, then handed it to the boy. "Be glad for what you're gonna get and take this back where it belongs."

Samuel opened the door and flung the straw outside. When he stepped into the kitchen again, he wore a smug expression on his face. "We've got us a batch of new kittens in the barn, did ya know that, Papa?"

Mary Ann jumped up from the table. "Were they just borned?"

Samuel shook his finger. "Born, ya *glotzkeppich* girl. Ain't ya learned nothin' in school?"

Mary Ann stuck out her tongue. "I'm not blockheaded, and I've learned aplenty." She pointed to the pictures still on the table. "See there, I know how to draw really good."

Abraham's patience was waning, and he'd had about as much as he could take. He clapped his hands together, and everyone in the room jumped, including Matthew, the oldest. "It riles me when my kinner can't learn to get along. Samuel and Mary Ann, you ought to be ashamed of yourselves."

Mary Ann hung her head, and Samuel dragged the toe of his boot across the floor. "Sorry," they said in unison.

"That's better. Now I have some gut news."

All eyes focused on Abraham.

"Is it about Zach or Naomi? Has either one been found?" Matthew questioned.

"I'm afraid not, although Fannie Miller came to the store today and showed me a notice in *The Budget* that gave me some hope Zach might be okay."

"Fannie Miller? Who's she, Papa?" Jake asked.

"She's the woman I met in Berlin, Ohio. The one who runs the quilt shop."

"Right," Nancy put in. "Papa told us about her after he came home."

Abraham nodded and pulled out a chair. "Why don't you all have a seat?"

Everyone did as he suggested, and Norman leaned forward, his elbows on the table. "What'd the notice say about Zach?"

Abraham gave his beard a couple of tugs before he answered. He wanted to be sure he worded it just the way it had been written in the paper. In his eagerness to get home, he'd left it at the store. "Let's see now. . . . It said something like: 'This is to notify the family of the

Amish baby who was taken from a farm in Lancaster County in June that the boy is fine. He's happy, healthy, and bein' well cared for.' "

Nancy's eyes were huge as the sugar cookies Naomi used to bake. "You think they were talkin' about our Zach?"

He nodded soberly. "I'm nearly sure. How many other Amish babies did you hear about bein' kidnapped from our area back in June?"

"None. Only Zach." Matthew rubbed his chin as though deep in thought. "Is there any way we can find out who placed that notice?"

"Fannie and I called *The Budget*, but nobody there knows. The ad was sent in the mail and paid for with cash. There was no return address on the envelope, and the postmark was smudged."

Jake let out a low whistle. "So near, yet so far away."

Abraham didn't need that reminder. He tapped his fingers along the edge of the tablecloth. "At least we know Zach's all right and not bein' mistreated or—" His voice trailed off. He couldn't bring himself to say the words.

"Did Fannie Miller come all the way from Ohio just to tell you about that ad?" Matthew asked.

Abraham shook his head. "She's in the area to attend her cousin's birthday party. She just happened to get ahold of *The Budget* before she left home. Said after she read it, she thought of me and my missin' boy. That's why she dropped by the store."

"Fannie must be a right nice woman," Nancy said.

"Jah, she is. Which brings me to another topic. She—uh—invited us to attend her cousin's party tomorrow night at six."

The room got so quiet that Abraham was sure he could have heard a feather land on the floor.

"Do we know Fannie's cousin?" The question came from Mary Ann, whose blue eyes were fairly gleaming. "We haven't been to a party in a long time, and I think it would be fun."

"I'm not sure whether we've met Edna Yoder or not. She lives up near Strasburg, so she could've come into the store if she was near

Paradise, but we don't actually know her."

"Why would ya wanna go to some woman's party you don't even know?" Norman asked.

"Because we were invited by Fannie, that's why."

"Well, the younger ones can go, but I'm stayin' home," Jake said with his arms folded across his chest.

"Me, too," Samuel agreed.

Abraham pushed his chair away from the table. "We're all goin', and that's the end of it. Plain and simple."

CHAPTER 24

Naomi was glad one of the restaurants she had circled in the newspaper yesterday was only a few blocks from Carla's apartment. She could walk and wouldn't have to bother Ginny or Carla for a ride. Besides, Ginny had just announced that they'd already made other plans for their Saturday.

"Carla and I are going shopping at the mall, then we plan to take in a show. If you've got any money, you're welcome to come along, Naomi," Ginny said as she grabbed a donut from the plate in the center of the table.

Naomi shook her head. "I had planned to see about a job today."

"That's a good idea." Ginny gulped down a glass of milk and wiped her mouth on a napkin. "I don't want to impose on Carla much longer, and in order for us to afford an apartment of our own, we'll both need jobs."

"Jah—I mean, yes, I know. A couple of restaurants are looking for waitresses, and one's not far from here, so I thought I'd check on it sometime today."

"That's great. I hope it works out." Ginny stood. "I'd better go see if Carla's out of the shower yet. She said she wanted to get an early start, and it's almost ten."

"Do you think I look all right?" Naomi asked. "I wasn't sure what to wear when I went lookin' for a job." She stared down at the blue jeans and white cotton blouse, on loan from Ginny. "If I had enough of my own money left, I'd buy a dress or skirt and blouse."

"I think what you're wearing is fine. After all, it's not like you'll be applying for a job at some fancy office where you'd be expected to dress up every day." Ginny balled up her napkin and tossed it across the room. To Naomi's surprise, it landed right in the garbage can. "Some restaurants provide their employees with a uniform anyway, so I wouldn't worry about what you have on today."

"Okay, I'll try not to worry."

Ginny started for the door to the living room but turned back around. "That's your biggest fault; do you know that?"

Naomi pushed her chair away from the table and grabbed her dishes. "What is?"

"You worry too much." Ginny left the room, and Naomi headed for the sink to wash her plate and glass.

Ginny's words stung like fire ants, but even so, she wondered if they might be true. Did she worry too much? Was it a fault? A passage of scripture from the book of Matthew came to mind. "Which of you by taking thought can add one cubit unto his stature? And why take ye thought for raiment?"

Naomi turned on the faucet and allowed a stream of warm water to pour over the dishes as memories of home flitted through her mind. She had left the Amish faith when she ran away from home, but the things she had learned about God were still embedded in her mind. She might be able to turn her back on the responsibility to her family, but Naomi didn't think she could ever reject God. Only trouble was, she felt like He had rejected her.

"Say, Caleb, are you going to the singin' on Sunday night? I hear it's gonna be out at Jacob Weaver's place."

Caleb handed Andy a piece of sandpaper for one of the new buggy wheels they had been working on. "Nope. Hadn't planned on goin'."

"Why not? Seems like all you ever do is work. You need to get out and have a little fun." Andy winked. "Maybe find a pretty girlfriend and start courtin'."

Caleb clenched his teeth. "Now you sound like Mom. She's always sayin' I should be married and raising a family by now."

"Maybe she's right. Ever think about that?"

Sure, he'd thought about it aplenty. Trouble was, there was no one he wanted to marry except Naomi Fisher, and that was about as unlikely as the moon falling from the sky.

Andy glided the sandpaper back and forth, and Caleb did the same with the other buggy wheel. "No comment?"

Caleb shook his head. "Nope."

"You're still pinin' for Naomi, aren't ya?"

He shrugged.

"Have you heard anything from her since she left home?"

"Not a word. 'Course I didn't really expect to."

Andy clucked his tongue. "Still can't believe she took off and left her family like that. Always thought Naomi was more dependable."

Caleb dropped the piece of sandpaper and frowned at his younger brother. "She is dependable. Naomi's a wonderful woman, who stood by her family long after her mamm died."

"That may be true, but what about now? Where's Naomi when her family still needs her?"

Andy's point was well-taken. Where was Naomi, and what had happened to drive her away? Caleb was sure it had happened that way. Somebody must have said or done something to make her run off with Ginny Meyers. It wasn't like Naomi to do something so rash.

Caleb noticed an unpleasant odor, and he wrinkled his nose. "Smell that? There must be a stinky old skunk nearby."

"Sure hope it's not someplace in the buggy shop," Andy said with a scowl. "If it sprays our equipment, we'll be in a fine fix."

"It's most likely outside, but it sure does stink." *Just like this whole mess with the storekeeper and his daughter*. If only Abraham Fisher had given Naomi the freedom to court, she might still be here. In fact, Caleb and Naomi could very well be published by now. If Caleb had been allowed to have his way, come November they would have become man and wife.

He grabbed a fresh piece of sandpaper and gave the wheel a couple of good swipes. He might not be able to do anything about his future with Naomi, but he sure enough had the power to make this wheel look as smooth as glass.

As Fannie checked her appearance in the mirror, she grinned at her reflection and patted her hair to be sure it was still in place. She felt like a teenager getting ready for her first suitor to come a-calling. It was silly, really. She was a grown woman, forty-two years old to be exact. Even though tonight wasn't a date, she hoped Abraham Fisher and his family would show up for Edna's party. There was something about the man that fascinated her.

Fannie had been thinking about Abraham ever since she'd gone to his store yesterday afternoon. She was worried about him and felt bad he couldn't get any answers from *The Budget* regarding the origin of that ad. Then there was the situation with his daughter leaving home. It really put Abraham in a bind. Who was helping care for his children, and what about the store? Was he able to run it by himself? If he did come to the birthday party, she planned to ask him those questions.

Abraham seems nothing like my husband was, she mused. Ezra had been short, a few inches taller than Fannie's five foot two. Abraham was tall, maybe six feet or better. Ezra was thin and wiry. Abraham had muscular arms, even though he was a bit portly around the middle. That didn't bother Fannie in the least, since she was on the plump side herself.

"You've got to quit comparin' the two men," she fumed. "Abraham lives here, and I make my home in Ohio, so there's no chance of us gettin' together, even if I might wish it were so."

Abraham's bearded face popped back into her mind. His eyes were so blue she felt she could drown in them.

Abraham's personality seems the opposite of my Ezra's, too. He appears to be strong-willed and a bit harsh, whereas Ezra was the quiet, placid type. She shook her head. *I loved my husband. Loved him a lot. So why am I fascinated with Abraham when he's nothing like Ezra? Besides, I barely know the man.*

A forceful knock brought Fannie's musings to a halt. "You about ready, Cousin?" Edna called through the door. "My guests will be arrivin' 'most any minute."

Fannie turned away from the mirror. "I'll be out shortly."

"Jah, well, don't take too long."

"I won't." Fannie smiled. Edna always had been the impatient one. Impatient but sure could be a lot of fun. It was a wonder she never married after Joseph died. Ten years Edna had been without a husband, but she seemed to be getting along okay. Shortly after Joseph passed away, their son Aaron got married, and Edna gave him the house. She and her two other children, Gretchen and Gerald, lived with Aaron and his wife, Irma, until the twins were both married. Once they were settled into homes of their own, Edna moved into the small house behind her place. Edna's grandparents had built the home many years before, but for a long time it sat empty. Edna was determined not to rely on family to care for her, so she supported herself by taking in sewing. She made a lot of head coverings for women in the area who didn't have time to sew for themselves.

Fannie sighed and picked up the quilted pillow she'd made to give her cousin as a birthday present. It was time to head outside for Edna's party.

By six o'clock, the serving tables on the lawn were covered with an array of delicious food. Friends and relatives had brought everything from baked beans and potato salad to pickled beets and dilled green beans. Fannie scanned the crowd of people. The only thing missing at this party was Abraham and his family. Had he changed his mind about coming? Maybe he'd been delayed or couldn't find the place. Edna's home was rather out of the way.

"You look as nervous as a bird tryin' to escape the claws of a cat on the prowl. What are ya pacin' for?" Edna asked, as she gave Fannie a nudge to the ribs.

"I told you I had invited a guest, remember?"

Edna nodded. "The storekeeper up near Paradise—isn't that what ya said?"

"Right. I told him to bring his whole family, so if they do come, we might need another picnic table."

"Not a problem. Aaron has more sawhorses in the barn, and he can always lay plywood over the top. In fact, I'll go ask him now if you're sure the man's comin'."

Fannie smoothed the folds in her dark green dress. "He never actually said he'd come, just that he'd try to."

Edna gave her a knowing look. "I'd say you're a mite smitten with the storekeeper."

"What makes you think that?"

"You've got the look a young woman gets when she's expectin' her beau to arrive." Edna wiggled her eyebrows. "If the love bug has bit you, then I guess there's still hope for me at my old age."

Fannie shook her head. "I haven't been bitten by love, and fifty's not old, Cousin."

"I guess not, if you consider I might live another fifty years yet." Edna chuckled. "You know what middle age is?"

"Turnin' fifty?"

"Uh-uh. It's when ya know all the answers, but nobody asks you the questions."

Fannie laughed. "You always come up with the silliest things." She fidgeted with the cape on her dress. "Think I look okay?"

"Of course you do."

"I don't look too fat?"

Edna's pale eyebrows drew together. "You ain't fat, just pleasingly plump, as my dear mamm used to say."

"I've put on a few pounds since Ezra died, and I've been trying to watch what I eat, 'cause I don't want to gain any more weight."

"Maybe you should try the garlic diet. I've got a friend who's been on it a year already." Edna giggled like a schoolgirl and slapped her knee. "She hasn't lost a pound, but she has a few less friends now, that's for sure."

Fannie shook her head. It was easy for Edna to make jokes about people being fat. She was skinny as a twig. Had been since they were young girls.

"Tell me now, how much do you weigh?" Edna whispered in Fannie's ear.

Fannie pondered that question a few seconds, then turned to her cousin and said, "Oh, one hundred and plenty."

Edna roared, and Fannie did, too. It felt wonderful to be having such a good time. Too bad Abraham wasn't here to share in the lively banter. With all his problems, he probably needed a good laugh.

Fannie glanced at the driveway and sighed. She so hoped he would show. "Well, guess I'll get some food and find myself a seat."

"Good idea. I'm headed that way, too."

Fannie followed her cousin to the serving table and had filled her plate half full when a vehicle pulled into the yard. It was a van driven by an English man, and when she saw Abraham Fisher get out of the passenger's side, Fannie almost dropped her plate. "He's here," she whispered to Edna.

"Then go greet him," her cousin said, giving Fannie a little nudge.

"Why don't you come with me? After all, this is your party, and I'd like to introduce him to the guest of honor."

"All right." Edna followed Fannie up the driveway, and by the time they reached the van, three young children, two girls and a boy, stood by Abraham's side. Then the back door opened, and three older boys, almost men really, climbed out of the vehicle.

"Abraham," Fannie said breathlessly. "I'm glad you could make it." She turned to Edna. "This is my cousin, Edna Yoder. She's the one havin' the birthday."

Edna smiled and held out her hand. Abraham shook it, but Fannie couldn't help noticing how he kept his focus on her. "It's nice to meet you, Edna. Happy birthday."

"Danki."

"How old are you?" the youngest girl asked.

Abraham raised his eyebrows. "Mary Ann, it ain't polite to pose such a question."

Edna laughed. "It don't bother me none. I'm fifty years old, but I'm not over-the-hill yet. Just runnin' a little harder, that's all."

Everyone but the younger ones laughed. Fannie figured they probably didn't know much about being over-the-hill. She smiled at the children. . .Abraham's kinner. It sure was nice to finally meet them.

"This is Matthew, my oldest," Abraham said. "Then there's Norman, Jake, Nancy, Samuel, and Mary Ann."

"It's good meetin' all of you," Fannie said. "Won't ya come fill your plates now? The rest of Edna's guests are already eatin'."

"I'll be right there. Just need to tell our driver what time he should come back for us." Abraham looked over at Edna, as though he was waiting for her to give the word as to when the party might wind down.

"Tell him to drop back around nine or so," she said with a nod.

"All right then." Abraham headed for the driver's side of the van.

"Why don't you wait for him?" Edna said to Fannie. "I'll take the rest of his brood over to the food." She started toward the tables, and the children willingly followed.

Fannie held back, feeling more nervous than ever. What did Abraham's children think of their father bringing them to a party for a woman they didn't even know? Had he told them how he and Fannie met? Did they think she might be after their daed?

Am I?

The question in Fannie's mind frightened her. She'd never been the kind of woman to throw herself at a man. Had she been too forward, asking him here tonight?

When Abraham stepped up beside her, she shivered.

"You cold?" he asked.

"No, no, I'm fine. You ready to eat?"

He nodded. "Jah, sure. Always ready for some gut food."

"Who's doin' the cookin' at your place now that your oldest daughter's gone?" Fannie asked as they strolled down the driveway, side by side.

"Nancy, but she's only ten and can't cook nearly as good as Naomi." He stopped walking and kicked a small stone with the toe of his boot. "Sure has been hard to keep things goin'."

"I'm sorry to hear that," Fannie said, feeling an ache in her heart for Abraham. "Do you have help at the store?"

He shook his head. "Not since Naomi left."

"That's a lot of responsibility for one man. I know, because I run my quilt shop with the help of my daughter. Don't know what I'd do if Abby ever quit helpin' out."

"I've thought about hiring someone, but I don't know who. It would have to be a person I could trust to do a good day's work and not fool around like some of the young ones are apt to."

"I understand," Fannie said. "Have you put the word out that you're lookin' to hire someone?"

"Nope. Thought I could manage on my own awhile yet. Been hopin' and prayin' Naomi might come to her senses and return home."

When Fannie looked into Abraham's blue eyes, she could see the depth of his pain. She wished there was something she could do to help. But what would it be?

As they continued walking toward the group of people gathered at the tables, an idea popped into Fannie's head. "Say, I was thinkin' maybe I could help at the store. Just 'til you're able to hire someone more permanent," she blurted out.

His eyes grew large, and he looked at her as though she'd offered him a special gift. "You mean it, Fannie?"

She nodded. "I'll phone the English gift shop next to our store tomorrow morning and ask them to get word to Abby. If she's agreeable for me to stay here a few weeks, I'll be free to help you."

He tipped his head to one side. "But if you're helpin' me, won't that leave your daughter alone at the quilt shop?"

Fannie pursed her lips. "My daughter-in-law, Lena, would probably be willing to help Abby during my absence."

A huge smile spread across Abraham's face. "Fannie Miller, I believe you're an answer to my prayers!"

CHAPTER 25

Fannie had never seen the time pass so quickly. It was hard to believe she'd left Ohio two months ago and had been helping Abraham ever since.

"I sure like your little house," Fannie said to Edna as the two women cleared their breakfast dishes one morning.

"Danki. I think it's kinda cozy and comfortable."

"It's nice you can live close to your family yet be off by yourself. It's not like it is with most *grossdaadihaus*—grandparents' houses—where you are right next door."

Edna grinned. "I'm afraid my family couldn't put up with me livin' that close. My joke tellin' and silliness might bother 'em to no end."

Fannie shook her head. "I doubt that, Cousin. I think your happy attitude is a real pleasure, and I've enjoyed our time together more than I can say."

Edna poured liquid detergent into the sink and turned on the faucet. "When you came for my birthday, I never expected you to stay so long."

"Have I been a bother?"

Edna clucked her tongue. "Goodness, no. I'm right glad you're still here." She leveled Fannie with a serious look. Too serious for Edna. "That storekeeper must have some hold on you, that's all I've gotta say."

Fannie grabbed a dish towel, in readiness for the clean dishes. "Abraham doesn't have any kind of hold on me. He needs my help, and since Abby's been more than willin' to let me stay on—"

"He couldn't have hired someone in the area to work at the store?" Edna interrupted.

Fannie shrugged. "Guess he likes the way I do things."

"*Humph!* I'd say it's you he likes."

Fannie's face heated up, but she didn't argue. Truth was, she had a hunch Abraham was beginning to see her as more than someone to help at the store. They'd become good friends, and she'd even gone to his house for supper a time or two. Of course, she usually ended up doing the cooking, since Nancy's meals were pretty bland.

If she were truly honest, Fannie had to admit she'd agreed to stay on longer for more than Abraham's need of help. She enjoyed the man's company and hoped. . . *What exactly am I hoping for?*

"Looks like it might snow," Edna said, breaking into Fannie's thoughts. "Sure is cold enough for it." She chuckled. "When my twins were little, they used to think the clouds were giant pillows leakin' feathers all over the earth."

Fannie smiled and nodded absently.

"Do you think it's safe to take my horse and buggy to the store today? I could always run next door and ask my Mennonite neighbor to drive you."

Fannie shook her head. "That's all right, Edna. I rather enjoy driving my own buggy, and I know how to get around in the snow, should the clouds decide to let loose of their feathers."

"You be real careful crossing Route 30, ya hear? There was a bad accident out there last week."

"I never go against the light, and I'll take every precaution."

The women finished the dishes as they engaged in light conversation, and a short time later, Fannie had Edna's horse and buggy hitched and ready to go.

"Take care, ya hear?" Edna called as Fannie got the horse moving down the lane.

"I will!"

A short time later, Fannie headed down Fairview Road toward Paradise. By the time she got to Paradise Lane, the buggy started shaking.

"Was is letz do—what's wrong here?" she mumbled, trying to hold the reins steady.

The buggy wobbled, lurched, then unexpectedly tipped to the right.

"Ach!" Fannie halted the horse and climbed down to evaluate the problem. It took only a moment to realize the right back wheel had fallen off and was lying in the ditch.

The frosty November wind whipped against Fannie's dress, and she shivered, wrapping her woolen shawl tightly around her shoulders. "This isn't good. Not good a'tall. I sure can't put the wheel in place, and even if I did know how, I have no tools to fix it."

Fannie climbed back into the buggy. At least she was out of the cold. She'd have to wait until someone came along who might be willing to help—wait and pray it would be soon. She'd left Edna's place later than planned and had no idea how long it might be before help arrived. She was going to be late showing up at the store, and Abraham would probably be worried.

Fannie closed her eyes and prayed. *Father in heaven, send someone who can fix my buggy. Help Abraham not to worry, and please be with his daughter and baby boy today.*

At the sound of a horse's hooves, Fannie opened her eyes. A young Amish man driving an open buggy pulled in front of her rig. He hopped down and came around to the right side where Fannie sat holding the reins. She opened her door and greeted him.

"Looks like you've got a problem with your buggy. Maybe I can help," he said with a smile.

"Oh, I surely hope so. I was travelin' along fine one minute, and the next, I'd lost a back wheel."

He extended his hand. "I'm Caleb Hoffmeir, the buggy maker in this area. I've got some tools in the back of my rig, so if the wheel's not badly broken, it shouldn't take me long to fix."

"I'd be much obliged," she said, stepping out of the carriage.

Fannie stood off to the side as Caleb picked up the wheel and set it in place. When he headed to his buggy to get some tools, she remembered something Abraham had told her one day at the store. "Caleb Hoffmeir, the buggy maker, wanted to court Naomi, but I wouldn't give my permission for her to even go to singings. If I'd allowed them to court, Naomi might still be with us," he'd said with a look of regret.

As she watched Caleb work on the wheel, Fannie decided they needed to have a little talk. "My name's Fannie Miller, and I own a quilt shop outside of Berlin, Ohio."

"I know the place. Was there awhile back and saw some English folks in front of your shop." He grunted. "Thought maybe the baby they had with 'em was Abraham Fisher's boy."

"Abraham told me. I've been helping in his store the last couple of months, but I don't believe I've met you before."

Caleb grunted. "I haven't been in Fisher's store for quite a while."

"Abraham's mentioned you several times."

"I bet whatever he said wasn't good. The storekeeper and me don't see eye to eye, especially concerning his oldest daughter."

Fannie shifted from one foot to the other, praying for the right words. "Actually, I think Abraham regrets not allowin' Naomi to be courted by you."

Caleb looked up from his job and frowned. "It's a little late for that, wouldn't ya say? Naomi's gone, and there's no chance of us ever courtin' now."

Fannie offered up another quick prayer. "Abraham believes if he'd given Naomi more freedom, she might not have run off like she did."

Caleb stood and pushed his hand against the buggy wheel. "Seems like it's in good shape now."

Fannie was amazed at how quickly he'd fixed it. She was also stunned by his lack of interest in what Abraham had to say. *Maybe it's not a lack of interest*, she decided. *I fear the young buggy maker has a bitter heart toward Naomi's father.*

"Danki, for fixin' the wheel. How much do I owe you?" she asked.

He shook his head. "No charge. I was passin' by anyhow, and I'd never leave anyone stranded."

She smiled. "I can see why Naomi was so taken with you."

He shrugged. "I ain't so sure about that. If she'd been taken with me, then she wouldn't have run off with her English friend. She left the Amish faith and her friends and family behind. Truth be told, I think she's probably much happier now."

Fannie wished there was something she could say to make Caleb feel better or at least offer him a ray of hope. She moistened her lips with the tip of her tongue and decided to make one last attempt. "I want you to know that I've been praying real hard—prayin' God will take this situation with Abraham's two missing kinner and turn it into something good."

Caleb's Adam's apple bobbed up and down as he swallowed, and Fannie could see he was struggling to keep his emotions in check. "That'd be right nice if God could make something good come from the whole mess, but to tell ya the truth, I ain't holdin' my breath for no miracle." He grabbed his tools and turned toward his buggy. "It was nice meetin' you, Fannie Miller."

"Same here," she called. "And I'll continue to pray for everyone concerned."

Naomi arched her back and wiggled from side to side, trying to dislodge the kinks that never seemed to go away. It was cold and raining outside, which Carla said was typical for November in Portland,

Oregon. Between the chilly rain and her aching back, Naomi had been tempted not to come to work today. However, she needed the money.

Naomi donned her monogrammed apron and massaged the muscles in her lower back. She was grateful for her job as a waitress here at Jasper's Café, but she hated the work. She had been waiting tables for the last two months and still hadn't gotten used to the expectations placed upon her. Naomi had plenty of chores to do at home, but she could do them as she found the time and was pretty much in charge of things. Here at the restaurant she had a boss telling her what to do and criticizing every time she messed up.

Of course, she reasoned, *I did have Papa tellin' me what to do—especially at the store.*

Thoughts of her family sent a wave of homesickness through Naomi so sharp she felt as if her knees could give way. She missed Mary Ann's silly questions, Samuel's curious nature, and even Nancy's sometimes defiant attitude. She longed to listen to Matthew's mellow voice, telling her things would work out all right, and she would give most anything to have a little chat with Jake, or even Norman, who often got on her nerves.

She sighed. *I miss Papa, too, even though he does blame me for Zach's disappearance. Maybe my daed was right when he said some of the English like Ginny are spoiled. Seems to me most of 'em I've met have way too many things to take up their time. I'd much rather be sittin' out on the front porch, eating homemade ice cream and visiting with the kinner and Papa than I would rushin' off to movies, dances, and whatever else Ginny and Carla do on the weekends.*

Naomi had thought she and Ginny would be able to pool their money and get an apartment of their own. But as it turned out, Ginny decided the kind of place she wanted was too expensive, so they were still staying at Carla's.

At least Naomi had her own bedroom, which was something to be grateful for. Ginny and Carla shared a room with twin beds, and that was fine with Naomi. She felt out of place around Carla, who drank beer and smoked cigarettes. Back in Pennsylvania, Ginny seemed to care about Naomi and acted like she wanted to be her friend. Here, she only seemed worried about her own needs and practically ignored Naomi unless she wanted something. Being able to escape to her room at the end of the day was one small comfort. For the most part, she felt removed from everything—like she didn't really belong.

Not only had Ginny and Carla become best friends, often leaving Naomi out of things they'd planned, they expected her to prepare most of the meals and keep the apartment cleaned and picked up. Already they were talking about Thanksgiving and Christmas and how they looked forward to the meals she would cook. Naomi wondered if she could make it through the holidays away from her family, while she catered to the whims of Carla and Ginny.

As she neared the restaurant's kitchen, Naomi smelled spaghetti sauce cooking. She closed her eyes and inhaled deeply. The aroma reminded her of the scalded, peeled tomatoes she and Mama used to make for homemade, savory tomato sauce. It was nothing like the plain old canned stuff that came from the grocery store.

"Sure wish I could go home," she mumbled.

"Are you gonna stand there all day rubbing your back and talking to yourself, or did you plan to start working sometime in this century?" Dennis Jasper's dark, bushy eyebrows drew together as he planted his beefy hands against his wide hips.

"I—I was only trying to get the muscles in my back to relax," Naomi replied, making no mention of the private conversation she'd been having with herself.

His thin lips turned into a scowl. "Make an appointment with a massage therapist, or see one of them bone crackers, but do it on your own time!"

Naomi nodded, grabbed her order pad, and headed for the dining room. This was not a good way to begin the day.

Jim had thought if he gave Linda more time, she would relax and not be so overprotective with their son. Two months had passed since he'd decided to take charge of things, yet so far he hadn't done a thing to let Linda know her actions were unacceptable and would only lead to trouble for Jimmy later on.

"Today's the day I lay down the law," Jim told himself as he headed across town to bid another job. "As soon as I get home tonight, I plan to tell Linda the way it's going to be from now on."

Jim's cell phone rang. "Probably the owner of the house I'm supposed to bid," he grumbled. "I'm only a few minutes late, but some customers can be so demanding."

"Scott's Painting and Decorating," he said into the phone.

"Jim, it's me."

He shook his head. Didn't she know by now that he recognized her voice? "What's up, Linda?"

"Jimmy fell and split open his lip. I think you should come home so we can take him to the emergency room for stitches."

"How deep is the cut?" Jim asked, feeling immediate concern.

"Not very deep, but it's bleeding."

"A lot or a little?"

"Well—"

"Linda, is the cut really bad or not?"

"I—I—think it could be."

"You think or you know?"

There was a pause.

"Linda?"

"I'm here. Just taking another look at Jimmy's lip."

"Is it still bleeding?"

"It does seem to be slowing up. I put a cold washcloth on it."

"That was a good idea."

"Are you coming home or not?"

"I really don't see the need." This was one of those times Jim wished his wife was willing to drive. It was ridiculous that she had to take the bus everywhere or call a taxi if Jim wasn't available to take her. Once in a while, she'd rely on a friend, but since they'd gotten Jimmy, she didn't socialize much anymore.

When Jim and Linda first got married, she had driven. But then she'd had an accident not far from their home. Even though it was only a fender bender and she hadn't been seriously hurt, Linda refused to drive the car from that day on.

"Please. . .Jimmy needs his daddy right now," she pleaded.

"Look, honey, if he was seriously hurt, I'd rush right home, but from what you've told me, it's just a little cut. Keep the washrag on it awhile longer, and if the bleeding stops, you'll know it doesn't need any stitches."

"Does that mean you're not coming home?"

He groaned. "That's exactly what it means. I'm on my way to bid a job, and I'm already late, so—"

"Fine then. If Jimmy bleeds to death, it will be your fault."

"He's not going to bleed to death from a split lip." Jim's patience was waning, and if he didn't hang up now, he knew he would say something he might regret later on. "I've got to go, Linda. I'll call you later and see how Jimmy's doing."

"But—"

He hung up before she could finish her sentence and clicked the button to silent mode. He may not have won the match, but he felt sure he'd won this round.

"You about ready to take a break for lunch?" Abraham asked Fannie as she reached under the counter and put the dust rag in place.

She smiled, and his heart missed a beat. Fannie had come to mean a lot to him. Truth of the matter, he'd been taken with her from the day they'd met at her quilt shop in Ohio. Since she'd been helping out at the general store, they'd had a chance to get to know each other. It still made him wonder why she'd been so willing to stay and help these past two months. In the beginning it was only supposed to be a couple of weeks—until he could find someone else. But the longer Fannie stayed, the more he wanted her to. She was a big help at the store, had a wonderful way with his kinner, and he'd fallen in love with her sweet, gentle spirit.

"You're lookin' at me awful funnylike," she said, pursing her lips.

He cleared his throat, feeling self-conscious all of a sudden. "I—uh—was admirin' your smile."

"Is that so?"

"Jah."

"I think your smile is nice, too."

"Danki. I'm also glad your bein' late today wasn't anything worse than a buggy wheel fallin' off."

"I agree."

"I was worried when you didn't show up at the usual time."

"I've got the buggy maker to thank for gettin' me back on the road again. If Caleb Hoffmeir hadn't come along, who knows how long I might have been stranded?"

Abraham's heart clenched at the thought of Fannie sitting on the road by herself on such a blustery November day. "I'd have come a-lookin' for you if you'd been much later," he said.

She offered him another smile. "I believe you would."

He grinned back at her.

"Now about lunch," she said. "Would you like to take your break first today? You look kind of tired, Abraham."

He shook his head. "Actually, I was thinkin' of closing down the store for an hour or so and takin' you to lunch at the Good 'n Plenty."

"Eat out? You and me together?"

He winked, feeling like he used to when he was a teenaged boy flirting with one of the girls in his community. "That's how I'd like it. Kinda like a date, don't ya know?"

She smoothed her navy blue dress as though there might be wrinkles. "Aren't we a bit old to be courtin'?"

He laughed. "Ask your cousin Edna what she thinks about gettin' old."

Fannie waved her hand. "I'm not askin' Edna anything, 'cause I already know how she stands on the subject of middle age."

"She's got a good attitude about things. Always positive and cracking jokes."

"That's true. It wonders me that she's never remarried."

"How about you, Fannie? How come you've not married again?"

She shrugged. "I could ask you the same question, Abraham Fisher."

He chuckled. "You got me there."

She touched her fingertips to the sides of her hips. Hips that were a little wide, but he didn't mind one bit. "Are you gonna say why or let me guess?"

He gave his beard a few pulls, the way he always did when he was thinking. "The truth is, I never found anyone I thought I could love as much as my Sarah."

She nodded. "Same with me and Ezra."

He took a deep breath and decided to throw caution aside. "Here of late, I've been feelin' differently, though."

Her dark eyebrows raised a notch. "Oh? How so?"

"You're bound and determined to make me say it, aren't you, Fannie Miller?"

"Say what?" she asked in a teasing tone.

He reached for her hand and was glad when she didn't pull it away. "I've come to care for you, Fannie. You've brought joy into my life and helped me learn to deal with the pain of losin' two of my dear kinner."

Fannie glanced at the floor, but then she lifted her gaze to rest on him. "I feel the same way, Abraham. I enjoy your company a lot."

"You think it might be possible you'd consider stayin' on here permanently so's we could do some courtin'?"

She held up two fingers. "I've already been here two months longer than I'd planned to be. I can't expect Abby to keep runnin' the quilt shop by herself."

"Why not? She's done well in your absence, ain't it so?"

Fannie nodded. "Jah, but she's had to rely on my daughter-in-law, Lena, when things have gotten real busy."

"Would Lena be willing to keep helping Abby—if you stayed here in Lancaster County, that is?"

"She might. I really couldn't say without speakin' to her first."

"Will you do that, Fannie? I surely want you to stay on." He wiggled his eyebrows. "I think my kinner are rather fond of you, too, and they'd probably turn cartwheels if I was to tell 'em you were gonna stay and maybe become their new mamm."

Fannie's mouth fell open, and she stood there gaping at him. "Are you sayin' what I think you're sayin'?"

A trickle of sweat rolled down Abraham's forehead and onto his cheek. Was he ready to answer that question? Should he have said anything about her becoming a mother to his children? "I—that is—if we were to court for a while, I think maybe we'd soon know if we're ready to make that kind of commitment to one another."

"I agree. We mustn't rush into anything."

"Right." He leaned forward, and with no thought for what he was doing, Abraham grabbed Fannie in a hug and kissed her right on the mouth.

She responded favorably, but when they pulled away, he noticed her face was as red as a ripe tomato.

"Sorry for takin' liberties that weren't mine," he mumbled.

She slapped his arm lightly. "No apology needed. I rather liked it."

Relief flooded his soul. Maybe there was hope for the two of them to start courting. Might could be Fannie Miller would one day soon become Mrs. Abraham Fisher.

CHAPTER 26

Abraham took a seat in the rocking chair near the woodstove. It was quiet here in the living room, and he hoped to spend a few minutes alone in prayer. Fannie had offered to cook their Christmas dinner, and she'd arrived early this morning. Ever since then, she and the girls had been in the kitchen.

He breathed in the aroma drifting through the house. A nice fat turkey as well as a shank of ham roasted in the oven. There would also be mashed potatoes, stuffing, creamed corn, pickled beets, chow-chow, and whatever else Fannie decided to place on the table. He had an inkling she'd brought a couple of apple-crumb pies, which he'd told her were his favorite. Yesterday, Nancy had made two pumpkin pies and one cherry cream, but unless her baking skills had improved here of late, he knew the crusts would either be burned or too tough.

Abraham patted his stomach, anticipating the meal that would be served in another hour or so. He'd been pleased when Fannie told him her daughter wouldn't be spending the holiday alone. Fannie had talked about returning to Ohio for Christmas, but Abby wrote and told her it would be fine if her mother wanted to be with Abraham and his family. Abby said she'd be having Christmas dinner with her brother and his wife, and she'd also mentioned she was being courted by a young man named Lester Mast, who Abraham figured might have more to do with her being okay with things as they were.

"Seeing as how Fannie's daughter is so happy and Fannie's here with me and the family, it's gonna be a much better Christmas than I'd thought it would be," he murmured. "Only thing that could make this day better would be if Zach and Naomi were home."

He leaned his head back, closed his eyes, and let memories of days gone by wash over him. Two years ago, his Christmas had been the best one ever. Sarah was pregnant with Zach and excited about the prospect of being a mother to the little one who'd be born in the spring. In Abraham's mind, he could see Sarah's sweet face as she sat in the same chair he now occupied. . . .

"You want another boy to help out on the farm, or would you be just as happy with a girl this time?" she'd asked when Abraham stepped into the room.

"I'll be content with whatever the good Lord gives us," he replied, bending over and kissing Sarah on the cheek.

She patted her bulging stomach. "Sure does kick a lot, this little one. Could be a feisty child, you suppose?"

He chuckled and took a seat on the couch across from her. "If he is, we'll have to give him twice as many chores so he doesn't have time on his hands to think up too many troublesome things to do."

"You said *he*." Sarah smiled. "I suspect that you're hopin' for another boy."

He shook his head. "It really don't matter. Just want the boppli to be healthy, that's all."

"Jah, me, too."

"Papa, you sleepin'?"

Abraham's reflections came to a halt as he opened his eyes. Samuel stood facing the woodstove, his hands held out so he could warm them.

"I—uh—was restin' my eyes." Abraham wasn't about to share his deepest thoughts with young Samuel.

"Well, I didn't hear no snorin', so I guess that means you weren't really asleep," the boy said with a snicker.

Samuel's my youngest boy livin' here now, Abraham mused. *His temperament isn't nearly as easygoin' as Zach's, but I sure do love him.*

"How old are ya now, boy?" he asked.

Samuel brought himself up to his full height. "Will turn nine soon, after Naomi's birthday next month."

A lump lodged in Abraham's throat. Naomi had been their New Year's baby, born one hour after the New Year. She'd be turning twenty-one in a week, but sorry to say, she wouldn't be celebrating the special day with her family.

Oh, Naomi, if only I could see you again and tell you the things on my heart. I've sought God's forgiveness for my mixed-up thinkin', but I need your forgiveness, too.

Thanks to Jacob Weaver's godly counsel, as well as Fannie's sweet spirit and love, Abraham had come to realize he could no longer hold Naomi responsible for Zach's disappearance. He'd forgiven the man who took Zach, too, and that hadn't been easy. The hardest person to forgive had been himself. He'd made so many mistakes since Sarah's death, but if God could pardon his sins, then Abraham knew he needed to forgive himself.

Matthew 7:1 said, "Judge not, that ye be not judged." Abraham had judged his daughter when he told God he thought Naomi might have left Zach outside with a stranger on purpose. That was wrong, and he was glad he'd finally seen the light. Only trouble was, Naomi didn't know he'd forgiven her. In Matthew 18:21, he was reminded of the way Peter had asked Jesus how many times he should forgive someone who had sinned against him. Jesus' reply in verse 22 was "seventy times seven." That was a lot of forgiving, and before Naomi left home, Abraham had refused to forgive her even once.

"Something sure smells good comin' from in there, ain't it so?" Samuel said with a nod in the direction of the kitchen.

Abraham pulled his thoughts away from the past. There was no point going over things that couldn't be changed. He had a sense of peace now, and if God allowed him to share the things on his heart with Naomi someday, he would be grateful. If not, then he prayed God would give Naomi the same feeling of peace and the knowledge she was both loved and forgiven.

"The smells are *wunderbaar schee*," he said, smiling at his freckle-faced son.

Samuel grinned. "Jah, wonderful nice. I'm gonna eat two helpings of everything today. Fannie says I'm a growin' boy, and she's a mighty good cook, don't ya think, Papa?"

"Jah, ever so gut."

Samuel turned around so his back was facing the stove. "Sure is gettin' cold outside. Me and Jake were out in the barn playing with the kittens awhile ago, and we nearly froze to death."

"Guess we could have ourselves a white Christmas," Abraham said.

"Sure hope so. I'm more'n ready to build a big snowman. Maybe a snow fort, too, so's I can hide behind it when Jake and Norman decide it's time for a snowball fight."

Abraham chuckled. Samuel could hold his own against his older brothers. He was a determined one; that was for sure.

Samuel moved over to the living room window. "Thought I heard a car door slam. Did ya hear it, Papa?"

"Nope, can't say I did. 'Course the wood from the stove is poppin' pretty good, so that might be what you heard."

Samuel wiped the moisture off the window and peered out. "It's a car all right. Looks like Mavis Peterson's station wagon. Wonder why she'd be comin' over here on Christmas Day."

Abraham shrugged. "Don't rightly know. Maybe she has somethin'

246

she wants to give you younger ones."

"You think so?" Samuel raced to open the front door before Abraham could respond. A few seconds later, the boy turned around, and his eyes were huge as pancakes. "You'll never guess who got out of Mavis's car."

Abraham craned his neck to see, but the view out the front door was out of his sight.

"It's Naomi, Papa! Naomi's come home for Christmas!"

Naomi trembled as she stepped out of Mavis's station wagon. What if her family wasn't happy to see her? How would she respond if Papa was still angry and blamed her for Zach's kidnapping? That was an issue she'd been dealing with for the last few weeks—ever since a customer left her a biblical tract along with his tip. The first verse of scripture that caught her attention was from Psalm 51:3: "For I acknowledge my transgressions; and my sin is ever before me." On the back of the tract was a verse from that same chapter of Psalms, verse 10: "Create in me a clean heart, O God; and renew a right spirit within me." That little piece of paper had been enough to make Naomi realize she needed to seek God's forgiveness and ask for a renewed heart. Returning home to ask Papa's forgiveness seemed like the next step to take. Besides, she was tired of the modern world and missed her family and friends here in Lancaster County.

"It's good to have you home," Mavis said, breaking into Naomi's thoughts. "Tell your family I said hello."

Naomi said she would and thanked Mavis for the ride from the bus station. She'd been grateful their English neighbor had agreed to come, this being Christmas and all.

Oh, Lord, Naomi prayed silently as she made her way to the house, *please give me the right words to say when I see the family. . .especially Papa.*

She'd only made it to the front porch when Samuel stuck his head out the door. She thought he'd seen her and might even come out, but instead, he ducked back inside.

Maybe I made a mistake coming home. Should I have bothered to save up my money for the long bus ride from Oregon to Pennsylvania?

Naomi had no more time to ponder the question. A chorus of voices was hollering for her to come inside out of the cold.

Matthew grabbed her suitcase, while Mary Ann squeezed her around the waist, and Nancy and Samuel clung to her hands. Norman and Jake stood off to one side, smiling like they were ever so glad she'd come home. She couldn't tell what Papa was thinking, as he just stood there with his mouth hanging slightly open.

Naomi took a tentative step in her father's direction. "Papa, I'm sorry about everything. I don't want to be English anymore, and I came here to beg you to let me come home." Her vision clouded with unshed tears. "Can you ever forgive my trespasses?"

He rushed forward, embracing Naomi and wetting the top of her head with his tears. "Oh, Naomi, my beautiful daughter, you're more than welcome here. As far as forgiving you. . .I've already done that, and now I'm the one who needs your forgiveness. That day in the barn, when you heard me talkin' to God, I was just spouting off. I spoke out of pain and frustration and wasn't thinkin' clear. I know you'd never leave Zach alone on purpose, and I'm sorry for what I said. Will you forgive me, Naomi?"

Overcome with emotion, Naomi could only nod. Tears coursed down her cheeks and ran onto her jacket, but she didn't care. Papa was glad to see her. That's all that mattered.

Papa held Naomi at arm's length. "Let me look at you. Oh, you've grown so thin."

She opened her mouth to reply, but everyone started talking at the same time.

"Where have ya been?"

"Why didn't you write?"

"How come you're dressed thataway?"

Naomi looked down at her blue jeans and heavy jean jacket. She'd wanted to wear her own clothes when she arrived home, but she no longer had any of her Plain dresses. When Naomi was at work one day, Ginny gave them to some charity organization. "If you're going to be English, you should set aside all your Amish ways. That means getting rid of those drab dresses and ridiculous white caps you were forced to wear back in Pennsylvania," Ginny asserted.

"Why don't you all come into the kitchen? Dinner's ready, and you can visit with your sister while we eat."

It wasn't until then that Naomi realized there was someone else in the room besides her and the family. A middle-aged, slightly plump Amish woman with dark brown hair and hazel-colored eyes stood off to one side. Had Papa finally hired a *maad*?

Papa withdrew a hanky from his pants pocket, blew his nose, and announced, "Naomi, this is Fannie Miller."

Fannie stepped forward and held out her hand. "I've heard so much about you, Naomi. I can see how happy your family is that you came home for Christmas."

"Fannie is Papa's girlfriend. We're all hopin' she's gonna be our new *mamm*," Mary Ann blurted out.

Papa's girlfriend? New mamm? So the woman wasn't a maid at all. But where had she come from, and why hadn't Naomi ever seen her before?

"I met Fannie at her quilt shop in Berlin, Ohio," Papa said. "Remember, I told you about her when I got back after goin' to see if I could find Zach."

Naomi did remember. It was their first ray of hope concerning her little brother, but nothing had come of it. Fannie had told Papa she didn't know the English couple with the little boy. Did her being here have anything to do with that? Could it be Fannie now remembered something and had come to Pennsylvania to tell Papa about it?

"Fannie's been helping at the store for the last couple months," Papa said before Naomi could voice any questions. "She came here in early September to attend her cousin's birthday party, and when she saw I needed help at the store, she stayed on." He smiled at Fannie and reached for her hand. "I—uh—well—since that time, we've come to care deeply for each other."

Fearful she might topple over, Naomi grabbed the arm of the nearest chair. How could so much have happened since she left home? Papa in love? How was this possible when he'd loved Mama so dearly?

"I'm afraid we're bombarding her with too much too soon," Fannie said softly. "Come, let's go into the kitchen and eat ourselves full."

For the next hour, the Fishers and Fannie sat around the huge wooden table in the kitchen, eating a wonderful array of foods and visiting. For now, Naomi decided to set her feelings regarding Fannie aside and enjoy the time spent with her family. She was glad she hadn't been baptized and joined the church yet, for if she had they would have surely shunned her.

"Tell us where you've been these nearly four months," Matthew said as he reached for another piece of apple-crumb pie.

"Out west—in Portland, Oregon."

"How'd ya get clean out there?" Jake asked.

"In Ginny Meyers's car. She has a friend who lives in Portland, so we were able to stay with her."

Papa leaned forward with his elbows on the table. "Where's Virginia now? Did she come back to Pennsylvania, too?"

Naomi shook her head. "Afraid not. Ginny's got a job workin' at a fitness center in Portland, and she seems to like it there."

"What about her folks? They're worried about her, ya know," Nancy put in.

"Ginny said she had contacted them, saying she'd decided to stay in Oregon for good."

Papa shook his head. "That's not what Bob Meyers told me. He said they'd not heard a single word from Virginia since she left a note saying she was going. They didn't even know you'd gone with her until I told 'em."

Naomi felt awful about that bit of news. At least she'd told her daed she was heading out with Ginny. Then she'd mailed him a postcard, but of course, that didn't make up for not writing again.

"How come you didn't send but one postcard?" Norman asked. "Don't ya know how worried we all were?"

Her face heated up, and she stared down at the table. "I'm sorry about that, but I convinced myself none of the family would want to hear from me again."

"That ain't true, Naomi," Samuel spoke up. "We've missed ya somethin' awful."

She lifted her head. "I've missed you, as well."

"Tell us what it's like out west," Matthew said. "Is Oregon much different than here?"

Naomi nodded. "It rains a lot there, and Portland's awfully crowded. I worked as a waitress in a café near Carla's apartment, and the traffic on that street was horrible."

Fannie pushed her chair away from the table and grabbed several pie plates. "Naomi's probably tired from her long bus trip, so why don't we let her rest awhile?"

Papa stood, too. "Fannie's right. Naomi, why don't you go upstairs and take a hot bath, then climb into bed? Tomorrow we can hear more about your adventures in the English world."

Naomi could hardly believe this was the same father she'd left a few months ago. He wasn't harsh or yelling at anyone. He didn't seem distant or irritable. He had said earlier that he'd forgiven her and asked for forgiveness in return. Something had happened to Papa since she'd been gone, and she had a feeling it had a lot to do with Fannie Miller.

Naomi picked up her plate and a few others, then hauled them over to the kitchen sink.

Fannie smiled and shooed her away. "Nancy and Mary Ann can help do the dishes. Why don't you go upstairs like your daed suggested?"

"Jah, maybe I will. I am kind of tired." Naomi started for the door leading to the stairs, but she turned back around. "Has there been any word on Zach?"

"Nothing a'tall," Nancy said. "I don't think he's ever comin' home."

Papa moved across the room and opened one of the cupboard doors, then reached up and withdrew a newspaper. "That's not entirely true. We have had some word."

Anticipation welled within Naomi's chest. "What do you mean?"

"When Fannie came for her cousin's party, she stopped by the store to give me this." He walked over to Naomi and handed it to her.

"*The Budget*? Fannie gave you a copy of the newspaper?"

He nodded. "Read what I've highlighted, right here."

Naomi studied the part where Papa's finger lay, the section he'd colored with a yellow highlighter pen. By the time she'd finished reading the notice, her heart was pumping extra hard. "This has to be Zach." She looked up at her father. "You think it's him, don't you, Papa?"

He nodded. "I do."

"Then the man who took him must have placed this notice." A ray of hope seeped into Naomi's soul, and she squeezed her eyes shut in prayer. *"Let it be Zach, Lord. May this be the tool that leads us to him."*

"I called *The Budget* as soon as I saw the ad," Papa said, "but they had no information to give me."

Naomi's hopes were dashed as quickly as they had soared. She blinked back tears. "All this tells us is that Zach's with someone, but we don't know who. Not very good news if you ask me."

"But it says Zach is okay and being well cared for," Papa said in a calm voice. "Somewhere out there among the English your little brother is living, and even though I still miss him terribly, this ad in *The Budget* is something to hold on to, don't you think?"

"I—I guess so."

"Even if we never see Zach again, at least we have the assurance he's not hurt or anything."

She nodded.

"I think this notice is an answer to prayer." Papa smiled, despite the tears in his eyes. "Our little boy is spending Christmas Day with someone who cared enough to place the ad so we wouldn't worry. Even though we don't know where Zach is, I feel peace in my heart about it." He nodded at Fannie. "I've come to believe, thanks to Fannie and Jacob's good counsel, that God will use this whole thing to bring something good for our family." He took Naomi's hand and gave it a gentle squeeze. "He brought you home, and that's one good thing. If He can give us a Christmas miracle like that, I'm gonna trust Him where Zach's concerned, too."

Naomi marveled at the peace she saw on her father's face. If he could rely on God like this, maybe she could, as well. He'd brought her home again, and Papa was right, it was like a Christmas miracle.

She handed the newspaper back to him. "I'll see you in the morning, for we've surely got a lot more catchin' up to do."

CHAPTER 27

"Naomi! Are you up?" A child's high-pitched voice, followed by the sound of determined knocking, roused Naomi from her sleep. Groggy and disoriented, she rolled over in bed, noticing a ray of light streaming through a hole in the dark window shade.

"Naomi?"

"Jah, I'm awake." Naomi recognized Nancy's voice and realized this wasn't a dream. She was home in her own comfortable bed. A renewed sense of joy flooded her soul as she burrowed deeper into the feather pillow she had missed for too many nights. It was much softer than the flat, lumpy pillow she'd slept on for the last several months. The heavy quilt that covered her was warm and invited Naomi to linger awhile. Even the pungent aroma of kerosene from the lantern she kept near her bed was comforting. How she'd missed this familiar room, their big drafty house, and especially the family whom she had never stopped loving.

"You comin' downstairs soon?" Nancy asked. "Or do ya want me to get started on breakfast without you?"

With great effort, Naomi sat up. She glanced at the clock on her dresser and grimaced. This was her first morning home, and she'd slept later than she had planned. "I'll be there as soon as I'm dressed," she called.

"See you in the kitchen." Naomi heard her sister's footsteps pad down the hall, and she smiled. Outside, the old rooster crowed raucously. These sounds were a lot more pleasing than the loud music Carla used to play every morning or the noisy cars that whizzed by in front of their apartment.

Naomi climbed out of bed and headed for the window. Lifting the shade, she peeked out. The ground below was covered with a blanket of radiant white. If more snow came, there would soon be bonfires, sledding, and sleigh rides. Courting couples in their community would be having all kinds of fun.

Naomi's thoughts went immediately to Caleb. Had he found someone to court during her absence? She couldn't blame him if he had. After all, Naomi had told Caleb on several occasions not to wait for her and to look for someone else. She'd often reminded him that as long as she was responsible for her family, there was no chance for them to court.

Naomi shook her head. *Leaving the way I did probably told Caleb I had no interest in him.* Naomi had never allowed herself to give in to the feelings she'd had for Caleb ever since they were kinner. There was no point in leading him on when they had no future together.

She blinked away sudden tears. Naomi hadn't written to Caleb even once while she was away, even though she'd been tempted to. "There was a good reason for that," she mumbled. Besides not wanting to give Caleb hope that she might care for him, Naomi had convinced herself she would never return to Pennsylvania. Until she'd found the tract left by a customer at Jasper's Café, she had given up hope of ever reconciling with God, herself, and especially Papa.

Has Caleb thought about me or missed the times he used to come into the store and talk to me when we were alone? She shivered against the cold and hugged herself. *Caleb deserves to be happy, so if he did find someone while I was gone, I'll make an effort to set my feelings for him aside and share in his joy.*

Tap. Tap. There was another knock on the door. "Naomi, are you in there?" This time it was Mary Ann calling to her.

"I'm about to get dressed. I'll be down in a few minutes."

Naomi knew there was no more time for reflections. Her family was waiting for breakfast, and she needed to hurry and see that it was on the table. "At least some things haven't changed 'round here," she said with a shake of her head. "But that's all right. I'm just mighty glad to be home."

Jim jerked the pillow over his ears in an attempt to drown out the shrill cry of their fussy child vibrating through the intercom. Yesterday, since it was Christmas, they had allowed Jimmy to stay up later than usual, playing with his new toys. Now Jim was paying the price for that decision. Linda's folks had come for the holidays, and all day, Jimmy had been passed from Grandma to Grandpa and back again. Between them and Linda, the kid was spoiled rotten. He'd received way too many gifts, eaten far too much junk, and had been up running around when he should have been sleeping.

When Jim heard Linda slip out of bed, he groaned. "What time is it?"

"Three in the morning," she whispered. "Jimmy's crying again."

"I'm well aware of that. The kid's been screaming every hour on the hour since he went to bed at eleven. Probably has a stomachache from all the candy he ate."

"Go back to sleep, honey. I'll tend to him."

Jim only grunted in response. If he didn't have to get up for work in three hours, he might not care about lost sleep or a screaming child in the room down the hall.

Jim had just dozed off again when he heard a familiar sound. "Da-Da-Da."

When he rolled over and sat up, Jim could see Linda's silhouette at the foot of the bed. She had Jimmy in her arms.

"What's he doing here?"

"I couldn't get him to settle down, so I thought he could sleep with us."

"That's not a good idea, Linda."

"Why not?"

"I've got to get a few hours' sleep before it's time to get ready for work."

"Which is exactly why I brought the baby into our room." She moved to her side of the bed, placed Jimmy between their two pillows, and crawled in beside him.

Jim turned on his side toward the wall. If this didn't work out, he might have to sleep on the couch.

"Da-Da."

"Yeah, right. Go to sleep, Jimmy. Da-Da needs his rest."

Jim had no more than closed his eyes when he felt a small foot connect to his ribs. "Ouch!"

"What's wrong, honey?"

"The kid's kicking me."

"Jimmy, no-no," Linda said sweetly.

Another jolt with the boy's toes.

Jim moaned. "Can't you move him to the other side of the bed?"

"He might fall out if he's not between us. Close your eyes and try to sleep."

"Ma-Ma-Ma! Da-Da!" A small, wet hand touched Jim on the back, and he jerked away.

"Take the boy back to his own room, Linda."

"He's lonesome, Jim. After the excitement of yesterday and being the center of attention, he needs us."

"And I need my sleep!"

"There's no reason for you to yell. You might wake Mother and Daddy."

"If they're not already awake, it's a miracle," he grumbled.

"You don't have to be sarcastic."

"I'm just stating facts."

"Our first Christmas with Jimmy was wonderful, wasn't it?" she asked, changing the subject.

"It was great."

"Wasn't it cute when the baby tried to give his bottle to the teddy bear my folks got him?"

"Yeah, real cute. Jimmy shouldn't be taking a bottle anymore."

"I think he still needs it. It offers him comfort."

"Then why isn't he taking one now?"

"I tried that, but he wasn't interested. He's probably full."

"Uh-huh." Jim's breathing slowed as the need for sleep overtook him. *Whap!* Jimmy's clammy little hand slapped the side of Jim's head. He bolted upright. "That's it. I'm putting the hammer down."

"The hammer? Jim, what on earth are you talking about? Are you having a bad dream?"

"No, it's more like a nightmare." Jim jumped out of bed, swooped Jimmy into his arms, and stumbled for the door.

"Where are you taking my baby, and what's all this about a hammer?" Linda shouted.

He halted and turned toward the bed. "My dad used to say he was putting the hammer down whenever he made up his mind to take control of a situation. So I've decided it's time for me to do the same, because this whole thing is totally out of control."

"I don't understand why you're so upset." Linda's voice shook with emotion, but he wasn't going to give in. Not this time. He'd done it too much in the past, and where had it gotten him? Jim usually took the easy way out, opting not to answer his cell phone when he knew it was Linda calling or sleeping on the couch when she was determined to bring Jimmy to bed with them. He was putting the hammer down once and for all, and it was going to stay down this time!

"Naomi, there was really no need for you to come in this mornin'," Abraham said as she moved around the store, lighting the gas lanterns.

"I figured you'd want to stay home and get caught up on your rest."

She shook her head. "I want to be here, Papa. I've missed helpin' you, and it's a lot nicer workin' at our store than waiting tables at a crowded, noisy restaurant."

"I doubt we'll have many customers today, what with it bein' the first Monday after Christmas and all." He nodded toward the closest window. "Besides, it's snowing like crazy, and folks aren't likely to brave the storm just to come into our store."

She smiled at him. "Then why'd we open at all today?"

"Out of habit, I guess." He chuckled, then shrugged. "Never know when someone might have a real need for somethin'."

"That's true. I remember last winter when it got so cold that folks were comin' in here to buy kerosene for their lanterns, woolen scarves, hats, and gloves. We sold plenty of snow shovels, too."

"Good point. Which is exactly why I felt I couldn't close the store today."

"When did you start selling quilts, Papa?" Naomi asked, as she fingered a stack of colorful coverings on the shelf a few feet away.

"Those are Fannie's. She made them, and I suggested she try selling 'em here." Abraham put the OPEN sign in the door window and grabbed the broom. "It wonders me so the way this place can get so dirty. Sure wish folks would learn to wipe their feet before comin' inside."

Naomi left the quilts and came to stand at his side. "Mind if I ask you a personal question?"

"Ask away."

"Just how serious are you and Fannie?"

He stopped sweeping and turned to face her. "I'm hopin' to ask her to marry me soon."

Naomi's mouth fell open. "I never thought you'd marry again. You and Mama—well, I know how much you loved her."

"I did, and there will always be a spot in my heart for her. You can't live with someone over twenty years and not keep that love in here."

He placed his hand against his chest.

"Do you love Fannie more than Mama?"

Abraham's throat constricted. The way he felt was hard to describe. He scuffed the toe of his boot against the floor. "What Fannie and I have is special. I won't deny it. As far as lovin' her more than your mamm—I don't think I could ever love anyone more than Sarah." He shook his head. "Maybe the same, but in a different way. Does that make sense to you?"

Naomi nodded, and her dark eyes filled with tears. "I—think so, Papa."

He set the broom aside and gave her a hug. "It's so gut to have ya home, Daughter. I surely did miss you."

"I missed you, too."

Abraham was going to say more, but the front door opened, and Fannie stepped into the room.

"Gude mariye," she said with an easygoing smile. "Sure is nasty out there." The top of Fannie's black bonnet was covered with white flakes, and Abraham was sorely tempted to brush them away.

Instead, he returned her smile and said, "Didn't expect you'd be in this mornin', what with the snow and all."

She waved a hand. "Wouldn't let a little bad weather keep me from comin' to the store when I figured you'd be here all alone."

He nodded toward Naomi. "Couldn't persuade her to stay home and rest up today."

Fannie removed her heavy shawl and bonnet and hung them on a wall peg. "Knowing Matthew, he'd probably have been grateful to give you the job of babysitting after school," she told Naomi.

Naomi's forehead wrinkled. "Matthew's been watchin' the kinner while I was away?"

"Only after school and on Saturdays," Abraham explained. "Nancy does most of the cooking and cleaning these days, but Matthew's good at keepin' the peace when the younger ones start scrappin'."

Naomi smiled. "Jah, I know how that can go."

Fannie cleared her throat. "Abraham, I was wonderin' if I could talk with you a minute—in private."

He glanced over at Naomi. "Would ya mind waitin' on any customers who might come into the store?"

"I'd be happy to, Papa."

Abraham took hold of Fannie's arm and led her to the back of the building. They stopped in front of a rack full of seeds and gardening supplies. "What's up?" he asked.

She shifted her weight from one foot to the other, kind of nervous-like. "I've been thinking that since Naomi is home now, maybe I should head on back to Ohio."

He stood there for several seconds, feeling numb and not knowing how to respond. "You want to go?" he finally mumbled.

She stared at the floor. "I've been gone for several months now, leaving Abby on her own at the quilt shop."

"I thought she was managing pretty well with Lena's help."

Fannie nodded. "She is, but—"

"And I thought you enjoyed workin' here with me." Abraham fingered his beard, wishing this conversation had never taken place.

"I do, but I miss my quilts, and—"

He pointed to the front of the store. "I cleared off a shelf so you could sell some of your quilts."

"I know, and I appreciate that." She smiled, but it never quite reached her eyes. "Your daughter's back, Abraham. You don't need me anymore."

With no thought of anyone seeing them, Abraham pulled Fannie into his arms. "I'll always need you, Fannie Mae. I love you and want to make you my wife."

Her beautiful eyes, which reminded him of acorns in the fall, filled with tears. "You really want to marry me?"

He kissed the top of her white head covering. "I thought you knew how I felt. I've told ya often enough lately that I love you."

"I know, but with Naomi comin' home and all, I thought you might feel you could get along without me now."

"I could never get along without you, Fannie. I want you to be my *fraa*."

She sighed against his chest. *"Ich lieb du*—I love you, Abraham Fisher."

"Does that mean you'll marry me?"

She nodded. "If Abby's willin' to take over the shop completely."

Abraham stiffened. "And if she's not?"

Fannie smiled and reached up to gently pinch his cheek. "I'll suggest she move here. Maybe we can find a building nearby and set up a quilt shop."

Suddenly, an idea popped into Abraham's head, and he snapped his fingers. "Say, I'll tell ya what."

"What's that?"

"I could add on to my store, then you'd have your own quilt shop. How's that sound?"

She tipped her head back and looked up at him. "It sounds wunderbaar gut to me."

Caleb couldn't believe his mother had sent him out in weather like this just to get some kerosene, which she'd said she was only low on. And why did it have to be him and not Andy or Marvin? Was it the fact that he was older, and she felt he knew better how to handle the horse and buggy in the snow?

Pop had hired a driver this morning to take him to a dental appointment in Lancaster, and both John and David had gone off to see their girlfriends. Since Mom had insisted Caleb head to the Fishers' store right away, he'd left Andy and Marvin at the buggy shop. They'd begun work on a new carriage for an English man in the area who ran a bed-and-breakfast and offered free buggy rides to the tourists. Caleb could only hope his brothers wouldn't mess up the job while he was away. Marvin was careless at times, and Andy tended to be accident-prone. No telling what might happen in Caleb's absence.

By the time he arrived at Fisher's General Store, Caleb was pretty worked up. He hadn't been to the store in many months. Not since Naomi left home.

Caleb stomped the snow off his feet and entered the store. A blast of warm air hit him in the face, and he rubbed his hands briskly together. It felt good to be out of the cold, even though he'd driven a closed-in buggy, which had a portable heater inside.

"Gude mariye," he said, nodding at Abraham, who sat behind the counter, looking at a large blue ledger.

"Jah, it surely is a gut morning."

Caleb shoved his hands into his pockets. *The storekeeper seems to be in an agreeable mood today. Don't recall that he's ever been so friendly to me before.*

"Did ya have a gut Christmas?"

"It was fine. How about yours?"

Abraham nodded and smiled. "Better than I ever expected."

Hmm. . .maybe the man's cheerful attitude has something to do with Fannie Miller. Caleb's mother had recently told him that she'd heard from her friend Doris, who knew someone acquainted with Fannie's cousin Edna Yoder, that Fannie and the storekeeper saw a lot of each other these days. Edna told her friend she thought there soon might be a wedding between Abraham and Fannie, and the word had been passed along.

"Me and the family had the best Christmas present," Abraham continued.

Caleb leaned against the counter. "What was it?"

The storekeeper pointed toward the back of the room, and Caleb's gaze followed the man's finger. Two Amish women stood side by side with their backs to him. One he figured was Fannie, but he didn't know whom she was waiting on.

Suddenly, the smaller of the two women turned around, and Caleb nearly passed out from the shock of seeing her. "Naomi!"

She made her way to the front of the store, and her radiant smile lit up the whole room. "It's nice to see you, Caleb."

"I—I had no idea you were back," he stammered. "How long have ya been here?"

"I came home on Christmas Day."

He studied Naomi intently. She was dressed in Plain clothes, although they hung loosely on her. She was obviously not English anymore or she wouldn't be here, dressed as an Amish woman. There were dark circles beneath her luminous brown eyes, but he thought she looked beautiful.

"Have you come home for good?" he asked hopefully.

"Jah, I've seen the error of my ways."

He smiled. "I'm so glad—about you comin' home, that is."

Abraham cleared his throat a couple of times. "Ah-hem."

Caleb whirled around. In his joy over seeing Naomi again, he'd almost forgotten her daed was right there. No doubt the man was scrutinizing everything he'd said, just waiting to ask Caleb to leave his store.

"I—uh—came by for some kerosene," Caleb mumbled. "Mom's almost out, and with the bad weather settin' in, she thought she'd better have plenty on hand."

"Makes sense to me." Abraham had a funny kind of grin on his face, and Caleb didn't know what to make of it.

Fannie joined the group then. "It's nice to see you, Caleb."

"Likewise." There was an awkward silence, then he asked, "How's that buggy wheel holdin' out? It didn't fall off again, I hope."

Fannie shook her head. "Been stayin' right in place."

"That's gut. Real gut."

Fannie glanced at Abraham and winked. "Don't ya have somethin' you want to tell the buggy maker?"

Abraham's forehead wrinkled. "I do?"

She went around the back of the counter and whispered in his ear, which quickly turned pink, while a slow smile spread across his face.

"Fannie reminded me of somethin' I told her awhile back. . .when Naomi left home and I wasn't sure if we'd ever see her again."

"What was that?" Caleb asked.

"I'd like to hear whatever it is, too," Naomi put in.

The storekeeper gave his beard a couple of yanks, leaned slightly forward, and announced, "Caleb Hoffmeir, I give you permission to court my daughter."

CHAPTER 28

Naomi pulled on a clean dress and secured her head covering in place. She'd been home a week already, and here it was New Year's Day—her twenty-first birthday. Would her family remember? Would they do anything special to celebrate?

She smiled at her reflection in the mirror. "It doesn't matter. Just being home with those I love is birthday present enough for me." She thought about Ginny and wondered if she ever missed home. Her first day back at the store, Naomi had gone to Meyers' Restaurant to see Ginny's folks. She felt they deserved to know where their daughter was living and that she was okay. They had appreciated the information but said their hearts were saddened by their daughter running off that way.

A knock on her bedroom door drove Naomi's thoughts aside, and she called, "Come in."

Nancy and Mary Ann stepped into the room, each with their arms held behind their backs.

"Hallich Neiyaahr un Hallich Gebottsdaag!" Mary Ann announced.

"Jah, Happy New Year and Happy Birthday!" Nancy echoed.

Before Naomi could respond, they both handed her a gift. Mary Ann's was in a white envelope, and Nancy's was inside a small brown paper sack.

Naomi struggled not to cry. Her sisters had remembered today was her birthday, and even if no one else in the family acknowledged it, this display of love was enough for her.

She took the gifts, went over to her bed, and seated herself. Her sisters followed and sat on either side of Naomi.

"Open mine first," Mary Ann said excitedly. "I made it myself."

Naomi tore the envelope open and withdrew a piece of heavy paper folded like a card. There was a picture of a tulip on the front, colored with red crayon. The words HAPPY BIRTHDAY were above it. Inside Mary Ann had written a note. "To my big sister: I'm glad you didn't stay gone like Zach. We all missed you! Love, Mary Ann." Tucked inside the card was a blue felt bookmark that had been cut out with pinking shears.

Tears sprang to Naomi's eyes as she hugged her little sister. "The card's so nice, and I'll put the pretty bookmark inside my Bible."

Mary Ann smiled. "I knew you'd like it."

"I do. Danki."

"Now mine," Nancy said, nodding at the paper sack Naomi had placed in her lap. "Fannie helped me make it."

Naomi reached inside the bag and pulled out a pot holder, quilted in various colors using a simple nine-patch pattern.

"It's for your hope chest," Nancy explained. "For when you and Caleb get married."

Naomi wrapped her arms around Nancy. "It's ever so nice. You did a gut job, and it would definitely go in my hope chest, if I had one." She sighed. "As far as me ever marryin' Caleb. . . Well, that remains to be seen. We only got permission to court a week ago."

Nancy nodded, looking suddenly grown up. "It'll happen, just you wait and see."

Naomi stood. "Right now the three of us need to head downstairs and get breakfast started. The menfolk will be in from chorin' soon, and if I know Papa and those brothers of ours, they'll be hungry as a bunch of mules."

Mary Ann and Nancy both giggled, and Naomi followed them out of the room.

"After breakfast is over, I'm gonna bake you a hurry-up cake," Nancy announced. "I've learned to cook since you were gone."

Naomi opened the refrigerator door and withdrew a carton of eggs. "I'm sure you've become right capable in the kitchen."

"Nancy can't make blueberry pancakes as good as yours," Mary Ann put in. "She always burns them around the edges."

Nancy stomped her foot. "Do not!"

"Do so!"

Naomi held up one hand to silence the girls before their disagreement got out of hand. "Let's not spoil the New Year by arguing, okay?"

"Yeah, Papa don't like it when he hears us yellin'," Mary Ann said as she began setting the table.

"Then don't yell," Nancy shot back at her.

Naomi was about to say something when the back door swung open and in walked Samuel, carrying a wicker basket with a strip of cloth draped over the top. Believing it was freshly collected eggs, she pointed to the refrigerator. "Set 'em in there 'til we've had a chance to be sure they're clean enough."

Samuel's eyebrows shot up. "I ain't puttin' your birthday present in the refrigerator. It'd kill him."

"Him?" Naomi moved to where Samuel stood by the table. "What have you got in there?"

Samuel grinned and handed her the basket. "This is my present to you."

Mary Ann and Nancy crowded around as Naomi pulled back the piece of cloth, and a ball of white fur poked its tiny head up. *Meow!*

"It's one of Snowball's kittens, ain't it so?" asked Mary Ann.

Samuel nodded, looking right pleased with himself. "I named this one Speckles 'cause he's white with gray spots on his legs and head." He touched the kitten's pink nose with the tip of his finger. "Ya like him, Naomi?"

She gently squeezed his shoulder. "He's real nice, Samuel. Danki."

"You better put that cat outside," Nancy said in her most bossy voice. "Papa don't like animals in the house; you know that."

Samuel started to protest, but Naomi came to his rescue. "I think it might be best if Speckles stays in the barn with his mother for a while, don't you, Samuel?"

He shrugged. "I guess so."

"He'll still be my pet, though," Naomi assured the boy. "I'll play with him whenever I'm in the barn, and when he's old enough to leave his mamm, he can run all over the yard."

Samuel grinned from ear to ear. "I like that idea." He took the basket from Naomi. "Speckles is gonna be one good mouser, you'll see."

"I'm sure he will be."

As Samuel headed out the door, Matthew, Jake, and Norman entered the kitchen. They were carrying something under a large piece of canvas.

"What have you got there?" Naomi asked, her curiosity piqued.

"It's your birthday present," Matthew said. "We've been fixin' it ever since you came back home a week ago."

Naomi crossed the room and lifted one corner of the canvas. Her breath caught in her throat when she saw what was underneath. "This is our mamm's old cedar chest, isn't it?"

Norman nodded. "You like what we did with it?"

"Oh, yes." Naomi knelt on the floor beside her mother's beloved hope chest. Her brothers had sanded away all the old scratches and gouges and given it a new coat of stain with clear varnish brushed over the top.

"We thought with you bein' courted by the buggy maker and all, you'd be needin' a hope chest now," Jake announced.

Tears slipped out of Naomi's eyes and rolled down her cheeks. "Caleb and me haven't had even one date yet, but I surely do appreciate all the work you three did on Mama's cedar chest." She stroked the lid, which felt as smooth as glass. "Even if I never marry, I'll treasure this all of my days."

"Why not start by fillin' it with this?"

Naomi looked up. Papa stood inside the door, holding a quilt in his hands. "This was your mamm's, and I want you to have it for your twenty-first birthday," he said with a catch in his voice.

Naomi stood. "Oh, Papa. Mama's Double Wedding Ring quilt has been on your bed ever since I can remember. Her mamm gave it to you as a wedding present. How can you part with it?"

He stepped forward, holding it out to her. "She'd want you to have it, Naomi, and I sure wouldn't think of sellin' it."

"Why would ya be sellin' anything of Mama's?" The question came from Nancy, who stood beside Naomi, fingering the edges of the blue and white quilt as though it were made of spun gold.

"Fannie and I have decided to get married in the spring, and it's customary for a widower to sell his wife's things before he remarries." Papa smiled at Naomi. "Of course, I'll be giving you and the sisters a chance to pick whatever you're wantin' first."

The joy of Naomi's birthday and all the wonderful presents faded as the stark reality set in that her daed really was planning to marry Fannie Miller. Soon Fannie would be in charge of the house, and since he'd said he wanted to add a quilt shop on to the store, it would probably mean Fannie would continue to work there, as well.

Wonder where that leaves me? Naomi asked herself. *From what I can tell, Fannie seems like a nice enough woman, but I don't really know her yet. The thought of her takin' Mama's place hurts real bad, and it would appear she'll soon be fillin' my shoes, as well. Even so, my burdens will be lighter once Papa and Fannie are married. Now there'll be a chance for me to finally think about marriage—should Caleb ask.*

"I have somethin' else for you," Papa said, forcing Naomi to set her thoughts aside.

"Oh, what's that?"

"It's right here." Papa handed Naomi a black Bible, which she recognized as also having belonged to her mother. "I thought, as the oldest daughter, this ought to go to you."

Naomi gulped back a sob. Everything was happening too fast, and she felt so confused about her father's plans to be married. She would treasure Mama's hope chest, quilt, and especially the Bible, but could she really accept Fannie as her stepmother?

As Caleb guided his horse and sleigh down the road, he kept glancing at the box on the floor by his feet. Inside was a delicate purple and white African violet, one his mamm had grown. She had a way with plants and things—had them growing in pots all over the sunporch and into her sewing room. Caleb had offered to buy the violet, telling his mother he wanted something special to give Naomi for her birthday. Mom flatly refused, saying he did so many favors for her—always running to town to fetch things and whatnot. Besides, there was no way she would take money from one of her sons for a plant she'd so easily grown. She only sold them to the customers who visited her booth when the farmers' market was open.

"Sure hope the cold doesn't get to the violet before I arrive at the Fishers' place. Wouldn't do to present Naomi with a dead plant for her twenty-first birthday," Caleb mumbled.

The horse whinnied as if in response, while the sleigh glided across the snow-packed road as easy as a duck sets down on water.

"This is gonna be the best New Year's," Caleb shouted into the wind. He'd been given permission to court the storekeeper's daughter, and nothing could be any better than that. Nothing but marrying Naomi, and he hoped that would come about next fall.

A short time later, Caleb pulled into the Fishers' yard, hopped down from the sleigh, and tied his horse to the hitching rail near the barn. He grabbed the box housing the African violet and chanced a peek inside. It looked fine, and he breathed a sigh of relief.

Caleb took the porch steps two at a time and knocked on the back door. It was still early, and he figured Naomi might be in the kitchen doing up the breakfast dishes.

The door swung open on the second knock, but instead of Naomi, it was Abraham who greeted Caleb. "Hallich Neiyaahr," he said with a nod.

"Happy New Year to you, too," Caleb replied. "Is—uh—Naomi at home? I came to wish her a happy birthday and give her this." He held out the box, feeling kind of nervous all of a sudden.

Abraham nodded and stepped aside, pushing the door all the way open. "Naomi, there's someone to see you."

Caleb still couldn't believe the change that had come over the storekeeper in the last few months. Mom had mentioned a few times that ever since Fannie Miller started helping at the store, Abraham had been much more agreeable. Now that Naomi was back home again, her daed seemed downright friendly. Caleb couldn't believe the man had actually given him permission to court his oldest daughter. It seemed almost too good to be true.

He shifted from one foot to the other, hugging the box close to his chest.

"Well, you comin' inside or not, boy?"

"I—uh—sure." *Guess some things haven't changed. Abraham still sees me as a boy, not a man.* Caleb stepped into the warm kitchen, and the sight of Naomi standing at the sink washing dishes made his heart pound. Her cheeks were flushed, and a wisp of golden brown hair had worked its way free from the bun at the back of her head. He stared at Naomi several seconds, imagining what it would be like to be married to her and come into their own house, knowing she was his and his alone.

"Happy birthday," he said, extending the box toward her.

She smiled and wiped her hands on a dish towel.

Nancy, who had been drying the dishes, spoke up. "You're sure gettin' a lot of presents today, Sister."

"Why don't you set it there?" Naomi said, motioning to the table. She finished drying her hands and joined him a few seconds later.

"Sure wasn't expectin' you to give me a gift," she said breathlessly. "What is it?"

He chuckled. "Open the box and take a look for yourself."

She lifted the flaps, and her sharp intake of breath made him wonder if she believed the plant was as pretty as he thought she was. "It's beautiful, Caleb. Danki."

"Sure can't put that gift in your hope chest," Nancy announced.

Naomi's face flamed, and she gave her sister a warning look.

"If you don't have other plans, I was hopin' you'd go for a ride in my sleigh," Caleb said, coming to Naomi's rescue. No doubt some of her other birthday presents had been meant for her hope chest.

Naomi glanced at her father. "Would that be all right with you?"

He nodded. "Jah, sure, as long as you're back in time for our afternoon meal. Fannie's comin' by soon, and she plans to fix us a big pot of sauerkraut and pork to eat around one o'clock."

"I'll have her back in plenty of time," Caleb assured him.

"But shouldn't I be here to help with the cooking?" Naomi asked. She looked kind of flustered, and Caleb wondered if maybe she didn't want to go with him.

Abraham shook his head. "Fannie can call on Nancy if she needs any help."

Naomi shrugged, but Caleb could see by the wrinkles in her forehead that she wasn't too happy. Did she prefer to be here cooking rather than go for a ride in his sleigh? Maybe she wasn't all that anxious to be courted by him.

"If you'd rather not go sleigh ridin', I'll head for home." Caleb held his breath and waited for her answer.

She shook her head and offered him a smile. "A sleigh ride sounds like fun. I'll get my heavy shawl and gloves." She left the room, and Caleb shuffled to the back door to wait for her.

Naomi returned to the kitchen a few minutes later, wrapped in a long black shawl and wearing her dark bonnet and a pair of heavy gloves. "I'm ready to go."

Caleb opened the door and followed her outside. Maybe her problem had more to do with Fannie Miller than it did him. He looked over his shoulder, calling, "We'll be back soon."

When Fannie drove into the Fishers' yard, she spotted Caleb Hoffmeir in an open sleigh. Naomi sat beside him, and as their rigs passed in the driveway, Fannie waved and called, "Hallich Neiyaahr!"

"Happy New Year to you, as well!" Caleb hollered in response.

Fannie grinned. Things were working out real nice for her and Abraham these days. Spring would be here soon, and after their wedding, she'd be living in his house permanently. *Sure hope everything works out equally well for Naomi and the buggy maker. After all this family's been through, there needs to be a time of peace and happiness.*

Fannie pulled her buggy beside the barn and climbed down. Before she had a chance to unhitch the horse, Matthew stepped out of the barn and took charge of things. "I'll put your horse away. That way you can hurry inside out of this cold."

"Danki. That's right nice of you," she said with a smile. "Some woman's gonna be lucky to call you 'husband' someday."

Matthew's face turned pink. Fannie figured it was a result of embarrassment rather than the cold weather. From what she'd been able to tell, he seemed kind of shy around women. Abraham had told her that so far Matthew showed no signs of wanting to pursue a serious relationship with anyone, either.

"I saw Naomi and Caleb heading out in his sleigh," Fannie said, changing the subject. "Looks like the beginning of their courting days."

"It would seem so."

"After all Naomi's gone through, I'm glad to see her finding some happiness."

"She's been through a lot; there's no denying that." Matthew stroked the horse behind his ear. "Uh—Fannie, I want you to know I'm real glad you and Papa are plannin' to get married come spring."

"Thank you for saying so," she said, a feeling of joy bubbling in her soul. "I hope to make your daed feel happy and content. He's been through more in the last couple years than many men face in a whole lifetime."

Matthew nodded. "You're right about that, too." He touched Fannie's arm, and she knew at that moment she'd made a friend. "Papa's changed a lot since he met you, and we're all grateful."

Tears sprang to Fannie's eyes, but she blinked them away. "It's God who gets the thanks, Matthew. He's done a mighty work in Abraham's life, but it's only because the man allowed God's Word to take root in his soul."

"I understand Jacob Weaver has shared a good many scriptures with Papa, too," Matthew said. "The verses and his friendship with Jacob have also been gut, but being in love with you has brought joy back into my daed's life."

"I love Abraham very much, and he's brought a good deal of happiness into my life, as well."

"Glad to hear that."

Fannie turned toward the house. "See you later, Matthew. And don't forget. . .pork and sauerkraut at one o'clock sharp!"

CHAPTER 29

The remainder of winter flew by like flurries of snowflakes, and spring was ushered in with blustery winds and a sprinkling of rain. Naomi had recently been baptized and joined the church. With a sense of peace, she enjoyed each moment, whether she was working at the store, doing chores at home, or having fun with Caleb in his courting buggy. They'd gone ice-skating, taken several leisurely drives, spent time at her house playing games and visiting, and attended a few singings. Tomorrow night, another one would be held, only this singing would be at the Fishers' place. Caleb wouldn't be driving Naomi to or from the young people's event, and Matthew, who was usually shy around women his age, would be there, since Papa had insisted on it.

Naomi couldn't believe her father had agreed to host the singing in their barn. It was the first time he'd ever allowed anything like that. There seemed to be a lot of "firsts" for Naomi's daed these days, and she was pretty sure Fannie Miller was the reason he'd become so agreeable.

As she moved away from her bedroom window, Naomi spotted the letter she'd received from Ginny Meyers that morning. This was the first Naomi had heard from Ginny since she'd returned to Lancaster County three months ago without her English friend.

She plucked the letter off the dresser and read it aloud.

Dear Naomi:

You've probably been wondering why I haven't written before now. To be honest, I was mad at you for leaving the way you did and then compounding it by giving out Carla's phone number to

my folks. I'm okay with that now, though. I talked to Mom and
Dad last week, and they've finally come to accept my wanting to
live out here and be on my own.

Naomi smiled as she reread that part. She was glad things were better between Ginny and her folks. At least they were keeping in touch now.

She drew her attention back to the letter and continued to read.

> *Since you left Portland, I've been dating Chad Nelson, the*
> *guy who manages the fitness center where I work. He's already*
> *talking about marriage and says he's hoping we can buy our own*
> *fitness center someday. That would be so great. As you know, I've*
> *wanted to have my own fitness center for some time.*
>
> *I want you to know that I harbor no ill feelings toward you.*
> *I'd hoped you would make it in the English world, but apparently*
> *you're not cut out for it.*
>
> *All the best,*
> *Ginny*

Naomi sighed and flopped onto her bed. It was late, and she should be asleep by now, but she wasn't tired. There were too many thoughts rolling around in her head. Things with Ginny seemed to be settled, but there was still one more item she needed to deal with.

"If only Mama were here," she whispered. "She was so full of wisdom and would surely have some answers for my confusion."

As Naomi rolled over, her gaze came to rest on the black Bible she kept on the nightstand by her bed. "Mama's *Biewel.* Maybe I can find a solution in there."

She reached for the worn, leather book but had no idea where to look for the specific answers she wanted. "Something to make me feel better about Papa marrying again," Naomi murmured. "Jah, that's what I'm needin' the most right now."

Naomi's mother had placed several bookmarks inside the Bible, so she opened to the place where the first one was marked. "Genesis chapter two, verse twenty," she read aloud. " 'And Adam gave names to all cattle, and to the fowl of the air, and to every beast of the field; but for Adam there was not found an help meet for him.' "

Tears slipped out of Naomi's eyes and rolled down her cheeks. She sniffed and wiped them away with the back of her hand. *Oh, Papa, you've been like Adam ever since Mama died. You had plenty to do but have been lonely and needed a help meet.*

Naomi knew Fannie would make a good wife for Papa. She'd proven that already by the way she'd helped out, both here at the house and working at their store. She had taught Nancy how to quilt, given Mary Ann and Samuel the love and attention they needed, become a friend to the older boys, and most of all—she loved Papa and made him happy. Naomi had also taken notice of Fannie's gentle, positive spirit, which she felt sure came from her deep devotion to God. Fannie was much more outgoing than Mama had been, but she had the same qualities in many other ways.

Naomi set the Bible aside and closed her eyes. *Heavenly Father, help me love Fannie the way the rest of my family does. I don't know what my future holds regarding workin' at the store, but help me learn to be content in whatsoever state I shall find myself.* She paused, about to close her prayer, when a vision of Zach popped into her mind. He would be two years old in a few weeks, probably celebrating his birthday with his new family—whoever they were. It was looking more and more like Naomi would never see her little brother again, but as long as she lived, she would not forget him.

And Lord, she continued, *please, protect Zach and let him know how much he's loved, even if it has to be through someone other than his real family. Give him a happy birthday and see that he gets plenty of hugs. Amen.*

As Naomi crawled under the covers, a sense of peace settled over her like a soft blanket. Things would work out in the days ahead. She felt certain of it.

"It's so good to have you home. I've missed you, Mom."

Fannie smiled at Abby and gave her another hug. "It's good to be here, but remember, it's only for a few weeks. I'll be returning to Pennsylvania soon to get ready for my wedding to Abraham."

Abby nodded. "I know, but I'll enjoy the time we do have together."

Fannie glanced around the quilt shop. She'd missed this place and all the activity of customers coming in to look at quilts, pillows, potholders, and wall hangings. Not only that, but one day a week, a group of Amish ladies from their community came here to spend several hours making quilts, which would then be sold. She and Abby had enjoyed many days with the women as they stitched and chatted about the weather and one another's lives.

"I wish you would consider moving to Lancaster County with me," Fannie said. "I think you'd like Abraham's family, and you could help me in the quilt shop Abraham plans on adding to his store."

Abby shook her head, and her cheeks turned slightly pink. "I have a boyfriend, Mom. If I left, what chance would there be for me and Lester to court?"

"There are many eligible young men in Lancaster, you know."

Abby sank to a chair in front of the quilting rack. "Oh no, Mom. I couldn't think of letting anyone else court me. Lester is special, and I—"

"He's not been comin' over to the house when you're alone, I hope," Fannie said, a feeling of concern welling up in her chest.

" 'Course not. With Harold and Lena livin' right next door, I always make sure Lester comes a-callin' at their place, which is where I've been taking my meals since you've been gone."

"That's gut. I wouldn't want anyone thinkin' ill of my daughter."

"You should know I'd never do anything to embarrass you." Abby's dark eyes shimmered with tears.

"I know you wouldn't, sweet girl." Fannie patted her daughter's hand. "However, I've been thinkin' it might be better for all concerned if you moved in with Harold and Lena. They can either rent out my place or close it up 'til you're married."

Abby's forehead wrinkled. "I'd miss the old house if I had to move out."

"It would only be temporary."

"Jah, okay. If Harold and Lena have no objections, I'll move in with 'em." Abby jumped up. "Now let's talk about your wedding plans, shall we?"

Fannie grinned. "The date's set for May nineteenth. I'm hoping you, Harold, and Lena can all be there."

Abby leaned over and kissed her mother's cheek. "I wouldn't miss it for the world, and I'm sure my big brother and his wife will feel the same."

"You'll like Abraham," Fannie said, pushing her chair back.

Abby smiled. "I've only met him once, when he came here to see about the English couple who had a little boy he thought might be his. He seemed like a nice enough man."

"Abraham and his family have been through a lot the past couple of years." Fannie's throat clogged, and she had to pause in order to gain control of her emotions. Just thinking about the pain Abraham had endured made her feel all choked up.

"From what you've said in your letters, he's come to grips with the loss of his son. Isn't that right?"

Fannie's fingers traveled over the top of a Lone Star quilt. "Don't rightly think he'll ever completely get over losin' Zach, but he is dealin' with it pretty well these days."

Abby touched her mother's arm. "I believe you might have somethin' to do with that, Mom."

"It's the Lord who gets the credit for Abraham's change of heart," Fannie asserted.

Abby grabbed a large cardboard box from under the counter. "Guess we've had ourselves enough of a chitchat. If you want to pick out some quilts to sell in your new shop, we'd better get to work, don't ya think?"

Fannie smiled. "I can sure tell who's in charge of this shop these days."

Abby's cheeks flushed a bright pink. "Sorry, Mom. Didn't mean to sound so bossy."

"It's all right. You're used to bein' on your own now, and that's perfectly understandable." Fannie pulled a Log Cabin quilt out of the stack and placed it inside the box. "Think I'll give this one to Naomi when she and Caleb get married next fall."

Abby's eyebrows shot up. "There's to be another wedding in the Fisher family?"

"It would appear so." Fannie shrugged. "But only time will tell what the future holds."

Caleb felt mighty good about going to the singing. Since the event would be held in the Fishers' barn, he wouldn't be driving Naomi home tonight, but he had every intention of spending time alone with her. In fact, he hoped to get the chance to discuss their future.

He clucked to his horse to get him trotting faster. Wouldn't pay to be late—not when he was planning to spend every minute with the woman he loved.

"Sure hope she feels the same way about me," Caleb said to the gelding. "I've waited so long to court Naomi Fisher, and I don't want us to waste one single moment."

When Caleb pulled into the Fishers' yard, he noticed there were already several buggies lined up beside the barn. He climbed down from his open rig and secured the horse.

"Hey, Caleb, how are you?" Norman called as he stepped around the corner.

"I'm gut. And you?"

"Doin' fine, and I'll be even better once all the girls get here."

Caleb chuckled. "Anyone in particular you're waitin' for?"

Norman shook his head. "Not really. Still lookin' for the right one."

"Jah, well, I wouldn't wait too long if I were you. You ain't gettin' any younger, ya know."

Norman snickered. "Look who's talkin'. If I'm not mistaken, we're not that far apart in age, and you ain't married yet, neither."

Caleb thrust out his chest. "I hope to remedy that soon enough."

"Ha! I'll bet I know who you're on the verge of askin', too."

"Never you mind," Caleb said, shaking his finger at Naomi's brother. He glanced around. "Where is she?"

"Who?"

"Don't play dumb. I'm talkin' about Naomi. Is she in the barn or still up at the house?"

Norman shrugged. "How should I know? I ain't my sister's keeper."

Caleb slapped Norman on the shoulder. "Very funny." He started to walk away, but Norman stepped in front of him.

"She's in the barn, if you must know. I believe she brought out a jug of lemonade."

"I worked up quite a thirst on the drive over here," Caleb said with a wink. "I think I'll head in there and see about gettin' myself a glass."

"You do that, Caleb." Norman leaned against the side of the barn. "I'm gonna stay out here and watch the rest of the buggies come rollin' in. That way I can check out the competition."

Caleb sauntered off, chuckling to himself.

Just inside the barn door, Caleb bumped into Matthew, who carried a bale of straw. "Need any help?" Caleb asked.

"No, I'm fine. Just haulin' this across the barn so there'll be more room." Matthew's face was kind of red, and Caleb noticed he seemed nervous and out of place. In all the time Caleb had been attending singings, he'd never seen Matthew at one. From what he knew of Naomi's oldest brother, Caleb doubted he was here to choose a girlfriend. Truth be told, Matthew's daed probably asked his son to hang around, since Matthew was a few years older than most of the young people who would be here tonight and could act as chaperone without being too obvious or intrusive.

Caleb spotted Naomi on the other side of the room. She held a glass in one hand as she visited with a couple of women her age. He felt funny about interrupting, but if he didn't say what was on his mind right away, he might lose his nerve.

"Caleb, I'm glad you could make it," Naomi said as he approached her. "Did some of your brothers come to the singing, too?"

He nodded and reached up to wipe the trickle of sweat dripping down his face. "Marvin and Andy said they were comin', but I didn't see any sign of their rigs when I pulled in. Guess that means I beat 'em here."

"You look flushed," Naomi said. "Would you like a glass of cold lemonade?"

"That'd be nice," he said, reaching out to take the glass she offered. "Danki."

Clara and Mabel, who stood next to Naomi, giggled, and she wrinkled her nose at them.

"Want to take a walk before things get started?" he asked, feeling his courage begin to mount. "I'd like to talk awhile, if it's okay with you."

"I'd like that." Naomi set her glass down on the wooden table, said good-bye to the two young women, and headed for the door.

Caleb gulped down a swig of lemonade, placed it on the table, and followed quickly. Once they were outside, he suggested they go to the creek behind the Fishers' place.

They walked in silence until they reached the water's edge. Taking Naomi's hand, Caleb turned to face her. He moistened his lips. This was going to be more difficult than he'd thought. Things always seemed simpler when rehearsed in one's mind, but when it came down to the actual saying, Caleb felt like his mouth had been glued shut.

"Sure is a nice night," Naomi said. "Looks like we'll have us a hot summer, what with spring bein' so warm and all."

"Yep."

"Hope we have a good turnout tonight."

"Uh-huh."

"I'm glad Matthew agreed to help out. It's good for him to be with young people other than those in his own family."

"Right."

Naomi sighed. "Caleb, you said you wanted to take a walk so we could talk. Only trouble is, I'm doin' all the talkin'."

He let go of her hand and bent over to scoop up a flat rock, which he promptly pitched into the water. "Guess I'm a bit nervous."

"How come? It's not like this is our first date or anything."

"I know, but it's the first time I've ever proposed to a woman."

Naomi's mouth dropped open, and her eyes were wide. "You mean propose marriage?"

He nodded. "If you'll have me, I'd be pleased to make you my wife come November."

"Really?"

"You don't believe me?"

She laughed lightly. "Of course. It's just so sudden. We've only been courting a few months."

Caleb took both of her hands this time. "You've known for some time how I feel about you, right?"

"Jah."

"I've loved you ever since we were kinner, but until the Monday after Christmas, when your daed said we could court, I never thought

284

I'd have the chance to ask you to marry me."

Naomi's eyes filled with tears. "To tell you the truth, I never thought I'd be asked to marry anyone."

He could hardly believe his ears. Naomi was everything a man could possibly want in a wife. She was beautiful, smart, a hard worker, and ever so sweet. "Well, I'm askin' now, and if you think you could love me even a little bit, it would make me the happiest man in all of Lancaster County."

Naomi smiled, and he thought he could drown in the joy he saw on her face. "Caleb Hoffmeir, I love you, and not just a little bit. I'd be honored to be your wife."

CHAPTER 30

"I don't see why you're making such a fuss over Jimmy's birthday. You bought enough balloons and crepe paper to decorate the whole house." Jim motioned to the pile of decorations Linda had placed on the kitchen table. "He's only turning two and won't even remember this day when he's grown up."

She frowned. "We'll take lots of pictures. He'll have those to look at and know his mommy and daddy cared enough to give him a party."

"Who are you inviting to this shindig?" he asked.

"Just my folks—and maybe my sister and her husband."

"No other kids besides Jimmy will be here?"

She shook her head. "He doesn't really know any children."

Jim groaned. "That's because you shelter him too much, Linda. The boy should be around kids his age."

Linda pulled out a chair and took a seat at the table. "He's too young for preschool, and he has no cousins living nearby, so how can you expect him to have other children to play with?"

He shrugged. "Why don't you enroll in an exercise class at that new fitness center across town? I hear they have a great nursery for kids." Linda opened her mouth, but before she could reply, Jim added, "It would be good for both you and Jimmy."

She scowled. "Are you saying I'm fat and need to exercise in order to lose weight?"

Now where did that come from? Jim rubbed his forehead, glad Jimmy was taking a nap and couldn't hear the shouting that was probably forthcoming.

"Is that what you were insinuating, Jim?" she asked, her voice rising a notch.

Jim took the chair opposite Linda and grabbed a package of blue balloons. "You're not fat, and I wasn't hinting you needed to lose weight."

"What then?"

"I just think you stay cooped up in this house too much. You and Jimmy need to get out more."

"I take him for walks to the park, and we go shopping when I feel up to catching the bus."

"I'm not talking about going for a trek to the park or shopping. You need to socialize more."

"I would if we still lived in Boise. All my friends and family live there."

Jim didn't need reminding. She'd told him often enough that she didn't like western Washington and wished they were still living in the town where they'd both grown up.

"We moved here because of my job," he reminded. "You said back then you were in agreement with me starting my painting business here."

She sighed. "I know, but I thought we'd have two or three children by now and would be so busy raising them that I wouldn't have time to miss my family back home."

"This is your home now, Linda, and you do have Jimmy to raise."

"But he's only one child. I'd like more. Wouldn't you?"

"We aren't able to conceive, remember?"

"I know, but we adopted Jimmy, so why can't we adopt more children?" She pushed her chair back and stood. "I can give our lawyer a call right now and ask him to get the proceedings started."

Jim jumped up, knocking his chair over but catching it before it hit the floor. "That's not a good idea!"

She whirled around. "Why not?"

"We've had Jimmy a couple months shy of a year. He needs more time as an only child."

"Why? Because you were?"

He squinted, feeling his defenses rise. Was she trying to goad him into an argument? "That's not what I meant, Linda, and you know it."

"Isn't it?"

"No. I think we need to allow ourselves and Jimmy the luxury of enjoying one another awhile." He motioned toward the boy's high chair. "When we first learned we couldn't have children, you said you'd be happy with just one child. . .that it would be enough if I agreed to adopt. Well, I got you a baby, so why don't you appreciate it and ease up on me?"

Linda's forehead wrinkled, and she tipped her head in question. "You make it sound as if you grabbed a kid off the street and presented him to me as some kind of peace offering."

Jim swallowed hard. Linda had nearly hit the nail on the head. He had taken their son, and there was no legal adoption involved whatsoever. The adoption papers in the safe were phony. He didn't even know when the boy's real birthday was. The Amish girl selling root beer had said her brother turned one in April, so he'd made sure the birth certificate listed April fifteenth as Jimmy's birth date. He had done everything involving Jimmy out of love for Linda. He wasn't simply trying to appease her.

Jim stepped around the table and took his wife into his arms. "Let's not fight, okay?"

"I didn't start it," she reminded.

"It doesn't matter how it started. We need to set this disagreement behind us and go on from here." Jim had been putting the hammer down on several things concerning Jimmy lately, but he figured he should back off on the issue of the boy's party.

Linda's chin quivered. "And where exactly is *here*?"

He kissed the top of her head. Those golden tresses that had enticed him when they were teenagers were still shiny and inviting. If he let her know how much she was loved, maybe Linda would calm down.

"You can have as big a party for Jimmy as you want," he relented, "but what would you think about me inviting a couple of my employees who have little kids? That way Jimmy will have someone to play with at the party."

"Are you saying my family isn't good enough for Jimmy?"

Jim blew out an exasperated breath. "I like your family, and I know your folks are good grandparents, but I wish you'd quit reading things into what I say."

Linda leaned into him. "I'm sorry, Jim. I'm feeling uptight right now."

"Yeah, I know." As much as Jim had come to care for that little boy asleep in his crib upstairs, there were moments like now when he wished he'd never driven onto that Amish farm nearly a year ago.

Abraham leaned the pitchfork against the barn wall and breathed in the scents he had enjoyed since he was a boy. All the while he'd been growing up, Abraham figured he would end up a farmer like his daed. He'd been one for a while—until he married Sarah and she took over her folks' general store after their passing. He couldn't let his wife run the place by herself. There were too many heavy boxes to lift, figures and bookwork that never seemed to end, and often more customers than one person could handle. Besides, when the kinner came along, Sarah had more duties at home than ever before, which meant she sometimes couldn't go to the store at all. Abraham had exchanged his pitchfork for a broom, and instead of riding an old hay baler pulled by a team of horses, he'd become co-owner of his wife's family business. At that time he'd changed the name from Raber's to Fisher's General Store.

"No point in thinkin' about the past or wishing for things that can never be," Abraham murmured as he settled himself on a bale of straw.

At the end of a long day, it was relaxing to come out to the barn and muck out the horses' stalls or feed them some hay. It wasn't the same as being out in the fields with his boys, but at least he could enjoy hearing the horses nicker, smell the aroma of hay bales stacked along one wall, and imagine he was a farmer again.

Speckles, Naomi's cat, jumped into his lap and began to purr.

"Matthew, Norman, and Jake are the farmers now—carryin' on a Fisher tradition that began many years ago when my ancestors first settled in Lancaster County," Abraham said, stroking the furry creature's head.

Speckles responded with more purring and a few licks to Abraham's hand with his wet, sandpapery tongue.

"Wonder if Samuel will follow in his brothers' footsteps and take to the plow, as well," he continued, as though the cat were listening to his every word. "The boy already helps in the fields whenever he's not in school. Seems to like it well enough, and might could be he'll also become a farmer."

The cat's only response was a faint *meow*.

"And what about Zach? If he were still livin' here, would he have grown up with a love for the fields? Or would my youngest boy have developed other interests, as so many of the young people in our area are now doin'?" Abraham closed his eyes as he scratched Speckles behind one ear. "I'll never know 'cause Zach won't be growin' up on this farm. His birthday's tomorrow, and he'll be turnin' two. Only he won't be celebrating with his real family, if at all."

Abraham's eyes snapped open. Did the folks who took Zach even know how old he was? Would they make up a birth date for the boy and celebrate it then?

A pang of regret stabbed Abraham's heart, as sharp as any pitchfork piercing a bale of hay. In just a few weeks, he would be marrying Fannie Miller, and she made him happier than he ever dreamed possible. However, there would always be a part of him that would remain empty and void—the chunk of his heart that had been ripped away when Zach was kidnapped.

Fannie slipped into the dark blue dress she had recently made. She could hardly believe today was actually here. Her marriage to Abraham Fisher would take place in a few hours, and she was as nervous as she had been when she married Ezra twenty-three years ago.

Edna had wanted to host the wedding, but her house was too small, even though only family and a few close friends had been invited. So Abraham agreed to have it at his place, which had a lot more room.

"Mom, you're shaking," Abby noted as she helped her mother with her cape and apron. "You're not havin' second thoughts about marrying Abraham, are you?"

Fannie turned away from the mirror to face Abby. "Of course not. I love that man dearly and can't wait to become his wife."

"Then why so nervous?"

Fannie twisted her hands together. "Guess I'm feelin' prewedding jitters like most brides do." Her vision clouded as tears gathered in her eyes. "I hope I can make him happy—and his family, too."

Abby hugged her mother. "You've been a wonderful mamm to me and Harold, and I know you'll do fine with Abraham's kinner, as well. And as far as makin' him happy. . . I've seen the look on that man's face whenever the two of you are together. I'd say he loves my mamm beyond measure."

Fannie dabbed at the corners of her eyes and smiled. "I'm glad you could be here to witness my special day. Havin' you, Harold, and Lena at the wedding will make it even more wunderbaar."

Abby sniffed and swiped at the tears running down her cheeks. "I love you so much, Mom, and it makes me glad to see you this happy."

"You don't think I'm being untrue to your daed by marrying again?"

"Definitely not. I know you'll always love Dad, but I think there's more than enough room in your heart to love Abraham, too."

Fannie nodded. "How'd you get so smart, anyway?"

Abby grinned and took hold of her mother's hand. "Guess it runs in the family, 'cause you're one of the smartest people I know."

Fannie clicked her tongue. "Go on with ya now."

"No, I mean it, Mom. You're the person who taught me how to quilt and run the shop so efficiently, and you instilled the love of God in Harold and me from the time we were little. I'd call that real smart."

"Someday you'll marry and do the same with your own children," Fannie said as she set her head covering in place.

Abby's cheeks turned pink, and her eyes glistened. "I hope it's Lester I marry, for I surely do care for him, Mom."

This time it was Fannie who initiated the hug. "God will show you if Lester's the one He wants you to wed. Pray about it, okay?"

"I will. You can be sure of that." Abby pulled back and studied her mother intently. "I'd say the bride's ready to meet her groom. Shall we go see if the others are all set?"

Fannie nodded. "If I know Edna, she's probably got the horse hitched to the buggy and is sittin' in the backseat, ready and waiting." She chuckled. "That fun-lovin' cousin of mine enjoys any kind of party. Truth be told, she's probably got all sorts of tricks up her sleeve to give me and Abraham a good laugh during our reception today."

Abby slipped her hand through the crook of her mother's arm. "Then we'd best not keep Cousin Edna waiting—or your groom, either."

Naomi stood in the living room, appraising each nook and cranny to be sure there wasn't a speck of dust. She'd been up since early this morning and had worked until late last night, making certain the house was clean and everything was ready for Papa and Fannie's big day.

Fannie and her daughter, Abby; her daughter-in-law, Lena; and her cousin, Edna had come over yesterday to help cook and clean. The women dusted, washed windows, scrubbed floors, and made huge pots of chicken corn soup, Papa's favorite. At the reception dinner, they would also serve potato cakes, cucumber salad, deviled eggs, and the spiced layer cake Edna had promised to bake. The meal wouldn't be nearly as elaborate as a first-time wedding, but the food would be tasty and filling, nonetheless.

Naomi thought about how Fannie's daughter had pitched right in and worked hard all day with a smile on her face. Naomi had taken a liking to Abby when they'd first met, and even though Abby was two years younger than she was, Naomi could tell the woman was mature and responsible. Abby wasn't quite nineteen, yet she had taken on the task of running her mother's quilt shop in Ohio, and according to Fannie, she'd done well with it, too. Now that Fannie was marrying Naomi's daed and would be staying in Lancaster County, where she'd be running the quilt shop Papa added to his store, Abby planned to remain in Berlin and keep that shop open.

Naomi shook her head. "As much as I love workin' at the store, I doubt I could run the place alone."

"You talkin' to me or yourself?"

Naomi whirled around. Her father stood by the bookcase with a huge smile on his face. "Papa, you scared me half to death. I didn't hear you come into the room."

He chuckled. "No, I expect you didn't or ya wouldn't have been chattering out loud."

A warm flush of heat spread across Naomi's cheeks. "You got me there."

"What makes you think you'll have to run the store by yourself?" Papa asked.

"I was thinkin' about how Abby's taken over her mamm's quilt shop in Ohio and marveling at how she's doin' so well with it."

"Jah, she seems like a capable young woman. A lot like her mother, I expect."

Naomi took a seat on one of the wooden benches that had been set up in the room. "You think everything looks okay, Papa? Is the place clean enough for this special day?"

He nodded and sat down beside her. "Looks gut to me, and I thank you for workin' so hard to make it just right."

She reached for his hand, noting the warmth and strength of it. "I'm so glad you and Fannie found each other, and I know you're gonna be real happy in the days ahead."

He sat there for several seconds as though contemplating something. Then he squeezed her hand and said in a shaky voice, "I'm lucky to have a daughter like you. You've done your best to keep the deathbed promise you made to your mamm, but now that commitment's been fulfilled. It's time for you to find happiness with Caleb, and I know when you two are married in the fall, you'll feel every bit as blessed and happy as me and Fannie."

Naomi swallowed around the lump lodged in her throat. "Oh, Papa, that's ever so nice of you to say."

He let go of her hand and slipped his arm around her back. "As the old saying goes, 'We grow too soon old and too late smart.' I'm sorry it took me so long to come to my senses."

She sniffed back the tears threatening to spill over. "That goes double for me."

Norman stepped into the room and planted his hands on his hips. "There you are, Naomi. I thought you'd be out in the kitchen fixin' breakfast. I'm hungry as a horse."

Papa stood. "Then why don't you march right out there and fix yourself somethin' to eat? Naomi ain't the slave around here, ya know."

Norman blinked, and Naomi stifled a giggle. In all her twenty-one years, she'd never heard Papa come to her defense thataway. She stood and headed for the kitchen. "I'll have breakfast on the table in thirty minutes, but I could use some help, if you're so inclined," she said with a smile in her brother's direction.

Norman coughed and sputtered, but she heard his footsteps right behind her. This day was sure beginning on a good note.

The wedding was more special than any Naomi had ever attended. Papa looked so handsome in his dressy black suit, and Fannie was radiant, although it wasn't just her crisp new dress that made her so attractive. It was her rosy cheeks, a smile that could melt a frosty snowman, and her twinkling hazel-colored eyes that made Fannie glow like a moonbeam.

As Papa and Fannie stood in front of Bishop Swartley repeating their vows, it was all Naomi could do to keep from sobbing out loud. The emotion with which her daed said, "Jah, I do," after the bishop asked, "Can you confess, brother, that you accept this our sister as your wife, and that you will not leave her until death separates you?" was enough to make anyone cry. And when Fannie replied, "Jah," to the similar question directed at her, Naomi knew without reservation her new stepmother would love and cherish Papa for all the days God gave them together.

At the end of Bishop Swartley's blessing, which closed with "This all in and through Jesus Christ. Amen," Papa, Fannie, and the bishop bowed their knees.

The bishop's final words were "Go forth in the name of the Lord God. You are now man and wife."

Papa and Fannie returned to their seats, grinning like children and radiating a blissful glow that fairly lit up the living room.

As several of the ordained ministers from their community gave a word of testimony, Naomi's gaze traveled across the room to seek out Caleb. When he glanced her way and gave her a quick wink, she felt her face flood with a penetrating heat. In six more months, the two of them would stand before Bishop Swartley, repeat their vows, and promise their love forever. She could hardly wait.

CHAPTER 31

It was another warm summer evening, and Naomi sat in the rocking chair on the front porch with a basket of mending in her lap. She and the girls had been so busy with canning all week that there hadn't been time for much else. Fannie had helped, too, when she wasn't working in her new quilt shop at the store.

Naomi glanced at her stepmother, who sat on the porch swing with her head leaning on Papa's shoulder. They looked as happy and content as a couple of kittens sharing a bowl of fresh milk.

Matthew, Norman, and Jake had headed for bed a few minutes ago, saying they were exhausted after another long day in the fields. Nancy, Mary Ann, and Samuel were frolicking in the yard, waiting for the first set of fireflies to make their appearance. Samuel had punched holes in the lid of an empty jar, ready to capture a few shimmering bugs.

"There's one!" Nancy shouted. "Get it, Samuel, before it flies away!"

Samuel took off across the yard, running this way and that, chasing the glowing insects, and missing every time he came close to one.

Papa kissed Fannie on the cheek. "Hold my spot; I'll be back soon." He ambled down the steps and into the yard. "Hand me that jar, Samuel, and I'll show ya how it's done."

"It ain't easy, Papa. Them bugs don't wanna be caught."

"*Humph!* I'll have you know, I was an expert at catchin' lightning bugs when I was a boy." Papa grabbed the jar, squatted down on the lawn, and waited. A few seconds later, several fireflies rose from the grass. As quick as a wink, Papa's hand swooped out and snatched a couple. When he dropped them into the jar, the children all cheered.

Naomi took another stitch on the sock she was darning, as she savored the moment of peace and happiness. Since Papa married Fannie, he'd been so relaxed and easygoing. Love and marriage were obviously good for him. Even the kinner seemed happier these days. Everyone in the family had taken to Fannie, whose gentle, sweet spirit wove its way straight into their hearts—even Naomi's.

The *clip-clop* of horse's hooves on the gravel drove Naomi's thoughts aside. She looked up and smiled when she saw Caleb step down from his open buggy.

He hopped onto the porch and handed her a loaf of gingerbread wrapped in plastic. "Mom baked today and had extra. I thought you might like this."

"Danki. It was nice of you to bring it by."

"I didn't come just to give you the bread."

"No?"

He shook his head. "I was hopin' to take you for a buggy ride."

"Now?"

Caleb leaned against the porch railing. "I know it's gettin' dark, but I'll turn my flashers on, and I'll stick to the back roads where there isn't much traffic."

"I'm not concerned about that." Naomi stared into the yard, where Papa and the children were still cavorting with the fireflies. "I've got to see about gettin' the little ones to bed soon."

"That's my responsibility now," Fannie said. "You go along with Caleb and have a gut time."

Naomi felt a twinge of resentment toward her stepmother. It used to be her job to tuck the younger siblings in, but now Fannie often did it. Realizing how foolish she was, Naomi grabbed hold of her thoughts and gave them a good shake. *I should be ashamed of myself. It's been nice to have Fannie take some of the responsibilities I used to resent off my shoulders. Besides, she's only trying to be nice.*

Naomi stood, holding the mending basket in her hands. "I guess

I could go, but I'll have to bring this along."

Caleb's eyebrows lifted. "On our date?"

"If I don't, I'll never get caught up."

Fannie left the swing and moved beside Naomi. "I've never heard of takin' work along on a date. Now you just leave that mending with me, and I'll have it done by the time you get home."

Naomi gave Fannie an impulsive hug. "Papa's not the only one lucky to have you."

"Sure is a nice night," Caleb commented as he guided his horse onto the main road. "Not nearly as hot as it was today." He glanced at Naomi and grinned.

"The last few days have been real scorchers," she agreed.

"How do you stay cool enough to work at the store?"

"Papa recently bought one of those battery-operated fans. It keeps the air moving pretty good."

"Might have to look into gettin' one of those," Caleb remarked. "It can get real hot inside my buggy shop."

"How's things going with your business?" she asked. "Are you keeping plenty busy these days?"

He reached for her hand. "I'm makin' a good enough living to support a wife and a family; that much I know."

She smiled and squeezed his fingers.

"Sure can't wait 'til November and our wedding."

"Me neither."

They rode in silence for a time, but Caleb was content to enjoy the camaraderie of being with the woman he loved without any conversation. It was relaxing to listen to the steady *clip-clop* of the horse's hooves against the pavement and know that Naomi sat right beside him.

When the sky grew dark, Caleb decided it was time to head back to the Fishers' place. It wouldn't be smart to upset the storekeeper by keeping his daughter out too late. Caleb figured he was in pretty good with Naomi's daed right now, and he aimed to keep it that way.

He'd no more than turned the buggy around when he heard a snap, followed by a thud. The buggy tilted to the right, and Caleb pulled sharply on the reins.

"What happened?" He could hear the note of concern in Naomi's voice.

"I think one of the back wheels fell off. I'd better have a look-see." Caleb jumped down and went around to survey the situation. A few minutes later, he returned to the buggy.

"It's busted real bad," he said with an exasperated sigh. "I've been so busy fixin' other people's buggies, I've neglected to keep my own up to snuff."

"Can it be repaired? Do you have your tools with you?"

Caleb thought about the day he'd met Fannie on the road to Paradise and how he'd put her buggy wheel back on with no problem at all. That was different, though. The wheel had only fallen off, not broken in two places like his had. "Tools won't help. It'll have to be replaced with a new wheel."

In the moonlight, he could see Naomi's eyes were wide. "What are we gonna do? We have no phone to call for help."

Caleb reached under his straw hat and scratched the side of his head. "Never thought I'd hear myself say such a thing, but at this moment, I wish I had one of those fancy cell phones so many of the young people carry with them these days. If I did, we'd be able to call someone to come get us." He skirted around the buggy to Naomi's side. "You think you can ride bareback?"

She tipped her head. "We're gonna ride double on your horse?"

"We could walk, but it would take much longer, and that would be pretty silly seeing as how we have Ben here to carry us back to your place."

"Will he be able to hold both our weight?" she questioned.

"He pulled my buggy with both of us in it, didn't he?"

"Jah, but that's him *pulling* our weight, not carrying it all on his back."

Caleb chuckled and helped Naomi out of the buggy. He unhitched Ben, gave her a boost onto the back of the animal, and climbed up behind her. Grabbing the reins, Caleb hollered, "Get up now, boy!"

He could feel the weight of Naomi as she leaned against his chest, and he breathed in the scent of her hair. It smelled like strawberries ripening in the sun. *Sure wish I could remove Naomi's head covering. I'd give most anything to let her hair down and run my fingers through those silky tresses.*

"This is kinda fun," she murmured.

"You think so?"

"Jah. A real adventure."

Caleb smiled. At least she wasn't mad at him for ending their date with a jostling ride on the back of his horse.

It was nearly an hour later when Caleb and Naomi plodded into the Fishers' yard. Abraham sat in the rocking chair on the front porch, but no one else was in sight.

"Sure hope I'm not in trouble with your daed," Caleb mumbled as he jumped down and helped Naomi to the ground.

As soon as her feet touched the gravel, Naomi's dad bounded off the porch. "Where have you two been so long, and what happened to your buggy, Caleb?"

Caleb quickly explained about the broken wheel and apologized for keeping Naomi out so late.

Abraham's bushy eyebrows drew together, but then he smiled. "Seems to me a buggy maker oughta take better care of his own vehicle. A broken wheel—well, I never!"

"Papa, I'm sure Caleb didn't know there was anything wrong with his wheel," Naomi said.

"Don't look so worried, Daughter. I was only kidding." Abraham sauntered off toward the house, chuckling all the way.

A sense of relief flooded Caleb's soul. The cranky old storekeeper surely had changed. He turned to Naomi. "I hear tell my mamm's plannin' a quilting bee at our house tomorrow. Are you gonna be there?"

She nodded. "Both Fannie and I have been invited, and Papa plans to take Mary Ann and Nancy to the store with him, so we'll be free to go."

Caleb smiled. "Maybe you can sneak away for a bit and come out to the buggy shop to say hello."

"I'll surely try."

Naomi fidgeted in her chair and glanced around Millie Hoffmeir's dining room table. She wasn't used to sewing for hours on end, the way she and the other twelve ladies had been doing since nine o'clock this morning. Truth be told, she'd much rather be working at the store than sitting inside a stuffy room with a bunch of chattering women. The only good thing about today was the hope she might get to spend a few minutes alone with Caleb. If she could figure out some reason to go to his shop, that is.

Fannie had seemed in high spirits all morning, but then quilting was a thing she enjoyed and did very well. She scurried about with a smile on her face, handing scissors, thread, and stick pins to anyone with a need.

"Won't be long now 'til your wedding," Jacob Weaver's wife, Lydia, said. She nudged Naomi gently in the ribs and grinned.

Naomi nodded but kept her concentration on the piece of material she was stitching.

"I'm hopin' Naomi and Caleb will bless us with many kinner," Millie piped up.

Naomi's cheeks warmed. She wished someone would change the subject to something other than her wedding or how many children she might someday have.

"Naomi's had lots of experience takin' care of little ones," Fannie chimed in from across the room. "I'm sure she'll make a real gut mamm."

"While Naomi and Caleb are waitin' for their own place to be built, I'll have the pleasure of her company right here in this house." Millie glanced at Naomi and sighed. "Lettie and Irma, my two youngest girls, can be quite a handful at times, and I'm not gettin' any younger. Maybe you can help keep them in line."

"I'll do whatever I can." Naomi glanced out the window and spotted Caleb and Andy maneuvering a broken buggy in the direction of his shop. She wondered if the Hoffmeir men would be invited to join the women for lunch or if Millie planned to fix something to take out to the buggy shop, where Caleb, Andy, and Marvin worked. If so, maybe she would volunteer to carry it out. That would be the excuse Naomi needed to see Caleb. *When it's time to stop for lunch, I'll ask Millie,* she decided.

Caleb eyed the clouds creeping in from the west. It was plenty hot today, and they could use a good rain to soak the parched ground. He leaned his full weight against the back of Mose Kauffman's mangled buggy. Andy was up front, pulling and guiding the rig into the shop. Too bad Marvin had quit helping awhile ago, but Pop showed up and announced that he needed an extra pair of hands to stack hay in the barn, so Marvin volunteered.

A couple more steps and the buggy rolled between the double doors of his shop. Caleb drew in a deep breath and stood back to eye the buggy. "Sure is a mess!" he said, shaking his head.

"Yep," Andy agreed. "Old Mose can count himself lucky he escaped that accident with only a few bumps and bruises."

Caleb nodded. Many times when a buggy was hit by a car, the driver wasn't so fortunate. Just the other day an Amish man had been killed when a truck on Route 30 bumped his rig.

"This is gonna take a powerful lot of work," Caleb mumbled. "I think Mose would be better off to let us make him a new buggy."

"You know how stubborn that man can be," Andy reminded.

"Jah, kinda the way Abraham Fisher used to be."

"Speaking of the storekeeper. . .isn't Naomi supposed to be here today? Mom said she'd invited her and Fannie to the quilting bee."

Caleb grabbed a wrench off the pegboard where some of his tools were kept. "Yep, that's what I understand."

Andy snickered. "I'm surprised you haven't come up with some excuse to go inside and see your girlfriend."

Caleb shrugged. "I've been thinkin' on it."

"Figured as much."

"Maybe I'll go up to the house at noon, but in the meantime, we've got plenty to do. So let's get busy."

Andy wrinkled his nose. "Whatever you say, boss."

Naomi glanced out the window again. Caleb and Andy had disappeared into his shop, along with the broken buggy they'd been pushing. *Sure wish I could step outside for a breath of fresh air.*

"Naomi, would you mind helping me in the kitchen?" Millie's question drove Naomi's musings to the back of her mind.

"Sure, I'd be happy to." Naomi followed Caleb's mother into the next room. "Will the menfolk be comin' inside to eat lunch today?"

Millie opened the refrigerator and withdrew a platter of sliced ham. "Don't think they'd feel comfortable in the presence of so many women. I thought maybe I'd take something out to the shop for Caleb and Andy, and one of them can haul lunch to the rest of the men workin' in the barn."

Naomi moistened her lips with the tip of her tongue. "I'd be willing to take their meal out. That is, if you want me to."

"That'd be much appreciated." Millie smiled. "I'm sure Caleb would be glad to see you."

Fifteen minutes later, Naomi stood in front of the buggy shop with two baskets of food. She set one on the stoop and rapped on the door. When no one answered, she decided the men were probably busy or didn't hear her knock, so she entered the building unannounced.

The front part of the shop, where Caleb did his paperwork, was empty, but she could hear voices coming from the back room.

"Hand me that screwdriver, would ya, Andy?" She recognized Caleb's voice, and her heart skipped a beat. Hearing her intended talk made her all the more eager to see him. She set the baskets on the wooden desk and started across the room.

Suddenly, there was a crash, followed by a muffled cry.

"Oh, no! Caleb!" Andy shouted.

With her heart pounding so hard it echoed in her ears, Naomi rushed into the next room. She'd barely stepped through the door when she bumped into Caleb's younger brother. His face was white as a sheet of blank paper, and Naomi knew something horrible had happened.

"What's wrong, Andy?"

"We were tryin' to get the wheel off Mose's buggy, and the whole thing collapsed." Andy's chin quivered. "I've gotta get help quick. Caleb's pinned underneath."

CHAPTER 32

Naomi stood on the Hoffmeirs' front porch, holding the book she'd brought for Caleb. Ever since he came home from the hospital, he had refused to see her. Mose Kauffman's mangled buggy could have cost Caleb his life, but he'd escaped with a concussion, several broken ribs, and a hand that had been badly crushed under the weight of the buggy axle. The doctors performed surgery, but Millie Hoffmeir told Naomi that Caleb would never again be able to use his left hand for repairing buggies. He wouldn't have enough strength, and two fingers were severely damaged. It looked as though Caleb would need to give up the buggy shop and learn a new trade, unless he wanted to oversee his brothers, who might be willing to take over the business.

Naomi drew in a deep breath and knocked on the door. She hoped she could see Caleb today. It wasn't good, him shutting himself away in his room like that, refusing to see her or even talk about the horrible accident.

Life was full of disappointments; Naomi knew that firsthand. But you didn't give up or shut your loved ones out when you needed them most.

Caleb's nine-year-old sister, Irma, answered the door. "Hello, Naomi. How are you?"

"Fine. I came to see Caleb."

Irma shook her head, her blue eyes looking ever so serious. "He don't wanna see anyone. He's only allowed our mamm and daed into his room."

Tears stung the back of Naomi's eyes, and she blinked a couple of times. "Is he feeling any better?"

Irma shrugged. "Don't rightly know."

Naomi transferred the book from one hand to the other. "This is for Caleb. Would you see that he gets it? It's a fiction novel set in the Old West. I thought he might enjoy reading it."

Irma took the book, and Naomi turned to go.

"Wait up, would you?"

Naomi recognized Caleb's mother's voice, and she spun around. "How's Caleb doing? Is he feeling any better than he was the last time I dropped by?"

There were dark circles under Millie's pale blue eyes, and her ash-blond hair seemed to have developed a few more gray strands than Naomi remembered. "Caleb's concussion is better, and his ribs will heal in time, but his hand will never be the same." Millie sighed. "I fear my boy's heart is crushed as badly as those wounded fingers that will no longer hold the tools of his trade."

Naomi stared at the wooden boards beneath her feet, unable to voice her emotions. If only Caleb would see her, maybe she could say something that would help him feel better or at least offer a ray of hope. His hand might be crippled, and he probably would have to give up fixing buggies, but one thing hadn't changed. Naomi still loved Caleb and looked forward to their wedding, only a few months away.

"Won't ya come in?" Millie prompted. "I took a shoofly pie from the oven a short time ago, and I could fix us a cup of hot tea."

Naomi pondered the invitation. Shoofly pie was a favorite of hers, and it would be nice to visit with Caleb's mother awhile. Maybe she could learn more about his condition and why he refused to see her whenever she dropped by. She nodded and forced a smile. "Jah, that sounds gut."

"Have a seat, and I'll get the teapot," Millie said when they stepped into the kitchen. "Would ya like cream or sugar?"

"I drink mine black, danki."

Millie scurried about the kitchen, and with Irma's help, soon they each had a cup of hot tea and a plate full of pie. Irma was about to take a seat in the chair beside Naomi, when her mother waved her away. "Why don't ya cut your sister a hunk of pie and take it to her?"

Irma's forehead wrinkled. "Lettie's outside playing. She probably don't want to stop for a snack."

Millie wagged her finger. "Don't be sassin' me now. Get some pie for both of you and head on out."

Irma did as she was told, but Naomi could see by the set of the young girl's jaw that she was none too happy about being forced to leave the kitchen. If Irma was anything like Nancy, she probably figured the conversation between the women at the table would be more interesting than entertaining her younger sister.

As soon as Irma left the room, Millie leaned forward and looked intently at Naomi. "I'm worried about Caleb, and I think it's important for the two of you to talk."

Naomi nodded. "I agree, but how's that ever gonna happen if he refuses to see me?"

Millie pushed her chair back and stood. "I'll go upstairs and tell him to come down to the kitchen and have a hunk of pie. He doesn't need to know there's someone waitin' to see him."

"He might not like it when he realizes I'm here."

Millie shrugged. "Maybe so, maybe not. The point is, he's put off seeing you long enough."

When Caleb's mother left the room, Naomi took a long drink from her cup. She hoped the herbal tea would help steady her nerves.

Caleb sat on the edge of his bed, staring at his bandaged hand. He clenched his teeth and struggled with the desire to holler at someone for the injustice that had been done to him. It wasn't fair. Why had the Lord allowed him to make such wonderful plans for the future, only to dash them away?

He thought about a verse of scripture the bishop had quoted from Isaiah chapter forty-nine, verse four during the last church service he'd attended. *"Then I said, I have laboured in vain, I have spent my strength for nought, and in vain: yet surely my judgment is with the Lord, and my work with my God."*

Caleb groaned. *I have labored in vain for several years while I tried to build up my buggy business so I could marry and start a family. I used all my strength, and it was for nothing. One little mistake under Mose's buggy cost me everything I loved so much.* A tear slipped out of Caleb's eye and rolled down his cheek. He wiped it away with his good hand, feeling angry with himself for giving in to his grief. All these months he'd waited for permission to court Naomi. They'd been on the brink of marriage, and now this!

A knock on his bedroom door drove Caleb's thoughts aside. "Who's there?"

"It's your mamm."

"Come in."

Mom opened the door and peeked in at him. "I made shoofly pie. How about comin' down to the kitchen and havin' a piece?"

He shook his head. "No thanks. I ain't hungry."

"Won't you do it for me?" she pleaded. "I'm sure you won't be disappointed."

Caleb blew out his breath and stood. He winced as pain shot through his side, but he tried not to show it.

"You okay?" Mom asked with obvious concern. "You look a mite pale."

He shook his head. "I'm fine. Let's go to the kitchen."

Caleb followed his mother and took the stairs carefully, holding onto the railing with his good hand. When he entered the kitchen a short time later, he halted inside the door. *Naomi.* What was she doing here?

She smiled, and it made his heart clench. "Hello, Caleb. It's good to see you."

Caleb's gaze darted to his mother, who stood off to one side with her arms folded. "Well, I think I'll head outside and check on the girls. You two have a nice visit, ya hear?"

The back door clicked behind Mom, and Caleb fought the desire to flee to his room. He didn't, though. Instead, he marched across the kitchen and took a seat at the table. *Might as well get this over with, 'cause if I don't, Naomi will probably keep coming around.*

"I'm sorry about your accident with Mose's buggy," she said. "I wanted to tell you sooner, but everything happened so fast the day it occurred, and after that, I was always told you weren't up to company."

Caleb just sat there, staring at the shoofly pie in front of him.

"How are you feeling?" Naomi prompted. "Are ya in much pain?"

He forced himself to look directly at her. He could see the questions on her face, the look of compassion in her eyes. He didn't want Naomi's pity or to have to answer any questions. He just wanted to be left alone, to suffer his grief in silence.

She tipped her head. "Caleb? Why aren't you sayin' anything?"

He shrugged. "There ain't much to say."

"I asked if you're in pain. You could start by answering that question."

He lifted his bandaged hand. "This will never work right again, did ya know that?"

She nodded, and tears welled up in her eyes.

"I can't make or repair buggies anymore."

"Jah, I heard."

He cleared his throat. "You know what that means, don't ya?"

"I—I guess it means you'll have to learn a new trade."

"There is no trade for this cripple, Naomi." Caleb slowly shook his head. "And since I can't do the work I've been doin', I won't be able to support a family."

310

"Oh, Caleb, you can't mean that. Surely one of your brothers will keep the buggy business going. Maybe you could do some light chores and keep charge of the books."

"Makin' and repairin' buggies is all I've ever wanted." He grunted. "Do you really think I could sit around doin' nothing while my two brothers took over the business I've worked so hard to build up?"

She opened her mouth to say something, but he cut her off. "I don't see how we can get married now, Naomi."

"Please, don't say such a thing. I love you, Caleb, and I'm sure we can work something out." Naomi reached out to touch his uninjured hand, but he pulled it away and stood.

"If I can't support a wife with honest work, I won't have a wife at all. It must not be God's will for us to be together, or He wouldn't have allowed the accident to happen." He turned toward the door.

"Caleb, wait! Can't we talk about this some more?"

"There's nothin' to be said. You'd better find someone else."

"I don't want anyone but you," Naomi said tearfully.

It almost broke Caleb's heart to know she was crying, but he couldn't back down now. "There will be no wedding for us." He nearly choked on his final words. No matter how much Caleb's heart ached to have Naomi as his wife, he would not take on that responsibility when he couldn't provide adequately for her. As he stumbled out of the room, the echo of the door slamming shut reminded Caleb that a chapter of his life had been closed for good.

Fannie stood at the kitchen stove, stirring a pot of bean soup. Today, things had been busier than usual at the store, and she was exhausted. Since Naomi left early to go over to the Hoffmeirs', and Mary Ann, Nancy, and Samuel were back in school, she and Abraham had been on their own all afternoon.

She added a dash of salt to the soup. *Sure hope Naomi made out okay with Caleb. I pray he agreed to see her this time.* She sighed. *That girl's been through enough, and she shouldn't have to hurt anymore.*

Fannie turned when she heard the back door open and click shut. Mary Ann and Nancy rushed into the room, their faces aglow.

"Guess what, Mama Fannie?" Mary Ann said breathlessly.

Fannie smiled. She liked how easily Abraham's youngest children had taken to her. "What's got you two lookin' so excited this evening?"

"There's a new batch of kittens in the barn," Nancy announced before Mary Ann could open her mouth.

"How many are there?" Fannie questioned.

Mary Ann held up five fingers.

"They're all white this time. Not a dark one in sight," Nancy said.

"Is that so?" Fannie got a kick out of the girls' exuberance. She'd always liked animals and could remember her own excitement over the birth of new arrivals on the farm when she was a young girl.

"When Papa comes in from feedin' the horses, I'm gonna ask if I can keep one of those cute little *busslin*," Nancy added. "Naomi has her own cat, so I think it's only fair I should have one, too."

Fannie chuckled. "We'll have to wait and see what your daed has to say about that. In the meantime, I'd like you girls to run upstairs and wash your dirty hands. I'll be needin' help with supper soon."

"What are we havin'?" Mary Ann asked.

"*Buhnesupp*—one of your daed's favorites."

Mary Ann wrinkled her nose. "Bean soup? I'd much rather have chicken noodle."

Nancy grabbed her younger sister's hand. "Aw, quit your gripin' and come with me."

The girls' footsteps resounded on the stairs as Fannie gave the soup a couple more stirs. When she heard a horse and buggy come prancing into the yard, she glanced out the window and saw it was Naomi. She'd no more than climbed down from the buggy, when Abraham stepped out of the barn and unhitched the horse. He led him away, and Naomi headed for the house, shoulders drooping and head down.

Fannie moaned. *It doesn't look like things went well for my stepdaughter this afternoon.*

A few minutes later, Naomi entered the kitchen through the back door. She hung her black bonnet on a wall peg and without a word went to the sink to wash her hands.

"You okay?" Fannie asked.

Naomi shook her head but made no verbal reply.

"Did you get to see Caleb this time?"

Naomi's shoulders trembled as she nodded.

Fannie turned down the gas burner and rushed to her stepdaughter's side. "What's wrong? What happened that's got you so upset?"

When Naomi reached for a hand towel, Fannie noticed how red the young woman's eyes were. She'd been crying—probably all the way home, from the looks of it. "Caleb called off the wedding," she said with a catch in her voice. "He doesn't want to marry me anymore."

"Come over to the table and have a seat," Fannie suggested. "Then you can tell me what happened, if you like."

Naomi shuffled across the room as though she was in a daze and sank into a chair. Fannie took the seat beside her, placing one hand on Naomi's shoulder.

"The doctors told Caleb his left hand will never be the same, and it means he can no longer work on buggies." Naomi sniffed and blinked a couple of times. "He said if he can't make buggies, he won't be able to support a wife, so there will be no wedding for us in two months."

Fannie's heart went out to Naomi. She looked so downcast and discouraged. If there was only something Fannie could say or do to make things better.

"Caleb thinks it must not be the Lord's will for us to be together, or else God wouldn't have allowed the accident to happen."

Heavenly Father, give me the right words, Fannie prayed. *Show me how to help Naomi through this ordeal.* She gently squeezed Naomi's shoulder. "I know things look bleak right now, but God has a plan for your life, and you need to wait and see what it is."

A muffled sob erupted from Naomi's throat. "I think maybe God's still punishing me for leavin' Zach on the picnic table last summer."

"No, no, you mustn't think that way," Fannie was quick to say. "You didn't do it on purpose. God knows that, Naomi."

Tears rolled down Naomi's cheeks. "I—I don't believe I can take much more."

Fannie reached out to wipe away the tears. "Sweet girl, the Bible says God won't give us more than we can handle. And Isaiah chapter twenty-six, verse four, says, 'Trust ye in the Lord for ever: for in the Lord Jehovah is everlasting strength.' "

Naomi pushed her chair back and stood. "I'm goin' upstairs awhile. Is that okay?"

"Jah, sure. Take as long as you like. Nancy and Mary Ann can help me get supper on."

Fannie watched helplessly as Naomi trudged out of the room. *Why, Lord? Why'd You have to let this happen now?* She swallowed against the burning at the back of her throat. It didn't seem fair for her to be so happy being married to Abraham when his oldest daughter was suffering so.

Fannie had just started mixing biscuit dough when Abraham stepped into the kitchen. At the same time, Mary Ann and Nancy entered the room.

"Would you two girls mind going back upstairs awhile?" Fannie asked. "I need to speak to your daed a few minutes."

The children didn't have to be asked twice. They raced for the stairs, giggling all the way.

Abraham kissed Fannie on the cheek. "You're lookin' awful somber for a new bride."

Fannie slapped him lightly on the arm. "Go on with ya now. We've been married over three months already, so I'm no longer a new bride."

He snickered and chucked her under the chin. "Our love will always be new to me, dear wife."

She set her mixing bowl aside and hugged him tight. "The Lord God was surely smiling on me the day you walked into my life."

"That goes double for me," he murmured.

"Sure wish things would go better for Naomi."

"What's wrong? She went to see Caleb today, didn't she?"

Fannie nodded. "She didn't share with you what happened when you were both outside?"

He shook his head.

"Then I'd best fill you in."

Abraham leaned against the cupboard with his arms folded. "Jah, please do."

Fannie quickly related all Naomi had told her and ended by saying she wished something could be done to get Caleb and Naomi's relationship back on track.

Her husband's bushy brows drew together as he squinted. "I'm goin' over there to have a talk with that boy."

"Now?"

He nodded. "No time like the present."

"But what about supper? I've made your favorite buhnesupp."

He kissed the tip of her nose. "Keep it warm for me, will ya, fraa?"

"Jah, and I'll be prayin' the whole time you're gone."

Naomi pulled another box of books over to the shelf she was stocking. She hadn't slept well last night and could barely function here at the store this morning, so it was good she wasn't waiting on customers. She probably wouldn't be able to think clear enough to make change, much less carry on a pleasant conversation with anyone today. In her gloomy mood, Naomi would more than likely drive customers away.

She tipped her head and listened as her father whistled a merry tune. *Papa's sure actin' peculiar today*, she noted. *Whistling and kissin' on Fannie whenever no one but us three are around.*

Naomi didn't resent her daed and Fannie's happiness, but it sure was a reminder of her own miserable circumstances. It seemed like every time things were beginning to look up, something else went wrong. It was enough to make her give up hoping anything would ever be right again.

After Naomi emptied the first box, she grabbed another. *I know I shouldn't be wallowing in self-pity. At least I'm able to keep workin' at the store and don't have to give up a job I enjoy. Poor Caleb has lost the one thing he likes so much, and now he has nothing to look forward to.* She squeezed her eyes shut in an effort to keep the tears at bay. Giving in to her grief wouldn't change the situation.

"You doin' okay?" Papa asked as he stepped up beside her. "You gonna make it through this day, Daughter?"

She nodded, feeling a sense of comfort knowing her father cared. "It took me some time, but I finally came to grips with losin' Mama and then Zach. So, with God's help, I'll try to accept that Caleb and I can never be together."

Papa patted Naomi's arm. "What God doeth is well done."

She swallowed hard. "You really think so?"

He nodded.

"You believe I'd be better off without Caleb? Is that what you're sayin', Papa?"

Her father opened his mouth, but the bell above the front door tinkled, and he motioned toward the front of the store. "Why don't you go see what that customer wants, Naomi?"

She pointed to the box of books. "I still have these to set out."

"I'll do 'em."

"But, Papa, I—"

"Please. I'm tired of dealin' with customers this morning."

She sighed but nodded. "All right."

Naomi made her way up front, but she halted when she saw Caleb standing near the door. *What's he doing here? I can't deal with seeing him just now.* She started to turn around but was stopped by Papa's deep voice.

Naomi looked up at him and was surprised when she noticed the serious expression on her father's face. Only moments ago, he'd been whistling. "Caleb came by to sign some important papers," Papa said.

She looked back at Caleb, and he nodded. "You got 'em ready for me, Abraham?"

Papa stepped around the counter, reached underneath, and withdrew a manila envelope.

Naomi took a tentative step forward but couldn't find her voice. What kind of important papers would Caleb be coming to the store to sign? It didn't make sense at all.

Papa laid the paperwork on the counter and handed Caleb a pen. "You'll need to put your signature here on this line."

Caleb gripped the pen with his good hand and wrote his name, then he turned to Naomi and smiled. "Naomi Fisher, will you marry me?"

She stood frozen to the spot, feeling like her brain was full of cotton.

Papa cleared his throat real loud. "I believe the young man asked you a question, Naomi."

She tried to speak, but her throat might as well have been glued shut.

Caleb set the pen aside and reached out to take Naomi's hand. "Your daed came over to our place last night and offered to sell me his store. I've decided to take him up on the offer."

Naomi's mouth dropped open. "What?" She looked at Papa. "Why would you want to sell this place when you've worked here so many years?"

Papa glanced into the next room, where Fannie was busy sewing a quilt. "I've never been truly happy running the store," he said. "I took it over when your mamm's folks died and left her the place." He gave his beard a couple of tugs. "Sarah loved this business, and I think she passed that love on to you, Naomi, but I only agreed to work here because I didn't want to see Sarah run the place alone. It's too much for one person to handle." He smiled, and there was a faraway look in his eyes. "To tell ya the truth, I'd much rather be farmin' my land with the boys."

Naomi could hardly believe her ears. In all the years they'd been running the store, she'd never heard Papa admit he would have preferred to be farming.

"And since Caleb needs a job he can do with mostly one hand, I thought he'd be the perfect person to ask about buyin' the store," Papa continued.

Naomi chanced another peek at Caleb and noticed there were tears in his eyes. "You—you're really wantin' this?" she stammered.

He nodded. "More than anything I want to be your husband. If it means sellin' my buggy shop and takin' over here, then so be it." He made a sweeping gesture with his bandaged hand. "I know how much you love this place, and if your daed could run it for twenty-some years because he loved your mamm, I'll find pleasure in doin' the same for you and our future kinner." He smiled and squeezed Naomi's hand. "What's your answer? Will you marry me come November?"

Tears rolled down Naomi's cheeks, and she nodded. "Yes, Caleb. I'll marry you."

Papa cleared his throat again. "What God doeth is well done."

Naomi smiled. She didn't know what the future held for her missing brother, and she had no idea what might lie ahead for her, Caleb, or the general store, but the storekeeper's daughter knew one thing for sure—what God had done, He'd done well.

the Quilter's Daughter

by
Wanda E. Brunstetter

BARBOUR
PUBLISHING

To my friend Katherine Baar,
who has walked through the fire and come out victorious.
To Betty Yoder,
a special friend with a spirit for adventure.
And to Donna Mae Crow,
a dear friend who is always there when I need a listening ear.

When thou passest through the waters, I will be with thee; and
through the rivers,
they shall not overflow thee:
when thou walkest through the fire,
thou shalt not be burned;
neither shall the flame kindle upon thee.
ISAIAH 43:2 KJV

PROLOGUE

A mysterious dark cloud hovered over Abby Miller's bed, pressing on her from all sides. Blinking against stinging tears, she drew in a ragged breath. An invisible hand pushed against her face, and she flung her covers aside. "*Ich kann nimmi schnaufe*—I can no longer breathe!"

Meow. Meow. Somewhere in the distance Abby heard the pathetic cry and knew she must save the poor kitten. With a panicked sob, she rolled out of bed, but the minute her bare feet touched the floor she shrank back from the intense heat. A paralyzing fear wrapped its arms around Abby, threatening to strip away her sanity. She lifted her hands to her face and rubbed her eyes, forcing them to focus. "Where are you, kitty? I'm coming, kitty."

Suddenly, she realized that her room was engulfed in flames —lapping at the curtains, snapping, crackling, consuming everything in sight. As the smoky haze grew thicker and the fire became an inferno, Abby grabbed the Lone Star quilt off her bed and covered her head. Coughing, choking, gasping on the acrid smoke, she stumbled and staggered toward the door. "*Feier*—fire! Somebody, please help me save the kitten!"

~

Abby bolted upright in bed. Droplets of perspiration dripped from her forehead, trickling onto her hot cheeks. Goose bumps erupted on her arms, and she realized that her cotton nightgown was soaking wet.

A howling wind rattled the windows with such force that

she was sure the house would come crashing down. Rain pelted the roof like a herd of stampeding horses, while thunderous roars pounded the night air.

Huddled under her patchwork quilt, Abby drew in a deep breath and tried to still her racing heart. She ordered herself to sit up and light the kerosene lamp on the small table by her bed. As the room became illuminated, she was able to see the cedar chest that had belonged to her grandmother at the foot of her bed. The wooden rocker Dad had made for her thirteenth birthday was positioned between the two windows, and her dressing table stood across the room where it always had. She'd been dreaming.

"*Jah*, that's all it was—the same horrible nightmare I've had before." Abby clutched the comforting quilt and wrapped it around her shoulders. "Oh, Lord, what does that night terror mean?"

*A*bby opened the front door of her quilt shop and stepped onto the porch. A gentle breeze caressed her face, and she inhaled deeply. She hadn't slept well the night before and awoke this morning feeling tired and out of sorts. She'd been haunted by that dreadful nightmare again, the one she'd had several times over the last few months. Fire and smoke. Unable to breathe. Paralyzing fear. What was the meaning of the dream, and why did she have it so often? Abby remembered reading an article in *The Budget* some time ago about a young Amish boy in Indiana who'd been trapped in his father's burning barn. She'd been filled with compassion for the child's parents and wondered what terrible pain the boy must have endured in the blazing inferno. Could that newspaper article have stuck in her brain and caused the reoccurring nightmares, or was there something more to it, something buried deep in her mind? And what about those pathetic cries of a kitten she'd heard in her dream? Had there been a cat in the barn with the boy that day? She didn't remember all the details of the article and had long since thrown that issue of *The Budget* away.

Abby reached into the mailbox and retrieved a stack of letters. *These negative thoughts aren't good for me. Lester Mast and I have finally set a date for our wedding, the sun is shining, spring is in the air, and my business is doing better than ever. There's so much to be thankful for.*

"Anything good in the mail?" Lena asked when Abby re-entered the shop a few minutes later.

Abby smiled at her sister-in-law and held up the stack of

envelopes. "Looks like a note from Mom." She placed all of the mail but her mother's letter on the desk and reached underneath to grab her metal lunchbox. "It's a beautiful day, and I think I'll go out to the picnic table so I can read Mom's letter and eat lunch. Can you handle things on your own for a while?"

Lena nodded and repositioned a blond tendril that had slipped from under her small white head covering. "Jah, sure, I've already eaten my lunch." She made a sweeping gesture with one hand. "As you can see, we are not so busy at the moment."

Abby nodded and hurried out the back door. She placed the lunchbox on the picnic table, seated herself on one of the wooden benches, and tore open the envelope. She was pleased to discover that Mom had enclosed a white handkerchief with the initials A. M. embroidered in one corner.

"I'll bet this is for my hope chest. Either that, or Mom thinks I've come down with a cold."

Laying the hankie aside, Abby read the letter.

Dear Abby,

The enclosed handkerchief is a gift from Mary Ann for your hope chest. She said she was glad you're en-gaged to a man with the same last initial as yours. That way, if you decide not to marry him, you can still use the hankie.

Abby chuckled. "Leave it to Mary Ann to say something like that. Never know what my youngest stepsister might come up with."

She diverted her attention back to the letter.

Things are going well here. Naomi's doing fine with her second pregnancy, and I think she and Caleb are hoping for a boy this time around. Samuel and Mary Ann are growing like weeds, and Nancy, who turned fifteen last month, is talking about courting and such. 'Course her dad would never allow it—not until she's sixteen.

Matthew, Norman, and Jake continue to help their

*dad on the farm, and my dear husband has never seemed so
content.*

*I have some news of my own, which I hope will bring
you as much joy as it has me. Abraham and I are expecting
a baby.*

Her mother having a *boppli*! Abby's eyes flooded with tears,
causing the words on the page to blur. Could this be true? After
all these years, was Mom, at age forty-seven, really going to
have another baby? Using the new hankie to dab her eyes, she
read on.

*Since Lena is helping you at the quilt shop, I thought you
might want to share the news with her and your brother.*

*Other than a queasy stomach, I'm feeling pretty good.
As you can imagine, Abraham is thrilled about this. Who
would have thought after being barren for so many years,
the Lord would bless me with another child?*

*I know you're busy planning your wedding, but I'm
hoping you can be here when the baby is born. Since that
will happen in late October, and your wedding is not until
the end of November, it shouldn't interfere with your big
day. With Lena there to help in the quilt shop, maybe you
can come a week or so before the baby is born and then
stay a week or two after? I'm sure I'll be able to handle
things on my own by then.*

Looking forward to hearing from you soon.

With love,
Mom

Abby thought about the day her *mamm* had left Ohio for
Pennsylvania. It had begun as a weekend trip to visit her cousin
Edna. But then Mom ended up staying to help Abraham Fisher
at his store, since his oldest daughter had run away from home
soon after his son was kidnapped. It didn't take long for Mom
and Abraham to fall in love, and soon they were married. Now,
after four years of marriage, they were expecting a baby. Such a

miracle it was!

"Yoo-hoo! Abby, are you done with your lunch yet?" Lena called from the back door of the quilt shop. "A busload of tourists just showed up, and I could use some help."

Unable to speak around the lump in her throat, Abby merely nodded and stood. She would have to wait until the tourists left to share Mom's unexpected news with her sister-in-law.

⁓

"You look tired today, *Fraa*. Are you doin' too much?"

Naomi Hoffmeir released a weary sigh. "Jah, Caleb, this wife of yours is a bit tired." She patted her bulging stomach. "This one's draining my energy more than Sarah did."

Her husband nodded toward their two-year-old daughter, toddling around the store, checking out everything within her reach. "I'd say our little girl's more than makin' up for her quiet ways when she was a boppli."

Naomi nodded. "You're right about that." She bent over and scooped Sarah into her arms. "I love you, sweet girl, even if you are a handful at times."

"Want me to put her down for a nap?"

"Sure, that's fine."

Caleb extended his arms, and Sarah reached out her hands. "Jah, that's right, come to your *daadi*."

"I hope she cooperates and falls asleep right away," Naomi said as father and daughter headed for the back room where they kept Sarah's playpen and a few toys.

"I think she will. Already her eyes are droopin'," he called over his shoulder.

Naomi sighed. *Sarah reminds me so much of Zach—full of energy and eager to investigate new things. How proud Mama would be if she were still alive and could see the precious granddaughter named after her.*

Naomi's gaze went to the calendar hanging near the counter by the front door. In just a few weeks it would be Zach's sixth birthday. Had her little brother been missing five years already?

A lump lodged in Naomi's throat as she reflected on all

that had happened since the boy's kidnapping. She had run off for a time, unable to cope with the blame she felt for Zach's disappearance. Then later, shortly after she returned home, Papa had married Fannie Miller. Naomi and Caleb's wedding took place soon after he'd injured his hand while repairing a buggy, and ever since their marriage, they'd been working at the store that had been in Naomi's family a good many years.

Despite the fact that Naomi led a busy yet satisfied life, she often found herself thinking of Zach, praying for him, and wondering if he was happy and safe. Except for that one notice they'd read in *The Budget* shortly after he was taken, there had been no word on her little brother.

Naomi lifted her gaze to the ceiling. *Thank You, Lord, for the healing You gave our family during such a difficult time. And bless my little brother, wherever he might be.*

"How's business today?" Fannie asked, stepping into the store from the adjoining quilt shop.

Naomi turned to face her stepmother. "No customers at the moment. How's it going with you?"

"Things are fine at my shop." Fannie tapped her stomach. "But my insides are still pretty unsettled."

Naomi nodded, for she knew exactly how Fannie felt. She had been sick for the first six months when she carried Sarah, but this pregnancy was different. Not one day of morning sickness so far, and since she only had four months until the baby came, Naomi figured she was in the clear. Her only complaint was frequent fatigue. "Have you told Abby your exciting news?" she asked Fannie.

"Jah. Sent her a letter a few days ago. She should have gotten it by now."

"I'm sure she'll be as thrilled as we all are."

Fannie's hazel-colored eyes filled with tears. "It's such a miracle, me bein' in my late forties and gettin' pregnant after all these years." She gave Naomi a hug. "I'm glad our little ones can grow up together."

"Jah. God is good, isn't He?"

"That's for certain sure."

"Papa's beside himself over this, ya know."

Fannie crossed her arms over her ample chest, and her forehead creased with concern. "This babe won't take the place of your missing brother. I hope you realize that."

Naomi sucked in her lower lip. "I know." But even as the words slipped off her tongue, she wondered if she believed them. *Would Papa be so caught up with the baby that he would forget he'd ever had a son named Zach?*

"Your *daed* deserves this chance with another child, don't ya think?"

"Of course he does, and so do you."

Fannie opened her mouth to respond, but an English woman entered the store just then. "I'll let you get back to work," she whispered. "And I've got a Log Cabin quilt that needs to be finished."

"Talk to you later then." Naomi turned toward the customer and smiled. "May I help ya with somethin'?"

⁓

Linda Scott aimed the digital camera she'd recently purchased and snapped a picture of her son. Jimmy had been playing in the sandbox, but he'd decided to try out the slide.

Jimmy takes after his dad, she mused. *He's not afraid of high places. Maybe he'll be a painter someday, too. I'm glad he's not like me—afraid of so many things.*

"Do you mind if I share your bench?"

Linda slid over as a woman with dark hair cut in a short bob took a seat beside her.

"I'm Beth Walters, and that's my son Allen."

Linda's gaze went to the dark-haired boy climbing the ladder behind her son. "My name's Linda Scott, and my boy's name is Jimmy."

"Do you and Jimmy live nearby? I don't recall seeing you at the park before."

"Our house is a few blocks away. We normally come here after Jimmy gets home from morning kindergarten. But since there's no school today, he wanted to play as soon as he finished breakfast."

"My son is in afternoon kindergarten, so mornings usually work best for us." Beth glanced at her watch. "We've only been living in Puyallup a few months, and my husband has a night job at a lumber mill in Tacoma. I try to occupy Allen with quiet games at home, or we come to the park so Eric can sleep."

Linda stared at the camera clasped in her hands. She couldn't imagine having to plan her and Jimmy's lives around Jim's work schedule. Since her husband owned his own painting business and had several employees, Jim could usually come and go as he pleased. Although, lately he'd been working so much, he was seldom at home. Linda figured he might be using his job as an excuse to avoid her and their frequent arguments. She and Jim hadn't gotten along well since they'd adopted Jimmy five years ago.

"Looks like our boys are making friends," Beth said, her words pulling Linda's thoughts aside.

She looked up. Allen sat on one of the swings, and Jimmy stood behind him, pushing.

"Be careful, Jimmy. Don't push too hard or too fast."

"Allen will be fine," Beth said with a nod. "He always hangs on tight."

Linda lifted the camera and snapped a few pictures of the children. *This should prove to Jim that I'm letting our boy make new friends.*

"Jimmy looks small to be in kindergarten. How old is he?" Beth asked.

"He'll turn six in a few weeks."

"Allen celebrated his sixth birthday in February." Beth smiled. "Since we both live in the same neighborhood, I guess our boys will be starting first grade together this fall."

Linda nodded, remembering how Jim had wanted her to homeschool their son but changed his mind shortly before Jimmy started kindergarten, saying he thought it would be better if the child went to public school where he could play with other kids.

"Your dubious expression makes me think you're not looking forward to sending Jimmy to school all day. Is he your youngest?"

"Jimmy's our only child," Linda said, feeling tears prick her eyes. She'd wanted to adopt another baby as soon as Jimmy was out of diapers, but Jim flatly refused. He'd said one child was enough and reminded Linda that since they argued so much it wouldn't be good to bring another child into an already troubled home.

"Eric and I have two older boys," Beth commented. "Ricky's eight and Brett's ten. Having three kids so close in age was hard when they were little, but now that they're older, it's gotten easier."

As the boys moved from the swings to the teeter-totter, Linda snapped a few more pictures.

"Maybe we can both bring our boys to the park next Saturday," Beth said. "It will give us all a chance to get to know each other."

The thought of making a new friend was pleasant. Linda hadn't made any real friends since she and Jim moved from Boise, Idaho, to Puyallup, Washington, several years ago. Maybe it was time to reach out to another person. She and Jim certainly weren't good friends anymore.

CHAPTER 2

$\mathcal{A}$nxious to read the letter she'd just received, Fannie closed the door behind Samuel and Mary Ann. She'd sent the two outside to weed the flowerbeds. They had been arguing ever since they got home from school, and she knew the only way to have any peace and quiet was to find something constructive for them to do.

Fannie reached for the pot of herbal tea brewing on the back of the propane stove and took a seat at the kitchen table. Then she poured herself a cup of tea and tore open Abby's letter.

Dear Mom,

The news of your pregnancy was quite a surprise—a pleasant one, of course. How thrilled you and Abraham must be, and I'm certain the rest of his family is happy, too.

I told Lena and Harold about the baby, and they're as excited as I am. Lena said she would get a note off to you soon, because you know how Harold is when it comes to writing letters.

I can't help but worry about you, Mom. Please take care of yourself and be sure to get plenty of rest.

In answer to your question about me coming there when the baby is born—I'd be happy to come. Fact is, you couldn't keep me from being there when my little brother or sister is born.

Things are fine here in Berlin. The quilt shop is doing well, and Lester and I have been talking about our upcoming marriage and where we will live. Since I've

17

been staying with Lena and Harold since you moved to Pennsylvania, our old house has been sitting empty when it's not had renters. So, if you have no objections, Lester and I would like to buy your house and live there.

Give my love to Abraham and the rest of the family. Please write back soon, for I want to know how you're doing. I'll be praying for both you and the baby.

Love,
Abby

Fannie clicked her tongue. "Silly girl. I wouldn't dream of lettin' you buy that old house. It'll be my wedding present to you and Lester."

Her eyes misted as she thought about her daughter getting married in November. Abby and Lester had been courting for four years and probably would have been married by now, except two years ago Lester's daed passed away unexpectedly, leaving Lester, the only son in his family, to care for his mamm and run their blacksmith shop. It had taken him awhile to get to the point where he felt ready to take on the responsibility of marriage.

Fannie smiled through her tears. *At least they've finally set the wedding date for November, although Abby could have had it sooner, since weddings in Holmes County aren't restricted to November and December the way they are here in Lancaster. But Abby's a thoughtful daughter, and she knows that by the end of November the harvest will be done and Abraham and the boys will be free to leave their work and accompany me and the girls to Ohio for the wedding.*

Fannie placed her hand against her stomach and massaged it gently. *So many things have changed in the last few years. First, my marriage to Abraham, Naomi and Caleb getting married and taking over the store, Abby's engagement to Lester, and now a new boppli will soon be coming into our lives.*

She bowed her head and closed her eyes. "Heavenly Father, please bless this child I'm carrying. Thank You for the miracle You've given Abraham and me. Let our little one be healthy, and grant me good health as well." Tears slipped out from under

Fannie's lashes and rolled onto her cheeks. "Lord, You know how much Abraham has gone through, first losin' his Sarah, and then Zach. I pray for Your mercy, and through me and this babe I'm carrying, I ask You to restore to my husband all he lost after his first wife and youngest son were taken."

A door slammed, and Fannie opened her eyes.

"I'm sorry. I didn't realize you were prayin'," Nancy said, as she moved toward the kitchen sink.

Fannie wiped the dampness from her cheeks and smiled. "It's all right. I was about done anyhow."

Nancy crossed the room and laid a hand on Fannie's shoulder. "I couldn't help but hear part of your prayer, Mama Fannie. But I wasn't eavesdroppin'. Honest. I just got done workin' in the garden and came inside for a glass of water."

Fannie patted Nancy's hand. "It's okay. I wasn't sharing anything with God that I'm ashamed of."

Nancy pulled out a chair and sat down. "Papa's doin' all right now. Even before he found out you were gonna have a boppli, he was dealin' with things pretty well."

"I know, but this babe will be like a reward for his patience and faithfulness. Kind of like Job in the Bible when he lost everything and God gave him even more in the end." Fannie reached for her cup of tea. "Of course, I'm not saying me and the child I carry could ever replace your real mamm or your little *bruder* who was kidnapped."

Nancy nodded, and her chin quivered. "I know."

"How'd you get so smart for a girl of fifteen?"

"Maybe it's from bein' around you so much."

Fannie was about to comment, but their conversation was interrupted when a ruckus broke out on the back porch.

"*Ach*, my! It must be Samuel and Mary Ann scrappin' again." Fannie pushed her chair back, ready to deal with the problem.

"Want me to tend to it?" Nancy asked.

"Would ya mind?"

"I'd be happy to. You just sit there and relax. Have yourself another cup of tea. I'll start supper as soon as I get things straightened out between the *kinner*."

Fannie appreciated her stepdaughter's willingness to help out. Nancy was a good girl, and a pretty one, too, with her light brown hair offset by a pair of luminous green eyes. Now that Naomi was married and had a family of her own, it was nice to have another pair of capable hands she could rely on, even though Nancy did tend to be a bit headstrong at times.

She yawned. "I think I'll take my cup of tea into the living room and stretch out on the sofa a few minutes. Call me when you need help in the kitchen, okay?"

Nancy nodded and scurried out the door.

Abraham blotted the sweat from his forehead, while he stomped his dirt-crusted boots against the steps on the back porch. He and the boys had accomplished a lot in the fields today. Much of the planting was now done. He'd sent Norman home to his bride, Ruth, whom he had married last fall. Jake and Matthew, still single and living at home, had gone to the barn to put the mules away.

When Abraham entered the house, he found Fannie slouched on the sofa in the living room with her feet propped on a leather stool. Her head leaned against a pillow, and her eyes were closed, but she opened them as soon as his boots touched the hardwood floor.

"Were ya sleepin'?" he asked, tossing his straw hat onto the coffee table.

"Just restin' my eyes."

He leaned over and kissed her forehead. "Did ya work at the quilt shop today?"

"Jah, only until two, though. Then I did a little shopping in Paradise and came home."

"You be sure to rest whenever possible," he said, taking a seat beside her.

She reached for his hand. "You sound like Abby. She's worried I'm going to do too much and said in her letter that I should get plenty of rest."

"Abby's a smart woman," Abraham said with a nod. "Takes after her mamm."

Fannie needled him in the ribs with her elbow. "Go on with ya, now. I'm gettin' too old to be taken in by such a flattering tongue."

"That'll be the day. And ya ain't old, neither." Abraham gently patted Fannie's stomach. "You think you'd have a boppli in there if you was old?"

Her cheeks turned pink, and she looked away. It made Abraham feel kind of good to know he could still make her blush. He rested his head on her shoulder and whispered, "I love you, Fannie Mae Fisher."

She brushed the top of his head with her lips. "I love you, too."

"You've made me so happy, and I know you'll make a *wunderbaar gut* mamm."

"I hope I'll be a wonderful good mom. I've wanted another boppli for such a long time, but I had given up hope that it would ever happen."

"God is full of grace and miracles, ain't it so?"

"Jah," she murmured. "He truly is."

Abby glanced at the small clock on her desk and frowned. What was keeping Lena? She should have been here by now.

Since Abby lived in the same house with Harold and Lena, the two women usually rode to work together in one buggy. This morning, however, Lena had said she was tired and wanted to stay in bed a little longer. She'd told Abby she would hitch up one of their other buggies and try to be at the quilt shop by ten o'clock. It was almost eleven now, and there was still no sign of Lena. Had her buggy broken down along the way? Could she have been in an accident?

Abby drew in a deep breath and tried to relax. There was no point in worrying. "Most things one worries about never come to pass," Mom had often told her.

She pushed her chair away from the desk and stood. "Maybe I should go look for Lena." Her gaze came to rest on the clock again. At eleven thirty several ladies from their Amish community would show up at the shop ready to work on a quilt and eat lunch together. Abby didn't want to leave the place unattended, so she decided to wait awhile longer. If Lena didn't arrive by the time the women did, she would go looking for her.

The bell above the front door jingled, and Abby discovered her friend Rachel had entered the quilt shop.

"I'm a little early," Rachel said cheerfully, "but I thought if I came over now it would give us a chance to visit before the others get here."

Abby smiled. "I always enjoy chatting, but I'm wonderin' if you could do me a favor."

"I will if I can. What is it?"

"Lena was supposed to be here by ten o'clock." Abby made a sweeping gesture with one hand. "As you can see, she's not. So, I'm thinking I should head in the direction of home, in case she's broken down somewhere or has been involved in an accident."

Rachel's forehead wrinkled, and concern showed in her dark eyes. "You think she's been hurt?"

"I hope not, but I'd feel better if I went to check on things. Would you mind watching the store while I'm gone?"

"Sure, I can do that." Rachel glanced around the spacious room. "I see there are no customers at the moment, either."

Abby nodded. "Things have been slow this morning, but if someone does come in, I'm sure you can handle it."

Rachel grinned, her cheeks turning slightly pink. "I'll do my best."

"Hopefully, I won't be gone too long. But if the others show up before I get back, please tell them to begin working on the quilt." Abby grabbed her black shawl and matching bonnet from the shelf under her desk and headed for the back door. "See you soon, Rachel. And please say a prayer that everything's okay with Lena."

"I surely will."

Abby murmured her own quick prayer and hurried out the door.

CHAPTER 3

$\mathcal{A}$bby's heart pounded when she discovered Lena's buggy, with a gentle mare hitched to the front of it, sitting in the front yard. She'd been relieved when she hadn't run into her sister-in-law on the road. But now, realizing Lena hadn't even left home caused her a different concern. Was she still sleeping? Could she be sick? This was so unlike Lena.

Abby took the steps two at a time and entered the house through the back door. "Lena! Are you here?"

Silence.

Abby peered into the kitchen.

The room was empty.

Her next stop was the living room, but Lena wasn't there, either. *Where could she be? Surely not still in bed. Why would the horse and buggy be out front if she were sleeping?*

Abby climbed the stairs to the bedrooms. "Lena!"

"I'm in here" came a muffled reply.

Abby hurried to Lena and Harold's room. The door was ajar, so she felt it would be okay to step inside. She found Lena fully dressed, lying on top of the bed. Her face looked pale, and dark circles shadowed her pale blue eyes.

"What's wrong? Are you sick?" Abby rushed to the bed and placed her hand on Lena's forehead. She felt relief to discover that it was cool.

Lena moaned. "I've been throwing up all morning."

"You must have the flu, although I'm sure you don't have a fever. Want me to get a cup of mint tea to settle your stomach?"

23

Lena shook her head. "It's not the flu."

"It couldn't be food poisoning. You, me, and Harold all had the same thing for supper last night, and I feel fine."

Lena pushed herself to a sitting position, leaning her head against the pillows that were propped against the headboard. "I—I think I'm in a family way. I missed my monthly, and for the last week I've felt awfully nauseous." She slowly shook her head. "Although today's been the worst."

Abby's mouth dropped open. She lived under the same roof with Harold and Lena and hadn't suspected a thing. How could she be so unobservant? Maybe those terrible nightmares she'd been having were making it hard for her to focus.

She sank to the edge of the bed, too numb to say a word. It didn't seem possible that Naomi, Mom, and now Lena were all expecting *bopplin* so close together.

"I thought the queasiness would pass, and that I'd be able to come into work. But soon after I got the horse hitched to the buggy, I had another round of vomiting." Lena gripped her stomach and drew in a deep breath.

Abby stood. "I'll go downstairs and fix you some mint tea. Maybe some saltine crackers would help, too."

"*Danki.*" Lena offered Abby a weak smile. "I'm planning to see the doctor next week, but I'm almost certain I'm pregnant."

"Guess I'll have to get busy and sew some little blankets," Abby said. "Between you, Mom, and Naomi, there will surely be a need for many baby things."

"Harold and I have been married a little over five years, and we were about to give up hope of ever having any kinner." Lena smiled. "This is such a happy surprise, and it seems like God is really blessing our family these days."

"Jah, I believe He is." Abby left the room and headed downstairs to the kitchen, but a shadow of fear crept into her soul; the same one she'd been fighting since she got the news of her mother's pregnancy. Now she had the worry of her sister-in-law, too.

The scripture verse found in Psalm 55:22 filled Abby's thoughts. "*Cast thy burden upon the Lord, and he shall sustain thee: he shall never suffer the righteous to be moved.*" She drew in a deep breath. "I will not worry, but will trust God in all things."

⌒

When Abby returned to her shop some time later, things were really busy. The women who had come to help with the quilt had already eaten their lunch and were hard at work in front of the quilting frame, exchanging stories and comparing thimbles. Abby noticed that some of the women's fingers had turned green from their skin interacting with the metal of the thimble. Mary Kaulp had a hole in her thimble and said it had worn through from so much use. "Sometimes the needle sticks through it, and that's sure a big surprise," Mary quipped.

Abby flinched as she thought of how many times she had pricked her finger while working on a quilt. Still, she wouldn't trade the work for anything. She glanced over at Lester's mamm, Deborah. The dark-haired woman sat in front of one of the treadle sewing machines, pumping her legs up and down as she folded over the lining of the quilt she was working on in order to stitch down the binding. Everyone kept busy, and there were several customers milling around the store. Three English women stood in line behind the counter, waiting for their purchases to be rung up. Rachel's cheeks were bright red, and her forehead glistened with perspiration.

"I'm glad you're back," she whispered when Abby slipped behind the counter. "Things have been kind of hectic."

"Sorry for taking so long, but I found Lena at home, and she wasn't feeling well." Abby helped her friend fold the Rose of Sharon quilt that an English customer had purchased. "I'll tell you more about it later."

"Jah, okay."

For the next hour, Abby and Rachel waited on customers, and in between they worked with the women on the Dahlia pattern quilt. At two o'clock Lester entered the store.

"I came by earlier hopin' to take you to lunch," he told Abby, "but Rachel said you'd gone lookin' for Lena because she didn't show up for work this morning."

Abby nodded. "I was getting worried about her."

"Did ya find her? Is she okay?" Lester's deep-set blue eyes revealed concern.

"She was still at home, not feeling well." Abby didn't think it would be right to tell Lester that Lena suspected she was pregnant when it hadn't been confirmed yet.

"Sorry to hear that. Is she gonna be okay?"

"Jah, I'm sure she will."

"Glad to hear it's nothing serious." Lester removed his straw hat and raked a hand through his wavy blond hair. "Have you eaten yet?"

She shook her head.

"Then why don't we go over to the Subway place?"

"What about your blacksmith shop? Shouldn't you be there right now?"

"My helper is takin' care of things, and we're pretty well caught up." Lester snickered. "Besides, I'm the boss. I can take off whenever I want, now that I've got Seth workin' for me. "

Abby smiled then glanced around the store. There were only a few customers now, and the quilters were doing fine on their own. Even so, she didn't feel right about imposing further on Rachel.

As if she could read Abby's thoughts, her friend spoke up. "Things are slower now. I'll be happy to stay and wait on customers if you'd like to have lunch with Lester."

Abby tipped her head, as she considered the offer.

"We won't be gone long," Lester coaxed. He glanced across the room. "My mamm's here, and I'm sure she'd pitch in to help Rachel if it was needed."

Rachel smiled. "That's right. I can ask any of the ladies if I get real busy, so go on now, and take your time."

"All right then." Abby stepped out from behind the counter, and Lester steered her toward the front door.

"I'll have her back within the hour," he called over his shoulder.

A short time later, Abby and Lester were seated at a booth inside the Subway place, sharing a turkey hoagie that had been made on a foot-long roll.

Leaning against the seatback, Abby began to relax. It was the first time all day that she'd really felt calm, but then she knew why. She always felt good whenever she was with Lester. She had known since their first date that she could spend the rest of her life with him. He was kind, gentle, and hard-working, the way her daed had been when he was alive.

Lester reached across the table and took her hand. "Your eyes are sure pretty, ya know that? I always did like the color of sweet, dark chocolate."

Abby smiled, despite the blush she felt cascade over her cheeks. Lester always knew the right thing to say. "Danki," she murmured.

"Is your family still plannin' to come to our wedding in November?" he asked, taking their conversation in a new direction.

She nodded. "I hope so. But it will depend on how well Mom's doin' by then."

Lester stared at her strangely. "What's wrong with your mamm?"

"I got a note from her the other day, saying she's expecting a boppli near the end of October."

Lester's jaw dropped. "Really?"

"It would seem that God has given Mom and Abraham a second chance."

He let out a low whistle. "That is great news. If the baby's due in October and we're not gettin' married 'til late November, then there shouldn't be a problem with them comin' to Ohio for the wedding, do ya think?"

"I'm sure there won't be." Abby toyed with her napkin. "I am concerned about Mom, though."

"How come?"

"She's not so young anymore. A lot could happen." She took a small bite of her sandwich, chewed, and swallowed. "When the time gets closer to Mom's delivery, I'll need to go to Pennsylvania to help out. Then I'll have to stay until after the boppli comes and I'm sure Mom can handle things on her own."

Lester grabbed his cup of iced tea and gulped some down.

"We've waited a long time to get married, Abby. I sure hope you're home in plenty of time for the big day."

"Oh, I will be," Abby assured him.

"Will Lena run the quilt shop in your absence, or do you think you'll have to hire a second person to help out?"

Abby nibbled on the inside of her cheek. Should she tell Lester about Lena's suspected pregnancy or wait until she knew for sure? "I'm hoping Lena can mind the store, but if that doesn't work out, I'll have to think about hiring someone else."

Lester stared at Abby as he swirled his straw around the inside of his cup. "I can see by your solemn expression that you're worried. Is it leavin' Lena in charge of the store, or are you frettin' over your mamm's condition?"

"A little of both," Abby admitted. "Mostly, I'm worried about Mom."

"Is she doin' okay so far?"

"Jah, but she's having some morning sickness."

"That's pretty common."

"True, but—"

Lester held up his hand. "Abby, please try not to worry. Women have been havin' babies for thousands of years."

She chuckled softly. "I know. Ever since Adam and Eve. But this is my mamm we're talkin' about."

He nodded with a look understanding. "She'll be fine; just pray."

"I am and shall continue to do so."

⁓

"Daddy, Daddy, guess what?"

Jim Scott set two paint buckets on the floor of his garage and turned to face his son. "What's got you so excited, Jimmy?"

"Me and Mommy went to the park again today. I saw my friend Allen there."

"Is Allen the little boy in the picture Mommy took last week?" Jim asked.

Jimmy's dark eyes gleamed as he bobbed his head up and down. "Me and Allen had ice cream."

"You did, huh?"

"Yep. Big chocolate cones."

Jim ruffled his son's chestnut-colored hair. "That's nice. I'm glad you've made a new friend." *And I'm happy my over-protective wife is finally giving you a bit of space to grow and learn.*

"Mommy said we could go to the park again soon."

Jim was about to comment when his cell phone rang. "I've got to get that, Jimmy. Find something to do until I'm off the phone."

"Okay, Daddy."

Jim flipped the phone cover open. "Scott's Painting and Decorating. Yeah, sure, Hank. What can I do for you?"

Absorbed in his conversation, Jim almost forgot about Jimmy until the boy wandered out of the storage closet holding a scrap of material. At first Jim thought it was a paint rag, but then he realized it was multicolored, not white.

"I've got to go, Hank. I'll call you back." Jim clicked off and turned to face his son. "What have you got there, Jimmy?"

When Jimmy opened the piece of fabric to its full length and held it out, Jim felt the blood drain from his face. It was a baby quilt—the same one Jimmy had been wrapped in the day Jim snatched him off the picnic table in an Amish family's yard.

"Where'd you get this?" Jim's hands trembled, but he tried to keep his voice calm as he moved toward his son.

Jimmy pointed to the storage closet at the back of the garage where Jim kept some of his painting supplies.

"You'd better let me have that."

The child stood there, unmoving.

"Give it to me, now!"

Jim barely realized he'd shouted until Jimmy's eyes filled with tears.

"Please, don't start bawling."

Jimmy sniffed and handed Jim the quilt.

I should have thrown this thing out years ago instead of stashing it away with my paint rags. If Linda ever sees the quilt, she'll start asking questions, and then I'll have some serious explaining to do.

"Jimmy, I want you to go inside the house and tell Mommy

I'll be ready for lunch in a few minutes."

"Okay." Jimmy hesitated a moment, then pointed to the quilt. "Can I have that, Daddy?"

"No! And don't mention it to your mother. Is that clear?"

Jimmy blinked, and for a moment Jim thought the boy was going to give in to his tears.

Jim held the quilt at his side as he squatted in front of his son. "This is just an old rag. It's nothing you'd want to play with. Understand?"

Jimmy nodded soberly, then turned toward the door leading to the house. His shoulders were slumped, and he hung his head as though he'd lost one of his favorite toys. Jim felt like a heel, but he couldn't let Jimmy have the quilt. "I'll be in soon," he called to his son's retreating form.

As soon as Jimmy was out of sight, Jim made a beeline for his work van. He snapped the back door open and stuffed the quilt inside, burying it under a canvas tarp. When he returned to work after lunch, he would ditch the incriminating piece of evidence.

"Out of sight, out of mind," Jim mumbled. But even as the words tumbled out of his mouth, he wondered if he would ever be free of his deception. Jimmy wasn't legally theirs, and no matter how hard he tried, Jim would never forget the day he had kidnapped the boy.

Chapter 4

*A*bby stretched her tired neck and shoulder muscles as she sank onto the wooden stool behind the counter where she waited on customers. For the past week she'd been working at the quilt shop alone. Lena had gone to the doctor, and her pregnancy had been confirmed. Since her morning sickness was not any better, Harold insisted she quit helping Abby at the store. He had asked his mother-in-law, Esther, to help Lena with some of the chores at home, saying that he wanted his wife to rest as much as possible. Abby had talked with Rachel about the possibility of her coming to work in the quilt shop, but her friend had just gotten word that her application at the Farmstead restaurant had been accepted. None of the women who regularly made quilts to be sold at the store seemed interested in working full time, and Abby wondered if she would ever find someone to take Lena's place. Soon it would be summer, and then even more tourists would flock to Holmes County, which meant her shop would often be full of people.

The bell above the front door jingled, and Abby glanced up to see who had come in. It was Lester, carrying a paper sack and wearing his usual cheerful smile.

"I knew you wouldn't be able to go out to eat today, so I brought you some lunch." He placed the sack on the counter and smiled.

Abby was happy she was betrothed to such a considerate man. "Danki. That was thoughtful." She reached for the sack. "What'd you bring?"

"Got us an order of fried chicken, coleslaw, and some hot

potato salad from the Farmstead restaurant. Saw your friend Rachel waiting tables."

"She started working there a couple days ago." Abby peeked inside the sack, and the pleasing aroma of warm chicken caused her to lick her lips. "*Umm. . .*it sure smells good."

"Want to eat here, or would ya rather go out to the picnic table in back of your store?" Lester asked.

"I guess we'd better stay put, in case a customer comes in."

"Jah, okay." Lester pulled another stool over to the counter, sat down beside Abby, and took her hand. They bowed for silent prayer; then he reached into the sack and withdrew their lunch.

Abby unfolded the napkins and placed the plastic silverware beside their paper plates, while Lester poured cups of iced tea from the thermos he'd brought along. They ate in companionable silence, until Lester wiped his mouth and announced, "My mamm's comin' by later on."

"Does she need some quilting material?"

He shrugged and gave Abby a quick wink.

"You're up to something. What is it?"

"I ain't up to nothin'."

Abby was sure Lester was teasing and would tell her if it was anything important, so she didn't press the issue.

A short time later, as they were clearing away the remains of their lunch, the front door opened and Deborah Mast walked in. "*Wie geht's,*" she said with a cheery wave.

"Good day to you," Abby replied. "What can I help you with?"

Deborah smiled and stepped up to the counter, casting a quick glance in her son's direction. "Lester tells me you're in need of a helper here."

Abby nodded. "Lena had to quit because she's got the morning sickness real bad. She and my mamm seem to be going through the same struggles right now."

Lester cleared his throat. "Uh—guess I'd best be gettin' back to work." He gave Abby's arm a gentle squeeze. "See you later."

"Have a good day," she said.

"And don't work too hard," Lester's mamm called to him.

When Deborah's son waved and disappeared out the door, she stepped up to Abby. "I was pleased to hear that your mamm's in a family way. She must be real *hallich*."

"Jah, she's happy as a springtime robin, and so is the rest of the family."

"I guess Lena must be excited about her pregnancy, too, since she and Harold have no kinner yet." Deborah leaned on the counter. "Speaking of Lena. . . Since you haven't found a replacement for her, I was wondering if you'd want to hire me to take her place."

Abby's lips curved into a smile. "I know you often come by to help the ladies work on a quilt once a week, but I didn't think to ask if you'd consider coming to work here."

"I would be happy to, if you think I'd be useful."

"Of course, you're a wonderful quilter."

Deborah grunted. "That doesn't mean I've got a head for business."

"I'm sure you'll do fine. You're friendly and outgoing, and that's what matters most when it comes to waiting on customers."

"Since I've been widowed these last two years and all my kinner but Lester are out on their own, I've got time on my hands." Deborah smiled. "How soon would you like me to start work?"

"How about right now?"

"That sounds good to me." Lester's mother made a sweeping gesture. "Where do you want me to begin?"

⁓

Abraham wiped the sweat from his forehead using a damp rag he'd left hanging on the pump behind the house. He and the boys had worked hard in the fields all morning, and he was more than ready for their noon meal.

"Sure hope Nancy and Fannie have lunch on the table," Jake commented. "I'm hungry enough to eat an old mule."

"Jah, me, too," Matthew agreed.

Abraham stood off to one side, watching two of his sons as they took turns washing up. Norman had gone to his own place for lunch, saying he wanted to spend a few minutes with his wife.

Abraham knew about that "in love" feeling; he'd been blessed with it twice. Even now, after being with Fannie four years, he felt like a lovesick schoolboy whenever she smiled at him in a certain way or said something to make him feel special.

"Hey, watch what you're doin', Jake!" Matthew's usual calm voice rose a notch, driving Abraham's musings to the back of his mind.

Jake grunted. "I'm washin' up; what do you expect?"

"I expect you to keep the soap and water on yourself, not on me."

Abraham shook his head. It was hard to believe Matthew was almost twenty-six years old and Jake had recently turned twenty, since they both were acting like a couple of schoolboys. "You two had better knock it off, or I'll make you eat in the barn."

Matthew grunted. "That'd be a good place for Jake, since he already smells like one of the sweaty horses."

Jake wrinkled his nose and slapped the wet rag against Matthew's arm. "You don't smell like no rose garden yourself. No wonder ya can't find a wife."

Matthew's ears turned crimson, but he made no reply.

"I think the real reason you're not married is 'cause you're scared," Jake taunted.

Matthew flicked some water in his brother's direction. "Let's drop the subject, okay?"

"I agree." Abraham nodded toward the house. "We'd best not keep the women waitin'. I'm sure they have lunch on the table by now."

"First one to the house gets two helpings of dessert!" Jake hollered as he took off on a run.

Matthew shook his head. "I wonder if he'll ever grow up."

Abraham thumped his eldest son on the back. "Why don't you try to set him a better example?"

"*Humph!* A lot of good that would do."

Abraham wondered if something was eating at Matthew, but he figured in time his boy would come to grips with whatever it was, so he said nothing as he strode toward the house.

Fannie placed a platter of ham on the table and yawned. She'd been unable to go to the quilt shop this morning because of her queasy stomach, and even though her nausea had subsided some, she felt too tired to do much of anything. All she really wanted to do was get the men fed, then collapse on the sofa awhile.

"Want me to ring the dinner bell again?" Nancy asked as she headed to the refrigerator to fetch a jar of pickles.

"I think I hear our menfolk comin' now," Fannie replied.

Sure enough, the *thump, thump* of men's boots could be heard on the back steps. A few seconds later, Abraham, Matthew, and Jake entered the room.

Fannie nodded at the table. "Everything's ready, so take a chair and eat yourselves full."

Abraham gave her a peck on the cheek and then pulled out his chair at the head of the table. Once everyone was seated, he bowed his head for silent prayer, and the others did the same.

Fannie folded her hands in her lap, and when the prayer was over, she stared at the food set before her. There were thick slices of the ham she had carved earlier, a heaping bowl of macaroni salad, deviled eggs, tangy pickled beets, dilled pickles, and a basket of fresh homemade bread for sandwiches. None of it appealed, but for the sake of the baby she carried, she knew she must eat.

"You okay, Fannie?" Abraham asked with a look of concern.

She forced a smile and nodded. "Fine and dandy."

"You look awfully *mied*. Are you still feelin' sick to your stomach?"

"Just in the mornings now, but you're right, I am a bit tired."

Abraham glanced over at Nancy, who sat beside Fannie. "After lunch, I want you to clear away the dishes and clean up the kitchen while my wife takes a nap."

Nancy nodded. "Okay, Papa."

"I take it you're not goin' to the quilt shop this afternoon," Matthew said around a mouthful of macaroni salad.

"Guess I'd better not," Fannie replied.

"I'm thinkin' we might need to close down the shop or find someone else to run it for a time," Abraham said.

Fannie sighed. It would be a shame to close the quilt shop. There were many women in the area who made quilts and sold them in her store. And what of the tourists who liked to shop there?

"Naomi's not up to working at the store and minding the quilt shop, as well," Abraham went on to say. "She's got her hands full taking care of little Sarah, not to mention her being in a family way again. Once her boppli's born, she won't be able to work at the store for a while, either."

"If you didn't need me in the fields, I'd be happy to work at the store while Naomi takes over Fannie's quilt shop," Matthew said.

Jake spoke up for the first time since they'd begun the meal. "Yeah, right. I can see my big brother tradin' in his plow for a broom and sittin' behind a cash register all day instead of workin' the mules out in the fields."

"It would be a sight better than puttin' up with the likes of you," Matthew shot back.

Abraham held up his hand. "Don't start scrappin' again. I've already had enough of it today, and I'm sure the womenfolk aren't in the mood to hear it, either."

"Maybe I'll pay Edna a visit this afternoon," Fannie said, taking their conversation in another direction.

"I thought you were going to take a nap."

"I'll go after I've rested awhile."

"Why do you want to travel all the way over to Edna's place in Strasburg?" Matthew asked.

"Cousin Edna's always full of good advice. Maybe she can come up with some idea to solve my dilemma."

Abraham grunted. "The only thing that fun-lovin' woman can come up with is a good joke or two."

Fannie shrugged. "That might be exactly what I need today."

CHAPTER 5

$\mathcal{A}$bby smiled as she watched Deborah wait on the English customer near the front of the store. She had been working at the quilt shop a few weeks now and was doing a fine job. The pleasant expression on the woman's face and the exuberance with which she went about her tasks let Abby know that Lester's mamm thoroughly enjoyed her work. It was almost time to close for the day, yet she was still pleasant and energetic. *She responds well to the customers, too. She also enjoys quilting and is good at it. I'm sure Deborah will be a wonderful mother-in-law.* Abby knew not everyone was blessed with a sweet mamm like hers and an easy-going *schwiegermammi,* like Deborah Mast would be.

Shortly after the last customer left the store, Lester showed up, informing his mother that he'd come by to give her a ride home.

"I'll be ready in a few minutes," she said. "Just need to put a couple things away."

"That's all right, Deborah," Abby was quick to say. "You've worked hard today, and if you want to head home, I can take care of anything else that needs to be done."

Lester moved in front of the treadle sewing machine where Abby sat. "Such a thoughtful daughter-in-law my mamm will be gettin'."

Abby smiled. "And how about you, Lester Mast? What kind of wife do you think I'll be?"

He chucked her under the chin and winked. "A mighty fine one, I'd have to say."

"I'll surely try, but you know I'm not perfect," she replied, taking pleasure in the feel of his calloused fingers against her skin.

"You're even-tempered, kind, considerate, and pretty. What else could a man ask for in a wife?"

Before Abby could reply, Lester leaned closer. "Say, how about you and me goin' out to lunch tomorrow? Maybe we can eat at the Farmstead restaurant this time."

Abby pursed her lips. "I'd like that, but things have been busy here all week. It's only May, yet every day we've had lots of customers. I wouldn't feel right about leaving your mamm alone when things are so hectic."

"I can manage," Deborah called from across the room. "You two have yourselves some fun. You deserve it."

Abby deliberated a few seconds. "I'll tell you what. How about I bring a lunch basket for us to share out back at the picnic table? That way I'll be close, in case your mamm needs help."

"Sounds fine to me." Lester grinned. "And I'll bring the dessert."

~

"Hey, Boss, where'd ya put that box of mudding tape?" Ed Munson called to Jim, who had just descended a six-foot ladder. Part of his crew had been painting the outside of a new apartment complex, while the rest of the men mudded and taped the new Sheetrock walls.

"The tape's in the back of my van." Jim wiped his hands on the paint rag protruding from his back pocket and glanced at the gray paint splattered all over the front of his white overalls. "If my wife could see me now, she'd have a fit."

Linda didn't approve of him working side-by-side with his paint crew, but there were times when they got busy and needed his help. At other times, Jim had to pick up supplies, bid jobs, or do paperwork, so the painting was left to his six employees.

"What's this?" Ed shouted to Jim. "You usin' some fancy paint rags these days?"

Jim's heart palpitated when he realized what Ed held in his hands. It was that baby quilt—the one he'd forgotten to dispose of. "Uh—it's just an old baby blanket," he stammered.

Ed's reddish-brown mustache twitched when he smiled. "You and Linda plannin' to adopt another baby?"

"This was something I picked up on our vacation to Ohio a few years ago." Jim snatched the quilt from the man who had been working as his foreman for the last two years. "I'm planning to get rid of it."

"I'm thinkin' my wife would like it," Ed said. "She's into quilts and that kind of thing. So if you're just gonna pitch it, I'd be happy to take it off your hands."

If it had been anything other than the Amish baby quilt, Jim would have let Ed have it. But this was the one piece of tangible evidence that linked him to the kidnapping of an Amish baby. If he gave it to Ed, and Ed's wife said something to Linda, Jim would have some serious explaining to do.

"I've—uh—already promised it to someone else," Jim lied. "In fact, I'll be taking the quilt to them as soon as I get off work today."

Ed shrugged and turned away. "Guess I'd best go back to the van and get that mudding tape."

Jim glanced at his watch. It was only two o'clock. Too early to call it quits for the day. However, this was something he felt couldn't wait, so he decided to take a drive to Tacoma, where he purchased most of his paint and supplies.

"I'm going to Parker Paint," he called to Ed as the man closed the van door and headed back with the box of mudding tape. "Make sure the guys stay on course while I'm gone."

"Sure thing, Boss," Ed yelled over his shoulder.

A short time later, Jim drove into downtown Tacoma. When he spotted a thrift store, he pulled into the parking lot, grabbed the quilt, and rushed inside.

The middle-aged woman at the front desk was busy waiting on a customer, so Jim stood off to one side until they had finished with their business. When the elderly gentleman left, Jim stepped forward and plunked the quilt down for the clerk's inspection. "Would you be interested in this?"

She slipped on her reading glasses and studied the covering

intently. "Why, this looks like an Amish quilt."

"Yeah, it is."

"Since the items we take in here are on a consignment-only basis, why don't you tell me how much you would like it to be sold for?"

Jim frowned. "Can't you just buy it from me outright?"

"Sorry, but that's not our policy."

This isn't going so well. I thought it would be easy to get rid of my albatross. He deliberated a few more seconds and finally pushed the quilt toward the clerk. "I guess you can have it then."

Her dark eyebrows rose a notch, and she squinted at him. "What?"

"I said, you can have the quilt, free and clear. I just need—I mean, I want to get rid of the silly thing."

The woman pursed her lips as she fingered one edge of the covering. "This is a very nice piece, sir. Are you sure you want to leave it with no payment in return?"

"I'm positive."

"Very well then. Let me write you a receipt."

Jim transferred his weight from one foot to the other. "No, no. That won't be necessary. Do whatever you want with the quilt, and I'll be on my way." He whirled around and rushed out of the store, feeling as though a heavy weight had been lifted off his shoulders. The only evidence linking him to a missing Amish baby was gone, and he never had to worry about it again.

~

Linda lowered herself onto the park bench, anxious to read the romance novel she'd recently purchased. It helped to immerse herself in someone else's complicated life, even if it was only fiction.

She glanced up at Jimmy to be sure he was okay. There were no other children at the park right now, so she hoped he would play happily by himself. Relieved to see that he seemed content to play on the slide, she opened her book to the first page. She'd only read a few lines when the sound of children's laughter pulled her attention away from her book. She looked up and saw Allen rush over to the slide where Jimmy was playing while his mother headed her way.

"Sure is a nice day. Won't be long and summer will be here," Beth said as she seated herself on the bench beside Linda. She took a sip from the Styrofoam cup in her hand. "Umm. . .this mocha latté is delicious. I would have bought two if I'd known you were going to be here."

"That's okay," Linda replied. "I prefer tea over coffee anyway."

"Have you ever tried an iced herbal raspberry tea?"

Linda shook her head. "I usually drink plain black or orange pekoe."

"Mommy, Mommy, watch me go down the slide on my belly!" Jimmy shouted, interrupting their conversation.

Linda stood and cupped her hands around her mouth. "Be careful, Jimmy! I don't want you to get hurt."

"I'll be okay!" The boy flopped onto his stomach and skimmed down the slide, giggling all the way. When he came to the bottom, he grabbed the edge of the slide and did a somersault to the ground.

"Boys will be boys," Beth said with a chuckle.

Linda inhaled deeply and blew out her breath in a quick puff that lifted her bangs off her forehead. "I wish I could wrap Jimmy in a bubble and keep him safe from any harm."

"That would be nice, but think of all the fun our kids would miss if we shielded them in such a way."

Linda dug her fingernails into the palms of her hands. Was she selfish for wanting to protect her child? From the first day they'd adopted Jimmy, Jim had accused her of being over-protective. She tried not to be, but Jimmy was their only son, and she loved him so much. When Jimmy turned six on April 15, in his excitement to see his cousins Cameron and Pam who lived in Idaho, he'd fallen off the porch and sprained his ankle. Linda had felt the child's pain as if it were her own.

"I'm glad I ran into you today," Beth said, breaking into Linda's thoughts. "I've been wanting to tell you about the vacation Bible school our church is having next month. I was hoping you would let Jimmy attend."

Bible school? Linda had attended vacation Bible school when she was a young girl, but she only went then to please her friend Carrie who lived next door. She'd been ten years old at the time and had received a Bible for memorizing five scripture verses and being there every day. *I wonder whatever happened to that old Bible? Did Jim throw it out after we got married, or is it buried somewhere on our bookshelf in the living room?*

"Anyway," Beth continued, "the sessions will be from ten in the morning until noon during the third week of June. There will be Bible stories, crafts, puppets, and snacks."

Linda was prepared to tell Beth that she didn't think Jimmy was ready for Bible school, when Beth added, "The classes are for preschool kids all the way up to the sixth grade. Since Jimmy and Allen are both in the same grade, they'll be together."

"I don't know—"

"If you'd like to come along, that would be great. We're always in need of helpers."

"It would probably be better than sitting at home feeling sorry for myself," Linda mumbled.

Beth touched Linda's arm. "Is something troubling you?"

Linda's only response was a slow nod.

"If you'd like to talk about it, I promise it won't be repeated."

"I—I appreciate that." Linda's voice shook with emotion, and she clenched her teeth. "My marriage is a mess."

"Would you care to explain?"

"Jim and I are unable to have children of our own. We adopted Jimmy five years ago, and ever since then our marriage has been strained." Linda shifted on the unyielding bench. She didn't know why she was unloading on a near stranger, but there was something about Beth's gentle voice and compassionate expression that prompted her to reveal what she had.

"Didn't your husband want to be a father?"

Linda's gaze came to rest on her child, happily sharing the teeter-totter with his new friend. "I thought he did. In fact, he seemed as excited about going to Maryland to get our son as I was."

"You went all the way to the East Coast to adopt a baby?" Beth's uplifted eyebrows revealed her surprise.

"Jim's attorney set it up with a lawyer he knew in Maryland. Since Jim's folks live in Ohio, we turned the trip into a vacation."

"I see."

"Everything seemed to be okay until we got home. Then Jim started accusing me of being overprotective of Jimmy." Linda's vision clouded with tears, and she sniffed. "Jim looks for excuses to be away from home, and to tell you the truth, I think he would rather be at work than with me or Jimmy."

Beth offered her a supportive smile. "Do you and Jim attend church anywhere?"

"No. Jim's opposed to anything religious, and I haven't been to church since I was a girl." A sharp throb cut across Linda's forehead, and she inhaled deeply, hoping to drive away the pain. She hadn't had one of her migraine headaches for several weeks, and she hoped she wasn't getting one now.

"Maybe vacation Bible school would be good for both you and Jimmy," Beth said.

"I—I don't see how it could do anything to help my stagnant marriage."

Beth gave her arm a gentle squeeze, and Linda felt comforted. "God can work miracles in people's lives."

"I think it would take even more than a miracle to fix my broken marriage." Linda paused, willing herself not to break down in front of Allen's mother. "I've asked Jim several times if we could go back east for another vacation, but he refuses to take us there."

"Has he said why?"

"No. He just reminded me that his folks have been out here to visit a couple of times and said there's no reason for us to make the long trip to Ohio."

"Men can be so stubborn," Beth said with a shake of her head.

"My husband can be downright obstinate. He says he loves Jimmy, yet he refuses to adopt another child. It makes no sense at all."

"I'm glad you've shared your concerns, Linda. It helps me know how to pray for you."

"I appreciate that, and I will think about letting Jimmy go to Bible school." Linda sniffed and swiped at the tears trickling down her cheeks. She'd given in to her unstable emotions and insecurities again, but at the moment, it didn't matter. Beth hadn't condemned her the way Jim always did, and she actually seemed to understand. Maybe this new friendship was exactly what Linda needed.

CHAPTER 6

$\mathcal{T}$he mail's here, Abby," Deborah called as she stepped into the quilt shop the following day. "I put it on your desk. Is that okay?"

"Sure, that's fine," Abby replied. She was busy placing some quilts on one of the shelves near the back of the store and would take time to go through the mail later on.

"Looks like there's a letter from your mamm." Deborah stepped up beside Abby and reached for one of the Tumbling Block quilts. "How's Fannie doing these days?"

"Her last letter said she was still having some morning sickness and felt awfully tired, but she's managed to work in her quilt shop a few afternoons a week."

"Bet she wishes you were there to help out," Deborah said as she straightened the corner of the quilt closest to her.

Abby sighed. "I wish I could be in two places at once, but it's not possible for me to run two quilt shops at the same time. Especially with one of them being in Pennsylvania."

"I'm sure Fannie will hire a *maad* to help out at home if she needs to."

"I suppose Mom could hire a maid, but she does have Abraham's two youngest daughters. Nancy is fifteen, and I'm sure she's capable of cooking and cleaning. Even Mary Ann, who's not quite eleven, can help with some things when she's not in school." Abby frowned, as another thought popped into her head. "It's the quilt shop Mom needs help with the most."

The bell above the door jingled before Deborah could comment. "Guess I'd better see what that customer needs," she said, motioning toward the front of the store.

"And I think I'll take the time to read Mom's letter. I really want to see how she's doing."

"Good idea."

Deborah moved toward the customer, and Abby hurried to her desk. She found the letter from her mother on top of the mail and quickly tore it open.

Dear Abby,

I went to the doctor yesterday, and he seemed concerned about the slight swelling I have in my legs. He told me to avoid salt and to stay off my feet as much as possible. Nancy's here to help out, and Cousin Edna offered to come by a few days a week, so I'm sure everything at the house will be cared for. It's the quilt shop I'm worried about. Since I'm not able to work there right now, I may have to close it down. Sure would hate to do that, though, since it's doing so well. But I suppose if there's no other way, I'll have to accept it.

I'm doing some better with the nausea now but still feeling drained of energy. Sure will be glad when I'm feeling better. It's hard to do nothing but rest. You know me—always puttering around, and not happy unless I've got something constructive to do.

Enough about me now. How are things going for you? I hope your quilt shop is doing well, and I'm looking forward to hearing from you soon. Tell that future son-in-law of mine I said hello.

Love,
Mom

Abby dropped the letter to her desk and let her head fall forward. If the doctor had ordered Mom to rest more, and she was having some swelling in her legs, he must be concerned about her losing the baby. Ever since Abby had learned of her mother's pregnancy, she'd been anxious. Now, she was more worried than ever.

Am I being selfish staying here in Ohio when my mamm needs my help there? Even if it means closing my own shop, I feel I must go to

Pennsylvania and keep Mom's shop open. She gave up one quilt shop when she moved from here; I can't let her give up another. Abby's fingers clenched as she thought about Lester, and how much she would miss him. It would be hard to be separated, but their relationship was strong, and she prayed he would understand.

With her decision made, Abby went to speak with Lester's mother. The woman she'd been waiting on had left the store, and Deborah now sat at one of the sewing machines, ready to begin a new quilt.

She glanced up when Abby approached. "Is somethin' troubling you, Abby? Your serious expression makes me think you have some concerns."

Abby swallowed past the lump in her throat. "I just read Mom's letter, and she's had some swelling in her legs, so the doctor advised her to get more rest. I fear she might lose the boppli if she doesn't follow his orders."

Deborah shook her head. "Fannie's no schoolgirl. She'll be careful to do as the doctor says."

"But she might have to close the quilt shop." Abby pursed her lips and drew in a deep breath. "I really ought to go and keep the place running for her."

"To Pennsylvania?"

"Jah."

"What would you do about your shop here?"

"I—I was hoping you might be able to take over for me. Maybe I could see if one of the ladies who does quilting for us could help you a few days a week."

"I could ask my sister, Clara. She still has two children in school, but they're old enough to fend for themselves when she's not at home."

"That would be wonderful if Clara's in agreement."

"How soon do you plan to leave, and how long will you be gone?"

"I'll go as soon as possible and would probably stay until the boppli is born and Mom can manage on her own."

"I understand why you feel the need to go." Deborah's face tightened. "But I don't think my son's going to take this news so well."

"It will be hard for me, too." Abby smiled through quivering lips. "I'm hoping Lester will understand."

"What will I understand?"

Abby whirled around. She hadn't realized anyone had come into the shop. "You scared me, Lester."

He gave her a quick hug. "I figured you'd hear the bell."

"Guess I wasn't paying attention."

"What were you two discussing?" Lester looked first at his mamm, then back at Abby. "I heard my name, so I suspect it must have somethin' to do with me."

"Actually, it has more to do with my mamm," Abby replied. "I'll tell you about it over lunch, okay?"

"Jah, that's fine." He held up a brown paper sack. "I brought the dessert, like I promised."

"I'll get the lunch I packed, and we can go out back to the picnic table." Abby turned to Lester's mamm. "Can you manage on your own for a while?"

Deborah waved a hand. "Jah, sure. You two go along; things will be fine here."

A few minutes later, Abby took a seat on the bench across from Lester, and they bowed their heads. When they'd finished their silent prayer, Abby reached inside her wicker basket and pulled out the meal she had provided—cold golden-fried chicken, tangy coleslaw, baked beans, and fluffy buttermilk biscuits.

"What were you gonna tell me about your mamm?" Lester asked around a mouthful of chicken.

"She's having a difficult pregnancy and will probably have to close her quilt shop so she can stay home and rest."

"Sorry to hear that."

Abby clutched her napkin, rolling it into a tight ball. "I've—uh—I think—I mean—" She paused and moistened her lips. Then, gathering up her courage, she began again. "I've decided that I should go to Pennsylvania to help out, and your mamm's agreed to run my quilt shop while I'm gone." There, it felt better to have gotten that out.

Lester's pale eyebrows squeezed together, and his mouth drooped at the corners. "You're leavin' me, Abby?"

She touched his arm. "It'll only be temporary. I'll be back

soon after the boppli is born."

"But how are we gonna plan our wedding if you're not around?"

"We can do it through letters. And if we need to talk, we can call each other. You know, I have a phone here at the shop now, and since Caleb and Naomi took over the general store in Paradise, they've put one in as well."

Lester didn't look the least bit convinced, but he made no comment.

Abby prayed for the right words that would help Lester understand. "I'll be back in plenty of time for the wedding."

"But the boppli's not due until October. That's four and a half months away."

"I wouldn't go so soon if I didn't think it was important for me to be with Mom right now. I'll not only be running her quilt shop, but I'll be at the house when I'm not working to make sure everything's going okay and that Mom's doing as the doctor says."

Lester's expression softened some. "I know you'll be doin' a good thing by goin' to help out, but I'll surely miss you."

"I'll miss you, too," she said, blinking against the tears clinging to her lashes.

Lester leaned forward, like he was about to kiss her, but a blaring siren sounded in the distance, and he pulled back. "Sounds like a fire truck."

Abby sniffed the air. "I smell smoke. Sure hope it's nothing serious."

"Think I'll run around front and have a look-see." Lester jumped up and disappeared around the side of the building.

"Whenever anything out of the ordinary happens, why is it that men always have to see what's going on?" Abby muttered. With an exasperated sigh, she rose to her feet and followed him.

Out front on the sidewalk, a group of people had gathered, pointing and chattering about the flames shooting out of the cheese store down the street.

"My friend Joe works there! I've got to see if he's okay," Lester shouted. He dashed away before Abby could stop him.

With her heartbeat matching the rhythm of her footsteps,

Abby raced down the sidewalk toward the burning building. She was panting for breath by the time she reached Lester's side.

One part of the store was engulfed in flames, and smoke bellowed from the roof like a teapot boiling over. Lester's eyes darted back and forth as he took in the situation. "I have to go inside and see if everyone made it out okay."

Abby grabbed hold of his arm. "You can't, Lester. Please. It's too dangerous."

His wild-eyed expression caused Abby to worry that he might ignore her warning and do something foolish. "What if Joe and the other workers are still inside? Someone has to see if they're all right," he argued.

"That's the firemen's job. They're here now, so please let them handle things."

Lester's gaze went to the burning building, then back to Abby. She clutched his arm tighter. "If you went in and something happened to you, I would be overcome with grief. Please, Lester, please stay put."

He nodded slowly. "I guess you're right."

Four firemen rushed into the building, and Abby released the breath she'd been holding. A few seconds later, Joe and several other people who worked at the cheese store emerged from the other side of the building.

"Is everyone out?" one of the firemen shouted.

Joe nodded. "Jah, we're all safe."

Abby breathed a sigh of relief, and she could see by the look on Lester's face that he was equally thankful. He grabbed his friend in a bear hug. "I'm sure glad you're okay. Wouldn't want anything to happen to one of my future wedding attendants." He glanced over at Abby with a questioning look. "That is, if there's still going to be a wedding in November."

She clicked her tongue. "Of course there will be. I'll be back from Pennsylvania in plenty of time."

CHAPTER 7

$\mathcal{N}$aomi arched her back and straightened with a groan. She'd been stocking shelves all morning and was paying the price for working too long without a break. She sank wearily to the stool behind the counter, relieved that Sarah was sleeping in the back room and she could finally have a few minutes to rest. Caleb had gone out to run some errands a few hours ago, saying he would be back before closing time, so she'd been on her own for quite a while.

Naomi glanced at the stack of envelopes piled on one end of the counter and decided now would be a good time to read today's mail. She discovered a letter from her old English friend, Ginny Meyers, who was now Ginny Nelson. Three years ago Ginny had married Chad, the young man who ran the fitness center where Ginny worked when she and Naomi ran off to Portland, Oregon. Ginny's letter said she and Chad had moved from Portland and now lived in Puyallup, Washington, where they'd opened a fitness center they planned to remodel soon.

Naomi smiled. *Ginny always did want her own place of business, and now she's gotten her wish. Too bad she doesn't come home to visit more often. I know her folks still miss her.*

Thinking about Ginny and the time they'd spent in Oregon made Naomi feel sad. Those had been stressful days, when she'd been homesick and thought she couldn't make it through another day. But God had seen her through the rough times. He'd brought Naomi home on Christmas Day, and her family had accepted her unconditionally.

Just the way God accepts wayward sinners, she mused. *He*

never turns anyone away who comes to Him with a repentant heart.

Naomi had just finished reading Ginny's letter when the front door opened and a customer stepped in. At least she'd thought it was a customer, until she looked up and saw Abby Miller standing on the other side of the counter, holding a small black suitcase.

"Abby, what a surprise! What are you doing here? Did Fannie know you were coming?"

Abby set the suitcase on the floor and smiled. "If I'd told her, she would have argued and insisted I not come."

Naomi rushed over to Abby and gave her a hug. "I'm sure Fannie will be happy to have you here for a visit."

"This is more than a visit," Abby said. "After reading Mom's recent letter and learning what the doctor said about her needing to rest more, I decided to take over her quilt shop until she's had the boppli and is ready to return to work."

Naomi's mouth fell open. "Why would you do that when you have your own place of business to run?"

Abby released a yawn as she leaned on the counter. She was tired from the long bus ride and hadn't slept well in the uncomfortable seat. She'd had another one of her frightening dreams, which hadn't helped, either. "I couldn't stay in Ohio, knowing Mom would likely have to close her shop here."

"That's so nice of you, Abby. I'm sorry to say it, but I'm not up to running both the store and the quilt shop. It'll be all I can do to keep helping Caleb until my own boppli is born." Naomi thumped her protruding stomach.

"I understand. How are you feeling? Are you doin' okay?"

"Jah. I'm healthy as a mule, but feeling awful top heavy these days. It's gettin' to where I can barely bend over." She leaned over as far as she could to demonstrate.

Abby offered her a sympathetic smile. "And how's little Sarah? Is she excited about becoming a big sister?"

"I think so, although I'm not sure she fully understands that a boppli's comin'."

"Your kinner will only be two years apart, so I'm sure she'll adjust real well."

"Probably so."

"Would you and Caleb be able to give me a ride to Abraham and Mom's place on your way home from work today?" Abby asked.

"I don't see why not. Caleb's running some errands, but he should be back soon. Then we can close the store early and head out to their place. I'm sure Fannie will be thrilled to see you."

Abby grinned. "I'm anxious to see her as well."

Fannie shifted, trying to find a comfortable position on the sofa. Only a few days ago she'd been given orders from the doctor to stay off her feet as much as possible. Already she felt as restless as a cat on a hot summer day. If there was only something constructive she could do instead of sitting here wishing she could be at the quilt shop. The only thing useful she'd done all day was knit on the little sweater she was making for the boppli. She patted her stomach and smiled. *The way this babe is growing so quickly, I have to wonder if the child will weigh a ton when he's born.*

"Want me to start supper yet?" Nancy asked, stepping into the living room with a cup of tea, which she held out to Fannie.

"Danki. This is just what I need." Fannie took the offered cup then glanced at the clock on the far wall. "It's not quite five, and I'm sure your daed and brothers will be out in the fields awhile, so there's no hurry gettin' things going in the kitchen."

"Even so, I think I'll start making a tossed salad, and then I'll put some chicken in the oven," Nancy said. "It can stay on warm if they don't come in by six o'clock."

"That sounds fine."

Nancy turned to go, but she'd no more than left the room when Fannie heard the back door open and click shut. She figured it was Mary Ann or Samuel, coming in from their chores, so she settled against the sofa pillows and took a sip of tea.

A few seconds later, she heard voices in the kitchen, followed by footsteps clomping down the hall. When Abby stepped into the living room, along with Caleb, Naomi, and Nancy, who held Sarah in her arms, Fannie nearly dropped her cup. "Abby!

What are you doing here, daughter?"

Abby rushed to Fannie's side, dropped to the sofa, and gave her a hug. "I came as soon as I got your letter."

"My letter?"

"The one saying you had to rest more, and that you would probably have to close the quilt shop."

Fannie's throat clogged with tears, and she couldn't speak.

"I'm here to take over the shop, Mom. And I plan to stay until the boppli's born and you're back on your feet."

"Oh, Abby, you're such an amazing daughter," Fannie said with a catch in her voice. "But, what are you going to do about your quilt shop in Berlin if you stay here and keep my store running?"

Abby smiled. "Lester's mamm and his aunt Clara will be minding the store until I get back."

Fannie was on the verge of telling Abby that her sacrifice wasn't necessary, when Naomi chimed in. "I think you should accept your daughter's offer and be thankful the Lord has provided her help." She touched Caleb's arm and smiled. "I surely appreciate it whenever someone helps me these days."

"That's another reason I need to be here," Abby said with a note of conviction. "When Naomi has her baby, someone will need to help Caleb at the store."

"I think Matthew might be plannin' to do that," Caleb announced. "He told me the other day that he's tired of farming and wants to try something new."

"But who will help Papa and the brothers in the fields?" Nancy asked.

Caleb shrugged. "Guess they'll have to hire someone, 'cause Matthew seems determined to get out of farm work."

Relief spread through Fannie like the warmth of her tea. "The good Lord is workin' things out, and we should rejoice and be glad."

"That's right," they all chorused.

It didn't take Abby long to get her suitcase unpacked and settled into the bedroom that used to be Naomi's when she lived at home. She took a seat on the four-poster bed and glanced around, noting the old wooden dresser on the opposite wall, with a small mirror hanging above it. The room looked similar to her room at home, only here there were dark green shades covering the two windows instead of white curtains. The oval braided throw rug on the hardwood floor was made of beige and brown material, and the Lone Star quilt on the bed was blue and white. If it hadn't been for the ache in Abby's heart from leaving Lester back in Ohio, she would have felt quite comfortable here.

"I think I'll go downstairs and see if there's anything I can do," she murmured.

A few minutes later, Abby found her mamm asleep on the living room couch, so she tiptoed out of the room and went to the kitchen. Nancy stood at the sink peeling potatoes, and Mary Ann was busy setting the table. "Need any help?" she asked the girls.

Nancy smiled. "We've got things well underway for supper, but if you'd like to go outside and bring in the quilts I've got airin' on the fence, that would be a big help."

"Sure, I can do that."

Abby opened the back door and stepped onto the porch. The late afternoon air was still warm, and a chorus of crickets sang to her as she wandered into the yard. She drew in a deep breath, savoring the pleasant aroma of peppermint growing in clumps along the edge of the garden.

The clip-clop of a horse's hooves drew her attention to the road out front. *Things aren't much different here,* she noted as the horse and buggy passed. *The buggies are gray instead of black, and I know some of their church rules are a bit different, but otherwise the Plain life in Lancaster County is pretty much the same as it is in Holmes County where I was born and raised.*

Abby spotted three colorful quilts draped over the split-rail fence that separated Abraham's farm from his son Norman's place. The beauty of the quilts on the fence with the red barn and white house in the distance looked like a picture postcard. Tears sprang to her eyes as she dropped to the grass and studied the striking scene. Abby loved everything about quilts, from the comforting warmth they provided on a cold winter night, to the unexplainable joy of putting one together by hand. Each quilt was unique, whether intricate or simple in pattern, and served a purpose. She had been quilting since she was a young girl and never tired of the tedious work or longed for any other occupation. Quilting was her life, and she couldn't imagine doing anything else.

Abby's attention was diverted when she heard a woman shouting, "Katie! Katie! Where are you, daughter?"

Smoothing the wrinkles in her long, green dress, Abby stood and turned around. A young Amish woman hurried up the driveway, frantically waving her hands. "Have you seen my little girl? She was playing in the yard while I fixed supper, and when I went outside to get her, she had disappeared."

Abby's heart clenched at the thought of a child who might have wandered onto the road, where cars often went much faster than they should. "I've only been out here a short time," she replied, "and I haven't seen any children playing nearby."

"I don't believe I know you," the woman said, tipping her head toward Abby.

"I'm Abby Miller—Fannie's daughter."

"Jah, jah. Your mamm's mentioned you, but I'm new to the community and haven't met you before." She extended her hand. "I'm Irma Hochstetler. My husband, Sam, and I moved here from Indiana a few months ago with our little girl, Katie. Sam's a painter, and he's been workin' for Jacob Weaver. But Sam's not home yet. If he were, he'd be out looking for our little *schtinker*, who likes to wander off." Irma glanced around the yard. "I've caught Katie over here several times, playing in the barn or bothering Mary Ann, so I'm hoping that's where she is now."

"Mary Ann's in the kitchen setting the table for supper," Abby said. "If your daughter did wander over, maybe we should take a look in the barn."

Irma nodded. "That's a good idea."

Abby led the way, and Irma followed. Inside the barn, they called Katie's name and searched in every nook and cranny. Abby was afraid to think of the outcome if the child wasn't found. She knew the little girl's mother was equally frightened, because Irma's voice trembled as she continued to call Katie's name.

"I think we should get some others to help us look," Abby suggested. "Maybe Katie wandered up the road to someone else's farm."

Irma nodded, and tears splashed onto her cheeks. "I'll never forgive myself if anything happens to my daughter. I should have been watchin' her closer—shouldn't have let her play in the yard alone, not even for a few minutes."

Abby gave Irma a reassuring hug, even though she didn't feel so confident right now. What if the child had been kidnapped? Could the same thing have happened to little Katie as happened to Abraham's boy, Zach? "Why don't you go back to your house in case Katie comes home?" she suggested. "I'll run out to the fields and see if I can enlist the help of Abraham and his sons."

Irma's chin quivered. "Jah, I'll appreciate all the help I can get."

As Abby headed into the fields, she sent up a prayer for Katie and one for Zach Fisher. Mom rarely mentioned him in her letters anymore, but she felt sure the boy's family had not forgotten him.

Abby had only made it halfway across the alfalfa field when she saw a small figure zigzagging her way. When she came upon the little blond-haired girl, she knew immediately that it must be Katie Hochstetler.

"Danki, Lord," Abby murmured. At least one of her prayers had been answered, and now she could take the little girl home, gather up the quilts that were on the fence, and return to the house knowing Katie's parents wouldn't have to suffer the way the Fishers had for so many years.

CHAPTER 8

$\mathcal{A}$bby could hardly believe she had been in Pennsylvania a whole month. She supposed the time had swept by so quickly because of her busyness. She had been working at her mother's quilt shop five days a week, and when she wasn't there, she was at home with Mom, making sure everything ran smoothly and offering her assistance whenever it was needed. Each night, Abby fell wearily into bed, often forgetting to pray or read her Bible. She'd been negligent about writing letters to Lester and Deborah, too, which she had been reminded of today when a letter from Lester arrived. With a pang of regret, Abby took a seat on the edge of her bed and reread his note.

> *Dear Abby,*
>
> *It's been almost two weeks since I've heard from you. I hope it's only because you've been busy and not because you've forgotten me. If things slow up at the blacksmith shop, I may catch a bus and come there for a few days. I miss you so much and feel the need to spend time with you. It would be nice to meet Abraham and his family, too.*
>
> *Mom says she hasn't heard from you in a while, either. She wanted me to tell you that everything is going well at the quilt shop. Lately, there have been a lot of tourists in town, but that's pretty normal for summertime, I suppose.*
>
> *Please write soon, and tell your mamm I'm prayin' for her and hope she's doin' okay. Mom says she's prayin', too.*
>
> *Always yours,*
> *Lester*

Abby hurried to her dresser and retrieved her writing paper and a pen. Tonight she would write Lester a letter, no matter how tired she felt. She loved Lester with all her heart and didn't want him to think she'd forgotten him.

She had just finished her letter to Lester and sealed the envelope when someone rapped on the door. "Abby, are you still awake?"

"Jah. Please, come in."

The door opened and Nancy entered the room, wearing a white cotton nightgown that brushed her slender ankles. The girl's golden brown hair hung loosely down her back, and its shiny luster offered proof that it had recently been brushed. "I hope I'm not disturbin' you, but I'd like to talk awhile, if it's all right."

Abby patted the edge of her bed. "Come have a seat, and tell me what's on your mind."

Nancy sat down with a groan. "It's Fannie's cousin."

"Edna?"

"Jah."

"What about her? Is Edna sick or something?"

"No, but she sure is bossy. The woman's always tellin' me what to do and complainin' because I don't do things exactly the way she wants 'em done." Nancy's forehead wrinkled. "Things were goin' along fine until she started coming over to help out. Can't you send her away, Abby?"

Abby knew her young stepsister was quite capable and probably felt like a failure in Edna's eyes. Even though she didn't know her mother's cousin well, from what Mom had said, she knew Edna was pleasant and liked to kid around. Maybe she was only funning with Nancy when she said or did certain things. The girl might be overly sensitive in that regard.

Abby took Nancy's hand and gave it a gentle squeeze. "It's possible that Edna doesn't think you're incompetent. Maybe she's just teasing when she makes little irritating comments."

Nancy pursed her lips. "Why would she do that? Can't she see how hard I work? Doesn't she realize I'm doin' the best I can?"

"I'm sure she does. My advice is to simply ignore Cousin Edna's remarks."

"You think if I didn't try to stand up for myself, things would go better?"

Ah, so that was the problem. Everything Edna said to Nancy was going against the grain, and the girl defended herself in return.

"Edna is older and wiser than you, Nancy," Abby said. "You've been taught to show consideration for your elders, isn't that right?"

Nancy's reply was a quick nod.

"Even if Edna's comments aren't meant in jest, you should never argue with her; it's not the respectful thing to do."

"You're right. I'm sorry."

"I think it's Edna you should apologize to, don't you?"

"Jah. I'll do that when she shows up tomorrow."

"And you'll try harder to ignore the things she says that get under your skin?"

"Uh-huh."

Abby gave her stepsister a hug. "I'm proud of you. Being willing to apologize shows how mature you've become."

"Danki." Nancy stood and started for the door, but turned back around. "Abby?"

"What is it?"

"I know you'll have to return to Ohio after the boppli comes, but if I had my way, you'd stay with us forever."

Abby smiled, wishing it were possible to be in two places at once. *At least I'll sleep well tonight,* she mused. *I've written Lester a letter and had a heart-to-heart talk with Nancy. Tomorrow will be a good day.*

A mysterious dark cloud hovered over Abby Miller's bed, pressing on her from all sides. Blinking against stinging tears, she drew in a ragged breath. An invisible hand pushed against her face, and she flung her covers aside. "*Ich kann nimmi schnaufe*—I can no longer breathe!"

Meow. Meow. Somewhere in the distance, Abby heard the pathetic cry and knew she must save the poor kitten. With a panicked sob, she rolled out of bed, but the minute her bare feet touched the floor she shrank back from the intense heat. A paralyzing fear wrapped its arms around Abby, threatening to strip away her sanity. She lifted her hands to her face and rubbed her eyes, forcing them to focus. "Where are you, kitty? I'm coming, kitty."

Suddenly, she realized that her room was engulfed in flames—lapping at the curtains, snapping, crackling, consuming everything in sight. As the smoky haze grew thicker and the fire became an inferno, Abby grabbed the Lone Star quilt off her bed and covered her head. Coughing, choking, gasping on the acrid smoke, she stumbled and staggered toward the door. "*Feier*—fire! Somebody, please help me save the kitten!"

Abby's eyes flew open as she sucked in a shallow breath. She was drenched in sweat, and her throat felt raw, as though she'd been screaming. She glanced around the room and, seeing everything was as it should be, realized she had only been dreaming. "It was that same horrible dream about a fire," she moaned.

Abby clambered out of bed and raced over to the window. She lifted the dark shade and jerked the window open, breathing deeply of the early morning air. The sun peeked over the horizon, its delicate shades of pink graduating into a fiery red. A burst of air swept suddenly into the room, and she shivered. "Oh, Lord, why do I continue to have that awful dream?"

Abraham stood outside the barn door, stretching his arms over his head and suppressing a yawn. He'd lain awake into the wee hours last night worrying about Fannie. Most days she had dark circles under her eyes, and her ankles were still slightly puffy, even though she had been following the doctor's orders and resting much of the time. He had heard of women who developed toxemia during their pregnancy and knew it could be serious. When he'd mentioned his concerns to Fannie last night, she'd made light of it, saying she had cut salt out of her diet and was sure that would help the swelling.

"If it doesn't, I'm takin' her back to the doctor," Abraham mumbled.

"What was that, Papa?" Matthew asked as he led one of their mules out of the barn.

Abraham's face heated. "Nothin'. I was talkin' to myself."

"You said something about going to the doctor. Does Fannie have another appointment today?"

"No, but I'll be takin' her in if she don't look better in a few days."

"Is she lookin' poorly?"

Abraham leaned against the side of the barn and groaned. "Haven't ya noticed the dark circles under her eyes?"

Matthew removed his straw hat and fanned his face with it a couple of times. "Can't say that I have, but then I've had a lot of things on my mind lately."

"Yeah, like quittin' work on the farm," Abraham grumbled. "If you hate field work so much, how come you never said anything before?"

"I don't hate it, Papa. To tell you the truth, until lately I didn't know I wanted to do something else."

"You think it could be runnin' a store?"

"Not necessarily, but if I try workin' there after Naomi has her baby, it might give me a better idea of what I want to be doing."

"*Humph!* You sure this change of attitude doesn't have more to do with some pretty face than it does with you not wantin' to farm?"

Matthew's ears turned pink, and he stared at the ground. "I don't know what you're talkin' about."

"Who, not what," Abraham corrected.

Matthew made no reply, just stood there making little swirls in the dirt with the toe of his boot.

"I've seen the way you look at Abby when you think no one's watchin'. You wouldn't have a crush on her now, would ya, son?"

" 'Course not. She's betrothed to some fellow in Ohio."

Matthew slapped his hat back on his head. "Guess I'd best get the other mule out, or we'll be late gettin' out to the fields."

"Where are Jake and Norman? How come they're not here helpin'?" Abraham asked.

"Norman hasn't shown up yet, and Jake had to drive Mary Ann and Samuel to school because they spent so much time arguing this morning, it made them late."

Matthew disappeared into the barn, and Abraham frowned. *Guess I'll need to have a little talk with my two youngest tonight.*

A buggy rolled into the yard, drawing Abraham's attention aside. He smiled and waved when he realized it was his good friend, Jacob Weaver.

"What are you doin' out so early?" he asked as Jacob stepped down from his buggy.

"I'm on my way to the buggy shop to see if the new rig I ordered has been finished yet."

The mention of the buggy shop sent Abraham's mind whizzing back to the past. It had been a sad day when Caleb had to give up buggy making because of his injury. His two younger brothers were running the place now, having become quite capable under Caleb's tutelage. Caleb seemed content to run the general store, which he had purchased from Abraham. He could do most things there with only one good hand, and the change of occupations had allowed him to marry Abraham's daughter. Everything had worked out for the best. At least that's the way Abraham saw it.

"Looks like you're headin' to the fields," Jacob said.

"Jah. Just waitin' for Matthew to bring the other mule out."

As if on cue, Matthew showed up, leading Bossy, their most headstrong mule. "Had a hard time gettin' her out of the stall," he complained. "I think she had her mind set on stayin' in the barn today."

Jacob chuckled. "Always did prefer working with horses."

"Horses can be a mite stubborn, too," Abraham put in. "Fact is, I've had some that were just plain *mehne.*"

"Jah. I've encountered a couple of mean ones over the years," his friend agreed.

"Papa, if you and Jacob want to jaw awhile, I'll head out to the fields with these two." Matthew nodded at Bossy and Barney.

"Sure you don't mind?" Truthfully, Abraham did want the chance to speak with Jacob a few minutes. His friend was always full of good advice, and if anyone could get Abraham thinking straight or help strengthen his faith, it was Jacob.

"Naw. We'll be fine, and Norman and Jake should be along shortly." Matthew grabbed hold of the mules' bridles and led them away.

"Want to sit a spell?" Abraham motioned to a couple of old barrels sitting near the barn.

Jacob nodded. "Jah, sounds good."

Once they were seated, Abraham decided to share his concerns about Fannie. "I'm glad you stopped by, Jacob, because I need to talk."

"Figured as much." Jacob grinned. "Felt a little nudge from the Lord as I was passing by your place this morning. Thought I should drop over and see how things are with you."

"Things are fine with me. It's Fannie I'm worried about."

Jacob's bushy eyebrows lifted. "What's the trouble?"

Abraham related his concerns about Fannie's pregnancy, and ended it by saying, "I want to believe God will bring her through this in good shape and that our boppli will be born healthy, but I've got a nagging feeling that something's not right." He reached under his straw hat and rubbed the side of his head. "I haven't shared this with anyone, but I'm afraid something bad is going to happen to our family again." He paused and moistened his lips. "Don't think I could stand it if I lost this wife or the child she's carrying."

Jacob sat there with his hands clasped in his lap, staring at the ground like he was mulling things over. After a few moments, he spoke. "In the book of Psalms, David went through many tribulations. Yet in chapter 31, verse 14, he was able to say this to God: 'But I trusted in thee, O LORD: I said, Thou art my God.'"

Abraham nodded. "I know I need to have more faith and learn to put my trust in God, but that's easier said than done. Especially when things ain't lookin' so good."

"Which is why you should pray every day and read God's Word. That's how my faith has been strengthened." Jacob clasped Abraham's shoulder. "Take one day at a time, my friend. Commit your wife and unborn child to God and enjoy each moment you have with your family. None of us knows when our time will come or what the future holds."

Abraham blew out his breath. "You're right about that. If I'd known my boy was gonna be kidnapped, I'd have stayed home from the store that day and watched his every move." He glanced over at Jacob and smiled. "I appreciate your friendship more than you know."

"And I appreciate yours," his friend said with a nod.

⸻

"Hope you don't mind me cleanin' the living room while you rest," Nancy said to Fannie, who reclined on the sofa.

"No, no, not at all," Fannie replied from her place on the sofa. "It is hard for me to lie here and watch you work, though."

Nancy shrugged. "It's nice to have your company. Edna will probably be here soon, then I'll have to let the two of you visit while I get some bakin' done."

"*Humph!*" Fannie scoffed. "Some company I am these days."

"Just because you're not able to get up and work doesn't mean you're not good company. I've always enjoyed visiting with you and hearing stories from when you were a girl." Nancy gave the broom a couple sweeps in front of the rocking chair, and then moved over to the couch.

"It has been fun doing some reminiscing," Fannie said with a smile.

Nancy swept under the sofa and Fannie cringed at the dust balls clinging to the broom. *I used to keep the house spotless, but Nancy probably didn't think to clean under there before.*

"Hey, what's this?" Nancy bent down and picked up an object, which she held out to Fannie in the palm of her hand.

"Looks like a wooden block."

Nancy squinted, and her forehead creased. "Why, I haven't seen this in some time. Must have been stuck under the couch."

"Whose block is it?" Fannie asked.

"It was Zach's." Nancy closed her fingers around it and slowly shook her head. "We'd best not let Papa see this."

Fannie swallowed around the lump in her throat. Was Abraham still grieving for his lost son? He rarely spoke of Zach anymore. Maybe talking about his missing boy brought back too many painful memories. Fannie figured her husband would always miss Zach, and so would the rest of the family. She squeezed her eyes shut. *Oh, Lord, let this child I'm carrying heal any remaining pain in Abraham's heart.*

CHAPTER 9

*I*f you're ready for lunch, maybe we can take our noon break together today."

Abby looked up from her quilting project and smiled at Naomi, who stood inside the door that separated their store from Mom's quilt shop. "Were you planning to go out or eat in?"

"Since Sarah's sleeping and things are quiet in the store at the moment, Caleb said it would be okay if you and I went out someplace to eat," Naomi replied.

"That's fine with me. I could use some fresh air to help wake me up."

"Didn't you sleep well last night?"

Abby set her sewing aside and shook her head. "I had a bad dream and couldn't get back to sleep when it woke me."

"Sorry to hear that. Some dreams can make you feel pretty rung out."

"Jah." Abby was tempted to reveal the details of her reoccurring dream, but she didn't want to bother her stepsister with it. Naomi had enough to deal with, having so much work to do at the store and another boppli coming in a few months.

"Should we go to lunch now?" Naomi asked.

"Jah, sure."

"We shouldn't be too long," Naomi said when Caleb took her place behind the counter.

He gave her arm a squeeze. "No problem; take your time."

Abby and Naomi were preparing to leave the store when the door swung open. A handsome Amish man, his wavy blond hair peeking out from under his straw hat, stepped into the store carrying a small suitcase.

Abby's mouth dropped open. "Lester! What are you doing here?"

"Came to see you."

When he gave her a lopsided grin and reached for her hand, the faint smell of peppermint tickled her nose. She spied two pieces of candy sticking out of his shirt pocket. "I—I had no idea you were coming." She stared up at him in disbelief.

"Wanted it to be a surprise."

"And what a surprise it is. Jah, for certain sure." Then, remembering her manners, Abby introduced Lester to Naomi and Caleb.

"It's nice to meet you, Lester," Naomi said. "We've heard a lot about you."

Caleb's head bobbed up and down. "Jah, Abby's mentioned you plenty of times."

Abby felt the heat of a blush, but she couldn't deny it. She had missed Lester so much and often talked about the fun things they'd done during their courtship. She and Naomi had also discussed her upcoming wedding and how the Fisher family planned to go to Ohio to witness the ceremony in November.

"Abby and I were about to head out for some lunch," Naomi commented. "But now that Lester's here, I think it should be him and Abby going instead of me."

"Maybe you and Caleb can join us," Lester suggested.

Caleb nodded toward the back of the store. "Our little girl is sleepin' in the other room, so I'd better stay put. My wife can go with you, though."

Naomi shook her head. "I'll stay here, and Caleb and I can eat the lunch I packed this morning."

Abby hesitated. "Are you sure you don't mind?"

"Not at all. I'll keep an eye on the quilt shop while you're gone."

"Danki."

Lester pushed his suitcase off to one side, opened the front door, then motioned for Abby to step out first.

"No need to hurry back," Naomi called.

A short time later, Abby and Lester sat at a corner table in the cozy restaurant down the street. Abby still couldn't believe he was here, and she just sat there staring at him.

He stared back, looking pleased as a child with a new toy.

"How long are you here for, and how'd you manage to get away from the blacksmith shop to make this trip?" she asked, pulling her gaze from his handsome face to glance at the menu lying before her.

"Probably be here a couple of days. I hired on another man a few weeks ago, so I'm sure my two helpers can handle things while I'm gone."

Abby still couldn't believe he'd come all this way just to spend a few days with her.

"I've missed you, Abby." Lester's voice had a soft quality about it, yet he spoke with assurance, and it gladdened her heart.

"I've missed you, too." She smiled. "How are things in Holmes County these days?"

"Fine. Mom sends her love and said to tell you everything's goin' great at the quilt shop."

"I'm pleased to hear it. How are Lena and Harold?"

"Last I heard, Lena was feelin' some better, but Harold still insists she stay home and not work too hard." Lester's eyebrows suddenly drew together, a stark contrast from his usual smiling face. "I wish I could speed up the hands of time and get that bruder or *schweschder* of yours born so you can come back to Ohio."

Abby took a sip from her glass of water as a film of tears obscured her vision. "The time will go quickly, you'll see."

He reached across the table and took her hand, making tiny circular motions with his rough fingertips. "It hasn't so far. Every day since you left Berlin has seemed to drag by for me."

She nodded in understanding, because she felt the same way. "This coming Sunday is an off-Sunday from church, and there's going to be a picnic and softball game over at the Beechys' place. I hope you can stay that long, because I know how much you like to play ball."

Lester let go of her hand and drummed his fingers along

the edge of the table. "Let's see now. . . Today's Thursday, so if I hang around 'til Sunday and catch an early bus on Monday, that should work out fine and dandy. I told my mamm and the fellows at work I'd probably be gone 'til early next week."

"I'll see if you can stay with Caleb and Naomi while you're here. They've got plenty of room at their place."

Lester nodded, and she was relieved that his smile had returned. "I'll stay wherever you say, just as long as I get to spend time with you," he said.

"I'll see that you do," she whispered as the waitress came to take their order.

With a weary sigh, Linda crawled onto her bed and stretched out in the middle. After lunch she'd put Jimmy down for a nap and had decided to take one herself. She was exhausted and couldn't believe she'd let Beth talk her into helping with crafts at vacation Bible school this week. However, it had been kind of fun.

She jabbed her pillow a couple of times, trying to find a more comfortable position, then rolled onto her side. Her gaze came to rest on the Amish quilt covering their bed, and she thought about the morning they had visited a quaint little quilt shop outside of Berlin, Ohio, over five years ago.

I've never understood why Jim doesn't have any interest in visiting Amish country again. I found it to be so fascinating. Her fingers traced the uniform, almost perfect hand stitches on the blue and white quilt done in the Lone Star pattern. *If I had more patience and better sewing skills, I might try my hand at quilting.*

She flipped onto her other side. *I wish I could convince Jim to take us to Ohio again. I'm sure Jimmy would enjoy the trip, and I know Jim's folks would love to have us visit.*

In an attempt to shrug away her irritation, Linda closed her eyes and pictured the beautiful Amish homes they'd seen when they were back east. Most were neat, orderly, and devoid of weeds in their bountiful gardens.

"Amish country," she murmured. "Where life is slower, and

the men come home to their families after work every night."

She squeezed her eyes tighter to keep threatening tears from escaping. It was pointless to wallow in self-pity. She'd done it too much, and where had it gotten her? Short of a miracle, Jim would probably never be the kind of husband she needed. The best thing to do was to keep busy and try not to dwell on their artificial marriage.

Maybe I should take Beth's suggestion and start taking Jimmy to Sunday school. We'd be around people, and it would be better than watching Jim snooze every Sunday until noon or sit in his recliner, focused on the TV.

Linda exhaled, as the need for sleep took over. *Jim needs church, too. He needs. . .*

Jim entered the house through the garage door. Except for the steady hum of the refrigerator, everything was quiet. He slipped off his work boots and left them sitting by the door, then sauntered across the kitchen to get a drink of water. Today had gone well. They'd finished painting the outside of a newly remodeled fitness center, and the general contractor had praised Jim's work and said he was impressed with how quickly his paint crew had finished the job.

Jim opened a cupboard door and grabbed a glass. "Wonder if there's any iced tea in the refrigerator? That would taste better than water."

After filling his glass with cold tea, Jim grabbed a handful of cookies from the ceramic jar on top of the china hutch then dropped into a chair at the table. It was nice to come home to a quiet house for a change. Usually Jimmy had the TV blaring or ran around the house making weird noises.

He shook his head. *That kid's imagination can sure run wild. One minute, he's a police car with a blaring siren, and the next, he's some silly ice cream truck. And then there's Linda. If she's not nagging me to fix something, she's asking me to take her somewhere. It's ridiculous that she won't drive. It's been years since she was involved in that little fender bender, and she wasn't even hurt.*

Jim bit off a hunk of peanut butter cookie and washed it down with a gulp of iced tea. He glanced at the clock. *I wonder if Linda and Jimmy are at the park. She's usually in the kitchen by now, starting dinner.*

"Oh, you're home," came a sleepy voice from the doorway.

Jim turned his head. Linda stood there, long blond hair in disarray and cheeks slightly pink. In the early days of their marriage he would have been pleased to see her. Now, he merely tried to be polite enough to avoid a confrontation.

"Have you been sleeping?" he asked.

She nodded. "I put Jimmy down for a nap after lunch and decided to take one, too. I didn't expect to sleep so late, though."

"What'd you do all day that made you so tired?"

Linda joined him at the table. "I've been helping with crafts at Bible school this week, remember?"

He grabbed another cookie. "Oh, yeah, that."

"You don't have to sound so disapproving. Jimmy's having fun, and he's with other children. That should make you happy."

Her tone was mocking, and it only fueled Jim's irritation. "Don't get smart, Linda."

"I wasn't trying to be."

"Yeah, right."

She sighed deeply. "Why is it that every time I try to have a sensible conversation with you, it ends up in an argument?"

He shrugged. "Who's arguing?"

No reply.

"Since you've slept the afternoon away, when do you plan to have dinner on the table?"

"We're having sandwiches tonight, so it won't take long." She toyed with a piece of her hair but made no move to get up. "Uh, Jim, I was wondering. . ."

He reached for his glass, which was almost empty. "What were you wondering?"

"Allen's mother invited Jimmy and me to come to Sunday school this week, and I was hoping we could go as a family."

Jim's forehead wrinkled. "You want me to go to Sunday school?"

She nodded. "I thought it would be something we could all do together."

He pushed away from the table and stood. "Count me out."

"Why?"

"Church is for weak people who are looking for something to make them feel better. It's a crutch, and if I needed one of those, I would rent a pair from Keller's Medical Supply."

"You don't have to be sarcastic."

He marched across the room and set his glass in the sink. "If you want to take Jimmy to Sunday school, I won't stop you, but it's not likely I'll step foot inside a church building unless it's for somebody's wedding or a funeral."

Jim glanced over his shoulder to gauge Linda's reaction. Her chin quivered as she stared at the table. He didn't care. She wasn't going to manipulate him with her tears or whining. She'd done that too many times in the past, and ever since the day he'd made up his mind to "put the hammer down," he'd been a lot happier.

Well, maybe not happier, but at least Linda knows who's in charge around here.

CHAPTER 10

$\mathcal{A}$bby reclined on the grass beside Nancy and watched the baseball game in progress. Lester had just made a homerun, and everyone cheered. She was glad the men in Abraham's family had made him feel welcome.

"Too bad Lester doesn't move to Lancaster County," Nancy said. "Then you could stay here for good."

Abby smiled. "It's nice to know you'd like me to stay."

"You're my big sister now, and I enjoy your company."

"Danki. I enjoy being with you, too."

Nancy sniffed. "Sure wish I could help at the quilt shop. I get tired of stayin' home all the time and doing nothing but housework and cooking."

Abby knew Nancy worked hard and rarely went anywhere for fun. "Maybe one day when Cousin Edna comes to help Mom you can drive into town and I'll take you out to lunch."

Nancy's green eyes danced with enthusiasm. "I'd like that."

Abby smiled. "I've always wanted a sweet sister like you."

Nancy shook her head. "It's you who's the sweet one. Everyone always says I'm stubborn and bossy."

Before Abby could comment, she heard a loud *smack*, followed by a groan. Her gaze went to the ball field, and she was shocked to see Lester lying on the ground, with Matthew and several others standing over him. She scrambled to her feet and raced over to the scene.

"Lester, are you all right?"

"Ball. Hit. Stomach," he gasped.

She looked up at Matthew. "Did you see it happen?"

He nodded. "It was my fault. Lester was up to bat and I got a little overanxious when I pitched the ball. Sure didn't mean to take him out."

Lester coughed and struggled to sit up. "I'm okay. Just knocked the wind out of me, is all."

Abby held her hand out to him.

"That's what I get for watching my *aldi* instead of the ball," he said, with a red-faced grin.

"That'll teach you not to make eyes at your girlfriend when you're supposed to be playin' a serious game of baseball," Caleb teased.

Jake chuckled. "As if you never made eyes at my sister when you two were courtin'."

"Are you sure you're not hurt?" Abby asked as she and Lester moved to the sidelines and took a seat on the grass.

"The only thing banged up is my pride," he replied with a grunt.

"It wasn't your fault Matthew's aim was off." Abby took a deep breath to settle her nerves. It had frightened her to see him lying on the ground like that. What if he'd been seriously injured? What if. . .

Lester leaned closer, and his warm breath tickled her ear. "Don't look so worried. I'm fine."

"I couldn't stand it if anything ever happened to you."

He touched the side of her face with his thumb. "You worry too much, Abby. I ain't goin' nowhere."

"Except back home. You're still leaving Monday morning, right?"

He nodded. "But it won't be long 'til your mamm has that boppli, then you'll be comin' home to Ohio." He caressed her chin, and Abby's skin turned to gooseflesh. She could hardly wait until November when she would become Lester's Abby.

⌒

"Sure is muggy tonight," Fannie said, squirming restlessly, while she tried to find a comfortable position on the porch swing. At least the swelling in her legs had gone down, and she felt some better. "It wonders me so that anyone would want to play ball in this heat."

Abraham chuckled. "When I was a young man I could do most anything in the hot weather. Now, by midday I'm feelin' ready for a cold shower and a tall glass of iced tea."

She glanced over at him with sudden concern. "You doin' okay in the fields?"

"Everything's fine."

"Do you ever wish you'd kept running the store?"

He nuzzled her neck. "Only when I'm missin' you."

She giggled, enjoying his attention and feeling like a schoolgirl again. "Need I remind you that I'm not at the quilt shop anymore? So, if you really find yourself missin' me, you can always take a break and come up to the house."

Abraham jiggled his bushy eyebrows. "Now there's a pleasant thought, and I just might do it more often." His brows drew together. " 'Course once Naomi has her boppli, and Matthew leaves the farm to help at the store, I'll be shorthanded in the fields. Gettin' away for breaks will be harder then."

"I'm sure you can find someone to fill in for Matthew."

"Maybe so, but what if he decides to give up farmin' altogether?"

She squeezed his arm gently. "You'll accept his decision and be glad he's found something he likes to do, same as you've done."

"Jah." Abraham sat there several seconds as he rested his hand on Fannie's stomach. Suddenly, he pulled back like he'd been stung by a bee. *"Was in der welt?"*

"What in the world, what?"

"Can't ya feel that?"

"Feel what?"

"The boppli kickin'."

Fannie chuckled. "Oh, sure. I feel it often these days. It's normal for a baby to kick, ya know."

"That wasn't just any old kick. It felt like a whole baseball team trompin' around in your belly."

She nodded. "I think our little guy likes to kick with his feet on one side of my stomach and punch me with his fists on the other side."

"Hope that don't mean he's gonna be a rambunctious one."

"If he is, we'll handle it, jah?"

"Sure. Always have with my other kinner."

"I know you're countin' on a boy, Abraham, but what if it's a girl instead?"

He kissed her cheek. "I'll love our child no matter if it's a *bu* or a *maedel*."

"I'm glad to hear that, because we sure can't send it back."

Abraham chortled. "You're such a hoot. I surely do love you, Fannie Mae."

"And I love you."

His face sobered. "For a while I was worried about your health, and the boppli's, too, but I finally committed things to God and decided to put my trust in Him."

She gave his hand a gentle squeeze. "Same here. I've learned that worry never solves anything. Fact is, it only makes one feel miserable."

Abraham pulled Fannie into his arms. "You're sure smart, ya know that?"

She smiled. "I must be, 'cause I was wise enough to marry you."

⁓

Abby had been home from the Beechys' for half an hour, and since she didn't feel ready for bed yet, she took a seat in one of the wicker chairs on the front porch to watch the sun set and enjoy the fireflies as they performed their nightly dance. It was still too warm for sleeping, and she just wanted to sit here and think about Lester. After the game and time of refreshments, he had borrowed Caleb's buggy and given her a ride home. Tomorrow would be their last day together until she returned to Ohio in early November.

Abby stood. *Maybe I'll take a walk to the barn and see how Callie's new kittens are doing.* She strolled through the yard, and a ray of light greeted her when she opened the barn door. She'd thought everyone in the family had gone to bed, but someone must be inside.

She moved across the straw-covered floor until she came to the source of light. Matthew was inside one of the stalls, grooming his buggy horse. "Sorry to disturb you," she said. "I didn't realize you were out here."

He held up the currycomb. "Thought I'd spend a little extra time on Bonnie tonight. And you're not disturbing me at all."

She smiled. "What made you choose that name for the horse?"

"Actually, it was Jake's idea, and I went along with it so he'd quit buggin' me."

"There's an English woman who comes into my quilt shop back home whose name is Bonnie."

Matthew chuckled. "This horse likes to prance around, and Jake said she looks like one of them Irish dancers he's seen on the neighbor's television set. He thought Bonnie was a good Irish name for her."

Abby rested her hands on the stall door. "I'm surprised your daed allows Jake to watch TV. Is he still going through his *rumspringa?*"

"I think my younger brother's been going through his running-around years since he was born." Matthew patted Bonnie's flanks. "One of these days he'll settle down and get baptized into the church. Maybe he'll find a woman desperate enough to marry him, too."

Abby smiled. "How come you're not married yet? And don't tell me it's because you haven't found a woman that desperate."

He snickered. "Haven't found the right one, that's all."

"I knew Lester was the man for me after our first date."

He lifted his head and gave her a curious look. "You could tell so soon?"

"Jah."

While Matthew continued to groom the horse, Abby glanced around the barn. She didn't see any sign of Callie or her kittens. They'd been inside a small wooden box the last time she was here, but now the box was empty. "Do you know what happened to the mama cat and her brood?"

Matthew shrugged. "Beats me. She probably got tired of Mary Ann and Samuel messin' with 'em and carted the kittens off to some other spot."

"That could be." Abby sighed. "That's why I came out here. . .to check on the kittens."

"Didn't figure you'd come out just to chew the fat with me."

Her only response was a self-conscious giggle. She was glad Matthew was her stepbrother. He was different than Harold, who hardly ever kidded around. Of course, Abby's brother had many other fine qualities.

"Don't believe I've told you this before, but I think it was real nice of you to leave your shop in Berlin and come here to help Fannie. You're a kind and caring woman, just like your mamm."

Abby's throat constricted. "I love Mom very much and would do anything I could to help her."

"Your boyfriend seems like a real nice fellow," he said, changing the subject.

"Jah, Lester has many fine qualities."

"Hope he knows how lucky he is to be gettin' someone as *wunderbaar* as you."

Abby lowered her lashes as heat flooded her face. "Danki for the kind words, Matthew, but I believe I'm the lucky one."

CHAPTER 11

On the last day of July, Naomi stepped out of the bathroom at the back of their store. "The boppli's coming, so you'd better find us a ride to the hospital," she whispered to Caleb.

He looked stunned. "You're kidding?"

"I'm not."

"But I thought you said your due date wasn't until August 15."

"Babies don't read calendars, Caleb, and this little one's comin' sooner than expected, so we'd better hurry."

"Have you been having contractions all morning and not said anything until now?"

"Just some aching in my lower back, but now my water's broke, and I'm feeling more pain."

"We'd better notify Abby so she can keep an eye on the store, as well as our sleeping daughter," Caleb said, moving toward the adjoining quilt shop.

"Maybe we should close the store and take Sarah home so your mamm can watch her."

He shook his head. "I'm expecting a supply of kerosene lamps, and if no one's here, the UPS man won't leave the box. Besides, driving Sarah home would take too much time."

Naomi leaned against the edge of the counter, as a painful contraction shot through her middle. "Tell Abby what's going on, then ask if she's willing to watch Sarah and take her to my daed's after work."

"Okay." Caleb rushed into the other room, and a few moments later he returned with Abby at his side.

"Caleb says you've gone into labor," she said with a look of concern. "Do you want me to call an ambulance?"

"Maybe we should," Caleb agreed. "That would get us to the hospital much quicker."

"And it would cost a lot of money." Naomi shook her head. "Just go to the gift shop down the street and see if Mary Richards is free to drive us."

Caleb's eyebrows drew together. "I don't know, Naomi—"

"I'll be fine. You'll see." She waved her hand. "Now *dummle*—hurry!"

Without another word, he gave her a quick hug and rushed out the door.

Abby paced in front of the store window. It had been two hours since Caleb and Naomi had left for the hospital in Mary Richards' car. They'd promised to send word as soon as the baby was born, but that could be hours yet. *If I'm this anxious over Naomi having her baby, I can only imagine how I'll feel when Mom's time comes.*

Abby was glad her mother had agreed to have the baby at the hospital in Lancaster rather than hiring a midwife like some Amish women chose to do. At least they would have plenty of doctors and emergency equipment available should a problem arise.

If I'm not mistaken, Mom had a doctor's appointment today. Seems she said the doctor planned to do an ultrasound, and I'm anxious to know how that turned out. Abby frowned. *I hope there's not a problem with her pregnancy.*

Abby's thoughts were halted when the front door opened and Matthew walked in. "I heard you were here by yourself and figured you could use some help." He removed his straw hat and hung it on a wall peg by the door.

"News sure travels fast. How'd you know Caleb took Naomi to the hospital?"

"Caleb called his brothers at the buggy shop, and Andy drove over to our place to give us the word."

Abby was about to comment, when she heard a muffled cry coming from the back of the room. "That must be Sarah. Can you mind the store while I get her up?"

"Sure, no problem."

Abby found Naomi's daughter standing in her playpen, tears streaming down her flushed cheeks and her golden curls in a tangled mass. She bent over and lifted Sarah into her arms. "Let's change your *windles*, and then you can go see Uncle Matthew."

A short time later, Abby carried the little girl up front and found Matthew sweeping the floor. When he spotted his niece, he set the broom aside and reached for her. "If Naomi has her boppli before the day's out, we can spread the news tomorrow at church," he said, glancing at Abby.

"That would save a lot of time in the telling," she agreed.

Sarah nuzzled Matthew's clean-shaven cheek, and he patted her back in a fatherly fashion.

Such a shame he's not married and raising his own family, Abby thought. *Naomi told me that Matthew's shy around women, but he doesn't seem so whenever he's with me.*

An idea popped into Abby's head. Why not invite her friend Rachel to come for a visit? Rachel had told her many times that she was looking for the right man. Maybe she and Matthew would hit it off. *That's exactly what I'm going to do. I'll write Rachel a letter and invite her to spend some time with me here.*

"I can't believe we still haven't had any word on Naomi," Fannie said to Abby as they sat at the kitchen table cutting lettuce and tomatoes for a tossed salad. This was one thing her mamm could do from a sitting position, and since the swelling in her legs had finally gone down, Abby figured it would be all right.

"I thought from the way Naomi talked, the boppli might be born soon after they got to the hospital," Abby said.

"Maybe she wasn't as close as she thought," Nancy put in from her place at the stove.

Mom frowned, and the wrinkles around her eyes seemed

more pronounced. "Sure hope when my time comes it'll go quickly."

"Speaking of your time, what'd the doctor say today? Did they do the ultrasound?" Abby questioned.

Mom nodded. "Jah, but I'd rather wait and tell you the results when Abraham and the rest of the family are here."

"Is there something wrong with the boppli?" Abby couldn't help but feel some concern.

Mom reached over and patted Abby's hand. "Not to worry, dear one."

Abby set her paring knife aside in order to scratch an irritating itch on her wrist. She didn't know why she felt so nervous. Maybe it was because she didn't like to wait for things, especially something as important as the news of her mother's ultrasound. This had been a day of waiting, and she felt rung out.

"Let's get the rest of our supper made," Mom suggested. "As soon as the men come in from the fields I'll tell you about my appointment."

Abby resumed her salad making, cutting a few more tomatoes and tossing them into the bowl. She was glad Mary Ann had volunteered to watch Sarah and had taken her outside to blow bubbles. As jittery as Abby felt right now, she wouldn't have made the best babysitter. She was about to head to the refrigerator for a bottle of salad dressing, when the back door opened and Matthew, Jake, Samuel, and Abraham entered the room. Matthew had gone to the barn after the two of them arrived home from the store, and from the looks of the dirt on the other three men's clothes, she guessed they must have just come in from the fields.

"Any word on Naomi yet?" Abraham asked as he bent to give Abby's mother a kiss on the cheek.

She shook her head. "No, but I have some news of my own to share."

Abraham's eyebrows shot up. "You'd better not have gone into early labor. The boppli's not due for three months yet."

She clucked her tongue. "No need to worry. I'm not havin' any contractions."

"That's a relief." He dropped into the chair beside her. "So, tell me what's on your mind."

"Would somebody please call Mary Ann? She took Sarah outside awhile ago, and I'd like her to hear my news, too."

"What about Norman?" Matthew asked. "He's already gone home for the day."

"Guess he'll have to wait 'til tomorrow to hear whatever Fannie has to say," his daed replied, "because I'm not waitin' any longer."

"I'll go get Mary Ann," Samuel offered. He scampered out the door and returned a few minutes later with Mary Ann and Sarah at his side.

"Samuel says you've called a family meeting," Mary Ann said. "Is somethin' wrong?"

Mom wagged her finger. "Not unless you think two bopplin would be wrong." Tears gathered in the corners of her eyes, and she brushed them away.

A muscle in Abraham's jaw quivered, and he blinked a couple of times. "Two bopplin? What two bopplin—Naomi's and ours?"

Mom placed one hand against her stomach and smiled. "I'm talkin' about the two bopplin I'm carryin' right here."

"What?"

"*Zwilling*—twins?"

"How do ya know?"

"That's wunderbaar!"

Everyone spoke at once, until Abraham held up his hands. "Let my fraa tell us the details of this great news." The adoring look he gave his wife put a lump in Abby's throat. *He must feel truly blessed.*

"As some of you already know, the doctor saw me last week and ordered today's ultrasound," Mom said. "He'd wanted me to have one done a few months ago, but I kept putting it off."

"Why'd he want the test?" Jake asked, as he took a seat at the table.

"Because he'd heard two heartbeats." Mom patted her stomach. "Now we know why I've gotten big so quickly."

Abby had to admit that her mamm's stomach had rounded considerably in the last few months, but she figured it was because she carried a big baby.

"So two babies showed up on the ultrasound? Is that what you're sayin', Fannie?" This question came from Matthew, who stood behind Abby's chair.

Mom nodded and swiped at the tears that had splashed onto her cheeks. "It's taken me some time to accept the idea of bein' a mother again, but this news is almost too much to comprehend."

"Thank the Lord for His goodness," Abraham exclaimed. "We're gonna have zwilling!"

A chorus of cheers went up around the room, and no one seemed to hear the pounding on the back door until Abby excused herself to answer it. Caleb's brother Marvin stepped into the room wearing a huge smile on his face. "It's another girl! Naomi's boppli was born an hour ago, and mother and child are doin' fine."

~

Linda was pleased that Beth's church was within walking distance, because she wasn't about to ask Jim for a ride. He'd been irritable and impatient with her and Jimmy last night. This morning, when she'd awakened him to say they were leaving for church, he'd nearly snapped her head off. She had tried one more time to get him to go with them, but he'd adamantly refused.

Now, as she and Jimmy walked up the steps to the church, she had second thoughts about her decision. *Maybe I should have only agreed to come to church and not Sunday school. It might have been best to work our way into things.*

"There's Allen!" Jimmy shouted, giving Linda's hand a tug. "See, right over there."

Linda turned and saw Beth, Allen, and Beth's other two boys coming up the sidewalk. A feeling of relief washed over her. She found comfort in seeing some familiar faces.

"I'm glad you could make it," Beth said, giving Linda a hug. "My husband wanted to meet your husband, but he came down with the flu last night and couldn't be here this morning."

Linda swallowed past the lump in her throat. "Jim won't be here, either. I'm afraid he's not interested in attending church."

"Maybe we can plan a barbecue sometime and get our men together that way," Beth said as they entered the building.

Linda's only response was a noncommittal shrug. She knew it wasn't likely that Jim would be willing to get together with her new friend's family. She couldn't get him to do much of anything she wanted these days.

"The boys' Sunday school class is downstairs," Beth said. "Allen knows the way, so he, Brent, and Ricky can take Jimmy there while we go to our class."

Linda halted at the top of the steps, clutching her son's hand. *Am I really ready for this?*

"They'll be fine," Beth whispered, as though sensing Linda's reservations.

Linda didn't admit it to Beth, but she was more nervous about going to the adult Sunday school class than she was about letting Jimmy attend his class without her. He had done well during Bible school and would be going to first grade in the fall, so she was sure he would be okay.

The boys bounded down the stairs, and Linda followed Beth down the hall. *Maybe I should have dropped Jimmy off at church and gone home to be with Jim this morning. We need some time alone, that's for sure.* She thought about her mother's comment when they'd gone to Boise to visit her family the last time. *"I can tell things are strained between you and Jim. Have you thought about seeing a counselor before things get any worse?"*

Linda had made light of it to her mother that day, but the truth was, she knew her marriage was in trouble. Later she'd mentioned counseling to Jim, but he'd blown up and said she could have her head shrunk if she wanted to, but he wouldn't be going.

As Linda and Beth entered a large, cheerfully decorated classroom, she forced her thoughts aside and drew in a deep breath to help steady her nerves.

"This is the Young Marrieds' class," Beth said with a sweeping gesture. "For the last few weeks we've been studying the book of Ruth."

Linda took a seat at the table next to Beth, and Ray and

Christine Bentley, a middle-aged couple who seemed quite pleasant, introduced themselves as the teachers.

For the next hour, Linda sat in rapt attention as she listened to the biblical account of Ruth and Boaz. She was amazed to learn what a caring man Boaz was and couldn't get over how Ruth had willingly gone with her mother-in-law to a strange country. By the time class was over, Linda felt a deep yearning to return to Sunday school next week and to read her Bible at home, which she had discovered yesterday near the back of their bookcase.

When she and Beth reached the sanctuary, they met Jimmy and Allen inside the door. Jimmy's face was flushed and beaded with perspiration.

"If you're running a fever, son, we'll have to go home," Linda said, reaching out to touch his forehead.

"I ain't sick," he insisted with a shake of his head.

She pulled her hand back, relieved to discover that his sweaty forehead was actually cool.

"I think the boys are just overheated from playing," Beth assured her.

Allen nodded. "We always have playtime after the Bible story and snacks."

"Are you ready for church?" Beth asked, turning to Linda. "Pastor Deming's sermon and the music during morning worship are always so uplifting."

Linda nodded, feeling almost hungry for spiritual things. The notion startled her. *If Jim were a better husband, I might not need anything else. But maybe I'll find what I'm looking for here at this church.*

CHAPTER 12

*A*bby rubbed her eyes, trying to relieve the gritty, burning sensation. She had worn herself out trying to run the quilt shop and help Mom as much as she could. Since Naomi had given birth to the baby, whom they'd named Susan, Nancy went over to Caleb and Naomi's place to help out whenever Caleb's mother wasn't available.

Cousin Edna dropped by to help Mom as often as she could, and Mary Ann would be around until school started in a few weeks. Even so, Abby felt compelled to pitch in whenever she could. The doctor had cautioned Mom again to stay off her feet as much as possible. But Abby knew how stubborn her mother could be, and she couldn't help but worry about her and the bopplin she carried. Abby continued to have more of those bad dreams and wasn't sleeping well, either, which only added to her exhaustion.

"You look tired," Matthew said, stepping into the quilt shop. "Maybe you should close the place up for the rest of the day and go home so you can get some rest."

Abby shook her head. "We're in the middle of tourist season, and there's much to be done."

He tipped his head, and a lock of dark brown hair fell over one eye. "Know what I think, Abby Miller?"

"What's that?"

"You work too hard, worry too much, and concentrate on everyone else's needs but your own."

Abby made no comment as she reached for a bolt of material on the shelf overhead. Matthew didn't understand how important it was for her to keep Mom's shop running smoothly.

"When was the last time you did something fun—just for you?" he questioned.

She whirled around, nearly dropping the cloth, but Matthew caught it before it hit the floor. "There's no time for fun right now. That will come later, after I'm married."

"You really think so?"

"Of course."

His face contorted. "Right. And split pea soup is little brother Samuel's favorite meal, too."

Choosing to ignore his sarcasm, Abby replied, "Once Lester and I are together again, everything will be back to normal."

Matthew cleared his throat. "Know what else I think?"

She shrugged. Why was Matthew going on and on about this? Was he intentionally trying to get under her skin?

"You've been self-sacrificing for so long, I don't believe you know any other way."

Abby opened her mouth to defend herself again, but Matthew cut her right off.

"I've seen how you rush around at home, always worried about your mamm and doin' things that don't really need to be done." He handed her the fabric. "What about you, Abby? Don't your needs count? Shouldn't you be plannin' your wedding instead of workin' so hard to care for your mamm? There are others who can help out, you know."

Abby stood there, too dumbfounded to say a word. What was wrong with her being self-sacrificing? Didn't the Bible teach that she should love others and be helpful? Besides, she owed it to Mom to be there when she needed her.

The bell above the general store door jangled, and Matthew turned toward the door separating the two places of business. "I'd better see who came in, because Caleb's not here at the moment."

As soon as he left the room, Abby sank into a chair in front of one of the quilting frames, tears clogging her throat. Matthew was right about one thing. She did care more about Mom's needs than her own. It was the only way she could keep her promise to Dad. She dabbed at her eyes with the handkerchief tucked in the band of her apron. *Things will go better once Mom's bopplin are born. And soon after that, I'll be on my way home.*

Fannie bunched a small pillow under her head and stretched out on the sofa. It was only one in the afternoon, and she was already exhausted. Right after lunch, she'd realized that she needed a nap but felt too tired to climb the stairs to her bedroom, so she'd decided to rest here awhile.

Her eyes drifted shut, and she was almost asleep, when she heard the back door open and close again. She knew it couldn't be Nancy, since she had gone to Naomi's to help out today. Mary Ann was supposed to be downstairs in the cellar washing clothes, so she figured it might be her sneaky husband, who'd come in from the fields to pay her a surprise visit.

Heavy footsteps sounded in the hall, and she turned her head in that direction. "Abraham?"

"No, Fannie, it's me." Matthew stepped into the room and removed his straw hat.

"What are you doing home in the middle of the day? You're not sick, I hope."

He shook his head. "Norman's back kinked up on him yesterday, and he's at the chiropractor's this afternoon, so Papa asked if I could help. Caleb said he could manage at the store without me this afternoon, so here I am."

Matthew's disgruntled look let Fannie know he would rather be anywhere other than on the farm right now. She thought he had seemed much happier since he'd begun working at the general store.

"Sorry your daed hasn't found anyone else to help in the fields yet," she said. "It seems like you're needed in two places at once."

He nodded and plunked down in the easy chair across from her, apparently in no hurry to get outside.

"I'm not the only one who's tryin' to cover all the bases these days," Matthew said, turning his hat over in his hands.

"Are you thinking of Abby?"

"Jah. I saw her this morning, and she looked exhausted."

"Abby always has been a hard worker." Fannie pulled herself to a sitting position. "Is there something more bothering you, Matthew?"

"I—I'm concerned about her. A couple of times this week I found her nearly asleep at the quilting frame."

Fannie shook her head as she exhaled deeply. "I didn't realize she was that tired. Whenever I ask how she's doing, she always says she's right as rain. Seems more interested in how I'm doing these days."

"Have you ever thought that your daughter might be too self-sacrificing?"

Matthew's words jolted Fannie to the core. Too self-sacrificing? Was that possible for a Christian?

"Right before I left the store to come here, Abby mentioned that she's been so busy she hasn't written to her future husband for a couple of weeks."

Fannie fiddled with the piping along the edge of the sofa, wondering why Matthew seemed so concerned about Abby's welfare. *He is her stepbrother,* she reminded herself. *Guess that gives him the right to speak on her behalf.*

"I'll have a talk with my daughter," Fannie promised. "If she's so overworked that there's no time for letter writing, then I'd best see if I can find someone else to help at the quilt shop or here at home."

Matthew stood. "I hope you don't think I'm buttin' into business that ain't mine, but I'm worried about Abby."

"I'm glad you told me, because she surely wouldn't have mentioned it."

"Okay then. Guess I'd best be gettin' out to the fields. See you at suppertime, Fannie."

She smiled and lifted her hand. "Have a good day."

⁀

Linda relaxed against the seat in the passenger's side of Beth's compact car. The more time she spent with her new friend, the more at ease she felt. And the more times she and Jimmy attended church, the more she desired for Jim to go.

Today she and Beth were on their way to visit the newly remodeled fitness center on the other side of town. When she'd mentioned the place to Jim this morning, he'd said that his shop had done the painting on the building and thought it was a good idea for Linda to go there because she needed some exercise. *Maybe if I firm up my flabby muscles, Jim will take an interest in me again.*

"There was a write-up about the fitness center in last night's paper," Beth said, pulling Linda's thoughts aside. "They have new owners now and are offering child care for those who bring their children along when they come to exercise."

Linda glanced over her shoulder at Jimmy in the backseat. "I'm not sure I want to leave my son with strangers."

"You could have left him at my mother's, along with my three boys."

"I—I feel better having him with me." Even though Linda had been trying not to be so overprotective, she still wasn't comfortable with the idea of leaving Jimmy with people she didn't know.

Beth pulled into the parking lot and had barely turned off the engine when Jimmy unbuckled his seatbelt and clambered out of the backseat.

"Wait for me," Linda called. "I don't want you running across the parking lot. You might get hit by a car."

Jimmy halted, and Linda grabbed his hand. The three of them headed for the main entrance, and once inside, they located the reception center. Beth stepped confidently up to the desk, but before she could ask any questions, the young auburn-haired woman behind the desk spoke up. "Hi, my name's Ginny Nelson. Welcome to Puyallup's newly remodeled fitness center. Here's some information on our facilities." She grinned and handed Beth a brochure. "Everything's free today, and there's fresh carrot and orange juice at the snack bar. If you have any questions, I'd be happy to answer them."

Linda was tempted to mention that it was her husband

who'd done the painting on the building, but she decided to let Beth do the talking.

"I understand you have child care here," Beth said. "It would be easier for my friend to try out some of your equipment if her boy had a safe place to play."

"The children's playroom is just down the hall." Ginny leaned forward, her long hair fanning her face. "Cute boy. How old is he?"

"My son is six," Linda replied.

Ginny squinted her jade green eyes and stared at Jimmy.

"Is—is there something wrong?" A sense of uneasiness crept up Linda's spine, even though she knew it was silly of her to feel so paranoid.

Ginny shook her head. "Nothing's wrong. It's just that—well, I know this will probably sound goofy, but your boy is the spitting image of Samuel Fisher, one of the brothers of an Amish friend of mine back in Pennsylvania. Of course, I haven't seen him for several years now and he would be much older than this little boy. Your boy is more the age of Naomi's other brother, the baby who was. . ." Her voice trailed and her eyes grew round with wonder. "I mean, he looks the way I would imagine little Zach would look if I saw him now—same hair color and eyes. Even his smile reminds me of the Fisher boys." Her face flushed. "Oh, never mind me. I am known as a motormouth around here. Talking is by far my favorite exercise." She fidgeted with the phone cord on the reception desk. "Isn't it funny how everybody reminds you of somebody else you know?"

"I guess we all have a double somewhere in the world." Linda offered a weak smile, but she felt uneasy in this gal's presence.

"Yes, I know what you mean. People always mistake me for a Karen or a Gayle," Beth said, nudging Linda's arm.

Linda pointed to the brochure Beth had been given. "Does this include a map of the center?" Linda asked. The fact that the young woman continued to stare at Jimmy made her feel more apprehensive, and she wanted to get away.

"Yeah, sure." Ginny smiled and nodded at Linda.

Beth opened her brochure and studied it. "Look, the map shows the children's center is right here." She pointed to a spot on the paper, but it barely registered with Linda. She grabbed Jimmy's hand and dashed down the hall.

"What's the hurry?" Beth asked when she caught up to Linda and Jimmy.

"I just want to look at the facilities and go home."

"I thought we were going to try out some of the equipment. We can drop Jimmy off, change into our exercise clothes, and see if we can work up a sweat."

Linda shook her head. "I don't feel like exercising. If you want to work up a sweat, go ahead. Jimmy and I can watch from the sidelines."

"You seemed enthused about checking out the fitness center. What's happened to change your mind?"

"I'm just not comfortable leaving Jimmy with strangers," Linda mumbled.

"Is it what that young woman at the reception desk said?"

Linda nodded. "She showed too much interest in Jimmy, and comparing him to an Amish child was so ridiculous."

"I'm sure she was just surprised that he reminded her of someone she used to know."

"But she kept staring at him, and it made me nervous." Linda shuddered. "Just the other day a child was kidnapped in the parking lot at the Tacoma Mall. There are too many nutty people in this world, and parents need to protect their kids."

"I understand. I'm concerned for my boys' welfare, too, but—"

"But you're not unreasonably mistrusting like me? Is that what you're saying?"

Beth blanched as though Linda had thrown cold water in her face. Linda knew her overprotective ways had driven a wedge between her and Jim, and she didn't want anything to spoil her new friendship. She had to set her fears aside and try to relax. The woman at the front desk was probably trying to be friendly so people would sign up for a membership.

"I'm sorry for acting so ridiculous," Linda apologized. "I'll put Jimmy in the children's room and we can exercise awhile."

"I think it will be fun." Beth offered Linda a reassuring smile. "And I'm sure your little guy will be just fine."

CHAPTER 13

$\mathcal{A}$bby stood in the middle of her mother's quilt shop, studying it from all angles. Thanks to several Amish and Mennonite ladies in their community, she had a lot more quilts to sell. That was good, since so many tourists flocked to Lancaster County and visited Fannie's Quilt Shop in Paradise. There was only one problem. Abby had run out of room to display all the quilts. "I would hate to start turning quilters away," she mumbled.

"Why would you have to do that?"

Abby spun around at the sound of Matthew's deep, yet mellow voice. "I have no more space to display quilts," she said, motioning to the crowded shelves along the walls and several racks in the middle of the room.

He stepped up beside her. "How did you display things at your shop in Berlin?"

"I had several wooden quilt racks scattered around, and some were draped across a bed we had set up in the middle of the room." Abby sighed. "Of course my shop there is much larger than this one."

"Seems to me what you need are some large hangers you could put on that bare wall with quilts draped over them." Matthew nodded toward the wall facing the adjoining general store.

"The only trouble with that is I have no such hangers."

"I saw some in a quilt shop over in Strasburg a few weeks ago. I like to fiddle with wood when I have the time, and I'm thinkin' I might be able to make you some hangers."

"That would be wunderbaar," she said with a burst of enthusiasm. "I'll pay you for them, of course."

He grinned at her, and the dimple in his chin became more pronounced. "How about in exchange for me making the quilt hangers, you take a day off and do something for yourself?"

She frowned. "I can't do that. Mom needs my help here and at home."

"But she's gonna need you a lot more once the twins are born." Matthew leaned on the table closest to him and stared at her. "If you know you'll be workin' harder in a few months, that's all the more reason you should take time to rest or do something fun now."

Abby drew in a deep breath. Matthew was right, as usual, although she hated to admit it. "Okay, I'll take a longer lunch break this afternoon and try to get caught up on my letter writing."

He chuckled while shaking his head. "Abby Miller, you're too much."

She plucked a bolt of material off the table. "I'd best get back to work now, and if I'm not mistaken, you've got some customers in the store needing help, too."

Matthew groaned, but there was a mischievous twinkle in his eyes. "Work, work, work. That's all you ever think about."

She poked him playfully on the arm. "See you later, big brother."

"Yep." He turned and sauntered out of the room.

⁓

Linda stood at the kitchen window, watching her son play in the backyard. She had given Jimmy a jar of bubbles after they finished eating breakfast, and for the last half hour he'd been keeping himself well entertained.

He's such a sweet, even-tempered boy, she mused. The woman in charge of child care at the fitness center had told Linda that Jimmy was an absolute pleasure to be around. He'd played well with the other children there and hadn't given the woman a bit of trouble.

Linda smiled and waved as Jimmy pranced across the lawn

in front of the window, wielding his wand and leaving a trail of rainbow-colored bubbles floating behind.

My fears about leaving him with strangers while Beth and I exercised were unfounded, and I'm sure the young woman at the front desk wasn't a threat, either.

"What are you staring at?"

Linda whirled around. "Jim! I thought you'd left for work already."

"I did, but I forgot something and had to come back for it."

"What'd you forget?"

"The little book I write my paint jobs in. Can't get any work done without that." Jim stepped up to the window. "I see our boy's getting his exercise for the day."

She nodded. "I got some yesterday, too."

"Oh? What'd you do, jog to the park and back?"

"Beth and I went to that newly remodeled fitness center you painted. They had an open house and offered free workouts."

Jim grabbed a glass from the cupboard and turned on the faucet at the sink. "You planning to go back?"

"Beth said she'd like to, but the membership fee is pretty expensive. I'm not sure she can afford it."

"Well, we can, so if you want to join, you have my blessings."

Linda shrugged. "I don't know. I'm not sure I'd want to go alone."

He gulped down the water and set the glass in the sink. "Don't get any dumb ideas about me going with you. I don't have the time."

She clenched her teeth. "I know that, Jim. You never have time for anything I want to do."

"That's not true. I took you to the grocery store last night, didn't I?"

"That was for necessities, not for the fun of doing something together."

"You think working out on some stupid rowing machine and getting all sweaty would be fun?"

"It could be, if we did it together."

"And what would we do with Jimmy if we ran off to the

health club to get healthy and fit?" he asked in a sarcastic tone. "We have no babysitter, as you may recall, because you don't like to leave Jimmy with strangers."

Linda moved away from the window and dropped into a chair at the table. "Beth was wondering if we could get together with her family for a barbecue sometime soon," she said, hoping the change of subject might relieve some of the tension between them.

"I don't have time to socialize right now. Need to get my outside painting jobs done while we've still got good weather."

"But, I thought—"

"I said no!" Jim stomped across the room and jerked open the refrigerator. "Have we got any beer? I told you to pick up a case last night."

She shook her head. "Sorry, I forgot." *I wish you wouldn't drink, Jim. It only fuels your agitation.*

He slammed the refrigerator door, causing the vase on top to tumble to the floor. It was plastic and didn't shatter, but Linda felt irritation that her husband could lose his temper so easily. Jim hadn't always been this testy, but in the last few years, he often exploded over the littlest thing.

"You could have gone into the store with me instead of waiting in the car," she mumbled.

"Yeah, right, and haul Jimmy in there so he could whine and beg for everything that caught his eye?"

"Jimmy doesn't do that whenever I take him to the store. He's very well behaved. In fact, the lady who watched him at the fitness center commented on what a nice boy he is."

Jim's features softened some as he bent to pick up the vase. "Jimmy's a good kid."

"And cute, too," she added with a smile. "The young woman at the front desk said Jimmy reminded her of a little Amish boy she used to know."

"What?"

"She said Jimmy had the same color hair and eyes as the little boy."

"What else did the woman say?"

"That's about all." Linda's forehead wrinkled. "I'll have to

The Quilter's Daughter

admit, it did make me kind of nervous the way she kept staring at Jimmy."

Jim's hand shook, and the vase crashed to the floor again.

"Jim, what's wrong? You're trembling like we've just had an earthquake."

"Nothing's wrong. I—I'm tired and need to get to work." He bent to pick up the vase for the second time and placed it back on the refrigerator.

"Are you sure you're okay?"

"I'm fine!"

Her spine went rigid, and she recoiled.

"I think it'd be best if you don't sign up at the fitness center right now."

Jim's wrinkled forehead and eyebrows drawn together let Linda know that he was uptight, but she didn't understand why. "A few minutes ago you said we could afford for me to go there."

"I've changed my mind!"

"You don't have to get so angry."

"I'm not angry." Jim glanced at his watch. "But I am late, so this discussion is over." He turned and rushed out the door.

Linda swallowed around the lump in her throat. Would things ever be right between her and Jim again? Maybe a few minutes in the fresh air with Jimmy would help calm her.

Naomi sat in the rocking chair holding baby Susan. Sarah knelt on the living room floor, playing with the wooden blocks her uncle Matthew had made for her second birthday. There was a knock at the front door, and rather than disturb the baby, Naomi called, "Come in."

A few seconds later, Abby stepped into the room, carrying a large paper sack.

"It's nice to see you," Naomi said with a smile.

"I thought I'd drop by on my way home from work and see how everyone's doing."

"We're doin' well." Naomi motioned to the sofa. "Have a seat. You look done in."

103

Abby flopped down and leaned against the throw pillows with a yawn. "It's been a busy day, and I didn't sleep well last night."

"Sorry to hear that. Maybe you should see about hiring a helper at the quilt shop."

"I've thought about it, but sooner or later Mom will take the place back over, and I'm sure I can keep things running smoothly until that time."

Naomi lifted the baby onto her shoulder and patted her gently on the back. "You really think Fannie will be up to running the quilt shop after she gives birth to twins?"

Abby shrugged. "She says she will."

"I thought I'd be going back to help at the store soon after Susan was born, but as you can see, I've got my hands full right here. If I tried to take my two little ones to work with me every day, I doubt I'd get much done." Naomi sighed. "Caleb would probably still need to hire someone, and the girls and I would just be in the way."

Abby lifted her brows. "Are you saying you're not going back to work at all?"

"I will when the boppli is a little older, but for now Caleb and I have decided that my place is at home.

"Guess that makes sense." Abby reached her hand out to Sarah. "What have you got there, *hatzli*—sweetheart?"

The little girl held up two wooden blocks and grinned. "*Ich schpiele gern.*"

"I know you like to play, Sarah." Abby smiled at Naomi. "She's learning to speak so clearly already."

Naomi chuckled. "Jah. Caleb thinks she gets her smarts from him. I don't have the heart to tell him that I started talking clearly before I was two. At least that's what Papa says."

Abby reached into the paper sack she'd brought along. "I made something for the boppli." She removed the baby quilt and handed it to Naomi.

"Oh, it's beautiful, Abby. Danki."

"You're welcome."

Naomi fingered the pink and white patchwork quilt done in

the Lancaster Rose pattern. Then she draped it across her knees and placed her infant daughter in the center of it.

"I hope you like it."

"It's real nice, Abby, and it will surely be put to good use." Naomi brushed at the tears splattering her cheeks.

"I'm sorry if I made you cry," Abby apologized.

Naomi shook her head. "I love the quilt, and I know Susan will, too, when she's older. Guess I'm just goin' through a bit of postpartum depression right now, and everything makes me feel weepy."

Abby offered Naomi a look of sympathy. "Is there anything I can do to help?"

"Just stop by once in a while for a visit when you have the time."

"I always enjoy being with you, and I'll come over as often as I can."

Naomi reached for a tissue from the box on the table beside her chair. "I don't know what we'd all do without you, Abby."

CHAPTER 14

*O*h, Matthew, these are perfect," Abby exclaimed.

Matthew beamed as he placed several wooden hangers on the table in Fannie's quilt shop. "Sorry it's taken me so long to get 'em done."

She waved her hand. "It's only been a few months since you agreed to make them for me, and I know you've been busy assisting Caleb in the store, not to mention helping out on the farm whenever you can."

"That's true. I'll be glad when things slow down a bit."

"I doubt if they will ever slow down once Mom has the bopplin."

Matthew chuckled. "Things will probably never be the same around our place after those little ones enter the world." His brown eyes seemed darker than usual, and a muscle on the side of his cheek quivered slightly. "I remember when Zach was born and everything seemed to be centered on him. He was such a cute little fellow, and even after all this time I still find myself missin' him."

Abby could only imagine how painful it must have been for the Fishers to lose their mamm in a terrible accident, and then have their boppli kidnapped just a year later. It had been hard enough for her and Mom to deal with things after Dad's heart attack. She winced as a stab of regret sliced through her. "The trials in life are never easy, but God gives us the strength to bear them."

He nodded. "Jah, and as time goes on, the pain lessens."

Feeling the need to change the subject, Abby motioned to the wall across from them. "Would you have time to put some quilts on the hangers you made and get them set in place?"

Matthew's eyes brightened. "For you, sister Abby, I'll make the time."

She smiled. It was nice to have another brother. Especially one that was so willing to help whenever it was needed.

Abby thought about her brother, Harold, and wondered how he and Lena were doing. It had been several weeks since she'd sent them a letter, and nearly that long since she had written to Lester. She'd received a couple of lectures from Mom about working too hard and was asked when the last time was she'd written to her intended. Her mamm had even suggested they might need to hire someone else to help at the quilt shop, but Abby had assured her that she was doing just fine.

"I'm going to try and get a couple of letters written, since there are no customers at the moment. So let me know if you need anything," she called to Matthew.

"Sure will."

Matthew headed to the storage closet to get a ladder, and Abby scurried over to her desk. She found Lester's most recent letter in the drawer and decided to read it again, so she could answer any questions he might have.

Dear Abby,

The news of your mother carryin' twins was sure a surprise. Mom's been talking about all the things she wants to make in duplicate. Guess it won't be long until those bopplin are born.

How are things at the quilt shop? Did Matthew ever make the hangers you mentioned in your last letter? If they work out well, maybe he could make some for your quilt shop here.

Speaking of your shop. . .Mom said to tell you that she and my aunt Clara are managing fine. There are still lots of tourists coming in every day, and the quilting ladies have continued to meet at the store once a week.

Please write soon. I'm looking forward to hearing from you.

Always yours,
Lester

Abby reached for her pen. Lester had probably been watching the mail every day, hoping for a letter. He might think she'd forgotten him by now or didn't care. She'd heard from her friend Rachel last week, too, and that letter would also need to be answered. In response to Abby's invitation to come to Lancaster County for a visit, Rachel had declined, saying she had no vacation time yet, since she hadn't been working at the restaurant in Berlin long enough.

If it's meant for Rachel and Matthew to meet, then God will work things out, Abby mused. *I've done the inviting. Now the rest is in His hands.*

She lifted her pen to begin Lester's letter, but had only written a few words when Jake rushed into the quilt shop, all red-faced and sweaty. "Fannie's gone into labor! Papa got one of our English neighbors to drive 'em to the hospital in Lancaster, and they left Nancy in charge of things at home."

Unable to respond, Abby just sat there, letting Jake's words sink in. *Mom has gone into labor. They were on their way to the hospital. Nancy was at home, overseeing the two younger ones.*

She glanced at the calendar on her desk. Mom wasn't due for another three weeks. The doctor had said that at thirty-seven weeks the babies would be fully developed. Everything should be okay.

Matthew scrambled down the ladder and rushed to Abby's side. "Want me to run over to the gift shop and see if someone can give you a lift to the hospital?"

"What about you? Don't you want to go?"

"I'd like to, but it wouldn't be fair to leave Caleb alone to run the general store and the quilt shop."

"Maybe I can put the CLOSED sign on the quilt shop door, and then he'd only have one store to watch."

"Say, why not let me stay here and help out?" Jake suggested.

"We're done in the fields for the day now that Papa's taken off."

Matthew ran a hand over his clean-shaven face. "You wouldn't mind?"

"Not at all."

"All right then." Matthew reached for Abby's hand. "Let's go find us a ride!"

❧

Abby paced the length of the waiting room, anxious to know how things were going in the delivery room. Mom had been taken in shortly before Abby and Matthew arrived at the hospital, and they hadn't heard anything since.

"You're gonna wear a hole in the carpet if you don't sit down," Matthew said.

She turned to face him. "I'm feeling kind of fidgety."

He patted the chair beside him. "You've got every right to be, but you really should try to calm yourself."

With a sigh of resignation, Abby sank to a chair and picked up a magazine, although she didn't know why. All she could think about was Mom. Was she doing okay? Would the babies be born healthy? Would they weigh enough so they could go home when their mamm did? And what were the bopplin—boys or girls? They could have found out the sex of the babies when Mom had the ultrasound done, but she'd been adamant about not wanting to know until the babies were born.

"Everything will be fine, you'll see," Matthew said in a reassuring tone.

Abby smiled, despite the doubts tumbling around in her head. "I hope so."

"God's in control."

"I know."

"And your mamm is in good hands."

Abby set the magazine aside. "You're a special friend, Matthew, and I'm glad you were able to come to the hospital with me."

"That's what a big brother should do," he said with a wink.

When a middle-aged nurse entered the room, Abby jumped to her feet. "Have you any news to give us on Fannie Fisher?"

The nurse nodded. "She just gave birth to a healthy set of twin boys. One weighs six pounds, and the other is six pounds two ounces."

"Two *buwe?*" Abby's heart swelled with joy.

"Wow! Papa and Fannie are doubly blessed," Matthew said. "God took one son and gave my daed two."

Abby wondered if Abraham would see it that way. Had God taken Zach from the Fishers? It seemed more like the sinful nature of the man who had kidnapped him than anything else.

"When can we see my mom and the twins?" Abby asked the nurse.

"As soon as your mother is back in her room and the babies have been cleaned up."

"Are they identical?" Abby questioned.

"It would seem so, but there are still some tests to be done."

"I need to notify Harold and Lena right away." Abby started for the door but turned back around. "I'm going down the hall to phone Lester's mom at the quilt shop in Berlin and ask her to get word to Harold and Lena—and, of course, Lester, too." She grinned at Matthew. "What a joyous day!"

CHAPTER 15

$\mathcal{N}$aomi halted inside the living room of her father and Fannie's house, awed by the sight that greeted her. She and Caleb had brought the kinner over to visit their twin uncles, who had just come home from the hospital. But now she wondered if they should have waited awhile. Papa and Fannie sat on the sofa together, each holding a baby. Fannie looked tired but happy as she rubbed her chin slowly against one twin's downy dark hair. Papa looked like a kinner with a new toy, rocking the other baby in his arms and crooning softly. It was a blissful scene. One Naomi felt deserved no intrusion.

"Bopplin! Bopplin!" Sarah hollered as she bounded across the room.

Papa lifted the baby to his chest. "Whoa, now! Don't go climbin' up here, little girl."

Caleb, who held baby Susan, reached down with his free hand and grabbed Sarah's arm. "Slow down once. You'll get your chance to see the bopplin soon enough."

"Come, let her sit beside me." Fannie patted the cushion next to her.

Naomi joined Sarah on one end of the couch and leaned over to get a better look at the babies. "They're beautiful, and they look exactly alike. How will you ever tell them apart?"

"They've still got their hospital bracelets on, so that's helping for now," Fannie replied. "We'll figure something else out soon enough, I expect."

"What have you named them?" Caleb asked, taking a seat in the rocking chair across the room and placing baby

Susan across his knees.

"This one is Titus," Fannie said, kissing the wee one on top of his head.

"And this here's Timothy." Papa held the baby up for everyone to see. "Did ya ever see any bopplin as cute as these two?"

Caleb cleared his throat. "Jah. Our Susan. She's wunderbaar!"

"Of course she is," Fannie was quick to say. "All babies are special, and ours don't hold no title to bein' cute."

"Sure they do," Papa said with a smirk. He cradled little Timothy in his arms and glanced over at his wife. "Fannie's made me so happy, and our twin buwe are the best."

"*Es bescht,*" Sarah said with a giggle.

"Jah," Papa agreed. "The boys are the best." He stared at Timothy with such a doting expression it made Naomi wonder about a few things. She was pretty sure her daed was only having fun with Sarah, but she couldn't help but feel a bit put out because he showed so little interest in either one of her girls. Not only that, but Papa seemed more enthralled with his twin boys than he ever had with Zach. Maybe it was just the newness of things. A few weeks from now everything would most likely be back to normal, with Papa out in the fields again and Fannie shouldering most of the responsibility of raising their sons.

"Where's the rest of the family?" Caleb asked. "I figured we'd find everyone crowded around the twins."

"Abby's out in the kitchen fixing supper," Fannie said. "Mary Ann and Nancy are helping her."

"Shortly after we got home, I sent Matthew out to the fields to check on Jake, Norman, and Samuel," Papa spoke up. "They've been handling things on their own for the last couple of days, what with me traipsin' back and forth to the hospital."

"Are you managing okay at the store on your own?" Fannie asked, giving Caleb a look of concern.

He nodded. "Matthew's still comin' in, and he's agreed to take care of things in the quilt shop so Abby can stay here to help you."

Fannie sighed. "There's so much to be done, what with me not able to do a lot yet. I wouldn't know what to do without

Abby's help, because caring for two bopplin means we'll need every available pair of hands."

"I understand," Naomi said. "I've got my hands full from sunup to sunset trying to keep Sarah out of mischief while I care for little Susan."

"We're thankful for the days when Nancy can help us," Caleb interjected, "but if she's needed here, we can probably call on my mamm."

"I think Abby's got things under control," Papa said. "She's real organized and seems willing to do whatever needs done."

A stab of remorse shot through Naomi. She felt as if Papa's remark had been directed at her. Many times after Mama's death, when Naomi had taken over household chores and helped at the store, Papa had accused her of not doing things right.

I'm just overly sensitive right now, she reminded herself. *Have been ever since Susan was born. I need to keep my eyes on God and quit worrying about what others say and do.*

"Abby's a good daughter," Fannie put in. "She's always had a servant's heart, and she's puttin' her wedding on hold because of me."

"What?" Naomi's eyebrows lifted. "You mean she's not getting married in November?"

"Well, she says—"

"Did I hear someone mention my name?" Abby asked, stepping into the room.

~

All eyes seemed to be focused on Abby as she took a seat on the arm of the sofa, close to Naomi. "We're having an early supper tonight," she said. "Since Mom just got home from the hospital, I'm sure she's tired and would like to go upstairs as soon as we're done eating." Abby touched Naomi's arm. "You're welcome to stay and eat with us."

"Oh, no, we wouldn't think of imposing. We just wanted to drop by and meet the twins, but we'll be on our way in a few minutes," Naomi replied.

"That's right," Caleb agreed. "As soon as I got home from

the store, I loaded my brood in the buggy and headed straight here. We were all anxious to see the little miracle bopplin."

Fannie nodded. "That's just what they are, too. After going without more children for so many years, I never expected to give birth at my age, let alone to identical twin boys."

"What were you talking about when I came into the room?" Abby asked, redirecting their conversation.

"I was telling everyone how you're planning to stay awhile longer, and that you've decided to postpone your wedding a few more months," her mother replied.

Abby nodded. "There's no way I could return to Ohio knowing my mamm and little brothers need me. I wrote Lester a letter yesterday, explaining things and saying we can be married sometime in January." She drew in a deep breath and exhaled it quickly. "I miss Lester, of course, but it's nice to be with all of you during this exciting time of so many bopplin being born."

"Isn't your brother's wife due to have a baby soon?" Abraham asked.

"Lena's due date is shortly after Mom's was supposed to be, so she's got another three or four weeks to go."

Mom sighed and reached up to straighten her *kapp*, which was slightly askew. "I wish there was some way I could be there for Lena, but I'll have my hands full right here for some time, I'm afraid."

"Which is exactly why I'm going to stick around until you're feeling stronger and can manage on your own," Abby asserted.

"Such a fine daughter I raised," Mom said with a smile. "I only hope I do half as well with these two boys."

"You're already a good mamm, and you'll do fine by our little fellows." Abraham gave her knee a pat. "The best thing that ever happened to this family was when you came along."

Mom blushed and swatted at his hand. "Oh, go on with ya now. I'm no saint, so don't make me out to be one."

Abraham chortled. "You're the next thing to it, Fannie Mae."

Abby glanced at Naomi and noticed her furrowed brows. Was she hurt by her daed's comments, maybe thinking of her own mamm and wondering if he loved his second wife better than the first?

I must have a talk with Naomi soon, Abby decided. *It wouldn't be good for hard feelings to tear this family apart now that things have been going so well.*

When Abby awoke on Sunday morning, her bed sheets were soaked with perspiration and so was she. She'd had that terrible dream about a fire again, and it had left her feeling physically and emotionally drained. What could it mean, and why had she had it so many times over the past several months?

Her hands trembled as she fumbled to undo the buttons on her nightgown. Would it help to tell someone about the dream? Maybe Mom could soothe her fears, the way she had when Abby was a little girl and had been frightened about something. *Jah, as soon as I get dressed I'll have a talk with Mom.*

A short time later, Abby found her mother in front of the kitchen sink, filling the teakettle with water. "You look tired, daughter. Didn't ya sleep well?"

Abby yawned, stretched, and lifted her choring apron from a wall peg. "I had a nightmare and didn't feel the least bit rested when I woke up."

"I'm sorry to hear that. Maybe it was somethin' you ate last night that caused the bad dream."

Abby shook her head. "I've been plagued by this same night terror many times, and I don't understand it, Mom."

"How come you've never mentioned it before?"

"I didn't want to bother you, and I figured it would go away."

Her mother pulled out a chair at the table and motioned for Abby to do the same. "Would you like to tell me about it?"

Abby nodded and flopped into the chair beside Mom. "In the dream I'm asleep in my bed, but something wakes me up. When I open my eyes, there's smoke and flames, and I can't breathe." She inhaled and blew out her air in a quick puff. "I hear a kitten's cry, and I call for someone to help me save it, but nobody ever responds."

Mom's eyebrows furrowed. "Does the same thing happen each time in your dream?"

"Jah, only sometimes I'm covering my head with the quilt on my bed."

"Hmm. . ."

"I've read in *The Budget* some articles about fires, and a few months back Lester and I witnessed a fire at the cheese place near my quilt shop." Abby pursed her lips. "Do you think the dream could have been a foreshadowing of what was to come? And if so, then why am I still having the horrible nightmare?"

Mom placed her hand on Abby's arm and gave it a gentle squeeze. "Dreams are often a combination of things we've heard or something we may have read about, but I think it's rare that they'd be a warning of what was going to happen in the future."

Abby groaned. "I wish there were something I could do to keep from having that dream. It's so frightening, and I wake up feeling as if something terrible is about to happen."

"I suggest that you pray about it, Abby." Mom gave her a hug. "Ask God to take away the dream and the fear you feel whenever it happens." She pushed back her chair. "And I'll be praying, too, dear one."

Sitting beside Beth on a pew that was three rows from the back of the sanctuary, Linda marveled at how relaxed she felt on this Sunday morning. Her son and Beth's three boys were in junior church, and she knew Jimmy was happy and comfortable, too.

"My sermon today is entitled 'Life's Disappointments,' " Rev. Deming began as he stepped up to the pulpit. "We all encounter disappointments in life, such as marital discord, trouble with our children, parents, coworkers, neighbors, or friends. People are human, and everyone has certain frailties. People often let us down—even those we are closest to."

Linda thought about Jim and how he seemed to take pleasure in disappointing her. Jimmy wasn't a disappointment, though. Adopting him was the best thing they had ever done. She glanced over at Beth and her husband, Eric. *They seem to be so happy. If Jim would just agree to get counseling, we might discover the kind of happiness they obviously share.*

"I'm reading from the book of Psalms, chapter 147, verse 3, New International Version," the reverend continued. " 'He heals the brokenhearted and binds up their wounds.' " He looked out at the congregation. "Are you brokenhearted? Do you have wounds that won't heal? Cast your cares on Jesus and give your troubles to Him."

Tears clouded Linda's vision, and she blinked several times, hoping to ward them off. But it was no use. She felt moisture on her cheeks and reached into her purse for a tissue to wipe the tears away.

Beth's hand closed around Linda's. "Are you okay?"

Linda could only nod in reply. Her throat felt clogged, like she had eaten a piece of dry bread and had nothing to wash it down. She knew if she uttered one word it would come out in a strangled sob.

As Rev. Deming continued his sermon, Linda felt as if every word, every verse of scripture was meant for her. For the first time in her life she realized how much she really needed God.

"Some of you have had a personal experience with Christ," the pastor said. "For you, it's as simple as recommitting your life to the Lord and letting Him take control of your circumstances." He paused and leaned slightly forward.

Linda's body went rigid, and her stomach churned like a blender on full speed. *Is he looking at me? Does he know my needs, my pain?*

"Some of you may never have made a commitment to Christ. You may be wondering what it takes to become a believer." Rev. Deming turned in his Bible to another passage. "Romans 3:23 says, 'For all have sinned and fall short of the glory of God.' "

Linda squeezed her eyes shut. She had never consciously admitted it, but she knew she was a sinner. She'd been devious in her relationship with Jim, often scheming to get her way. She had argued, pouted, and martyred herself in the hope of making him give in to her demands. Her thoughts were often negative, and she'd spent hours pondering ways to get even. Sometimes, when she and Jim argued, she shouted and called him names.

"Christ died on the cross for you and for me. His shed blood

119

is the atonement for our sins, and the only way we can come to the Father is through His Son, Jesus." The pastor stepped down from the pulpit and stood behind the wooden altar in front of the communion table. "As our organist plays 'Just as I Am,' I would like to invite anyone who wants to be free of their burdens and find forgiveness for their sins to kneel at the altar."

The music began, and the congregation sang softly, "Just as I am, without one plea. . .but that Thy blood was shed for me. . .and that Thou bidd'st me come to Thee, O Lamb of God, I come! I come!"

"All you need to do is step out of your pew and walk down the aisle," Rev. Deming said in a soft, pleading voice. "Jesus is waiting for you."

Linda heard Beth's harmonious voice beside her, singing, "Just as I am and waiting not. . .to rid my soul of one dark blot. . .to Thee whose blood can cleanse each spot, O Lamb of God, I come! I come!"

The words on the hymnal blurred, and Linda's hands shook so badly she was afraid she might drop the book. She couldn't sing. Couldn't think. Couldn't breathe. Her soul ached to kneel at the altar and ask God to forgive her sins. She wanted desperately to let Jesus take control of her life. But could she go forward in front of all these people? What would they think of her? Would they look down their noses or cast judgment?

"Just as I am," the song continued, "tho' tossed about. . . with many a conflict, many a doubt. . .fightings and fears within, without, O Lamb of God, I come! I come!"

Come to Me, Linda. Come to Me just as you are. The voice in Linda's head gave her the confidence she needed. On shaky legs she made her way slowly down the aisle. She'd been living in fear for too long. Her life was full of conflict and doubts. It was time to find rest for her weary soul. It was time to meet Jesus.

CHAPTER 16

$\mathcal{L}$inda hummed as she stirred a kettle of homemade chicken gravy. The meal she prepared would be a surprise for Jim. She and Jimmy had been home from church about an hour, and Jim was still lounging in bed. She hoped the tantalizing aroma of fried chicken and biscuits would rouse him. She'd thought about sending Jimmy up to get his father but didn't want to chance him snapping at the boy. Besides, Jimmy was playing happily in the backyard, and there was no point in disturbing him.

Linda was anxious to share her altar experience with Jim. Since she had confessed her sins and accepted Christ as her Savior, she felt like a new person.

If only Jim would find the Lord, I'm sure we could get our marriage back on track. Maybe I should speak to Rev. Deming about counseling with us. If we started going to church as a family, I know we'd be happier.

Jim sauntered into the room, halting Linda's thoughts. "What's cookin'? I could smell something all the way upstairs."

She turned from the stove and offered him a smile. "I've made fried chicken, buttermilk biscuits, mashed potatoes, and your favorite gravy."

"What's the occasion? Most Sundays you usually fix something simple and quick."

Linda turned down the stove burner and moved to his side. "I'm celebrating, Jim, and I wanted to fix your favorite meal in honor of the new me."

Jim looked her up and down. "Same hairstyle. Same amount of makeup." He squinted. "Is that a new outfit you're wearing?"

She laughed and smoothed the skirt of her knee-length navy blue dress. "No, it's not new, but I am."

"I hate it when you talk in circles." He pushed past her and headed for the refrigerator. "Is there any beer left?"

Linda slumped and turned back to the stove. Jim didn't even want to know how or why she had changed. She could hear him rummaging around in the refrigerator, and she fought the urge to remind him that he sometimes drank too much and certainly shouldn't be drinking so early in the day.

The refrigerator door slammed shut. "There's no beer," he grumbled. "Guess I'll have to run to the store for more."

She whirled around. "Now?"

Jim dragged his fingers through the back of his thick, dark hair. Hair that she used to enjoy running her own fingers through. "Any objections?" he snarled.

Linda knew they would only argue if she mentioned how uneasy she felt whenever he drank. "Could you wait until after dinner to go to the store?"

He shrugged. "Maybe. How soon will it be ready?"

"Ten minutes."

"Yeah, okay. I'll hang around 'til after we eat." Jim gave her an odd look. "Say, there *is* something different about you today. Are you sure you didn't change your makeup or buy a new dress?"

She moved to his side and touched his arm, glad when he didn't recoil. "When I said I was new, I meant I've found Christ."

Jim's eyebrows lifted, and his mouth turned up at the corners. "I didn't realize He was missing."

Linda stiffened and fought the urge to say something catty in return. "No, Jim, Christ isn't missing. He's very much alive— right here." She placed her hand against her chest.

He shook his head. "Have you lost it, or what?"

"No, I've found it. I've found the Lord Jesus as my personal Savior."

"What's He saving you from? I didn't know you were lost, Linda."

"I knelt at the altar this morning and asked Jesus to forgive my sins."

He stared at her, and his expression was stony. "Your sins, huh?"

"That's right."

"Have you done something bad, Linda?"

Was he mocking her? Linda closed her eyes, praying for the right words. When she opened them a few seconds later, her courage was renewed. "During church today, the pastor spoke about disappointments in life."

Jim grunted. "He's right about that. There's a ton of 'em!"

"Rev. Deming said we're all faced with disappointments, but God can help us through them if we know Him personally."

He held up his hand. "That's enough, Linda. If I'd wanted a sermon today, I would have gone to church or turned on the TV and listened to one of those boring televangelists."

Tears clouded Linda's vision as her gaze dropped to the floor. *Help me, Lord. Help me make him understand.*

Jim pulled out a chair and took a seat at the table. "Cut out the 'poor little Linda' routine. Your tears and pathetic looks don't work on me anymore."

"I'm not trying to get my way on anything. I just wanted to share my newfound faith, and I'd hoped you might consider going to church with me and Jimmy next week."

Jim's fist came down hard on the table, scattering several napkins to the floor and clattering the silverware Linda had placed on the table earlier. "If you need religion in order to get through the disappointments in life, then go to church all you want. Just don't expect me to follow like an obedient puppy."

With a heavy heart, Linda shuffled back to the stove. She'd been foolish to believe that because she had changed, Jim might consider her request to attend church.

Give him time, a voice in her head seemed to say. *Pray for your husband and set a good example.*

She swallowed around the constriction in her throat. *I'll try, Lord, but I'm going to need Your help.*

Abby placed a plastic tub filled with warm water on the kitchen table. It was time for the babies' baths. First she would give Titus his bath, and then Mom would dress him while she washed Timothy. While Abby dressed that baby, Mom would feed Titus. The routine seemed easy enough, but both boys were howling in their cradles across the room. Mom had gone upstairs to change clothes, because she'd spilled a glass of goat's milk all over the front of her dress, leaving Abby alone to begin the twins' baths. The only problem was, she couldn't decide which infant to bathe first.

She leaned down and scooped Titus into her arms. At least she thought it was Titus. Abraham had removed their wristbands last night, saying he thought they might become too tight as the babies continued to grow. He'd also said he could tell the boys apart, pointing out the fact that Timothy's right eye was slightly smaller than his left eye, while Titus's looked to be about the same size.

Abby squinted at the twins, still kicking their feet and waving their arms like a windmill. To her, it looked like both boys' eyes were the same size. She picked Titus up, and his crying abated, but as soon as she placed him on the oversized towel she had spread on the table and began to remove his sleepers, the howling began again. To make matters worse, the other twin was still crying, too.

"I hope your mamm comes downstairs soon," Abby crooned. She hurried through the bathing process, anxious to get Titus back in his cradle so she could wash Timothy. She had no sooner carried baby number one across the room than a knock sounded at the back door.

Abby placed Titus in his cradle and hurried to answer the door. When she opened it, she was surprised to see Cousin Edna on the porch, looking thinner than ever. The last thing she'd heard was that Edna had the achy-bones flu and wouldn't be coming over this week. From the looks of the dark circles that rimmed her pale blue eyes, she figured the woman should be home in bed.

Abby glanced over her shoulder at the wailing babies. She knew it would be rude not to invite Edna in, but she didn't want to chance the twins getting sick if Edna was still contagious. "Um. . .we didn't expect you this week."

Edna pushed the door fully open and strolled past Abby. "I'm feeling some better, so I thought I'd come by and see if you needed any help today."

"I think Mom and I can manage on our own all week. Mary Ann's here, too. She's gone out to the chicken coop to check for eggs."

"The bopplin are crying." Edna started across the room. "How come they're howlin' like that? Do they need to be fed or have their windels changed?"

"I just gave Titus a bath, so he has clean diapers," Abby replied.

"Even so, it never hurts to check. I remember when my twins were little. They went through so many diapers every day, and it seemed like all I did was wash baby clothes." Edna moved closer to the twins, but Mom's shrill voice stopped her as she stepped into the room.

"What are you doin' here, Cousin?"

Edna whirled around. "Came over to help. What do ya think?"

Mom clucked her tongue. "I think you look tired and pale, and I'll not have my favorite cousin havin' a relapse on my account." She brushed past Abby and took hold of Edna's bony arm. "Now you get on back home where you can rest. I insist."

Abby held her breath and waited to see what would happen next. To her amazement, Edna nodded and headed for the back door. "You're right, Fannie. I do feel a bit weak and shaky yet. Probably would be best if I waited 'til next week to offer my assistance."

"Abby and I will manage, but I appreciate your comin' by," Mom said as she followed her cousin outside to the porch.

Abby chuckled softly and moved over to the twins. She was surprised Mom had been able to convince Edna, who clearly had a mind of her own, to go home. She glanced over at the babies and was pleased to see that Titus had settled down and was sucking contentedly on his fist. Timothy, on the other hand, was still howling like there was no tomorrow. "There now, little guy. You'll feel better once we get those dirty windels off and you're all cleaned up." She placed the baby in the center of the quilt, quickly undressed him, and was surprised to see that his diaper was clean and dry. "Guess you're not as messy as your twin brother was this morning."

Abby had just finished bathing and dressing Timothy, when her mother returned to the kitchen. "That cousin of mine is such a character. She kept tellin' one joke after the other, and I finally had to remind her that I was needed inside. Sure hope she doesn't have a relapse by comin' over here today."

Abby placed Timothy in his cradle, noting that Titus was fussing again. "I only hope she didn't expose you or the twins to that flu bug she's had."

"Since I'm nursing, that's supposed to help the babies' immune system. I'm sure they'll be fine." Mom moved to Abby's side. "Did you get them both bathed?"

"Jah. Now I think they'd like to be fed."

Mom bent down and scooped Titus into her arms. "Eww. . .he feels wet. Didn't you say you bathed and changed him already?"

"I did, but—" A light suddenly dawned, and Abby broke into the giggles. "You know what, Mom?"

"What's that?"

"I think I may have bathed Titus twice. The boppli you're holding is probably Timothy, and he's most likely wet through his clothes because he hasn't been bathed or changed at all."

Mom grinned and handed Abby the baby. "Guess you'd better see to that while I feed Titus."

"Good idea," Abby agreed. "And afterwards, I believe we should put on our thinking caps and come up with some way to tell these two apart."

CHAPTER 17

$\mathcal{J}$im gripped his paintbrush and swiped it across the wood siding of the house he'd been hired to paint.

"Hey, Boss, you'd better watch what you're doing," Ed called from several feet away. "You're sloppin' paint all over the place this morning, and we'll end up with a mess to clean up if you're not careful."

"Let me worry about that," Jim snapped.

"Sorry, but you've been so testy lately, and it's beginning to show in your work."

Jim gritted his teeth. "If you had to put up with my wife, you'd be testy, too."

Ed moved closer to Jim. "What's the trouble?"

"Linda flipped out a couple weeks ago and went religious on me. Even suggested the two of us start seeing her preacher for some *Christian* counseling." Jim dipped his brush into the bucket and slapped another round of paint on the siding in front of him.

"Why does she believe you need counseling?"

"Guess she thinks if she gets me into that Bible-thumper's office he'll talk me into going to church with her and Jimmy."

"You got somethin' against church?"

Jim shrugged. "Not church per se, just the hypocrites who sit in the pews."

Ed flipped the end of his mustache. "Guess there's hypocrites nearly everywhere."

"Are you saying I'm a hypocrite?"

"I'm not saying that at all. I just think it's easier to see other

127

people's faults than we do our own."

Jim let Ed's words roll around in his head as he wondered if his own actions were really so bad. He tried to be honest and aboveboard in his business dealings. He was fair with his crew and paid each one what they were worth. He was a decent husband and father, even if Linda didn't think so. He didn't need church or some holier-than-thou preacher pointing out his sins.

Of course, I have told a lot of lies over the last few years, and if I went to church or started counseling with the preacher, sooner or later he might drag the truth out of me about Jimmy's phony adoption.

Jim grimaced. He knew it had been wrong to kidnap Jimmy, but he'd convinced himself it was an act of love—done in Linda's best interest. And look how she was thanking him for it!

"Going to church would only make things worse," he muttered.

"What's that, Boss?"

"Nothing, Ed. I'll be fine once we quit work for the day and I can stop somewhere for a couple of beers."

~

A knock at the front door drew Abby's attention away from the quilt she was working on. The twins were asleep in their cradles on the other side of the living room, and Mom was upstairs taking a nap. Abby had decided to use this quiet time to get some quilting done.

When Abby opened the door she was surprised to see nine-year-old Leona Weaver on the front porch. There was something unique about the young girl, and it was more than her luminous green eyes and matching dimples placed evenly on both cheeks. Leona had a quality about her—sweet, even-tempered, and spiritually mature for one so young. The child probably got it from her father, whom Abraham had said was not only a good friend, but was full of wisdom and godly counsel.

"What brings you over here on this Saturday afternoon?" Abby asked the child. "Do your folks know you're here?"

"Papa's out there, talking with Abraham about doin' some

painting on his barn." Leona pointed across the yard.

Abby squinted against the glare of the afternoon sun. Sure enough, there was Jacob Weaver's buggy parked next to the barn.

"I thought I'd have a look at the twins, if ya don't mind," Leona announced.

Abby opened the door fully and bid the girl to enter. "They're asleep in their cradles, but if we're quiet, they'll probably keep on sleeping."

"My little cousin Amos could sleep through most anything when he was a boppli," Leona said.

"Jah, most bopplin do, but for some reason the twins seem to be light sleepers."

Abby led Leona across the living room and stopped in front of the cradles. One twin had kicked his covering off, so she pulled it up under his chin. The days were getting colder now, and it wouldn't do for the babe to take a chill.

"They're so *schee*," Leona murmured.

"They are quite pretty," Abby agreed.

"I can't wait 'til I'm grown up and can get married and have some bopplin of my own." The child grinned, and her dimples seemed to be winking at Abby.

Abby thought about her upcoming wedding and how she'd felt compelled to postpone it in order to stay in Pennsylvania so she could care for Mom and the twins. Lester hadn't been happy about moving the wedding date to January, but after a few letters of encouragement, he'd finally agreed.

Abby motioned to the sofa. "Would you like to sit and visit until your daed's done talking to Abraham?"

Leona nodded and followed Abby across the room. They sat next to each other on the sofa, and Abby picked up her quilting squares again.

"Titus and Timothy look so much alike," Leona said. "How do you ever tell 'em apart?"

Abby chuckled. "That has been kind of tricky. I thought I had the problem solved when I tied a blue ribbon around Titus's ankle. That worked fine until I bathed him once and forgot to remove the ribbon."

"What happened?"

"The ribbon became soggy and fell off. By the time I got the boppli dried and dressed again, a ruckus broke out in the yard between Samuel's dog and Mary Ann's cat. So I placed Titus back in his cradle and went outside to see about it."

Leona covered her mouth with the palm of her hand and giggled. "Don't tell me—when you came back inside, you thought Titus was Timothy. Am I right?"

Abby nodded. "That's exactly what happened, only this time I figured it out before I gave the same baby a bath."

"You mean that's happened before?"

Abby told Leona the story about her bathing the same baby twice and how this time, she'd discovered Timothy's dirty diaper right away and realized it was he and not Titus. "It's been a job for Mom and me to keep the boys straight, but Abraham thinks we're silly."

Leona's eyebrows lifted. "Why's that?"

"He says Titus has one eye slightly larger than Timothy's, so he always seems to know which twin he's holding." Abby shrugged. "I've never noticed much of a difference in the shape of their eyes, but I wish there were something I could do to identify one from the other without it washing off in the bath water."

Leona smiled. "I know what you could do."

"What's that?"

"Why not take some waterproof paint and make a dot on one twin's toe? Since Papa's a painter, he uses paint to mark lots of things."

Abby reached for the child's hand. "Leona Weaver, you're one smart girl. I wouldn't be surprised if you didn't grow up to be a schoolteacher someday."

Leona's eyes brightened. "You really think so?"

"Might could be. None of us knows what the future holds."

~

"The weather's been dry, so I think my paint crew can start workin' here sometime next week," Jacob Weaver said as he studied Abraham's barn.

"Sounds good to me," Abraham replied. "It's been too many years since the barn's had a new coat of paint, and as you can see, it's peelin' and chippin' all over the place. I should have had you do it much sooner, but I kept puttin' it off."

Jacob stroked his long, full beard, which was beginning to show a few signs of gray. "What color are you thinkin'? Want it to be white again?"

Abraham nodded.

"White it is then." Jacob lowered himself to a bale of straw sitting in front of the barn. "Mind if I sit a spell? We haven't had ourselves a little chat in some time."

"You're right about that," Abraham agreed, and he also took a seat. "Between me and the older boys tryin' to get the harvest done, and you and your son havin' so many paint jobs, we rarely see each other except on preaching Sundays."

"I imagine you're kept busy with those zwilling of yours, too," Jacob commented.

Abraham grinned. Just thinking about his identical twin boys brought a smile to his face. "The truth is, Abby and Fannie do most of the work. I mostly get to hold and cuddle my sons, but that's fine by me."

"Sure is a miracle the way God gave you those boys."

"Jah. It's like He took one son and gave me two."

Jacob frowned, and his bushy eyebrows drew together. "I wouldn't say God took Zach away, my friend. It's more likely He allowed free will to be done."

"That's what I meant to say." Abraham decided it was time for a change of subject. Otherwise, Jacob would end up giving him a full-fledged sermon. "When you first showed up, I saw your daughter go into the house. I'll bet she wanted to see Titus and Timothy."

"Leona loves bopplin and is real good with 'em. She'll make a fine mamm someday, I expect."

"She sure has a good-natured disposition. Kind of reminds me of Abby, who's always so agreeable."

Jacob gave his earlobe a couple of pulls. "I've never told ya this before, but I used to hope my Leona and your Zach would end up marrying each other some day."

Abraham stiffened. Jacob's comment was a painful reminder that he had not only been cheated out of seeing his son grow up, but would never know if Zach got married or to whom.

"Even if my boy hadn't been snatched away, it ain't likely our two would have ever gotten married," he mumbled.

"Why not?"

"Leona's almost three years older than Zach."

"*Humph*! Who worries about a little thing like that?" Jacob stood and arched his back. "I hear tell our bishop's five years younger than his second wife."

"Really? Didn't know that." Abraham shrugged as he also stood.

Jacob yawned. "Guess I should round up my daughter and get on home. I've got some paintin' of my own that the wife's been after me to do for some time."

Abraham chortled. "Isn't that the way? Seems like the last thing on our list of things to get done is usually at the top of the list our wives are keepin'."

"That's how it goes once a body's been married awhile." Jacob patted Abraham on the back. "Before I go, mind if I take a look at those growin' boys of yours?"

Abraham clasped his friend's arm as they began walking toward the house. "Don't mind at all. Fact is, I'd be pleased to show 'em to you."

Jacob halted, and Abraham almost ran into him. "Oh, I nearly forgot. I stopped by the general store yesterday afternoon and spoke with Caleb."

"How are things going there? Are he and Matthew managing okay?"

Jacob's expression turned serious, and for a moment Abraham was afraid he was about to receive news that his old business was failing.

"Caleb's concerned for Naomi and asked me to pray about things."

"What's wrong with Naomi? Is she sick?"

Jacob shook his head. "She's not sick, just seems kind of

depressed." He paused and slid his tongue across his top teeth. "I hesitate to say anything, but I think you have the right to know."

"Know what? If there's somethin' you're not tellin' me, then please do so."

"Well, Caleb thinks Naomi's hurt because you show the zwilling so much attention."

Abraham's mouth fell open. "What? They're my twin boys. Why wouldn't I give 'em lots of attention?"

Jacob cleared his throat a couple of times. "It's fine to love on your little ones, Abraham, but Naomi's concerned you may have forgotten about Zach and believes the twins have replaced him in your heart."

Abraham clapped his hands together. "That's *lecherich*! I'll never forget Zach."

"It may seem ridiculous to you, but Naomi's hurtin' just the same. I think she feels you haven't shown her daughters much attention, either."

Abraham felt a sense of irritation well up in his soul, but as he mulled things over, he realized he might have been remiss in showing enough love to his granddaughters. He supposed he could have said or done a few things to make Naomi think he cared more about Titus and Timothy than he did Zach, too.

"I'll drop by Naomi's place soon," he promised. "There were enough hard feelings between us after Zach was kidnapped, and I don't want anything gettin' in the way of our relationship now."

CHAPTER 18

$\mathcal{N}$aomi had just started supper when she heard a knock on the back door. She glanced at the wall clock above the refrigerator. Caleb wasn't due home from the store for another hour. Besides, he wouldn't be knocking on his own door.

She turned down the burner on the propane stove and went to the door. When she opened it, she was surprised to see her father standing on the porch. Since Nancy hadn't come over today, he obviously wasn't here to pick her up.

"Papa, what are you doing here? Is everything all right at home?"

"Everything's fine. I dropped by so we could talk." He glanced over her shoulder. "Is this a good time?"

She nodded and stepped aside. "I'm just heating some bean soup, but it can warm on the stove while we visit. The kinner aren't up from their naps yet, so if you'd like to go into the living room, we can visit there."

Papa removed his straw hat and hung it on a wooden peg by the door. "Why don't we sit at the kitchen table? That way you can keep an eye on your soup."

"Okay." Naomi pulled out a chair, and her father did the same. "What'd you want to talk about?"

He cleared his throat a couple of times and gave his beard a quick tug. "I—uh—it's come to my attention that you think I've forgotten about Zach."

Naomi stared at her hands, folded in her lap. "Who told you that?"

"It don't matter who told. The question is, do you believe it?"

Naomi lifted her gaze. "I have noticed the way you dote on the twins, and you hardly ever speak of Zach these days."

Papa didn't respond at first; just sat there fiddling with the stack of paper napkins nestled in the wicker basket on the table. Finally, he leaned forward and leveled her with a most serious look. "Zach's gone, Naomi. Unless God performs a miracle, he ain't comin' back."

"I know that, and I was dealing with things fairly well until the twins were born. That's when I began to wonder—"

He held up his hand. "Zach's not here, but the zwilling are. Don't ya think I should be giving them my love and attention instead of pining for the child I lost and can't bring home?"

Tears clouded Naomi's vision, and the lump in her throat prevented her from answering his question.

"I still love Zach, and I always will," he went on to say. "I pray for him often, too."

"So do I." Naomi almost choked on her words, and she swallowed hard. "I miss my little brother. There are times when I still feel guilty for leaving him on that picnic table five years ago."

Papa shook his head. "The past is in the past; it can't be changed. What counts is what we do with the days God gives us now."

"I know that, but—"

"God's blessed you with two little girls, so rather than dwellin' on the things you wish could be changed, why not focus on Sarah and Susan? They need you, and so do my twin boys."

Naomi grabbed a napkin and blew her nose. "Why would Titus and Timothy need me when they have you and Fannie?"

"You're their big sister, and your kinner are their nieces." Papa paused and gave his beard a couple more quick pulls. "Each member of our family is important, and we need each other. Don't you agree?"

She nodded.

"At times it may seem like I'm favoring my twin sons, but they're still little and need all the love and attention Fannie and I can give 'em right now." He smiled. "Just as your kinner need you and Caleb to shower them with love."

Naomi drew in a deep breath and released it quickly. "What about you, Papa? Is there enough love in your heart to show my girls a little attention once in a while?"

"Of course there is." Papa pushed back his chair, and it scraped across the hardwood floors. "If you'd like, I'll go upstairs right now and see which one of them is howlin' like a stuck pig."

Naomi jumped up. One of the girls was crying? She'd been so engrossed in their conversation she hadn't even heard it.

"Please let me go," Papa said, starting for the door that led to the stairs. "Why don't you check on that good-smelling soup, and I'll find out which girl needs tendin' to?"

"Danki, Papa." Naomi turned toward the stove, her heart filled with gratitude that she and her daed had been able to talk things through. She knew he was right about Zach, and with God's help Naomi would try to pray more, love more, and live each day to the fullest. She must leave Zach in God's hands and move on with her life.

Abby turned down the burner under the pot of savory stew that was simmering on the stove. Then she opened the oven and slipped a baking dish filled with biscuits inside. Supper was nearly ready, Mom would be up from her nap soon, and when Abraham returned from Naomi's and the men came in from the fields, they could eat.

She glanced at the windowsill, where the letter lay that she'd received from Lester today. Mom had received a letter from Harold, too. He wanted to let them know that three days ago Lena had given birth to a healthy baby boy they'd named Ira. Abby wished she could be there to help her sister-in-law, but she was needed here. Lena did have her own mamm living nearby, so she was sure there would be plenty of help at Harold and Lena's place, and that made her feel some better.

Abby turned her attention back to Lester's letter. She'd been too busy to read it until now. She opened it and took a seat in the rocking chair near the stove so she could keep an eye on things.

Dear Abby,

I'd thought about making another trip to Lancaster County to see you, but things have gotten real busy at the blacksmith shop, and it would be hard to get away at this time.

I wish you could come home right now, but I know that's not possible, since you've got your hands full caring for the bopplin, and helpin' your mamm with the things she needs to have done. Even though January is only two months away, it seems like a long ways off to me. I'm tryin' to be patient, though.

Say hello to the family there, and please write soon. Your letters don't come as often as I'd like them to.

Always yours,
Lester

"I wish I had time to answer his letter right now. But I'd no sooner get it started and it would be time to serve supper." Abby opened her mouth and released a noisy yawn, causing her jaw to pop. She'd been so busy since she came to help Mom that she barely had any time to herself. There were days when she wished she could be alone, to write letters, read a book, work leisurely on a quilt, or take a walk to the creek. She missed spending time with Lester and longed to go for buggy rides, picnics, or simply walk by his side. *Lester might not realize it, but I'm as anxious as he is to marry and begin our family. Being around Naomi's little girls and my new twin brothers has made me yearn even more to be a wife and a mother.*

Abby glanced at the calendar tacked on the wall next to the refrigerator. If things had worked out differently, she and Lester would be getting married in a few weeks. Now they had two more months to wait, and that was only if Mom could manage on her own by then.

Abby's mother was slowly getting her strength back, but she still needed one or two naps every day. Mary Ann helped out when she wasn't in school, and Nancy alternated between their home and Naomi's. Then, there was dear Cousin Edna, who'd been more than willing to help at first, but she'd been fighting a cold after her bout with the flu, so she'd been unavailable to come over for the last several weeks.

Abby grimaced as she thought about the prospect of having to postpone her wedding a second time. How would Lester take the news if she decided to stay even longer? Would he be angry and break their engagement? She prayed he would understand. After all, he'd put off setting a date for their wedding for a couple of years due to his daed's passing and him trying to get the blacksmith shop running smoothly on his own. It wasn't until he'd hired an employee and gotten him trained to do things the way he and his daed had done that Lester felt ready to make the commitment to marriage.

"Guess I'd best not borrow trouble," Abby said, tucking Lester's letter inside the mending basket at her feet. "I'll have to pray harder and trust that Mom's strength will fully return before January."

A shrill cry, followed by another one equally high-pitched, alerted Abby that the twins were awake and needed her attention. She pushed herself out of the rocker and started across the room. *My own needs must be set aside. All that's important right now is caring for Mom and those baby brothers of mine.*

Linda hung up the phone then quickly dialed Jim's cell number. "Guess what?" she said when he answered on the second ring.

"Beats me."

"I just got off the phone with my mother. She and Dad are coming for a few days' visit, and they'll be staying through Thanksgiving."

"That's nice."

Linda moved to the living room with the cordless phone so she could check on Jimmy, who'd gone there a short time ago to watch Saturday afternoon cartoons.

"Is that all you wanted?" Jim asked in an impatient tone. "I'm really busy."

She grimaced. Why did he always seem so irritated with her?

In the early years of their marriage, he'd never minded when she called him on the phone.

"I won't keep you long," Linda said, clicking off the TV and heading back to the kitchen. Jimmy had fallen asleep on the couch. "I was wondering if you might be able to take some time off while Mom and Dad are here. Maybe we could make a trip to the ocean. It's usually nice there in late fall."

"Get real, Linda," Jim snapped. "I've got a ton of work lined up clear into January. The only time I'll be taking off that week will be on Thanksgiving Day."

Tears stung the back of Linda's eyes, but she willed herself not to cry. Jim hated it when she gave in to her emotions—as he'd so often said. "It was only a thought," she mumbled. "I'll let you go so you can get back to whatever you were doing."

"I'm painting, Linda. That's what I do for a living." She flinched, feeling as if he'd thrown cold water in her face. It seemed that no matter how hard she tried to be sweet and set the example of a Christian wife, Jim responded negatively. She and Beth had recently begun attending a women's Bible study on Wednesday mornings. The fellowship and lesson helped some, but Linda felt she needed something more, something that would teach her how to respond to Jim's nasty attitude and eventually lead him to Christ.

Maybe I'll speak to Rev. Deming after church tomorrow. He might have the answers I need.

CHAPTER 19

"Mom! Dad! I didn't expect to see you until later in the day." Linda grabbed her parents in a hug, as the three of them stood inside the hallway outside her living room.

"We left Boise yesterday afternoon and drove as far as Yakima," her father said, running his fingers through the back of his thinning brown hair. "Then we got a hotel for the night and left early this morning to come here."

"I'm glad you're early." Linda smiled, feeling happier than she had in a while. She missed her family and wished they lived closer. "Have you had breakfast yet?"

"Just one of those continental things the hotel provided," her mother replied. "But if you haven't eaten, I'm sure we could eat again."

"Since it's Saturday, Jimmy and I slept in this morning, so I haven't fixed anything yet. Jim left for work before we were up. He probably grabbed a donut and a cup of coffee somewhere on the road."

Dressed in his pajamas, Jimmy padded out of the living room, where he'd been watching TV. "Grandpa! Grandma!"

Linda's father bent down and scooped Jimmy into his arms. "Look at you! I think you've grown at least a foot since we were here in the summer."

Jimmy giggled and nuzzled his grandfather's cheek. "I only grew a few inches. My daddy said so."

Dad set Jimmy on the floor again. "Say, how come Jim's working on a Saturday? Doesn't that man ever stay home?"

Linda sighed. "He's trying to get a group of condos painted

before Thanksgiving, so he and his crew have been working a lot of overtime."

Mom slipped an arm around Linda's shoulder. "Why don't we let Grandpa and Jimmy carry our bags upstairs while the two of us go to the kitchen to see about fixing breakfast?"

"That's a good idea." Linda looked down at Jimmy, who was already racing for the front door. "Get your jacket, and don't try to carry anything too heavy."

Her father frowned. "You're just like your mother, Linda. You worry too much. I won't let the boy do anything I wouldn't have done at his age."

Mom's gaze went to the ceiling. "That's what she's afraid of, Thomas."

Linda led the way to the kitchen. She would have to trust her father not to let Jimmy carry anything heavier than he could handle. "How's my big sister and her family?" she asked. "Are they still going to Dean's parents' for Thanksgiving?"

Mom nodded. "Cheryl and the children have all had colds, but I'm sure they'll be well enough to drive up to Lewiston to share dinner with her husband's family."

"It would have been nice if they could have come here," Linda said wistfully. "Jimmy hasn't seen his cousins since his birthday in April, and I know he would have enjoyed playing with Cameron and Pam." She smiled. "Of course, I realize they have to spend some holidays with the Pattersons."

"That's true," her mother agreed. "So, how are you doing, dear? The last time we were here you looked kind of down, but this morning you seem happier and more at peace."

Linda pulled out a chair and motioned her mother to take a seat at the table. "I am feeling peaceful about my spiritual life, and it's all because of Christ."

Her mother squinted her pale blue eyes. "What do you mean?"

"Jimmy and I have been going to church, and awhile back I accepted Christ as my personal Savior." Linda took a seat on the other side of the table. "I wrote you about it, don't you remember?"

Her mother shrugged and started folding napkins into

perfect triangles. "You may have mentioned something about it, but I figured it was only a passing fancy."

Linda released a sigh. "It's not a passing fancy, Mom. I've made a decision to follow the Lord, and—"

"What were you planning to have for breakfast, dear? Shouldn't we get it started?"

Linda pushed her chair back and stood. "I guess we can talk and prepare the meal at the same time." She went to the refrigerator and took out a chunk of ham and a carton of eggs. "Do you want your eggs scrambled, poached, fried, or boiled?"

"Scrambled is fine. Would you like me to make some toast?"

"Sure. There's a loaf of bread in the refrigerator. Do you remember where the toaster is?"

"I'll find it."

Linda placed the ham and eggs on the cupboard and decided to broach the subject of her newfound faith again. "There's going to be a Thanksgiving service at my church on Thursday morning. I was hoping we could go."

Her mother whirled around. "All of us?"

She nodded. "First there will be a program about the pilgrims and how they came to America to find religious and political freedom. That will be followed by some singing, and then Rev. Deming will deliver a short message."

"What about dinner?"

"I can put the turkey in the oven before we leave. I'm sure we'll be home in plenty of time to get everything ready so we can eat by one thirty or two."

"If your father is willing to go, I will be as well." Mom reached up to fluff one side of her blond hair, which she wore in a short bob. "I really should see about getting my hair done if I'm going to church, and maybe I should buy a new dress, too."

Mom and Cheryl are just alike. All they ever think about is how they look and how much money they can spend on new clothes. Linda cracked an egg into the bowl she'd placed on the cupboard. "There's no reason for a trip to the beauty shop or a new dress, Mom. I'm sure whatever you brought to wear on Thanksgiving Day will be fine."

"But it might be fun to go on a shopping spree, don't you think? How does tomorrow afternoon sound, dear?"

Linda nodded. "Sure, Mom, that would be fine." Maybe she would have the opportunity to talk about Christ later on.

⁓

"It's been almost two months since the twins were born, and I'm sure I can handle things on my own now," Fannie told Abby as the two of them began lunch preparations for themselves and the crew of men who were painting Abraham's barn. "I think it's time for you to return to Ohio."

Abby shut the refrigerator door and turned to face her mother. "Not before Thanksgiving, Mom. You'll need help with the dinner, and I've been looking forward to spending the holiday with my family here."

Fannie took a large, enamel kettle from the bottom drawer of the stove and placed it on the cupboard. "Wouldn't you like to be with Lester for Thanksgiving?"

Abby handed her mother the container of chicken noodle soup they had made last night. "Of course I would, but Lester and I will be together at Christmas. Soon January will be here and then we'll be getting married. After that we can spend every holiday with each other—some here and some in Ohio."

Fannie nodded. As much as she wanted to have her daughter with them for Thanksgiving, she felt bad for Lester. He'd been without Abby for several months and had to postpone his wedding because of the twins being born and Abby staying to help. She was glad he and Abby would finally be together for Christmas.

"If you're feeling up to being on your own for a few hours, I thought I'd go into Paradise after we serve lunch to Jacob Weaver's painting crew. I'd like to see how things are going at the quilt shop," Abby said.

"That's a fine idea. You work too hard around here, and it will give you a chance to see which of the quilts you might want to take home to Berlin."

"I'm not sure I should take any of the quilts back with me,"

Abby said as she began setting the table.

"Why not?" Fannie poured the soup into the kettle. "You've made a couple of nice ones since you've been here, and I would think you'd want to try and sell them in your own shop."

Abby grabbed a handful of napkins and placed them beside each plate. "I'm sure Deborah has plenty of quilts we can sell, but if it would make you feel better, I'll take a look at them when I go there after lunch."

Fannie smiled and turned down the stove burner. The soup was already beginning to simmer, and the pleasant aroma of chicken broth tickled her nose and made her stomach rumble.

"I'm going to miss you," Abby said, coming to stand beside her mother.

"I'll miss you, too. Fact is, I'm sure the whole family will."

"Everyone's been so kind and helpful. I can't get over the way Matthew has been willing to help at the quilt shop now that Naomi's working at the store again." Abby moved back to the table. "He's been like a big brother to me, and it means a lot."

Fannie sighed. "Matthew's a fine man. I wish he'd find a nice wife and settle down."

"I invited my friend Rachel to come here for a visit, but she hasn't been able to get away," Abby said. "I'd planned to introduce her to Matthew and hoped they might hit it off."

"Maybe when we come to Ohio in January for your wedding, they'll have a chance to meet."

Abby moved to the cupboard and took a loaf of bread from the breadbox. "You don't think Matthew's afraid of getting married, do you?"

Fannie chuckled. "I doubt that. He probably hasn't found the right woman yet."

Abby nodded. "Guess I'll have to pray that the Lord sends my stepbrother just the woman he needs."

When Abby arrived at the general store later that afternoon, she found it full of customers. Caleb was waiting on an Amish man buying a new shovel, and Naomi was kneeling in front of a shelf, restocking it with rubber stamps.

"Looks like business is booming," Abby whispered as she wandered over to Naomi. "I'll bet Caleb's glad you're back at work again."

Naomi nodded. "Jah, things have been busy today, both here at the store and in your mamm's quilt shop. I'm glad Matthew is able to help out."

Abby glanced around. "Where are your girls? Did you leave them at home with Caleb's mamm?"

"They're in the back room sound asleep."

"I wonder if Mom will be able to work in her quilt shop soon and bring the twins along," Abby said. "She suggested I return to Ohio, saying she could manage on her own, but I think she only meant at home."

Naomi nodded toward the adjoining room. "I believe Matthew's got things well under control in the quilt shop. Now that I'm not needing Nancy's help so much at home maybe she can help him there."

"That makes sense. If Nancy were to come to the store every day, she could help Matthew and would be available to watch your kinner whenever it's needed."

"That's what I thought." Naomi smiled. "Are you here for anything in particular today?"

"Just came by to see how things are going, and Mom suggested I look over some of the quilts I've made and decide if I want to take any home with me next week."

"I can't believe you're actually leaving." Naomi stood and gave Abby a hug. "I'm going to miss you, sister."

Abby fought the urge to cry, but she refused to give in to her threatening tears. She would be going home to Lester soon, and that was something to be happy about.

"I'll miss everyone," Abby said. "But it won't be long before you'll be coming to Ohio for my wedding."

"Jah. January's not far off at all, and we're looking forward to the big day."

"Guess I'd best go see about those quilts." A few seconds later, Abby entered the shop and was surprised to see that

Matthew had hung several more of his quilt hangers on the wall opposite the door. A few English women were shopping in the store, and since Matthew was busy waiting on a customer, she decided not to bother him.

Matthew must have seen her come into the room, for he gave her a friendly wave. Abby smiled and headed over to the box where she'd put some of the quilts she had made. She was about to open it when Naomi called out to her.

"Abby, Caleb just answered the phone, and it's someone from Ohio. They asked if you were here and said they needed to talk to you."

Anxious to speak with anyone from home, Abby hurried from the room. She slipped behind the counter and took the phone from Caleb. "Hello. This is Abby Miller."

Her forehead wrinkled as she tried to make sense out of the jumbled words on the other end of the line. "Deborah, is that you? I can barely hear what you're saying. Can you speak a little louder, please? What was that?"

There was a long pause, and Deborah's high-pitched voice came on the line again.

Abby's mind reeled as she tried to digest everything that was being said. She wished Deborah would slow down. She wished. . .

"A fire! At the quilt shop? Wh–what did you say?" Abby gripped the edge of the counter as the room began to spin.

Chapter 20

"Abby, Abby. Wake up!"

"Is she okay?

"She hit her head."

"It's bleeding."

"Better get a clean towel."

"Maybe we should call 9-1-1. She might have a concussion."

"Let's wait a few minutes and see if she comes around."

Somewhere in the distance, Abby heard muffled voices. Where was she? Why did it seem so dark? She tried to open her eyes, but her head hurt too much. She tried to think, tried to focus. Had she fallen into a deep, dark pit, or was this another one of her horrible nightmares?

Something cold touched her forehead, and a stinging sensation followed. Abby flinched.

"Abby, please say something."

She recognized Matthew's voice and struggled to open her eyes.

"She's coming around."

Someone's cool hand touched the side of her face. She blinked and tried to sit up, but a heavy weight seemed to be pressing her down.

"Wh–what happened?" she murmured, as the faces of Naomi, Caleb, and Matthew came into view.

"You were talking on the phone one minute, and then you fainted." Naomi held a small wet towel against Abby's forehead.

Matthew clasped her hand. "You must have hit your head on the edge of the counter when you went down."

Abby's mind whirled like tree branches swishing in the wind as she forced herself to remember the conversation she'd had with Lester's mamm.

"The phone. Where's Deborah? I—I need to speak with her." Tears blurred Abby's vision, and she attempted once more to sit up.

Caleb knelt beside her, placing a gentle hand against her shoulder. "When you passed out, the phone went dead. Was it Lester's mamm you were speaking to?"

Abby nodded, and the room tipped precariously. She swallowed the bitter acid taste in her mouth. *No, no, it can't be. I had to be dreaming. That's all it was—that frightening nightmare I've had about fire and smoke and a kitten being trapped with me.*

Abby trembled and squeezed Matthew's hand. "It—it wasn't a kitten that was trapped; it was Lester."

"What are you talking about?" Naomi gave Abby's arm a gentle shake. "Please, tell us what Deborah said."

Abby turned her head away. "Fire. The quilt shop."

"Did your shop in Berlin catch on fire? Is that what Deborah told you?" Caleb asked. Obvious concern creased his brow as he leaned closer to Abby.

She nodded and drew in a quivering breath as her stomach churned like a boiling pot on the stove.

"What happened? Was anyone hurt?" Naomi questioned.

Abby rolled her head from side to side, while the realization of what Deborah had said became clearer. She gazed at the gas lamp that hung overhead and wished she were dreaming. "He's gone."

Matthew leaned closer. "Who's gone?"

"My Lester. He's dead." Abby choked on a sob and fell into Matthew's arms.

⌒

Fannie paced the living room floor, anxious for some word on Abby. Matthew had brought her home from the quilt shop half an hour ago, and they'd called Dr. Frazier, who lived nearby. He'd been kind enough to make a house call and was upstairs with Abby right now.

"Fannie, won't you please sit down?" Abraham said, taking hold of her arm. "I'm sure we'll hear something soon."

She turned and looked up at him, tears flooding her eyes. "I can't believe this has happened. Why would God allow it, Abraham?"

He pulled her gently to the couch, and they both took a seat. "Many times I've asked God that same question. First, when Sarah died, again after Zach was kidnapped, and once more when Naomi was gone for several months." Abraham took hold of Fannie's hand and massaged her fingers. "My friend Jacob has reminded me many times that God's ways are not our ways. He allows certain things to happen, which often become a testing of our faith."

"But Abby deserves to be happy," Fannie wailed. "She was planning to return to Ohio right after Thanksgiving, and she and Lester were going to be married in January." She dabbed at the moisture on her cheeks. "I should never have let my daughter stay here so long."

"Fannie, you can't blame yourself for this."

"Abraham's right," Matthew spoke up. He'd been sitting in the rocking chair across the room ever since Abby had been taken upstairs. "It was an accident, plain and simple."

"If I had only insisted that Abby return to Ohio sooner, the fire might not have happened and Lester would still be alive." Fannie's chin trembled. "My dear girl should be returning to Ohio to marry Lester, not bury him."

Abraham squeezed her hand. "Please, don't talk that way. It ain't your fault. Abby came here to help because she wanted to. I know she would never cast the blame for this terrible loss at your feet."

Fannie just sat there, too numb, too full of remorse to comment.

"I still don't understand how the quilt shop caught fire or why Lester was in there and couldn't get out," Matthew said.

"We won't have the answers until we speak with Deborah Mast. Even then, I'm not sure she will have all the details," Abraham replied.

Fannie stood. "Dr. Frazier's been with Abby long enough. She needs me."

"Give them a few more minutes." Abraham reached out to her, but she bolted from the room.

Just as Fannie reached Abby's door, the doctor stepped into the hall. "There's a small cut on her forehead, but no concussion from what my examination showed. I think with a few days' rest she'll be fine."

"Fine? How can my daughter be fine? She's just received news that the man she was planning to marry has been killed in a fire that destroyed her quilt shop."

Dr. Frazier shook his head. "I was talking about her physical condition, Fannie. Abby's in shock right now."

"I need to see her." Fannie pushed past the doctor, rushed over to Abby, and took a seat on the edge of her bed.

Abby lay quietly, her eyes shut and a small bandage taped to her forehead. Her cheeks were chalky white and stained with tears. It nearly broke Fannie's heart to see her sweet daughter that way.

Fannie took Abby's hand and squeezed it gently. "My dear girl, I'm so sorry this happened. If there were a way I could shoulder your pain, I surely would."

Abby's eyes opened, and Fannie studied her through the dim circle of light cast by the oil lamp at her bed. She not only looked pale, but her brown eyes appeared faded, as though her tears had washed some of the color away. There was no question about it— Fannie knew her daughter's heart was broken and bleeding.

"He's gone, Mom. Lester is gone." A strangled sob escaped Abby's lips, and she moaned.

Fannie nodded and swallowed around the lump in her throat. "I know, dear one." A deafening silence hung in the air, separating them like a shade at the window. *If only I knew what I could say to comfort my girl. If I could just take this dreadful pain away.*

"Why? Why'd this happen now, when I was ready to go home? What was Lester doing at my quilt shop, and how did it catch on fire?"

Fannie shook her head. "Caleb and Naomi are making phone calls to Ohio. After they've spoken with Deborah, we'll know more of the details."

Abby struggled to sit up. "I need to go home. Need to be there for Deborah, to attend Lester's funeral, and see about the quilt shop."

Fannie wrapped her arms around Abby and held her tight. "We can talk about all that later. You don't have to think about any of this right now."

Abby released a shuddering sigh. "It's—it's my fault Lester is dead."

"No, no. You mustn't say that."

"It's true. I know now what those dreams I've been having meant."

"You do?"

Abby nodded. "Don't you see, Mom? The kitten in my dream represented Lester, and I was supposed to save him."

"Oh, Abby, I don't think—"

"The dreams were a warning of what was to come. I should have returned to Ohio sooner. I might not have been able to keep the fire from happening, but I could have prevented Lester from going in after my quilts."

"You can't know that," Fannie argued. "Once a man determines that he's going to do something, there's little a woman can say that will change his mind."

Abby shook her head. "He listened to me when the cheese place caught on fire. He'd wanted to go inside the building to see if his friend Joe was all right, but he didn't, because I asked him not to."

Unsure of what to do or say to ease her daughter's pain, Fannie held Abby, and they wept together.

⟶

Naomi sat on the wooden stool behind the counter in their store, waiting for Caleb to get off the phone. He had called his cousin Henry, who ran a buggy shop outside of Berlin, asking for the phone number of Lester's blacksmith shop. Now he was talking with one of Lester's employees, trying to get some details about the fire and Lester's death.

Oh, Lord, Naomi prayed, *please help Abby during this difficult time. She's so sweet and kind, always caring for others while she sets her own needs aside. Show me how I might help her.*

Caleb hung up the phone and groaned.

"What is it, Caleb? What did you find out?"

"The cause of the fire is still unclear, but there was a witness who overheard Lester say he was going inside to save Abby's quilts." Caleb shook his head, and his eyes darkened. "The first time he went into the burning shop, he was able to bring out a couple of quilts. But when he went in the second time, he didn't make it out again. By the time the firemen were able to get inside the store, Lester was dead."

Naomi covered her mouth with the back of her hand as mist welled in her eyes. She dropped her hands to her lap and looked at her husband. "How will Abby get through this, Caleb? What can we do to help her?"

Caleb squeezed her shoulder. " 'I will instruct thee and teach thee in the way which thou shalt go: I will guide thee with mine eye,' saith the Lord."

She nodded, remembering the passage of scripture from Psalm 32:8 that their bishop had quoted in church a week ago. Oh, how they required God's instruction—this needy family, who'd already been through so much pain.

CHAPTER 21

*A*bby sat on a wooden bench, waiting for the early Monday morning bus to depart. Abraham had hired an English driver to take her to the station in Lancaster. Mom had wanted to send Nancy along on the trip, but Abby insisted she would be fine and preferred to go alone. She had told her mamm that going back to Ohio was something she must do on her own, and she'd meant it.

She clutched the straps of her black purse and drew in a deep breath, as she struggled for control. She felt all stirred up. Her insides burned like hot coals. *I can do this. Deborah needs me. Lord, give me the strength.*

When the bus pulled into the station a few minutes later, Abby climbed aboard. She looked for a seat at the back of the bus, hoping she wouldn't have to sit next to anyone. She didn't want to make polite conversation. She didn't want to think or even feel. Sleep. That's what she needed right now.

Abby leaned her head back and squeezed her eyes shut against the tears that were so determined to fall. Controlled by an irrational need to hear Lester's voice, she allowed her thoughts to carry her away.

A vision of Lester inside his blacksmith shop popped into her mind. She could smell the pungent aroma of hot metal being forged and feel the heat of glowing embers beneath the anvil. His green shirt and tan suspenders accentuated the crimson flush on his face. Lester smiled in that easygoing way of his; then he reached out his hand. The memory was painful, yet strangely soothing.

Suddenly, Abby saw herself inside her bedroom, with fire and billowy smoke threatening to choke her to death. Lester was by her side, grabbing the quilt off her bed. Their fingers intertwined as they pulled on the doorknob, but it didn't budge. Abby and her betrothed were trapped in the inferno and would perish together.

Abby's eyes snapped open, and her trembling fingers trailed along the narrow ties of her black bonnet. Had she fallen asleep and been dreaming again? She sat for a few minutes in the company of her bitter regrets, then decided she must forcibly rearrange her thoughts. She stared out the window, attempting to focus her attention on the passing scenery, but it was no use. All she could think about was Lester, and how he wouldn't be waiting for her when she arrived in Ohio. He'd given his life trying to save her quilts, and she should have been there to stop him.

Abby gripped the edge of her seat, as tears blinded her vision. *Oh, Lester, how can I go on living without you? I'll never forgive myself for causing your death.*

<hr />

Jim entered the kitchen, switched on the overhead light, and glanced at the clock. It was four in the morning, and he didn't have to get up for work until six, yet he hadn't been able to sleep. He'd gone to bed late last night, tossed and turned for hours, then finally gotten up.

"Why did I let Linda talk me into attending church with her folks on Thanksgiving morning?" he groused as he ambled over to the refrigerator. He pulled out a container of apple juice, grabbed a glass from the cupboard, and filled it to the brim. *If I go to church on Thanksgiving, will Linda keep nagging me to attend services with her and Jimmy on Sunday mornings?*

He gulped the juice down, placed the empty glass in the sink, and snapped off the light. *Might as well see if I can sleep a few more hours. Maybe I'll just crash on the couch.*

Jim headed for the living room and tripped over a pair of Jimmy's sneakers on the way. He cursed and gave one shoe a swift kick. It flew into the room and hit the coffee table with a thud.

He dropped to the couch but jumped up when something sharp jabbed his hip. He groaned when he realized it was a toy truck. "If I've told that kid once, I've told him a hundred times, not to leave his things lying around." Jim grabbed the truck, pitched it across the room, and flopped down with his head on a throw pillow.

He lay there with his eyes closed, hoping sleep would come quickly. A few seconds later, Jim heard a *click*, and he bolted upright. A ray of light coming from the hallway streamed into the room. Who would be milling around this early in the morning?

Jim heard the sound of running water coming from the kitchen, so he decided to investigate. He found Linda's father, clad in a pair of navy blue flannel pajamas, standing at the sink.

Thomas whirled around. "Jim! You scared the daylights out of me. What are you doing up at this hour?"

"I could ask you the same question."

"Woke up to use the restroom and decided I was thirsty."

"Same here. I mean, about the thirsty part," Jim said with a snicker. "I bedded down on the couch, hoping I could get a little more sleep before it was time to get ready for work."

Thomas raised his dark, bushy eyebrows. "Are you and Linda getting along okay?"

"Sure. Why do you ask?"

"Just seems as if there's some tension between the two of you. And then with you sleeping on the couch I figured there might be some serious problems."

Jim grunted and flopped into a chair at the table. "She didn't kick me out of our room, if that's what you're getting at, Tom."

Linda's father shook his head and took the seat opposite Jim. "That's not what I meant to imply." He grinned. "And thanks for not calling me Thomas. I've hated that name since I was a boy, but it's what most people call me, and it's kind of late in the game to start using a nickname."

Jim fingered the edge of the blue vinyl tablecloth. "It's never too late for anything."

Tom cleared his throat. "About you and Linda. . ."

"Yeah?"

"Are you having some problems?"

Jim compressed his lips. Just how much should he tell Linda's dad? Would he be in for a lecture if he voiced his complaints? It was only natural that a father would defend his daughter, and it wasn't likely that his father-in-law would take Jim's side.

"Whatever you tell me won't go any further than these kitchen walls," Tom said with a nod.

Jim drew in a deep breath and decided to plunge ahead. "To tell you the truth, things haven't been good between Linda and me for some time."

"I see."

"Linda has always been somewhat needy, and after we got Jimmy, she became overprotective and whiny, always wanting her own way." Jim grimaced. "This doesn't feel right, me talking about my wife to her father."

Tom shook his head. "That's okay. I'm not so naïve as to think my daughter has no faults."

"I appreciate your understanding."

"How is Linda acting now?"

"She's done an about-face." Jim popped a couple of his knuckles. "Awhile back, she began going to church with some religious friend of hers. Ever since then she's been syrupy sweet and way too compliant. It makes me wonder if she has some ulterior motive."

"Such as?"

He shrugged. "Maybe getting me to go to church with her and Jimmy. Maybe adopting another child."

"But you're going to church on Thanksgiving, right?"

"Yeah, against my better judgment."

"And you don't want more children?"

Jim blew out his breath. How could he explain things without Tom asking a bunch of questions he wasn't prepared to answer? "I think Jimmy's enough for us. And since Linda and I don't see eye-to-eye on many things that pertain to raising the boy, I can't feel good about bringing another kid into our home."

Tom nodded. "I think I understand. Claire tended to be overprotective with both our daughters when they were growing up, but Cheryl has always had an independent spirit and has pretty much done as she pleased since she's been out on her own. Linda, on the other hand, was afraid of everything when she was a child, and she's never had much confidence, not even as a young adult."

"Yeah, I know. She has improved in that area some, but we still have a lot of problems."

"Have you considered seeing a counselor?"

Jim clenched his teeth. Not the counselor thing again. He shook his head. "Don't need a counselor. Things will be fine. You don't need to worry." He pushed away from the table. "I think I'll go upstairs and get ready for work."

"So soon? It's only five o'clock."

"Might as well get an early start. Since I'll be losing a whole day on Thursday, I need to get as much done these next few days as I can."

"Linda thinks you work too hard, and I'm inclined to agree with her."

Jim frowned. "How else can I provide a decent living for us if I don't put in long hours? Can't pay the bills and buy the things Linda might want if I sit around the house all day."

"That's true, but—"

"Gotta run, Tom. I'll see you after work this evening." Jim rushed out of the room before Linda's father could say anything more.

⌒

Fannie sat at the kitchen table watching a wisp of steam as it curled and lifted from her cup of tea, then vanished into the air. Abby had only been gone a few hours and already she missed her. Would her daughter be all right on her own? Could she handle the pressure of going back to Ohio and facing the remains of her shop, knowing Lester had been killed trying to rescue her quilts? The thought sent a shiver tingling down Fannie's spine. So many hopes for the future had been dashed away in a single moment. If there was only some way to change the past, she surely would.

"Are you okay, Mama Fannie?"

Startled by the sound of Nancy's voice, Fannie whirled around. The young girl stood off to one side, and Fannie realized Nancy must have slipped into the room while she was deep in thought. "I was just havin' a cup of tea," she mumbled.

"Mind if I join you? The twins are down for a nap, and I could use a little break."

Fannie nodded at the pot sitting in the center of the table. "It's probably empty. I've already had three cups."

Nancy reached for the teapot and carried it over to the stove. "I'll add some hot water and another tea bag. Would ya like some zucchini bread to go with it?"

Fannie shrugged. "I'm not so hungry right now."

A few minutes later, Nancy joined her at the table. She poured them each a cup of tea and passed the plate of zucchini bread to Fannie. "You need to keep up your strength."

Fannie glanced at the clock on the wall across from her. "Wonder how Abby's doing. Sure hope she'll be able to sleep on the bus. She's had a rough couple of days, and I hated to see her leave for Ohio so soon."

"She did have a pretty nasty bump on the head."

"I wasn't talking about that. I was referring to the trauma of Lester dying."

Nancy nodded. "I can't imagine how she must feel, losin' her entire quilt shop and the man she was plannin' to marry."

"It's always hard to lose a loved one, but having them die in a tragic accident is ever so sad." Fannie took a sip of tea and hoped it would push down the lump that seemed to be stuck in her throat.

"I remember how we all felt when our mamm was hit by a car," Nancy said. "It was like a part of us died that day."

Before Fannie could comment, Nancy reached across the table and patted her hand. " 'Course, havin' you as our new mamm has helped to heal that pain."

Fannie's eyes filled with tears. "Bein' married to your daed and helpin' him raise his brood has filled a void in my life, too."

Nancy leaned her elbows on the table. "You think Abby will ever find love again?"

"It's too soon to be thinking of such things. Abby needs time to grieve and put her memories to rest before she can consider love or marriage again."

"She sure is brave, going back to Ohio by herself."

Fannie nodded. "Brave and determined to do what's right by Lester's mamm."

"Abby's a real special woman, ain't it so?"

"Jah, but I wish she would learn to care for her own needs."

"Doesn't the Bible teach that we should love others and do to them as we would have done to us?"

"It does, but it also teaches that we need to love ourselves."

"Where's it say that?"

"In the New Testament Gospels, Jesus tells us that the second greatest commandment is to love thy neighbor as thyself." Fannie smiled. "How can we love others if we don't love ourselves and take care of our own needs?"

Nancy took a sip of her tea. "And you don't think Abby does that?"

"Most of the time she's worried about everyone else and tries to meet their needs instead of her own. Many times, my daughter has done without or given up her plans for me. She did that when she came to help during my pregnancy." Fannie shook her head. "To tell you the truth, Abby's been overly self-sacrificing ever since her daed died of a heart attack when she was sixteen."

"When she stayed on after the twins were born, it made sense, but then after you seemed strong enough, I figured she would go right back to Ohio," Nancy said.

"Exactly. Now I'm wishin' I had insisted she go sooner. If she had, Lester might still be alive."

Nancy's dark eyes showed obvious concern. "You can't blame yourself for that, Mama Fannie. Abby came here of her own free will, and she stayed because she wanted to. I'm sure she doesn't blame you for what happened to the quilt shop or to Lester."

"That's what Abraham says." Fannie sighed. "About all we can do now is pray for Abby. Pray that in the days ahead she will find comfort from us, as well as the Lord."

CHAPTER 22

*A*bby's heart thumped like a trapped animal as she stood on the sidewalk, holding Deborah's hand, in front of the remains of her quilt shop. A pile of ashes and charred timber was all that was left. It had been burned beyond repair. *If only there was a way to turn back the hands of time. If I just hadn't gone to Pennsylvania to help Mom. If I had only returned to Ohio a few days sooner. If I had understood the meaning of my dream, this would not have happened.*

Abby's chest heaved, and her throat burned, but she wouldn't give in to the tears stinging the back of her eyes. She needed to be strong for Lester's mamm. She needed some answers.

"Did the firemen say why the store caught fire?" she asked Deborah.

Deborah's shoulders lifted, and she drew in a shuddering breath. "I—I—believe it's my fault, Abby. I think I'm the cause of my son's death."

"Wh–what are you saying?" Abby couldn't imagine that Lester's mamm could be responsible for this tragic accident.

Deborah sank to a nearby bench, and Abby did the same. "A cat got into the shop the afternoon before the fire and hid. I tried to find him but finally gave up." She sniffed and dabbed at the tears trickling down her cheeks. "I completely forgot about the cat when I closed up the shop and went home. I thought about it after I made it to the house, but I figured I'd just find him and shoo him away in the morning."

"I don't understand," Abby said. "What would the cat have

to do with the fire?"

"The fire chief said they found the remains of a kerosene lamp overturned." Deborah gulped on a sob. "I—I—think I may have forgotten to turn it off, and the cat—"

"Knocked it over," Abby said, finishing Deborah's sentence.

"Jah. Then the following morning, Lester came through Berlin before any of the other stores had opened. He said they had a lot of work to do at the blacksmith shop, and he wanted to get an early start. He must have passed by your store on the way and caught sight of the fire. Instead of waiting for help to arrive, he went inside with the hope of saving some of your quilts."

"How do you know this?" Abby asked with a catch in her voice.

"Some carpenters who'd come to work on the cheese shop down the street saw it all. They'd already called the fire department, and one man said he had cautioned Lester about going inside." Deborah drew in a quick, shaky breath. "I was told that the first time Lester entered the store, he came out with four quilts. But then, foolishly, he went back for more. That was when the roof caved in, and he was knocked unconscious. By the time the firemen arrived, my son was dead."

The haunting memories of Abby's dream crept into her mind and tightened its grip. It wasn't just an ugly dream as Mom had suggested. It really had been a warning, and maybe the cat in the dream represented the one that had gotten into her quilt shop.

"I'm ever so sorry, Abby," Deborah wailed. "Sorry for the loss of your shop, and sorry for the loss of my boy, who would have been your husband soon if this hadn't happened."

The silence between them was thick and draped around Abby like the heavy shawl she wore. She sat there awhile, picking at the cuticle on her index finger until it bled. Her life had been cut back like a pruned vine, but she didn't hold Deborah responsible for the accident. Many times at the end of the day she had been distracted or overly tired. She could have easily left one of the gas lamps burning, the way Deborah thought she had done. Abby could see herself doing the very same thing with the cat. No, she couldn't allow Lester's mamm to carry the blame for this. It was Abby's fault the shop was now a pile of rubble. She was to blame for Lester's horrible death. It had been her decision to go to Pennsylvania. It was she who'd decided to stay so long. And she had not heeded the warning of her recurring dream.

She reached for Deborah's hand. "You're not to blame. If I had returned to Ohio sooner, Lester would still be alive." The words stung, but she had to say them. "If I had been here, he wouldn't have gone inside."

"You can't know that."

Abby nodded. "Jah, I'm certain of it."

Deborah's dark eyes shimmered with tears. "No matter who's to blame for this tragedy, I know my son loved you, Abby. He loved you enough to risk his life to try and save some of your quilts."

Abby sniffed back tears that threatened to spill over. "I know."

"The four quilts Lester managed to save are at my house. Maybe you'd like to get them after Lester's funeral service."

Deborah's last statement was nearly Abby's undoing. She didn't think she could ever look at another quilt without feeling guilty and remembering her loss. Yet she knew she couldn't leave the quilts with Deborah. Maybe she would have them shipped to Mom's house. When and if she felt ready, she might decide to sell them.

~

"I wish I could have gone with Abby to Ohio," Naomi told Caleb as they opened the store for business. "She's going to need someone to help her get through Lester's funeral."

"Lester's mamm is there, and so are Abby's brother and sister-in-law," Caleb reminded her.

"I know, but I wish I could be there for her."

"You can be, when she returns to Pennsylvania."

"Do you think Abby might decide to stay in Ohio? It is her home, you know."

Caleb turned on the gas lamp hanging above the counter. "What's left for her there? The quilt shop's gone, and Lester is dead. I'm sure she'll want to get away from all those unpleasant memories."

"You're probably right." Naomi opened a sack of toys for Sarah and went to put baby Susan in the crib at the back of the room. When she returned, she found Caleb struggling to open a carton of books. She was tempted to offer her help, but then she reminded herself how important it was for him to be independent. Caleb had given up a lot when he'd sold his buggy shop and purchased the store. She knew he'd done it so they could be married and he would have a way to support them. Most things in the store he could do fairly well, but the forefinger and middle finger on Caleb's left hand had been badly crushed when Mose Kauffman's buggy gave way. Since that time Caleb had only limited use of his hand.

Naomi was relieved when Caleb found a utility knife and finally accomplished his task. She knew he wouldn't have liked it if she'd stepped in to help. Not unless he'd asked her to.

Naomi headed to the quilt shop, where Matthew was opening for business. He looked sad today, probably feeling Abby's pain and wishing he could do something to ease it for her.

"Anything I can do to help you here?" she called to her brother.

Matthew turned from his job of lighting the gas lamps. "Unless we get a lot of customers, I think I can manage on my own today."

"With Thanksgiving only a few days away, I doubt we'll get too many customers in the store or the quilt shop."

"You're probably right. Most women are at home getting ready for the holiday." Matthew's eyes darkened, and he released a groan. "Sure won't be much of a Thanksgiving for Abby this year. Do you think she'll spend it in Berlin or come back here to be with our family?"

Naomi shrugged. "I'm guessing she'll want to stay in Ohio a few days after the funeral. Abby's worried about Lester's mamm, and I'm sure she'll offer Deborah as much support as she needs."

Matthew's gaze went to the ceiling. "Abby thinks too much of others and not enough about herself. She should have gone back to Berlin several weeks ago, like Fannie wanted her to."

"Abby's a caring woman, and she was only doing what she felt was best for her mamm and little brothers. You can't fault her for that, Matthew."

"Don't fault her. I was just voicing my thoughts, that's all."

Naomi knew it was best to drop the subject. Truth be told, she had a hunch Matthew cared a great deal more for Abby than he let on. It made her wonder if somewhere down the line, after Abby had time to heal, there might be a chance for her and Matthew to become a courting couple.

Better not mention that, Naomi decided. *It's too soon after Lester's death to even be thinking such things.* She turned toward the door leading to her and Caleb's store. "If you need me for anything, be sure and let me know."

Linda rolled out of bed, fumbling around for her robe. She thought she'd heard Jimmy calling, and when she tried to rouse Jim she discovered his side of the bed was empty.

She snapped on the light to check the alarm clock and realized it was only six in the morning. Had Jim left for work already, or had he slept on the couch again? He'd been doing that a lot lately. But surely he wouldn't do it with her parents here.

Since her conversion, Linda had made every effort to restore peace to their household, but Jim seemed to be growing more distant as the weeks went by, and she didn't know what to do. She knew he was angry because she had convinced him to attend church on Thursday morning.

"I'll go this once," Jim had muttered when they got ready for bed last night. "But don't think I'm going to make a habit of it."

I need to commit this situation to God, while I pray, set a good example, and leave everything in His hands. Linda opened the door and headed down the hall to Jimmy's bedroom. A quick peek let her know he was still sleep. Probably just dreaming. She shut the door again and returned to her room.

Wide-awake and not wanting to go back to sleep, she took her Bible from the dresser and curled up on the bed to read a few chapters. The first passage she chose was 1 Peter 3:1–2. "Wives, in the same way be submissive to your husbands so that, if any of them do not believe the word, they may be won over without words by the behavior of their wives, when they see the purity and reverence of your lives."

Linda closed her eyes. "Lord, I'm trying to be that submissive wife, but it gets harder all the time. If Jim would only show some response, it would give me a ray of hope. I want him to know You personally, and I know that without You in the center of our lives, our marriage will never be what it should."

A knock on the bedroom door caused Linda to jump. "Jim?"

"No, honey, it's me."

"Come in, Dad," she called.

The door opened, and Linda's father poked his head inside. "You alone?"

She nodded.

"I thought I heard you talking to someone."

"I—I was praying."

Her father frowned. "At six in the morning?"

"There's no special time to pray, Dad." Linda smiled. "Did you need something?"

He shook his head. "I was heading downstairs to get a glass of water and heard Jimmy crying, so I thought I'd better let you know."

She jumped off the bed. "Is he okay?"

"Don't know. Figured I'd let you handle things."

Linda started for the door. "I checked on him a few minutes ago, and he was sound asleep."

"He's probably having a bad dream."

"I'm sure that's all it is, but I'd better make certain he's not sick."

"I'm going downstairs to start a pot of coffee," her father said. "Call if you need me. I think Jim's already gone to work."

"I figured as much," Linda said as she slipped past him.

When Linda entered Jimmy's room, she found him awake and crying. "Honey, what's wrong?" She brushed Jimmy's hair aside and felt his forehead. No fever. That was good.

"I've got a stomachache. Can I stay home from school? I wanna be here with Grandma and Grandpa all day."

Linda kissed his soft cheek. "Thursday is Thanksgiving, and there's no school for the rest of this week, remember?"

Jimmy's eyes brightened, and he bounded off the bed. "Yippee! Me and Grandpa can go to the park. Maybe Allen will be there, too."

She smiled at her son's exuberance. Not more than a minute ago he'd complained of a stomachache, and now he was bouncing all over the place, excited about going to the park. *At least one of my men is happy about my folks being here. Jim's been so aloof since Mother and Daddy came, it's downright embarrassing.*

She reached for Jimmy's hand. "Let's go downstairs and see about making some blueberry pancakes."

"Can we do the kind with faces?"

She released his hand and ruffled his hair. "Sure, sweetie. If that's what you want."

Jimmy scampered out of the room, and Linda followed, thanking the Lord for the joy this little boy had brought into her life.

~

Huddled beside the other mourners who stood near Lester's plain, wooden casket, Abby struggled to keep her emotions in check. Her chest burned and her nose ran, but she held her breath until the urge to cry diminished. When someone took her hand, she felt the warmth and comfort flow all the way to her bones.

"I'm sorry for your loss," her friend Rachel whispered. "If there's anything I can do, please let me know."

"Danki. I'll be fine." Except for the tears Abby had shed in her mother's arms the day she'd received the news of Lester's death, she had not truly wept. She glanced over at Deborah, sobbing uncontrollably and leaning on one of her daughters' shoulders. Emma had come from Indiana for her brother's funeral, and Lester's other two sisters, Bernice and Hattie, who lived in Florida, were there, too. Deborah had told Abby earlier that day that she would be moving to Indiana soon to live with Emma. Abby figured it was just as well, since there was nothing left for Deborah here, now that her only son was gone.

Abby had been tempted to stay in Berlin in order to see to Deborah's needs, but she knew it would be too painful for her or Lester's mamm if either of them stayed. She had promised to spend Thanksgiving with Harold and Lena, but as soon as she'd fulfilled that commitment, she would be on a bus bound for Pennsylvania.

CHAPTER 23

$\mathcal{A}$braham entered the living room and went to the wood-stove to add another log. It had been a fairly pleasant day, with most of their family gathered around the table sharing a delicious Thanksgiving meal. Fannie had put on a happy face, cooking the dinner, with Naomi, Nancy, and Mary Ann's help, and then serving it as though everything was normal. However, Abraham knew, even though his wife smiled on the outside, she hurt on the inside. He was sure Fannie missed Abby and wished her daughter could have been with them today. Fannie was a good mamm, and if she could shield Abby from the trials of life, he knew she would. But that wasn't possible. Fannie needed to rely on God and leave things in His hands the same way Abraham had done countless times.

He opened the woodstove door, tossed the log inside, and then moved across the room to check on the bopplin—first his youngest granddaughter, asleep in her portable crib, then his twin sons, lying in their cradles. "So young and innocent," he murmured. "I pray none of you will ever know the heartaches I have had to endure. I pray each of you will grow up healthy, happy, and relying on God to meet all of your needs."

Abraham's thoughts went to Abby. She had phoned Naomi at the store yesterday and said she planned to catch a bus to Pennsylvania late this evening. She would arrive in Lancaster early tomorrow morning, and Abraham had arranged for one of their English drivers to pick her up.

Some people never find the joy I know, Lord, he silently prayed. *Some lose a loved one and spend the rest of their lives grieving. I pray it won't be so with Abby.*

Abraham meandered back to the wood-burning stove, where it was warm and comforting. *Lord, please be with Fannie's daughter. Give her a safe trip to Pennsylvania, and grant her healing, peace, and comfort in the days ahead.*

Fannie stepped into the room just then and joined him in front of the stove. "Would you care for a piece of apple crumb pie and a cup of coffee?" she asked, slipping her arm around his waist.

He shook his head. "I'm still full from that big dinner we had. Sure was a good meal, and I thank you for it."

She smiled, although he could tell it was forced. "Everyone ate plenty of ham and turkey, not to mention all the trimmings that went with it."

He thumped his stomach a couple of times. "That's for certain sure."

Fannie glanced across the room. "I see the boys and little Susan are still sleeping. Guess that means they'll be wide awake half the night again."

"I hope not. You and Naomi both need your sleep."

"That is so true." She lowered herself into the rocker. "Mary Ann took Sarah upstairs to play with her doll, the menfolk went out to the barn to look at Jake's new horse, and Naomi and Nancy are doing the dishes. I was planning to help, but they said I'd done enough and insisted I come out here to rest awhile."

Abraham took a seat on the sofa across from her. "Guess I raised some smart girls."

She nodded. "Jah. They take after their daed."

"Your daughter's smart like her mamm, too."

Fannie smiled, but even from where Abraham sat, he could see the tears in her eyes. "I'm glad Abby's comin' back to Pennsylvania. There are too many memories for her in Berlin. It will be easier for her to heal if she's not living close to the heartbreaking reminder that Lester's dead and her store is gone." She sniffed and reached for a tissue from the small box on the table beside her chair. "I wish I could take away her pain, Abraham. If I could fix this hurt the way I used to fix her scraped knees and bruised elbows, I surely would."

"Just be there for her," Abraham said. "Love Abby, pray for her, and let the Lord do His work in her life. It's the only way."

She nodded. "I know."

⌒

Jim shifted uncomfortably on the pew near the back of the church, where they sat. Not only were the pews too hard and the music too loud, but the pastor's sermon was boring. So far all the man had talked about was how people should be thankful and give praise to God for the blessings He had given them.

Any blessings I've got came about because of my own doing, he thought ruefully. *I work hard, and everything we have is due to the long hours I put in. I've never understood why some people think they need God in order to feel good about their successes.*

"So on this Thanksgiving Day," the pastor said, breaking into Jim's thoughts, "I want to remind you to give thanks for your family."

Jim glanced down the pew. Linda sat on his right, with Jimmy squeezed in between them, and Linda's parents were on the other side of her. *We look like a model family, all decked out in our best clothes. But are any of us really happy?* He studied his son, nestled against his arm. *Jimmy seems happy most of the time. As happy as any kid could be, I suppose.*

Jim gave his shirt collar a couple of tugs and loosened the knot in his tie. *I've got everything a man could want—a beautiful wife. . .a successful business. . .and a son who practically idolizes me. Then why do I feel as if something is missing?*

His gaze came to rest on the crude wooden cross, nailed to the wall behind the pulpit.

Jimmy's not yours. You stole him.

As Jim stared at the cross, he wondered if he might be losing his mind.

You need to confess. The truth will set you free.

Jim reached into his jacket pocket and pulled out a hankie to wipe the sweat dripping from his forehead. *Now I'm hearing voices in my head? If this is what happens when you attend church, I don't want any part of it.*

He forced his gaze away from the cross and focused on his hands, clenched in his lap. *Guess I didn't get my nails clean enough when I showered this morning. I've still got paint under some of them.* He turned his wedding ring over. No paint there, but then he didn't wear it whenever he painted. The only time Jim put the band of gold on his finger was when they went out, and then it was only to please Linda. *I've spent a good deal of our marriage trying to please that woman, and look where it's gotten me—a seat on a hard pew in a church that's seen better days.*

He glanced around the room. The off-white walls looked like a blind man had painted them. There were roller marks in numerous places and several runs here and there. Sloppy work, that's what it was.

Jim jerked when Jimmy's elbow connected with his ribs. "Daddy, you're supposed to stand up."

"Huh?"

"Church is over. It's time to pray."

Heat flooded Jim's face as he stood. *Free at last. Now to go home and carve that fifteen-pound bird. A few helpings of turkey and some mashed potatoes, and I'll be good as new.*

~~~~~

"I wish you didn't have to leave so soon. You barely touched your Thanksgiving dinner, and now you're heading home when you could have waited until morning."

The chilly November wind whipped at Abby's black woolen shawl, and she gave her brother a hug. "There's nothing here for me anymore. I have no reason to stay."

"You've got Lena, me, and your new nephew, Ira," Harold reminded. "You could stay and be part of our family."

Abby shook her head and blinked against the burning behind her eyes. She wouldn't give in to the threatening tears. Not here in front of Harold. One life had been taken, and another had recently entered the world. It was part of life, and she must learn to deal with it.

"Well, if you're set on leaving, tell Mom and all of Abraham's family that we send our love," Harold said, hugging Abby one last time.

"I'll do that." Abby offered him her bravest smile and stepped onto the bus. She found an empty seat near the back, and a few minutes later, the bus pulled out of Dover.

Abby leaned back and closed her eyes, but uninvited visions flashed through her mind—the charred remains of the quilt shop—Lester's gloomy funeral service—the dinner afterwards at Deborah's house—Thanksgiving with Harold and Lena. Abby didn't know how she had gotten through any of it without falling apart, but she'd managed to put on a courageous front and remain strong for Deborah's sake. It was the least she could do to make up for the poor woman's loss.

Abby felt as if a black cloud had settled over her heart, and she knew it wasn't good to hold her grief inside. But she was afraid if she gave in to the emotions swirling throughout her body, she might never stop crying. Her shoulders ached from the pressure and stress of holding everything in these last few days, and the emptiness in her heart threatened to envelop her.

She gripped the armrest on her seat, forcing her gaze to the scenery whizzing past her window. *I can get through this if I don't take time to think. When I get back to Mom's place, I'll keep busy helping her, the way I did after Dad died. Surely, in time, the pain will get better.*

CHAPTER 24

"Come sit with me awhile, Abby," Fannie said, patting the sofa cushion beside her. "We can have a cup of tea and look at the schee—pretty—snow out the living room window."

Abby swished her dust mop back and forth across the hardwood floor like there was no tomorrow. "I don't have time, Mom. I've got bread rising in the kitchen, clothes needing to be washed, more cleaning to do, and babies to bathe when they wake up from their morning naps." Her eyes looked hollow and tired, like she hadn't slept in many days, and Fannie couldn't help but feel concerned.

"We've got all day to finish our chores, daughter," she said softly. "And you don't have to do everything yourself."

"Jah, well, the work won't get done if we sit around watchin' the snow fall, now will it?" Abby said sharply, holding her body rigid.

The air between them felt thick like butter, and Fannie's muscles coiled tight. It wasn't like her sweet girl to be so rude. Abby was usually soft-spoken and kind, no matter what the circumstances. "Are you feelin' all right this morning?"

"I'm fine." Abby squinted and massaged her temples, like she might have a headache. "If you need to relax, then please do, Mom."

"It's you who needs to relax. Ever since you returned from Ohio three months ago, all you've done is work."

Abby held the dust mop in midair. "The floor's dirty from the kinner tracking in mud and snow; there's always lots to be done."

"That's true, but you don't have to do it alone."

"You still tire easily, and it's my responsibility to help."

"Why do you feel it's necessary to care for me, Abby?"

Abby blinked. "Because—because Dad asked me to before he died."

Fannie's eyebrows lifted. "What?"

"He asked me to see that your needs were met if he didn't make it, and I'm keeping to that promise."

Tears clouded Fannie's vision, while guilt gnawed at her stomach. She should have had this discussion with Abby sooner. "Oh, Abby, I'm sure your daed didn't mean for you to work yourself to death in an effort to meet my needs. He would have wanted you to build a life of your own and take care of your needs, too."

Abby sniffed. "It's too late for that, Mom. I gave up bein' with Lester to come here, and now he's gone." She quickly ran the dust mop across the floor near the woodstove. The hiss and crackle of the logs burning should have offered comfort, but they seemed only to fuel her frustration.

Fannie reached for her cup, sitting on the coffee table in front of her. Should she say what else was on her mind, or would it be best to let it go? "I'm thinkin' your needing to work has more to do with you tryin' to forget the past than it does with keeping your promise to your daed," she blurted.

Abby compressed her lips and kept right on sweeping.

Fannie sent up a quick prayer, determined to try one more time. "I was wondering if you'd be willing to work at the quilt shop on Monday of next week. Naomi's made a doctor's appointment for the boppli that day."

Abby's eyebrows drew together, and the floor creaked under her feet. "Is Susan sick?"

"It's just for a checkup, and I suppose it might include a shot or two if the doctor says it's time."

Abby moved to the other side of the room, swishing the dust mop along the baseboard near the wall.

"Would you be willing to manage the quilt shop for Naomi that day?" Fannie persisted.

"I can't, Mom. You know I can't."

"It's hard for Naomi to haul both girls into town and try to watch them, plus help Caleb in the store, and wait on customers in the quilt shop, too."

"I'm sorry about that." Abby pushed the mop under Abraham's favorite rocker, and then did the same to the chair beside it. "Can't Matthew be there on Monday?"

"He's got a dental appointment that day. Besides, now that he's planning to open a woodworking shop—"

"I didn't realize he was."

Fannie nodded. "He's been talking about it for some time. Haven't you heard him mention it?"

Abby shrugged. "I thought he enjoyed working at the quilt shop."

"He's only been filling in, and I doubt he'd be happy doing that for the rest of his life."

"What about Nancy? Can't she work there on Monday?"

"Nancy started working as a maad for Anna Beechy last week. Have you forgotten?"

"Maybe you should close the shop until you're ready to work full time again," Abby said, making no comment on Nancy's new job.

"That might not be for a while, if ever." Fannie took a sip of tea, savoring the pleasant mint flavor and hoping it would help her relax. She wasn't getting anywhere with her daughter and didn't know if anything she could say would get through to her. "The twins are a handful, and I'm not sure how well it would work for me to take 'em to the quilt shop every day."

"Naomi does it."

"I know, but her girls are further apart in age than my two little fellows."

"I can watch Timothy and Titus while you go to the quilt shop."

Fannie shook her head. "You're at home too much as it is. Wouldn't you enjoy workin' among the quilts again?"

Abby's winced as though she'd pricked her finger with a needle. "I can't."

"Why?"

"You know why, Mom. If Lester hadn't tried to rescue my quilts, he wouldn't have been killed." Abby sucked in a deep breath and released it with a moan. "I doubt I'll ever have the desire to make another quilt, much less run a quilt shop."

"Don't you think it's time to begin moving on with your life, Abby?"

"I am moving on."

"No, you're not. You stay cooped up here most of the time, minding the twins and working until you're ready to drop."

With no further comment, Abby headed for the door, holding the dust mop in front of her. A few seconds later, she stepped outside.

A blast of cold air whipped through the open doorway and Fannie shivered. She glanced out the window and saw Abby on the porch, shaking the mop so hard she feared the head might fly right off. *Lord, please intervene on my daughter's behalf. I fear if she doesn't soon deal with her pain she'll likely cave in.*

Abby reentered the living room a few minutes later, leaned the mop in one corner, and grabbed the dust rag from the table where she'd placed it earlier. She swished it across the front windowsills and worked her way around the room, dusting every nook and cranny.

"Naomi told me that Gladys Yutzy and Rhoda Lapp were by the quilt shop the other day," Fannie commented. "They both asked about you."

No response.

"I think they'd like to get together and do some quilting."

Still nothing from Abby.

"Rhoda thinks it would be fun to make a friendship quilt."

"They can do that without me."

"Gladys mentioned a quilt auction that's to be held in Kentucky this spring. They're looking for Amish quilts from all over the country, so I thought maybe we could send a few from my shop."

"Whatever you want to do, Mom. It doesn't concern me."

Fannie set her cup on the coffee table and stood. "Oh, Abby, if you'd only get back into the routine of things maybe you would—"

"I won't work at the quilt shop, and nothing is going to change my mind!" Abby whirled around and fled from the room.

Fannie flopped onto the couch with a groan. "Oh, Lord, what's it gonna take to reach her?"

⁓

"Why do you have to leave for work so early this morning?" Linda asked Jim as he turned off the alarm clock and crawled out of bed.

"I've got an early job, and I told you that last night. Just go on back to sleep."

"I'm already awake, so I may as well get up with you," she murmured, although it was tempting to stay under the warmth of their cozy Amish quilt.

"I can make my own lunch. There's no reason for you to get up," he insisted.

"And let you leave the house with nothing but a thermos full of black coffee and a couple of donuts?" Linda pushed the covers aside and reached for her fuzzy yellow robe, lying on the chair near her dressing table.

"Yeah, okay, whatever."

While Jim headed for the bathroom, Linda put on her slippers and padded down the hall. She stopped long enough to peek into Jimmy's room and was relieved to see that he was still asleep.

A short time later, she and Jim were in the kitchen. He stood in front of the coffeepot while she worked at the counter making a ham and cheese sandwich. "Would you like me to fix some scrambled eggs?" she asked. "I can put some of this ham in with them."

"Nope."

"A bowl of oatmeal?"

"I'm not hungry."

"Well, how about—"

"I said no!"

Linda recoiled, feeling like she had been slapped. "You don't have to be so mean."

"I get tired of you hounding me about things," he muttered.

"I don't do it on purpose." She turned her attention back to the sandwich, hoping he wouldn't see the tears clouding her vision.

"You push too hard and try to smother me the way you do with Jimmy," he grumbled.

Linda grabbed a knife and slathered some mayonnaise on the bread, willing herself to keep quiet. Since she'd become a Christian, she had tried harder to please Jim, but she often fell short. In fact, it seemed that nothing she did or said was good enough. Jim had become critical, finding fault with even the smallest things.

"I think if you found something constructive to do, we'd all be happier," Jim said with a grunt.

She whirled around to face him. "What is it you think I should be doing?"

He eyed her critically. "You've gained a few pounds since Christmas. It might not be a bad idea if you started exercising so you can shed some of it."

Linda's hands went immediately to her hips. Had she put on weight? Maybe a little. "I could enroll in the fitness center you painted. If you've changed your mind about me going there, that is."

Jim's face turned red, and his forehead wrinkled. "Forget I said anything. The fitness center's a bad idea."

"Maybe I could buy an exercise tape and get together with Beth to work out."

"You already spend too much time with that religious fanatic!" He stomped across the room, jerked open the refrigerator door, and grabbed a carton of milk. Then he turned, marched over to the cupboard, and reached around her to retrieve a glass.

"I'm sorry you don't approve of my new friend," Linda said, her defenses rising further. "If you weren't so unwilling to get together with Beth and her husband and weren't too stubborn to attend church regularly, you might realize there are more important things in life than painting twelve hours a day or hanging out with the guys at the pool hall when you aren't working!" Linda's hands shook, and she berated herself for losing her temper. This was no way to set a Christian example for Jim.

He slammed the glass down hard on the counter, and she was surprised it didn't shatter. "Don't start with me this morning, Linda. I'm not in the mood!"

She moved slowly toward him, praying they might be able to resolve this before he left for work and hoping their shouting hadn't roused Jimmy. "Let's not argue, Jim. I love you, and—"

"Then get off my back!"

A knot formed in Linda's throat as her eyes flooded with tears. What had happened to their storybook romance? Had they both changed so much over the last few years that everything they said to each other turned into a disagreement?

She slunk back to the cupboard to put Jim's sandwich in some plastic wrap as a feeling of despair weighed her down. As soon as she got Jimmy off to school, she planned to give Rev. Deming a call. She'd put it off long enough.

⟿

Abby leaned over the crib and pinned Timothy's diaper in place. Titus would be next, and then she planned to take the boys downstairs to the parlor, where Mom was working on a new Sunday dress.

Titus began to cry, thrashing his arms and legs. In the process, he bopped his brother on the nose, and Timothy started to howl.

"Hush now; I'll be done in a minute." Abby's patience was beginning to wane. She loved her little brothers, but there were times when they got on her nerves. Of course, she'd never let Mom know that.

Abby finished diapering the other twin and reached into the crib. Timothy had settled down, so she figured he could wait a few minutes while she carried Titus downstairs. She had no more than picked the boy up, when Timothy let loose with an ear-piercing wail. "I can't carry you both at the same time," she said, remembering when they were newborns and she'd been able to manage two at once. But the boys had been growing quicker than summer grass and were turning into a couple of chunks.

Timothy let out another yelp, and Abby felt as if she could scream. She hurried out of the room and down the hall.

Downstairs, as she put Titus in the playpen, she could still hear Timothy's desperate cries.

"I'd better get that little fellow," Mom said, looking up from her sewing project at the treadle sewing machine.

Abby shook her head. "I'll do it." She rushed up the stairs and stopped at the top long enough to catch her breath. A pulsating throb in her right temple let her know a headache was forthcoming, and a wave of heaviness settled on her shoulders. *Keep going. Keep working. Don't stop. Don't take time to think.*

The baby's cries seemed to bounce off the walls and echo into the hallway. Abby lifted her shoulders and sucked in a deep breath. "I'm coming, Timothy!"

I'm glad we decided to visit my daed and the family today," Naomi said to Caleb as they loaded the girls into their sleigh. "We haven't spent much time together since Christmas."

Caleb nodded. "Jah, and since this is an off-Sunday and there's no preaching, it's the perfect time to get in a good visit." He reached over and took her hand. "Besides, a sleigh ride in the snow is pretty romantic, don't ya think?"

She chuckled. "It used to be, when we were courting."

"Still can be," he said with a wink. "We've just got ourselves a couple of chaperones now."

"I hope Abby's willing to sit awhile and visit with us," Naomi said, changing the subject. "The last time I dropped by, she kept running all over the place, fiddling with this, fixing that, and fussing over the twins. If she doesn't slow down, I fear she'll end up sick in bed."

"Each person deals with their grief in a different way," Caleb said, picking up the reins. "Giddyup there, boy!"

"You think that's why Abby works so hard and won't go to any social functions?"

"Yep. Most likely she's still pinin' for Lester."

"But it's been three months since he died, and she never talks about her pain."

Caleb shrugged. "Remember what I was goin' through when I crushed my hand under Mose Kauffman's rig and knew I could never work on buggies again?"

"Jah. You refused to see me or even talk about what had happened."

"I thought if I didn't discuss it, I wouldn't have to deal with the agony. But after your daed set me straight on a few things, I finally came to realize that life goes on, despite the trials that come our way. It's what we do about our situation that makes the difference." Caleb gave Naomi a lopsided grin. "I'm glad I listened to Abraham and bought his store. Otherwise we might not have gotten married or become the parents of such *siess* little girls."

Naomi glanced at the baby in her arms and then looked over her shoulder at their other daughter. "Jah, Sarah and Susan are both mighty sweet. Two more precious girls cannot be found in all of Lancaster County."

"My advice is for you to continue being Abby's friend, pray for her, and encourage her to get back to quiltin' again."

"You're right, that is what she needs," Naomi agreed. "Fannie confided in me the other day that Abby won't work on quilts and has tried to take over the care of Timothy and Titus so much so that Fannie feels as if she's not able to raise her own boys."

"Can't say as I blame her for feelin' frustrated. I wouldn't want someone else takin' over the care of our kinner, would you?"

Naomi shook her head. "Not unless I was sick or injured and couldn't do it. But Fannie's been feeling fine for some time, so there's no logical reason for Abby to take over the way she has."

"No reason except she's drivin' herself in order to keep from dealin' with her pain."

"I asked Fannie to speak with Abby about filling in for me tomorrow while I take Susan to her doctor's appointment."

"You think she'll do it?"

Naomi shrugged. "Guess I won't know 'til we get to their place and I've had a chance to speak with her."

⁓

Abby glanced out the kitchen window and saw the Hoffmeirs' sleigh pull into their yard. The realization that she would never experience the joy of bundling up in the snow with her husband and children hit her like a vicious stab to the stomach. When her quilt shop went up in flames so did her hopes and dreams.

When Lester was killed so was her chance to marry and raise a family.

"Naomi's here!" Mary Ann hollered from across the room. "Now I get to play with my nieces."

Abby was tempted to hurry upstairs to her room so she wouldn't have to socialize, but she knew that would be rude. Instead, she scooted over to the stove and flicked the propane switch on. She would heat water for tea and serve it to their guests, along with the apple crumb pie she'd made yesterday.

A short time later, the adults gathered around the table, and Nancy, Mary Ann, and Samuel went to the living room to entertain the little ones.

"Umm. . .this is sure good pie," Matthew said, smiling at Abby.

"Danki."

Naomi nodded. "Apple crumb pie and hot cinnamon tea hits the spot on a cold, snowy day."

Abraham chuckled and thumped his stomach. "I can eat pie most any time of the year. Or any time of the day or night for that matter."

Abby's mamm reached over and jabbed him in the ribs. "I knew you would say something like that, husband."

He tickled her under the chin. "You know me so well."

Tears pricked Abby's eyes, and she blinked to keep them from spilling over. All this happy talk was one more reminder of her great loss.

"My favorite pie is cherry," Jake said, swiping a napkin across his chin.

"Mine's peach, although I don't get it as often as I'd like." Caleb gave Naomi a sidelong glance, but she just ignored him.

Mom pushed away from the table. "I think I hear my boys crying."

Abby jumped up, nearly knocking over her chair in the process. "I'll see to them. You stay and visit with your company."

"But they might need to be fed," her mother said firmly. "Besides, our company came to see you, too." She hurried out of the room before Abby had a chance to argue the point.

Feeling like a caged animal, Abby grabbed her shawl off a wall peg and made a beeline for the back door.

"Where ya goin'?" Abraham called after her.

"Just need a bit of fresh air."

Outside, Abby stepped carefully over the ridges of frozen snow as she made her way to the barn. The ground was slippery beneath her feet, and she knew she mustn't run. A few minutes later, she opened the barn door and stepped inside, relieved to discover a lantern had been lit and a fire blazed in the woodstove. She took a seat on a bale of straw and leaned her head against the wall. *Everyone must think I'm terrible, but I couldn't stay in there a minute longer.*

A fluffy gray and white cat rubbed against Abby's legs and purred. When she was a young girl, she'd enjoyed playing with the kittens in their barn and found comfort in holding one close and letting it lick her nose with its sandpapery tongue. Not anymore. Abby felt irritation as soon as the cat showed up.

She stood and moved closer to the stove. *What's wrong with me? Why can't I enjoy any of the things that used to bring me pleasure?*

The door squeaked, and Abby turned to see who had entered the barn. It was Naomi.

"I came to see if you're all right," Naomi said, crossing the room.

"I'm fine."

"Would you mind if I stay awhile so we can talk?"

Abby shrugged. "I'm not good company today."

"That's okay; you don't have to be." Naomi motioned to the bale of straw. "Let's have a seat, shall we?"

Abby didn't want to hurt her stepsister's feelings, so she lowered herself to one of the bales.

"Did Fannie ask you about filling in for me at the store tomorrow?"

"Jah, but I can't do it. Sorry."

"How come?"

"There's too much to do here, and it wouldn't be right to leave Mom with all the work."

"I'm sure she could manage for one day."

Abby just sat there, hoping Naomi would change the subject. "Your mamm's concerned about you. We all are."

"No need to worry about me," Abby mumbled.

"I'm not trying to tell you what to do, but I think it might help if you talk about the accident and the pain of losing Lester."

Abby clenched her fingers until they dug into the palms of her hands. Didn't Naomi realize that talking about the fire wouldn't make her feel better? It wouldn't bring Lester back, either.

Naomi reached over and took Abby's hand. "Keeping things bottled up isn't a good thing. Your pain will never leave until you've come to grips with it."

Abby's face grew hot, and she looked away. "That's easy for you to say. The man you love isn't dead."

Naomi didn't reply. She merely sat there quietly, and Abby did the same. The only sounds were the gentle nicker of the buggy horses and the crackling wood from the nearby stove.

Finally, Naomi spoke again. "You're right, Abby. I don't understand what it's like to lose the man I love, but I do know the pain of losin' my little brother."

Abby grimaced. She hadn't meant for Naomi to think about her past. "I—I know it must have been hard for you when Zach was kidnapped."

"Jah, it was hard on the whole family. I blamed myself for a time, but I sought forgiveness and finally came to realize that I couldn't undo the things I had done."

"There's no point in talking about this," Abby mumbled.

"I think there is. I believe that in time—"

"Have you lost all hope of Zach ever coming home?" Abby interrupted.

"I still pray for my little brother, but I know, short of a miracle, it's not likely we'll ever see Zach again."

"But there's still some hope, right?"

"There's always hope. Fact is, the Bible teaches that *mir lewe uff hoffning*—we live on hope."

Abby knew what the Bible taught, but it didn't apply to her situation. "If Zach is still alive, then there might be hope of

189

him coming home some day. Lester's dead, though, so there's no chance for him to return."

⁓

Fannie had no more than finished diapering the twins when she heard a horse and buggy roll into the yard, making crunching noises against the hard-packed snow. She went to the bedroom window and peeked out. There was Edna, stepping down from her buggy.

Fannie hurried from the room and leaned over the banister. "Come on up!" she hollered as Edna stepped into the hallway. "I'm about to nurse the twins, but we can visit while I feed them."

"Be right there!" Edna called in response.

Fannie slipped back to the boys' room and seated herself in the rocking chair with Timothy in her arms. Titus seemed content to suck his thumb for the moment, but Timothy had been fussing ever since she'd come upstairs.

Soon Edna entered the room, her cheeks rosy and her eyes aglow. "Wie geht's?" she said, flopping to the end of Fannie's bed.

"I'm fine, and you?"

Edna rubbed her hands briskly over her arms. "At the moment, I'm cold, but other than that, I'm right as rain." She giggled. "Make that right as snow."

Fannie smiled.

"How are our growin' boys?" Edna asked. "Are they sittin' up by themselves yet?"

"No, but I expect it won't be long in comin'."

"How's Abby these days? And where is she? I didn't see her downstairs with the others."

"She must have gone outside. She was pretty worked up earlier." Fannie shook her head. "I'm really worried about her, Edna. All my daughter does is work, and she won't even consider making quilts or helpin' out at the shop. Not even part time."

Edna clucked her tongue. "It's never easy to lose a loved one, but when you're Abby's age and on the brink of marriage, I think it hurts even more."

"She blames herself for the fire, you know."

Edna's dark eyebrows rose. "How so? She wasn't there. She didn't knock over that kerosene lantern."

"You and I know it wasn't her fault, but my daughter thinks otherwise."

Fannie finished nursing Timothy, then after he had burped, she put him back in the crib. Now it was Titus's turn to be fed. "Abby believes if she'd gone back to Ohio sooner the accident wouldn't have happened. Also, she told me that she'd had a recurring dream about a fire, and she thinks it was some kind of warning—one she should have heeded."

"But if it was Lester's time to go, nothing Abby said or did could have prevented the fire or him gettin' killed."

Fannie shook her head. "I know some believe that's the way things are, but I've never been so sure about it."

Edna shrugged and moved over to the crib, reaching through the slats and tickling Timothy's bare toes. Apparently she didn't want to debate the issue.

"To tell you the truth," Fannie went on to say, "I'm beginning to wonder if Abby will ever get over Lester's death and become part of our world again."

"She's not pinin' away in her room or givin' in to fits of tears, is she?"

"No, but she keeps everything bottled up and works from sunup to sunset." Fannie sighed. "Won't even talk to her own mamm about things."

Edna walked away from the crib, and Timothy howled. She scooted back across the room and picked him up. Taking a seat on the bed, she rocked the baby in her arms.

"Say, I have an idea," she said in an excited tone.

"What's that?"

"I'm wonderin' if it might help Abby if she went away for a while."

Fannie blinked. "Away? Where would she go?"

"Give me a minute, now. I'm thinkin' on that."

Fannie hated the idea of Abby going anywhere, but she'd be willing to send her to the moon if it would help with the depression.

"*Hmm. . .*"

"What?"

"My late husband's sister is a widow who lives in a small Amish community in northern Montana."

"And?"

"Elizabeth's been through a lot, losin' both her husband and son in the same accident."

"How'd she deal with it?"

"Better than you can imagine."

"Do you think she might be able to help my daughter?"

Edna shrugged. "It's worth a try, don't ya think?"

"Maybe so, but how are we going to convince Abby to go to Montana to visit a woman she's never met?"

Edna's smile stretched ear-to-ear. "Just leave that up to me."

CHAPTER 26

*L*inda fidgeted with the straps on her purse as she sat across the desk from Rev. Deming, waiting for him to get off the phone. *Should I have come here this morning? Will the pastor be able to help me?* She gripped the armrest of the chair. *If Jim finds out, he'll be furious.*

Rev. Deming hung up the phone a few minutes later. "That was my wife calling from the church's daycare center. They're shorthanded today and she can't get away, so I'll ask my secretary to join us, if you don't mind."

"Your—your secretary?" What was the man planning to do, ask Mrs. Gray to take notes during their counseling session?

He nodded. "My wife usually sits in whenever I counsel with women."

"Can't we leave the door open or something?" Linda leaned forward, her shoulders stiffening. "I wouldn't feel comfortable discussing my problems with anyone but you or Mrs. Deming."

The pastor sat there several seconds. Finally, he nodded and reached for his Bible. "The door stays open. How can I help you, Linda?"

She drew in a deep breath. "My—my husband needs the Lord but he refuses to come to church."

"I believe he was here for our Thanksgiving service and the children's Christmas program."

"Yes, but he only came out of obligation, and it was obvious that he was miserable."

"Perhaps in time he will feel more comfortable about attending on a regular basis."

She shook her head. "Unless things get better at home, I doubt he'll ever agree to come to church with me and Jimmy on Sunday mornings."

Pastor Deming placed his hands on top of the Bible and leaned slightly forward. "Would you care to explain?"

"Jim and I were high school sweethearts, and during the first few years of our marriage we got along well."

"And now?"

"Ever since we adopted our son, things haven't been right between us. Jim works long hours and is rarely at home. When he is there, he's edgy and often says harsh things to me. We hardly ever do anything just for fun, and whenever I've suggested we go back east to visit his folks, he flatly refuses." Linda paused and licked her lips. "At first I thought it was my fault that our marriage was falling apart, because I tend to be overprotective of Jimmy. But then, after I became a Christian, I made more of an effort to please my husband and not be so overbearing where our son is concerned."

"How does Jim respond to that?"

"It's made no dent in his moods. If anything, I think he's become more impatient with me. There are times when he seems so agitated, and I'm afraid he might—" Tears clouded Linda's vision, and she sniffed, hoping to keep them from spilling over.

Pastor Deming opened a drawer in his desk and pulled out a box of tissues. "Take your time, Linda. I know this is hard."

"Thanks." She wiped her eyes and blew her nose. "I have no proof, but I've got a terrible feeling that Jim might be hiding something from me."

"Do you think he could be involved with another woman?"

Linda trembled. "Oh, I hope not. But I suppose—" Her voice faltered. What if Jim was having an affair? How would she cope if he wanted a divorce? She had no job, no way of supporting herself and Jimmy. And what if he tried to get custody of their son? "Do you think I should hire a detective?"

The pastor ran his fingers through the back of his thick gray hair. "That's your decision, of course, but if your husband found out he was being followed, it could make things worse."

"You're probably right. Besides, how would I pay for a detective without Jim knowing?"

"I'd like to give you a list of scriptures to read," the pastor said. A few minutes later he handed her a slip of paper. "I would also suggest you keep praying and try to set your husband a good example." His bushy eyebrows drew together. "Do you think Jim might be willing to come in for counseling, either by himself or with you as a couple?"

She shook her head. "I've suggested that, but he flatly refuses."

Rev. Deming offered to pray with Linda before she left, and she nodded in agreement. At this point, she knew God was the only One who could save her marriage.

Abby stood at the kitchen sink, peeling potatoes for tonight's supper. She had struggled with guilt ever since she'd turned down Naomi's request to fill in for her at the quilt shop today. Even so, she knew there was no way she could go there without falling apart.

She cut up the potatoes and dropped them into the pot of stew, then glanced out the kitchen window when she heard a horse and buggy pull into the yard. It was Cousin Edna, and she was heading for the house. Abby hurried to open the back door.

Edna stamped the snow off her boots before entering the kitchen. "Whew! Sure is a blustery day! I wish spring would hurry and get here."

"I'm surprised you would make the trip from Strasburg in this kind of weather," Abby commented.

Edna hung her heavy black shawl and matching bonnet on a wall peg, then went to warm herself in front of the woodstove. "I don't enjoy drivin' the buggy in the snow, but I needed to speak with you today."

"I thought it was Mom you came to see."

"Nope." Edna glanced around. "Where is Fannie, anyway?"

"Upstairs feeding the twins."

"And the menfolk?"

"They're out in the barn." Abby thought her mother's cousin was acting kind of strange, but then Edna always had been a little different than most. "Would you like a cup of hot apple cider or some mint tea?"

"Jah, that sounds good."

"Which one do you want?" Abby asked, feeling a bit impatient. She had things to do and didn't have time for a visit with her mamm's happy-go-lucky cousin.

Edna shrugged and pulled out a chair at the kitchen table. "It doesn't matter. Just as long as it's hot. Need somethin' to warm my insides, don't ya know?"

Abby poured them both some hot water and added a tea bag to each cup. She placed Edna's in front of her and took a seat across from the woman. "Would you care for something to eat? I believe there's still half a shoofly pie left over from this morning."

Edna patted her stomach. "I'd better pass on the pie. Think I gained a couple of pounds over the holidays."

Abby studied the woman's slender figure. Even if she had gained a few pounds, it wouldn't be a bad thing. From all that Mom had said, Edna had never dealt with a weight problem. Not the way Mom struggled with it, that was for certain sure.

"So, what'd you want to talk to me about?" Abby asked.

Edna took a sip of tea and smacked her lips. "Umm. . .this surely hits the spot."

An uncomfortable silence passed between them, and Abby glanced at the door leading to the hallway. She wished Mom would come downstairs and rescue her. In fact, if Edna didn't say what was on her mind in the next few seconds, Abby might leave the table and cut more vegetables for the stew simmering on the stove.

"I've been in touch with my sister-in-law who lives near Rexford, Montana," Edna announced. "She's wantin' me to come there for a visit, but it would mean I'd have to travel by train."

Abby had no idea what this had to do with her, but she waited to hear what else Edna had to say.

"I've never been on a train before, and to tell ya the truth, I hate the idea of travelin' alone." Edna paused and took another swallow of tea. "So, I was wonderin' if you'd be willing to accompany me."

Abby squinted. "You want me to make a trip to Montana?"

"Jah."

"But that's clear across the country."

"It's not so far by train."

"I can't leave Mom and the kinner. Surely there must be someone else you can ask."

Edna shook her head. "Can't ask my daughter. She's got three little ones to care for. Gerald, my son, has his dairy farm to run."

"What about Gerald's wife? Couldn't she go with you?"

"Mattie helps Gerald with the cows. Besides, she's got four kinner still living at home."

Abby's head began to throb, and she massaged the bridge of her nose, hoping to ward off the headache she felt was forthcoming.

"It would mean a lot to me if you'd agree to be my traveling companion," Edna persisted. "To tell you the truth, I think it might do you some good, too."

Abby's hand trembled as she reached for her cup. She gulped some tea and scalded her lips. "Ouch!"

"You okay?"

"Just drank it too quickly."

"Want me to get you a glass of cold water?"

"No, no. I'm fine." Abby grimaced. *Liar. You're not fine. Your hands are shaking, and your cheeks feel hot as the stove.* The thought of leaving this safe haven made her stomach feel like it was tied up in knots.

Edna just sat there a few seconds, staring at Abby. For the life of her, Abby couldn't imagine what her mother's cousin was thinking.

"If your mamm says she can get along without you, would ya be willing to go?"

Abby opened her mouth to decline, but before she got a word out, Mom stepped into the room.

"What's all this about me gettin' along without Abby?"

Abby breathed a sigh of relief. Mom would set Edna straight on things.

"My sister-in-law, who lives in Montana, has invited me to come there for a visit," Edna said, motioning her mom to join them at the table. "I've invited Abby to go along, since I'm nervous about ridin' the train by myself."

Mom helped herself to a cup of tea, pulled out the chair beside Abby, and sat down. "I think the idea of you going to Montana is a fine one, daughter."

"What?" Abby could hardly believe her mother would say such a thing. Didn't Mom realize how hard it would be to get along without her help?

"Nancy and Mary Ann are capable of helping in your absence, and I think the trip would do you a world of good." Mom gave Edna a quick wink. "Besides, I'd never sleep nights if I thought my favorite cousin was travelin' all that way by herself."

Abby squirmed in her chair, feeling like a helpless bug trapped in a spider's web. *Tricked might be a better word for it,* she thought ruefully. *I wouldn't be surprised if Mom and Cousin Edna didn't cook this whole thing up in order to get me away from here.* She took another sip of tea, this time being careful not to burn her lips. It wasn't good for a body to get so worked up, and she knew she probably wasn't thinking clearly. Truth was, she hadn't had many clear thoughts since Lester died.

"How about it, Abby?" Edna persisted. "Will you go with me to Montana?"

Abby glanced at Mom, then over at her cousin. Both women wore expectant looks, and Abby figured if she didn't say yes, she would be forced to sit here all day and listen to their arguments. She sighed and set her cup on the table. "Jah, okay. I'll go."

CHAPTER 27

*Y*ou're lookin' mighty glum, Matthew," Naomi said to her brother when he entered the store with a frown on his face. "Did you have trouble navigating the snowy roads on this cold Friday morning, or did you get up on the wrong side of the bed?"

Matthew brushed the snow off his heavy woolen jacket and hung it on the closest wall peg. "Neither one."

"Then why the long face?"

He shrugged and removed his black felt hat, hanging it over the top of his jacket.

Naomi skirted around the counter and stepped up beside him. "Come now, brother. I know something is bothering you, and I won't stop asking 'til you tell me what it is."

Matthew grunted and leaned against the front of the counter. "It's Abby. She's gone."

"Gone?"

He nodded.

"What do you mean? Where'd she go? Not back to Ohio, I hope."

"No, she left for Montana. Caught an early morning train with Fannie's cousin, Edna."

Naomi's mouth fell open. "This is the first I've heard of it. Why would they go to Montana?"

"Yeah, why would they?" Caleb asked as he strolled across the room with Sarah toddling beside him and Susan snuggled in his arms.

"Guess Edna has a sister-in-law who lives near Rexford, and she's decided to go visit her," Matthew replied.

"In the dead of winter?" Caleb's eyes were wide.

"Jah."

"But why'd Abby go with her?" Naomi questioned. "Ever since Lester died, she hasn't wanted to do much of anything except hang around my daed's place and help Fannie."

Matthew reached up to scratch the side of his head. "From what I gathered, Edna's afraid to ride the train alone. She practically begged Abby to go along."

Naomi smiled as a revelation came to her. "I believe Edna and Fannie might have cooked this up in order to get Abby off someplace where she could rest and allow her broken heart to mend."

"Makes sense to me," Caleb put in. He handed the baby to Naomi. "I think she's wet."

Naomi squinted at him. "Would it kill you to change a windel once in a while?"

"It might." He wrinkled his nose. "Especially if it was a dirty one."

She groaned. "You're such a *hatzkauer*."

"I ain't no coward."

"Prove it."

"All right, I will." Caleb took the baby from her. "Is it all right if I leave Sarah here with you?" he asked with a grin.

"Jah, sure. She can play with her doll while Matthew and I finish our discussion."

Caleb headed for the back room, while Naomi found Sarah's faceless doll and got her settled on the braided throw rug behind the counter. Then she called to Matthew, who had headed in the direction of the quilt shop. "Where are you going?"

"I'm workin' here today."

Naomi followed him into the next room and waited until he had all the gas lamps lit. "Are you planning to tell me why you're so upset about Abby going to Montana?"

He shrugged his broad shoulders. "Just don't think it's a good idea. What if she likes it there and decides to stay?"

"Ah, so that's the problem. I've been suspicious for some time that you cared for her."

Matthew moved to the window and lifted the dark shade. "Of course I care. She's part of our family."

Naomi studied her handsome brother.

"Why are you starin' at me like that?" he asked, moving to the wooden counter in the center of the room.

"You're in love with Abby, aren't you?"

Matthew's ears turned red, and the color quickly spread to his face. "Wouldn't do me no good if I was."

"Why do you say that?"

"She's in love with Lester."

Naomi shook her head. "Lester's dead."

"Don't ya think I know that?" Deep creases formed above Matthew's brows. "Abby doesn't see me as anything more than a big brother. So even if her pain should heal, I doubt she could fall in love with me."

Naomi's heart went out to Matthew. She knew well the frustration of being in love with someone and thinking things would never work out. Yet God had worked a miracle in her life where Caleb was concerned, and He could do it for Matthew and Abby, too.

Naomi touched her brother's arm. "My advice is to pray about a relationship with Abby and keep being her friend."

He grabbed a stack of invoices from under the counter. "No problem there."

Abby leaned her head against the back of the seat, a sense of relief washing over her. Edna had finally drifted off to sleep, after spending the last several hours talking nonstop and telling one joke after another. All Abby wanted to do was watch the passing scenery and be left alone with her private thoughts. Her mind spun with the details of Lester's death and fueled her anxiety. Snippets of her last letter from him rolled around in her mind. He'd been anxious for her to return home—anxious for their wedding.

Clickety-clack, clickety-clack, the train rumbled over the tracks, taking them farther and farther away from all that was familiar to her. What would Montana be like? How long would

Elizabeth expect them to stay? Would there be something for Abby to do there so she wouldn't have to think about Lester or the quilt shop in Ohio that no longer existed? She swallowed around the perpetual lump in her throat and closed her eyes. *I mustn't allow myself to think about Lester or what might have been. Maybe a nap would be good for me, too. When I wake up, I hope my headache is gone.*

Abby had just nodded off when someone bumped her shoulder. She opened her eyes and turned her head toward the aisle. A tall, dark-haired man, wearing blue jeans, a fancy red-and-white western shirt, and a black cowboy hat, smiled down at her. "Excuse me, ma'am," he said in a slow, lazy drawl. "I was tryin' to get something outta the overhead luggage rack, and I sure didn't mean to wake ya."

"I—I wasn't sleeping," she stammered.

He nodded toward Edna, who leaned against the window with her mouth slightly open. "Guess I didn't wake your mama, either."

"Oh, she's not my mamm. Edna's my mother's cousin."

He grinned. "Where ya headed?"

"Rexford, Montana."

"What's up there?"

"Edna and I are goin' to visit a relative of hers."

"Amish, like you?"

Abby nodded.

"Didn't realize there were any Amish out west."

"There aren't that many, but—" Abby stopped in mid-sentence. She didn't care for the way the cowboy was looking at her, with his dark eyes narrowed and his lips curled in a crooked smile. It made her feel like a feeble mouse about to be pounced on by a hungry cat. Truth was, she felt as out of place talking to this friendly cowboy as a prune in a basket of apples.

As the train rounded a curve, it rocked from side to side, and Abby gripped her armrest. "Maybe you should take a seat so you don't topple over," she told the man.

"Aw, I'm a professional bull rider; I've been up against worse than this." He winked at her.

Abby squirmed in her seat, feeling more uncomfortable by the minute. She was tempted to wake Edna.

"Well, guess I'd best be gettin' back to my seat. Nice jawin' with ya, ma'am." The man tipped his hat and shuffled across the aisle.

Abby's only response was a brief nod as she breathed a sigh of relief.

~

Abraham entered the kitchen and found his wife sitting at the table, sobbing. He hurried across the room and touched her shoulder. "Fannie, what's wrong? Are ya sick? Has somethin' happened to one of the twins?"

She looked up at him, her cheeks flushed like ripe cherries. "The boys are fine, and I'm not sick."

Abraham pulled out a chair and sat beside her. "What is it then?"

Fannie sniffed. "I'm missin' Abby and wondering if we did the right thing by sending her away."

"We? Who's *we*, Fannie?"

"Me and Edna."

He gave his beard a couple of quick pulls. "You and Edna set up this whole Montana trip to get Abby out of town?"

She lifted her shoulders in a quick shrug. "We thought it would be good for her to get away. To tell you the truth, I'd begun to resent the way she took over the bopplin's care and so many of my chores around the house."

Abraham let his wife's words sink in before he said anything. He'd known she was worried about Abby's depression, but he had no idea she'd felt so frustrated over her daughter's help.

"Don't get me wrong," Fannie said, as though she could read his mind. "I'm not sayin' I didn't appreciate all the things Abby did around here. She was a big help, especially when the twins were first born."

Abraham took her hand and gave it a gentle squeeze. "You don't have to explain. I know you love Abby. It just never occurred to me that you might be feelin' resentful about not bein' in charge of your house anymore. You should have said something. I could have spoken to Abby about it."

She shook her head. "That would have only made things worse, Abraham. Abby's still going through troubled waters and needs to be handled with tender loving care."

"I expect you're right about that."

"When I shared my concerns with Edna, she came up with the idea of taking Abby with her to Montana. She said her sister-in-law has been through the fire herself, so she's hoping Elizabeth might be able to help Abby through this difficult time." Fannie groaned. "I sure have failed in that regard."

"Don't be so hard on yourself, my love. You've done your best by Abby."

"You think so?"

Abraham nodded. "However, Edna might be right about Abby needin' some time away." He gave his beard another good tug. "Got any idea how long they'll be gone?"

Fannie offered him a sheepish grin. "Edna plans to come back in a few weeks, but she's not told my daughter that. She hopes to fix it so Abby will stay on through the rest of winter and into the spring awhile."

He frowned. "How come so long?"

"In June there's to be a big auction in the Rexford Amish community, and one of the main things they auction off is quilts. So Edna figures—"

"But Abby's been sayin' she wants nothing to do with quilts," Abraham interrupted.

She sighed. "I know, but if she's ever to move on with her life, then she's got to work through her grief. I'm hoping someday she'll enjoy quilting again, too."

"What if that doesn't happen?"

"Then I'll keep praying for her." Fannie's voice broke. "Oh, Abraham, I can't bear the thought of my daughter spending the rest of her life in such grief."

Abraham's mind drifted back in time. Back to when his first wife had been killed, and then on to when his baby boy was kidnapped. If he hadn't finally let go of his pain, he wondered where he might be today. Certainly not sitting here with his sweet Fannie Mae. He'd probably still be a cranky old storekeeper who felt sorry for himself and yelled at his kinner when he should have been loving on them.

He leaned over and kissed Fannie's cheek. "We need to put Abby's future in our heavenly Father's hands."

Fannie smiled through her tears. "How'd ya get to be so smart, husband?"

He chucked her under the chin. "Guess bein' around you so much has caused some of your wisdom to rub off on me."

She swatted him playfully on the arm. "Go on with ya now."

A piercing wail drifted down the stairs, and Abraham tipped his head. "Sounds like the boys are awake."

"I'd best go see to them." Fannie started to stand, but Abraham beat her to it. "Let me get 'em while you fix yourself a cup of tea."

She lifted her shoulders in an exaggerated shrug. "What are you tryin' to do, Abraham, take over where Abby left off?"

He winced as though she'd wounded him, but then followed it with a quick wink. "You're right, Fannie Mae. Far be it from me to take over your chores."

She gave him a quick hug, then rushed out of the room. Abraham decided he would head back to the barn, because that's where he did his best praying.

CHAPTER 28

$\mathcal{L}$inda tried to relax, curling her legs underneath her and pushing against the sofa cushions. It was Saturday, and she was alone. Jimmy had gone over to Allen's to spend the day, and as usual, Jim was working. She'd decided this was a good time to reread the verses of Scripture Rev. Deming had given her earlier in the week.

Linda opened her Bible and turned to 2 Timothy 1:7. " 'For God did not give us a spirit of timidity; but a spirit of power, of love and of self-discipline,' " she read aloud.

The reverend must have realized that I'm full of fears. Fear that Jim will leave me. Fear that I won't be able to love him as I should. Fear that he will never find the Lord as his personal Savior.

Linda turned to the next verse of scripture, which was found in Galatians 5:22.

" 'But the fruit of the Spirit is love, joy, peace, patience, kindness, goodness, faithfulness, gentleness and self-control. Against such things there is no law.' " She squeezed her eyes shut. *Lord, I need the fruits of the Spirit—especially peace and patience. In my frustration over our relationship, I've often become impatient and said things to Jim out of anger. Help me become the kind of wife he needs, and help him see You living in me.*

The telephone rang, and Linda jumped. She hurried across the room and grabbed the receiver, hoping it might be Jim. "Hello, Scott residence."

"Linda, this is Marian. Is my son at home? I need to speak with him."

Linda frowned. Couldn't Jim's mother have asked how she

and Jimmy were doing before demanding to speak with her son? "Jim's working today, Marian. May I take a message?"

"I have something important to tell him, and I'd rather he hear it from me."

"I suppose you could call his cell phone. Do you have that number?"

"I thought Jim had given it to me, but I can't seem to find it."

Linda gave her mother-in-law the phone number slowly, then repeated it.

"All right, thanks. Be sure to give Jimmy a hug from his grandma and grandpa Scott."

"Yes, I will. Good-bye, Marian."

Linda hung up the phone, wondering what Jim's mother wanted to tell him that she couldn't have said to her. She hoped it wasn't bad news, but if it was anything serious, she felt sure Jim would call and let her know.

"Fannie is really missing Abby," Naomi told Caleb as the two of them set out some rubber stamps that had been delivered to the store a short time ago. "I hope she and Edna won't be gone too long."

Caleb grunted. "I would think Fannie might be glad to have her house back. Abby pretty much took over after the twins were born."

Naomi nodded. "That's true, but she was only trying to help. After Lester died, the poor thing needed something to keep herself busy."

"Let's hope that when Abby returns to Pennsylvania she'll feel better about things and will be willing to work at the quilt shop again." Caleb motioned toward the adjoining store. "We can't keep buying quilts from the Amish and Mennonite ladies in our community to sell in the shop and expect Matthew to work there. He's trying to get his woodworking shop going, you know."

"I've not heard him complain."

"Men don't complain, Naomi."

She slapped him playfully on the arm. "Is that so?"

"Hey, quit that!"

She snickered. "See, you're complaining now."

He chuckled and pushed the last box of stamps over to her. "Here you go. Someone just came into the store, so I'd better go see who it is."

"Okay, you wait on the customer, and when I get done with these stamps, I'll go to the back room and check on our sleeping girls."

Caleb gave her a peck on the cheek and headed up front.

As Naomi set the last of the stamps in place, she thought about Ginny Meyers and how she used to come into the store to buy rubber stamps for her scrapbooking projects. It had been some time since Naomi had heard anything from Ginny, and she wondered how her old friend was doing. Ginny had only come home once since she'd headed west with Naomi, and that was just for a short visit with her folks one Christmas. To Naomi's knowledge, Ginny's family had never even met Ginny's husband.

How sad, she thought, *that some families rarely see each other and live so far away. If I had stayed out west, I would have surely missed my family.*

"Got any new stamps?"

Naomi jumped at the sound of a woman's voice. She turned her head while rising to her feet. "Ginny?"

"Yep, it's me."

"Ach, I was just thinkin' about you." Naomi gave her friend a hug. "How are you? What brings you to town? How long are you here for?"

Ginny laughed. "Slow down, Naomi. I'm only good for one question at a time."

"Jah, okay. I'm just so surprised to see you. Did your folks know you were coming?"

"No. Today's Mom's fiftieth birthday, so Chad and I flew in for the surprise party my brother and his wife are putting on." Ginny smiled. "I decided to stop by and see you first. Thought maybe there might be something in your store I could buy for Mom."

Naomi nodded toward the adjoining room. "How about a nice quilt from my stepmother's quilt shop?"

Ginny shook her head. "That won't work. Mom already has an Amish quilt."

"Maybe a wall hanging or pillow then?"

"She might like a couple of throw pillows."

"Follow me and I'll see what's available."

A few seconds later, they were inside the quilt shop. Ginny wandered around the room, commenting on how beautiful the quilted pieces were, as Naomi pointed out various pillows she thought Ginny's mother might like.

"You mentioned your stepmother's shop in one of your letters, but I had no idea it was so big," Ginny commented.

"Papa added onto the store shortly after he and Fannie were married."

"So where is Fannie? Doesn't she work here?"

"She does all her quilting at home these days, because she's got her hands full takin' care of the babies."

Ginny ran her fingers over a beige and green pillow with the Lone Star pattern. "Ah, yes, that's right. Your dad and Fannie have twins; isn't that what you told me in one of the letters?"

"Jah. Timothy and Titus, and they're identical." Naomi grinned. "Took us the longest time to tell 'em apart, but we finally figured out who was who."

"So now you have two little brothers."

"And two little girls of my own." Naomi nodded toward the back room. "They're both down for naps at the moment."

Ginny's auburn eyebrows drew together. "I remember when Zach used to sleep in that room."

Naomi stared at the floor as memories cascaded over her like a broken dam. Even though it had been almost six years, she could still picture her baby brother's sweet face. He was such an agreeable child, always giggling and making everyone laugh.

"Sorry if I upset you by bringing up Zach." Ginny touched Naomi's shoulder. "I don't imagine you've heard anything more since his disappearance?"

Naomi shook her head. "Not since we saw that ad in *The*

Budget letting us know he was all right. I doubt we'll ever see my little bother again, but I still pray for him and trust that whoever took Zach is taking good care of him."

"I think about the little guy sometimes, too."

"You do?"

Ginny nodded. "One day a couple of women came into the fitness center, and one of them had a little boy who made me think of Samuel when he was that age. I'm guessing he's exactly how Zach would look about now."

"In what way?"

Ginny shrugged. "He had Samuel and Zach's same dark chocolate eyes and golden brown hair. And the boy was about the age Zach would be these days, too."

"Did you happen to look behind his right ear?" Naomi didn't know why she was asking such a silly question. The idea that the boy Ginny saw could be Zach was ridiculous, despite his familial resemblance to her brothers.

"I never got close enough to see behind the kid's ear. Why do you ask?"

Naomi shook her head. "Never mind. It was only a silly notion that popped into my head."

"As I recall, you always were one for silly ideas." Ginny picked up the Lone Star pillow. "I think I'll take this one, and maybe I'll get a wall hanging for Mom, too."

"Jah, okay." Naomi led Ginny to the wall hangings on the other side of the room. She was glad to see her old friend again but wished the subject of Zach had never come up. He was gone, and no amount of wishful thinking could bring him back.

As the train pulled into Whitefish, Montana, Abby breathed a sigh of relief. It had been a long two-day journey, and she was exhausted not only from the trip, but from being forced to make conversation with Edna. The only time the woman didn't talk was when she was asleep.

Abby knew her mother's cousin was trying to be friendly, but Edna's silly jokes and idle chatter grated on Abby's nerves.

Another thing that had set her nerves on edge was the cowboy sitting a few seats away. She'd caught him staring at her on several occasions, and a couple of times he'd tried to make conversation. Edna said the man was probably lonely or curious about their Plain clothes, but the way his dark eyes bore into Abby made her feel uneasy.

She shivered thinking about all the questions the cowboy, who'd said his name was Bill Collins, had asked her. She'd not given him any more information than her name, where she was from, and where she and Edna were going. Truth was, he seemed more interested in talking about himself, and he'd told her that he'd been traveling to various rodeos across the United States ever since he had graduated from high school. Bill said he was going to Whitefish to visit a relative, and then would be boarding the train again to go to McCall, Idaho, where his folks lived. Unlike most Englishers, the cowboy admitted that he hated to fly and preferred to travel by bus or train.

Abby couldn't imagine traveling all over the country, much less living the life of a rodeo cowboy. Until her trip to Pennsylvania, she'd never been out of the state of Ohio. This trip to Montana seemed like a real adventure. One she'd rather not be a part of.

When the train came to a stop, Abby slipped out of her seat and reached overhead to open the luggage compartment where their carry-on items were stowed.

"Let me help you with those," the cowboy offered as he stepped up beside her.

"I—I can manage." Abby quickly pulled Edna's black satchel out and handed it to her.

"Danki," Edna said as she scooted over to the seat Abby had previously occupied.

Abby reached for her own carry-on and noticed that the strap was wrapped around someone else's piece of luggage, which was near the back of the compartment and out of her reach. She struggled with it a few seconds, until she felt someone touch her shoulder. When she turned around, she realized the cowboy still stood there wearing a silly-looking grin on his face.

"I'm taller than you and can reach that better," he drawled. "Besides, it's my bag your strap's stuck on, so it's my duty to free it for you."

"I'm sure I can get it," she argued.

"Let the nice man help," Edna said. "Our driver's probably waitin' inside the station, and we don't want to keep him any longer than necessary."

With a shrug, Abby stepped aside. She knew Edna was anxious to see her sister-in-law. Truth be told, she, too, would be glad once they were headed for Rexford and the Amish community they would be visiting. At least there she wouldn't feel so out of place, and she wouldn't have to deal with any overfriendly cowboys.

A few seconds later, the man handed Abby her satchel and retrieved his as well.

"Danki—I mean, thank you." She stepped farther into the aisle so Edna could join her.

Bill nodded. "Glad to be of service, ma'am. Will ya be needin' help with your other bags?"

Edna opened her mouth as if to say something, but Abby cut her off. "No thanks. I'm sure our driver will help us gather the ones we checked through."

"All right then. You ladies have a nice drive to Rexford." Bill tipped his hat and gave Abby a quick wink. "It's been nice meetin' ya."

"And you as well," Edna said.

Abby merely nodded and hurried to exit the train. The sooner she got away from Cowboy Bill, the better she would feel.

CHAPTER 29

*A*bby couldn't get over all the trees that scattered the hills and bordered Lake Koocanusa in the Kootenai National Forest of northern Montana. Tim Hayes, their middle-aged driver who was an English neighbor of Elizabeth's, had informed his passengers that there were a variety of trees in the area—noble fir, stately pine, tamarack, and cedar. Homes made of logs dotted the land, and Tim was quick to point out that the local Amish men had made some of them. "In fact," he said, as they drove past the general store, run by an Amish family, "building log homes is how a few of the Amish men support themselves. Others make log-type furniture, which is a good business for many of them."

"I hear that the yearly Amish auction also brings money into the community," Edna commented.

He nodded. "That's true. The auction's held in June, and more than a thousand people come to West Kootenai to buy and sell that day."

Edna glanced at Abby as they sat in the back seat of Tim's minivan, and she smiled. "Your mamm might be interested in sendin' some of her quilts to be auctioned off, don't ya think?"

Abby's only response was a quick shrug. She had come here with the hope of getting away from quilts and didn't want to think about them, much less talk about the ones in her mother's quilt shop.

"This is Elizabeth King's place," Tim said, as he pulled onto a graveled driveway and stopped in front of a small log home set well off the main road. "She'd have ridden with me to

Whitefish, but I had a few stops to make along the way, and I guess Elizabeth thought she could use that time getting ready for her two houseguests instead of waiting on me." He chuckled and massaged the top of his balding head. "She's quite an independent woman, living here by herself and doing some teaching at the Amish one-room schoolhouse in the past."

Abby looked over at Edna. "I thought you'd mentioned that your sister-in-law is married and has a little boy."

Edna's pale eyebrows drew together. "Jah, but Dan and their son Abe were killed a few years ago. Don't you remember, as we traveled here I told you the story of how the car they were riding in slid on a patch of ice and was hit by a truck."

Abby's brain felt dull and fuzzy. Truth be told, she remembered very little of what Edna had said to her on the train.

"Oh, there's Elizabeth now," Edna said excitedly. Without waiting for Abby to respond, she opened the van door and hopped out.

Abby watched out the side window as Edna ran up the path and was greeted with a hug by a tall, dark-haired woman who looked to be in her late thirties.

"I'll get your luggage," Tim said, looking over his shoulder.

Abby nodded and drew in a deep breath. Whether she liked it or not, it was time to meet Elizabeth King.

~

"Slow down, Mom. I can't understand what you're saying." Jim shifted his cell phone from one ear to the other as he moved away from two of his painters who worked in the hallway of a new apartment complex on the east side of Puyallup.

"I said your father hasn't been feeling well, but he refuses to see the doctor." She sniffed. "Will you talk to him, Jim? He'd be more apt to listen to you than he would me."

"Sure, Mom. I'll give him a call when I get home from work this evening."

"I wish you and the family could come here for a visit. You and Dad used to be so close, and I'm sure if he saw you he wouldn't say no to your suggestion that he see the doctor."

Jim grimaced. He cared about his dad and would do his best to talk him into going in for a physical, but he'd have to do it by phone. Besides, knowing Mom, she was probably making more of this than there really was. In all likelihood, Dad only had a touch of the flu. Give the man a few more days, and he'd probably be good as new.

"Look, Mom," Jim said patiently, "I can tell that you're worried, but it's impossible for me to get away right now. I promise I'll call Dad as soon as I get home."

"If you're short on money, I'd be happy to pay for your plane ticket," she offered.

He cringed. Didn't his mother realize he was making a good living at his profession? Did she think he was too poor to buy a plane ticket and that was the reason he hadn't been back to Ohio since they'd gotten Jimmy? *If Mom only had an inkling of the real reason I've stayed away from home. What would she think if she knew her son was a kidnapper who'd taken an Amish baby from Pennsylvania?* Jim knew he was probably being paranoid by refusing to visit his folks. After all, Millersburg, Ohio, was several hours from Lancaster, Pennsylvania. Still, Amish people lived there, and one of them might know Jimmy's real family. If someone saw Jimmy and recognized him. . .

"Jim? Did you hear what I said? I'd be happy to—"

"I can afford the ticket, Mom. I'm busy right now with a couple of big paint jobs, and since Dad's not critically ill, I see no reason to make the trip. Maybe this summer we can come for a visit," Jim lied. *Tell her what she wants to hear and she'll get off my back. That usually works with Linda.*

"Your father could be dead by then." There was a brief pause. "Oh, I wish we had stayed in Boise and not moved to Ohio. He surely could have found a job as a high-school principal in Idaho as easy as here."

He lifted his gaze to the ceiling. A ceiling that still needed to be painted.

"Jim, are you there?"

He blew out his breath. "Yes, Mom, I'm still here."

"I guess if you're not willing to talk to your dad in person, I'll have to be satisfied with a phone call." There was another pause. "Please don't tell him I called about this."

"I won't even mention that we talked."

"Thanks, son."

"Let me know what the doctor says."

"I will. Good-bye, Jim."

"Bye, Mom."

Jim clicked the phone off and slipped it inside the leather case he wore on his belt. He was sure there was nothing to worry about, but he would feel better once he talked to Dad.

⌒

Linda paced the living room floor as she waited for Jim. His foreman had called around six o'clock, saying Jim wouldn't be coming home for dinner and that he wasn't sure when they would be done for the day. It irritated Linda that her husband couldn't have told her himself. Avoidance seemed to be the way he dealt with things these days.

She glanced at the grandfather clock on the opposite wall. It was almost nine, and she'd put Jimmy to bed half an hour ago. "This is ridiculous," she fumed. "It's bad enough that Jim has worked every Saturday for the past two months, but lately he's been working so many long hours, he has no time to spend with Jimmy." A lump lodged in her throat, and she blinked against the smarting tears that threatened to spill over.

Linda sank to the couch and picked up her Bible from the coffee table. She turned to another passage her pastor had recently given her—this one in Lamentations—and read it aloud. " 'The LORD is good to those whose hope is in him, to the one who seeks him.' Lamentations 3:25. " She closed her eyes. *At least I know I'll always have You, Jesus. If only Jim would see his need, too.*

When a car door slammed shut, her eyes snapped open. A few minutes later Jim appeared, dressed in his white painter's overalls and wearing a matching hat. "Sorry I'm late, but we ran into a problem with the paint we were using."

She left the couch and rushed to his side. "Did your mother get hold of you? I gave her your cell phone number when she called here earlier today."

Jim nodded and ran his fingers along the white speckles of paint dotting his chin.

"What did she say?"

He tipped his head and stared at her in a peculiar way. "Didn't Mom tell you what she wanted?"

"No. She asked to speak with you, but her voice sounded strained. I got the impression it was something important."

Jim flopped into the closest chair and released a puff of air.

"I hope you don't have any fresh paint on those overalls," Linda said, stepping forward. "I wouldn't want—"

"It's dried paint, Linda, so don't worry."

She recoiled, feeling that familiar hurt whenever he snapped at her. "Sorry."

"Do you always have to look for something to complain about?"

"I—I wasn't."

He pulled the hat off his head, flopping it over one knee. "Do you want to hear what Mom said or not?"

"Of course I do."

"Then have a seat."

Linda returned to her spot on the couch and waited for Jim to continue.

"Mom said Dad hasn't been feeling well, and she wanted me to talk him into seeing the doctor. Since I knew I'd be working late, I gave Dad a jingle during my dinner break."

"What did he say?"

"Not much. He made light of the whole thing and guessed that Mom had put me up to calling."

Linda felt immediate concern. If Bob was anything like most men, she figured that his making light of it meant he was sicker than he was admitting. "I hope it's nothing serious."

"Guess we won't know until he sees the doctor."

"Do you think we should go to Ohio, Jim? I mean, just in case—"

He shook his head. "I can't get away from either of the jobs I'm on right now. I'm sure Dad will be fine."

"But how can you be certain of that when he hasn't been to the doctor yet?"

"Trust me, I know my dad. If he says he's feeling better, he probably is." He stood and started for the door leading to the hallway.

"Where are you going?"

"Upstairs to bed. I'm exhausted."

Linda watched Jim's retreating form, wishing he would stay awhile and visit with her. In the days before her conversion, she would have probably whined and begged. But now, as a Christian wife trying to win her husband to the Lord, she knew the best thing to do was keep silent. She hurried to turn off the living room lights and followed him upstairs. Since tomorrow was Sunday, maybe they could spend some time together as a family after she and Jimmy got home from church.

Abby stood at the window in the small loft above Elizabeth's living room. This would be her sleeping quarters for the next few weeks, until she and Edna headed back to Pennsylvania. It was a pleasant room, just high enough for her to stand without bumping her head. Against one wall was a single bed made of knotty pine. A matching dresser sat against the other wall, and a wooden rocking chair was positioned near the window. The moon shone bright and clear tonight, casting rays of golden light against the snowy yard below. She was keenly aware of how quiet and isolated it was here in the mountains. *It's almost eerie*, she thought. *I wonder how many wild animals are out there lurking about?*

Abby shivered and rubbed her hands against the sleeves of her long flannel nightgown. She needed to focus on something else, or she would be awake all night, thinking some strange creature would sneak into the house and attack her while she slept.

Her thoughts went to Edna and Elizabeth, who had stayed up until after eleven, chattering and getting caught up on one another's lives. Not wishing to appear impolite, Abby had joined the conversation by providing a listening ear and answering any questions that had been asked of her. Elizabeth seemed like a nice enough woman, and she was much younger than Abby had expected. She also seemed to be full of energy and exuberated with the kind of joy Abby had once known.

She leaned against the windowsill and sighed. *If Elizabeth lost her son and husband, how can she be so cheerful and positive?* She turned from the window and flopped onto the bed. *Maybe it's an act, to make people think she's doing okay, the way I've done with Mom and Abraham's family. Maybe deep down inside, Elizabeth is hurting as much as I am and doesn't want anyone to know it.*

Abby closed her eyes, hoping sleep would come quickly. She had given up saying her nighttime prayers. Truth was, since Lester died she'd only pretended to pray before and after meals, as well as during church. There wasn't much point in praying when God didn't answer her prayers. She'd prayed for Lester and asked the Lord to keep him safe and bless their upcoming marriage. And what good had that done?

Grief rose in her throat like bile, and scalding tears seeped under Abby's lashes, rolling onto her cheeks. She leaned over the bed and reached into her small satchel, pulling out a handkerchief— the same one Mary Ann had made her several months ago—the one with the initials A. M. embroidered in one corner.

Abby dabbed at her eyes and blew her nose. *Oh, why couldn't it have been me who was killed in that fire instead of Lester?*

~

Linda had just drifted off to sleep when she was awakened by the sound of deep moaning. She turned her head and saw Jim writhing about and punching his pillow. She was tempted to wake him but thought better of it, remembering how irritable he got if his sleep was disturbed.

"No, baby. Put the Amish quilt back," he mumbled. "No. I said, no."

Amish quilt? Baby? What was Jim talking about? Linda knew he must be dreaming, and since they had an Amish covering on their bed, the fact that he'd mentioned a quilt did make sense. But she couldn't figure out what would cause him to dream about a baby. Had he recently been watching a rerun of *Witness* on TV?

No, there were no babies in the movie that she recalled. Maybe Jim's dream was a combination of things locked away in his subconscious. The Amish quilt, which Linda had wanted a long time. The baby they had adopted when they'd gone to the East Coast and toured Amish country. That's all it was. . .just a silly dream full of blended things that had occurred in the past.

Linda was relieved when Jim's moaning subsided and turned to soft snores. Maybe now she could get some sleep. In the morning, if she didn't forget, she would ask if Jim remembered the dream.

CHAPTER 30

$\mathcal{A}$bby proceeded down the lane on foot, heading to the general store and mindful of the snow that still lay in patches. She couldn't believe she had been in Montana two weeks already. She was beginning to like it here. The trees seemed greener, the air fresher, and other than Cousin Edna, no one knew her situation.

Although Abby still felt empty inside, at least she didn't have the pressure of trying to measure up to what others expected of her. She'd always been a hard worker, but truthfully, she was getting tired of doing chores all the time in order to keep from thinking about Lester and what her quilt shop had done to him. All she wanted to do was rest and saturate her mind with the things of nature, the way she could do here in the Kootenai National Forest, where it was ever so peaceful and quiet.

When Abby reached the mailbox at the end of the driveway, she slipped her hand into her jacket pocket and retrieved the letter she'd written to her mother last night. She knew Mom was worried about her; she could read it between the lines of the letter she'd received last week. Mom probably hoped Abby wouldn't be gone too long, but Cousin Edna seemed in no hurry to leave, and that was fine with Abby.

When Abby opened the mailbox, she was disappointed to see that the mail had already come. If she put the letter to Mom inside now, it wouldn't go out until tomorrow. Still, it was better than taking it back to Elizabeth's house and trudging down here again in the morning. So, she placed the envelope inside the metal box and lifted the red flag.

Thumbing through the stack of mail that had been delivered, she noticed a letter for Edna bearing her daughter Gretchen's return address. *Should I take the mail up to the house now or continue on to the store?* Abby decided on the latter, figuring the letter for Edna was probably nothing important and that she could wait another hour or so to read it. She dropped all the mail into her black canvas satchel and kept walking.

A short time later, Abby stepped inside the general store, feeling a rush of warm air that quickly dispelled the chill she had encountered on her trek over here.

"Can I help ya with somethin'?" the young Amish girl behind the counter asked.

Abby rubbed her hands briskly together and shook her head. "I just need a couple of items, but I think I can find them."

"All right then. Let me know if you need help findin' anything."

"Jah, I will." Abby proceeded to the back of the store, where the notions were kept. She was almost out of writing paper and planned to buy a new tablet and maybe some colored pencils for drawing. Elizabeth had asked her to pick up two spools of white thread, as well.

When that was done, Abby decided to climb the stairs and see what might be up there for sale. She'd been in the store a couple of times since her arrival but had never thought to look in the loft above.

At the top of the landing she spotted a couple of men's black felt hats lying on a chest of drawers that was also for sale. There were several other pieces of Amish-made furniture—two rocking chairs, a small table, and a couple of straight-backed chairs. To the left, four quilts hung on a makeshift clothesline. The sight of them almost brought Abby to the floor in a pool of tears, but she gritted her teeth and looked away. She knew it was silly to feel so anxious whenever she looked at a quilt, but she couldn't seem to help herself. Quilts were part of the Amish life. They were warm and cozy, and she had covered up with one nearly every night since she was a child.

Guess it's not the quilt itself that bothers me so much, but the sight of one hanging in a store reminds me of my own quilt shop and the grief it caused the day it burned to the ground.

Abby moved slowly around the small upstairs and finally headed back down, deciding there was nothing she needed.

Up front, near the counter, stood a refrigerated dairy case where Abby found a brick of Swiss cheese, her favorite kind. She was surprised to see that it had been made by one of the cheese places near her hometown in Berlin. Abby missed Ohio, especially the times spent with Lester during their courting days.

For a moment her sorrow dissipated, as she allowed memories of Lester to bathe her in warm thoughts. They had gone to the cheese store down the street from her quilt shop on several occasions, sampling the various cheeses, laughing, and talking with others they knew. Seeing the cheese now was a painful reminder that Lester was gone, yet in some ways it was comforting to find something so familiar here.

Abby drew in a deep breath. *At one time I thought Lester and I would be together as husband and wife for many years, and that our love could withstand anything, even time spent apart. But now he's gone, and others expect me to move on.* She blinked against the tears clinging to her lashes. Despite her resolve to push thoughts of Lester aside, Abby often dreamed of him. Not the nightmare with fire and smoke, but dreams of happier days, when they'd been courting. *Help me, Lord. Help me let go of Lester if I need to, and show me if there's any meaning in life.*

With a determination not to give in to her tears, Abby turned and set her purchases on the counter.

"Will you be needin' anything else?" the young woman asked, as she rang up the three items.

Abby shook her head. "That'll be all. Danki."

The girl opened her mouth, like she might be about to say something, but the telephone rang and she reached for it.

Abby counted out the money for her purchases and left it on the counter, not wanting to interrupt the phone conversation.

Fannie didn't know what had possessed her to load both boys into the buggy and drive over to Caleb and Naomi's store. She could have left them at home with Nancy, who wasn't working at Anna Beechy's today, but decided the fresh air would do them some good. Besides, there were a few things she needed from the store, and she didn't want to wait until Abraham was free to bring her.

Just a short ways from the house, Titus started to holler, and then Timothy joined in. Fannie figured they probably wanted her attention and felt frustrated because they were confined in the buggy.

"Calm down!" Fannie clutched the reins and tried to keep her focus on the road. The last thing she needed was to get in an accident while trying to settle her fussy sons.

The boys howled all the way to Paradise, and it wasn't until Fannie took Titus out of the buggy that he finally stopped crying. She was relieved when Caleb, who'd been sweeping the store's front porch, spotted her and came to offer his assistance.

"Danki," she said as Caleb reached into the buggy and scooped Timothy into his arms. "These two are sure gettin' to be a handful these days."

Caleb nuzzled the top of Timothy's downy dark head. "I hope Naomi and I are blessed with a couple of boys some day." He gave Fannie a sheepish grin. "Not that I'm unhappy with Sarah and Susan, you understand."

Fannie chuckled. "Jah, I know. Most men want at least one son to carry on their name."

He nodded and lifted his left hand. "With this bein' practically useless, it'd be nice to have a boy's strong arm when there's heavy stuff to be done at the store."

Fannie followed Caleb into the building, wondering if he ever regretted his decision to buy Abraham's store and sell his buggy shop to his two younger brothers. Of course, she knew he'd done it because of his love for Naomi.

So many sacrifices some folks make in order to care for their loved ones, she thought. *Look at what Abby sacrificed on my behalf. And what's she got to show for it but a lot of heartaches and regrets?*

"It's nice to see you," Naomi said, stepping out from behind the counter and giving Fannie a hug. "Have you come alone, or is one of the girls with you today?"

"It's just me and the twins."

Naomi touched Titus's rosy cheek. "Looks like he's been crying. Is everything all right?"

Fannie motioned with her head toward Timothy, still held in Caleb's arms. "They carried on somethin' awful the whole way here. Guess they wanted my full attention and were determined I should know about it."

Naomi exhaled with a groan. "I can relate to that. Bringing our girls to the store every day can present some problems whenever one of them acts up."

"Where should I put this little fellow?" Caleb asked, stepping between Naomi and Fannie. "I'd hold him all day, but I've got some boxes on the back porch that need to be brought inside."

Fannie glanced around. "Matthew's not working here today?"

"Nope. Said he had some things to do in his woodworking shop at home."

"I didn't see him at all this morning. He never even showed up for breakfast."

"Maybe he had errands to run," Naomi put in.

"That could be." Fannie motioned to the back room. "Are the girls down for their naps right now?"

Naomi shook her head. "Susan's in her playpen, but she's not sleeping. Sarah's seated on a throw rug by the bookcase with some of her favorite children's books. I'll get Susan out of her playpen and set her next to her big sister, and then you can put the twins in the playpen while you shop. Would that work?"

Fannie smiled. "Sounds fine to me."

A few minutes later, the twins played happily in the playpen, while little Susan sat on the floor beside Sarah. Fannie smiled at the older girl, pretending to read to her eight-month-old sister. Even though the girls weren't Fannie's grandchildren by blood, she'd become quite fond of them.

She thought about Harold and Lena and the baby boy they now had, wishing they lived closer and wondering when they might come to Pennsylvania for a visit. It wasn't easy making a trip by bus or train when you had a baby or, in her case, two babies to care for.

"You think you might want to run the quilt shop again?" Naomi asked, driving Fannie's thoughts to the back of her mind.

"I'd like to, but with the boys keeping me so busy, I believe it's best that I do my quilting at home and leave the store to someone more capable."

"Wish I could do more," Naomi said, leaning her elbows on the counter. "But I've got my hands full helping Caleb in the store, and about all I can do for the quilt shop is ring up folks' purchases and answer a few questions."

Fannie nodded. "I understand, and I don't expect you to do any more than you're already doing now. Things will just have to stay as they are until Abby returns and we see how she feels."

"Have you heard anything from her lately?" Naomi asked.

"Got a letter from her last week. She seems to like it in Montana, and I believe the change is good for her."

Naomi opened her mouth as if to comment, but her words were cut off by an earsplitting crash. "*Himmel*—heavens! What was that?"

Both women headed to the back of the store, and they'd just reached the spot where Sarah and Susan sat when both girls started to howl.

"*Der bichler!*" Sarah sobbed, pointing to the stack of books strewn on the floor.

"Susan must have pulled one out, and then they all tumbled down," Naomi shouted over the noise of her daughters' weeping.

Titus and Timothy began to holler then, and Fannie clicked her tongue. "See why I can't come back to work?" She headed for the storage room. "I'm comin,' boys. Jah, your mamm's right here."

Linda sat at the kitchen table with a cup of hot apple cider in one hand and her open Bible before her. She'd seen Jimmy off to school a few minutes ago, and Jim had left for work before she'd gotten out of bed. He'd been leaving early almost every morning and coming home late. It was hard to have any family time with him gone so much. Linda hadn't even been able to ask about the dream he'd had a few weeks ago, when he'd mumbled something about a baby and an Amish quilt. In fact, she'd forgotten about it until now.

"I'm supposed to focus on God's Word, not worry about some silly dream," she muttered. "It probably didn't mean anything other than Jim had eaten too much junk food before going to bed. Unless he has the dream again and talks in his sleep, I won't bother to ask him about it."

The phone rang, and Linda placed a bookmark inside the Bible to indicate the spot in 1 Corinthians where she wanted to begin reading. She hurried across the room and picked up the receiver. "Hello, Scott residence."

"It's Marian, Linda. Is Jim there?" Jim's mother's voice sounded even more strained than the last time she had called, and Linda felt immediate concern.

"No, he's not. He left for work early this morning. Can I take a message?"

There was a brief pause. "I guess I'd better try his cell phone then."

Linda glanced at the kitchen counter, where Jim had left his phone. This was the second time in the past week he'd forgotten to take it with him. She wondered if he'd become forgetful because he wasn't getting enough sleep.

"Sorry, Marian, but Jim forgot to take his phone this morning. Would you like him to call you when he gets home?"

"I've got bad news, and it can't wait until then." Marian's voice caught on a sob.

"What is it? What's wrong?"

"Bob's in the hospital and may be faced with open-heart surgery. It could be serious, Linda."

Linda's forehead wrinkled as she felt her mother-in-law's pain. "I'm so sorry. Jim will be upset when he hears, and I'm sure he'll want to fly out to Ohio right away."

"I was hoping he would. And you and Jimmy, too, if you can get away."

Linda nodded, even though she knew Marian couldn't see her. "As soon as I hang up, I'll see about getting some plane tickets. Jim will call you tonight and let you know when we'll arrive in Millersburg, then you can give him more details on Bob."

"Okay." Marian sniffed and blew her nose. "There's one more thing. . ."

"What's that?"

"I know from your letters that you go to church and believe in God. So if you could offer a prayer on Bob's behalf, I'd really appreciate it."

"Of course. I'll call our church and get it put on the prayer chain, too."

"Thanks. See you soon."

Linda hung up the phone with a sense of frustration be-cause she didn't have any idea where Jim was working today. She wouldn't be able to speak to him until he came home, whenever that might be. She could, however, purchase their plane tickets and pray for Jim's dad.

~

"I picked up the mail, Elizabeth," Abby said when she entered the cozy log house after her walk to the store. "There's a letter for you, too, Edna. I think it's from your daughter."

Edna took the letter, and Abby handed Elizabeth the rest of the mail. Then she went to the loft to put away her jacket, scarf, and gloves. When she returned, she found Edna sitting at the kitchen table, shaking her head, and staring at the letter she had received.

"What's wrong? It's not bad news, I hope," Abby said with concern.

"All three of my granddaughters are down with the chicken pox, plus Gretchen has the flu. Looks like I'm gonna have to re-turn home as soon as possible, because my daughter could surely use some help."

Abby nodded. "I'll run down to the store and use their phone to see about getting us some train tickets."

"There's no need for you to go, Abby," Edna said, pursing her lips.

"What do you mean, there's no need? I thought you were afraid to travel by yourself."

Edna folded Gretchen's letter and stuck it inside the band of her apron. "I think I'll be fine on the train now that I've done it already."

Abby leaned on the cupboard, wondering what she should do. Truth be told, she wasn't ready to return to Pennsylvania, but would it be right to stay on without Edna? She'd only met Elizabeth a few weeks ago and hesitated to ask if she could stay longer.

Elizabeth spoke up as though she could read Abby's thoughts. "I'd be happy if you stayed on awhile, Abby."

"Really? You wouldn't mind?"

"Not at all. I'd like the opportunity to get to know you better."

Edna smiled. "I'm glad that's all settled." She nodded at Abby. "Now if you want to run to the store again to use their phone, I'd be much obliged if you'd book me a ticket home."

CHAPTER 31

"I still can't believe you booked us a flight into Akron/Canton without bothering to check with me first." Jim released the tray in front of his seat on the plane and grimaced. He dreaded going to Ohio again. What if Linda wanted to extend their stay and drive to Pennsylvania in order to tour Amish Country? They hadn't seen much of it the last time they were there, and she'd been after him to go back ever since. And what if someone from Jimmy's Amish family spotted him and Jim ended up behind bars on kidnapping charges?

Linda looked at him and frowned. "Do you have to keep bringing this up? Ever since you got home last night, all you've done is complain about the trip. If I didn't know better, I'd think you didn't want to see your dad."

"It's not the trip I'm upset about. It's the fact that you planned everything without my knowledge." Jim glanced over at their son, asleep in his seat next to the window. "Before we adopted Jimmy, you left everything up to me, but in the past year or so you've gotten pretty independent."

"Do you see that as a bad thing?"

"It is when you usurp my authority."

She folded her arms and stared straight ahead. "I was not usurping your authority. I did what needed to be done because you weren't there to do it."

"*Humph!*" Jim snapped the tray shut. Where was that flight attendant? It had been at least ten minutes since she'd said she would be serving a snack, and he could really use a drink.

"Don't you realize how important it is to see your father

before he goes into surgery?" Linda asked. "What if he doesn't make it? What if—"

"He will make it. He has to, Linda. Mom couldn't survive without Dad."

Linda turned to look at Jim again, and her face softened. "I know you're worried about him, but all the worry in the world won't change a thing. What Bob needs is prayer, and I've been doing that ever since I talked to your mother on the phone."

Jim squeezed his fingers into a tight fist, until his nails bit into his flesh. "Right. Like prayer is going to change anything."

"It can, and it has."

"Yeah, whatever." He blew out his breath. "I don't see why you and Jimmy had to come along on this trip. Our son should be in school, not thousands of miles from home, mingling with strangers."

Linda's forehead wrinkled. "That's the silliest thing I've ever heard you say. Jimmy's only in first grade, so if he misses a few days of school, it won't be the end of the world. Besides, your parents aren't strangers. They've been out to visit us several times since we adopted Jimmy."

He shrugged. "You're right, as usual."

"This isn't about being right." Linda reached for his hand. "Your parents are my family, too. I want the three of us to be there to offer support as they go through this stressful ordeal."

Jim leaned his head against the seat and closed his eyes. *Guess I'm worried for nothing. Even if Linda decides she wants to tour Amish Country in Pennsylvania, all I have to do is say no. I'll just tell her there are plenty of Amish in Ohio we can see. I know I'm being paranoid when I worry about someone finding out the truth of Jimmy's heritage. Just like with that woman at the fitness center who mentioned to Linda that Jimmy reminded her of an Amish child she used to know. It was irrational for me to think the woman knew the Amish boy I took. Jim drew in a deep breath and tried to relax. I need to remember that Jimmy's not a one-year-old baby anymore. His Amish family or anyone who knew him back then could probably look him right in the face and not even know it was their child.*

Abraham's boots crunched through the gravel as he headed to the small outbuilding Matthew used for his woodworking shop. The two of them had both been busy lately and hadn't said more than a few words to each other. He figured a good visit was long overdue. Besides, there was something specific he wished to discuss with his eldest son.

Inside the shop, Abraham found Matthew bent over a table, sanding a mahogany quilt hanger. "Got a minute?"

Matthew looked up and grinned. "Sure. Always have time for you, Papa."

Abraham removed his black felt hat and hung it on a wall peg near the door. "Fannie says you never came to the kitchen for breakfast yesterday morning. She figured you'd gone into Paradise to work at the quilt shop, but she and the boys stopped by there, and Naomi said you hadn't been in."

Matthew blew some dust off the piece of wood he was sanding. "Had some errands to run in Lancaster, so I hired a driver and we grabbed a bite to eat at a fast-food restaurant on the way."

"Ah, I see." Abraham took a seat on a sawhorse sitting a few feet away. "Mind if I ask what kind of business you were tendin' to?"

"Just ordering some supplies and checkin' out a few furniture stores to see what's selling well."

"You thinkin' of adding more to your line than just quilt racks and hangers?"

Matthew nodded. "Yep."

Abraham glanced around. "This building's not very big. How you gonna fit a bunch of furniture inside?"

"Thought I'd work on one piece at a time, then take 'em to the quilt shop and try to sell 'em there."

"You're becomin' quite the businessman these days, ain't it so?"

"I'm workin' on it." Matthew's eyes twinkled, and his grin stretched ear-to-ear. "I think I've found what I've been lookin' for all these years, Papa. Never did enjoy workin' in the fields, and the feel of wood and sandpaper under my fingers brings me much pleasure."

"I know what you're saying, son. Workin' at the store wasn't my idea of fun, but bein' back in the fields is like honey on my tongue. Sure am glad Norman's brother-in-law, Willis, came to work for me after you gave up farming completely."

"Jah, it's good he was able and willing, Papa," Matthew said with a nod.

Abraham chewed on the inside of his cheek as he contemplated his next words.

"You got somethin' else on your mind, Papa? You're lookin' kind of thoughtful there."

Abraham grunted. "Guess you know me too well."

Matthew straightened, reaching around to rub a spot in his lower back. "Why don't you just say whatever it is that brought you out here? I have a feelin' it's more than just a friendly visit."

"Well, truth be told, I've been wonderin' about something."

"What's that?"

Abraham left the sawhorse and moved to stand beside his son. "I'm a little concerned because you spend so much time alone."

Matthew's fingers moved from his back up to his forehead, where he made little circular motions. "Don't know what you're talkin' about. I live in the same house as you, and I'm around the family a lot."

"Not anymore. You spend most of your waking moments out here or in town at the quilt shop."

"And when I'm there I'm around customers, so I'm not alone."

Abraham gave his beard a couple of sharp pulls. This conversation wasn't going nearly as well as he'd hoped. Maybe he should be more direct with Matthew, instead of thumping around the shrubs. "Okay, let me give it to you straight. . . . I'm worried because you don't have a steady girlfriend." He shrugged. "For that matter, as far as I know, you've never had more'n a few dates since you turned sixteen and got your courtin' buggy. I know you're kind of shy around women you don't know well, but most men your age are married and have several kinner by now."

Matthew's forehead wrinkled. "There's a reason for that, Papa. I haven't found the right woman yet."

Abraham released a puff of air and tapped Matthew on the shoulder. "How hard have ya been lookin'?"

Matthew's hand fluttered, like he was batting at an annoying fly. "Ah, Papa, do I have to go lookin' for a wife? Can't I just pray about it and let the good Lord bring the right woman when the time's right?" He sobered. " 'Course, maybe I'm not cut out for marriage or raisin' a family."

"*Puh!* That's plain *eefeldich*—silly. Of course you're cut out for it. You're a good man, with a lot of love to give a wife and a brood of kinner." Abraham shook his head. "Maybe you're just too picky. Have you thought of that?"

"Maybe so, but I won't settle. Not for anything."

"Don't expect ya to settle. Just make a little more effort, that's all. Surely there has to be someone you could become interested in."

Matthew's face turned crimson, and he moved swiftly back to his workbench.

Abraham followed. "There is someone, isn't there?"

"Maybe, but she don't know I'm alive."

"How do you know that?"

"Because she only thinks of me as her big brother." The red in Matthew's cheeks deepened, and he started sanding the piece of wood again, real hard.

Abraham smiled. *Ah, so it is Abby my son's come to care for. Who else would be looking on him as though he were her brother? Better not say anything, though. No point embarrassing Matthew more than I already have. Truth be told, Abby and Matthew would be good for each other, but I guess that's not my place to be sayin'.*

"Well, I'd better head up to the house for some lunch. Fannie's probably wonderin' what's keepin' me." Abraham turned for the door and grabbed his hat off the wall peg. "You comin', son?"

"In a few minutes."

As Abraham headed up to the house, his brain swirled with ideas. . .things he might do to get Abby and Matthew together.

Of course, she would have to come home before anything could happen.

⁓

Abby stood at the end of Elizabeth's driveway, waving good-bye to Edna. She'd been picked up by the same English driver who had met them at the train in Whitefish when they first arrived in Montana. She couldn't believe how quickly she had been able to get Edna's train ticket. Coming here, they'd only purchased one-way tickets, since they weren't sure how long they would be staying, and those had been bought several days in advance.

"Shall we go inside and have a cup of hot tea?" Elizabeth asked, touching Abby's arm.

"Jah, that sounds good."

As they started up the driveway, a multitude of doubts tumbled around in Abby's mind. Should she have let Edna go home by herself when she knew how the woman felt about traveling alone? Was Abby really staying because Elizabeth was lonely, or had she made this decision because of her own selfish needs? She'd never felt like a selfish person until she'd come here. In fact, she'd always looked out for others before thinking of herself.

Elizabeth draped her arm over Abby's shoulder. "Edna's gonna be fine, and you did the right thing by stayin' here." She grinned, and the dimple in her left cheek seemed to be more pronounced than usual.

"I hope so."

They entered the house and removed their wraps then headed to the kitchen. Elizabeth turned on the back burner of the propane stove, and Abby took two empty mugs and a couple of tea bags down from the cupboard.

"Would ya like some banana bread to go with the tea?" Elizabeth asked.

"That would be nice."

A few minutes later they were both seated at the table with steaming cups of raspberry tea and a plate of moist banana bread set before them.

"Edna tells me you're quite a quilter," Elizabeth commented.

"I—uh—used to be." Abby took a sip of tea, hoping their conversation would take another direction.

"Edna also told me about your quilt shop burning and how your future husband tried to rescue some of the quilts but perished in the fire."

Abby swallowed the tea in her mouth and nodded. This was the first time this subject had come up since she'd been here, and she was afraid if she spoke, she might break down and cry. Just thinking about the fire that had destroyed her dreams made her feel weepy. Talking about it was nearly unbearable.

"How long ago did it happen?"

"Right before Thanksgiving," Abby mumbled.

"And you're still grieving as though it were yesterday. I can see the sorrow in your eyes and hear the anguish in your voice."

Abby nodded. "I wonder if the pain will ever go away."

Elizabeth reached across the table and patted Abby's hand in a motherly fashion. "Of course it will. This kind of grief takes time to get over."

"I understand that you lost your son and husband in a car accident," Abby ventured to say.

"That's true. It happened two winters ago, when the vehicle they were riding in skidded on a patch of ice. The English driver's car smashed into a truck traveling in the opposite direction, and only the truck driver survived the crash."

Abby shook her head. "How awful for you. I can't imagine how it would feel to lose two loved ones at the same time."

"It was difficult, and it took me a good while to get over the hurt and to stop askin' God why He'd taken my husband and boy." Elizabeth's dark eyes filled with tears, and Abby's did as well. "But life goes on, and I have learned, in whatsoever state I am, therewith to be content." She smiled. "That's found in the book of Philippians, chapter 4, verse 11."

Abby nodded.

"God allowed the accident that took my husband and son, and it's not for me to question why or spend the rest of my days grievin' over what can't be changed. I have chosen to get on

239

with the business of living and have found a purpose for my life again."

Abby leaned forward, her elbows resting on the table and her chin cupped in the palm of her hands. Elizabeth's calm voice was like a strong rope tying Abby fast when she had no strength left to hold on. "What purpose have you found?" she asked.

Elizabeth pushed her chair away from the table. "I can best show you that." She scurried from the room and returned a few minutes later carrying a cardboard box, which she placed on one end of the table.

Curious to know what was inside, Abby left her chair and came to stand beside Elizabeth. "What have you got in there?"

Elizabeth lifted the flaps on the box and withdrew a partially made Log Cabin quilt in hues of beige and brown. Abby's heart clenched. How could she ever get over the pain of losing Lester when there seemed to be quilts everywhere, reminding her of the loss she had endured?

"I don't claim to be the best quilter in the world," Elizabeth said, "but I like the work, it keeps my hands busy, and I've found a good reason to do it."

Abby tipped her head. "Oh? What's that?"

"As I'm sure Edna has told you, our community has an annual auction in June."

Abby nodded.

"One of the biggest things we auction off is the quilts. In fact, we receive many quilts from women in other Amish communities, as well. Ten percent of the proceeds go to help support our school." Elizabeth pursed her lips. "If my son had lived, he would have gone to our one-room schoolhouse for his learnin'. I find great pleasure in knowing the quilts I have worked on all winter help support our school so other Amish kinner can learn to read, write, and do sums." She paused as her fingers traced the edge of the quilt. "Up until this year, I was teaching at the schoolhouse regularly, but after a bad bout with the flu, Myra Lehman took over. So after I got better, I decided to let her finish out the school year."

"Looks like you still keep busy, though," Abby said, nodding at the quilt.

"Jah."

Abby glanced at the cardboard box and spotted another quilt inside with the Tumbling Block pattern, done in various shades of blue. "Are you working on more than one right now?"

"I can't take credit for this one," Elizabeth said. "I found it in a thrift shop in Tacoma, Washington, while I was on vacation with a couple single ladies in our community." She smiled. "We went there to see Mount Rainer and what's left of Mount St. Helens."

Abby noticed right away that the quilt was small, probably made for a baby, and she felt a sharp prick of emptiness as she studied it. Reaching out to touch the covering, her eyes filled with unwanted tears. *Lester is gone and so are my plans to be married. I will never have any bopplin, so there will be no need for me to make a quilt such as this. Elizabeth might have been able to set her pain aside and find meaning in life, but I don't see how that could ever happen for me.*

CHAPTER 32

"Come in, come in. You look exhausted," Fannie said as she opened the back door for Edna.

"Jah, just a bit." Edna removed her black shawl and draped it over the back of a chair. "Things have been pretty hectic at our place this past week."

"I can only imagine." Fannie nodded toward the kitchen table. "Have a seat and tell me how your granddaughters are doing."

"Much better now. Gretchen is over the flu, and the girls aren't feeling nearly as sick."

Knowing her cousin's taste for mint tea, Fannie poured them both a cup and handed one to Edna. "Does that mean they don't need your help now?"

Edna took a sip of tea before answering. "I still plan to check in from time to time and see if there's anything Gretchen needs me to do. But for the most part, I'm back in my own cozy little home, makin' head coverings and workin' on other things for people who don't have the time to sew."

Fannie added a dollop of cream to her tea, picked up her spoon, and gave it a couple of stirs. "Are you wishing you could have stayed in Montana longer?"

"Not really. I think it's best that Abby spends time with Elizabeth alone, and I didn't even have to come up with a reason to leave early. God worked everything out, and I'm sure if anyone can get through to your daughter, it's my dear sister-in-law."

"I pray that's so, and I hope it happens soon." Fannie sniffed. "Even though I often felt that Abby was taking over too many of

243

my responsibilities, I do miss her and wish she were home with us right now."

"You missin' her company or all the help she gave you?" Edna asked with a wink.

Fannie chuckled. "A little of both. I've been praying every day, asking the Lord to heal Abby's heart and send her home with a joy for living."

"I'm sure she'll return when she feels ready, and I know the Lord wants only the best for Abby."

Fannie opened her mouth to reply, but the piercing wail of a baby's cry halted her words. She sighed. "Guess one of the boys is awake and wantin' to be fed. He probably needs to be diapered, too." She pushed her chair aside and stood. "I'd better tend to him before he gets the other brother howlin' like crazy."

"Want me to come along? I can change one babe's windel while you nurse the other."

"Jah, sure. That would be appreciated. We can visit while Titus and Timothy take turns eating."

"Sounds good to me." Edna rose from her seat. "I never seem to get in enough visiting, Cousin."

As Abby headed down the lane toward the mailbox, she reflected on the church service she'd gone to yesterday with Elizabeth. It was much the same as the ones she attended in Ohio and Pennsylvania, but there were fewer people, since this was a smaller community of Amish. The house where they met was much different, too, being made of logs and set among so many trees. The people had been friendly during the light meal afterwards, and Abby had been pleased to spend a little time visiting with Myra Lehman, who reminded her a bit of Rachel.

I wonder how my dear friend from Ohio is doing these days, Abby mused. *I haven't heard from her in some time. Of course, I haven't been good about keeping in contact, either. Truth is, I haven't been much of a friend to anyone since Lester died.*

Abby thoughts returned to yesterday's church service, and a verse of scripture one of the ministers had quoted popped into her head, from Isaiah, chapter 43, verse 2. *"When thou passest through the waters, I will be with thee; and through the rivers, they shall not overflow thee: when thou walkest through the fire, thou shalt not be burned; neither shall the flame kindle upon thee."* Abby grimaced. *I feel as though I've been through the fire, but I've been burned so badly my wounds will never heal.*

Sometimes, when Abby was alone in her room at night, she would close her eyes and try to imagine what it must have been like for Lester during the last moments of his life. In her mind's eye she would put herself in the scene, hugging him and being consumed by the flames together. The thought of dying in the arms of the man she loved seemed more pleasant than living a life without him.

"Lester should not have died alone," she moaned. "He shouldn't have perished on account of me."

Abby's thoughts went to the colorful quilt Elizabeth said she had purchased at a thrift shop in the state of Washington. *A year ago I thought I'd be making plenty of baby quilts in the days ahead. Some would be for Lester and my kinner, and others would be given to family members who were blessed with children.* She drew in a deep breath, determined to focus on something else. As she neared the mailbox, she heard the flutter of birds in the trees nearby and caught sight of a clump of yellow crocus. Spring was almost here, and this used to be her favorite time of year. Since Lester died, no time was her favorite. In fact, she barely noticed the changing seasons at all.

She pulled the mailbox flap open. *I will not give in to tears. Crying won't change a thing, and neither will dwelling on the past.* She thumbed quickly through the stack of mail and noticed a letter from her mother.

Abby leaned against a tree and tore open the letter. She missed Mom, her little brothers, and all of Abraham's family. Even so, she wasn't ready to return to Pennsylvania just yet.

Focusing on the letter in her hand, Abby read it silently.

Dear Abby,
I hope this finds you well and enjoying your visit with

Elizabeth. Edna made it safely home and said she wasn't the least bit afraid. Can you imagine my outgoing, silly cousin afraid of anything? It wonders me that she doesn't travel all over the place, the way some folks do when their family is grown.

She's been busy caring for her granddaughters who have the chicken pox and her daughter who is down with the flu, and I think she enjoys being needed.

I'm sorry to say that Bishop Swartley passed away a few weeks ago, so there's been another funeral in our community. You'll never believe who the lot fell on to take his place—Jacob Weaver. Abraham's been sayin' for years that he thought Jacob would make a good bishop, and now it's actually happened. Jacob seems fine with the idea, but I'm not sure how his wife and kinner are taking all of this. Guess it will be quite an adjustment for everyone in the family.

Mary Ann and I dropped by the store the other day. (Jah, Abraham kept the boys by himself for a few hours.) When I was there, Naomi mentioned the auction that would be held in the Rexford Amish community in June. I'm not sure if you'll still be there by then, but even if you're not, I thought it would be good if I sent some quilts to auction off. If you'd like, I could box up the ones Lester rescued from your quilt shop in Berlin and send those, too.

Tears welled up in Abby's eyes and distorted her vision. Would it help to get rid of those quilts? Maybe putting them up for auction was a good idea. It would be like burying her past once and for all. She swiped a hand across her damp cheeks and sniffed. "Guess I'll head back to the house and answer Mom's letter."

~

"Do you really think we should be leaving so soon after your father's surgery?" Linda asked Jim as they drove away from Millersburg in their rental car.

"We've been here a week, Linda, and you heard what the doctor said. Dad's recovering nicely."

"I know, but—"

"We need to get home. I talked to my foreman yesterday, and he's lined up another set of apartments for us to paint."

She sighed. "I was hoping we could have a little vacation time before we head back. Maybe spend a day or two touring the area and seeing some of the Amish again."

Jim pointed out the front window. "There's one now. See the Amish buggy ahead of us?"

From his seat in the back of the car, Jimmy piped up, "What's an Amish buggy, Daddy?"

"The Amish are a group of Plain people living much like the pioneers used to," Linda said, before Jim could respond. "They drive carriages pulled by horses, and they don't use electricity in their homes."

As they drove around the horse and buggy, Linda glanced over her shoulder to gauge her son's reaction. Jimmy had his nose pressed against the window, and when a young boy at the rear of the buggy waved, Jimmy giggled.

"We haven't been anywhere but at the hospital and your parents' house since we came here, Jim. Couldn't we at least take time to stop in Berlin so I can go into that little shop where we bought the quilt for our bed?" Linda pleaded.

"No."

"Why not? We don't have to be at the airport for several hours, and I'd like to see about buying a couple of quilted throw pillows or maybe a wall hanging." When Jim made no reply, she added, "I promise it will only take a few minutes."

"I suppose if I don't stop, I'll have to hear about it all the way home," he grumbled.

Linda smiled. "Thank you, honey."

A short time later, they pulled into the town of Berlin. Jim found a parking place near a drugstore and informed Linda that she could walk to the quilt shop while he went inside to get some aspirin.

"I'll take Jimmy with me," she said.

Jim shrugged. "Yeah, okay."

Jimmy scrambled out of the backseat and hopped onto the sidewalk, and Linda took hold of his hand. "We'll meet you back here in half an hour," she called to Jim.

"Don't be late." He sauntered up the walk toward the drugstore, rubbing the back of his neck as he went.

"How come Daddy's so cranky?" Jimmy asked.

"I think he's got a stiff neck, and I'm sure he's worried about Grandpa," she replied.

"Is Grandpa gonna be okay?"

Linda gently squeezed his hand. "The doctor said if he does everything he's supposed to do, he should be fine."

"I'm glad."

"Yes, so are we."

As they reached the end of the block, Linda halted. She thought Fannie's Quilt Shop was on this corner, just across the street, but it wasn't there. All she saw was a vacant spot next to another store. "That's odd."

"What's wrong, Mommy?"

"Nothing, Jimmy. I think maybe I'm on the wrong street." Linda looked to the left, then back to the right. Even though it had been several years since they'd been here, many things looked familiar. *Where is that quilt shop?*

A middle-aged woman stepped out of the gift shop next to the vacant lot, and Linda walked up to her. "Excuse me; I'm looking for someone who's familiar with this area who could tell me where Fannie's Quilt Shop is located. Are you from around here?"

"I'm from New Philadelphia, but I live close enough to shop here often, and I'm well acquainted with many of the local stores. Fannie's was right there," the woman said, motioning to the empty lot. "The shop burned to the ground right before Thanksgiving." She clucked her tongue. "Such a shame it was, too. All but a few of the quilts were lost, and a young Amish man died trying to rescue the rest."

Linda sucked in her breath. "Oh, that's so sad. What about Fannie, the woman who owned the shop? Was she inside when it caught fire?"

The woman shook her head. "From what I've been told, Fannie moved to Pennsylvania some time ago. Her daughter, Abby, took over the quilt shop, but she was away helping her mother, who'd given birth to twins."

"I bought a quilt from Fannie several years ago, and I was hoping to buy a couple of pillows." Linda stared at the empty lot with a feeling of regret. "I wish she was around so I could offer my condolences."

"Actually, it's Abby who's to be pitied. She and the young Amishman were engaged to be married, so the loss of her store was devastating for more than one reason."

Tears welled up in Linda's eyes as she considered how Fannie's daughter must have felt when her boyfriend died trying to save her quilts. She thought about Jim and wondered if he would do anything that heroic on her behalf. *Not that I'd want him to die for me. It would just be nice to know that he loved me that much.*

"I guess we'd better head back to the car, Jimmy," Linda said, shaking her thoughts aside. She glanced down, and panic gripped her like a vise. Jimmy was gone.

CHAPTER 33

$\mathcal{L}$inda looked up and down the street, hoping for some sign of Jimmy, but the only children she saw were two small Amish boys standing beside a black buggy parked up the street a ways. She cupped her hands around her mouth and screamed, "Jimmy! Jimmy, where are you?"

Nothing. No sign of her son anywhere.

Where could he have gone? He was here a minute ago, standing right beside me while I spoke with that woman coming out of the gift shop.

Linda's heart thumped fiercely, and she placed both hands on her chest while drawing in a deep breath. *What if someone has kidnapped my boy? I should never have let go of his hand or taken my eyes off him for even a second. What am I going to tell Jim?* She breathed in and out slowly, trying to calm her nerves. *Think, Linda, think. Don't panic. Maybe Jimmy walked back to the car and is with his daddy right now.*

She whirled around and dashed up the sidewalk.

Jim was just coming out of the drugstore when he spotted Linda running toward him. Jimmy wasn't with her, and he figured the boy had already gotten into the car.

As Linda drew closer, he noticed that her cheeks were pink and several strands of blond hair had come loose from her ponytail.

"Jimmy's missing," she panted. "I called and called but he didn't answer."

"What? He can't be missing, Linda. He was with you."

She let out a deep moan. "I know that, but when I got to where Fannie's Quilt Shop used to be and realized it wasn't there anymore, I asked a woman coming out of a gift shop about it, and—"

Jim held up one hand. "Slow down. Just tell me what happened with Jimmy."

"I'm trying to." Linda blinked and swiped at the tears running down her cheeks. "Jimmy was standing beside me when I started talking to the woman about the fire that destroyed the quilt shop, and when I looked down, he was gone."

"He's probably in there." Jim motioned to their rental car several yards away.

"How could that be? You locked the car before you went into the drugstore, remember?"

Jim's heart began to pound, matching the escalating throb he had felt in his head for the last hour. "Jimmy couldn't have gone far, Linda." He tried to keep his voice calm, even though he felt like he could jump right out of his skin. "Maybe Jimmy saw something in one of the store windows and went inside to check it out."

"Oh, I hope that's the case."

"You search the stores on this side, and I'll look in the ones over there," he said, motioning across the street. "Let's meet back here in twenty minutes."

"What if we still can't find him?" Linda grabbed Jim's arm and squeezed it so tight he felt her fingernails dig into his skin.

"Then we'll look on the next block, and the next, and the next, until we do find him."

Her chin quivered. "Maybe we should call the police."

"No. Absolutely not. He hasn't been missing long enough for that."

She sniffled. "We'd better start looking then."

Jim bolted across the street, fear gnawing at his stomach. As much as he hated to admit it, there was a possibility that Jimmy had been kidnapped. Truthfully, he knew how easily it could be done.

A cold chill spiraled up Jim's spine. *Am I being punished for taking Jimmy from his Amish family? Is this how they felt when they discovered he was missing?* He shook his head and darted into the first store. *No, I did that family a favor. They had too many kids and no mother. Linda wanted a baby, and I gave her one. Besides, we've given Jimmy a good home, and through an ad in* The Budget *I notified his Amish family that he was okay.* Reason, mixed with guilt and gut-wrenching fear, threatened to suffocate him. *I wish I knew how to pray.* He lifted his gaze toward the ceiling. *Dear God, if You're up there, please help me find my boy.*

Half an hour later, Jim returned to their vehicle, without Jimmy. His hands trembled as panic swelled in his chest and left him short of breath.

A few minutes later, Linda showed up, but Jimmy wasn't with her, either. "I didn't see him in any of the stores, and the people I asked said they hadn't seen a little boy matching Jimmy's description," she said tearfully. "Oh, Jim, what are we going to do?"

"Let's move to the next block." It was the only thing Jim could think to do, short of calling the police. And that would only be done as a last resort. He grabbed Linda's hand and they'd just started up the street, when he halted.

"What's wrong? Why are we stopping?"

"Look!" Jim pointed to an Amish buggy parked on the other side of the street. Three little boys had their heads sticking out the back opening. Two wore straw hats, and one child, who sported a Dutch-bob, wore no hat at all.

"Jimmy!" Linda hollered. "Oh, Jim, he must have been playing with those Amish boys the whole time."

Jim could only nod, as words stuck in his throat. Relief turned his muscles to jelly. Their son was one of the children wearing a straw hat, and if he hadn't been able to see Jimmy's yellow sweatshirt, Jim would have sworn the kid was actually Amish.

He is Amish, his conscience reminded him. As quickly as the thought came, he dashed it away.

Linda raced across the street, with Jim on her heels. She

rushed to the open buggy and leaned inside. "Jimmy! Oh, I'm so glad to see you, honey."

Before Jimmy could respond, Jim shook his finger in the child's face and shouted, "What do you think you're doing? We've been searching everywhere for you. Don't you know how scared we were when we couldn't find you?"

Jimmy's dark eyes filled with tears. "I just wanted to play with these boys, Daddy. They're Amish. Can ya tell?"

Jim blew out his breath with an exasperated groan. "Take that hat off and get out of the buggy right now!"

"You don't have to be so harsh," Linda said, reaching inside to take Jimmy's hand. "Come on, sweetie. You need to come with us now."

Jimmy removed the straw hat and handed it to the towheaded Amish child. "Here ya go. Thanks for lettin' me play in your buggy."

The two Amish boys waved and said something in Pennsylvania Dutch, while Jim lifted his son to the ground.

"You scared me when you disappeared," Linda said, leaning down and stroking Jimmy's cheek. "Please don't ever do that again."

"We need to get to the airport." Jim glanced at his watch. "Or we're going to miss our plane."

As they walked back to their car, Linda glanced over her shoulder. "Those two little Amish boys are sure cute, aren't they, Jim?"

"Yeah, I guess so."

"If it weren't for Jimmy's yellow sweatshirt and short hair, he would have looked like he was one of them, don't you think?"

Jim merely shrugged and kept on walking. There was no way he would admit to Linda that he'd thought the same thing. And he certainly wasn't about to tell her that the boy they'd supposedly adopted from the state of Maryland was actually an Amish child whose real family lived in Lancaster County, Pennsylvania.

Abby took a seat at the kitchen table, prepared to write Mom a letter. When she'd returned from the mailbox, she had spoken with Elizabeth about her mamm's request to send some of her quilts for the auction in June. Abby also mentioned that she would like to auction off the remaining quilts from her shop in Ohio and said she hoped it might help her put the past behind her. Elizabeth agreed that it was a good idea. Now Abby needed to let Mom know so she could set the wheels in motion.

"Does this mean you'll still be here during auction time?" Elizabeth asked as she pulled out a chair and took the seat opposite Abby.

Abby nodded. "If you don't mind me staying that long."

Elizabeth waved her hand "Not at all. In fact, I'd enjoy the company as well as the help."

"I'll be happy to help you and the other ladies in the community fix the meal that you'll be serving to those who attend the auction, but I'd rather not have anything to do with the quilts," Abby said with a lift of her chin.

Elizabeth shrugged her slim shoulders and smiled. "I wouldn't want you to do anything you're not comfortable with."

"Danki."

"So, now," Elizabeth said, pushing away from the table. "What should we have for lunch? I can get started on it while you write your letter."

"Are you sure you don't mind? I can help with lunch and write to Mom later on."

"Don't mind a bit. You keep on writing 'til you're done." Elizabeth grinned. "I thought, maybe, later this afternoon we could take a bike ride over to the Lehmans' place. Myra and you seemed to get along pretty well the other day, and I'm thinkin' the two of you might like the chance to get better acquainted."

"That sounds nice, but I haven't been on a bicycle since I was a young girl. I doubt I could still ride."

"Oh, sure you can. Once you've learned how to ride a bike, you never forget." Elizabeth stared across the room with a faraway look in her eyes. "I remember how my little brother and I used to ride our bikes back in Indiana where we grew up. We had some of our best visits when we rode into town to do errands." She smiled. "I think next to walking, riding a bike is the best way to travel, because you're able to see more scenery along the way. In a buggy you have to keep the horse in line and make sure you stay on your own side of the road."

"Do you have more than one bike?" Abby asked.

Elizabeth nodded. "I've got my own, plus the one my husband used to ride. I'll let you take mine, since you haven't ridden in a while. You might have trouble with the bar in the middle of the man's bicycle."

"That's nice of you, but—"

"Now, I insist."

"Jah, okay. I'll give it a try."

Naomi had just gotten her girls down for a nap and was planning to go over the receipt ledger when Lydia Weaver and her youngest daughter, Leona, entered the store.

"Wie geht's?" Naomi asked.

"Doin' fine, and you?"

"Other than being awfully tired, I can't complain."

"I've got some finished quilts out in my buggy," Lydia said, her blue eyes twinkling. "Me and my two oldest daughters recently finished several, so they're ready to sell in Fannie's quilt shop." She glanced around the room. "Thought maybe if Caleb or Matthew was here, I could talk 'em into bringing the boxes inside the shop for me."

"Caleb's getting one of our horses shoed, and Matthew's laboring at home in his woodworking shop."

"Guess I can manage on my own then." Lydia chuckled and pushed a strand of light brown hair back into her bun. "I loaded the quilts by myself, since Jacob and Arthur had already left for their paint job before I decided to come into town. So, if I could get the boxes into the buggy, I'm sure I can get 'em back out."

"I'd be happy to unload them for you," Naomi offered. She stepped down from her wooden stool and started for the front door, but the sound of her youngest daughter's wail halted her footsteps. "Ach! There goes Susan. I hope she doesn't wake her sister."

"Can I play with the boppli?" Leona asked. "I could keep her company while you and Mama bring in the quilts."

"I guess that would be all right." Naomi glanced at Lydia for her approval. Leona was almost ten years old and seemed quite capable.

Lydia nodded and headed for the door.

Naomi reached under the counter and handed Leona a small faceless doll. "If you give this to Susan, I'm sure she'll settle right down."

Leona took the doll and scampered off toward the back room.

"Be careful you don't wake Sarah," the child's mother called after her.

"I won't."

Naomi and Lydia stepped onto the front porch and down the steps. A few minutes later, they stood at the back of Jacob Weaver's market buggy.

"Have you heard anything from Abby lately?" Lydia asked, shielding her eyes from the sun.

"Had a letter from her a few days ago, and she seems to be doin' okay."

"When's she planning to come home?"

Naomi shrugged. "Don't know. Fannie seems to think she'll stay on at least until June, which is when the Amish community near Rexford holds its annual auction."

Lydia reached into the buggy and picked up the first box, and Naomi lifted the second one out.

"Sure would be nice if Abby decided to run the quilt shop for Fannie when she gets home," Lydia commented as they started for the store.

"I'm not sure Abby will ever work around quilts again. She's still grieving for Lester and the loss of her quilt shop. So far, nobody's been able to get through to her."

Lydia clicked her tongue. "It's such a shame when someone as young as Abby loses a loved one and can't come to grips with it." Her forehead creased as she shifted the cardboard box in her hands. " 'Course, I'm no expert on the subject of grief, since life has been pretty good to me and Jacob these twenty-two years we've been married."

"Guess nobody knows how they would handle things until it happens," Naomi said.

"That's for certain sure."

They were on the porch now, and Naomi leaned one edge of the box against the side of the store as she reached out to grab the handle on the screen door. She held it for Lydia, but the woman nodded for her to go ahead. Naomi had only taken a few steps when she halted. "Was in der welt—what in the world?"

In the middle of the floor sat two little girls with chocolate on their faces and various size candy wrappers surrounding them. It was a comical scene, and Naomi didn't know whether to laugh or cry.

"Ach, Leona," Lydia scolded, "I thought I could trust you not to get the baby up, and what's all this with the candy now?"

The child stared up her mother, and tears quickly filled her green eyes. "I couldn't get Susan to quiet down, and when Sarah woke up, she asked for some candy."

"Jah, well, that didn't give you the right to give her any, and especially not the boppli. She's too young to be fed chocolate."

"I figured she was hungry."

Naomi bent down and scooped Susan into her arms, then she grabbed hold of Sarah's hand. "I'd better take these two into the other room and get them cleaned up. When I come back, we can see about setting out those quilts."

"Jah, okay."

I sure hope the rest of this week goes better than today, Naomi thought as she and the girls headed to the back of the store. *For I surely don't have the energy to deal with much more.*

CHAPTER 34

*A*bby couldn't believe how well she had adapted to riding a bicycle again. For the past two months she'd been pedaling all over the area, visiting her new friend Myra, making trips to the country store, and going for rides simply for the enjoyment of spending time alone in the beautiful woods. Her depression had lifted some, but she still blamed herself for Lester's death, and even though Elizabeth kept coaxing Abby to make a quilt, she flatly refused.

"I can't believe the auction is only two days away," Abby said to Elizabeth as they rolled out pastry dough for some of the pies that would be sold to those attending the big event. "Don't know where the time has gone since I first came here to visit."

"Time does seem to move along rather quickly." Elizabeth smiled. "I've enjoyed your company and will miss you when you're gone."

Abby stared at the floor. She wasn't sure she wanted to return home. Being in this small Amish community was like a quiet respite.

"You're welcome to stay on even after the auction," Elizabeth was quick to say. "I'm sure I speak for others in our community when I say we'd be glad to have you stay here permanently."

Abby smiled. "That's nice to know, but it wouldn't be fair to my mamm."

"If you returned home, would it only be to please her?"

Abby pondered Elizabeth's question before she answered. Truth be told, she had spent most of her life trying to please her mamm, especially after Dad's death. It wasn't that Mom had asked Abby to make sacrifices. The two of them had always been close, but Abby had felt a sense of obligation to her mother that went beyond simple respect or willingness to help out. She'd been trying to fulfill her promise to her daed and had given up a lot in the process of trying to please Mom and see that her needs were met. Even now Abby wondered if she'd been selfish for staying here so long. Her mother had told her several months ago that Dad's request didn't mean Abby should be so self-sacrificing and put her own needs on hold. She'd also been reminded that since Mom was married to Abraham now, it was his job to look out for her.

"I'm feeling confused about things," Abby admitted. "I miss my family and want to be near them, but I've enjoyed being here with you, too."

Elizabeth nodded and measured out some lard as she prepared to make another batch of dough. "For now let's concentrate on gettin' ready for the auction. When that's behind us, you'll have time to decide what you want to do."

"That's true, and we do have a lot to get done before Saturday morning."

"I'm thinking about putting that small quilt I found awhile back into the auction," Elizabeth said, taking their conversation in a different direction. "There's not much point in me hanging on to it, because unless God brings another man into my life soon, it's not likely I'll have the need for a baby covering. I'm not gettin' any younger, ya know."

Abby grinned. "You never know how things will go. Look at my mamm. None of us expected her to marry again, much less become the mother of twin boys at her age."

Elizabeth clucked her tongue. "Poor Fannie. I can't imagine raisin' a couple of zwilling at any age."

"The twins can be quite the handful, but they're sure cute little fellows."

"I'm sure they are."

Abby sobered. "I hope Mom is managing okay without my help. She relied on me pretty heavily for a time."

"What do her letters say about how she's gettin' along in your absence?"

Abby grabbed the rolling pin and flattened the mound of pie dough in front of her. "Says she's doing fine, but then my mamm's never been one to complain."

"And how's your stepsister these days? Didn't you mention that she said in her last letter that she's pregnant?"

Abby nodded. "Naomi and Caleb have two little girls, and I think they're hopin' for a boy this time."

"Say, I've got an idea," Elizabeth said excitedly. "Why don't I give you the baby covering? You can present it to Naomi, if you like. I'm quite certain it's an Amish quilt, and I'd like to see it go to someone who would appreciate it."

"I suppose I could take it to her, and I'd be happy to pay you for it."

"I wouldn't think of takin' your money," Elizabeth said with a wave of her hand. A dusting of flour from her fingers drifted to the countertop, and she chuckled. "It'll be my gift to your new niece or nephew."

Abby smiled. "All right then. I'll take the quilt to Naomi whenever I decide to go home."

Linda walked slowly down the hospital corridor, feeling as though a hive of bees had taken up residence in her stomach. She'd discovered a breast lump last week and had gone to the doctor for a thorough exam. This morning she'd received a mammogram in the hospital's diagnostic lab. Depending on the results, she might be faced with a biopsy. *Oh, Lord,* she prayed, *please don't let this be cancer.*

Linda thought about Jimmy and how much he needed her. He'd turned seven two months ago and wasn't ready to be without his mother. She thought about Jim and how it might affect their marriage if the lump was cancerous. He had so little patience with her anymore, especially when she was sick or emotionally wrought. Would he want to be saddled with a wife who had serious health problems? *And what if I were to die before Jim finds the Lord as his Savior? I want our son to grow up knowing Jesus, and if Jim remains set against religion, he probably won't see that Jimmy goes to church or receives any religious training.*

Linda drew in a deep breath and tried to relax. She knew she was worrying about things that hadn't even happened yet.

*Please calm my heart, Lord, and if this does turn out to be cancer,
then all of us will need Your help in the days ahead.*

⌐

"You're lookin' awful tired these days," Fannie said, when she
discovered Naomi bent over an empty shelf in the store, swishing
a dust rag back and forth.

Naomi looked up and wiped the perspiration from her
forehead. "I do seem to tire more easily with this pregnancy than
I did with my other two. Guess it's because I have a lot more to
do now than I did before."

Fannie gave Naomi a hug. She had come to care deeply for
the young woman and hated to see her working so hard when
she obviously didn't feel well. "Why don't you bring the girls
over to our place each morning on your way to work? That way
you won't have so much responsibility here at the store."

Naomi smiled but shook her head. "I couldn't ask you to
watch my kinner. You've got your hands full takin' care of your
own two active boys."

"They can be a handful at times," Fannie admitted. "As
I'm sure you know, Nancy's still working as a maad for Anna
Beechy, who's been feelin' poorly for some time. Even though
I can't count on Nancy's help much these days, now that Mary
Ann's out of school for the summer, she's home most of the
time. That young girl has been a big help to me lately, and I'm
sure she wouldn't mind helpin' care for your girls."

"You really think so?" Naomi straightened and reached
around to rub her lower back.

"I do. Besides, Sarah and Susan would be good company for
Timothy and Titus." Fannie chuckled. "Might keep 'em occupied
so Mary Ann and I could get more chores done around the house.
I may even find more time for quilting."

"Did you leave the twins with Mary Ann this afternoon?"

Fannie nodded. "Jah, they were both sleeping soundly when
I decided to come to town, so I figured she'd have no problem
with 'em while I was gone."

"It's good for you to get away once in a while."

"It does feel kind of nice." Fannie shifted from one foot to the other. "What do you think about my offer to watch the girls?"

"I'll speak with Caleb about it as soon as he gets back from his dental appointment," Naomi said. "If he has no objections, maybe we could bring the girls by on Monday of next week and see how it goes."

Fannie smiled. "Sounds good."

"Did you come by for anything in particular?" Naomi asked. "Or did you stop to check on the quilt shop?"

"Both. I need some sewing notions, but I wanted to see how many quilts are in stock right now. If we're running low, I might have to ask a few more women to do some quilting for us." Fannie nodded toward her shop. "Now that it's summer, things can get busy when the tourists start comin' in."

"That's true, even here in the store." Naomi headed to the quilt shop, and Fannie followed. "Have you heard anything more from Abby?"

"I got another letter from her last week, and she mentioned that the auction will be held this Saturday. I'm guessin' my daughter's been helping the women in the community get the food ready that they plan to sell that day."

"From what Abby said in her last letter to me, it sounded like they'll have to feed at least a thousand people."

Fannie nodded. "I'm hopin' once Abby sees our quilts auctioned off, she'll be ready to come home. I miss her something awful."

"I'm sure you do. I'll be glad when Abby's back in Pennsylvania, too."

Fannie let her hand travel over a stack of queen-sized quilts. "I'm beginning to wonder if I should just sell the quilt shop and be done with it."

Naomi frowned. "Why would you want to do that? I thought you loved quilting?"

"I do enjoy making quilts, but I have no desire to drag the boys into town every day and try to run this place by myself."

"We need to keep praying about the matter," Naomi said. "I'd hate to see the quilt shop close."

Fannie shrugged. "If Abby returns and still refuses to work here, then I'll probably be forced to sell."

Linda glanced at Beth, who sat behind the wheel of her compact car. "Thanks for driving me to my appointment this morning. It was easier to have the biopsy done knowing you were waiting for me in the other room."

"I was praying, too." Beth tapped the steering wheel with her fingertips. "I still don't understand why your husband couldn't take time off to be with you. Surely he must realize how serious this could be."

"Jim doesn't care about anyone but himself," Linda said, as the bitter taste of bile rose in her throat. *I will not give in to tears. It won't change a thing.*

"I can see why you're frustrated, but we need to be patient and let the Lord work in Jim's life." Beth's voice was low and soothing, and in that moment, Linda almost believed her.

"What if this turns out to be cancer?"

"Then you'll do whatever the doctor suggests." Beth reached over and squeezed Linda's hand. "Our whole church will be praying for you."

"What scares me more than the disease is wondering what will become of Jim and Jimmy if I should die."

"Let's trust the Lord and take things one step at a time. The results of the biopsy could be negative, and then you will have been worried for nothing."

Linda nodded as tears blurred her vision. "I know I should trust God more, but sometimes it's hard, especially when I don't get answers to my prayers."

"God always answers," Beth said with a note of conviction. "Sometimes it's yes, sometimes no, and sometimes He says to wait. Regardless of how God answers, we must accept it as His will."

"I know," Linda murmured.

"No matter how this turns out," Beth said with an encouraging smile, "we'll get through it together. . .you, me, and our heavenly Father."

CHAPTER 35

$\mathcal{A}$bby sat on a backless wooden bench inside the quilt barn, observing the auctioneer as he hollered, "The bid's at three hundred dollars for this Lone Star quilt. Do I hear four hundred?"

In the row ahead, an English woman's hand shot up as she lifted the piece of cardboard with her bidding number on it.

"Four hundred dollars. Do I hear five?" The bidding went on until the Amish man finally shouted, "Sold at seven hundred dollars!"

Abby was amazed at how many quilts hung inside the tent. What seemed even more astonishing was the amount of people that had crowded into the area to watch the proceedings or bid on a quilt or wall hanging. She recognized the quilt being bid on now and leaned forward. It was one of her mamm's, and she figured the king-sized covering with various shades of blue would go for a tidy sum. She wasn't disappointed. It sold for nine hundred dollars. The other quilt her mother had sent was queen-sized, made in the Dahlia pattern with hues of maroon, pink, and white. Soon it was also gone—sold for seven hundred and fifty dollars.

Abby's spine went rigid when the two young Amish women standing on the raised platform held up one of her quilts—a Double Wedding Ring pattern, with interlocking rings made from two shades of green on a white background.

Tears stung her eyes as she thought about her and Lester's wedding plans and the quilt she'd been working on before she left Ohio. If she had finished the quilt and they'd gotten married as planned, it would have been covering their bed right now. All that remained of Abby's previous life as a quilter were the four double-sized quilts about to be auctioned off.

Her heart clenched when the auctioneer shouted, "Sold for six hundred dollars!"

The Amish women held up the second quilt Abby had made. This one was designed in the Distelfink pattern, which had been a favorite among the English who'd come to her shop in Berlin. In short order, it was sold for five hundred dollars.

Tears trickled down Abby's face, and a sob worked its way up her throat. *Oh, Lester, I loved you so much. You sacrificed your life to save my quilts, and I gave you nothing in return.*

The third and fourth quilts were then bid on and sold, and Abby swayed as a wave of nausea coursed through her stomach. She'd hoped that seeing her quilts auctioned off would bring release, but it only added to her grief. She stood on trembling legs and pushed her way through the crowd. Outside, she rushed behind the barn where her bicycle was parked. She needed to be alone—to go somewhere and find a quiet place to sit and calm down.

Abby pedaled across the open field, dodging the throng of people shopping at the various booths and weaving in and out of parked cars until she found her way to the main road. She kept the bike moving faster, taking her farther and farther away from the noisy auction and those painful memories of her beautiful quilts.

By the time Abby reached a turnoff for Lake Koocanusa, she was panting for breath. She braked and let her feet drop to the ground, then sat motionless, staring at the vast body of water below while she fought to gain control of her swirling emotions.

A hawk soared overhead, and Abby caught sight of a turkey hen and her chicks stepping out of the brush. The darker leaves of the trees surrounding the lake contrasted with the lighter bottle-green grass growing nearby. It was quiet and peaceful, which was just what she needed right now.

Feeling a need to be closer to the lake, Abby guided her bike slowly down the hill, following a narrow trail and being careful not to get her long dress caught in the bushes. When she reached the bottom, she noticed a young English boy sitting on a boulder with a fishing pole. He appeared to be alone, for she saw no one else in sight. Not wishing to disturb the child, she took a seat on one of the downed trees.

Clasping her hands around her knees, Abby lifted her face to the sun. She tried to pray, but no words would come. A verse of scripture popped into her mind. It was one Elizabeth had shared with her this morning from 1 Peter 1:7. *"That the trial of your faith, being much more precious than of gold that perisheth, though it be tried with fire, might be found unto praise and honour and glory at the appearing of Jesus Christ."* That was the second verse about fire Abby had heard since coming to Montana, and she wondered if God might be trying to tell her something. Abby knew her faith had been tried, but she felt as if her trials had done nothing to bring honor or praise to the Lord.

If only I could know peace and happiness again. If I could just be free from the overwhelming guilt I feel because of Lester's death. If only my life had some meaning.

Splash!

Abby's eyes snapped open.

"Help! Help!"

She jerked her head to the left, and her breath caught in her throat. The little boy she'd seen fishing had obviously fallen into the lake, and he was in trouble.

Abby scrambled off the log and jumped into the lake, giving no thought to the clothes she wore. Her father had taught her and Harold how to swim when they were little, but she hadn't gone swimming in several years. Even so, she soon discovered that, like riding a bike, she hadn't forgotten what to do in the water.

The boy continued to fight as he flailed his arms. His head bobbed up and down in the water. Abby reached out and grabbed the edge of his shirt, pulling him closer to her. She wrapped her arms around his chest, but the child floundered around as he fought to remain afloat.

"Calm down. Don't panic. I've got you now." Abby hoped he would soon relax, for if he kept thrashing like this, they might both drown. "Dear God, help us!" she shouted above the boy's screams.

The child went limp, making it easier for her to swim while she pulled him to shore. A short time later, they both lay on the grassy bank, the boy coughing and sobbing, Abby gulping in deep breaths of air. She was aware that her kapp was missing, her bun had come loose, and a clump of soggy hair pushed against her shoulders. Her dress was soaked, and so were her sneakers, but she didn't care. The child was safe, and that's all that mattered.

The boy stared at her with brown eyes, huge as chestnuts. "You—you saved my life."

She smiled. "What's your name?"

"Peter. I live up the hill."

"I'm Abby, Peter, and I think I'd better take you home."

He hiccuped on a sob. "Mama's gonna be real mad, 'cause she's told me never to come to the lake by myself."

Abby's heart went out to the child, but she knew what had to be done. "My bicycle is parked up the hill. We can ride double. How's that sound?"

Peter nodded, and she helped him to his feet. "I think I lost my pole," he whimpered.

"A fishing pole can be replaced, but you can't. Your mother will be happy to know you're okay."

Sometime later, with Peter riding on the handlebars in front of her, Abby pedaled into the boy's yard. A young woman with dark brown hair worn in a ponytail rushed out of the log home and onto the driveway. "Peter! Where were you, and why are your clothes all wet?"

"I—I went fishin', and I fell into the lake when a big one grabbed hold of my line," the child answered.

Peter's mother lifted him from the handlebars and hugged him tightly.

"I heard the splash and realized he was in water over his head and couldn't swim," Abby said.

The boy's mother stared at Abby. "Who are you?"

"Abby Miller, and I—"

"She jumped into the water and saved me, Mama," Peter interrupted, as his mother set him on the ground. "I would've drowned if she hadn't come along."

Abby's cheeks warmed as Peter threw himself into her arms. "I'm glad I was there," she whispered.

Peter's mother gave Abby an unexpected hug. "I'm Sharon Beal, and I thank you for saving my son."

"You're welcome."

"Why don't you come into the house and dry off? You're probably cold."

Abby shook her head. "I'm all right."

"At least let me get you a towel."

Abby glanced at her dress. She'd wrung it out the best she could, but it was sopping wet and stuck miserably to her skin. "Jah, I'd appreciate a towel."

Sharon patted her son on the head. "Run into the house and get some towels for you and Abby."

"Okay." Peter hesitated a moment, offered Abby a toothless grin, and scampered away.

"You were in the right place at the right time; there's no doubt in my mind," Sharon said to Abby. "God was watching out for my boy and brought you along at the exact moment it was needed."

Abby stared at the ground, puzzled by the woman's remark. Had she really gone to the lake because God had ordained it? If that were so, then why hadn't—

"Are you okay? You seem troubled."

Abby lifted her gaze to meet Sharon's. "I was wondering why God would send me to rescue Peter but let the man I was supposed to marry die."

Sharon tipped her head as a look of confusion clouded her dark eyes. Before Abby could explain, Peter came running toward them with a towel draped around his neck and another one in his hands. He handed the second towel to Abby. "Here ya go."

"Thank you."

"Now run inside and change into some dry clothes," his mother said.

Peter bounded off again, offering Abby a quick wave before he departed.

"Before my son came out, you said something about the man

you were supposed to marry dying," Sharon said. "Do you mind if I ask what happened?"

Abby rubbed the towel briskly over her arms and legs. She didn't know why she felt compelled to tell this near stranger about the fire that had snuffed out Lester's life, but she found herself pouring out the whole story. "If I'd only realized that the dream I kept having was a warning and returned to Ohio sooner, Lester might still be alive," she said with a catch in her voice.

Sharon's forehead wrinkled. "Is that how you see it?"

Abby nodded.

"There's a passage of scripture in Ecclesiastes 3:1 that says, 'To every thing there is a season, and a time to every purpose under the heaven.'" Sharon touched Abby's arm, and Abby felt warmth and comfort. "I believe God allows us to experience certain things in life that help us grow and learn to rely on Him. Even if you had returned to Ohio sooner, the fire might still have destroyed your quilt shop, and you could have been the one killed. Or perhaps both you and Lester would have perished."

Abby trembled as a rush of emotions spiraled through her body. "I've often wished I had been burned in the fire. It would have been better to have lost my own life than to have endured the pain of losing the man I loved."

Sharon slipped her arm around Abby's shoulder. "If you had died in the fire, you wouldn't have come to Montana. And if you hadn't come here, you would not have been at the lake this afternoon to save my boy."

"I—I guess you're right." Abby drew in a deep breath and released it slowly. "I've spent these last seven months feeling sorry for myself, wallowing in guilt, and trying to drown out the past by working so hard, when I should have been trying to deal with things."

"It's all right to grieve, Abby, but you must remember that the Lord is near to those with a broken heart. It says so in Psalm 34:18. All you need to do is call out to Him, and He will give you comfort, whether it be through His Word, by helping others, or in something as simple as a child's touch."

"Thank you," Abby said tearfully. "I've strayed so far from God these past several months, and I surely needed that reminder."

The two women hugged again, and Abby handed the wet towel to Sharon. "I must be going now or my friend Elizabeth will wonder where I am."

"Good-bye, Abby, and may God bless you in the days ahead."

As Abby pedaled her bicycle toward the auction barn, the verses of scripture Peter's mother had shared played over and over in her mind. Seeing her quilts auctioned off had put an end to the reminder of her quilt shop, but it had not put an end to the pain of losing Lester or lessened her guilt. However, a few simple passages from the Bible and the kind words of a grateful mother had helped Abby see the truth. For the first time since Lester's death, she was glad to be alive.

Abby drew in a deep breath, savoring the clean mountain air. She noticed the budding wildflowers growing along the edge of the road, and joined the birds in song as they warbled a happy tune from the trees overhead. Jah, it was wunderbaar gut to be alive!

A car whizzed past, and Abby gripped the handlebars, moving her bike to the edge of the road. *Guess some things aren't so different even here in the woods.* She glanced at a covey of quail running into the bushes, and smiled, refusing to let the speeding motorist spoil the moment. She could hardly wait to tell Elizabeth all that had happened after she'd left the quilt barn. Surely her new friend would share in this joy. Abby thought about Mom and the rest of the family waiting in Pennsylvania. *I'll send them a letter right away.*

Abby's attention was drawn back to the road when she heard a noise, and two female deer stepped out of the woods. She swerved to keep from hitting them, but her back tire spun in the gravel and she lost control. The last thing Abby remembered was the trunk of a cedar tree coming straight toward her.

CHAPTER 36

*A*bby moaned as she squinted against the ray of light streaming into the room. Her head ached, her vision was fuzzy, and nothing seemed familiar. *Where am I?* She tried to stretch and winced when a throbbing pain shot through her leg. *Oh! What's happened to me?*

"I'm glad you're finally awake. You've been in and out for the last couple of days."

Abby didn't recognize the woman's voice. She turned her head and blinked at the middle-aged woman with short auburn hair who stood beside her bed. She wore a nurse's uniform. "Wh—where am I?" she rasped.

"You're in the hospital. You were brought to Libby by ambulance late Saturday afternoon."

Abby tried to sit up, but the dull ache in her head prevented her from doing so.

"Better lie still," the nurse instructed. "You've had a serious concussion, and your leg is broken." She touched Abby's arm. "From what I was told, you took quite a spill, so it could have been a lot worse."

Abby squeezed her eyes shut, trying to remember what had happened. Saturday morning she'd gone to the auction and had watched her quilts being auctioned off. Then, unable to bear the pain of it all, she had ridden Elizabeth's bike down to the lake. There'd been a little boy there. He'd fallen into the water, and she'd rescued him. When Abby took Peter home, his mother had shared some verses of scripture and words of wisdom, helping her realize that life did have meaning, and because she had come to the lake when she did, Sharon's son had been saved.

And last, Abby remembered getting back on her bike and heading toward the auction. There were two deer on the road, and. . .

Her eyes snapped open. "I—I skidded in some gravel and must have hit a tree."

The nurse nodded. "That's what the paramedics figured had happened, although you were unconscious when they arrived and so, naturally, you weren't able to tell them anything."

"Who found me, do you know?"

"A man and woman who were driving to the Amish auction spotted you lying alongside of the road. They called 9-1-1 on their cell phone, and after the ambulance arrived, they drove to the auction and told someone what had happened."

Abby curved her fingers under her chin. "Oh, my! Elizabeth must be so worried. She probably wonders why I never came back and doesn't know where I am."

"Elizabeth King?"

"Jah."

"I guess with the description the English couple gave to the people in charge, they were able to figure out it was you who had been hurt. Elizabeth is here now, in the waiting room."

Abby drew in a deep breath. "Can I see her?"

"Certainly. I'll send her right in." The nurse left the room, and a few minutes later, Elizabeth entered with a worried expression on her face.

"Oh, Abby, I'm so glad you're going to be all right." She rushed to the side of Abby's bed. "When the doctor told me you'd had a concussion, I was terribly worried."

"The nurse said my leg's broken, too."

Elizabeth nodded and took a seat in the closest chair. "What were you doing out there with my bike?"

"I—I decided to go for a ride."

"But I thought you were going to help me and the other ladies serve the meal after you'd watched some of the quilts being auctioned off."

"I had planned on that."

"When it came time to get things set out, you were nowhere to be found, but it wasn't until later that I really began to worry."

Abby's eyes filled with tears. "I'm sorry for causing you to worry."

"It's you I'm concerned about." Elizabeth reached for Abby's hand. "What made you decide to go for a bike ride?"

"I had hoped if my quilts sold, it would put an end to my past and make me feel better."

"Did it?"

Abby shook her head. "I felt worse, and the only thing I could think to do was get off by myself for a while." She went on to tell Elizabeth about the boy who had fallen into the lake and how she'd saved him. Then she relayed what Peter's mother had said when she'd taken him home and how the woman had helped her see things more clearly. "I was planning to share this with you when I got back to the auction, which was where I was heading when I ran into a tree."

Elizabeth's eyes watered, yet she smiled. "I'm glad you've come to grips with the past and are ready to face the future."

"Sharon reminded me that if I hadn't come to visit you, I wouldn't have been at the lake Saturday afternoon to save her son." Abby brushed her tears away. "God showed me some other things, too."

"Such as?"

"All this time I've been feeling guilty for not returning to Ohio sooner, and thinking I could have spared Lester's life, when I should have been trusting God and allowing Him to heal my pain." She paused and moistened her lips with the tip of her tongue. "Peter's mother was right. If the fire hadn't happened at my quilt shop, I never would have come to Montana. I realize now that even if I had been there when my shop caught fire, I might not have been able to talk Lester out of going in. It was an accident—one I wish hadn't happened, but it did, and—" Abby couldn't go on and her voice broke on a sob.

"God used you in a mighty way when you saved that boy from drowning. I'm happy you've decided to trust Him again, and I know He is, too." Elizabeth plucked a tissue from the small box on the nearby table and blew her nose. "I know Edna and your mamm will be glad to hear this good news, too."

"Do they know about my accident?"

Elizabeth nodded. "When I heard what had happened, I used a friend's phone to call your stepsister's store in Paradise. Naomi said she would get word to your mamm and the rest of the family."

"I'm ready to go home to Pennsylvania, Elizabeth. I mean, as soon as I'm able to travel."

"I figured you might be."

"I don't know what the future holds for me, but I want to do something worthwhile—something that will help others and let them know God cares for them."

Elizabeth reached into her purse. "I wonder if you might be interested in this."

"What is it?"

"It's some information I recently received from a friend who lives in Indiana. Some of the women in her community are making quilts to send to people in Haiti, where there's a need for warm blankets."

Abby thought about what Elizabeth had shared. Until Saturday afternoon she'd given up on the idea of quilting again. But now she was being offered the opportunity to make quilts and give them to others who had so little. She was certain it was what God wanted her to do.

⁓

"What do you mean, you're going to Montana?"

"You heard me. I'm going there as soon as Abby gets out of the hospital and feels up to traveling." Matthew looked at Naomi like she'd taken leave of her senses, but she thought it was him who was talking crazy.

"Shouldn't it be someone else's responsibility to go after Abby?" she questioned.

He leaned across the counter until his face was a few inches from hers. "Think about it Naomi. Fannie can't go; she has the twins to care for. Abraham, Norman, Jake, and Samuel are in the middle of plantin' the fields. And you—well, you're in no condition to go anywhere now that you're in the family way again. Besides, you've got two little girls and a store to look after. I'm the only one with the time to go."

Naomi smiled. "So I've been right all this time, jah?"

"Right about what?"

"You're in love with Abby, and don't deny it, because I see the light shinin' in your eyes."

"What light's that?"

"The light of love."

Matthew's ears turned pink, and the color spread quickly over his face. "I've told you before, Abby thinks of me only as her big brother."

Naomi shrugged. "That could change."

He grunted and took a step back. "We'd best wait and see how it goes."

"You're still willing to go after her, even though you don't know if there's a future for the two of you?"

"Jah. She needs me."

Naomi skirted around the counter. "Matthew Fisher, you're a wunderbaar man."

⁓

Jim stared into his cup of coffee and tried to focus his thoughts on the paint job his crew was scheduled to do this morning. But no matter how hard he tried, he couldn't keep his mind on work. Linda's hurtful expression and slumped shoulders when he'd come home Friday night had made him feel like a heel. *She's upset because I didn't go with her when she had the biopsy done. She thinks I don't care.*

He pushed his chair away from the kitchen table and stood. *I do care. I just couldn't go, and it wasn't my job keeping me away, like I told her. I can't let Linda know how scared I am that she might have cancer. What would Jimmy and I do if she were to die?*

Jim glanced at the clock above the stove. It was almost six thirty, and he needed to get on the road. The paint job they'd be doing today was in Renton, a good hour away if traffic was heavy on the freeway. He'd thought about waking Linda before he left and apologizing to her. But she and Jimmy usually slept in now that he was out of school for the summer, and he didn't want to disturb her. *I should have apologized this weekend, but I couldn't seem to get the words out. Maybe I'll leave her a note.*

Jim opened the rolltop desk in one corner of the kitchen and pulled out a sheet of paper and a pen. He hurriedly scrawled an apology, said he would bring home pizza for dinner tonight, and left the note on the kitchen table. At least now he could go to work without feeling so guilty.

CHAPTER 37

$\mathcal{L}$inda hung up the phone and sank to the couch as shock waves spiraled through her body like a spinning top. The pathology report wasn't good. The doctor said there was a cancerous mass in her left breast, and he wanted to schedule Linda for a mastectomy as soon as possible.

She squeezed her eyes shut and tears rolled down her cheeks. "Oh, Lord, help me deal with this. Give me strength in the days ahead, and no matter what happens, please help my faith to grow stronger."

"Mommy, why are you crying?"

Linda's eyes snapped open. She didn't know Jimmy had come into the living room. For the last hour, he'd been upstairs playing. She sniffed and swiped her hand across her damp face. "Come sit beside me so we can talk."

Jimmy did as she asked and snuggled against her side. "Are you mad at Daddy? Did he yell at you again?"

"No, Jimmy." How could she tell her boy the truth without frightening him? And shouldn't she let Jim know what the doctor said before she told Jimmy anything about her going to the hospital?

"Why were you crying, Mommy?"

She kissed the top of his head. "I'll explain things after your daddy gets home."

"Okay."

Jimmy scooted away, but she reached out to him. "Don't go yet. I'd like to ask you something."

"What?"

"It's about Sunday school."

He grinned. "I like my teacher, and Allen and I always have fun during playtime."

"I'm glad." Linda fingered the edge of her Bible lying on the table to her right. "Will you promise to keep going to church, even if Mommy can't go?"

Jimmy's eyes were wide. "How would I get there if you didn't take me?"

She swallowed hard, afraid she might break down in front of him. "I'm sure Allen's mother would be happy to pick you up."

His forehead wrinkled. "Why can't you keep takin' me to Sunday school?"

"I—I will, Jimmy, for as long as I'm able." She moistened her lips with the tip of her tongue. "I just meant that if Mommy got sick and couldn't take you, I'd want you to go anyway."

Jimmy nodded soberly. "You're not sick, are you, Mommy?"

Linda drew a deep breath, praying for the right words. "Why don't the two of us go into the kitchen and see about having some lunch? We can talk about this later. How's that sound?"

"Can I have chicken noodle soup?"

"Yes, of course." Linda leaned over and kissed Jimmy's cheek. *Oh, Lord, please give me many more years with this precious boy.*

❧

"Are you excited to get home?" Matthew asked Abby as they rode in the backseat of their English driver's van, heading for Abraham and Fannie's place.

"Jah, I surely am. I never could have made the trip alone, and I appreciate your comin' to get me."

"I'm glad I could do it." He grinned at Abby, and her eyes flitted from his firm, full mouth to his serious brown eyes. The thick, dark hair covering his ears gleamed in the sunlight, and for the first time since she'd met Matthew, Abby realized how handsome he was.

"You've been kind to me the whole way here," she said, taking the apple Matthew had just handed her.

"It's easy to be kind to someone as sweet as you." Matthew looked straight ahead, but Abby noticed that his ears had turned slightly red. He embarrassed easily. She'd discovered that soon after moving to Pennsylvania.

She hesitated before responding to his last statement, not sure how she should interpret the words. Could it be that Matthew saw her as more than a little sister? If so, why hadn't he said anything to let her know? He was probably just speaking kindly in a brotherly way, the same as he always had. Still, if there was a chance that. . .

"On the train we talked about lots of things," Abby said hesitantly, "but there's one thing I didn't tell you."

"What's that?"

"Even though I will always have memories of Lester with me, I'm ready to move on with my life."

Matthew's eyebrows shot up so high they disappeared under the brim of his straw hat. "Oh?"

She nodded. "I know that when the time is right, someone will come into my life who will love me as much as Lester did, and I shall love him in return."

Matthew shifted in his seat. "Uh—Abby—I hope I'm not speakin' out of turn, but I was wonderin'—"

She reached over and touched his arm. "What were you wondering?"

He glanced at her, then looked quickly away. "Do you—uh—think you could ever be interested in someone like me?"

The rhythm of Abby's heartbeat picked up, and she shifted on the seat beside him. "Jah, I believe I could."

Matthew's face broke into a wide smile, and he reached for her hand, sending unexpected warm tingles up her arm. "I won't rush you into anything, because I know you've still got a lot of healin' to do, but I would like the chance to court you whenever you're ready."

She nodded. "I'd like that, too."

The van pulled into the Fishers' graveled driveway, and Matthew jumped out. He came around to help Abby down, then handed the crutches to her.

Abby's heart swelled with emotion. "I'm so excited to see everyone." She nodded at her suitcase, which their driver, Walt Peterson, had taken from the backseat. "I've got something to give Naomi for that boppli she's carrying."

Matthew chuckled. "Caleb's hopin' for a boy this time. Guess he feels a bit outnumbered with only girls around their place."

Walt set their suitcases on the front porch and said good-bye.

Matthew helped Abby up the steps, and they were almost to the front door when it swung open and a chorus of voices shouted, "Welcome home!"

"And I'm ever so glad to be here," Abby said in return.

Mom, Abraham, Mary Ann, Nancy, Jake, Samuel, Norman, and his wife, Ruth, all crowded around, but Mom was the first to hug Abby. "Come inside and have a seat. You must be exhausted."

Abby nodded. "It was a long trip, and my leg's beginning to throb."

Abraham took Abby's crutches and helped her over to the couch. After she was seated, Matthew pulled up a footstool and slid it under her leg.

"How much longer will ya have to wear that thing? It looks mighty heavy," Mary Ann said, leaning over to study Abby's cast.

"Three more weeks." Abby reached for her mother's hand as Mom took a seat beside her. "Where are the twins? I'm anxious to see how much they've grown."

"They're upstairs taking their afternoon naps, but it's nearly time for them to wake up," Mom replied.

"Mary Ann and I will go fetch them." Nancy grabbed her younger sister's hand, and they raced out of the room.

"Will Naomi and her family be over soon?" Abby asked.

Mom nodded. "They plan to stop by after they close the store for the day. I invited them to have supper with us."

"I'm glad. It will be nice to have the whole family together again."

Abby spent the next half hour answering questions and offering explanations about Montana, the Amish auction, how she had saved the little boy from drowning, and her bicycle accident. "I'm happy to say that soon after my cast comes off, I'll be ready to take over your quilt shop." She smiled at her mother. "That is, if you still want me to."

Mom's eyes shimmered with tears, and she sniffed a couple of times. "I'd like that very much. It's truly an answer to prayer."

"I'm hoping to enlist the help of several women in our

community to make quilts that will be sent to needy people in Haiti. Elizabeth told me about the special project," Abby said.

"That sounds like something a group of women are doing over near Strasburg, where Edna lives." Mom pursed her lips. "Only I believe they're sendin' their quilts to Africa."

Mary Ann and Nancy entered the room carrying Titus and Timothy. But Abby didn't mind the interruption to the conversation. She was happy to see her little brothers, who had grown so much in her absence. "Bring those precious boys here so I can love on them a bit," she said, motioning for the girls to come over to the couch.

"Be careful now," Abraham said with a chuckle. "Titus and Timothy have more energy than five boys their age, and we don't want 'em bumpin' that leg of yours."

Mom waved her hand. "Oh, husband, how you exaggerate." She reached for Titus and plunked him in Abby's lap, then took Timothy and seated him between her and Abby.

Abby kissed and hugged on the boys awhile, then Ruth asked Mom if it was time to start supper. Mom agreed but was reluctant to leave Abby.

"Ah, she'll be fine by herself," Jake said with a snicker. "Probably would enjoy bein' away from all the noise for a while."

Abby shook her head. "I don't mind the noise one bit."

"I'll take the twins outside to sit on the porch swing." Abraham gathered up his sons, while Mom, Ruth, and the girls headed for the kitchen.

"I think the rest of us ought to go outside, too," Matthew said, looking at Norman, then Jake, and finally down at young Samuel. "Abby needs some quiet time before the rest of the family arrives, don't ya think?"

"I'm okay, really," Abby spoke up.

"Even so, it would make me feel better if you rested awhile."

"Yes, Dr. Matthew," she said with a smile.

He grinned, like he was pleased with himself, and carefully lifted Abby's injured leg, helping her to lie on the couch. "Close your eyes, and we'll let you know when Naomi and her family arrive."

Abby settled against the pillows with a sigh. It was ever so nice to be home.

"It's good to see you again, Abby. You were surely missed," Naomi said. Supper was over and the two of them had come to the living room for a visit.

"I'm glad to be here." Abby nodded at her suitcase, sitting near the woodstove. "Would you mind bringing that over to me? I've got something for you."

"You didn't have to bring me anything."

Abby smiled. "Actually, it's more for the boppli you're carrying."

"I see." Naomi placed the suitcase on one end of the couch, and Abby scooted closer to it. She snapped the lid open and lifted the baby quilt, holding it out to Naomi. Naomi stood there a few seconds, staring at the quilt with a puzzled expression. Finally, with shaky fingers, she reached out and took it, examining each little square and touching every corner. Tears streamed down Naomi's cheeks, and she sank into a chair near the couch. When she lifted one end of the quilt and pressed it against her cheek, her whole body trembled.

Abby felt concern and wondered if giving the baby covering to Naomi had been a bad idea. "I was hoping you would like the little quilt."

Tears coursed down Naomi's cheeks. "Oh, I do, Abby. I just need to know where you got it."

"Elizabeth gave it to me. She said she'd found it at a thrift store when she and some other women from her community were on vacation."

"Where was it, Abby? Did she tell you where they had gone?"

Abby sat there a few seconds, trying to recall what Elizabeth had said about the trip. "I—I think it was somewhere in the state of Washington. Why do you want to know, Naomi?"

"Because this was my little brother's quilt."

Abby leaned slightly forward, unsure of what her stepsister had said. "What was that?"

"This quilt belonged to Zach. Our mother made it for him before she died."

"But—but how can you be sure it's the same quilt?"

Naomi held up the covering. "See here, there's a small patch that doesn't fit the Tumbling Block pattern. The quilt got caught in Zach's crib rails one morning, and I was in such a hurry I didn't do a good job patching it." She slowly shook her head, and more tears fell. "I would recognize this anywhere. It's Zach's, I know it is."

Abby gasped. "Do you know what this means?"

Naomi nodded. "It means my little brother must be living in the state of Washington somewhere." She stood and began to pace in front of the woodstove. "I've got to tell Papa about this. He needs to know Zach is still alive."

Abby opened her mouth to protest, but she closed it again. Finding the quilt was no guarantee that Abraham's son was still living. For that matter, the fact that Elizabeth had found the quilt in Washington didn't mean Zach was there. Whoever had kidnapped the boy could have sold the quilt or thrown it out. It might have passed through many hands before it ended up in the thrift store. *How do I say this to Naomi without upsetting her further? If I'd known this little covering was going to cause her such pain, I would have left it with Elizabeth.* As the words flitted through her head, Abby quickly changed her mind. *The quilt is a link to Naomi's missing brother, maybe an important one. Who am I to dash away any hope Naomi has of seeing Zach again?*

Naomi started for the front door, and Abby figured she was heading for the barn where the men had gone after supper. Her hand touched the doorknob, but suddenly she whirled around. "I can't show Papa the quilt. Not now. Maybe not ever."

"Why not?"

"He's been through so much over the years, I won't see him hurt again. This would only get his hopes up." Naomi flopped back into her chair, draping the quilt over her knees. "Even if Zach is living out west, we have no idea in which city or who his kidnapper is. Zach's not a baby anymore, either. He would be seven years old by now. Why, he could walk right up to us and we probably wouldn't even know it was him."

"I'm sorry for upsetting you," Abby apologized. "Maybe it would have been better if I hadn't given you the quilt."

"No, no, I'm glad you did." Naomi buried her face in the quilt. "It might be hard to understand, but holding this actually brings me comfort."

"Are you sure about not telling your daed?"

Naomi stood. "Someday, maybe. For now I'll keep it in my boppli's room as a reminder that somewhere my little bruder is still living among the English and I need to keep praying for him."

Abby nodded. "I'll be praying, too."

"I'm going to the kitchen to get a paper sack to put the quilt in, so none of the others will see it."

"Do you want to put it back in my suitcase for now?"

"That's a good idea." Naomi placed the quilt inside the suitcase, shut the lid, and then hurried from the room.

A few seconds later, Matthew showed up. "Whew, it's still mighty warm out there. Looks like we're in for some hot weather." He wiped the perspiration from his forehead and smiled at Abby. "Before this summer's over, you might wish you had stayed in Montana where it's cooler."

"I don't think so." She patted the cushion beside her. "Have a seat."

He grinned, and his ears turned pink. She had embarrassed him again, but that was okay. The fact that Matthew blushed so easily was part of who he was, and she rather liked it.

"How'd you like to go on a picnic with me one day next week?" he asked, lowering himself to the couch. "That is, if you're feelin' up to it."

"I'd like it fine, and I'm sure I'll be feeling good enough to go." Abby chuckled. "Of course, you'll probably have to bring a chair for me to sit in. It might be easy enough for me to drop to the ground, but gettin' back up would be a lot harder."

Matthew reached over and took her hand, giving her fingers a gentle squeeze. "Why don't you let me worry about that?"

Abby leaned against the sofa cushions and sighed. *I know my faith has been tried and withstood the flames. And regardless of what happens with Zach, the Fisher family, or between Matthew and me, I'm confident that God will see us through.*

the
Bishop's
Daughter

by
Wanda E. Brunstetter

BARBOUR
PUBLISHING

To Arie, Sue, Betty, and Ada Nancy—
four special women who have taught Amish children.

*Suffer little children to come unto me, and forbid them not:
for of such is the kingdom of God.*
LUKE 18:16 KJV

PROLOGUE

"I—I want you to promise me something."

Jim cringed when he thought of all the times he had reneged on a promise he'd made to his wife. "What do you want me to promise, Linda?"

"Would you see that—" Her voice faltered. "I—I want to be sure Jimmy continues to go to church—after I'm gone. Will you take him?"

A knot formed in the pit of Jim's stomach, and he nodded.

"I'm glad we adopted Jimmy. He's brought such joy into my life." Linda fingered the edge of the Amish quilt tucked around her frail form. "I—I know we agreed not to tell him that he's adopted while he's too young to understand." She paused. "But I want you to tell him about the adoption when he's older. He needs to know the truth. It—it wouldn't be right to keep it from him."

"Yeah, I know."

"And you won't tell him until he's old enough to handle it?"

"I promise I won't." Jim gritted his teeth. *Should I tell her the details of Jimmy's adoption? Would it be wrong to let Linda die without revealing the truth?* He dropped his head forward into his open palms. *It would be cruel to tell her what I did when I know she's dying. The news in itself might kill her, and it would certainly add to her agony. And for what purpose? Just to ease my guilty conscience? I did what I did because I loved her and wanted to give her a child, so I can't let her die with the truth of my betrayal on her mind.*

"What is it, Jim? Are you all right?"

He lifted his head and reached for her hand. "I will tell Jimmy about his adoption when I think he's old enough."

"Thank you." Tears matted Linda's lashes, speckling her pale cheeks. "I love you and Jimmy so much, and—and I pray you'll find comfort in knowing that I'm going home soon—to be with my Lord."

Jim's only response was a brief nod. The motion was all he could manage. He knew Linda believed in God and thought she would go to heaven, but he'd never been sure about all that religious mumbo jumbo. He only went to church when he felt forced to go—whenever Jimmy was in some special program. Even then, he always felt uncomfortable. Linda had said many times that she thought God had an answer for everything. But where was God when Linda had been diagnosed with breast cancer five years ago? And where was God when the cancer came back and spread quickly throughout her body?

Linda drew in a raspy breath. "Will you and Jimmy be able to manage on your own—after I'm gone?"

Jim groaned. He didn't need these reminders that she was dying or that their son would be left with only one parent. "We'll get along. I'll raise him the best I can."

"I know you will."

He leaned over and kissed her cheek. *If it were within my power, I would move heaven and earth to keep you from dying.*

CHAPTER 1

$\mathcal{T}$ears welled in Leona Weaver's eyes as she glanced around the one-room schoolhouse where she'd been teaching the last four years. Her days of teaching would have been over in two weeks, when the school year ended. The school board would have then selected a new teacher to take Leona's place in the fall, due to her plans to marry.

"But that won't be happening now," she murmured. "I'll be teaching in the fall again—not getting married."

Leona closed her eyes as she relived the shocking moment when she had been told that Ezra Yoder, the man she was supposed to marry, had been kicked in the head while shoeing a horse and had died.

"Uh—Leona, I've got something to tell you."

"What's that, Papa?"

"The thing is—"

"You seem kind of naerfich. *Is there something wrong to make you so nervous?"*

Papa pulled in a deep breath as he motioned for Leona to take a seat on the sofa. "There's been an accident, daughter. Ezra is—"

"Ezra? Has Ezra been hurt?"

He nodded soberly. "I'm sorry to be the one havin' to tell you this, but Ezra is dead."

Dead. Ezra is dead. Leona sank to the sofa as her daed's words echoed in her head.

Papa took a seat beside her, and Mom, who'd just come into the room, did the same.

9

"How did it happen, Jacob?" Mom asked, reaching over to take Leona's hand.

"Ezra was shoeing a skittish horse and got kicked in the head. His brother, Mose, saw it happen."

The tightness in Leona's chest interfered with her ability to breathe. "Ezra can't be dead. I just spoke to him last night. We were making plans for our wedding, and—" Her voice trailed off, and she gulped on a sob.

Papa kept his head down, obviously unable to meet her gaze. "The Lord giveth, and the Lord taketh away. It must have been Ezra's time to go."

Her daed's last words resounded in Leona's head. The Lord taketh away. It must have been Ezra's time to go. She gripped the edge of the sofa and squeezed her eyes shut. No, no, it can't be! I love Ezra. Ezra loves me. We are going to be married in the fall!

When Leona opened her eyes, she saw a look of pity in her mamm's eyes.

"You'll get through this, daughter. With the help of your family and friends, God will see you through."

As the reality of the situation began to fully register, Leona's body trembled. "The Lord giveth. The Lord taketh away," she murmured. "Never again will I allow myself to fall in love with another man."

Bringing her thoughts back to the present, Leona pushed her chair away from her desk and stood. She saw no point in grieving over what couldn't be changed. Ezra had been gone for almost three months, and he wouldn't be coming back. Leona would never become a wife or mother. She must now accept a new calling, a new purpose for living, a new sense of mission. She would give all of her efforts to being the best schoolteacher she could be.

"Maybe a few minutes in the fresh spring air might clear my head before it's time to call the scholars into the schoolhouse from their morning recess," she murmured. "Maybe I'll even join their game of baseball."

As a young girl, Leona had always enjoyed playing ball. Even now, with her twenty-fourth birthday just a few months away, she could still outrun most of her pupils and catch a fly ball with little effort.

She opened the door, stepped onto the porch, and hurried across the lawn. She stepped up to home plate just as Silas, Matthew Fisher's ten-year-old boy, dropped his bat and darted for first base. Sprinting like a buggy horse given the signal to trot, Silas's feet skimmed the base, and he kept on running. His teammates cheered, and the opposing team booed as the boy made his way around the bases.

When Naomi Hoffmeir's eleven-year-old son, Josh, nearly tagged Silas with the ball, the exuberant child skidded to a stop and slid into third base. Sweat rolled down the boy's forehead as he huffed and puffed, but his smile stretched ear to ear.

"It's my turn," Leona called to Emanuel Lapp, the pitcher. She grabbed the bat, bent her knees slightly, and planted both feet with toes pointing outward. "Get ready, Silas, 'cause I'm bringing you home!"

"And she can do it, too," Leona's niece, Fern, shouted from the sidelines.

Leona glanced at Fern, her older brother's eleven-year-old daughter. Several wisps of the girl's golden blond hair had come loose from her white *kapp*, and it curled around her ears. *She reminds me so much of her daed,* Leona thought. *Ever since Arthur started working for Papa, he's always said exactly what he thinks. Truth be told, Arthur probably can't wait for Papa to retire from painting so he can take over the business.*

Fern lifted her hand in a wave, and Leona waved back. *She's so sweet. I'd hoped to have a child like her someday.*

Her thoughts went to Ezra again. *But there will be no* kinner *for me. Ezra's gone, and I'll never know what our children would have looked like. I'll never. . ."*

Forcing her thoughts back to the game, Leona gripped the bat and readied herself for Emanuel's first pitch. She knew the twelve-year-old had a steady hand and could throw straight as an arrow. He was also known to pitch a good curve ball, which she would have to watch out for. If the Amish schoolteacher got anything less than a good hit, she would never live it down. *Keep your eye on the ball,* she reminded herself. *Don't give Emanuel an edge, and don't think about anything except playing this game.*

The pitch came fast and hard, but it was too far to the right. Leona held on to the bat but didn't swing.

"Ball one!" Harley Fisher hollered from the place where he crouched behind her, ready to catch the ball.

She shifted uneasily as her metal-framed glasses slipped to the middle of her nose. She mostly needed them for reading or close-up work and should have left them on her desk. But it was too late to worry about that. She had a ball to hit.

Leona took one hand off the bat and pushed her glasses back in place. *Whish!* The ball came quickly, catching her off guard.

"Strike one!" Harley shouted.

Leona pursed her lips in concentration. *If I hadn't tried to right my glasses, I could have hit that one. Might have planted it clear out in left field.*

Setting her jaw as firmly as her determination, she gripped the bat tighter, resolved to smack the next one over the fielders' heads and bring Silas home.

Emanuel pulled his arm way back, and a sly smile spread across his face.

"Teacher, Mary's bein' mean to me!"

Leona's gaze darted quickly to the left. When she saw it was only a skirmish over the swings, she turned back. But before she could react, the oncoming sphere of white hit her full in the face, sending her glasses flying and causing her vision to blur. She swallowed as a metallic taste filled her mouth. When she cupped her hand over her throbbing nose, warm blood oozed between her fingers. The ground swayed beneath her feet, and the last thing Leona remembered was someone calling her name.

"How come you wanted to go out for lunch instead of dinner tonight?" Jimmy Scott asked his dad. They had taken seats in front of the window at a restaurant overlooking Commencement Bay and given the waitress their orders.

"I thought it would be easier to get a table with a view of the water when they aren't so busy." Jimmy's dad pulled his fingers through one side of his dark hair, which over the last couple of years had become sprinkled with gray. "Maybe after lunch we can take a ride to Point Defiance Park, or would you rather do something else to celebrate your birthday?"

Jimmy chuckled. "I won't turn twenty-one until Sunday, Dad. I had hoped the two of us could attend church together and then maybe play a round of golf in the afternoon."

His dad's dark eyebrows furrowed, causing the wrinkles in his forehead to become more pronounced. "I planned it so we could take today off, figuring you'd want to spend Sunday with your friend, Allen, or some of the young people from your church."

Jimmy stared out the window as disappointment rose in his chest. Dad had never gone to church that often, not even when Mom was alive. Since her death nine years ago, all his dad had ever done was drop Jimmy off at church, and he'd even stopped attending the special holiday programs. What would it take to make the stubborn man see his need for Christ, and why hadn't Mom been able to get through to him? She'd tried plenty of times; Jimmy had heard her almost beg Dad to accept the Lord as his Savior. But Dad always said he didn't need church or anything God had to offer.

Jimmy studied a passing sailboat, which glided through the bay with ease and perfect rhythm. *If only life could be as serene and easy to handle as a boat skimming along the water on a calm spring day.* He thought about his mother's untimely death and how sad he had been when the ravages of cancer had taken her from them. *Still, it was because of Mom that I found a personal relationship with Christ. She set a Christian example, saw that I went to church every Sunday, and read me Bible stories when I was a boy.* He reached for his glass of water and took a drink. *At least Mom was set free of her pain, and I'm sure I'll see her in heaven someday.*

"So, have you made any plans with Allen for Sunday?"

Dad's question drove Jimmy out of his musings. "Uh—no, not really. I guess if you want to celebrate my birthday today and don't plan to go to church with me on Sunday I'll do something with Allen and his family."

"That's a good idea. I've got a lot of paperwork to do, and it'll take me most of the weekend to get it finished."

Sure, Dad, if this weekend is like so many others, you'll probably be camped out in some bar instead of at home doing paperwork. "Yeah, okay. I understand," Jimmy mumbled.

Dad reached across the table and handed Jimmy a small box wrapped in white tissue paper. "Happy birthday, son."

Jimmy took the gift and tore off the wrapping paper. When he opened the lid, he discovered an expensive-looking gold watch.

"So you're always on time for work," his dad said with a grin.

"Thanks. Even though I already own a watch, it'll be nice to have a new one I can wear when I'm not working and don't want to get paint all over it." Jimmy had started working part-time for his dad when he was a teenager, and he'd continued painting after he'd graduated from high school. The only time he hadn't worked for his dad was when he'd taken a couple of classes at the community college in Tacoma.

"The watch belonged to my father, and I thought you might like to have it," Dad said.

Jimmy studied the heirloom. If it had been Grandpa Scott's, then he felt proud to own it, even though he'd barely known his dad's father. Mom's parents came to visit often, and Jimmy's folks had driven to Boise to see them several times over the years. But Grandma and Grandpa Scott lived in Ohio, and the only times Jimmy remembered going there was when Grandpa had been in the hospital having open-heart surgery and again five years ago when Grandpa died. Jimmy's grandparents had come to Washington a few times for short visits, but after Grandpa's health began to fail, their trips to the West Coast stopped; he hadn't seen Grandma since Grandpa's funeral.

"Do you like the watch?" Dad asked, breaking into Jimmy's thoughts.

"Sure. It's a beauty. I'll take good care of it."

Their waitress approached, bringing champagne for Dad and lemonade for Jimmy.

"To your health and to many more birthdays," Dad said, lifting his glass in a toast.

Jimmy cringed as their glasses clinked, leaving him with a sick feeling in the pit of his stomach. "I wish you wouldn't use my birthday as a reason to drink."

"Can't think of a better reason." His dad gulped down the whole drink and smacked his lips. "That wasn't the best champagne I've ever tasted, but it's good for what ails you."

Jimmy made no comment, just turned his gaze to the window again. There would have been harsh words on both their parts if he had reminded Dad that he drank too much or mentioned that if Mom were still alive, she would have gotten on to him about ordering champagne in the middle of the day. When Jimmy was a boy, he'd known that his dad drank some, but after Mom died, it had gotten much worse. Jimmy thought his dad might be using her death as an excuse to drown his sorrows or bury the past, but he also knew the way to deal with one's pain wasn't found in a bottle. Dad needed the Lord.

"Oh, I almost forgot," Dad said, halting Jimmy's thoughts. "This came in the mail for you this morning. It has a Boise postmark on it, and I'm guessing it's a birthday card from your grandparents."

Jimmy reached across the table and took the envelope, stuffing it inside his jacket pocket.

"Aren't you going to open it?"

"Naw. I think I'll wait until Sunday, so I have something to open on my actual birthday."

Abraham Fisher had just entered the barn when he heard a horse and buggy pull into the yard. He glanced through the open doorway and smiled. His friend Jacob Weaver had come to pay him a visit.

"Wie geht's?" Abraham asked, extending his hand when Jacob joined him inside the barn a few minutes later.

Jacob offered Abraham a strong handshake and grinned, causing the skin around Jacob's hazel-colored eyes to crinkle. "I can't complain. How are you this warm April afternoon?"

Abraham nodded toward the bales of straw piled along one side of the barn. "I was about to clean the horses' stalls and spread some of that on the floor."

"By yourself? Where are those able-bodied *buwe* of yours?"

"Norman, Jake, and Samuel went home to their families for the day, and I sent the twins inside to wash up." Abraham shook his head. "Titus pulled one of his pranks, and he and Timothy ended up with manure all over their clothes."

"Phew! Sure am glad I missed seeing those two." Jacob removed his straw hat and fanned his face with the brim. "Can we sit and talk a spell, or would ya rather work while we gab?"

Abraham gave his nearly gray beard a quick pull. "Me and the buwe worked hard in the fields all morning, so I think I deserve a little break." He motioned to a couple of wooden barrels. "Let's have a seat."

Jacob lowered himself to one of the barrels and groaned. "You oughta get some padding for these if you're gonna keep using 'em for chairs."

Abraham snickered. "*Jah*, well, if I got too comfortable out here in the barn, I might not appreciate my old rockin' chair in the house."

"You've got a point."

"How come you're not working on some paint job this afternoon, and what brings you out our way?" Abraham asked his friend.

"I'm headed to Bird-in-Hand to bid on a paint job for the bank there, and I thought I'd drop by to see you first." Jacob's fingers traced the side of his prominent nose. "I know today is Zach's twenty-first birthday, and I figured you might be feeling kind of down."

Abraham leaned his head against the wooden planks behind him. It always amazed him how Jacob seemed to know when he needed to talk, and his friend's memory for dates was even more astonishing. Ever since Abraham had known Jacob Weaver, he'd been impressed by the man's wisdom and ability to offer godly counsel. When Jacob had been chosen as their new bishop some fourteen years ago, he'd become even more knowledgeable and helpful during times of need. Everyone in the community seemed to admire, respect, and appreciate the way Bishop Jacob Weaver led his flock.

"You're right," Abraham admitted. "I did feel a pang of regret when I got up this morning and looked at the calendar." He drew in a deep breath and expelled it with a huff. "For many years, I prayed that my son would be returned to us, but after a time, I came to accept the fact that Zach's not comin' home. Even though I don't talk about him much anymore, I've never forgotten my boy or quit praying that God would protect Zach and use his life for good."

Jacob reached over and touched Abraham's arm. "I've prayed for your missing son all these many years, too."

"Jah, I know." Abraham cleared his throat. "Truth is, even if Zach were to come home now, he wouldn't know us, and we wouldn't know him. We'd be like strangers." He gave his beard another good tug. "Just wish I knew how he was gettin' along out there in the English world. It would have helped if we'd have gotten more than one message in *The*

Budget from the man who stole Zach—something that would have let us know he was still doin' all right."

"You must remember that God's ways are not our ways. He has His hand on Zach," Jacob reminded.

"I realize that, and rather than dwelling on what can't be changed, some time ago I made up my mind to get on with the business of livin' and enjoy the family I have right now."

"That's good thinking." Jacob thumped Abraham on the back and stood. "Guess I should be on my way."

Abraham walked his friend out to his buggy, and Jacob was about to climb in when another horse and buggy rolled into the yard. Abraham's grandson Harley was the driver, and as soon as the horse came to a stop, he jumped down from the buggy and dashed over to the men.

"What are you doin' out of school?" Abraham asked, placing his hand on the boy's shoulder.

Rivulets of sweat trickled off Harley's forehead and onto his flushed cheeks. "I went by Jacob's place, but nobody was at home, so I decided to come over here, hopin' you might know where Jacob was."

"And so you found me," Jacob said. "What can I do for you, Harley?"

"It–it's Leona," the boy panted. "She got hit with a baseball and has been taken to the hospital."

CHAPTER 2

"Miss Weaver, can you hear me? Try to open your eyes if you can."

Leona forced one eye open and blinked against the invading light that threatened to blind her. The other eye wouldn't cooperate. It felt as though it were glued shut. She tried to sit up, but the blurry-looking middle-aged English woman dressed in a white uniform laid a gentle hand on Leona's shoulder.

"Wh—where am I?" Leona rasped in a nasal tone. Her nose seemed to be plugged, and she needed to open her mouth to breathe.

"You're in Lancaster General Hospital. You were brought here a few hours ago."

Leona pushed against the pillow as memories rose to the surface of her thoughts. She'd gone outside during afternoon recess hoping to clear her head of the painful memories concerning Ezra's death and had planned to play ball with her students. She remembered Silas standing on third base, and it had been her intention to hit a good ball and bring him on home. Someone had called her name, and she had looked away. Then. . .

"How—how bad am I hurt?"

"Your nose is broken, one eye is swollen shut, and you have a slight concussion," the nurse replied. "You were unconscious when the ambulance brought you to the hospital, and you were moved to this room after your injuries were diagnosed and treated. The doctor wants to keep you overnight for observation."

Leona squinted her one good eye and tried to focus. "My glasses. Wh—where are my glasses?"

"I've not seen any glasses," the nurse replied. "I suspect they were broken when the ball hit your face."

Leona groaned. "I need them in order to teach. I don't see well enough to read without them."

"You probably won't be able to return to work for a few weeks, and I'm sure you'll be able to get a new pair by then."

"But—but school will be out for the summer soon." Leona fought against the tears clogging her throat. "I—I must be able to teach my students."

"I'm sure you will in due time. You'll just need to be patient." The nurse patted Leona's hand. "Your folks are in the visitors' lounge waiting to see you. Should I show them in?"

"Please."

The nurse left the room, and a few minutes later, Papa's bearded face stared down at Leona. "Ona, what's happened to you?"

"I—I got hit in the face with a ball I should have seen coming. That's what I get for thinking I'm still a young girl." Despite her discomfort, Leona managed a weak smile. She always felt better whenever she and Papa were together. The use of her nickname let her know that he was as happy to see her as she was to see him.

Papa reached out to stroke the uninjured side of her face. "No matter how old you get to be, you'll always be my little *maedel*."

Tears sprang to Leona's eyes. "Oh, Papa, your little girl has gone and broken her glasses, and I can't possibly teach school without 'em."

"One of your students found them in the dirt, but they were busted up pretty bad," Leona's mother said as she stepped up to the bed.

"I—I knew it." Leona sniffed, then winced as a sharp pain shot through her nose. "There's only a few more weeks 'til summer break, and—"

"A substitute teacher will be taking your place," Papa interrupted.

Leona shook her head, ignoring the pain radiating from her forehead all the way down to her chin. "I'll be all right in a few days. I'll need new glasses, though."

Papa clicked his tongue. "If you could see how swollen your nose and left eye are right now, you'd realize you're not gonna be wearin' your glasses for some time yet." He reached for her hand and gently squeezed her fingers. "The best thing you can do is rest and allow your body to heal. The school board will find someone to fill in for the rest of the year."

Leona shook her head again, but a jolt of pain shot through her nose, and she winced. "I—I must teach, Papa. It's all I have left now that Ezra's gone."

"Oh, Leona, don't say that." Mom patted Leona's arm. "One of these days, the pain of losin' Ezra will lessen, and then—"

Leona shook her head again, this time more slowly. "*Nee.* I just want to teach my students. They are all I have now."

This has not been a good day. Not a good day at all, Naomi Hoffmeir thought as she stood in front of her propane cookstove preparing to cook her family's supper. First thing this morning, Kevin, her youngest, had spilled syrup all over his clean trousers. Then Millie fussed and fretted because she wanted to accompany her parents and older sisters to the store rather than stay with Grandma Hoffmeir for the day. Next, a tour bus unloaded a bunch of Englishers in front of their general store, and Naomi, Caleb, and their two oldest girls had been bombarded with a whole lot of questions. Even Naomi's sister-in-law, Abby, who ran the quilt shop next door, had been busy all morning with the curious tourists. Around one o'clock, when Naomi had finally taken the time to eat lunch, she'd glanced at the calendar and realized that today was Zach's twenty-first birthday. For twenty years, her little brother had been missing, and her heart still ached whenever she thought of him.

Hardly a day's gone by that I haven't said a prayer for my missing bruder, she thought ruefully. *Is he happy and doing well among the English? Does he have a job? A girlfriend? Could he even be married by now?* Of one thing Naomi felt sure: If God had seen fit to return Zach to them, He would have already done so. Papa and all Zach's siblings had moved on with their lives, and she was sure Zach didn't know any of them even existed. How could he? He'd only been a year old when a stranger snatched him from their yard. And it wasn't likely that the kidnapper had told Zach about them.

"Mama, guess what happened at school today?"

"Jah. You'll never believe it."

Naomi turned from the stove to greet her two sons, who had just rushed into the kitchen, faces flushed and eyes wide open. It appeared as if they had run all the way home from school. "Have a seat and tell me what happened," she said, motioning to the table.

"Teacher got hit in the face with a ball," nine-year-old Nate announced.

"That's right," his older brother, Josh, agreed. "Emanuel Lapp was pitchin', and he smacked her right in the *naas*."

"You should've seen it, Mama," Nate said, his dark eyes looking ever so serious. "Never knew a person's naas could bleed so much."

Naomi pulled out a chair across from the boys and sat down. "I'm sorry to hear about Leona. I hope she wasn't hurt too bad."

Josh's blond head bobbed up and down. "Teacher passed out soon after the ball clobbered her. One of the Englishers who lives near the school called 9-1-1, and Leona had to be taken to the hospital in an ambulance."

Naomi gasped. "How *baremlich*."

Nate nodded in response. "Mama, it will be terrible for *all* of us if Teacher isn't in school tomorrow."

"From the sounds of it, she's not likely to be there, but we'll have to wait and see. In the meantime, we need to pray for her."

The boys agreed, their faces somber.

"Can we have some cookies and milk?" Josh asked, abruptly changing the subject. "I'm starvin'!"

"Sure. You can get the milk from the refrigerator while Nate brings some glasses from the cupboard." Naomi pushed her chair away from the table and stood. "I'll run upstairs and get Kevin and Millie. I'm sure they'd like a snack, too."

"I hope you don't mind if I'm not here for dinner tonight," Jimmy said as he and Jim entered the house through the garage entrance. "Allen called earlier and asked if I'd like to go bowling. We'll probably grab a hot dog or something at the snack bar there."

Jim shrugged. "Not a problem. I'm still full from that huge platter of oysters and shrimp I wolfed down during lunch."

"Yeah, I can relate. I ate more than my share of fish and chips." Jimmy hung his jacket on the coat tree in the hallway. "Sure am glad I didn't grow up anywhere but here in the Pacific Northwest. Everyone I know says we've got the best fish around."

"Yeah, nothing better than our fresh-from-the-sea food."

"I guess I'll head upstairs and take a shower," Jimmy said. "I told Allen I'd meet him at six."

"Sure, go ahead." Jim was glad he would be home alone all evening. It would give him time to think things over and decide whether he should broach the subject of Jimmy's adoption, as he'd promised Linda he would do when Jimmy was old enough.

An hour later, with a bowl of clam chowder and a stack of saltine crackers piled on a tray, Jim settled himself on the couch in the living room, prepared to watch TV while he ate. When Linda was alive, she would have pitched a fit if he'd wanted to eat in the living room, but she wasn't here to tell him what to do; and since Jimmy had left to go bowling a short time ago, Jim didn't have to answer to anyone.

"I still miss you, Linda," he mumbled. "Even though we had our share of problems, I always loved you."

Jim thought about the day of Linda's funeral and how his folks had flown in from Ohio and Linda's parents and sister had driven to Puyallup from their homes in Idaho. Both sets of parents had suggested that Jim move closer to them, saying it would be good for Jimmy to be near his grandparents. But Jim had refused each of their offers. Linda's mother was a control freak, and he knew she would have tried to take over raising Jimmy. Besides, there was his painting business to consider. Jim had worked hard to establish a good relationship with the general contractors in the area, not to mention the jobs he got from individual home owners. If he were to sell his business and move to Idaho or Ohio, it would mean having to start over, and he had no desire to do that.

A curl of steam lifted from the bowl of chowder, letting Jim know it was probably still too hot to eat. He grabbed the TV remote and pushed the ON button. *Jimmy and I have done all right by ourselves since Linda died. In fact, if she could see our son now, she'd be real proud. Jimmy's a good kid, and he's a dependable worker. One of these day, when I'm ready to retire, I hope to turn my painting business over to him.*

Jim clicked through several channels, hoping to find something interesting to watch, but it was no use. All he could think about was

Jimmy and the promise he'd made to Linda to tell their son the truth about his adoption.

His gaze came to rest on the photo album lying on the coffee table, and he leaned over and picked it up. Turning to the first page, he saw pictures of Jimmy during his first year with them, surrounded by little sayings and drawings Linda had made. *Jimmy takes his first step. Jimmy cuts a tooth. Jimmy turns two.*

He flipped a couple more pages. *Jimmy's first Christmas. Jimmy playing in the mud. Jimmy eating chocolate ice cream.*

There were pictures of Jimmy on his first day at school, learning to ride a bike, helping Jim rake leaves in the backyard, running through the sprinkler, and so many others depicting the boy's life over the twenty years he'd been with them. He'd been a happy child, always eager to please and ready to help out. For the first several years, Jimmy had been a mama's boy, but Linda had finally let go and allowed their son the freedom to find himself.

"I guess she found herself, too," Jim murmured. "At least she said she had after she started going to church with Beth Walters." He set the photo album aside. Beth's husband, Eric, had tried to befriend Jim after Linda died, but Jim didn't want any part of a holier-than-thou religious fanatic. He had let Jimmy continue to go to church because he'd promised Linda that he would, and for a while, Jim had gone to Jimmy's church programs, but he didn't care to go any further with religion.

He reached for his bottle of beer and took a long drink, hoping it would help him relax.

When he'd finished the beer, he leaned against the sofa, no longer in the mood for the chowder, which had now grown cold. A wave of heaviness settled on his shoulders like a five-gallon bucket of paint. *Maybe when we finish the paint job we're doing on the new grocery store across town, I'll sit Jimmy down and tell him he's adopted. I need all my workers for that job, and I won't take the risk of Jimmy getting upset and walking out on me before it's done.*

CHAPTER 3

$\mathcal{L}$eona eased onto the front-porch swing and tried to relax. It had been almost a week since she'd been hit in the face, and still her nose and one eye were swollen. She still had no glasses to wear, either. A new pair had been ordered from the optical shop in town, but they hadn't come in. Even if they had, she knew she would never be able to put them on. Her nose was too sore, and there was so much inflammation.

Cinnamon, the Irish setter Leona had been given for her twelfth birthday, moved closer to the swing and laid her head in Leona's lap. It was as if the dog knew she needed sympathy, and Leona had always found comfort in being able to tell Cinnamon her troubles. Sometimes Mom accused her of caring more for the dog than she did for people, but Leona knew that wasn't true. She simply liked being able to bare her soul to one who wouldn't sit in judgment or tell her what to do.

"You know whenever I need a listening ear, don't you, girl?" Leona patted Cinnamon's head and situated herself against the pillow she'd positioned in one corner of the wooden swing. She missed her students—missed teaching them and preparing for the last day of school when they would have a picnic on the lawn. Leona's friend Mary Ann Fisher had been hired to take Leona's place for the remaining weeks of the school year. That had worked out well for Mary Ann, since Anna Beechy had passed away three weeks ago, leaving Mary Ann without her job as Anna's maid.

A warm breeze eased its way under the eaves of the porch, and Leona sighed.

"Mail's here," Mom said, waving a stack of envelopes as she stepped onto the porch.

Cinnamon wagged her tail and let out a *woof*.

"Anything interesting today?" Leona asked.

"Looks like more letters from your pupils." Mom smiled and took a seat beside Leona. "Seems they're really missin' you, jah?"

Leona nodded and blinked back stinging tears that threatened to spill over. She'd been weepy ever since Ezra's death. "Will you read the letters to me?" she asked, knowing she couldn't see well enough to read them without her glasses.

"Of course." Mom opened the first one and announced that it was from Emanuel Lapp.

Dear Teacher Leona,
  I'm sorry about the ball hitting you in the face. Maybe my brother will bring me by to see how you're doin' on Sunday since it's an off-week and there won't be any preaching.

"It wasn't Emanuel's fault I didn't have enough sense to keep my eye on the ball. I should have called the kinner in from recess instead of trying to join their game of baseball."

"Accidents have a way of happening when we least expect them. We can't stop living for fear that something bad will happen." Mom reached over and patted Leona's arm.

Cinnamon added her agreement by placing one huge, red paw in Leona's lap.

Leona groaned. "My accident was one that could have been avoided if I hadn't been so eager to join the game."

A horse and open buggy rolled into the yard just then, interrupting their conversation and causing Cinnamon to bark. The driver pulled up beside the barn, jumped down, and secured his horse to the hitching post. Then he sprinted for the house.

Even without clear vision, Leona could see that it was Abner Lapp, Emanuel's older brother. Abner worked at a furniture shop in Strasburg and had been overseeing his young sibling ever since their daed had been killed in a buggy accident last winter.

"Wie geht's, Leona?" Abner's heavy black boots clunked noisily over the wooden planks as he stepped onto the porch. "I was on my way home from work and decided to stop and see how you're doing. I'd meant to do it sooner, but I've been workin' a lot of overtime lately."

Cinnamon released a throaty growl, and Leona laid a firm hand on the dog's head to let her know everything was okay. "I'm feeling a little better, although I still don't have my glasses and my nose is pretty swollen yet."

"Sorry to hear that." Abner shied away from Cinnamon and took a seat in the chair beside Leona. He studied her so intently that she felt like a horse being inspected on auction day. "You're right about your naas being swollen. Looks awful painful to me."

Leona nodded, and when Cinnamon let out another little *woof*, she leaned down to pat the dog's silky head. "It's okay, girl."

Abner glanced over at Leona's mamm, and when he smiled, the corner of his mouth lifted in a slight slant. "How're things with you, Lydia?"

"Can't complain." She stood and smoothed the wrinkles in her dark green dress. "I think I'll take this mail inside and get something cold to drink. Would either of you like a glass of iced tea?"

"That sounds good to me," Abner was quick to respond. "It's a warm day, and somethin' cold would feel mighty good on my parched tongue."

"All right then." The screen door squeaked as Mom stepped into the house. Cinnamon released a grunt and flopped onto the porch beneath Leona's feet.

Abner removed his straw hat and placed it over one knee. Then he lifted his hand to run long fingers through the back of his thick brown hair. "I feel real bad about my brother hittin' you in the naas. Was he foolin' around with the ball? 'Cause if he was, then I'll see that he's punished."

"Nee. He wasn't fooling around. I just wasn't paying close enough attention, that's all."

"That's good to hear. I mean, the part about Emanuel not foolin' around." Abner's clear blue eyes clouded over as he slowly shook his head. "Ever since Pop died, Emanuel's sure been a handful."

Leona nodded. "His grades were down for a while, too, but he's been doing better lately."

"I'm glad of that."

They sat in silence, Leona rocking back and forth in the swing, and Abner fanning his face with the brim of his hat and tapping his boot in rhythm with each forward motion of the swing. "You—uh—think you'll be goin' back to teaching soon?" he finally asked.

Leona touched the bridge of her nose and cringed when her fingers made contact with the tender, bruised flesh. "Well, I'm hoping—" She let her words trail when her mamm stepped onto the porch with two glasses of iced tea.

"Here you go." Leona's mamm handed one to Abner and one to Leona, then turned back toward the house.

Leona wished Mom would stay on the porch. Being alone with Abner, or any single man, made her feel about as comfortable as a hen setting on a pile of rocks. She hoped he would gulp down his tea and head for home soon.

"You done messing with pictures?" Jim asked when Jimmy entered the living room.

"Yeah. For now, anyway."

Jim yawned. They'd gotten off work early this afternoon, thanks to an unexpected rainstorm that had wreaked havoc with the outside paint job they'd been doing on the Save-U-More grocery store. He and Jimmy had eaten a late lunch, and while Jim spent the rest of the afternoon reclining on the couch with a bag of pretzels and a couple bottles of beer, Jimmy had hidden out in his darkroom downstairs. It made no sense that the kid would want to mess around with an antiquated camera and a bunch of chemicals to develop pictures when he could snap some decent-looking shots with a digital camera and print them off on his computer.

Jimmy took a seat in the rocking chair across from Jim. It had been Linda's favorite chair, and Jim remembered all the nights she had rocked Jimmy to sleep when he was little.

His heart twisted as he thought about the lullabies she used to sing to their son. When he closed his eyes, he could almost smell her rose-scented perfume and feel the softness of her long blond hair between his fingers. *I should have been a better husband. Should have spent more time with her and Jimmy.* In the nine years since Linda had been gone, Jim had only gone out with a couple of women, and those had just been casual dates. His mother had mentioned once that she thought Jimmy needed a mother, but Jim didn't see it that way. It would have been stupid to get married again just so Jimmy could have a new mom. No one could ever love the boy the way Linda had.

"You drifting off to sleep, Dad?"

Jim's eyes snapped open. "Nope. Just doing a bit of reminiscing."

"Thinking about Mom?"

"Yeah."

"It's hard to believe she's been gone nine years, isn't it?"

"Yep. Nine long years." Jim sat up and reached for a freshly opened bottle of beer and took a long swig.

At the same time, Jimmy reached for the newspaper lying on the coffee table between them. "Wonder if there's anything good playing at the movies this week," he said. "Allen wants me to go on a double date with him and Sandy on Friday night."

"Speaking of Allen. . . What'd the two of you do on Sunday to celebrate your birthday?"

"Nothing spectacular. After church, I went over to his house, and his mom fixed my favorite meal—stuffed cabbage rolls and mashed potatoes. And, of course, Beth had baked me a birthday cake."

Jim grimaced. "Ugh. I hate cabbage rolls." He took another swallow of beer. "Doesn't sound like a very exciting day to me."

"It was quiet but nice. I always enjoy spending time with Allen's family."

"Your mom liked to hang around those religious fanatics, too."

"Dad, they're not—"

"So what was in that birthday card your grandparents sent? Did they give you a hundred dollars like last year?"

"Oh man!" Jimmy jumped up and dashed over to the coat tree near the front door. "I put that envelope you gave me in my jacket pocket when we had lunch last Friday, and I forgot all about it."

Once Jimmy was seated in the rocker again, he ripped the envelope open. It was a birthday card all right—with a sailboat on the front and a check for a hundred dollars. There was also a smaller envelope tucked inside, and Grandma had scribbled a note to Jimmy on the bottom of the card, explaining that the note had been written by his mother and that she'd asked Grandma to see that Jimmy got it on his twenty-first birthday.

"How much money did you get?" Dad asked, his words slurring a bit.

"Same as last year, only Grandma included a letter Mom wrote before she died." Jimmy squinted as he silently read the note.

Dear Jimmy,

I'm sure by now your father has told you the truth about your adoption, but he isn't always good about sharing details, so I wanted to be sure you knew and understood the whole story.

First, I want you to know that the reason we didn't tell you from the beginning that you were adopted was because we wanted to be sure you were old enough to understand.

The words on the page blurred as Jimmy reread the first two lines. Could it be true that he was adopted? He'd never suspected it, and neither Mom nor Dad had ever let on. He blinked a couple of times and forced his eyes to focus, determined to finish reading the letter.

Your dad and I were unable to have children of our own, and when we decided to adopt, it was because we both wanted a child and knew we could offer that child a good home with all the love he or she would need. So when Max Brenner, our attorney here in Puyallup, told us that a lawyer friend of his in Bel Air, Maryland, had contact with a single mother who couldn't care for her one-year-old son, we jumped at the chance to adopt you. After Max set the wheels in motion on this end, we drove to the East Coast to pick up our baby.

As it turned out, I ended up with one of my sick headaches and had to stay behind in the hotel while your dad went to Carl Stevens's office in Bel Air.

Oh, Jimmy, I can't tell you how excited I was when I held you for the first time. It was as though you had always been mine. Raising you has been such a joy and a privilege. I couldn't love you more had you been my own flesh-and-blood son.

Your dad loves you, too, although I know he has an odd way of showing it sometimes. He may come across as harsh and indifferent, but I think he hides behind his brashness in order to cover up his true feelings. I believe the reason he sometimes drinks is because he can't deal with certain things.

I thank God for leading me to church, and I'm grateful you've found a personal relationship with the Lord, too. Even though I've never been able to convince your dad that he has a need for Christ, I've continued to pray that he will someday come to know Him as we do. Maybe you will be the one to show him the way, so please continue to pray for your dad.

Always remember that I love you, Jimmy, and I have ever since that amazing day when I first held you in my arms.

All my love,
Mom

With tears clogging the back of his throat, Jimmy lifted the piece of paper. "Mom told me the whole story in this letter."

"The—the whole story? What whole story is that?" Dad plunked the beer bottle on the coffee table and clambered off the couch.

"About me being adopted. She thought you would have told me by now. Why haven't you, Dad?"

"I—I was going to, Jimmy." Dad's face had turned red, and a trickle of sweat rolled off his forehead and onto his cheek.

"Mom said the two of you drove back East to get me and that you went to the lawyer's office alone."

"Yeah, that's right. Your mother had one of her migraines that morning." Dad leaned over Jimmy's shoulder and stared at the letter. After a few minutes, he straightened, and his face seemed to relax. "She's right, Jimmy. We both loved you, and the only reason we didn't tell you about your adoption sooner was because—"

Jimmy waved the letter in front of his face. "I know all that. What I don't understand is why you didn't tell me yourself. Why'd I have to find out like this?"

"I'm sorry about that, but I—I just kept putting it off." Dad shrugged. "I would've gotten around to it sooner or later."

"Really? I'm not so sure."

"So I'm not perfect. You know about the adoption, and you know we both loved you. Now let's get on with our lives, okay?"

Jimmy sprang to his feet, and Dad staggered backward. "Get on with our lives? I just found out I'm adopted, and now you want me to get on with my life like nothing's any different than it's always been?"

"I—I said I love you, and I loved your mother, too. Loved her enough to—" Dad sank to the couch, and with shaky fingers, he reached for his beer.

"Yeah, that's right, Dad—the answer to everything is in that bottle, isn't it?" Jimmy rarely spoke to his dad like this, but he was getting tired of covering for him when he didn't show up at work and tired of putting up with his drunkenness and hearing all his lame excuses for why he drank. Learning that he'd been adopted and realizing his dad was supposed to have told him made Jimmy feel things he'd never felt before and say things he'd always wanted to say but had kept bottled up inside.

Dad gulped down some more beer and wiped his mouth with the back of his hand. "I—I need something to take the edge off. You know, to help me calm down."

"Yeah, right. Whatever." Every muscle in Jimmy's body tensed, and his head swam with so many unanswered questions—things he wanted to know—things he needed to understand. But now wasn't the time for more questions. He had to be alone. He was afraid that if he stayed here one more minute, he might explode.

Driven by a force he didn't question, Jimmy sprinted across the room and rushed out the front door.

CHAPTER 4

*L*eona remained on the swing with Cinnamon's head in her lap as she watched Abner head for his buggy. He seemed like a lonely person, and she wondered why he didn't have a girlfriend by now. Maybe he'd been hurt by someone and had decided to remain single. Or maybe he stayed single so he could better care for his mamm and little bruder. His only other siblings were two married sisters who each had families of their own to care for.

"I sure miss my students," she murmured, thinking about Emanuel and the other children she'd come to care about. "I wish I was at the schoolhouse cleaning the blackboard right now, not sitting here like a lazy lump of clay."

Cinnamon whimpered and nudged Leona's hand with her cold, wet nose. "And too bad I can't see well enough to read without my glasses," she added.

Leona stared at the lawn, and as she watched the tall blades of grass shimmer in the breeze, she thought about the letters from her students that had come in today's mail. After reading only the one note from Emanuel, Mom had taken them inside when Abner showed up.

She reached for her glass of tea, which she had set on the wide porch rail, and stood. "Guess I'll go inside and see if Mom has the time to finishing reading me the mail."

Cinnamon followed Leona to the door, but Leona didn't allow the dog to go inside. Papa had never been keen on pets in the house, and Cinnamon was no exception.

The sizzle of strong-smelling onions and the hiss of their propane stove greeted Leona when she stepped into the kitchen a few seconds later. She spotted Mom in front of the sink peeling potatoes.

"I didn't realize you were starting supper already. You should have called me," Leona said, moving quickly across the room.

Mom lifted the potato peeler. "Thought I'd get an early start, and I didn't want to interrupt your conversation with Abner." She smiled. "He seems to be a right-nice young fellow."

"Jah. Abner's a good bruder, too. He's concerned because Emanuel has been rather unruly since their daed died last spring, and he was worried the boy might have been fooling around when the ball hit me in the face."

"Did you set him straight on that?"

"I did. Accidents happen, and I'm sure Emanuel was only trying to strike me out, not break my naas." Leona opened a drawer and withdrew a paring knife. "Want me to cut up the potatoes for you?"

"Without your glasses? You might end up cutting yourself."

"I mostly need them for reading, Mom, but if it would make you feel better, I'll peel, and you can cut."

"That's fine by me."

For the next few minutes, they worked in silence as Mom cut potatoes and checked on the cooking onions while Leona peeled potatoes and thought about her students' letters. When the last potato was peeled, cut, and placed in the frying pan to cook with the onions, Leona turned to her mamm and said, "Since Papa won't be home for a while, would you have time to read me the other letters that came from my students today?"

"Jah, sure. I can do that right now." Mom pulled out a chair at the table, and Leona did the same. As her mamm read letters from Josh and Nate Hoffmeir, Elmer and John Fisher, and Leona's youngest student, Selma Stauffer, Leona sat with her eyes closed, basking in the pleasure of hearing what her students had to say and picturing each of their precious, youthful faces.

When the last letter had been read, Leona released a yawn. "Sorry about that, but I feel kind of sleepy all of a sudden."

"Why don't you go upstairs and lie down awhile? I'll call you when it's time to get the rest of supper going."

With a deep sense of appreciation, Leona gave her mamm a hug. "*Danki.*"

"You're welcome."

As Naomi guided her horse and buggy up the Weavers' driveway, Leona's dog rushed out to greet her, barking her usual friendly greeting.

Naomi halted the buggy in front of the hitching post near the barn, climbed down, and bent to pet the dog. "Hey, Cinnamon, how are you doin' this afternoon?"

Cinnamon responded with two quick barks and lots of tail wagging.

"That good, huh?" Naomi reached into the buggy and withdrew a wicker basket that contained the shoofly pie she'd baked last night. The dog sniffed the cloth draped over the top of the pie and released a pathetic whine.

Naomi shook her finger. "I baked the treat for Teacher Leona, not for you, girl." She started toward the house, and the dog slunk toward the barn with her tail drooping.

Naomi hurried around the back side of the house. When she stepped onto the porch, it creaked beneath her feet. *Guess our bishop's got so much to do these days that he can't keep up with things around here.*

She knocked on the edge of the screen door, and a few seconds later, Lydia made an appearance, bidding her to enter.

"How nice of you to stop by. What have you got there in the basket?" the older woman asked with a mischievous twinkle in her blue eyes.

Naomi smiled. Lydia had always been one to get right to the point, but that's just who she was. Everyone knew it. "I brought over a shoofly pie for Leona. It's a gift from my two oldest boys, who of course had nothing to do with the baking of it."

Lydia laughed and motioned to the kitchen counter. "You can put it over there. If you're not in a hurry, maybe you'd like a glass of iced tea or some lemonade."

Naomi set the basket down, lifted the pie, and placed it on the counter. "I was hoping for the chance to visit with Leona, and I'd very much appreciate a glass of cold tea. It's way too warm for the end of May."

"Leona's upstairs resting right now, and I hate to disturb her. So if you don't mind my company, maybe the two of us can visit awhile."

"Sounds good to me." Naomi took a seat, while Lydia scurried over to the refrigerator. A few minutes later, they both held tall glasses of iced tea in their hands.

"How's Leona doing?" Naomi asked. "Is there any chance of her going back to teach before the school year is out?"

Lydia shrugged. "Her new glasses aren't ready yet, and without those, she can't see well enough to read, which means she can't return to teaching 'til they come in. The bridge of her nose is still real sore, so even if she did have her glasses, I doubt she could wear 'em for long."

Naomi swallowed the cool liquid in her mouth, savoring the delicate flavor of Lydia's homemade mint tea. "Sure was a shame about the ball hitting her in the face and breaking her naas. Josh said Emanuel blamed himself for the whole thing, but it sounded like it wasn't really the boy's fault."

"Leona says she was in the wrong for not paying closer attention."

Naomi shook her head. "Seems like most folks have a way of blaming themselves when things don't go right. I guess it helps make some sense out of the tragedies in life if we've got someone to blame." She sucked in her bottom lip. "It's been twenty years since my little bruder was taken from us, and sometimes I still find myself going over the details of that day and putting the blame on my shoulders again. Then I'm reminded of how God forgives our sins and doesn't want us to beat ourselves over the head because of our mistakes. It's the lessons we learn that matter most, and you can be sure I learned a powerful lesson the day Zach was kidnapped."

Lydia reached across the table and touched Naomi's arm. The tender look on the woman's face made Naomi realize how much she sympathized with her pain.

"Last week was Zach's twenty-first birthday, and I had to wonder if Papa wasn't hurting that day as much as I was. Of course, he never said anything about it to me."

"I don't believe any parent ever gets over the loss of a child," Lydia said in a near whisper. "Whether it's from a kidnapping or having them taken in death."

Naomi recalled hearing that Lydia had lost a baby boy due to crib death a few years before Leona was born. She figured there were probably times when Lydia still mourned her loss, which was only natural. She knew, too, that a few months ago Leona had lost the man she'd planned to marry, and no doubt she still grieved that loss.

"I'm thankful Papa had a friend like Jacob to help him through the rough days after Zach was taken," she commented. "Your husband's a good man, and we're fortunate to have him as our bishop."

"Jacob would say, 'That's what friends are for,' and I'm sure Abraham would do the same for my husband if he had such a need." Lydia smiled. "What God doeth is well done."

Naomi nodded. "Absolutely."

As Jim began painting the back of the store he and his crew had been working on, he gripped the paintbrush so hard his fingers ached. It was difficult to keep his mind on the job when he knew Jimmy was upset with him.

Last night, after Jimmy left the house, Jim had stayed up late, waiting, hoping for his son's return. He needed the chance to explain things better and make his son realize why he hadn't told him about the adoption before. But Jimmy hadn't returned home all night, or this morning, either.

He gritted his teeth. *How can we clear things up if Jimmy doesn't come home so we can talk about all this?*

This morning, Beth Walters had phoned, saying Jimmy had slept at their place last night but that he'd left soon after breakfast. She'd also mentioned that Jimmy seemed upset about something and asked if Jim knew what it could be. Jim assured Beth that it was nothing to worry about. The last thing he needed was for that religious fanatic to stick her nose in where it didn't belong, the way she had done countless times when Linda was alive.

Jim released a noisy yawn. He'd spent most of last night pacing the floor, sulking over the mistakes he'd made during the last twenty years, and drinking one beer after the other until he'd finally fallen asleep in a stupor. When he'd awakened on the couch this morning, he had such a pounding headache he didn't know if he'd be able to make it to work or not. But after two cups of coffee, a couple of aspirin, and a warm shower, he'd managed to pull himself together.

I wish Linda wouldn't have written Jimmy that letter. It should have been me telling him that he was adopted, not her, he told himself. *Maybe she didn't trust me to keep my promise.*

Jim dipped the paintbrush into the bucket sitting near his feet and tried to concentrate on the job at hand. It was no use. All he could think about was the look of confusion on Jimmy's face when he'd read his mother's letter. *The kid must hate me now, and I guess I can't blame him. If Jimmy would just come home so I can explain things better, everything would be all right.*

"What's wrong, boss? You look upset, and you're dripping on the sidewalk—not to mention all over those new work boots you're wearin'."

Jim glanced down. Ed was right. A puddle of white paint had collected on the sidewalk, and a long streak dripped across the toe of one boot. "I—I didn't sleep well last night," he mumbled. "I've got a splitting headache, and I'm having trouble staying focused this morning."

"You can say that again." Ed shook his head. "A couple of the guys said they'd tried to ask you some questions earlier, and you never did answer any of them."

"I've got a lot on my mind." Jim frowned. "Besides, you're the foreman. Why didn't they ask you?"

"They did ask. After they got no response from you. Is there a problem?"

Jim dipped his brush into the paint again but made no comment. He shouldn't have to answer to anyone. He owned this business, could do whatever he wanted, and had the right to speak or not to speak whenever he felt like it. If Ed couldn't handle things, then he could—

"Where's Jimmy this morning?" Ed asked suddenly.

Jim shrugged. "Beats me."

"I hope he shows up soon. We need every available painter if we're gonna get this store done before the weekend."

"I doubt we'll see Jimmy today," Jim muttered, refusing to make eye contact with his foreman.

"How come? Is the kid sick or something?"

Jim fought the urge to rail at his faithful employee, but he knew none of this mess with Jimmy was Ed's fault. "He's not sick, and we'll manage fine without him today."

Ed squinted, gave his mustache a quick pull, and sauntered away without another word. Jim had a sinking feeling that this was going to be a long, grueling day.

"It's so good to finally have my new glasses," Leona said to her mother as the two of them sat next to each other in the backseat of Vera Griffin's station wagon. Vera, their English driver, had taken them to the optical shop in Lancaster in the morning, and after they'd picked up Leona's glasses, they had stopped at a fast-food restaurant for a quick lunch. Then they'd done a bit of shopping until Mom insisted it was time to go home because Leona looked tired. Leona had argued, saying she felt fine, but truthfully, she was happy to be heading for home. Today was the first day she'd been away from the house since her accident, and her nose was beginning to throb.

"How do the new glasses feel?" Mom asked. "Are they too heavy for the bridge of your *naas?*"

"They felt okay when the optician adjusted the earpieces and put them on my face, but they've been hurting a little ever since." Leona shrugged. "Maybe he didn't get them fitted just right."

"And maybe your *naas* is still too tender to wear the glasses for long," Mom said with a shake of her head. "It may take another week or so 'til you can wear them all day. You'll need to be patient."

Leona was tired of being patient and tired of staying home when she should be at school. She removed her glasses and gingerly rubbed the bridge of her nose. "I have no more time for patience."

Her *mamm's* pale eyebrows drew together, and her lips formed a frown. "What's that supposed to mean?"

"Friday's the last day of school, and I need to be there."

"Why would you need to be there for the last day of school?"

"Because we always have a picnic that day, and I want to spend some time with my pupils and say good-bye for the summer."

"I see."

Leona thought about Emanuel Lapp and how his brother had brought him by the house to see her last Sunday afternoon. He'd said several times how sorry he was for hitting her in the face with the ball.

Leona smiled as she pictured the sincere expression on Emanuel's youthful face when he and his older brother presented her with a birdhouse that Abner said he had made. Abner seemed pleased when Leona thanked them and said she would enjoy watching to see if any birds made a nest in it.

"I really think you should stay home and take it easy for the rest of the week," Mom said, breaking into Leona's thoughts. "You look awful tired right now, and I doubt you'd be able to make it through the whole day at school."

Leona felt her defenses begin to rise. "Mary Ann will be there to help. Besides, we'll be having a picnic, and school will get out early, so there won't be much work for me to do." She clenched and unclenched her fingers. *Why is Mom so overprotective? Sometimes she treats me as if I'm still a little girl. We would get along much better if she saw me as a grown woman, the way Papa does.*

Leona could tell by the determined set of her mamm's jaw that she was tempted to argue further, but they had just pulled into their yard and her daed was waiting for them on the front porch, so the discussion ended.

Cinnamon was there, too, lying on the porch beside her daed's favorite wicker chair. While Mom paid Vera for their ride, Leona hurried over to greet Papa and Cinnamon.

"How'd your appointment go at the optical shop?" Papa asked as soon as she stepped onto the porch.

"I got my new glasses." Leona bent over to pat Cinnamon's head, and the dog responded with a muffled grunt.

"Are they *aagenehm*?"

"I'm sure the glasses will be comfortable enough once the soreness leaves my nose." Before her daed could respond, she added, "I'm going back to school on Friday; I want to be there for the last day."

His forehead wrinkled slightly. "You think you're ready for that?"

"Jah."

He nodded slowly. "I'll drive you then."

"Danki, Papa." Leona was glad he hadn't tried to talk her out of going and that he'd agreed to take her to school. *At least Papa doesn't try to smother me as Mom often does. If I had half as much wisdom dealing with people as my daed does, I'd be the best schoolteacher in all of Lancaster County.*

CHAPTER 5

$\mathcal{A}$s Jimmy steered his small truck toward Point Defiance Park, all he could think about was the letter he'd read from Mom yesterday evening. It had been a shock to discover he was adopted. He found the news all that much harder to accept after learning that his dad was supposed to have told him about his adoption long ago but didn't. After Jimmy had left the house, he'd gone over to Allen's to spend the night but, unable to talk about his adoption, he had merely said that he'd had a disagreement with his dad and needed some time away.

Beth and Eric Walters were good people, and they'd raised three of the nicest boys Jimmy had ever known. He knew they wouldn't think any less of him if he told them he'd been adopted, but he needed more time to think about all this before he discussed it with anyone.

His hazy mind swept over the events of last night one more time, and he gritted his teeth in an attempt to control his swirling emotions. Maybe some time at the beach would make him feel better. Ever since he'd gotten his driver's license, he had often gone to Owen Beach or someplace along the waterfront to think and pray, and he'd always felt closer to God whenever he was near the water.

A short time later, Jimmy drove into the park and headed through the stretch of road known as Five Mile Drive. He let his pickup coast down the hill leading to the beach. When he found a parking place not far from the water, he parked, turned off the engine, and stepped out of the truck.

As the salty, fresh air teased Jimmy's senses, he drew in a deep, cleansing breath. For one brief moment, he felt as if things could be right in his world again. But then he thought about Mom's letter, and his confusion resurfaced.

He hopped across a couple of logs and jogged up the rocky beach, hoping to work off his frustrations. The brackish air blew against his face and felt invigorating, yet it was almost painful. "I wish I could splash paint thinner over the last twenty-one years of my life," he hollered into the wind. "If only Mom and Dad had told me I was adopted from the very beginning."

On and on, Jimmy ran, trying to block out the pain and focus his thoughts on something other than his adoption. Finally, in a state of emotional and physical exhaustion, Jimmy halted below the pier. Eager fishermen leaned against the railing with their fishing poles hung over the sides. He drew in a breath and bent over at the waist, trying to calm his racing heart.

His stomach growled as the smell of deep-fried fish and steamed butter clams tickled his nose. He glanced at the deck outside Anthony's Restaurant. People sat around tables eating with friends and admiring the view of Commencement Bay. Jimmy realized then that he hadn't had anything to eat since breakfast. He was tempted to grab a bite at the restaurant but decided against it.

"I doubt I could keep anything down," he mumbled. "What I need more than food is some answers." He turned and started back up the beach. "It's time to go home. It's time for a serious talk with Dad."

As Jim passed the health food store near the entrance of the Tacoma Mall, his thoughts turned to Linda. In conjunction with chemotherapy, radiation, and several surgeries, she had tried various kinds of vitamins, herbs, and homeopathic remedies during her bout with cancer. While nothing had cured her disease, she had found some relief from her pain, and he figured the vitamins she'd taken might have helped strengthen her immune system, which had given her a bit more time.

He glanced at the stack of bodybuilding nutrients displayed in the store window. *Maybe I should go inside and see if they have anything to help calm my nerves.* He'd thought about stopping somewhere after work for a couple of drinks, but in case Jimmy decided to come home this evening, Jim wanted to be sure he was sober and able to carry on an intelligent conversation.

"Yeah, right. Like anything I've ever done was intelligent," he mumbled.

"May I help you, sir?"

Jim studied the woman who had been stocking shelves near the front door. Her skin was smooth, with barely a wrinkle, and her short blond hair was shiny and thick. If she was as healthy as she looked and it was due to the products sold here, then he figured he had come to the right place. "I—uh—do you have anything that might help a person relax?" he asked.

"I sell several herbal preparations that seem to work pretty well." She smiled, and her pale blue eyes appeared to scrutinize him. "Say, you look familiar. Aren't you Jimmy Scott's dad?"

Jim nodded. "How do you know my son?"

"We go to the same church, and I believe I've seen you there for some of the programs Jimmy's been in." She extended her hand. "I'm Holly Simmons, the owner of this store."

Another religious fanatic, no doubt. He forced a smile and shook her hand. "My name's Jim."

Holly motioned to the back of the store. "The herbal and homeo-pathic remedies are right this way."

"Did Leona go inside?" Lydia asked her husband when she stepped onto the front porch.

"We visited a few minutes, and then she said she was going to get supper started."

"Did she show her new glasses to you?"

"Jah, the optical shop sure took their time gettin' them done, wouldn't ya say?"

Lydia shrugged. "It's just as well if you ask me. If our daughter had gotten her glasses any sooner, she'd have insisted on going back to teach at the schoolhouse."

He nodded. "I think you're right about that."

"Did she tell you she's planning to go there on Friday?"

"Jah."

"I hope you told her it wasn't a good idea."

"Now why would I say that?"

"Because her naas still hurts, and I'm sure she can't last the whole day with those glasses on her face," Lydia said with a click of her tongue.

"Maybe she won't have to wear 'em all day."

"What do you mean?"

"There's to be a picnic on Friday, so she won't be expected to teach the whole day. If her naas starts hurtin', she can take the glasses off. Besides, I'll be drivin' her to and from school, so she won't have to worry about that, either."

Lydia pursed her lips and shook her head. "I think Leona pushes herself too hard. She uses her job of teaching to cover up the pain of losing Ezra, too."

"It's good for her to keep busy, and she needs a purpose, Lydia." Jacob bent over and scratched Leona's dog behind its ears.

"I suppose you're right. I just hope she works through her grief soon." Lydia trudged across the porch, gave the screen door handle a sharp pull, and went inside.

Jimmy entered the house through the back door, figuring his dad would be in the kitchen eating dinner by now. He was right. Jim sat at the kitchen table with a bowl of soup in front of him. A couple of store-bought rolls were wedged on a plate, and a glass of milk sat to the right of it. At least it wasn't a bottle of beer this time.

As soon as the door clicked shut, his dad turned around. "I'm glad you're home. We need to talk."

"Yeah. That's why I'm here." Jimmy struggled with the desire to rush downstairs and hide out in his darkroom, but there were too many questions he needed to have answered. He strode across the room, pulled out a chair, and took a seat at the table.

"I was worried about you last night when you didn't come home," Dad said. "I wish you would have called."

"I spent the night at Allen's."

"So I heard."

Jimmy didn't bother to ask who had told. He figured Allen's

mother had probably phoned to let Jim know where he was. That's how Beth was—always thinking of others. She'd been a real help to Mom—especially during her illness.

"Did you tell the Walters about being adopted?"

Jimmy shook his head. "I haven't told anyone yet."

"I'm sorry about the way you found out, Jimmy. I should have kept my promise to your mother and told you sooner." Dad lifted the glass of milk to his lips and took a drink. "You were probably old enough to hear the truth by the time you were sixteen."

"Sixteen? Why didn't you just tell me the truth as soon as I was old enough to understand the concept of adoption? What'd you think I was going to do—run away from home?"

Dad shrugged. "I—I don't know. We were just afraid you wouldn't understand or might think we didn't love you as much because—"

"Because I wasn't your flesh-and-blood son?"

"Yeah."

"I've always known you and Mom loved me." Jimmy shifted on his chair and inhaled slowly. "I've thought about this a lot in the last twenty-four hours, and I need some answers, Dad. I need to know who my birth mother was."

"She lived in Maryland, just like your mother's letter said." A muscle in Dad's cheek quivered, and Jimmy realized he wasn't the only one struggling with a bundle of emotions.

"I think I'd like to try and find her, and see if I can learn who my real dad is, too."

Jim's forehead wrinkled as his eyebrows pulled together in a frown. "I—I hope you're not planning to go looking for them. That would be a huge mistake, Jimmy."

"Why would it be a mistake?"

"Think about it. If they gave you up, then it's pretty obvious that they didn't want any contact with you."

"They didn't love me? Is that what you're saying?"

"I'm not saying that at all." Dad pushed away from the table and headed over to the refrigerator. He removed a can of beer and flipped open the lid.

Jimmy's fist came down on the table. "Can't we have this conversation without you having to get liquored up?"

Dad sank to a chair and took a swig from the can. "I'm not *liquored* up. This is the first beer I've had all day."

They sat there for several minutes, both staring at the table, and the silence that permeated the room felt like a heavy fog creeping across the waters of Puget Sound bay. Wasn't Dad going to tell him anything? Didn't he want him to know any of the details of his adoption?

"I don't know what I'm going to do," Jimmy said, "but if I decide to search for my roots, I'll need to have as much information as you can give me."

Dad's next words came out slowly, almost as though he had rehearsed them. "I don't know the name of your biological parents. The lawyer said your mother was a single parent and couldn't provide for you."

"What about my father? What'd he say about him?"

"Nothing much—just that your birth mother had severed ties with him and that he'd married someone else and was living in another state. Oh, and that he had signed away all parental rights to their baby."

Jimmy swallowed and slowly released his breath. He couldn't imagine anyone giving up their paternal rights, but then he'd never been put in the position his real parents had been in, either. "Maybe I ought to call your lawyer here and see what he can tell me."

"Max moved several years ago, and I'm not even sure he's still alive." Dad placed his fingertips against his forehead, moving them up and down, then back and forth in a circular motion.

"Then maybe I should call the lawyer in Maryland. Do you have his phone number?"

"I—I—uh—it might be in the safe with your adoption papers."

"Can you get it for me?"

Dad dropped his hands to the table, clenching and unclenching his fingers. "Uh—well—"

"I need some answers, Dad."

"Yeah, yeah, I know you do." Dad stood and grabbed up his dishes, hauling them over to the sink.

"Are you going to help me with this or not?" Jimmy asked, feeling more frustrated with each passing moment.

"I'll see what I can do."

"You'll let me look through the safe for those adoption papers?"

"No!"

"Why not?"

Dad moved back to the table. "How about this—I'll look for the lawyer's phone number, and then I'll give him a call and see what I can find out for you. How's that sound?"

Jimmy shrugged. "I—I suppose that would be okay. It's a start, anyway."

Dad nodded, then took a long drink of beer. Jimmy cringed. *If he doesn't keep this promise, then I'm going to take matters into my own hands.*

CHAPTER 6

*L*eona was nearly finished helping Mom with the breakfast dishes when a knock sounded at the back door. She dried her hands and went to answer it.

"Guder mariye," Abner said when she opened the door.

"Good morning," she responded. "What brings you by here so early?"

"Emanuel and I came to give you a ride over to the schoolhouse."

Leona wondered how Abner knew she had planned to go to school this morning but didn't bother to raise the question. "I appreciate the offer, but my daed will be taking me."

Abner shook his head. "I ran into him on my way home from work last night, and he asked if I could come by and get you—said he had to be in the town of Blue Ball early this morning to bid on a paint job."

She stared at him, dumbfounded. "Papa never mentioned anything to me about leaving early today, and I'm sure he would have said something if he hadn't been able to drive me to school."

"Jah, well, he must have gotten busy and forgot to tell you." Abner lifted his straw hat from his head and shifted his weight from one foot to the other. "Maybe he figured you'd find out from me."

Leona leaned against the doorjamb as she tried to piece everything together. It wasn't like Papa to be so forgetful or promise to do something and then not follow through. She was about to say that she would need to speak with her daed about this, when she remembered that he had left the house right after breakfast. She figured he'd gone out to the barn to do a few chores, but maybe Richard Jamison, his English employee, had come by in his van. He and Papa could be halfway to Blue Ball by now.

Abner nodded toward his open buggy, parked alongside the house, and she noticed Emanuel sitting in the back. "Are you about ready to go then?"

Leona wished she could drive herself to school today, but she knew neither one of her folks would condone that idea. Not with the headaches that snuck up on her when she least expected them. "I'll need to speak to my mamm first and see if she knows whether Papa's left for work or not," she said.

He nodded. "Okay. I'll be waitin' in the buggy with my brother then."

Jim removed a five-gallon bucket of paint from the back of his van and glanced over his shoulder. Jimmy and two of his employees stood on scaffolding as they sprayed one side of the grocery store they had been painting this week. He'd felt a sense of relief when Jimmy said he would be here today, but he cringed when he thought about the promise he'd made to his son about calling the lawyer in Maryland. *I'll wait a couple days, and then I'll tell him I called the lawyer but that he had no information to give. Maybe then Jimmy will stop asking questions and give up on the idea of trying to find his biological parents. He needs to let it drop, that's for sure. And I'll need to make sure that he does.*

Jim had fought to get to sleep again last night but finally found some relief when he took the herbal tablets he'd bought at Holly Simmons's health food store. A shot of whiskey would have done the trick just as well, but he was already pushing his luck with Jimmy and couldn't risk angering him by getting caught guzzling a drink.

"Where do you want this paint to go?" Jim's foreman asked.

"You can take it to the guys working on the other side of the building," he mumbled.

"Sure thing, boss." Ed started to walk away but turned back around. "It's good to see Jimmy at work this morning."

Jim's only reply was a brief nod.

"The kid's been acting kind of quiet, though. Do you know if there's something wrong?"

Yeah, plenty, Jim thought while shaking his head to indicate the opposite. "Everything's fine, Ed." He clenched his fists. "Never been better."

"I hope you won't be late for work because you took the time to drive me to the schoolhouse," Leona said, glancing over at Abner in the driver's seat of his open buggy.

"He took the day off so he could come to the picnic with me," Emanuel chimed in from his seat in the back.

"Yeah, and if you should get tired and need to leave early, I'll be there to take you home," Abner added.

Leona clung to the edge of her seat as they jostled down the driveway heading to the main road. "That's kind of you, but I'm sure I'll be fine."

"Maybe so. Maybe not."

Irritation welled up within her. It was bad enough that the humidity this morning was stifling. Now her emotions were getting the best of her, too. Abner had no reason to be worried about her. She was tempted to tell him to turn around and take her back home, but that would mean she would miss seeing her students today.

"There's sure been a lot of corn goin' into the ground this past week," Abner said as they passed a neighboring farm where an Amish man and his son worked side by side in the field.

Leona nodded but made no reply. She wasn't in the mood for small talk. *Why did Papa have to leave early this morning? And why did he ask Abner to drive me to school? He should have at least told me about it.*

"Oats, hay, and wheat are growin' nicely now," Abner droned on. "It won't be long 'til the womenfolk in our community can start cannin' peas and strawberries."

Emanuel smacked his lips. "I sure can't wait for our mamm's strawberry pie. She makes the best in all of Lancaster County, ain't that right, Abner?"

"Jah, she sure does," his brother agreed. "And strawberries should be getting ripe by the middle of June."

Leona's head had started to throb, and her nose quickly followed suit. The pain couldn't be blamed on her glasses resting too heavily on the spots that were still tender, because she'd put them in her purse before she left home. *I wish we would hurry up and get there. It's times like this when I'd like to be riding in a car.*

49

Half an hour later, they pulled into the school yard. Several children milled about, some on the swings and others playing on the set of teeter-totters. The sight brought tears to Leona's eyes. Oh how she had missed her pupils these past few weeks!

Hannah Fisher bounded up to the buggy as soon as Abner stopped the horse. "Teacher Leona, it's so good to have you back!"

"That's for sure," Emanuel chimed in.

"It's good to be here." Leona climbed down from the buggy. "Danki for the ride, Abner."

He nodded. "I have a couple of errands to run in town, so I'll take care of those now, but I'll be back in time for the picnic."

"My mamm's comin' to the picnic, too," Hannah said, bouncing up and down.

Leona nodded at Hannah and then Emanuel. "Shall we go inside now?"

"Jah," they said in unison.

At noontime, Jimmy decided to take his lunch to the park, which wasn't far from the store they had been painting. It would be a welcome relief to get off alone for a while, and it would be better than sitting around with the guys trying to make idle conversation. The morning had gone by quickly, and for that he was glad. He'd made an effort to keep busy and had tried not to think about anything other than the job they were doing. He still hadn't made up his mind about what to do concerning his search for his birth family once his dad contacted the lawyer.

Jimmy had just grabbed his lunch pail from the back of his pickup and closed the tailgate when his dad showed up. "Where are you going, son?"

"I thought I'd walk over to the park to eat my lunch."

"Want some company?" Brad, one of the new painters, called out.

"I'd—uh—rather be alone. Maybe some other time." Jimmy hurried down the sidewalk, and a short time later, he entered the park and took a seat on a bench. He flipped open his lunch pail and stared at the contents—a tuna sandwich he'd made this morning and a couple of store-bought cookies. Neither appealed, so he grabbed his thermos of milk and poured some into the lid. When he took a drink, the cool liquid felt good on his parched throat. However, it did little to relieve the tension that seemed to be working its way through every muscle and nerve in his body.

Jimmy stared across the playground at the swings and spiral slide. It made him think of the park close to home—the one he and Mom had visited many times when he was a boy. He'd met Allen there, and it hadn't taken long for the two of them to become friends. Mom and Allen's mother had hit it off, too, and soon after that, they'd started going to the same church the Walters family attended.

"Those were happy times," Jimmy murmured. "Wish I could slip back to those days and stay there."

A horn honked, and his gaze went to the parking lot where a black sports car had pulled in. "What are you doing here?" he called as Allen exited the car.

As his friend sauntered up to him, a lock of dark brown hair fell across his forehead. "I didn't have to work at the lumber mill today, so I stopped by the grocery store where your dad's paint crew has been working."

"How come?"

"I was looking for you, and your dad told me you had come to the park to eat your lunch."

Jimmy nodded. "I needed to be alone for a while."

Allen took a seat on the bench beside him. "I know there's something bothering you, Jimmy. You wouldn't have stayed overnight at my house on a weeknight if not. And you wouldn't have been acting like your best friend had just died, either."

Jimmy smiled in spite of his dour mood. "You're my best friend, and I'm thankful you're still very much alive."

Allen pointed to the lunch Jimmy hadn't touched. "Just one more proof that something must be eating you."

Jimmy groaned. "You're right, there is. And it's a *big* something."

"Want to talk about it?"

"No. Yes. Well, I guess maybe I should."

"If it's something you don't want repeated, you can count on me to keep my mouth shut."

"I know. You've never blabbed anything I've told you in confidence."

Allen snickered. "Yeah, like you've ever told me anything exciting enough to want to blab."

Jimmy shivered despite the sun's warming rays. "What I have to say wouldn't be considered exciting. It was a pretty big shock, though."

His friend leaned closer and squinted his blue eyes. "You'd better spill it then, 'cause I can't stand the suspense."

CHAPTER 7

$\mathcal{I}$t was all Leona could do to help her mother fix supper that night. Not only was she exhausted from her long day at school, but her nose hurt something awful, as well. She removed her glasses and set them on the window ledge, then went to the refrigerator to get out the ingredients she would need for a tossed salad. It would go well with slices of cold ham, leftover baked beans, and potato salad. The day had turned out to be quite warm, so they'd decided not to heat up the kitchen any further by cooking a hot meal this evening.

"How'd the school picnic go?" Mom asked as she set the ham on the cupboard and began to slice it.

"It went fine. Everyone seemed to have a good time."

"And you, daughter? How'd you get along today?"

"I did all right." Leona placed the vegetables on the table, pulled out a chair, and sat down. If she were being completely honest, she would have to admit that things hadn't gone nearly as well as she'd hoped they would. She'd suffered with a headache most of the day, even though she hadn't been wearing her glasses. She didn't want her mamm to know that, though. Mom would only have reminded Leona that she'd returned to school too soon, and then there would have been tension between them.

Things will go better next term, when the scholars go back to school in late August, Leona thought. *Then again, though my nose will feel better by then, I'm not sure my broken heart will ever mend.*

Leona had just finished making the salad when Papa showed up. He looked tired, yet despite the slump of his shoulders and his slow-moving gait, he wore a smile on his suntanned face. "How'd your day go, Lydia?" he asked, setting his metal lunchbox on one end of the counter.

Mom held a piece of ham out to him. "It went well enough."

"Danki," Papa said, eagerly accepting it. He wandered over to the table and took a seat beside Leona. "How was your day? Were the kinner happy to see you at school?"

She nodded and placed the bowl of salad greens on the table.

"I see you're not wearin' your glasses. Is your naas hurtin' again?"

"A little." She shrugged. "Besides, I don't need them for salad making."

"Is there something bothering you? You seem awfully sullen this evening."

A few uncomfortable seconds passed between them before Leona wiped her hands on the dish towel lying in her lap and said, "If you must know, I'm a little upset because you arranged for Abner to pick me up this morning without telling me about it."

Papa's bushy eyebrows drew together. "I had to leave for work early, and I thought I was doin' you a favor by asking Abner. I ran into him yesterday on my way home from work, so he seemed like the likely one to ask."

"You weren't trying to play matchmaker, were you, Jacob?" Mom chimed in from across the room.

Leona clasped her hands tightly around the towel as she looked at her daed. "Is that what you were doin', Papa?"

He gave his earlobe a quick tug. "Well, I—"

"Papa, Abner seems nice enough, but I'm not looking for another man, because I won't be thinking of marriage ever again."

"Oh, Leona, you don't mean that," her mamm said. "You're still hurting from losing Ezra, and it's too soon for you to think of anyone else courting you, that's all."

"I enjoy teaching school, and that's enough for me," Leona said. "I don't need love or marriage."

Papa grunted. "That's just plain *lecherich*. Teaching's a fine vocation, but you should concentrate on finding a suitable husband so you can begin a life of your own as a *fraa* and *mudder*."

So now her father thought she was being ridiculous? Tears welled up in Leona's eyes, and she blinked to keep them from spilling over. She had wanted to be a wife and mother when she'd thought she was going to marry Ezra. But those plans had dissolved the day Ezra died, and she couldn't even think of loving another man or risk losing him.

"Our daughter will find someone when her heart has had time to heal," Mom said, touching Papa's arm.

He pushed his chair aside and stood. "I'm sure she will, but closing her mind off to love and marriage isn't a good thing."

Leona gritted her teeth. Her folks were talking about her as if she wasn't even in the room. And Papa seemed determined that she forget about Ezra and find someone else to marry. *Well, at least Mom stood up for me this time,* she thought. *Guess that's something to be grateful for. I just hope Papa has no more plans of trying to get Abner and me together.*

Jimmy was glad his dad was out on the deck soaking in the hot tub. It gave him a chance to be alone. After supper, he'd decided to come into the living room so he could look through a couple of old photo albums.

He settled himself on the couch and reached under the coffee table to grab an album off the shelf. It was full of pictures that had been taken of him from the time he was one-year-old up until his first day of school. Jimmy grinned when he spotted a picture of himself holding one end of the garden hose. Water squirted out of the hose, just missing his face, and a puddle of mud lay beneath his feet. His light blue overalls were wet clear up to the waist, but he wore a smile, nonetheless.

The next picture that caught Jimmy's eye was one of him bent over a branch on their Christmas tree, trying to blow out the twinkle lights. There were several pictures that had been taken on his second birthday, with blue balloons and matching crepe paper decorating the dining room. Jimmy sat in his high chair staring wide-eyed at a clown cake and clapping his chubby hands.

He turned the page, and his gaze came to rest on a picture of himself sitting in the middle of his parents' bed, on top of Mom's colorful Amish quilt. A pang of regret surged through him, and he snapped the album shut. *I miss her so much, and I wish she'd been able to tell me about my adoption in person so we could have discussed the details face-to-face. Well, at least I was able to talk about my feelings to Allen this afternoon.*

Jimmy leaned against the back of the couch and closed his eyes as he reflected on the information he'd shared with his best friend while they were at the park today. . . .

"I'm not who you think I am," Jimmy said in a near whisper.

"What are you talking about? You're Jimmy Scott, a great photographer and the truest friend I've ever had." Allen squeezed Jimmy's shoulder.

"I'm not Jim and Linda Scott's son. I was born to someone else."

Allen's forehead wrinkled. "Oh, you mean you were adopted?"

Jimmy nodded.

"Well, that's no big deal. Lots of kids are adopted."

"I know, but I've only known the truth for a few days."

"You mean your dad just told you? Is that why you spent the night at our place?"

"Yeah, and I found out about the adoption only because of a letter Mom wrote me before she died." Jimmy paused and pinched the bridge of his nose to ease the strain he felt between his eyes. "The letter came in a birthday card from my grandparents. I guess Mom asked her mother to see that I got the letter on my twenty-first birthday."

Allen's mouth hung slightly open. "That must have been a real shock, learning it that way."

Jimmy nodded. "I guess Dad was supposed to tell me, but he conveniently never got around to it."

"Do you think he kept it from you on purpose?"

"Maybe."

"Could be that he was worried you might not understand, or maybe he thought you'd think he and Linda didn't love you as much as your real parents might have."

"Mom loved me, I'm sure of that, and I guess, in Dad's own way, he loves me, too."

Allen nodded. "I don't think he always knows how to express himself, but I've never doubted his love for you." He gave Jimmy's shoulder another squeeze. "What now? Are you going to try and find out who your real parents are?"

"I want to, and Dad's promised to call the lawyer who set up the adoption for them and see what information he can get."

"Isn't there some kind of client confidentiality that would keep a lawyer from divulging that information?"

Jimmy shrugged. "Maybe, but it's the best place I can think of to start looking."

"I'll be praying that you find the answers you're seeking," Allen said in a sincere tone.

Jimmy clenched his hands so tightly that his fingers dug into his palms. "While you're at it, you'd better pray that my dad won't renege on this promise."

The irritating buzz of a lawn mower as it zipped across the yard next door brought Jimmy's thoughts back to the present. He opened his eyes and looked around. This had been his home for as long as he could remember. He'd watched television in this living room, played games, put puzzles together, listened as Mom read him Bible stories, and wrestled around on the floor with his dad. In all of his wildest dreams, he'd never imagined that they weren't his real parents.

Jimmy swallowed around the lump clogging his throat. *Mom was worried about me being old enough to deal with the truth about my adoption; yet here I am twenty-one years old, and I'm still not dealing with it well.*

Jimmy exhaled and closed his eyes, knowing he needed to pray. *Dear Lord, even after all these years, I still miss Mom so much. She was the only mother I've ever known, and I'll always love her. If only she were here now to tell me what to do. What should I do, Lord? What should I do?*

When Jim entered the living room after changing from his swimsuit into his sweatpants, he spotted Jimmy sitting on the couch, his head bowed and eyes closed. *The kid's just like his mom,* he thought as irritation welled up in his chest. *Every time he turns around, he's praying about something.*

Jim cleared his throat, and Jimmy opened his eyes.

"I'm glad you've come inside because I need to ask you something, Dad."

Jim took a seat in the rocking chair across from Jimmy. "What's up?"

"I was wondering if you were able to call that lawyer in Maryland today."

Jim groaned inwardly. "Nope. I was too busy. I'll do it later in the week."

"Are you sure?" Jimmy's expression was as stoic as a statue.

"Of course I'm sure. And don't start pressuring me. You know how busy we've been at work." He stood and moved toward the door leading to the hallway.

"Where are you going?" Jimmy called after him.

"Out to the kitchen to get a beer so I can unwind."

"I thought that was why you had gone in the hot tub."

Jim whirled around. "It was, but it wasn't enough to make me relax."

Jimmy grimaced. "You shouldn't have to drink in order to relax, Dad. I don't think you realize how much you're drinking these days. I'm worried that you'll lose your business if you don't get some help. Maybe you should consider going to AA."

"Alcoholics Anonymous?"

Jimmy nodded.

"You've got to be kidding!"

"I'm serious, Dad. There's a lady from church who's a recovered alcoholic, and she says she's gotten a lot of help from AA. She spoke to our young adult Sunday school class last week and told us that, even though she's been dry for years, she still goes to those meetings as often as she can."

"If she's recovered, why would she need to keep going?"

"Partly to remind herself that she is and always will be an alcoholic. But I think the main reason she goes is to help others who are new to the group and need some support."

"Each to his own, I guess."

Jim had almost made it to the hallway door when Jimmy called out, "Would you like me to see when and where the next meeting is going to be held?"

"No!"

"How about going to church with me this Sunday? I can introduce you to—"

Jim squinted as he looked over his shoulder at Jimmy. "What part of *no* don't you understand?"

"If it weren't for me and Ed covering your back at work much of the time, you might have lost your business by now. Have you considered that?"

Jim whirled around. "I'm not an alcoholic—and with or without Ed's and your help, I would not have lost my business!"

As Leona prepared for bed that night, her head pounded like a herd of stampeding horses. *I should have listened to Mom when she suggested I not go to school today. It was good to see the kinner again, but I'm not sure it was worth the headache I'm left with now.* She moved across the room to stand in front of her bedroom window. *If I had stayed home, Papa wouldn't have felt the need to ask Abner to give me a ride, either.*

She leaned wearily against the window frame. *I can't believe he actually thought I might be interested in courting someone when it's only been a few months since Ezra died.*

Woof! Woof! Woof!

Leona glanced into the yard below. There sat Cinnamon, staring up at her as if begging to be let in. Leona opened the window and leaned her head out. "You know you can't come inside the house. You'd better go out to the barn or find a comfortable spot on the porch to sleep."

Woof! Woof!

"Hush up, Cinnamon. You'll wake Papa and Mom with all that barking."

Woof!

"Okay, okay, you win. I'll be right down." Leona smiled as the dog wagged its tail and swaggered toward the porch as though she'd won a prize.

Grabbing her cotton robe from a wall peg, Leona slipped quietly out of her room, tiptoed down the stairs, and hurried out the back door.

A chilly wind met her as she stepped outside. She shivered, wrapping her arms around her chest. It might be plenty warm during the day, but nighttime was another matter.

Cinnamon pranced up to Leona, licking her hand as she bent to pet the dog. "I can't stay out here long, but we can sit awhile and listen to the crickets sing if you promise to be real quiet."

The dog answered with a soft whine, then flopped down beside Leona when she took a seat on the top porch step. Without an invitation, Cinnamon laid her head in Leona's lap.

"Did you miss me today, girl?" Leona asked, scratching the dog behind its left ear.

Cinnamon released a quiet grunt.

"I missed you, too." Leona closed her eyes and reflected on the days of her youth when Cinnamon had been her constant companion. With her sisters and her brother being several years older than she, Leona had little in common with Peggy, Rebecca, and Arthur. Sometimes Leona had felt like an only child, especially after both sisters had gotten married and moved to Kentucky. Arthur always seemed to be busy helping Papa with the painting business. Truth was, even if he had been around home more before he married Doris, Leona was sure he wouldn't have wanted his little sister tagging after him all the time. So, from the time Papa gave her Cinnamon, Leona and the dog had been best friends. Leona rather liked it that way. A dog wasn't likely to place demands on you the way people sometimes did. And a faithful dog loved unconditionally, which was more than could be expected from a lot of folks.

As Cinnamon's heavy breathing turned to soft snores, Leona opened her eyes and stared at the sky. The silver pinpoints of stars overhead reminded her of the Lone Star quilt on her bed. She sat there several minutes watching the stars twinkle, talking to God, and wondering what her future might hold.

"Sure is nice that you and your family could join us for supper to-night," Abraham said, thumping his friend on the back as they followed Lydia and Leona toward the house.

"I'd never pass up a free meal." Jacob chuckled. "Especially not when one of Fannie's delicious turkey potpies is involved."

"We're having banana cake for dessert," Abraham announced. "So be sure you don't eat too much supper."

Lydia glanced over her shoulder and smirked at him. "Oh, you can be sure my husband will eat more than his share this evening." She laughed, along with the others.

When they entered the house, Abraham noticed that Fannie and Mary Ann were scurrying around the kitchen like a couple of excited chickens.

"What can I do to help?" Leona asked, stepping up to Abraham's youngest daughter.

Mary Ann smiled and motioned to the table. "The glasses need to be filled with water."

"Okay."

"And what would you like me to do?" Lydia questioned.

"How about cutting some radishes? They're fresh from the garden," Fannie replied.

"Sure, I can do that."

Abraham leaned close to his wife. "Call us when supper's ready."

"Jah, we sure will," she said with a nod.

Abraham brushed Jacob's shoulder as he pointed to the living room. "Make yourself comfortable, and I'll go round up my youngest sons."

A short time later, Abraham sat at the head of the table with Jacob at the other end. The women took their seats on Abraham's left, and his twin sons, who would turn fifteen in the fall, found their way to the bench on the other side of the table. All heads bowed for silent prayer. When Abraham finished his prayer, he cleared his throat and said, "Now, let's eat ourselves full!"

"I know I'll eat my share," Titus announced. At least Abraham thought it was Titus. Sometimes, when the boys were in a teasing mood, they would pretend to be the other twin, wearing each other's clothes and answering to the other brother's name.

He leaned to the left, hoping to get a good look at his son's eyes. Titus had one eye a little bigger than the other.

The boy turned his head before Abraham could get a good look and confirm which twin was speaking. "Say, Bishop Weaver, I've been wonderin' about something."

Jacob forked a couple of Fannie's homemade bread-and-butter pickles onto his plate. "What do you want to know, Timothy? It is Timothy, right?"

"Nope. I'm Titus."

"All right then. What do you want to know, Titus?"

Timothy snickered, and Titus jabbed him in the ribs. "Knock it off!"

Fannie gave both boys a warning glance, and Abraham did the same. "You two had better quit fooling around and eat," he said sternly.

"I was eating 'til my *mutwillich bruder* decided to stick his bony elbow in my ribs."

"Jah, well, it hasn't only been your brother who's been playful—you've been pretty rambunctious yourself all day, and I've had enough of it." Abraham passed the platter of radishes over to Titus. "Why don't you have a couple of these? They ought to cool ya down some."

"No thanks. I'm sure they're too hot for me."

Jacob chuckled behind his napkin. "Now what was that question you had for me, Titus?"

"I was wonderin' if you're too poor to put a front window glass in your buggy?"

"Don't be rude, son," Abraham said with a shake of his finger. "You surely know that a missing front window is one of the things that distinguish a bishop's buggy from others in this community."

"Are ya *dumm*?" Timothy asked, giving his twin a sidelong glance.

"I ain't dumb," Titus shot back.

Timothy looked over at Jacob and said, "Say, I've got a question of my own."

"What's that?"

"I was wonderin' if anyone's ever fallen asleep during one of your long sermons."

Jacob slid his finger down the side of his nose and squinted. "Hmm. . . Well, there was this one time when Harley King dozed off. Deacon Paul sat near me, so I leaned over and whispered in his ear, 'Would ya please wake up the brother who's fallen asleep?' "

Timothy plunked his elbows on the table and leaned slightly forward. "What happened then?"

Jacob grunted. "The helpful deacon looked me right in the eye and said, 'It was you who put him to sleep, so you're the one who oughta wake him up.' "

A round of laughter went around the table.

"I'd like to know something else," Titus piped up.

"That'll be enough with the questions." Abraham stared hard at his son, for this time he had a clear view of the boy's eyes. Neither one looked any bigger than the other did, so he knew it must be Timothy sitting closest to him, not Titus. "Say, are you two tryin' to pull a fast one?"

"What do you mean, Papa?" Timothy asked, rather sheepishly.

"I know which of you is which, so you can quit trying to fool everyone. And since you've been actin' silly all day, you can both clear the table and wash the dishes after we're done eating."

Titus opened his mouth to protest, but another jab to the ribs from his brother kept the boy quiet.

Abraham stuck his spoon in his potpie and popped a piece of turkey into his mouth. There were times, like now, when he wanted to throttle his youngest sons. Even so, he was glad the good Lord had given him and Fannie such a miracle when the twins were born. They hadn't taken Zach's place, but they'd sure filled a big hole in his heart, and he loved them dearly.

During the drive home from the Fishers', Leona reflected on the pleasant evening they'd had. Other than the twins acting like a couple of silly kin-ner, there had been amiable conversation around the table during supper, and for most of the evening, she'd been able to think about something other than how much she still missed Ezra.

When the meal was over, the women had gathered on the front porch to chat, while the men retired to the living room for a game of checkers. Titus and Timothy had spent the remainder of their evening in the kitchen but didn't finish with the dishes until it was time for dessert.

Leona smiled to herself, thinking what it was like when she'd had the twins in her classroom. On more than one occasion, they had both tried to pass themselves off for the other brother. Sometimes they'd managed to fool the entire class—including their teacher. The boys liked to pull a few pranks now and then, too, but they'd never done anything harmful, which was a good thing.

As soon as they pulled into their yard, Leona realized another buggy was parked near the barn.

"Looks like Abner Lapp's rig," Papa commented.

Leona made no reply. She just held onto her skirt and climbed down from the buggy. *I hope Papa didn't set this up.*

Abner waved and stepped off the front porch, where he'd obviously been waiting. "Came by half an hour ago," he said, heading toward them with his usual jerky, bowlegged walk. "Figured since it was gettin' dark, you'd be home most anytime."

Papa headed quickly for the barn, leading the horse, and Mom glanced over at Leona with raised eyebrows. Leona started for the house, mumbling a quick hello to Abner as she approached the spot where he stood. "Papa's gone to the barn."

Abner smiled. "It's you I came to see, Leona, not your daed."

Leona looked at her mamm, who had just caught up to her. She hoped Mom might come to her rescue, but she only smiled, shrugged, and went inside the house.

Not wishing to hurt Abner's feelings, Leona seated herself on the porch swing. Abner followed suit. "I came by to see if you knew about the wood-stacking bee that's to be held next Saturday at my grandpa Lapp's place," he said.

She kept her gaze on the sky. It was a pale yellow flushed with pink on the rim of the horizon. "I heard something about it."

"Were you planning to go?"

"I'll have to wait and see." Leona scanned the front yard, wondering if Cinnamon might show up. She didn't think Abner cared much for the dog. If Cinnamon made an appearance, maybe Abner would make a hasty exit.

Abner leaned toward her as though he might be about to say something more, but just then, Leona's mamm opened the screen door. "I hate to interrupt, Leona, but I need your help with something."

Leona stood, releasing a sigh of relief. "You'll have to excuse me, Abner. Maybe we can visit some other time."

"Jah, sure. Guess I'll head out to the barn and say hello to your daed." He stood, shuffled his feet a few times, and mumbled, "Hope to see you on Saturday."

Leona's only reply was a quick nod. Then she scurried into the house.

As soon as his dad left the room, Jimmy reached for the cordless phone, which had been lying on the small table near the end of the couch. He punched in Allen's number and headed to the basement while he waited for one of the Walters to answer his call.

He had just entered his darkroom when Allen's voice came over the phone. "Hello?"

"Hi, it's me."

"Hey, buddy, it's good to hear from you. How's it going?"

"Not so great. My dad still hasn't phoned that lawyer, and we nearly got into an argument when he said he was going to the kitchen for some beer."

"Has he been staying sober lately?"

"Yeah, but he has to have a drink or two almost every night."

"Did you talk to him about going to AA or ask if he'd see our pastor for some counseling?" Allen asked.

Jimmy sank to the stool in front of the desk where he kept all his negatives. "He won't even admit he's got a drinking problem, much less agree to get any help."

"Sorry to hear that. Guess there's not much you can do except to pray for him."

"I'm afraid he's going to lose his business if he doesn't get his life straightened out soon."

"Some people have to hit rock bottom before they'll admit they have a problem and be willing to get help."

"I know." Jimmy released a moan. "He uses every excuse in the book to drink, and I'm not sure how much longer I can keep covering for him at work."

"You shouldn't have to cover for him. He's a grown man and needs to be responsible for his own actions." There was a brief pause; then Allen added, "Remember when Holly spoke to our Sunday school class?"

"Yeah."

"She mentioned that those who live with alcoholics are often enablers and that they have to practice tough love."

"I remember."

"So that's what you need to do, Jimmy. You've got to quit covering for your dad and allow him to sink or swim."

"Yeah, maybe so." Jimmy paused. "Well, I'd better go. I want to get a few pictures developed, and then I'm going to bed. We're still working on that big grocery store, and I'm sure Dad will want to get an early start again tomorrow morning."

"Okay. Keep looking up. And remember, I'll be praying for you and your dad."

"Thanks, I appreciate that." Jimmy hung up the phone and closed his eyes. "Oh, Lord, give me the courage to do whatever I need to do concerning my dad—and show me what to do about finding my birth parents."

CHAPTER 9

$\mathcal{I}$'m heading to Tacoma to run some errands. I told Ed if he has any questions, he can ask you."

Jimmy set his paint roller over the top of the bucket at his feet and turned to look at his dad. "Won't you have your cell phone on?"

"Yeah, sure, but I don't want to be bothered with twenty questions."

"How long will you be gone?"

"I don't know. All depends on how long it takes me to get everything done."

"Will you be back by noon?"

"Probably. See you later, Jimmy."

"Oh, hey, wait a minute."

"What? I'm in a hurry." Dad started walking and didn't even look back.

Jimmy left his job and rushed to his dad's side. "I was wondering if you called the lawyer in Maryland this morning."

"Not yet. I haven't had time. I'll do it later."

"East Coast time is three hours ahead of us," Jimmy reminded. "So you'd better make the call before—"

Dad screeched to a halt and glared at Jimmy. "I'm not stupid! I know how to tell time."

"I—I never said you didn't. I just wanted to be sure you—"

"I said I would call, so get off my back!" Dad climbed into his van and slammed the door before Jimmy had a chance to respond.

"Whew! He's sure testy today, isn't he?" Ed stepped up beside Jimmy as his dad peeled out of the parking lot. "Or maybe I should say he's testier than usual today."

Jimmy nodded and mumbled, "He needs help."

"What was that?"

"Oh, nothing. I'd better get back to work. This store won't paint itself."

"Guder mariye," Leona said as she and her friend Mary Ann walked up the path leading to Herman and Bertha Lapp's home, where there was to be an all-day wood-stacking bee.

"Good morning." Mary Ann smiled, her evenly matched dimples looking more pronounced than usual. "I'm doin' all right. How 'bout you?"

"Okay, I guess."

"Are you still having those headaches?"

"Jah, but they've gotten some better since I started seeing Mom's chiropractor. He thinks my neck went out of alignment when that ball hit my face."

"Guess that makes sense." Mary Ann leaned closer. "Are you dealin' with Ezra's death any better yet?"

Leona winced as though she'd been slapped. "How could I? I doubt my heart will ever be mended."

Mary Ann turned her palms upward and shrugged. "Of course it will. Once an open wound has turned to a scar, it's not so hard to deal with."

Leona made no reply but kept on walking. Mary Ann didn't know what it felt like to lose the man she loved. In fact, she'd never gotten serious enough about any of the men who had courted her to want to get married. Some said she was too particular, but Leona figured Mary Ann was either holding out for the right man or she just preferred to remain *en alt maede*—an old maid—at twenty-five years of age. On one hand, the thought seemed absurd, but most Amish women her age were married by now. *Of course*, Leona reminded herself, *I'm not so far behind my friend, so I guess we'll both be old maids together.*

Mary Ann gave Leona's arm a gentle squeeze. "Let's try to have fun today, okay?"

"Jah, sure."

"Oh, I almost forgot to tell you that starting Monday I'll be working in Abby's quilt shop."

"That's good. You've become an expert quilter, so I'm sure you'll do real well there."

"I hope so. Abby says they're so busy now that she and her daughter, Stella, can hardly keep up." Mary Ann pivoted toward the Lapps' house, which was connected to the home where their eldest son, William, lived with his wife and six children. "Guess we'd best get into the kitchen and see what needs to be done."

Leona followed Mary Ann up the steps and onto the back porch. She was about to go inside the house when someone called her name.

"Leona. I'm glad to see you made it today."

She turned and saw Abner stroll up the walk, pushing a wheelbarrow filled with split poplar wood. His face was red and sweaty, and streaks of dirt dotted his blue shirt.

"I came to help in the kitchen."

"Figured that's what you were here for."

She dipped her head. "Well, I'd best be getting inside."

"Okay. See you at noon if not before." Abner headed for the growing stack of wood piled alongside the shed.

Leona hurried into the house, anxious to get to work—and as far away from Abner as possible.

As Naomi put the OPEN sign in the store window, she thought about the wood-stacking bee that was probably going full force by now. She'd been hoping to go and help serve food to the men, but tourist season had already begun in Lancaster County, and they'd had an abundance of customers in the past few weeks. It wouldn't be right to leave Caleb alone to run the store, even if she had left the children behind to help out. All hands were needed on the busiest days, and Saturdays, especially during the summer months, were the most hectic of all.

Naomi glanced into the adjoining quilt shop where Abby and Stella were stacking bolts of fabric onto shelves. *I wonder if Abby wishes she could have taken the time to attend the wood-stacking bee. She's been so busy lately that she hardly has time for a lunch break, so it's a good thing my little sister will begin helping her and Stella next week.* She folded her arms and smiled. *I'm glad to have someone as sweet and kind as Abby for a sister-in-law. Poor thing went through a lot when she first came to Pennsylvania to help her mamm, and it's good to see her so happy now.*

Abby was a good wife to Naomi's older brother, and the Lord had blessed them with five special kinner. Naomi knew that if Abby hadn't allowed God to heal her heart after she lost Lester she and Matthew might never have gotten together.

"You gonna stand there all day starin' into the other room with a silly grin on your face, or do ya plan to help me unload those boxes of books that came in yesterday afternoon?" Caleb touched Naomi's arm as he spoke.

She turned to face him and smiled. "I was thinking about the past and how God has taken so many bad things that have happened to our family and turned them into something good."

"That's because God is good and full of blessings."

Naomi nodded. "Jah, no truer words were ever spoken."

Leona pushed a wayward strand of hair away from her face where it had worked its way loose from under her kapp. She and the other six women who'd come to cook for the men had been busy all day. Besides the two stockpots of homemade noodles and a kettle of wieners they had served for lunch, they'd taken turns running back and forth with jugs of water, coffee, and iced tea for the men to drink whenever they needed a break from the woodcutting, hauling, and stacking. For dessert there had been store-bought ice cream and some of Bertha Lapp's delicious peanut butter cookies. By three o'clock, most of the wood had been hauled over to the pile, and the remaining pieces were now being stacked by the men while the boys and young women began a game of volleyball.

"Looks like they're havin' fun out there," Mary Ann said, staring wistfully out the kitchen window as she and Leona finished up the last of the dishes needing to be washed and dried.

Bertha stepped between them. "There's no reason the two of you can't join the game. Fannie's still here, so she and I can finish up."

"That's right," Fannie agreed. "You two go have yourselves a little fun in the sun."

"You can play ball if you want to," Leona said to her friend. "I think I'll just watch from a chair on the porch."

Mary Ann tipped her head. "I thought you liked to play volleyball. Always did when we were kinner."

"I do enjoy playing, but I won't chance getting hit in the face with the ball and reinjuring my naas."

"That makes sense." Mary Ann dried her hands on a towel, and she and Leona scooted out the door.

For the next hour, Leona sat in a wicker chair, alternating between watching the game in progress and staring at the sky, which had suddenly grown dark.

"Looks like we might be in for a storm."

Leona jumped at the sound of Abner's deep voice. "Jah, the wind's picked up considerably in the last few minutes," she said, wrapping her arms around her middle and suppressing a shiver.

Abner tromped up the steps, his knees bowed slightly, and his black work boots clomp-clomping. When he reached the porch, he dropped into the chair next to Leona's and looked over at her with a crooked grin. "Wonder if we'll get some *wedderleech* and *dunner*."

"I hope not. It will be hard enough to drive home in the rain, and if there's lightning and thunder, my horse will become skittish, the way she always does in a storm."

"Guess everyone will have to hang out here 'til the storm passes."

"How come you're not out there playing ball with the others?" she asked.

He shrugged and ran his fingers through the sides of his dark hair. "Aw, I'd probably just make a fool of myself."

Leona opened her mouth to comment, but a clap of thunder sounded, cutting off her words. Suddenly, a burst of wind came up, lifting the trampoline that was used by the Lapps' grandchildren high into the air. She watched in horror as it sailed over the woodshed, making two holes in the roof and landing upside down on the ground several feet away. Everyone who'd been playing ball rushed toward the house, and the men who'd been stacking wood made a mad dash for the barn.

"That was unbelievable!" Abner shouted, rising to his feet. "I've never seen anything like it before, have you?"

Leona shook her head.

"Guess we'd better wait awhile before we head for home," Mary

Ann said as she stepped onto the porch.

Leona stood. "Think I'll go in the house and see if my help is needed. Bertha might have some refreshments she wants to serve." She hurried away, leaving Abner to stand beside Mary Ann.

As Jimmy pulled his pickup into the driveway, he frowned. Dad's van was here, parked at an odd angle. He'd either been in a hurry when he got home or he was drunk. Jimmy suspected the latter, because his dad hadn't returned to the job site today, nor had he answered any of Jimmy's phone calls. It was his usual pattern whenever he decided to go on a bender; only sometimes Dad didn't come home until the next morning, and then he would be out of sorts and worthless for days.

Jimmy gritted his teeth. "He'd better not be drunk, because if he is, I'm going to—" What was he going to do? Go to work tomorrow morning and cover for his dad, the way he'd done countless other times? Tiptoe around the house, sidestepping Dad and cleaning up the mess he always made when he drank himself sick?

"I'm getting tired of this," Jimmy mumbled as he exited his truck. From what he could remember, when Mom was alive, his dad's drinking hadn't been so bad. Dad had always been one to have a few too many beers now and then, but he never used to come home drunk or allow his work to become affected by his drinking. Dad's drinking binges had become more frequent in recent years, and it had fallen on Jimmy's shoulders to hold everything together—at home as well as on the job.

Maybe this time will be different, he thought. *Dad may have forgotten to turn his cell phone on, and he may have had more errands to run than he first thought. He could be in the house right now, starting supper.* He let himself in through the back door and soon discovered that the kitchen was empty. There was no sign of his dad's lunch box on the cupboard, which was where he usually left it. "Dad, I'm home!" Jimmy called, stepping into the hallway.

No answer, just the steady *tick-tock, tick-tock* of the grandfather clock.

"Where are you, Dad?" Jimmy stepped into the living room and halted. There lay his dad on the living room floor with five empty beer bottles on the coffee table and another one in the curled fingers of his hand.

Jimmy groaned and dropped to his knees beside his dad. *Well, at least he's still breathing.* He shook the man's shoulders. "Wake up, Dad. You need to get off the floor. Come on, I'll help you get upstairs to bed."

His dad's head lulled to one side, and he moaned. "I—I did it for you, Linda. You wanted a baby—so I gave you one—the only way I knew how."

Even though the words were slurred, Jimmy knew what his dad had said. He'd obviously been using the fact that Jimmy knew about his adoption as an excuse to get drunk. *Dad must feel guilty because he couldn't give Mom any children of his own.*

"Come on, Dad. You've got to get up."

No response, except for a loud hiccup.

"You can't stay on the floor all night." Jimmy shook his dad's shoulder again, but the only reply he got was a plea for more beer. "I'm not getting you anything more to drink. You need to sleep this off, but not here on the living room floor."

Dad closed his eyes, and his heavy breathing turned to loud snores.

Sometimes family members can be enablers. You need to practice tough love. His friend's recent admonition echoed in Jimmy's ears. "I know Allen's right, but it's a lot easier said than done," Jimmy mumbled. He squeezed his eyes shut and opened them again. Then, rising to his feet, he grabbed the lightweight throw from the couch, threw it across his dad's chest, and left the room. It was time for Dad to sink or swim. It was time for Jimmy to make a decision.

CHAPTER 10

*J*im's eyelids felt heavy as he struggled to sit up. He blinked against the invading light streaming in through the window and glanced around the living room. *What am I doing here, and what's that horrible smell?* As his eyes began to focus and reality set in, he realized that he was wearing the same white shirt and painter's pants he'd had on yesterday, and the putrid smell was his own body odor, combined with the pile of vomit not far from where he lay.

Where's Jimmy? Why didn't he put me to bed like he always does whenever I can't make it there on my own?

Jim moaned as he stood on shaky legs. There seemed to be no way to hold his head that didn't hurt. *I need some coffee and a couple of aspirin. I need—* He glanced at the mess he'd made on the carpet and grimaced. *I need Jimmy—where's Jimmy?*

He stumbled out to the kitchen, figuring Jimmy might be there making coffee, even though his nose told him otherwise. Maybe Jimmy was still in bed or had left for work already, figuring Jim would be too hung over to make it today.

When Jim realized Jimmy wasn't in the kitchen, he staggered over to the coffeemaker and was about to reach for the pot when he saw an envelope lying on the counter with his name on it. *Jimmy must have left me a note so I'd know he's gone to work without me.*

He got the coffee going, took a seat at the table, and ripped open the envelope.

> *Dad,*
>
> *I think I know what triggered this recent bender, but it's still no excuse. I've got a feeling the reason you still haven't called that lawyer in Maryland is because you're afraid if I find my real*

parents that I won't love you anymore or might not come home.

Jim moistened his lips and squinted at the page. *Come home? Has Jimmy gone somewhere?*

He read on.

> *Last night after I found you passed out on the living room floor, I made a decision. Since I'm the one who was adopted, it's really my job to search for information about my biological parents, not yours. So I left for Maryland early this morning. I'll let you know as soon as I find out anything.*
> *Take care, Dad. I'll be in touch.*
>
> *Love,*
> *Jimmy*

Jim let the note slip to the floor as he dropped his head to the table. "Oh, Jimmy, what have you done?"

On Monday afternoon, Leona entered the schoolhouse and glanced around the room. She'd come to see what all needed to be done before the school year began in August. As soon as she had lit a kerosene lamp, she pulled out the chair at her desk, took a seat, and opened the top drawer, withdrawing a tablet and pen. She wrote the following list:

1. *Outside and inside of building need to be painted.*
2. *Roof leaks and needs to be patched.*
3. *Need a new blackboard—one of those white ones that use an erasable marking pen rather than chalk.*
4. *Floors and desks need to be cleaned and polished.*

Leona's list making came to a halt when a horse and buggy trotted into the school yard. The horse's hooves clip-clopped against the gravel, and the animal neighed as it came to a stop. Leona pushed away from her desk and went to the door, pleased to discover Mary Ann climbing down from her buggy.

"Wie geht's?" Leona called.

"I'm doing good, danki."

"What brings you out here in the middle of the day?" Leona asked when her friend joined her on the porch. "I figured you'd be working at the quilt shop all afternoon."

"Actually, I am working today. I'm on my way over to Margaret Byler's place to pick up some quilts she has ready to sell."

Leona opened the door and led the way into the schoolhouse. "How come Margaret didn't bring them to the store herself?"

"Yesterday at church, her granddaughter mentioned that Margaret had come down with the flu and was home in bed."

"That's a shame." Leona clucked her tongue. "I hope you won't be exposed to the bug by going over to the Bylers' house."

"I won't be there long, and someone in the family will probably have the quilts ready when I arrive." Mary Ann smiled. "Changing the subject. . . I was wondering if you're planning to go to the singing this Sunday night. It's to be held in my daed's barn, you know."

Before Leona could formulate a response, Mary Ann added, "You've missed the last couple of young people's gatherings, and I think it would be good for you to get out and do something fun for a change."

"I'll probably be busy that night."

Mary Ann squinted, causing the skin around her eyes to crinkle. "Want to know what I think?"

"What's that?"

"You work too hard and need to socialize more."

Leona took a seat at her desk and motioned to the tablet lying before her. "Busy schoolteachers always have something to do."

"But it's summer, and you shouldn't be working here now."

"I'm making a list of the things that need to be done before school starts, and there's also some cleaning and organizing I want to do yet."

Mary Ann placed one hand on the desk. "But you won't be working on Sunday, and when it's time to get the schoolhouse ready, the students' parents will help with much of the repairs and cleaning. So there's no excuse for you not to come to the singing or any other social event that might be held this summer."

"I don't feel much like socializing these days, but I'll think about it."

"Jah, okay." Mary Ann turned toward the door. "Guess I'd best be on my way or Abby will wonder what's taking me so long."

Leona lifted her hand in a wave. "See you later then."

Jim left the house around noon after phoning Ed to say he would be late. Then he headed for the Tacoma Mall, hoping to stop at the health food store again to see what else they might have for his nerves. He'd tried to call Jimmy several times but had only gotten his voice mail. He needed to talk to Jimmy before he got to Maryland.

A short time later, he pulled his van into the mall parking lot and turned off the engine. When he entered the health food store, he discovered Holly was waiting on a customer. Not wishing to interrupt, he wandered up and down the aisles looking at various vitamins and herbal preparations.

"It's nice to see you again, Jim. May I help you with something?" Holly asked as she stepped up to him a few minutes later.

He smiled, feeling rather self-conscious yet pleased that she had remembered his name. "I'm—uh—feeling kind of shaky today, and I was hoping you might have something else I could try for my nerves."

"Didn't that homeopathic remedy you bought help any?"

"It did at first, but I'm still having a hard time sleeping, and—well, I'm kind of going through a rough time right now, so I really could use—"

"I know all about the problem of not sleeping," she said. "Plus I've dealt with a host of other things that affected my health for some time."

Jim studied the woman a few seconds. Her eyes were a pale blue, and her blond hair, worn short and fringed around her cheeks, looked even healthier than he had remembered. He couldn't imagine that she'd ever had any kind of health problems.

"I'm a recovered alcoholic," Holly said. "I'm not proud of my past, but with God's help and the support of Alcoholics Anonymous, I've remained sober for the past ten years."

Jim's mouth dropped open. He never would have guessed that this pretty, pleasant woman had ever had a drinking problem. *I wonder what got her started? Could she have had a troubled marriage or been dealing with guilt from her past, like me? Could Holly be the recovering alcoholic Jimmy had mentioned not long ago?*

"You seem surprised by my confession." Her lips curved into a smile. "Just because I go to church every Sunday doesn't mean I've lived my life on Easy Street. Accepting Christ as my Savior was the first step to my recovery, but I had to do many other things to help myself, too."

Jim thought about his own problem with alcohol, but it was nothing he couldn't control; he wasn't about to tell someone he barely knew that had awakened on the living room floor this morning because he'd had a few too many beers last night.

Holly pointed to the shelf in front of her. "I've got several things here that might help you sleep, but, of course, none of them will be as strong as what a doctor might prescribe."

"That's okay. I don't need any more drugs," he mumbled.

"What was that?"

"Nothing. Just give me some herbs to help me relax, and I'm sure I'll be good to go."

Jimmy loosened his grip on the steering wheel and tried to relax. He'd never made a trip this far alone. For that matter, he and his folks had never driven any farther than to one of the ocean beaches or down to Boise to see his mom's parents.

"They've never really been my grandparents," he muttered, squinting against the glint of the morning sun on his truck's window. "And neither were Grandma and Grandpa Scott." He clicked on the radio, hoping to diffuse his thoughts with some mellow music. The only stations he could pick up either played repetitious country songs or broadcast the local news. Remembering that he'd brought along some of his favorite Christian CDs, he finally popped one into the CD player. "Ah, that's better."

Jimmy hummed along with the music for a while, keeping his focus on the road and his thoughts off his unknown future. If he were to find his birth mother, then what? He couldn't just march up to her and announce, "Hi, my name's Jimmy Scott, and I'm the son you gave up for adoption twenty years ago." He'd never been in a situation like this before, and he had no idea what he would say or do if he were to meet either his real mother or father face-to-face.

Jimmy drew in a deep breath and tried to relax. There was no point thinking about any of this until he had something to go on. "I need to trust God to give me the right words—if and when the time comes for me to meet my real parents."

CHAPTER 11

*W*hat are you doing home in the middle of the day?" Lydia asked when her husband stepped into the kitchen around three o'clock.

Jacob grinned and hung his straw hat on a wall peg near the door. "My crew's paintin' Daniel King's barn, and since it's not so far from here, I thought I'd run home and give my fraa a great big hug." He took a few steps toward her, and Lydia went willingly into his arms.

"I've always known you were a fine painter, Jacob Weaver," she said, closing her eyes and leaning against his chest. "And ever since the day you were chosen by lots to be our new bishop, I was sure you would be a good one." She gave him a squeeze. "But to my way of thinking, the thing you're the best at is being a loving, *schmaert* husband and father."

He leaned down and kissed her gently on the mouth. Then Lydia opened her eyes and reached up to stroke his long, full beard, which seemed to have more gray than brown in it these days. She felt blessed to be married to such a caring, considerate man. He had not only looked out for her needs these nearly thirty-six years they'd been together, and to their children's needs, as well, but he guided, comforted, and befriended his entire flock.

"So, then, have ya got anything cold to drink for your smart old man?" Jacob asked. "It's sure a hot, sticky day out there. Can't believe how warm it's gotten already this year."

Lydia eased out of his embrace and tipped her head to one side. "Ah, so that's the reason you came by the house. I'll bet you were hoping to have a few cookies to go with that cold drink, *jah*?"

His hazel eyes twinkled, and he chuckled, which made his beard jiggle up and down. "Some cookies and a cool drink would be good, but that's not the only reason I dropped by to see you, my love."

Lydia clucked her tongue as she headed across the room to the refrigerator. "We aren't a couple of young sweethearts anymore, so you don't have to say things like that to get me to pour you a glass of iced tea." She glanced over her shoulder. "Or would you rather have some cold goat's milk?"

Jacob ambled across the room and pulled out a chair. "Milk and cookies would be fine and dandy."

A few minutes later, they were both seated at the table with tall glasses of milk set before them, along with a plate piled high with molasses cookies.

"Umm... These cookies are sure tasty," he said, smacking his lips and lifting his bushy eyebrows until they nearly disappeared into his hairline.

"Danki. I'm glad you like 'em."

"What's our youngest daughter up to today?" Jacob asked. "I figured she might be out workin' in the garden this afternoon, but I didn't see any sign of her when I pulled into the yard."

"She went over to the schoolhouse soon after lunch. Said she wanted to do some cleaning and make a list of things that need to be done before school starts."

He nodded. "It won't be long 'til the kinner's summer break is over. I'm thinkin' the outside of the school will need to be painted before then. That will no doubt be on her list."

"Jah, I'm sure you're right about that."

"You think our daughter's gonna be okay, Lydia?" Jacob asked as he rubbed the bridge of his nose.

"Well, I know she's still havin' some headaches, but I believe after a few more visits with the chiropractor, she'll be good as new."

He shook his head. "I wasn't talkin' about her physical condition. I was referrin' to her broken heart. She's not really been the same since Ezra died."

Lydia opened her mouth to reply but was interrupted by a knock at the back door. Her chair squeaked as she pushed it aside. "I'd best see who's come a-calling."

When she opened the door a few seconds later, she was surprised to see Abner Lapp standing on the front porch. "Is Leona here?" he asked.

"She's not at home just now."

His dark eyebrows lifted under his straw hat as he frowned. "She ain't, huh?"

"Sorry, no."

"Mind if I ask when she might be home?"

"She's gone over to the schoolhouse to get some work done, and I doubt she'll be here much before supper."

Abner nodded. "Guess I'll drive on over there, 'cause I need to talk to her about Emanuel."

Lydia pursed her lips. "Your little bruder isn't still blamin' himself for Leona's accident, is he?"

Abner shrugged. "I'm not sure, but all of a sudden, he's sayin' he doesn't want to go back to school when it starts up again in August, and I'm hopin' Leona might have some idea what I can do to persuade him. Short of me takin' a board to the seat of his pants, that is."

Before Lydia could respond, Jacob joined them at the door. "Maybe I should have a talk with the boy. I was always able to get through to my kinner—even Arthur, my headstrong one—without having to resort to physical punishment."

Abner smiled. "That'd be much appreciated. Since I'm only Emanuel's big bruder and not his daed, it's hard on our relationship when I have to discipline too much."

"I'll drive on over to your place sometime this week and have a little heart-to-heart with Emanuel then," Jacob said with a nod.

"Danki." Abner turned and started down the porch steps. "Tell Leona I'm sorry I missed her," he called over his shoulder.

Lydia watched Abner climb into his buggy and drive away, and then she turned to Jacob and said, "*Er is en erschtaunlicher mann*—he's an astonishing man. He seems a bit shy, but he's sure devoted to his family, and in my estimation, that says a whole lot." She sighed. "I know it's probably too soon for Leona to think about courting, but maybe in the days ahead, she and Abner will get together."

Jacob grinned and reached for her hand. "That's what I've been thinkin', too."

When Leona opened the schoolhouse door, about to empty the bucket of water she'd used to clean the floor, she was surprised to see Abner Lapp climb down from his buggy. She had been so busy scrubbing that she hadn't heard him drive up.

"I stopped by your house to see you," he called, "but your mamm said you were over here."

She set the bucket on the porch. "Jah, I'm doing a bit of cleaning."

He stepped onto the porch and removed his straw hat. "I thought a group of parents would be doin' that."

She nodded. "Several are planning to come by in the next week or so to help with some other cleaning and repairs, but I thought as long as I was here I'd do a few things on my own."

"I see." Abner shuffled his boots a couple of times and stared down at the porch. "Wanted to tell you that Emanuel's been sayin' he doesn't want to attend school next term." He leaned against the porch railing and folded his arms. "But your daed said he'd have a talk with him, so that might be enough. I sure don't want to have to force the boy to go, but I will if it becomes necessary."

If you think Papa speaking to Emanuel will be enough, then what are you doing here? Leona wondered as a sense of irritation rose in her chest. *Did Papa send Abner out to the schoolhouse in the hopes of getting the two of us together?*

Before Leona could comment, Abner spoke again. "I wasn't going to bother you with this, since your daed gave his offer to help, but I wanted you to know what's going on, too."

She pursed her lips. Emanuel had given her a few problems after his daed died, and though she knew the boy didn't like to study, she'd had no idea he disliked school so much that he didn't want to come back for the next term. "Maybe it's me Emanuel doesn't like."

"Now why would you be sayin' that?"

"I was thinking—if he got in trouble with either you or your mamm because of the ball that hit me in the face, maybe he's blaming me for whatever punishment he received." Leona's pupils were all she had now that she was destined to be an old maid, and the thought of any of them not liking her sent shivers up her spine.

Abner shook his head. "I never really punished the boy, except to give him a lecture on being careful where his aim was whenever he acted as pitcher. Besides, he felt really bad about your naas gettin' broke, and if he didn't like you, I doubt he would have kept askin' me to drive him over to your place so's he could see you."

A sense of relief came over Leona as she thought it all through. Emanuel had seemed genuinely sorry for throwing the ball, and other than being a bit unruly during school, he'd never given her any reason to believe he didn't like her.

"Guess I should be gettin' on home," Abner said. "Danki for takin' the time to talk to me, Leona."

"I'll try to think of some ways to convince Emanuel that he needs to come back to school—just in case my daed doesn't get through to him," she said.

Abner smiled, and his cheeks turned a light shade of pink. "Wish I'd had a teacher as nice as you when I attended school."

Unsure of what to say to that comment, Leona merely nodded and mumbled, "See you at preaching service on Sunday, Abner."

As Jimmy drove into the town of Bel Air, his stomach tumbled like a cement mixer. He'd gone online and done a search for the lawyer's address and phone number before he'd left home, and then he had called and made an appointment for four o'clock this afternoon.

What if he refuses to give me any information? What if he doesn't know where my real mother is? Jimmy's head swam with unanswered questions, and as he pulled into the parking lot in front of Carl Stevens's office, he knew he had to pray.

"Dear Lord, please slow my racing heart. Put the right words on my tongue. Let me leave here with enough information to begin my search for the woman who gave birth to me. Amen."

Jimmy climbed out of the truck and entered the building feeling a little less anxious than he had before his prayer.

"May I help you?" a middle-aged, redheaded woman asked when Jimmy stepped up to the reception desk.

He nodded and wiped his sweaty palms along the sides of his jeans. "I'm Jimmy Scott, and I have a four o'clock appointment with Mr. Stevens."

She glanced at her computer screen and said, "Mr. Stevens is running a little behind this afternoon, but he'll be with you shortly." She motioned to a group of chairs sitting against the far wall. "You can wait over there."

"Okay, thanks." Jimmy took a seat and picked up a magazine from the nearby table. He thumbed through a couple of pages and glanced at his watch—the one his dad had given him for his birthday. *I hope Dad understands why I haven't answered any of the messages he's left on my voice mail. I can't deal with talking to him right now. He'd only try to convince me to come home.* Jimmy grimaced. *If Dad had called Mr. Stevens like he said he was going to, I might not have felt the need to come here on my own.*

"Mr. Scott?"

Jimmy's thoughts came to a halt when the receptionist called his name. He stood.

"Mr. Stevens isn't ready to see you yet, but I was wondering if you would like a cup of coffee or something cold to drink?"

"Uh—yeah, I guess so."

"Which would you like?"

"Something cold would be great."

"We have several kinds of soda. Do you have a favorite?"

When Jimmy said any kind of soda would be fine, the receptionist opened a small refrigerator behind her desk and handed him a bottle of grape soda. "Would you like a glass?"

"No, thanks. This is fine." Jimmy opened the lid and took a big gulp.

He'd just finished the last of the soda when the receptionist said, "Mr. Stevens will see you now." She opened the door to her left and motioned Jimmy inside.

A young man with dark hair and metal-framed glasses greeted Jimmy when he stepped into the office.

"I—I have an appointment with Carl Stevens," Jimmy said, glancing around the room. If Dad had met Mr. Stevens twenty years ago, then he knew the man standing before him couldn't be the same lawyer.

"I'm Carl Stevens."

"But—but, I was expecting a much older man," Jimmy stammered.

The young man smiled, and his blue eyes twinkled. "Did you think you'd made an appointment with Carl Stevens Sr.?"

"I—I guess so."

"That would be my father. He's retired now. I'm Carl Stevens Jr., and I took over Dad's practice five years ago."

Jimmy felt as if the wind had been knocked out of him. If this wasn't the lawyer who had initiated his adoption proceedings, then he had probably made the trip for nothing.

Carl nodded to the straight-backed chair in front of his desk. "Have a seat, and you can tell me why you're here."

Jimmy sank to the chair, and Carl seated himself in the leather chair behind a mammoth oak desk. "I—uh—I'm not sure you can help me, but my dad—my adoptive dad—came here twenty years ago to get me." He felt moisture on his forehead and reached up to swipe it away. "Your dad—Carl Stevens Sr.—was the lawyer handling the adoption case."

Carl Jr. nodded. "I see."

Jimmy squirmed restlessly, trying to find a comfortable position and wishing he knew what to say.

"So what is it you want from me?"

"Actually, it was your dad I wanted information from, but since he's no longer practicing law, maybe you might—would you still have the adoption records that took place twenty years ago?"

"I'm sure we would, but you should know up front that a lawyer is bound by client confidentiality, so even if I were to find those records, I wouldn't be able to tell you the name of your birth parents."

Jimmy's heart felt as if it had dropped clear to his toes. Had he driven all this way for nothing? "Isn't there anything you could tell me? Maybe what hospital I was born in, or—"

"I'll tell you what," Carl interrupted. "Let me go in the back room and check through some old filing cabinets, and I'll see if I can come up with anything helpful for you."

"Thanks, I'd appreciate it."

Carl grabbed a pen and a tablet from his desk. "What are your adoptive parents' names, and when was the date of the adoption?"

"Jim and Linda Scott, and it took place twenty years ago. It was sometime in June, but I'm not sure of the exact date. I was one year old at the time."

"Okay. Be right back." Carl stood and exited the room.

While Jimmy waited, he reached into his jeans and pulled out his pocket change; determined to keep his mind busy and his hands from shaking, he began to count the coins. Once he'd counted the fistful of money, he glanced at his watch, wondering how long it might take Carl to find the information he'd gone looking for.

When he'd confirmed the amount of loose change in his pockets at least ten times and the lawyer still wasn't back, he stood and began to pace between the window and the watercooler. Traffic was steady on the street out front, and he wondered if it would take him long to find the hotel where he'd made reservations to spend the night.

He stopped in front of the watercooler and was thinking about getting a drink when the door opened. Carl stepped back into the room with a nod. "Sorry to keep you waiting."

"That's okay." Jimmy took a seat again, and the lawyer did the same.

"I'm afraid I've got bad news," Carl said. "I did find a Jim and Linda Scott in our database, but the adoption my dad had begun on their behalf fell through when the birth mother changed her mind and decided to keep her baby."

Jimmy's mouth dropped open, and once more his lungs felt breathless. "But that can't be. My mom—my adoptive mom—wrote me a letter before she died. She said my dad had come here alone to pick me up because she'd had a headache that day. She told me how excited she'd been when Dad came back to the hotel with me in his arms." He stared at the lawyer. "How could that have happened if there'd been no adoption?"

Carl shrugged. "I have no idea, but if there was an adoption, it didn't take place in this office." He tapped his pen along the edge of the desk. "But even if there were another adoption, then it couldn't have happened the same day your dad came here. It would have taken some time for him to find another lawyer and begin new adoption proceedings."

Jimmy just sat there, too numb to move, too confused to respond. *If I'm not the baby Dad came to pick up that day, then who am I, and where did he get me?*

CHAPTER 12

*L*eona reclined on an old quilt by the pond near their home. With Cinnamon lying contently by her side, she stared at the sky, noting the pale blue graduating to a deeper color. She relished the peace and quiet after her private picnic lunch.

A cool breeze tickled her nose, and she breathed in the fresh scent of the wildflowers growing nearby. She reached over and patted Cinnamon's head. The Irish setter responded with a grunt and rolled onto her back. "You want your belly rubbed, don't ya, girl?"

Cinnamon's head lulled to one side as Leona massaged the animal's soft stomach. While she continued the rhythmic motion, she thought about Abner Lapp's visit to the schoolhouse yesterday afternoon and wondered when Papa would visit with Emanuel. She hoped things would go well and that he'd be able to convince Emanuel that school was a good place to be. She knew the boy would be forced to attend, regardless of whether he wanted to or not, but it would be easier on both teacher and student if Emanuel wanted to be there.

She moved her hands up to Cinnamon's ears, stroking them both at the same time. "Teaching is all I have left, and I want to be the best teacher I can be." She closed her eyes, enjoying the gentle warmth of the sun's healing rays. For the last couple of days, the weather had been mild and not the least bit muggy. She wished every day of summer could be this way.

An approaching buggy crunched against the hard-packed dirt and halted Leona's thoughts. She opened her eyes and saw Naomi Hoffmeir and her youngest daughter, Millie, climb down from their buggy. "What brings you two out here today?" she asked as they neared the quilt where she sat.

"We were on our way home from a dental appointment and

decided to stop at the pond to see if there were many mosquitoes,"
Naomi explained. "Our family hopes to have a picnic supper later this
evening. That is, if there aren't too many nasty bugs here to bite us."

Leona shook her head. "I haven't seen any mosquitoes at all."

"That's good to hear."

Leona smiled at Millie. "I'm looking forward to having you in my
class when school starts up in August," she said in their Pennsylvania
Dutch language, knowing Millie wouldn't learn English well until she
started the first grade.

Millie nodded and gave her soon-to-be teacher a shy grin. Then she
flopped down beside Cinnamon. When the dog licked the child's hand,
Millie giggled and patted the animal's head.

"How much longer do you think you'll teach?" Naomi asked, taking
a seat on the edge of the quilt.

"For a long time, I hope," Leona replied.

"Maybe you'll be Kevin's teacher when he starts school in two
years."

"I should be."

"He's content to stay with his grandma Hoffmeir while Caleb and
I are at the store every day, but I'm sure he will enjoy going to school
once he's old enough." Naomi smoothed her long green dress over her
knees and wrapped her hands around them. "Abner Lapp's mamm
came into the store the other day, and she said something about Abner
having been over to your house to see you a few times."

Leona nodded.

"So, if Abner's courting you, maybe you won't be teaching as long
as you think."

Leona sat up straight, her back rigid. "I don't know where you got
the idea that Abner and I are courting, but it's not true. He dropped by
the house a couple of times to see how I was doing after my nose got
broke, and then he came once to talk about his brother."

"Guess I was wrong then." Naomi plucked a blade of grass from a
patch growing nearby and twirled it around her fingers.

Leona glanced at her dog. The critter nuzzled Millie's hand, and the
young girl seemed to be eating it up.

"Looks like my Millie has made herself a new friend," Naomi
commented.

Leona stroked the dog's floppy red paw. "Jah, and the feeling seems to be mutual."

Naomi smiled. "Dogs make *wunderbaar* pets, but they can't take the place of a loving, caring husband."

"That may be true for some," Leona said with a shrug.

Jim's alarm clock blared in his ear. He rolled over with a groan, wishing he could sleep a few more minutes. The hangover headache he'd had most of yesterday had finally abated, but he'd stayed up until late last night trying to call Jimmy. "That kid must have shut off his cell phone," he mumbled into his pillow.

Just then, the telephone on the table beside his bed rang, and Jim quickly reached for it. "Scott residence. Jim here."

"Hi, Dad, it's me."

"Jimmy! Where are you? Why haven't you been answering your phone? Did you get the messages I left?" Jim sat up and swung his legs over the side of the bed.

"Slow down, Dad. I can only answer one question at a time."

"Well, you can start by telling me where you are."

"I'm in Bel Air, Maryland, and I just checked out of my hotel."

"You—you drove all the way to Maryland by yourself?"

"I'm not a little kid, Dad, and I told you I was coming here in the note I left on the kitchen counter. You did get my note, didn't you?"

Jim stretched one arm over his head and yawned. "Yeah, I got it, and I was pretty upset when I discovered you were gone."

"Sorry about that, but you were passed out on the floor in the living room when I left, so—"

"Don't remind me," Jim said with a groan. He still couldn't get over the fact that his son had left him there. And it wasn't like Jimmy to take off on a trip by himself—not to mention that he'd left in the middle of a big paint job, which had affected Jim's entire paint crew.

"I went to see Carl Stevens yesterday," Jimmy said.

"You—you did?"

"Yeah, only it wasn't the Carl Stevens you had dealings with. It was his son, Carl Jr., who took over his dad's practice five years ago."

Jim breathed a sigh of relief. If Jimmy had only met the lawyer's son, then maybe he was still in the clear. It wasn't likely that the son would know anything about what had gone on in his dad's office twenty years ago. Still, there might have been some records kept on the prospective adoption. "Wh–what'd the lawyer say?"

"He looked your name up in his database and discovered that the birth mother of the baby you'd gone there to adopt had changed her mind and decided to keep the child." There was a brief pause. "Is that true, Dad? Did you leave Carl Stevens's office without a baby?"

Jim stood and ambled across the room. He pulled back the curtain and stared out the window. It was a sunny day, but inside his room, a dark cloud was hanging over his head.

"Dad, did you hear what I said?"

Jim leaned against the window casing and closed his eyes. "Yeah, I heard your question."

"So what's the answer?"

"I—uh—no, I didn't leave there with a baby." Jim's eyes snapped open as the truth hit him full in the face. He was caught in his own web of deceit, and there didn't seem to be a way out, short of telling Jimmy what had really happened that day. But could he risk losing his son forever by revealing the truth?

"If you didn't leave the lawyer's office with a baby, then how could you have shown up with me at the hotel where Mom was waiting?"

Jim glanced around the room as a feeling of panic threatened to overtake him. He needed a drink—needed something to give him courage and calm his nerves. His gaze came to rest on the bottle of herbal tablets he'd bought at the health food store yesterday. They'd helped him get to sleep last night, but it had taken almost an hour for them to take effect. He didn't have that kind of time now. He needed something that would work fast.

"Dad, are you still there?"

"I'm here. Just thinking is all."

"Thinking about what—the next lie you're going to tell me?" Jimmy's tone was sarcastic, and Jim knew he'd better think fast and come up with something good if he was going to keep Jimmy from knowing the truth. But what could he say—that he'd gone to some other lawyer's office and adopted another baby? He swallowed around the lump lodged in his throat. "The—the truth is—we did get another baby—"

"The same day?" Jimmy's voice had raised a notch, and Jim could tell his son was feeling as much frustration as he was. "How about the truth, Dad? Think you could handle that?"

"Well, I—"

"The truth is always better than a lie."

"This truth might not be."

"What are you talking about?"

"Are you sitting down, Jimmy?"

"Yeah, I'm in my truck."

"Good, because what I'm about to tell you is gonna be a real shock." Jim stumbled back to the bed on shaky legs and flopped down. "I—I hardly know where to begin."

"Why not start at the beginning?"

"Yeah, okay. I guess it's time you knew the truth about your real family."

"You mean my birth parents—the ones you adopted me from?"

"No. There was no adoption."

"Huh? I don't get it. If there was no adoption, then how—"

"Stay with me, Jimmy." Jim drew in a deep breath, hoping it would give him added courage. "The day I went to pick up our adopted son at the lawyer's office in Bel Air, I was told that the birth mother had changed her mind and decided to keep her one-year-old boy. Needless to say, I was pretty upset and didn't know what I was going to tell your mother when I got back to the hotel."

"So if you didn't get the baby you'd gone there to adopt, then how did I—"

"I'm getting to that." Jim shifted on the bed as he tried to form his next words. "When I drove out of Maryland, I was in a state of panic, and by the time I got back to Pennsylvania, I could barely function. I drove up and down some backcountry roads for a while. There were a lot of Amish farms there, and when I spotted a sign advertising home-made root beer, I pulled into the driveway." He paused and swiped his tongue across his chapped lips. "A young Amish woman came out of the house holding a baby, whom she said had recently turned one." Another pause. "That baby was you, Jimmy. You were born in Lancaster County, Pennsylvania. Your real family is Amish."

Lancaster County, Pennsylvania? Amish? Jimmy sat there several seconds, allowing his dad's words to sink in. His brain felt numb, like he might be dreaming. He couldn't be Amish. He'd grown up in Puyallup, Washington, and his parents were Jim and Linda Scott. But then, he'd recently learned that he was adopted, so they weren't really his parents.

"After I asked the young woman for some cold root beer, she left you on the picnic table and went back inside to get it," his dad continued. "I expected her to return right away, but she didn't. Then you started getting restless, and I picked you up because I was afraid you might fall off the table. And then I ran to the car and drove off."

"Dad, have you been drinking this morning?"

"No, of course not. I haven't had a drop to drink since the night before last."

"Then why are you making up this crazy story? Do you really expect me to believe that you kidnapped some Amish baby and that the kid you took was me?"

"Yeah, that's right. I did it without thinking. But then as I drove away, everything started to make sense."

"How could kidnapping a child make any sense?" Jimmy didn't actually believe his dad's wild story, but if he was going to make him admit he was lying, then he needed to ask the right questions.

"I—I guess it didn't really make sense, but it's the truth, Jimmy. As odd as it might sound, I believed finding you was a twist of fate and that it was meant to be."

Jimmy's face felt like he'd been out in the sun too long. Could the person on the other end of the phone—the man he'd called Dad for the last twenty years—really be a baby snatcher? He shook his head. *No, it's not possible. Dad has to be making this story up to discourage me from searching for my birth family.*

"The young Amish woman told me there were eight kids in the family and that her mother was dead," Dad continued. "I figured I might have done them a favor by giving them one less mouth to feed."

Jimmy set the phone down on the seat and leaned forward, resting his head on the steering wheel. A spot on the side of his head began to throb as his thoughts ran wild. After several seconds, he sat up again and picked up the phone. "I've got to go now, Dad. I'll call you later, once you've sobered up and are ready to tell me the truth." He clicked off the phone before his dad could respond.

CHAPTER 13

*L*eona stepped into the kitchen the following morning and found her mamm cutting thick slices of ham. Mom looked at her and smiled. "Did your daed tell you he stopped by the Lapps' place last night and had a little talk with Emanuel?"

"No, he never mentioned it."

"He was awful tired last night. Maybe that's why he forgot to say anything."

"So how did it go?" Leona asked as she moved over to the cupboard and removed three plates.

"Guess it went well. Emanuel said the reason he didn't want to go to school this fall was because he thought he should get a job and help support his mamm."

Leona shook her head. "That's ridiculous. The boy's too young to be going to work yet, and besides, Abner's taking care of his mamm and little bruder just fine with what he makes at the furniture shop in Strasburg."

"That may be true, but apparently, Emanuel feels he should be helping out, too."

"So what'd Papa tell him?"

"Said he needed to learn all he could while he's young so he knows more when he's older and can do a better job of whatever type of work he chooses."

Leona smiled. "Papa's just like Solomon in the Bible—full of good wisdom."

Mom nodded. "Jah, my Jacob's been blessed with a special gift, all right."

"I'm going to see the chiropractor this afternoon," Leona said, taking their conversation in another direction. "So if you have any errands you'd like me to run, I'll be happy to do them for you."

"I do have a quilt finished that I'd like to have dropped off at Abby's quilt shop. Will you be going near there?"

"It won't be a problem. I'll go by the quilt shop on my way home after seeing Dr. Bowers."

"Are his treatments helping any with your stiff neck or headaches?" Concern showed on her mamm's face.

"My neck's feeling better, but the headaches are still there. That ball must have done more damage than I realized."

"Or maybe the headaches are from tension. You're still grieving over Ezra, and I know—"

"I'm not grieving, Mom," Leona said a bit too sharply, and she winced at her own snappish words. "Sorry, I didn't mean to sound so testy. It's just that I'm getting tired of being reminded that Ezra's dead. How am I ever going to get over him if everyone keeps bringing him up?"

"Your heart will heal in time, daughter, regardless of how many times you hear Ezra's name." Mom moved away from the cupboard and drew Leona into her arms. "Sooner or later, some other man will come along and win your heart, and then you'll look forward to getting married again."

Leona leaned her head on Mom's shoulder and let the tears flow. If she lived one hundred years, she didn't think she would ever stop loving Ezra, and she wasn't about to open her heart to love again.

As soon as Jimmy clicked off his cell phone, he put the truck in gear. His dad's kidnapping story was the most ridiculous thing he'd ever heard, but just to prove his dad was lying, he would drive over to Lancaster County, Pennsylvania, and check things out. If an Amish child had been kidnapped from there twenty years ago, someone in the area should know about it. And if the trip turned up nothing, then he would call Dad again and demand to know the truth about how he came to live with them.

Two hours later, as Jimmy headed down Route 30 in Lancaster, he spotted an Amish buggy. It looked similar to the ones he'd seen in Ohio during one of the few trips he and his folks had made to see Grandpa and Grandma Scott, only this buggy was gray instead of black. Traffic was a lot heavier than he'd thought it would be, and he noticed a multitude of shopping malls, restaurants, and tourist attractions on almost every block.

I wonder how the Amish manage with their horses and buggies in all this congestion, he thought as he turned into the parking lot of a visitors' center.

Inside the building, Jimmy found a rack near the front door full of brochures advertising Pennsylvania Dutch restaurants, authentic buggy rides, Amish country tours, hotels, and many local attractions.

"Guess I'd better start by finding a place to stay," he muttered.

"How long will you be in the area, and would you like a couple of recommendations?" the young, dark-haired woman behind the information desk asked.

Jimmy scratched the side of his head. "I'm not sure how long I'll be staying, but I'd appreciate any ideas you can give me."

She pulled out a brochure from the stack on her desk and handed it to him. "There's a nice bed-and-breakfast in Strasburg that has fairly reasonable rates. It's run by a Mennonite couple and comes highly recommended."

Jimmy studied the information, noting the picture of the tall, stately looking white house. It was surrounded by farmland, and an Amish buggy was shown heading up the road in front of the bed-and-breakfast.

"Thanks. I should be able to find the place with these directions," he said as he studied the map on the back of the brochure.

"Can I help you with anything else?" the woman asked.

Jimmy leaned on the counter. "Well, I'm—uh—looking for a place that sells homemade root beer. Would you know of any in the area?"

"There's lots of homemade root beer sold around here. You might find some at the farmer's market in Bird-in-Hand."

He shook his head. "The place I'm looking for is an Amish farm. I was told they had a sign out front by the road advertising root beer."

"Many Amish families have begun supplementing their income by selling produce and various other items from roadside stands or shops built near their homes. I think I've seen a couple of places selling root beer near Strasburg, so you might ask the folks at the B and B."

Jimmy started to turn away but hesitated. "I don't suppose you'd know about any Amish babies being kidnapped in the area?"

The woman's forehead wrinkled. "How long ago?"

"About twenty years."

"Sorry, but I wasn't living in Lancaster back then. You'll have to ask someone who's lived in the area that long."

"Okay. Thanks for your time." Jimmy put the brochure in his shirt pocket, along with a few others he'd plucked off the stand. He would head over to the bed-and-breakfast and see about getting a room. He'd then spend the rest of the day taking pictures of whatever he saw that interested him while searching for an Amish farm selling homemade root beer, which he felt sure was a complete waste of time.

"I'll be taking off early today," Jim told his foreman. "You and the rest of the crew can keep working if you want, or you can quit at noon, like I plan to do."

"I thought you wanted to get this job done by Monday."

"I did, but after starting it yesterday, I've come to realize that there's too much work involved for us to be able to finish today. We may as well quit for the weekend and get an early start on this old, peeling house come Monday morning." The house really would take longer to paint than Jim had figured, but the real reason he wanted to quit work early was so he could spend the rest of the day at his favorite tavern, drowning his sorrows and trying not to think about the confession he'd made to Jimmy earlier today.

"I don't think we should quit working for the day just because we can't get the job done until next week, and I can't believe how much work you've missed lately." Ed released a grunt and squinted at Jim. "I hope you're not hitting the bottle again."

"What I do on my own time is my business!"

"Okay, okay, don't get so testy." Ed lifted his hands. "You can take off whenever you want, and since you're the boss and this is your business, I'll just look the other way when your business folds." He started to walk away but turned back around. "Of course, that will mean I'll be out of a job, so I'd like to suggest something to you."

"What's that?"

"I have a brother-in-law who's a recovered alcoholic, and he's gotten a lot of help from AA."

Not the AA thing again. Jim gritted his teeth. *Is everyone out to see me reformed?* "I'm not an alcoholic, Ed, so get off my back."

"Whatever you say." Ed studied Jim intently. "Mind if I ask you something else?"

"What now?"

"I'm curious to know why Jimmy hasn't been at work all week, and I'm wondering why you've been late almost every day."

"Not that it's any of your business," Jim said gruffly, "but Jimmy's back East."

Ed's bushy eyebrows lifted on his forehead. "Back East? What's he doing there when we need him here?"

"He's on a quest."

"What kind of quest?"

"To find his biological parents."

Ed's mouth dropped open. "Huh?"

Jim glared at his foreman. "Well, as you know, we got Jimmy from the East Coast twenty years ago."

"Yeah, and you asked me not to mention Jimmy's adoption to anyone because you wanted to tell him when he was old enough and you didn't want him finding out some other way."

"Right."

"So now he knows?"

"Yeah, and he's determined to find his birth mother." *Which, of course, he won't be able to do because she was Amish, and his sister said their mother was dead.* Jim grimaced. *I wonder if Ed knew what really happened if he'd blow the whistle on me.*

"Do you know when Jimmy might be coming back?"

Jim rubbed his hand down the side of his face, wishing he and Ed weren't having this conversation. "I'm not sure. Guess it all depends."

Ed shrugged. "Guess we'll just have to get along without him until he gets back then."

Jim cringed. *Yeah, if he ever does come back.*

"Maybe I should take one of those buggy rides I saw in a brochure

I picked up on Saturday," Jimmy said to himself as he snapped on the radio. He had checked into the bed-and-breakfast and had driven around Strasburg and the outlying area, but so far he'd seen no Amish farms selling root beer. He'd talked to a couple of people and asked if they knew about an Amish baby who'd been kidnapped twenty years ago, but no one had any helpful information to give him.

A short time later, Jimmy parked his truck near Aaron and Jessica's Buggy Rides, outside the town of Bird-in-Hand, and waited on a bench with several other tourists for the next buggy. When his turn finally came, he climbed into the front of a closed-in buggy, taking a seat beside the gray-haired driver whose long beard matched in color. The man said he wasn't Amish but belonged to some other Plain group living in the area. The couple who had been waiting with Jimmy took the backseat, situating their little boy between them.

Jimmy removed his camera from its case.

"No pictures allowed on this trip," the driver announced. "We'll be stopping by several Amish farms and meeting some of the people who live there. It goes against their religious beliefs to have their pictures taken, so we ask that you respect those wishes."

"I read an article in the newspaper that said their opposition to having their pictures taken has something to do with the scripture about not making any graven images," the woman sitting behind them said.

The elderly man nodded and picked up the reins, guiding the horse to move forward. Jimmy slipped his camera back into its case.

Once they'd left the parking lot, they traveled at a fairly good pace down a narrow country road. The wind whipped at Jimmy's body through the open windows, and the rhythmic *clip-clop, clip-clop* of the horse's hooves echoed against the pavement.

Soon, they pulled onto a driveway leading to a well-kept farmhouse. An Amish woman and a little girl stepped out of the house and approached the buggy, each holding a tray filled with cookies and homemade bread.

"This is Mary and her daughter, Selma," their driver explained. "They make extra money for their family by selling bakery items to the tourists I bring along my buggy route."

Jimmy reached into his pocket and pulled out his wallet. "I'd like to buy a loaf of bread and six cookies, please."

Just before the horse started moving again, Jimmy leaned out the window and said to Mary, "Would you happen to sell any root beer here?"

She shook her head. "Just baked goods, that's all."

Jimmy slouched against the seat. He should have known it wouldn't be so easy to find an Amish farm selling root beer—if there even was such a place. *I'm sure Dad made this whole kidnapping thing up just to throw me off course. He's been a control freak for as long as I can remember, and I'm almost sure there's more to my adoption than he's willing to tell.* He studied the tall barn behind the Amish house as they pulled out of the yard. *Maybe I ought to see about getting a job in case I decide to stay in the area awhile. It will give me a chance to ask around some more before I call Dad again.*

After the buggy ride was over, Jimmy spent the next few hours driving along the back roads, taking pictures of barns, Amish men and boys working in the fields with their draft mules, and children playing in their yards.

By late afternoon, he was tired, thirsty, and thoroughly discouraged, so he pulled into the parking lot of a place called Hoffmeirs' General Store, hoping he might find something cold there to drink.

Naomi was busy dusting empty shelves near the back of the store when she heard the bell above the front door jingle. Knowing that Caleb and the children had gone out to run an errand and hadn't returned, she left her job and went to see who had come into the store. She discovered a young English man with light brown hair standing near the counter. "Can I help you?"

He nodded. "I was wondering if you sell anything cold to drink in this store."

She shook her head. "Except for some candy, we don't sell any food or drink items. I do have a few bottles of soda in the cooler I keep in the back room, though."

He moistened his lips with the tip of his tongue. "Would you be willing to sell me some of that? It's awfully hot and humid today, and I could sure use something cold to drink."

"I'd be happy to give you some soda. So, if you'll wait here, I'll be right back." Naomi hurried off, and a few minutes later, she returned with a bottle of orange soda, which she handed to him.

"Thanks. What do I owe you?"

"Nothing. Nothing at all." She studied the man, thinking he looked kind of familiar and wondering if she had met him before. "Mind if I ask where you're from?"

"I grew up in Puyallup, Washington." He took a drink and a dribble of orange liquid ran down his chin. He swiped it away with the back of his hand. "This is sure good."

"So, you're from out West then?"

He nodded and took another drink.

Naomi's thoughts went to her days of living in Oregon, and she reflected on how much she had missed her home and family during that stressful time. "Are you here on vacation?" she asked.

"Kind of." He finished the last of the soda and handed her the empty bottle. "Are you sure I can't pay for this?"

She shook her head. "No payment's necessary. Is there anything else I can help you with?"

He ran his fingers through the back of his wavy hair and shuffled his feet a couple of times. It reminded her of the way Matthew acted whenever he was mulling things over.

"I've been looking for a place that sells root beer, but I haven't had any luck so far."

Naomi opened her mouth to tell him that the ice cream shop down the street sold several kinds of soda and made root beer floats, but she was interrupted when Leona Weaver entered the store with a Dahlia-pattern quilt draped over her arm.

CHAPTER 14

As Leona stepped into the Hoffmeirs' store, she almost bumped into a young English man who stood near the front counter. He smiled. She returned the smile but then glanced quickly at Naomi, who stood nearby. "I came by to drop off a quilt my mamm finished for Abby. I also wanted to see if you'd gotten those rubber stamps in that you ordered for me awhile back. I'm planning to do some art projects with my students when we start back to school in August, and I thought I'd let them use the stamps."

"I'm expecting the order any day." Naomi motioned toward the back of the store. "I've got a couple of empty shelves dusted and all ready for them."

Leona skirted around the Englisher and moved toward the connecting quilt shop. "Guess I'll stop by another time to check on the stamps. Right now I need to give this quilt to Abby."

"Abby's not there, but you can leave it on her desk; when I see her tomorrow, I'll let her know it's from your mamm."

"Where is Abby?"

"She closed the shop for the rest of the day."

Leona halted. "How come?"

"She had to take all five of her kinner to the dentist for checkups."

"What about Mary Ann? Isn't she working today?"

"I talked with Fannie earlier. Seems my little sister's come down with the flu and is home in bed."

"I'm sorry to hear she's *grank*. I'll either stop by your folks' place and check on her or drop by here again later in the week."

The Englisher cleared his throat, and both women turned around. "I didn't realize you were still here," Naomi said. "Did you need something else?"

He shuffled his leather sandals across the wooden floor. "I just wanted to say thanks again for the pop—I mean, soda. It was real refreshing."

"You're welcome."

He started for the door but turned back around. "Say, I was wondering if you would know of anyone in the area who might be looking for a painter."

Before Naomi could respond, Leona stepped forward. "Have you had any experience?"

He nodded. "My dad owns his own painting business in the state of Washington, and I've been working part-time for him since I turned sixteen. When I graduated from high school, I painted during the summer when I wasn't taking classes at our local community college."

Leona took a few minutes to deliberate as she sized up the English man. He looked nice, dressed in a pair of blue jeans and a light blue, short-sleeved shirt. There was something about his serious brown eyes and the way he smiled that made her believe he was trustworthy. "My daed—I mean, dad—owns his own business, too," she said. "He mentioned the other day that he has a lot of work right now and might need to hire another painter."

The young man smiled. "Would you mind giving me the name of your dad's business or tell me where I might meet him to talk about the possibility of a job?"

"It's called Weaver's Painting, and I think Papa's got his crew working on the outside of a restaurant down the street. So if you head over there now, you might catch him."

"What's the name of the restaurant?"

"Meyers' Home Cooking. Just ask for Jacob Weaver—that's my dad."

"Thanks. I'll go there right away."

As Jimmy headed down the sidewalk toward the restaurant that the young Amish woman had mentioned, he was plagued with nagging doubts. How long would he stick around Lancaster County? Did he really need a job, or could he manage on the money he'd brought along? Was there even any point to him being here? Since he was here, and since he didn't want to return to Washington without some definite answers, he may as well stay awhile and get to know the area. Besides, he found the Amish culture kind of interesting.

Jimmy cleared his throat as he approached a middle-aged Amish man who knelt in front of a can of paint, stirring it with a flat stick. "Excuse me, but do you know where I might find Jacob Weaver?"

The man squinted and tipped his head to one side. "I'm Jacob Weaver. Do I know you from somewhere?"

Jimmy shook his head. "My name's Jimmy Scott, and I'm looking for a job."

"As a painter?"

"That's right. I spoke to your daughter over at Hoffmeirs' General Store, and she said you might be looking to hire someone."

Jacob placed the paint stick on the edge of the bucket and stood. "Have you had any experience?"

Jimmy nodded. "My dad owns a paint contracting business out in Washington."

Jacob pursed his lips and stared at Jimmy. "So you're not from around here, then?"

"No, I came to Lancaster County to. . ."

"Jacob, can you come here a minute?" A young Amish painter who was working nearby motioned to Jacob. "I'm having some problems getting this new paint to cover."

"Excuse me a minute." Jacob nodded at Jimmy. "I'll be right back."

Curious to see what the problem with the paint might be, Jimmy followed Jacob around the side of the building, where a couple of other Amish men stood painting with brushes.

"It might go on better if you used a roller rather than the brushes," he suggested.

"What makes you think so?" one of the fellows asked.

"You can cover a larger area quicker using a roller instead of a brush."

Before the young Amish man could reply, Jacob stepped forward, placed one hand on Jimmy's shoulder, and said, "Son, you're hired."

Jim's cell phone rang. He pulled it from his belt clip and frowned. "Now what?" he mumbled with irritation. "If this phone keeps ringing, I'll never get to the tavern. And it had better not be another disgruntled customer wondering why we haven't started working on their house yet." All morning, he'd had complaints, and he was tired of the interruptions. He hadn't even left the job site yet because he kept getting phone calls.

He checked the caller's number showing in the screen on his phone. When he realized it was Jimmy, he answered right away. "Hi, Jimmy. I'm so glad you called. After our last conversation, I was afraid you might—"

"I'm in Lancaster County, Dad," Jimmy interrupted. "I've spent all day driving around looking for Amish farms selling root beer, but as you may have guessed, I haven't found one."

"Jimmy, I—"

"You made that kidnapping story up, didn't you?"

"No, no, it's the truth." Jim leaned against the side of his van. "It took every ounce of courage for me to tell you the truth, Jimmy, and now that the story's out, I'm really scared."

"Scared of what?"

A trickle of sweat rolled down Jim's forehead and dribbled onto his cheek. "If you find your Amish family and tell them who you are, they might press charges against me. I could end up in jail."

"Come on now, Dad."

"No, really. Why do you think I kept this story a secret all these years?"

"Because you were afraid of going to jail?"

"That's right, and if your mother were still alive and knew about this, she'd be scared to death that if this leaks out I might be charged with kidnapping."

"What are you saying—that Mom didn't know the adoption had fallen through or that you'd snatched an Amish baby out of his own backyard?" Jimmy's tone was mocking, and Jim's frustration escalated.

"I couldn't tell her. It would have broken her heart."

"So you just let her believe I was the one-year-old kid you had planned to adopt?"

A muscle in Jim's cheek quivered. "Right. I did it because I loved her and wanted to give her the child she'd been wanting for so long. And if you could have seen the expression on your mother's face when

I returned to the hotel with you in my arms, you'd know why I did it. She was ecstatic."

There was a long pause, and Jim wondered if Jimmy had hung up. "Jimmy? You still there?"

"Yeah, Dad. I'm just trying to piece this all together. If you really did take me from an Amish farm, then I need to know exactly where it was."

"I—uh—I'm not sure where it was." Jim opened the door to the van and climbed in. If Jimmy stayed in Amish country long enough, there was a good chance he might find his Amish family. And if that happened, Jim felt sure he would be arrested. Worse than that, Jimmy might never return to Washington. Jim had already lost his wife, and the thought of losing his son was almost unbearable. "When are you coming home, Jimmy?" he ventured to ask.

"Look, Dad, I'm really not convinced that you're telling me the truth, but I think I'll stick around here awhile anyway."

"Do—do you need me to send you some money?"

"No, I found a job today—working for an Amish painter."

Jim grimaced. "Why would you need a job? I just told you, I'll send money if you need it."

"Working for Jacob Weaver will not only provide me with a paycheck, but it'll give me the chance to get to know some of the Amish people. Maybe I'll learn something that might lead me to my real family—if you're telling the truth about that."

Jim massaged his throbbing temple. "How many times do I need to say it, Jimmy? I'm not lying—I kidnapped you from your Amish family, just like I told you yesterday when you called from Maryland." He paused. "Uh, Jimmy—have you told anyone the reason you're there?"

"Not yet. It wouldn't make much sense for me to walk up to some Amish man and blurt out, 'Oh, and by the way, Jimmy Scott's not my real name. I'm actually the kidnapped child of an Amish family who live somewhere in Lancaster County.'"

"You're right, it wouldn't. Besides, they might not like you prying into their personal business. They may even think you're a reporter trying to get a story on them or something, and I'm sure that wouldn't be appreciated."

"I doubt they would think that. It isn't likely that a reporter would take a job working as a painter, Dad."

Jim shifted the phone to his other ear. "What if you do find your real family and they have me arrested, Jimmy? What if I have to spend the rest of my life in jail?"

"Listen, Dad, I've got to go. The battery on my phone is running low, and I need to get back to the B and B and get it charged."

"Okay, but listen, Jimmy—"

The phone went dead, and Jim moaned as he leaned against his seat. A part of him wanted Jimmy to find his real family because it might relieve his guilt. But another part wished he could turn back the hands of time—back to the way things had been when Jimmy was a boy and knew nothing about his past.

CHAPTER 15

$\mathcal{J}$immy had been working for Jacob Weaver a little over a week, and already he felt accepted by his easygoing boss. Jimmy was impressed with how well Jacob got along with all his employees—Amish and English alike.

This morning, Jimmy had been asked to work with Eli Raber, one of Jacob's young Amish painters. They were scheduled to begin painting a one-room schoolhouse in the area. Jacob said he was pleased to have another English painter working for him who owned a truck. That would make it even easier when he had equipment that needed to be hauled to the job sites.

As the two young men headed down a narrow road, jostling up and down in Jimmy's small pickup, Jimmy took the opportunity to get to know Eli better.

"Have you been working for Jacob Weaver long?" he asked.

"Started a year ago. How long have you been in Lancaster County?"

"A little over a week. Got here a few days before Jacob hired me." Jimmy turned on the air conditioning, noting that the cab of his truck had become stuffy on this warm, summer morning.

"You just passin' through, or are ya plannin' to stick around?"

Jimmy shrugged. "It all depends on how things go."

"You mean with your job?"

"That and a few other things."

"Where you stayin'?"

"At a bed-and-breakfast in Strasburg. But I'll need to make other arrangements, since it looks like I might be here awhile."

"My folks have a trailer out behind our place that they've decided to rent. If you're interested, you can come by after work and take a look."

109

Jimmy nodded. "That sounds good to me."

"I think you'll enjoy workin' for Jacob," Eli said.

"He seems like a nice man who is respected by his employees."

Eli nodded, and his blond hair bobbed up and down. "He's highly thought of—not only as a paint contractor but also as the bishop of our community."

Jimmy's mouth dropped open. "Jacob's a bishop?"

"Jah. Has been for a good many years."

"I didn't realize Amish bishops worked as tradesmen."

"Some do. Others farm for a living."

"So they don't get paid for their position in the church?"

"Oh no. When they're not fulfilling their preachin' duties, they work, same as the rest of us Amish men do."

Jimmy pursed his lips. "Guess there's a lot I don't know about the Amish way of life. Would you be willing to teach me?"

Eli smiled and nodded enthusiastically. "Jah, sure. I'll tell ya anything you wanna know."

When Leona heard a vehicle pull into the school yard, she glanced out the window. A small red truck was parked in the graveled lot, and two men were climbing out. She hurried to the other side of the schoolhouse and opened the door. She recognized one of the men as Eli Raber, who worked for her daed. Eli wore a pair of blue jeans and a white short-sleeved shirt, which was typical work attire for an Amish man who hadn't yet joined the church. The other man was an Englisher, also dressed in blue jeans and a white shirt, but he wore a painter's cap on his head. When the two men came up the walk, she realized that the Englisher was the same man she'd met at Caleb and Naomi's store a week ago. Apparently, he'd taken her suggestion and asked her daed about a job. From the looks of the equipment she saw piled in the back of his pickup, he'd obviously been hired.

"Wie geht's, Leona?" Eli asked, stepping onto the porch.

"I'm fine. How are you?"

"Feelin' hot and sticky, but that's to be expected for this time of the year." He turned to the English man at his side. "This is Jimmy Scott.

Your daed recently hired him, and we've come to paint the outside of the schoolhouse."

Leona nodded. "If Papa didn't own his business, the schoolhouse would be painted by my students' parents. But he figured his men could get the job done much quicker."

Jimmy smiled and reached out his hand to her. "We met at the general store in Paradise last week, remember?"

"I do remember, and it's nice to see you again," she said, shaking his hand.

"Thanks for suggesting I speak to your dad about a job. He hired me right away, and I really appreciate it."

Leona was about to comment when Eli said, "How come you're at the schoolhouse today? I didn't figure anyone would be around the place."

"I came to do some cleaning and organizing inside, so I won't be in the way of your painting the outside of the building."

"Will the inside walls need to be painted, too?" Jimmy asked.

She nodded. "Probably so. It's been a few years since they've had a new coat of paint."

"By the time we're done, this old schoolhouse will look as good as new." Jimmy grinned at Leona.

"Well, I'd best be gettin' back to work," she said, feeling kind of flustered. "Give a holler if either of you should need anything."

"Danki," Eli said, before Jimmy could comment.

Leona stepped inside the schoolhouse and quickly shut the door. Leaning her full weight against it, she released a quiet moan. *I can't figure out why I feel so jittery all of a sudden. Maybe it's the heat, or maybe I had too much coffee this morning. Jah, that must be it.*

As Jimmy's paintbrush connected with each wooden board, he thought about the Amish world here in Lancaster County and wondered if he'd really been kidnapped when he was a baby. As farfetched as Dad's story seemed, Jimmy couldn't help but wonder if he had been born Amish what he might be doing at this very moment. Would he have become a farmer like some Amish men in the area, or might he have learned a trade the way Eli and the others who worked for Jacob had done?

I can't believe I'm even considering this, he thought with a shake of his head. *But if there's any possibility that my dad's crazy story about me being Amish is true, then maybe I need to keep looking for answers. I wonder if Eli would know anything about an Amish baby being kidnapped in Lancaster County twenty years ago.*

Jimmy squinted against the hot sun and pulled the bill of his painter's cap over his forehead. *Probably not, since he would have been a baby himself back then. And the Amish schoolteacher doesn't look much older than Eli or me, so she probably wouldn't know anything, either. But if I start asking questions and discover there really was a kidnapping, then Dad might go to jail.* He gripped the paintbrush a little tighter. *Mom wouldn't want that—I know she wouldn't.*

Forcing his thoughts back to the job at hand, Jimmy decided that the best thing to do was get better acquainted with the Amish, learn more of their ways, and ask questions only when he felt the time was right.

Abraham was about to leave Naomi and Caleb's store when he bumped into his best friend, who was heading inside. "*Gut daag,* Jacob. How are things with you?"

"Good day to you, too, friend. Everything is fine and dandy as far as I'm concerned," Jacob said with a grin. "I hired me a new painter last week, and things are workin' out real good."

"Does that mean you've got lots of work these days?"

"Jah, and I'm gettin' more jobs all the time. Counting myself and Arthur, I've got a crew of seven men now, and two of 'em are English."

Abraham stepped to one side. "Guess you've got to have some Englishers so they can haul your equipment around in their rigs."

Jacob nodded. "That's right. As you know, Richard Jamison has worked for me a good many years, and we've been using his van all that time. Jimmy Scott, the new fellow I hired, drives a small pickup, so that will also come in handy."

Abraham was about to comment when Naomi called out to him. "Papa, Edna Yoder's daughter is on the phone. She has a message for Fannie. I figured it would be best if you spoke to her since you're about to head for home and will see Fannie sooner than I will."

"Excuse me, Jacob," Abraham said, giving his friend a quick nod.

"Go right ahead," Jacob replied. "I'm gonna get what I came for and head out to the schoolhouse to see how things are goin' with the paint job there."

Abraham went around the other side of the counter and picked up the telephone. "Abraham Fisher here."

He listened for several seconds to the distraught voice on the other end. "I'm sorry to hear that. I'll be sure to let Fannie know. I'm certain you'll be hearing from her soon."

Abraham hung up the phone and turned to face Naomi, who stood on the other side of the counter with a worried expression on her face. "I don't know how I'm gonna tell my dear wife this distressing news, but her cousin Edna passed away this morning, apparently from a heart attack."

Naomi's eyes filled with tears. "Oh, how sad. Edna was such a fun-loving person. She will surely be missed."

He nodded. "I'd best be on my way. I know Fannie will fall apart when she hears about Edna, and she'll no doubt need a shoulder to cry on." Abraham hurried out the door, whispering a prayer for all of Edna Yoder's family.

"Hello, Papa," Leona said, when her daed entered the schoolhouse shortly before four o'clock. "Did you come to check on the painters?"

He nodded solemnly. "I'll be going by the Fishers' place when I'm done here."

"How come? Are they needing some painting done?"

He shook his head. "When I dropped by Hoffmeirs' General Store a bit ago, I learned that Fannie's cousin Edna died this morning."

Leona gasped. "I'm sorry to hear that."

"I wonder how Gerald and Rachel are taking the news. First they lose their son, and now Gerald's mamm."

A vision of Ezra flashed into Leona's mind, and she winced. *If he were still alive, he'd be at his grandma's funeral service, and I'd be there to offer him support and comfort.*

"Fannie and her cousin Edna were so close," Papa went on to say. "So I'm sure Fannie will take this pretty hard."

"You're probably right." A stab of remorse shot through Leona as she thought about Ezra's funeral. It had taken all her willpower not to break down in front of everyone. Ezra's mamm had been so distraught, and Leona had kept her emotions in check that day to keep from causing Rachel further pain.

"Abraham left the store soon after I arrived, and he was planning to tell Fannie right away," Papa continued. He combed his fingers through the ends of his long beard as he slowly shook his head. "I'll need to go by and see her as well as those in Edna's immediate family. So whenever you decide to go home, would you mind tellin' your mamm what's up?"

"Sure, Papa. Should we hold supper for you?"

He shook his head. "Tell your mamm to keep something warm, but the two of you should go ahead and eat without me. I don't know how long I'll be."

"Okay." Leona pondered the idea of volunteering to go along with her daed, but the thought of trying to offer comfort to the Yoders was too much to bear right now. She figured it would probably bring back a flood of painful memories for her, and even though she knew she would have to work through it on the day of Edna's funeral, she just couldn't deal with that today.

Papa's eyes narrowed as he studied the room. "Looks like these walls are gonna need a good coat of paint after the outside gets done."

"I've been thinking that, too." Leona's gaze went to the front window, where she caught a glimpse of Jimmy taking two cans of paint from the back of his pickup. "Will the same painters you have doing the outside work do the inside, as well, or should we let some of my students' parents do that painting?"

"I'll probably ask Jimmy and Eli to do it, and the parents can do some of the cleaning and repairs you still need to have done." He grinned. "I'm real happy with that new English fellow. He says his daed owns his own painting business out in Washington. Evidently, Jimmy started workin' for his father when he was a teenager. 'Course, the young fellow ain't much more than that now."

"He does look young," Leona agreed, "but he seems to know a lot about painting."

"That's what I thought, too."

"What else do you know about Jimmy Scott?" she questioned. "I mean—other than he comes from the state of Washington."

Papa shrugged and leaned against one of her pupil's desks. "That's about all."

Leona glanced out the window again, but Jimmy was now out of view.

"Guess I'd best be going." Papa leaned over and kissed Leona's forehead. "See you later this evening."

She nodded. "And don't worry about any of your chores in the barn. I'll see that all the animals are fed and watered if you're not back in time."

"Danki, Leona. You're a real good *dochder*." He headed for the door, calling over his shoulder, "And you're gonna make some lucky fellow a mighty good wife some day."

Leona's gaze went to the ceiling. *I'm glad he thinks I'm a good daughter, but I sure hope he gives up soon on that idea of me being any kind of a wife—good or otherwise.*

Sweat beaded on Jimmy's forehead and trickled onto his cheeks. This hot, sticky weather was a lot harder to deal with than the milder climate he was used to on the West Coast. Even during the warmest days of summer, they never had to endure humidity and heat such as this. He wondered if the people who lived here ever got used to this kind of weather.

He reached into his back pocket and pulled out a rag. He wiped his damp face with it and groaned. "Guess I'd better head for that water pump out behind the schoolhouse," he told Eli, who kept right on painting. Apparently, the man didn't mind the heat at all. "I drank my last bottle of water when I ate lunch. Sure wish I'd thought to bring a few more along."

"The water from the pump will have to do then," Eli said, moving past Jimmy to grab another bucket of paint. "I can't believe we're on our second coat already. These old boards sure have soaked up the paint."

Jimmy was about to head around back when Leona showed up carrying a thermos, two paper cups, and a few cookies. "You two have been working hard all day, and I thought you might want to take a break," she said.

Jimmy nodded appreciatively, noticing the way her green eyes sparkled when she smiled. Apparently, she didn't mind the heat, either. "Thanks."

"Danki, Leona," Eli said with a nod.

"You're welcome." She took a seat on the top porch step, opened the thermos, and poured them each a cup of cold tea. Then she removed the plastic wrap from the cookies and offered those to the men. "If I'd known anyone was coming to paint the schoolhouse today, I'd have brought more treats. These cookies were supposed to be my snack, but I've had all I can eat."

Jimmy took two cookies and popped one into his mouth. "Umm. . . they're really good. Peanut butter is my favorite kind." He took a seat beside Leona, but Eli remained standing as he gulped down his iced tea.

"This tea is real *gut*," the Amish man said.

"The word *gut* means 'good,' right?" Jimmy asked.

"Yes, it does," Leona replied before Eli could answer.

"I took a year of German in high school, so I know a few words." Jimmy grinned. "Of course, I'm not very fluent in the German language, and I don't understand most of the Pennsylvania Dutch that you Amish speak."

"I think it's best learned by listening," Eli said. "Hang around me awhile, and by the end of summer, you'll have learned a lot more of our *Deitsch*."

CHAPTER 16

$\mathcal{W}$hen Abraham entered the house, he found Fannie and the twins sitting at the kitchen table eating pieces of apple crumb pie with tall glasses of milk. It was a happy scene. He hated to interrupt, but the news he had to share couldn't wait.

He cleared his throat twice, and Fannie glanced over her shoulder. "I didn't expect you'd be back so soon, Abraham. Figured you and Naomi might get to gabbing or that you'd want to spend a little time with those *kinskinner* of yours."

Abraham moved over to the table and pulled out a chair. "Sarah and Susan were helping their mamm in the store, but I don't know where Naomi's other four kinner were today."

"Nate and Josh were probably out behind the store playing," Titus spoke up. "They like to hang out there and pretend like they're carin' for the buggy horse they keep in the small corral."

"That's so they don't have to do any work in the store," Timothy put in. "I'd like to see those two follow us around in the fields all day. A couple of hours out there in the hot sun, and they'd understand what hard work's all about."

"Josh is only eleven, and Nate just turned nine," Fannie said with a shake of her head. "They should be allowed to play once in a while. Besides, their daed owns the general store. He doesn't farm for a living."

"Looks like you two are pretty good at finding ways to take a break." Abraham leaned over and poked Titus on the back. "For a couple of strong teenagers, you can sure figure out ways to get out of doin' a full day's work."

"Ah, Papa, we ain't sloughing off," Timothy said with a grunt. "We got hot out there in the fields and decided to come up to the house to get somethin' cold to drink."

"Jah, and when Mama saw us standin' out back at the pump, she invited us inside for pie and milk," his twin brother added.

Abraham smiled despite the sad news he had to share. "I think you've had enough of a break for now. If you eat more of your mamm's pie, you won't want supper."

"I'll be able to eat again by supper time," Timothy announced.

"Even so, I want you to get back to work, because there's a lot to be done in the fields yet today."

Titus slid his chair back and stood. "You comin', Papa?"

Abraham shook his head. "I've got something I need to say to your mamm first."

The boys gave him a questioning look, but neither one said a word. They gulped down the last of their milk, grabbed their straw hats from the pegs by the back door, and rushed out of the house.

Fannie turned to Abraham and smiled. "What'd you need to speak to me about?"

Abraham took hold of her hand. "I'm afraid I've got bad news."

Fannie's face registered alarm. "What is it, husband?"

"While I was at the store, I received word that Edna had passed away this morning. They think she had a heart attack."

Fannie covered her mouth and gasped. "*Nee, nee*, she can't be dead. I saw Edna last week at a quilting bee, and she looked just fine."

Abraham sat there a few minutes waiting for his announcement to register fully. He knew his wife well enough to realize that she needed more time to process this distressing news.

After a few minutes, Fannie spoke again. "Ever since I moved to Pennsylvania, Edna and I have been best friends. How can I go on without my dear cousin?" Her chin trembled as tears gathered in the corners of her eyes.

Abraham quickly wrapped his arms around her. "You've been through worse in years past, and you'll get through this, too. With God's help, we can survive any of life's tragedies."

"I appreciate you goin' to the Fishers' place with me," Leona's daed said as the two of them headed down the road in his buggy the following day.

"Since Mom's coming down with a cold and wasn't feeling well enough to accompany you, she asked me to come along in her place."

Papa glanced over at her and smiled. "I know I've said this before, but you're gonna make some man a real good wife someday."

Leona's face heated, and she quickly changed the subject. "When you went over to see Fannie yesterday, did you feel that she had accepted her cousin's death?"

"Afraid not," Papa said with a shake of his head. "Fannie was so distraught, and nothing either Abraham or I said seemed to offer much comfort, so I thought I'd try again today. We need to get her feeling as if she can cope better before Edna's funeral service."

"Now that she's had a few days to mourn, maybe she's calmed down some."

He nodded. "I'm eager to know if that's the case."

"How are Ezra's folks coping with Edna's death?" she asked.

"As well as can be expected. I spoke with Gerald's sister, Gretchen, too, and she's holding up pretty well."

They pulled into the Fishers' yard then, and Papa parked the buggy near the barn. Leona reached behind the seat and retrieved the wicker basket she'd brought. Then she climbed down from the passenger's side. As soon as Papa had the horse tied to the hitching rail, they strode toward the house, arm in arm.

Mary Ann greeted them at the back door. "I'm glad you've come," she whispered, glancing over her shoulder. "Mama Fannie's not been herself since heard about Edna, and I'm worried about her."

"Where is she now, and where's Abraham?" Leona's daed asked.

"Papa's out in the fields with my brothers. Mama Fannie's in there huddled on the sofa." Mary Ann motioned to the door that led to the living room. "I found her that way when I got home from the quilt shop awhile ago."

"Maybe she's tired and needed a nap," Leona suggested.

Mary Ann shook her head. "She's heartsick over losing Edna."

"I'll have a word with her." Papa turned to Leona. "Why don't you stay in the kitchen with Mary Ann? You two can visit while I speak to Fannie."

"That might be best." Mary Ann pulled out a chair at the table. "I'll pour us some lemonade."

Papa left the room, and Leona took a seat. "How are things at the quilt shop?"

"Busy as usual for this time of the year. Abby says she's glad she hired me to help out because there's just too much work for her and Stella to do by themselves. Besides, once the school year begins, Stella will be back in school and won't be able to help Abby at all." Mary Ann went to the refrigerator and took out a pitcher of lemonade, which she placed on the table. Bringing two glasses with her, she sat in the chair across from Leona. "I'm sorry you haven't made it to any of the young people's functions so far this summer. I think it would be good for you and help take your mind off—"

"Edna's funeral will be hard for many to get through," Leona interrupted. She didn't want to talk about her going to any young people's functions.

Mary Ann reached over and patted Leona's hand. "It's bound to bring back memories of Ezra's funeral, but you'll get through it, Leona."

"Let's talk about something else, okay?"

"Jah, sure. So, how's the painting on the schoolhouse comin' along?"

"Good. The outside's done, and Jimmy and Eli will be starting on the inside tomorrow or the next day."

Mary Ann filled the glasses with lemonade and handed one to Leona. "Isn't Jimmy that English fellow your daed hired?"

Leona nodded and took a sip of her cool, tangy drink.

"I wasn't working at the quilt shop the day he came into the general store, but Naomi told me later that he reminded her of someone."

"Really? Who?"

"She didn't say. Just thought he looked kind of familiar."

"I don't see how he could be anyone she knows," Leona said. "He's from the state of Washington."

"I've heard it said that everyone has a double somewhere." Mary Ann glanced at the door leading to the living room. "Sure hope your daed can get Mama Fannie calmed down."

"If anyone can, it will be him." Leona knew it was wrong to be full of *hochmut*, yet she couldn't help but feel a little pride in her daed's abilities to minister in such a gentle, caring way.

"I need to run over to Naomi's place," Abraham told his twin boys after they had quit work in the fields for the day. "Would one of you let your mamm know I'll be a few minutes late for supper?"

"Sure, Papa," Titus said with a nod.

"How come you're goin' over to our big sister's?" Timothy questioned. "Won't ya be seein' her at the funeral in a few days?"

"Jah, but I'm needing something from Naomi right now." Abraham headed for the stable to get one of their buggies. He didn't say anything to the boys, but the reason he was going over to his oldest daughter's was to see if she had a homeopathic remedy that might help Fannie get through the funeral service. Naomi often used natural remedies, and she had told him once about a particular one that was used for calming. He figured it was best not to mention it to the boys. No point getting them all worried about their mamm.

Half an hour later, Abraham guided his horse and buggy up to Caleb's barn. He entered the house through the back door, and seeing no one in the kitchen, he cupped his hands around his mouth and called, "Are ya at home, Naomi?"

"Mama and Papa aren't back from the store yet; I'm upstairs, and so are the two younger ones."

Abraham recognized Susan's voice. "You comin' down, or should I come up there?"

"Come on up," she hollered. "I'm busy changing sheets."

Wonder why she'd be changing sheets at this time of the day? Abraham made his way into the hall and up the flight of stairs. He found Susan in Naomi and Caleb's room stripping sheets off the bed.

"What's goin' on?" He grimaced as the sour smell of *kotz* greeted him.

"Kevin and Millie both came down with the flu and have been throwing up all morning," she replied. "So I stayed home from the store to care for them, and Sarah, Josh, and Nate went in with the folks today. Grandma Hoffmeir usually watches the younger ones, but she's got the flu, too."

"Sorry to hear they're sick. I take it the kinner must have been sleeping in this room."

Susan nodded and pushed a strand of ash-blond hair away from her face where it had worked its way from under her kapp.

"How come they weren't in their own beds?" he questioned.

"They were, but they both missed the bucket and ended up vomiting on their sheets. While I was changing their beds, I put them in Mama and Papa's room." She frowned. "By the time I was done and had their beds made up again, they'd thrown up in here, too."

Abraham shook his head, remembering the days of raising his own kinner and thinking about how when one had come down with the flu, the others usually followed. "I dropped by to see if your mamm has a homeopathic remedy that might help Fannie get through Edna's funeral without falling apart," he said. "Do you know where she keeps that kind of thing?"

Susan nodded toward the bathroom across the hall. "It could either be in the medicine chest or on the top shelf of the linen closet. I think Mama keeps some remedies there."

"Danki. I'll take a look." Abraham rushed out of the bedroom, anxious for some fresh air. The disagreeable odor of kotz had always made his stomach churn.

The bathroom didn't smell much better, giving proof that the children had probably gotten sick in there, as well. He searched quickly through the medicine chest but found no homeopathic remedies.

Frustrated, Abraham hurried into the hall and opened the linen closet. He discovered a stack of towels on the bottom shelf. There were a few bottles of aspirin and a jar of petroleum jelly on the top shelf, but he didn't see any remedies there, either. He was about to give up when he noticed a colorful piece of cloth sticking out of a box, also on the top shelf. Curious, he pulled it out, and his breath caught in his throat. *Why, this was Zach's quilt! I haven't seen it since the night before he was kidnapped, when I tucked him into bed, but I would recognize this anywhere.*

"Papa, what are you doing?"

Abraham whirled around and faced Naomi. He hadn't heard her come up the stairs. "I was looking for a homeopathic remedy that might calm Fannie's nerves." He thrust the quilt out to her. "Is—is this Zach's?"

Naomi nodded as tears clouded her vision. She reached out a trembling hand and touched the edge of her brother's quilt. "Jah, Papa, it's his."

His steely blue eyes seemed to bore right through her. "How'd you get this, and how long have you had it?" he demanded.

A sense of guilt, mixed with deep regret, pricked Naomi's heart. "Abby gave it to me when she returned from her trip to Montana several years ago. She said Elizabeth, the woman she'd stayed with there, had found it in a thrift store somewhere in the state of Washington."

"But Abby came back to Pennsylvania fourteen years ago. If you've had Zach's quilt that long, why have you been keeping it from me?" Papa's hand trembled as he held the quilt against his chest.

"I—I was afraid of getting your hopes up."

"Why would I get my hopes up?" He grimaced, and a shadow passed across his face. "My son's been missing for twenty years, Naomi. Don't ya think I had the right to know the quilt had been found?"

"Jah. You had the right. I was wrong." Tears streamed down her cheeks, and she hung her head, unable to meet his piercing gaze. At the time Naomi had decided to keep the quilt hidden from her daed, she had felt that she was doing the right thing. She'd planned to put the quilt in her baby's room but had changed her mind and stuck it in the linen closet instead. She'd almost forgotten about it until now. "I should have shown it to you right away. It would have saved us both this awkward, painful moment," she murmured, lifting her head.

Her daed blinked a couple of times as though he was struggling not to cry. His protruding Adam's apple bobbed up and down. "Do you suppose this means Zach is dead?"

She gasped. "Oh no, Papa! Surely, it doesn't mean that. Abby told me once that she thought the man who took Zach must have sold the quilt to the thrift shop—probably to get rid of any evidence that he'd taken an Amish baby."

"Maybe so. Maybe not." Papa buried his face in the folds of the quilt and sniffed deeply. "All these years I've prayed for Zach, asking the Lord to watch over my boy and bring him safely back home." His shoulders trembled, and his voice cracked. "I—I guess God's answer was no. Otherwise, your little bruder would have returned to us by now."

Naomi didn't know how to respond. Maybe Papa was right. God's answer to their prayers for Zach's safe return must have been no.

"The time for talking about my missing son must end right now."

Papa stared hard at Naomi, and his eyes glazed over. "Zach's gone for good, and it only hurts to keep bringing him up. It's over and done with, and I'm not going to discuss him with you or anyone else ever again." He threw the quilt on the floor, whirled around, and hurried down the stairs.

Naomi released a sob as she bent over to retrieve the small covering. "I'm so sorry, Papa. Sorry for all the grief I've brought to this family."

CHAPTER 17

*L*eona scurried about the kitchen helping Edna's daughter, Gretchen, and several other women serve the funeral dinner. She noticed that Fannie, wearing a placid expression, kept busy filling platters and plates for the younger women to carry outside to the tables. During the funeral service, which had been held in the barn, and again at the graveside committal, Fannie had appeared to be in control of her emotions.

It must be due to Papa's visit with her the other day, Leona thought. Her daed seemed to have a calming effect on everyone—herself included. She certainly needed some calming today, after spending time with Ezra's family and, despite her determination not to do so, reliving the day of Ezra's funeral in her mind.

Leona's thoughts halted when she glanced across the room and noticed Naomi sitting at the kitchen table and staring at a bowl of salad greens as if in a daze. Surely, Naomi couldn't be taking Edna's death harder than Fannie was. Edna wasn't a blood relative of Naomi's, and as far as Leona knew, Naomi had never been that close to her stepmother's cousin.

Leona wiped her hands on a dish towel and moved across the room. She stopped behind Naomi's chair and placed one hand on the woman's trembling shoulder. "You doin' okay?"

Naomi's only reply was a quick shake of her head.

"Would you like to go outside for a while? The fresh air might do you some good."

"I'm not sure the air's so fresh out there, but I guess it must be less stuffy than it is in here," Abby interjected as she passed by the table. "I think the men have all been served their meal now, so why don't the three of us find a place to eat our lunch where we can visit?"

Naomi made no move to get up. "I'm really not hungry."

"Oh, but you've got to eat," Leona insisted. "Once you walk up to that table and see all the good food that's been provided for this meal, I'm sure you'll find something that will appeal."

"Jah, okay." Naomi released a sigh, pushed her chair aside, and followed Abby and Leona outside.

The other women had already gathered at the tables that had been set up in the yard, so Leona filled her plate and found them an empty table under the shade of a leafy maple tree. Abby sat beside Naomi, and Leona took the bench across from them.

"Your mamm seems to be doing well today," Leona said to Abby.

Abby nodded. "Abraham gave her some kind of a natural remedy he got from the health food store. Between that and whatever your daed said to her when he stopped by their place yesterday afternoon, Mom's been able to get through the day pretty well."

Leona glanced at Naomi, wishing she knew what was troubling her. *Should I come right out and ask?*

"Abraham said he stopped by your place the other day," Abby said, turning to Naomi. "He mentioned that Millie and Kevin had come down with the flu."

"Jah."

"Are they still sick?" Leona asked. She hadn't seen Naomi's two youngest children here today.

"They're doing some better, but Sarah stayed home with the sick ones so that Susan, Josh, and Nate could come to the funeral with Caleb and me," Naomi replied.

Abby's wrinkled forehead revealed her obvious concern. "I hope no one else in your family comes down with the flu. You've got enough to keep you busy this summer without having to care for sick kinner."

Naomi stared at her plate full of food but made no effort to take a bite, and she gave no reply to Abby's comment.

Something is troubling her, and I've got a hunch it's more than sorrow over Edna Yoder's passing. Leona, having experienced her own sort of pain today, could hardly stand to see the gloomy expression on Naomi's face. She was about to express her concerns when Naomi scooted off the bench and stood. "I think I'll take a walk down to the creek." She hurried off before either Leona or Abby could say a word.

Naomi trembled as she knelt on the grass near the edge of the water. *Papa will hardly look at me today. I was wrong to keep the truth from him about Zach's quilt. I should have told him as soon as Abby gave it to me. Will I ever learn?* Tears stung the back of her eyes, and she gulped on a sob. *If I could change the past, I surely would—starting with that horrible day I left Zach sitting on the picnic table.*

Naomi felt the pressure of someone's hand on her shoulder, and she turned her head. Leona and Abby stood behind her, both wearing looks of concern.

"What's wrong, Naomi? Why'd you run off like that?" Leona questioned. "Why are you crying?"

"I've wronged my daed, and now he's upset with me," she said with a moan.

Abby knelt beside her, and Leona did the same. "What did you do? Or would you rather not say?" Abby asked.

Naomi swallowed hard and fought for control. "Papa dropped by our house yesterday, and he discovered Zach's quilt."

Abby's mouth dropped open. "How did that happen? I thought you had decided not to show it to him."

"I put it in a box in the linen closet some time ago, never thinking Papa would have any reason to look there."

Leona toyed with the strings on her kapp as she stared at the ground in front of her. "Maybe I should go. This sounds like something I'm not supposed to hear."

Naomi shook her head. "You don't have to go. The secret's out now, so I suppose it doesn't matter who knows."

Abby reached for Naomi's hand and gave it a gentle squeeze. "I'm sure once your daed thinks things through he will realize why you didn't tell him that I'd given you the baby quilt."

"How'd you end up with Naomi's little brother's quilt?" Leona asked, giving Abby a curious look.

Abby quickly relayed how she had acquired the quilt, and then Naomi explained that the reason she hadn't wanted Papa to know about it was because she was afraid seeing the quilt and not knowing where Zach was would have opened old wounds. "And now Papa wants everyone to stop talking about Zach. He thinks it's time to lay the past to rest once and for all."

"I understand that reasoning." Leona put her arm around Naomi and gave her a hug. "Things will work out between you and your daed. I'll be praying that they will." She stood and brushed a chunk of grass off her skirt. "I think I'll head on back to the house now. I need to speak with Ezra's folks again before my family heads for home."

"Danki for your concern," Naomi said with a nod. It came as no surprise to her that the bishop's daughter would have such compassion and understanding.

When Jimmy finished work for the day, he decided to drive down a few of the roads he hadn't been on yet so he could take more pictures and continue his search for an Amish farm that sold root beer.

He stopped at a covered bridge near Highway 222 and took several shots. Then, seeing nothing else that interested him, he headed up Highway 23. He'd only gone a short distance when he spotted a sign nailed to a tree near the end of a driveway that advertised root beer. He turned in, and his pickup bounced along the narrow, graveled road until he came to a makeshift stand several feet from the house. Jimmy turned off the engine and got out of his truck. *Was Dad telling me the truth? Could this be the place he told me about?*

He walked up to the stand and, seeing no one in sight, gave the bell on the wooden counter a good shake.

A few minutes later, a freckle-faced Amish boy came out of the house and slipped behind the counter. "Are ya wantin' a jug of root beer?" he asked with a friendly grin.

"Do you sell it by the glass?"

The boy nodded. "Got some paper cups right here. You want a small one or large?"

"Uh—large, I guess." Jimmy paid the boy, and while he waited for his root beer to be served, his gaze roamed over the spacious farmyard where cows grazed in the pasture and chickens ran about clucking and pecking at one another. *Could this have been my home? Is it possible that I was stolen from this yard?*

"Here ya go."

Jimmy snapped his attention back to the boy. He reached for the paper cup and took a drink. "This is real tasty root beer."

"My daed makes it."

Could your daed be my daed? Jimmy shifted his weight and took another swallow of the mellow, tasty beverage. "I—uh—need information."

"Are ya lost?" the boy asked with a tilt of his head. "Some folks who stop by here needin' information are on the wrong road and don't know how to get to where they're goin'."

"No, I'm not lost."

"Then what do ya need to know?"

"I was wondering if—has anyone here ever lost a baby?"

The boy blinked a couple of times and then gave a quick nod.

Jimmy set the paper cup on the wooden counter and wiped his sweaty palms along the sides of his jeans. "Really? How long ago?"

" 'Bout a year, I'd say. Lost my baby goat when its mamm wouldn't feed it. The poor thing up and died."

At first Jimmy felt irritation. Then he realized the boy must have misunderstood his question. "I wasn't talking about an animal. I was referring to a baby boy—about a year old."

The child's auburn-colored eyebrows lifted so high they nearly disappeared under the brim of his tattered straw hat. "Is somebody missin' a baby?"

"Not now. It was about twenty years ago. A man supposedly went to a root beer stand and kidnapped an Amish baby."

The boy looked at Jimmy like he'd taken leave of his senses. "You sure you got the right place? Ain't no baby been taken from here. If there was, my folks sure woulda said somethin' about it."

"I guess I must have the wrong place." Jimmy turned and started toward his truck as a feeling of frustration threatened to knock him to the ground. Was all this hunting for an Amish farm selling root beer a waste of his time? Was there any point in continuing to look?

"Don't ya want the rest of your root beer?" the boy called after him.

"No thanks. I'm not thirsty anymore." *Maybe what I'd better do is call Dad again. If he really did kidnap me, then he's got to give me some better answers. And if he's made the whole story up, then he'd better tell me the truth.*

CHAPTER 18

Jimmy climbed into his truck and pushed his painter's hat down on his head as he waited for Eli to come out of the house. A lot had changed for him in the last few weeks. Thanks to Eli's parents, Jimmy now rented a small trailer at the back of their property. And because of his new friend's patient teaching, he had learned a few words of Pennsylvania Dutch and was beginning to feel more comfortable with his surroundings here in Amish country. He and Eli had finished up the job on the schoolhouse a few weeks ago, and then, with the other men in Jacob's crew, they had painted a couple of houses and the outside of a gift store in Lititz. Today they would begin work on Mark Stauffer's barn.

Jimmy had learned from Eli that Mark was married to Nancy, one of Naomi Hoffmeir's sisters. He'd been told that the couple had three children and lived next door to Mark's folks, Elmer and Mandy. It seemed like everyone in this community was related somehow.

"Guder mariye," Eli said, climbing into Jimmy's pickup.

"Guder mariye to you, too." Jimmy grinned. "Did I say 'good morning' right?"

Eli nodded. "You're catchin' on real good to the Deitsch."

Feeling rather pleased with himself, Jimmy turned on the engine and steered his vehicle down the driveway. A short time later, they arrived at the Stauffers' place.

Jimmy noticed right away that the barn had already been scraped and primed. With a crew of five painters working on the building, including the bishop, it should take them only a few days to complete the job.

Jacob gave everyone instructions, telling the men to begin work on the shaded side of the barn. He asked his son, Arthur, to work with

Jimmy on the back side, while Eli and Richard painted the doors and trim around the windows.

"I'll climb the forty-foot ladder and do the high spots," Jacob announced. "That way, I can look down and see how things are goin'."

"Why don't you let me or one of the younger men do that, Pop?" Arthur suggested. "You're gettin' too old to be up on a tall ladder."

Jacob leveled his son with a most determined look and shook his head. "I ain't old, and since I'm the boss, I'll decide who gets to do what."

Jimmy bit back a chuckle and looked the other way. He got a kick out of the bishop's spunky attitude. *I'll bet my dad will be that way when he gets to be Jacob's age. He has always liked to be the one in control.*

Thinking about Dad caused Jimmy to worry a bit. He'd tried several times in the last few days to reach his dad by phone, and all he ever got was the answering machine at home or voice mail on his cell. *I hope he's not on another drinking bender. If he is. . . Oh, man, I wish I'd thought to bring Ed's number with me. Maybe I'll give Allen a call when I get off work today and ask him to check up on Dad.*

Jim rolled over in bed, grabbed the extra pillow beside his head, and covered his ears. Even so, his alarm clock continued to blare in his ear. He knew it was 6:00 a.m., and he also knew he was supposed to leave for work in one hour. But he didn't know how he would make it. He'd been drinking steadily for nearly a week—sometimes not even bothering to come home at night. Last night, he'd finally sobered up enough to realize he needed a bath and a good night's sleep, so he'd left his van parked at The Gold Fish Tavern and called a cab to take him home.

I've missed a week's worth of work, too, he thought ruefully. *But then I'm sure Ed's been keeping our jobs going.* He moaned and swung one leg, then the other, over the side of the bed. "Oh, my head's killing me."

Jim rubbed his blurry eyes, and as his vision began to focus, his gaze came to rest on the picture sitting on the dresser across the room. It was the last picture of Jim, Linda, and Jimmy together, taken a year before Linda died.

He grimaced, remembering how he'd put up a fuss when Linda told him about the appointment she'd made with the portrait studio across town. He'd said he was too busy to go but had finally relented when Linda reminded him that she might not have much longer to live. "I was such a lousy husband. Never could do anything right, and I guess I still can't."

He thought of all the times Linda had tried to get him to go to church, and how her friends, Beth and Eric Walters, had attempted to be his friend after she'd died. But he'd continued to reject all forms of religion, and he sure didn't need any Bible-thumping friends of Linda's to hold his hand.

A feeling of sadness and deep regret swept over him like a heavy fog as he thought about Jimmy and how he had failed him, too. *If I hadn't kidnapped the boy when he was a baby, he wouldn't be on a quest to find his rightful heritage now, and I wouldn't have to worry about the possibility of going to jail.*

Jim stood on rubbery legs and ambled across the room toward his closet. *I don't care whether he believes me about the kidnapping or not. Maybe if he thinks I made up the whole story, he'll stop searching for his real parents and come home.*

Feeling the need for some kind of comfort, he halted when he reached his dresser and grabbed the half-empty bottle of beer he'd left sitting there the night before. "At least I've got one friend I can count on," he mumbled as he lifted the bottle to his parched lips.

As Leona drove her horse and buggy down Harristown Road toward Nancy and Mark Stauffer's place, the sounds of summer engulfed her. The buzz of insects, the *click-click-click* of sprinklers, and the continual chirp of birds overhead—all brought a sense of peace she hadn't experienced in many days.

She thought about the conversation she'd had with Naomi when she stopped by Hoffmeirs' General Store yesterday afternoon. Naomi had mentioned that things were still strained between her and her daed, and she said she was sure that, even though many years ago Abraham had said he'd forgiven her for leaving Zach alone, he'd never truly let it go.

"So much pain and distress some people must endure." She inhaled deeply, savoring the pleasant aroma of freshly cut hay. Then she glanced across the road to see where the smell came from. There she spotted the newly mowed field bordering the Stauffers' place, and in the distance, she could see their stately white house with the faded red barn sitting behind it.

As Leona drew closer, she caught sight of Papa's crew painting on one side of the barn. She directed the horse onto the graveled driveway and stopped near the house where there would be less chance of getting paint on the buggy.

Jimmy waved to her, and she lifted her hand in response. Then she climbed down from the buggy, secured the horse to a maple tree, and headed for the barn.

"What brings you over here today?" Jimmy asked as she drew near.

"I brought my daed's lunch. He left it on the kitchen counter when he went to work this morning."

"Pop must have been in a hurry to get over here and begin working on Mark's barn," Arthur interjected as he came around the corner carrying a bucket of paint.

"I think so," Leona said with a nod. "Where is our daed, anyhow?"

Arthur turned and pointed to a ladder leaning against one side of the barn. "Up there."

Leona shielded her eyes from the glare of the sun and tipped her head to get a better look. There stood Papa on the third-to-the-last rung of the ladder with his paintbrush zipping back and forth faster than she could blink. She sucked in her breath. "*Ach*, my! He shouldn't be on that tall ladder."

"He insisted on doing the high painting," Arthur said, shaking his head. "I tried to talk him out of it, but he reminded me, like always, that he's the boss."

Leona knew how stubborn her daed could be when it came to anyone telling him how to run his business—including his only son.

"Jacob's doing fine so far." Jimmy's long legs filled the space between them. "I'm sure he would have let one of the younger men do the high painting if he didn't think he was capable of doing it himself."

Leona looked over at Jimmy and was about to comment when

her daed hollered down, "Can someone run up to the house and see if Nancy's got some *weschp* spray? There's a wasp's nest up here, and some of them critters have been buzzin' me real good." The ladder wobbled as he lifted his straw hat from his head and waved it in the air. "Get away from me, you crazy weschp!"

"Be careful, Papa, the ladder is—" Leona gasped as the ladder lurched and her daed lost his grip, falling straight to the ground.

Every man dropped his brush and rushed to their boss's side, but Leona just stood there, too numb to move.

"Pop! Can ya hear me?" Arthur looked at Leona with a pained expression. "He's out cold, and there's blood coming out of his ears. Someone with a cell phone had better call 9-1-1!"

CHAPTER 19

"$\mathcal{D}$ear Lord, why did You allow such a terrible thing to happen? How will we ever get through this?" Leona lamented as she stood in front of her bedroom window and stared out at the gray skies. It had been raining steadily since yesterday evening. Leona was exhausted, and her eyes burned from lack of sleep. The dismal, dark clouds that hid the sun matched her melancholy mood to a T this morning. She leaned against the window casing, tears coursing down her cheeks as she thought about that fateful morning two weeks ago when their lives had been changed in one split second—the moment Papa took his hand off the ladder to swat at a buzzing wasp. Jimmy Scott had been the one to call for help, using his cell phone. Then he'd covered her daed with a blanket and instructed everyone not to move him. After the ambulance took Papa away, Jimmy had given Leona, her mother, and her brother a ride to the hospital. The rest of the day had been spent waiting and praying for some word on Papa's condition. Leona's two older sisters, who lived in Kentucky, had been notified and said they would come as soon as they were able to secure transportation. Jimmy had remained at Leona's side the entire day, although she barely remembered anything he'd said to her.

Leona closed her eyes as she relived that day in the hospital, after all the tests had been done and the doctor had taken the family aside to give them his prognosis. . .

"Jacob has had a severe trauma to the brain, and there's a good deal of swelling," Dr. Collins told the family as they stood just inside the door of Papa's room. "Amazingly enough, he has no broken bones—just scrapes and bruises

on his arms and legs, but the blow to his head seems to have caused an acute memory lapse that has taken him all the way back to his childhood."

"Will my husband ever be the same?" Mom asked as she clutched the doctor's arm. "Please say he will recover from this."

Dr. Collins's gaze went to Papa lying in the bed with his eyes closed. Then he looked back at Leona's mamm. "There's no way of knowing at this point, Mrs. Weaver. Once the swelling goes down, Jacob could regain all or part of his memory. Or he might remain this way for the rest of his life."

"We need to pray for a miracle," Arthur interjected. "Jah, that's what we surely need."

Mom nodded as tears matted her lashes and trickled onto her cheeks. "God is able to do all things, and if it's His will, then He'll make my husband whole again."

Leona leaned against the wall with her arms folded and her lips pressed together, her eyes closed. God, You could have prevented this from happening. Why didn't You? Don't You care about Papa? Doesn't it matter that he is Your servant and so many people depend on him?

"Jacob will need to go through some therapy here at the hospital before he's released," Dr. Collins continued. "And of course, there are things you can do at home to help him adjust."

Mom nodded once more. "We'll do all we can."

Leona clenched her fists so tightly that her nails dug into her palms. Adjust? How can my daed adjust to anything when he thinks he's a little boy?

Leona shuddered and moved away from the window, allowing her thoughts to return to the present. She was thankful Papa was alive. However, the thought of him spending the rest of his days as a child in a man's body was unthinkable. How could he run his painting business or do the chores he normally did around their place? And what of his position as bishop? He could hardly preach or minister to the people if he thought like a child. Poor, confused Papa didn't know he'd ever been their bishop or that he owned a successful painting business. He thought his wife was his mamm, and he believed Leona and her brother were his siblings. He hadn't known his oldest daughters, Peggy or

Rebecca, at all when they'd come to visit soon after the accident.

Leona held her arms rigid at her side. Resentment welled up in her soul like a cancer. She fought the churning sensation in her stomach. *Unless God provides a miracle, Papa might never know any of us again.* She stumbled across the room, flopped onto her bed, and covered her mouth in an effort to stop the tears. *It isn't fair. This terrible tragedy never should have happened!*

Jimmy had just stepped out of his truck and placed a bucket of paint on the porch of Norman Fisher's house when his cell phone rang. He removed it from the clip on his belt and lifted it to his ear. "Hello."

"Hi, Jimmy, it's Dad. I—I haven't heard from you in a while, and I was getting worried."

"You were worried? Do you know how many times I've tried to call you? And all I ever got was the answering machine at home or your voice mail on the cell."

"Sorry, but I wasn't up to taking any calls."

"Have you been sick?"

"Yeah—well, sort of."

Jimmy groaned. "You've been on another drinking spree, haven't you, Dad?"

"So what if I have? It's my life, and I don't need you or Ed telling me what to do."

Jimmy knew Dad's foreman was aware of his drinking problem, and he figured Ed might be getting tired of covering for Dad and had probably given him a lecture about how he might lose his business if he didn't straighten up. *Guess there's not much point in me doing the same, because it's obvious that he isn't going to listen. Maybe Allen was right when he said Dad might have to hit rock bottom before he ever admits he has a problem or is willing to seek help.*

"Are you still there, Jimmy?"

"I'm here."

"How are things going? Have you found your Amish family yet?"

"No, but I did find an Amish farm selling root beer, and the kid looked at me like I was nuts when I asked about a stolen baby."

"You must have been at the wrong place."

"Yeah, well, what's the *right* place, Dad?"

"I—I don't know. I told you before that I was almost in a daze that day, and I don't remember what road I was on, or even what part of Lancaster County I was in."

"Are you sure you're not making this story up to confuse me?"

"Why would I do that? I put my neck in the noose when I admitted that I'd kidnapped you." There was a pause, and he added, "I—I've been keeping this secret for twenty years, Jimmy, and it's taken a toll on me."

"On you? What about the family you took me from?" Jimmy's own words echoed in his head as he allowed the truth to sink in. *Dad really did kidnap me. He wouldn't be so worried about going to jail if he hadn't committed the crime, and he wouldn't be going on long drinking benders if he wasn't dealing with guilt and fear.*

"It's true, isn't it?" he squeaked. "You stole me from an Amish farm twenty years ago."

"That's what I've been trying to tell you. I—I did it for your mom. I did it because I thought it was meant to be."

"How could stealing a child ever be right or 'meant to be'?" Jimmy's voice shook with unbridled emotion as he struggled with the anger he felt toward the man he'd thought, all but the past few weeks of his life, was his dad.

"Wh–what are you going to—to do, Jimmy?" Dad's tone sounded desperate, and his words were shaky.

"I'm going to stick around Lancaster County awhile longer."

"To look for your family?"

"That and to help the Weaver family."

"Who is this Weaver family, and why do they need your help?"

Jimmy quickly shared the story of how Jacob had fallen off the ladder and how his head injury had left him with amnesia. "Jacob's home from the hospital now," he ended by saying. "And since his son wants me to keep painting for them, I'll be around to help the Weaver family deal with Jacob's injury." Jimmy pulled a rag from his back pocket and wiped the perspiration from his forehead.

"So this is the Amish fella who hired you to paint for him?"

"Right. The doctor told Jacob's family that, short of a miracle, he might never fully recover."

"That's too bad, Jimmy. You're a good kid for wanting to help."

"I'm not a kid anymore. I just turned twenty-one, remember?" A sudden, sinking feeling hit Jimmy with such force he thought he might topple over. "You don't even really know how old I am or when I was born, do you, Dad?"

"I—I don't know the exact day you were born, but your Amish sister said you had recently turned one, so when I had your phony birth certificate made up, I asked my friend to give you an April birthday."

Phony birth certificate? A made-up April birthday? Jimmy sank to the grass. This whole kidnapping thing was getting thicker and sicker. He gave his forehead another swipe with the rag. "Listen, I—uh—need to get back to work."

"Okay. I'll talk to you again soon, son."

Jimmy clicked off the phone without even saying good-bye.

"I don't see why we had to tag along with you this morning," Titus complained from his seat at the back of Abraham's buggy. "Shouldn't we be helpin' our older brothers work in the fields today?"

"Yeah," his twin brother agreed. "I feel funny around Jacob Weaver since he fell on his head and turned into a kid. It's hard to know how we should act around him."

Abraham glanced over at Timothy, who sat beside him. "Don't you be talkin' that way. Jacob can't help that he's lost his memory. Since he's not able to do many of the things he used to do, his family needs all the help they can get. Just act like yourselves and help me with some chores that need doin'." Abraham thought of all the times Jacob had helped him in the past. He'd offered his friendship and spiritual counsel when it was needed the most, so now Abraham wasn't about to let his friend down in his hour of need. He would help the Weaver family as long as it was required.

"Can't the bishop's son help him?" Timothy questioned.

"I'm sure Arthur's helping as much as he can, but he has his daed's business to run now, which is a full-time job."

Titus leaned over the seat and tapped his father on the shoulder. "What about Leona and her mamm? Aren't they gonna be helpin' out?"

Abraham groaned. "Of course they are, but they have their own chores to do; there are some tasks only a man can manage."

Timothy snorted. "Jacob might be thinkin' like a little kid now, but he's still got the body of a man. I'm sure he could handle most of the chores if he was told what to do." He folded his arms and looked straight ahead. "Me and Titus have been doin' our share of chores ever since we could walk."

"Yeah, that's right," his twin agreed. "I've been haulin' wood in our old wheelbarrow since before I can remember."

Abraham clenched his teeth. It was bad enough that things between him and Naomi were strained. He didn't need two complaining teenagers to deal with this morning. "I'm sure there will be certain chores that Jacob's capable of doing, but the doctor wants him to take it easy and give his body a chance to recover from that nasty fall." He looked at Timothy, then over his shoulder at Titus. "I don't want to hear another word about your not wantin' to help. Is that clear?"

"Jah," the twins said in unison.

A short time later, Abraham guided his horse and buggy onto Jacob's property and pulled back on the reins, halting the horse in front of the rail near the barn. *Oh, Lord,* he silently prayed. *Please give my good friend his memory back.*

Chapter 20

*L*eona glanced at the other side of the barn where the men sat on backless, wooden benches during their Sunday preaching service. This week's service was being held at Jake Fisher's place. She spotted Papa sitting beside Arthur. On the other side of him sat Abraham Fisher. Abraham was a kind yet determined man, who had gone through many trials over the years, and Leona knew he cared about her family. He had proven that by all he'd done since her daed's accident—coming over to do some of the more difficult chores, bringing dishes of food Fannie had prepared, and letting Mom know that he and his family had been praying. Others in the community had been kind and offered their assistance and prayers, as well.

Leona stared at the veins protruding from her clenched hands as her thoughts continued to drift. Jimmy Scott had also been a big help since her daed's mishap. He often dropped by the house, offering to do chores and spending many hours with Papa. They talked, went for walks, and even played with the animals in the barn. Papa seemed to enjoy being around the barn animals, and he'd even made a pet out of one of the baby goats.

It's nice that Jimmy wants to be with Papa, but I don't know what they would have to talk about, she thought. *With Papa thinking he's a little boy, it's not likely that he'd have much in common with Jimmy or any other grown man, Amish or English, and yet he carries on as though he's known Jimmy all his life. Maybe Jimmy reminds Papa of one of his childhood friends. Jah, that's probably it.*

Leona remembered how distressing it had been the first day her daed came home from the hospital and saw his face in Mom's hand mirror. He'd clutched Mom's hand and begged her to take away that old man with the beard who stared back at him with such a curious expression. No matter how much explaining Mom did, Papa couldn't seem to grasp the concept that he was a grown man with a family, even though he had seen himself in the mirror several times since then.

Leona heard a scuffle on the other side of the room and glanced over to see what was going on. She was shocked to discover her daed standing in the aisle with his hands on his hips, staring at Leona's brother. "I need a drink of water. I told ya three times already—I'm thirsty," he said, his voice a little too loud.

Arthur's face turned cherry red, and he reached out and grabbed hold of Papa's hand. "Sit back down, please."

Papa jerked his hand away and took a step backward. "Mama said I could have some water whenever I feel thirsty!"

Leona quickly scanned the room. Everyone seemed to be watching Papa instead of Matthew Fisher, the song leader for the day. She knew if her daed were really a little boy, and not their bishop who'd lost his memory, he would have been taken outside for a good tongue-lashing or maybe even a sound *bletsching*. Amish children were taught at an early age to sit quietly during church, and no parent would allow an outburst such as this. Although her daed couldn't lose his title as bishop, he wouldn't be required to do any of his previous duties right now. Even so, he should be expected to sit still during the three-hour service, like all the kinner who were present.

Papa gave Arthur's hand another tug, and finally, Arthur grunted, stood, and led their daed out of the room.

Leona breathed a sigh of relief and forced her gaze back to the songbook resting on her knees. *"The innermost life of the true Christian shineth, tho' outwardly darkened by trials on hand."* The words on the page blurred, and she closed her eyes.

The following morning, Leona awoke with a headache. She hadn't slept well last night, and the weather had turned hot and muggy after a heavy rainfall, which didn't help her mood any. Her stomach growled, yet she didn't feel hungry. It was as though her body and mind waged a war on one another these days.

Despite the pounding in her temples, Leona knew she must wash up and get dressed because Mom was probably in the kitchen already and would need help making breakfast. She lifted herself off the bed and started across the room, but every move took courage and stamina she didn't seem to have.

Sometime later, she descended the steps and was on her way to the kitchen when the back door flew open and a baby goat trotted into the house. Papa followed, his face all red and sweaty.

"You'd better get that animal out of here before Mom sees him. And you're tracking mud into the house with your wet feet." Leona crossed her arms and glared at him. It seemed odd to be speaking to her daed in such a way, but if he was going to act like a child, he needed to be treated like one.

"I ain't got wet feet. I'm wearing my *gammschtiwwel*."

Before Leona could scold him about wearing his rubber boots inside, the goat darted into the living room, circled the rocking chair a couple of times, and then leaped onto the sofa. Papa laughed as he chased after it, angering Leona further. "This isn't funny, Papa. The living room is no place for a goat!" She could hardly believe the same man who had been so adamant about no pets in the house all these years could now be entertaining a goat—and right here in the living room, of all places!

"I'll take him upstairs to my bedroom." Papa grabbed hold of the goat's underbelly, lifted the squirming animal into his arms, and started across the room.

Leona positioned herself in front of the staircase. "That animal belongs outside in his pen, so please take him there now."

He glared at her defiantly. "You're not my boss, sister."

"I'm not your sister, but if you don't do as I say, I'm going to call Mom."

Papa's lower lip jutted out, and his forehead wrinkled. "Everything is out of kilter for me."

"I know," she said, her anger abating.

Papa hugged the struggling goat tighter and sauntered over to the front door. "Want me to make the door shut?"

"Jah, please."

Just as his hand touched the knob, he called over his shoulder, "Ya know what? You're not much fun, Ona!"

His words stung, but Leona kept quiet.

The door closed behind Papa, and as his final word registered in her brain, Leona stood there, too numb to move. He'd called her "Ona"—the nickname he had given her when she was a little girl. Did her daed know who she was now?

She rushed out the door after him. "Papa, wait up!"

He halted at the bottom of the steps, glanced around the yard, and then turned to face her. "Where's Papa? I don't see him nowhere. How come our daed's never around anymore?"

A weary sigh escaped Leona's lips, and she felt as if her heart had dropped all the way to her toes. If Papa had momentarily remembered her, his memory had already vanished. "Papa's gone away," she said with a moan. "Papa's gone away and might never come back."

Her daed squinted and stared at her. Then unexpectedly, his face broke into a wide smile. "Ah, you're just kiddin' with me, ain't ya, Mary?"

He thinks I'm his sister again. Leona gulped in a deep breath and released it quickly. "Jah. I'm just kidding." With her shoulders slumped and a heart full of regrets, she turned toward the house. *I'm a schoolteacher, and I should be accustomed to children's silly ways. But dealing with the mind of a child inside a man's body is an entirely different matter.*

"Would ya mind stoppin' by Hoffmeirs' General Store on our way to the next job site?" Eli asked as he and Jimmy drove into the town of Paradise. "I'm needing a new lunch pail, and Caleb usually keeps a pretty good supply on hand."

Jimmy shrugged. "Sure, I guess we have time to stop." A few minutes later, he pulled his truck into the parking lot next to the store and turned off the engine.

When the two men entered the store, Eli headed straight for the shelves where the lunch pails were kept. Jimmy glanced around the room and was surprised to see Jacob standing in front of the candy counter with a look of longing on his bearded face.

"How are you doing today?" Jimmy asked, stepping up beside the bishop.

"I'd be better if I had some candy." He looked over at Jimmy and blinked a couple of times. "Licorice is my favorite kind."

Jimmy reached into his pocket and withdrew a dollar. "Pick out a few hunks, and I'll buy them for you."

"Really?"

Jimmy nodded.

Jacob glanced around, kind of nervouslike. "You think my mamm will care?"

"Maybe we should ask. Where is she?"

Jacob pointed toward the adjoining quilt shop. "She and Mary went in there."

Jimmy knew the confused man was referring to Leona, since the other day she'd told him that her dad still thought she was his sister."

"Why don't you wait here? I'll go speak to Lydia about the candy."

Jacob's eyebrows furrowed. "Who?"

He patted the bishop's arm. "I'll speak to your mamm."

"Jah, okay. Hurry back."

Jimmy found Leona and her mother talking to Abby Fisher, who sat at a table in the middle of the room working on a quilt. The vivid blue colors and unusual star-shaped pattern reminded him of the quilt that had been on his parents' bed during his growing-up years. After Mom passed away, Dad had put the quilt in a closet, saying it brought back too many painful memories. At the time, Jimmy thought he meant the covering reminded him of Mom. But since he'd been told about his kidnapping and had now accepted the story as truth, he wondered if the fact that the quilt had been Amish-made was what really had bothered Dad.

Jimmy thought about last Saturday and how he'd driven all over the area around New Providence looking for a place that sold root beer. It had been a waste of time, just like all the other places he'd already looked. Even though Jimmy felt discouraged and realized that he might never locate his real family, he'd begun to wonder if God might have brought him to Lancaster County to help the Weavers, not to find his Amish roots. In fact, that was all that seemed important to Jimmy right now.

"Can I help you with something?" Abby asked.

Jimmy blinked and pushed his musings aside. "I—uh—was wondering if Lydia would mind if I bought Jacob some licorice."

Lydia smiled. "I have no problem with it. He is a grown man, after all."

Jimmy nodded, then glanced over at Leona, but she seemed preoccupied as she fiddled with the spool of thread she held in her hands. He looked back at Lydia. "How are things going this week? Is Jacob showing any signs of improvement?"

Lydia shook her head, and even though a look of sadness swept over her face, he sensed her determined spirit to look on the brighter side of things. "I haven't lost faith," she murmured. "If it's God's will for Jacob's memory to return, then it surely will."

Leona grunted and moved over to stand by the window. Jimmy was tempted to follow and offer some words of encouragement, but he decided against it. The last time he'd stopped by the Weavers' place and mentioned the idea of putting Jacob to work on some of the schoolhouse repairs, Leona seemed upset. In fact, she'd stared at him in obvious disbelief and said, "You can't be serious. My daed would never be able to help with repairs. He may look like he's capable of a man's work, but he thinks like a child, so he can't be expected to do anything more than a boy would do." The decided edge to her voice and the look of defeat he'd seen on her face let Jimmy know Leona still wasn't dealing well with her father's accident. His heart went out to her—and to everyone else in Jacob's family.

A short time later, as Eli and Jimmy were about to climb into his truck, he overheard Lydia, who stood near her closed-in buggy, ordering Jacob to get in. Leona sat in the driver's seat, and her deep frown conveyed her frustration. Jimmy knew he couldn't drive off without offering to help.

"Is there a problem?" he asked, stepping between Lydia and her husband.

She nodded, and a tear trickled down her cheek. "Jacob refuses to get into the buggy."

"Is that true?" Jimmy asked. He looked at the bishop, who stood with his arms folded in an unyielding pose.

"Mama won't let me have more candy."

"I bought you some licorice. Did you eat it all?"

"Jah, it's gone." Jacob patted his stomach and gave Jimmy a sheepish-looking grin.

"It will soon be time for lunch," Jimmy said, taking hold of the man's arm. "You don't want to spoil your appetite by eating too much candy, do you?"

Jacob lowered his bushy eyebrows and stared at the ground. "My eatin' went away."

Jimmy glanced over at Lydia and shrugged. He had no idea what the man was talking about.

"I think he means that his appetite has left him."

"And no wonder, what with him eating candy so close to lunch," Leona chimed in from her seat in the front of the buggy.

"Would you like me to stop by your house later tonight? We can play with your goat if you like," Jimmy said, hoping to get Jacob's mind on something else.

"That'd be nice."

Jimmy nodded at the buggy. "Then climb inside, and I'll see you later on."

Without a word of argument, Jacob climbed into the back, smiling like a happy child.

"Thank you, Jimmy." Lydia took a seat beside her daughter and lifted her hand in a wave.

"I'll see you later this evening," Jimmy called as the buggy pulled out of the parking lot.

Eli, who had been standing beside Jimmy's truck during the whole ordeal, shook his head. "That was sure somethin' the way you handled things with our bishop. You've got a way with him that no one else seems to have, that's for certain sure."

Jimmy opened the truck door. "I only wish I could do more."

CHAPTER 21

$\mathcal{J}$immy had just placed his breakfast dishes in the sink when his cell phone rang. He glanced at the clock on the wall and wondered who would be calling him so early. When he pulled the phone from his belt clip to check the incoming number, he was relieved to see that it wasn't his dad. "Hey, Allen," he said. "Why are you calling so early? It's seven o'clock here, which means it's only four on the West Coast."

"I know it's early, but I'm going with some of the young people to the Oregon coast today, and we want to get an early start," Allen explained.

"Sounds like fun. Wish I were going with you."

"Yeah, me, too." There was a brief pause, then, "Hey, it's sure good to hear your voice. It's been awhile."

"I know. I've been really busy."

"Are you still painting for that Amish bishop you told me about?"

"Yeah, but since Jacob's memory hasn't returned, he's no longer able to run his business. And since he doesn't remember hiring me, it's really his son, Arthur, I'm working for now."

"It's too bad about him falling off the ladder. I've still got our church's prayer chain praying for him."

"Thanks. Jacob and the rest of his family need all the prayers they can get."

"Oh, by the way, I wanted you to know that I did try to get ahold of your dad," Allen said. "He hasn't answered the door or his phone whenever I've dropped by the house or called. Have you heard anything from him since the last time we talked?"

"I spoke to him the other day, and as much as I hate to say this, I've decided that he's telling the truth about kidnapping me."

"Seriously?"

"Yep."

"You think he really took you from an Amish farm?"

"That's what he says, and he's scared to death that if I find my real family he'll end up in jail."

"The information I got off the Internet said the Amish don't sue. So I doubt they would press any kind of criminal charges against your dad," Allen said.

"Jim. His name is Jim. He's not my dad—not even my adopted dad," Jimmy muttered as he moved across the room and grabbed his lunch pail off the table.

"I know your dad's not a Christian and he can be kind of hard to deal with sometimes, but I can't picture him walking onto an Amish farm, snatching you away, and then passing you off to your mom as the baby they'd gone to Maryland to adopt."

Jimmy groaned. "It was hard for me to accept at first, too, but now that I've had a chance to think things over and have talked with Da—Jim again, I'm beginning to understand why he drinks so much and didn't want to go to church with me or Mom."

"He's probably been eaten up with guilt all these years. I'll bet he's fallen under conviction, which means there's still hope that he will—"

"Look, Allen, I've got to go. I'm going to work for Arthur part of the day, and then I'll be stopping over at the Weavers' place to see Jacob."

"Oh, okay. I need to head out, too."

"I'll call you soon." Jimmy grabbed his painter's hat off the wall peg near the back door of his rented trailer and started to leave the kitchen.

"One more thing," Allen said before Jimmy clicked off his cell phone.

"What's that?"

"I sensed some anger in your voice when you were talking about your dad."

"As I said before, he's not my dad."

"He might not be your flesh-and-blood father or your adopted father, but he is the man who raised you."

"Mom had more to do with raising me than he did." The feelings of bitterness Jimmy felt since his last conversation with Jim mounted higher, and he swallowed against the taste of bile rising in his throat.

"You've got to find a way to deal with this, Jimmy. If you don't, it will eat you alive."

"I'm not sure I'll ever come to grips with what that man did to me, Mom, and my real Amish family." He clenched his teeth so hard that his jaw ached, as he jerked open the door. "Can you imagine how my sister must have felt when she returned to the yard with a jug of root beer and discovered I was gone? It gives me the chills just thinking about it."

"I'll bet even after all these years they're still missing you."

Jimmy said nothing as he walked across the yard and opened the door to his truck, which he kept parked near the Rabers' barn.

"So, are you going to look for your real family?"

"I started looking for them—even before I fully believed Jim's story."

"So what else will you do to try and find them?"

"I'm not sure. Guess I'll have to rely on the Lord to help me."

"You don't really think God's going to help you find your real family as long as you continue to harbor anger and hatred toward Jim, do you?"

Jimmy halted. "I—I don't know."

"I'm sure you don't need to be reminded what the Bible says about forgiveness. The only way you'll ever have any peace is if you forgive your dad."

Jimmy grimaced. He knew Allen was right, but he wasn't sure he could forgive. "I'd better go. Talk to you later, Allen."

"Bye, Jimmy. I'll be praying for you."

Since school would be starting in a few weeks, Leona spent most of her free time at the schoolhouse getting things ready. At least that was her excuse for being here—as she was today. The truth be told, she'd begun to look for ways to get away from her daed and his childish antics. Her faith in God, which had once been strong, was faltering in the midst of all her disappointments.

It helped some whenever Jimmy came over and kept Papa occupied. In fact, the young English man seemed to be Papa's best friend these days, which Leona felt sure her daed needed. However, she had a hunch Papa's friendship with Jimmy had hurt Abraham's feelings. Papa had not only forgotten who Abraham was, but he didn't perk up whenever

Abraham came around the way he did with Jimmy. Leona had noticed the last couple of times Papa's old friend had dropped by, her daed acted kind of strange. She figured Papa's friendship with Jimmy might be the reason.

Leona glanced around the schoolhouse, wondering what she should do today. The walls had been painted, so no cleaning would need to be done on them. With the help of several parents, the desks had been cleaned and polished and a new blackboard had been put up—the kind Leona had requested.

"Maybe I should clean and organize my desk," she said, turning in that direction. "Anything to keep my hands and thoughts occupied."

Leona had only been working a few minutes when she heard a vehicle rumble into the school yard. She hurried to the front door and saw Jimmy and Papa climb out of Jimmy's truck. *I wonder what they want. I hope they're not planning to stay long. I don't need this interruption.*

"Hi, Mary," Papa said with a cheery wave. "We come to give you some wood."

Leona glanced at Jimmy, who grinned at her and said, "I figured you'd be needing some firewood cut and stacked before school starts."

"Actually, my students' parents usually take turns bringing wood over during the school year."

"That's okay. This is something your dad can do, so I guess you'll have some extra wood this school term."

Papa shuffled his feet a few times and looked at Jimmy as if he'd taken leave of his senses. "I ain't Mary's daed. I'm her bruder."

Jimmy shrugged, and Leona looked away. They had tried several times to explain things to Papa about his accident. Sometimes he seemed to grasp the fact that he had lost his memory, but other times he would only give them a blank stare. Even though Papa had called her "Ona" on a few occasions, he was still insistent that he was her little bruder, not her daed.

"Where would you like us to stack the wood once we get it cut?" Jimmy asked, halting Leona's thoughts.

She motioned to the side of the building. "Are you sure it's safe for him to be handling an ax? I mean, if he doesn't remember how to use it. . ."

"I'll do the cutting, and he can haul the wood over to the building and stack it."

"I guess that would be okay." Leona turned toward the door. "I'll be inside if you need me for anything."

When she returned to her desk, she noticed that her hands were shaking, and she clasped them tightly together. *If stacking wood would bring my daed back to me, I'd ask for a ton of wood and let him stack all day.*

Lydia sank into a chair on the front porch as a feeling of relief swept over her. For the first time in several days, she had some time alone. Ever since Jacob had come home from the hospital, she'd felt as if she were playing the role of babysitter rather than that of a wife who'd been married almost thirty-seven years. She released a sigh and reached for the glass of iced tea sitting on the small table beside her. *I probably should be out working in the garden or doing some cleaning, but it's awfully nice to sit here and relax awhile.*

Lydia closed her eyes and leaned her full weight against the wicker chair. It was peaceful this afternoon, with the birds chirping in the nearby trees and an occasional grunt coming from Leona's dog, which lay on the porch a few feet away. For the first time in many days, Lydia felt God's presence. Maybe she'd been too busy these past weeks to realize He'd been there all along, helping her cope with Jacob's handicap. *Will my husband always be this way, Lord? Is there more we can do to help his memory return?*

The *clip-clop* of a horse's hooves and the rumble of buggy wheels brought Lydia's prayer to a halt. She opened her eyes and saw Fannie Fisher climb down from her buggy.

"Wie geht's?" Fannie called with a wave.

"I'm fair to middlin'. How about you?"

"Still missin' Edna, but otherwise doin' okay." Fannie strolled across the yard and stepped onto the porch. "I was on my way home from town and thought I'd drop by and see how you're getting along."

Lydia motioned to the empty chair beside her. "I'm taking some time off from my chores, so have a seat, and we can visit awhile." She started to get up. "Can I get you something cold to drink?"

Fannie waved a hand. "I'm fine. I had a bottle of cold root beer out of the vending machine down the street from my daughter's quilt shop not long ago."

Lydia smiled, remembering how delicious the root beer was that Abraham used to make. "Don't suppose that husband of yours has made any of his own root beer lately?"

"In all the years we've been married, Abraham's only made it a couple of times." Fannie slowly shook her head. "I think every time he's made root beer it's reminded him of the day his little boy was stolen, although he never speaks of it anymore."

Lydia clicked her tongue. "Sometimes when I'm feeling sorry for myself because of Jacob's accident, I think about all you and Abraham have been through, and I have to stop and count my blessings."

"Abraham, Naomi, and my daughter, Abby, they're the ones who've really had their faith put to the test." Fannie reached over and patted Lydia's arm. "Keep trusting God; He will see you through."

Lydia nodded as tears clouded her vision. It was easy enough to say God was in control, but when one's faith was put to the test, it was another matter.

"Is Jacob getting any better?" Fannie asked.

"Not really. Some days he's hard to deal with because of his silly antics. Other days he seems calmer and more cooperative." Lydia drew in a breath and released it with a huff. "He's called Leona by her nickname a couple of times, which gave me some hope that he might remember she's his daughter. But then he goes right back to calling her Mary again. Leona gets set down pretty hard whenever her daed doesn't respond to things the way she would like."

"It has to be *hatt* for you, Leona, and Arthur to see Jacob like that and know there's nothing you can do but pray and try to be there for him."

"Jah, it's difficult, to be sure. Our other daughters, Peggy and Rebecca, are concerned, too. But with them both living in Kentucky, they only know what I write them and don't get to see it firsthand." Lydia forced a smile. "Jacob's birthday is this Saturday; he'll turn fifty-nine."

"Are you planning a party for him?"

"I hadn't given it much thought, but maybe I should. Might do him some good to have his family and close friends gathered together." Lydia shrugged. "Who knows, it may even be helpful in bringing back his memory."

"I think it's a fine idea."

"You, Abraham, and your whole family are invited, of course,"

Lydia said, feeling a surge of excitement she hadn't felt in a long time. "Maybe we can have a barbecue with cake and homemade ice cream for dessert."

Fannie licked her lips. "Sounds good to me. Just tell me what time the party will begin and what I can bring."

CHAPTER 22

$\mathcal{J}$immy whistled as he drove down the road toward the Weavers' place. He seemed to be fitting in more all the time and was pleased that Lydia had invited him to attend the barbecue in honor of her husband's birthday. It would give him a chance to get to know some of the others he hadn't become well acquainted with yet. Abraham Fisher was one of those he had met on a few occasions but didn't know so well. Abraham always kept his distance, and Jimmy wondered if the man might be prejudiced against him because he was English. Or maybe Abraham felt threatened by Jimmy's friendship with the bishop. Leona had mentioned once that her dad and Abraham used to be good friends before Jacob's accident. Now that he'd lost his memory and didn't know who Abraham was, they had little to talk about. Of course, Jacob didn't remember meeting Jimmy before the accident, either. But for some reason, he seemed taken with Jimmy and had quickly become his friend.

When Jimmy pulled into the Weavers' yard a short time later, he noticed several Amish buggies lined up beside the barn with their shafts resting on the ground. The horses had been unhitched, and he could see them moving around the corral.

"I hope I'm not late. I thought Lydia said six o'clock, and it's only two minutes after that now," he mumbled, glancing at his watch—the one his dad had given him for his birthday. He flinched, realizing once more that he still hadn't come to grips with the anger he felt over Jim's deceit. The only way he'd been able to keep from thinking about it was to stay busy and concentrate on helping Jacob. In fact, that had become his primary focus. Looking for his family had taken a backseat. *Of course,* he reasoned, *there's a part of me that's afraid to find my family, because I know that if Jim went to jail for kidnapping, I would feel disloyal to the only mother I've ever known.*

The pungent aroma of meat cooking on the grill drew Jimmy's thoughts aside, and when he stepped out of the truck carrying a paper sack with the gift inside that he'd bought for Jacob, his stomach rumbled. He hadn't eaten anything since breakfast, figuring he would make up for it tonight.

Jimmy hurried around to the back side of the house and discovered several people, including Leona and her parents, seated at two oversized picnic tables. They were already eating, and he glanced at his watch again. The time was the same as it had been a few minutes ago, and he realized then that his watch had stopped.

"Sorry I'm late," he said, stepping up to the table where Lydia and Jacob sat. "Guess the battery in my watch is dead."

Jacob grinned up at him. "Hi, Jimmy. Glad ya could make it to my party."

Lydia smiled and nodded. "You're not so late."

"We just started eating a few minutes ago," Arthur put in from across the table. "Grab yourself a burger from the grill and have a seat."

Jimmy handed Jacob the paper sack. "This is for you. Happy birthday."

Jacob's smile widened. "What is it?"

"Open the sack and take a look."

Jacob pulled it open and peered inside. "Umm. . .licorice." He smacked his lips. "That's my favorite candy."

Jimmy nodded. "There's something else in there, too."

Jacob stuck his hand into the sack again and withdrew a paintbrush. He gave Jimmy a quizzical look, then turned to Lydia and swished the brush against the tip of her nose. "Does that tickle, Mama?"

She chuckled and looked over at Jimmy.

"I thought it might help spark a memory for him," he said.

She nodded. "Maybe so."

Jimmy glanced around, wondering where would be the best place to sit.

"There's a vacant spot next to Mary," Jacob said, pointing to the bench where Leona sat.

Jimmy smiled, and Leona offered him a brief smile in return. "You're welcome to sit here if you like," she said.

Jimmy didn't have to be asked twice. He enjoyed Leona's company and thought if he was Amish or she was English, he might even be interested in dating her. *I'm almost Amish,* he reminded himself. *After all, I was born to an Amish couple.* He forked a juicy burger onto his plate and took a seat, hoping to focus his thoughts on something other than his past—a past he'd thought he had known about until he'd learned the truth concerning his so-called adoption.

"I'm glad you were able to come to the party," Leona said as she passed him a package of buns. "Would you like some ketchup or mustard to put on your meat?"

"I'd like both, please."

"How about lettuce, tomatoes, or onions?"

"Yeah, all three." He wiggled his eyebrows, and Leona giggled. It was good to see her in better spirits tonight. She had been sullen ever since he'd met her, and even more so since her dad's accident. She hadn't actually said so, but the way she acted whenever she was around her dad made Jimmy think she was embarrassed by her father's juvenile actions. The other day at the schoolhouse, Jacob had dropped a hunk of licorice Jimmy had given him, and he'd bent down, picked it up, and popped it into his mouth. Leona looked mortified, gave him a lecture about the ground being full of germs, and barely said more than two words to her dad after that.

"Would you like some potato salad?" Leona asked, touching Jimmy's elbow with her hand.

He felt a strange tingling sensation, and he gave his arm a quick once-over to see if some bug might have landed there. Relieved when he didn't see anything, he bit into his burger and mumbled, "Sure, I'd love some."

Abraham folded his arms and leaned back in the wooden chair where he'd taken a seat on the Weavers' front porch. A game of croquet was being played in the yard, and most of the young people were involved in it—everyone except Jacob's youngest daughter, that is. Leona and that young English painter who Jacob had hired awhile back left the yard a few minutes ago.

Abraham's gaze went to the driveway where Leona walked between

Jimmy and Jacob. *Not only is my good friend taken in by that young Englisher, but his daughter seems to be, as well. I need to nip this in the bud, because I'm sure Jacob's not going to do anything about it. Most of the time, he doesn't even realize Leona is his daughter, much less show any concern for her welfare.*

He reached under the brim of his straw hat and scratched his forehead. *Just who is this Jimmy Scott, and why's he been hanging around Jacob so much? No one seems to know a lot about him other than the fact that he paints and comes from the state of Washington.*

"You ready for some ice cream?"

"Huh?" Abraham looked up at his wife. She held a heaping bowl of vanilla ice cream in her hand. "Jah. Danki, Fannie."

"How come you're sitting here by yourself?" she questioned. "I figured you'd be visiting with the birthday boy."

Abraham took the bowl from her and groaned. "That's exactly what Jacob is, too. He might be fifty-nine years old on the outside, but inside he's just a kid." He pointed to the game in progress. "Did you see him out there earlier, snappin' that ball around and hollering like he don't have a lick of sense? Now he's walking down the driveway with Leona and that Englisher like they're the best of friends."

"You need to calm yourself down, husband," Fannie said, easing into the chair beside him. "It's not Jacob's fault he can't remember how old he is. Maybe if you talked to him more about the things you used to do together, it might help jog his memory."

Abraham spooned some ice cream into his mouth, savoring the rich, creamy taste and mulling over what his wife had said. Finally, he swallowed and cleared his throat. "I have tried talking to him some, but so far nothin' I've said has made any difference."

"Try to be patient and remember to keep praying."

"I have been praying." His gaze went to the driveway again. Jimmy, Leona, and Jacob had disappeared. No doubt they'd decided to walk up the road apiece.

"What are you looking at?" she questioned.

"Nothin'," he mumbled. "Just thinkin' about what I might do to make things better for my good friend."

"Maybe you should concentrate on trying to make things better between you and Naomi." Fannie shook her head. "I know you're still angry with her for hiding Zach's quilt, but giving her the cold shoulder whenever she's around isn't the way to handle it. It's not God's way, either."

"I know, but what she did was wrong."

"That may be, but is your trying to punish her the right thing to do?"

"I'm not trying to punish Naomi," he said, furrowing his brows. "I just can't trust her anymore, plain and simple."

As Jim approached the Tacoma Mall on his way back from picking up some paint and other supplies, he decided to drop by the health food store. Holly Simmons had mentioned during his last visit there that she was a recovered alcoholic. Maybe he could talk to her about the way he felt.

This is probably a dumb idea, he told himself as he climbed out of the van and headed across the parking lot. *She'll probably think I'm a hypochondriac who keeps coming back to her store to look for something to help calm his nerves.*

Despite his doubts, Jim kept on walking. Once he was inside the mall, he hurried to the health food store before he changed his mind. As soon as he walked in, he spotted Holly behind the counter and was relieved to see that there were no other customers.

Holly noticed him right away and stepped out from behind the counter with a friendly smile. "How's your son doing, Jim? I heard from someone at church that he'd taken a trip to the East Coast and might be gone awhile."

Jim nodded with a grimace.

"You look upset. Is everything all right?"

He started to nod again but shook his head instead.

"Are you still having trouble sleeping?"

"Yeah, that—and a few other things."

"Is there something in particular I can help you with?"

He shifted from one foot to the other, trying to work up the nerve to say what was on his mind. "I—I was wondering if you— Well, if you haven't had your lunch break yet, would you be interested in going somewhere with me to eat?"

"Kim and Megan, my helpers, should be back from their break

soon," Holly said. "So if you have the time to wait, we could go to one of the restaurants in the mall as soon as they get back."

He nodded. "That would be great."

A short time later, Jim and Holly sat across from each other at a table inside a restaurant not far from her store.

"So what did you want to talk about?" Holly asked after they'd placed their orders.

Jim cleared his throat a couple of times, searching for the right words. "Well, uh—the last time I came into your store, you mentioned that you—uh—used to have a drinking problem."

She nodded. "I'm a recovered alcoholic. I haven't had a drink in ten years."

He reached for his glass of water and took a sip. "So—uh—how did you get on top of your drinking problem?"

"AA helped a lot. So did the support I got from my pastor and friends at church."

Jim frowned. There was that *church* word again. First Linda, then Jimmy, and now the health food store owner. It seemed like he could never get away from religious fanatics.

"Is there a reason you're looking at me with such a glum expression?" Holly asked.

Jim drew in a breath and blew it out quickly. "Jimmy thinks I have a drinking problem."

She leaned her elbows on the table and studied him intently. "Do you?"

"I do have a few drinks now and then—whenever I'm feeling uptight and need to relax."

"Do you ever get drunk?"

Unable to meet her probing gaze, he stared at the table. "Yeah, sometimes."

"Has your drinking affected any of your personal relationships?"

"I—guess it has."

"What about your job? Have you ever lost time from work because you were drunk or hung over?"

He lifted his gaze to meet hers. "Maybe a couple of times, but I have a great foreman, and he's always taken over when I'm not there."

She pursed her lips. "You mean he *covers* for you?"

"I wouldn't put it that way," Jim said, feeling his defenses begin to rise. *This was a mistake. I shouldn't have come here. I'll bet Holly thinks I'm a worthless drunk who shrugs his responsibilities and then drops the ball in someone else's lap. She probably thinks I'm a lousy father, too. She might even believe Jimmy took off for Pennsylvania to get away from me.* He reached for his glass of water and took another drink. *If she only knew. . .*

"Have you ever considered attending an AA meeting?"

His only reply was a quick shake of his head.

"If you'd like to see what one of the meetings is like, I'd be happy to go with you."

The idea of spending more time with this attractive woman was kind of appealing, but the thought of going to an AA meeting and listening to a bunch of strangers talk about their drinking problems scared Jim to death. "I appreciate the offer," he mumbled, "but I'm not an alcoholic, and I can quit drinking anytime I want."

*A*s Jimmy turned onto Oak Hill Drive and headed toward the job he would be doing all week, he thought about Eli, who wouldn't be working with him today because he'd had all four of his wisdom teeth pulled yesterday. Eli would not only miss a few days of work, but he was worried that he might not be able to see his girlfriend on Saturday. Lettie Byler was an Amish schoolteacher who lived near Strasburg. Eli had told Jimmy that he and Lettie had been courting for the last six months.

Thinking about Eli and his girlfriend led Jimmy to mull over the way he felt about Leona. He reflected on Saturday night and the fun he'd had with her during Jacob's birthday party. He'd enjoyed visiting with many of the people—but none as much as the bishop's daughter. During the walk they'd taken with Jacob after their meal, it had been obvious by the way Leona had responded to some of her dad's comments that she felt uncomfortable whenever he said or did something childish. While Jacob chased fireflies, Leona had told Jimmy about her fiancé dying and how her faith had been badly shaken then—and that it had weakened even further after her dad's accident.

Jimmy could understand why her faith had been shaken. His faith had been strong until he'd learned about his kidnapping. Yet, despite his own problems, he still felt concern for Leona. The sadness he'd seen in her eyes had tugged at his heartstrings. He'd also seen a look of determination on Lydia's face and noticed the confusion Jacob experienced whenever he was asked to do a task that might be expected of a man. Such things made him even more determined to stick around Lancaster County and offer his help. The Weavers didn't deserve this kind of pain—no one did.

Jimmy's mind drove him unwillingly back to the day he'd learned of his mother's cancer diagnosis. He had been afraid of losing her then.

And, a few years later, when he was told that she was going to die, he felt as if his world had been turned upside down. But with God's help and the encouragement of his pastor and friends, Jimmy had made it through the darkest days.

Too bad Jim didn't do as well, he thought ruefully. *Drinking until he's too numb to care seems to be the only way that man can deal with anything. It's amazing that he hasn't lost his business by now, and if he keeps up the way he's going, he might lose it yet.*

Jimmy shook his head. *I can't worry about that anymore. I did all I could to get him to go to church, and he flatly refused. I covered for him whenever he couldn't go to work because he was on a drinking binge or suffered a hangover. Now it's time for him to sink or swim.*

A fast-moving semitruck whipped around Jimmy, and he had to steer his pickup toward the shoulder of the road to avoid being sideswiped. "Slow down! You shouldn't be going so fast," he grumbled. "Don't you know there could be an Amish carriage on this road?"

Since Jimmy's arrival in Lancaster County nearly two months ago, he'd read several accounts of buggy accidents in the newspaper. One had caused a tragic fatality, and another had left an Amish man paralyzed.

"People need to relax and not be in such a hurry," he continued to fume. "Drive slower, share the road, and more accidents will be prevented."

When Jimmy rounded the next bend, he caught sight of a team of horses pulling an empty wagon and running down a driveway at full speed. As soon as his truck came to the entrance of the drive, he put on the brakes, blocking the horses from gaining access to the road. Two men who he recognized as Jake and Norman Fisher ran behind the wagon, and their red-faced father wasn't far behind. *This must be the Fishers' place.* Jimmy had never had a reason to come here, so he hadn't been sure where they lived.

By the time Jimmy got out of his truck, Norman and Jake had grabbed hold of the horses' bridles. "Danki," Norman called. "If these critters had managed to pull the wagon out on the road, there's no telling what might have happened."

"How'd they get away from you?" Jimmy questioned.

Jake opened his mouth to reply, but Abraham spoke first. "My two youngest boys were supposed to be keeping an eye on the team while Jake, Norman, and I got the sickle-bar mower ready to cut hay. Instead of doing as I asked, Titus and Timothy were foolin' around with those dumb yo-yos they bought the last time we stopped by the general store."

Jimmy glanced up the driveway and noticed Abraham's twin boys heading for the barn with their heads down and shoulders slumped. "I'm glad I happened along when I did," he said.

Abraham made no reply. Instead, he nodded at his older boys and said, "Why don't you fellows get the horses and wagon turned around and back into the field?"

"Sure, we can do that," Norman replied.

"What about you, Papa?" Jake asked. "Aren't you comin'?"

"I'll be along soon." Abraham looked back at Jimmy. "I need to have a few words with this young man first."

A trickle of sweat rolled down Jimmy's forehead, and he swiped it away with the back of his hand. Abraham's furrowed brows and tightly compressed lips made Jimmy wonder if the man might be perturbed. "I need to get to work," he said, taking a step toward his truck. "We're starting a new paint job today, and—"

Abraham clasped Jimmy's shoulder. "I won't keep ya long."

"Well, okay." Jimmy leaned against the side of his truck and folded his arms, hoping he looked calmer than he felt. There was something about the tall, slightly overweight Amish man that made him feel nervous.

Abraham cleared his throat. "I know you're working for the son of my friend, Jacob Weaver, but I'm wondering why you've been hangin' around their place so much."

"I care about Jacob and want to help him in any way I can."

Abraham moved closer. He was so close that Jimmy could actually feel the man's hot breath. "And what about Jacob's daughter?"

"Leona?"

"Jah."

"What about her?"

"I'm wondering exactly what your relationship is to her."

"Leona's a good friend, and I'm concerned about her as well as Jacob's wife and son. They've all been under a burden since Jacob lost his memory, and they need help from all their friends."

Abraham's steely blue eyes seemed to bore right through Jimmy as he stared at him with pursed lips. "I'm wonderin' if you might not care more for Leona than you ought to. I've seen the way you eyeball her whenever you think no one's lookin'."

Jimmy couldn't deny that he did have feelings for the bishop's daughter. He just wasn't sure how deep those feelings went—or what he should do about them.

"When I was going through rough times some years ago, Jacob was always there for me," Abraham continued. "He's the best friend I've ever had, and I won't stand by and watch you make his life more complicated than it already is."

Jimmy dropped his arms to his sides and clenched his fists. He didn't think he had done anything to deserve this lecture, and he told Abraham so.

"Jah, well, I needed to be sure you knew how things were. You're not Amish, ya know, and Leona ain't English. So, for the good of everyone, it would be better if you backed off and didn't hang around their place so much."

Jimmy was tempted to tell Abraham the reason he'd come to Pennsylvania, but he held his tongue. Even though he was still angry with Jim for his dishonesty, a part of him felt some sense of loyalty to the man who'd raised him. And if there was a chance that Jim would go to jail if the truth were revealed, Jimmy wasn't sure he wanted to be responsible for that. Besides, Abraham might not believe his story. In all likelihood, the irksome man would think Jimmy had made it up in order to get close to Leona.

Turning toward the truck and grasping the door handle, Jimmy mumbled, "You don't have to worry. I'd never do anything to hurt Jacob or anyone in his family."

For the first time in many days, Leona had felt a sense of excitement when she'd gotten out of bed. Today was the first day of school, and she looked forward to teaching her pupils again. Besides, it gave her a good excuse to be away from the house.

As she finished up the dishes, she glanced over at Mom, who sat at the table helping Papa read a book. *He should be in school. But then, I guess that wouldn't be good, since the kinner would probably make fun of a grown man coming to school for learning.*

She dried her hands, grabbed her black bonnet from the wall peg, and placed it over her smaller white covering. "I'm heading out now, Mom."

"All right, Leona. Have a good day."

"Jah, Ona. Have a good day," Papa added.

Ona one day, Mary the next. Will Papa's memory ever return? Leona opened the back door and stepped onto the porch, gulping in a breath of air. She could feel the first hints of fall as crisp, clean air filled her lungs. It made her appreciate being outdoors. She felt so confined whenever she was in the house, especially if her daed was in the same room asking ridiculous questions or acting like a silly child.

Leona leaned against the porch railing and squeezed her eyes shut. *What's wrong with me, Lord? Why can't I accept everything that has happened to my family and me these past months and go on with the business of living?*

As usual, there seemed to be no answers from the heavenly Father. It was as if God had stepped away—or maybe it was the other way around. Leona knew she was guilty of not spending much time in prayer, and she'd all but given up on reading the scriptures.

Pushing the despairing thoughts aside, Leona entered the barn to fetch a buggy horse. Filling her lungs with the sweet smell of hay, she bent over to pet Cinnamon, who'd been sleeping in a patch of straw. The dog responded with a flick of one ear and a lazy whimper.

"You be good today, you hear? No chasing chickens. And you'd better stay away from Papa's silly goat!"

Jim moaned as he tripped over his shoe and kicked it across the room. He'd been out drinking the night before, and now, even after a couple of aspirin and two cups of coffee, his head felt like it was the size of a basketball.

"There's no way I'm going to be able to work today," he muttered as he stumbled back to bed. He glanced at the clock on the nightstand.

It was still early, so he could set the alarm, sleep a few hours, and call Ed right before he started work. *Or maybe I should call him now so he has enough time to set out everything he'll need for the day.*

Jim reached for the phone and, in so doing, knocked over a picture of Jimmy that had been taken during his senior year of high school. He'd kept it near his bed ever since Jimmy left, but instead of offering comfort, it only reminded him of the mess he'd made of his life and Jimmy's.

He bent over and retrieved the picture, thankful the glass wasn't broken. "Oh, Jimmy, don't hate me for what I did," he blubbered. "I'd do most anything if I could make things right between us."

He gulped in a deep breath and flopped onto his pillow. "Dear God, if you're as real as Linda always said You were, then bring my son home to me."

CHAPTER 24

*L*eona leaned wearily against the front of her desk as the students filed out of the schoolhouse. For the most part, this had been a good day. The majority of her scholars had been eager to learn, but she was exhausted.

"See you tomorrow, Teacher," Norman Fisher's son, John, said as he sauntered past her desk.

"Have a good evening," she replied.

"Are ya coming over to our place for supper on Friday night with Grandma and Grandpa?" Arthur's daughter Jolene questioned.

"I'm hoping to." Leona smiled at her six-year-old niece. She was the one child who had been the most attentive today. Not like Millie Hoffmeir, who hadn't shown a bit of interest in learning to read or write.

Maybe it's because this was her first day of school, Leona thought. *I'm sure once Millie gets used to being here, she'll become more attentive.* She glanced at her niece, who was actually skipping out the door. *This was Jolene's first day of school, too, and she showed a lot more interest in learning than Naomi's daughter did.*

When the last child left the building, Leona headed over to the blackboard to erase the day's assignments as she pondered the situation with Millie. *If things don't go better by the end of the week, I'll have a talk with Millie's folks.*

A few minutes later, she heard the front door open and click shut. Thinking one of her pupils had forgotten something, she kept on cleaning.

"How'd the first day of school go?"

Leona whirled around at the sound of Abner Lapp's deep voice. "Oh, it's you. I thought maybe one of the kinner had come back."

Abner removed his straw hat and grinned. "Just came by to pick up my bruder." He scanned the room. "Looks like I got here too late, though."

She nodded. "The scholars left several minutes ago. If Emanuel didn't cut through the Zooks' cornfield, you might catch him along the road on your way home."

Abner shuffled his feet a couple of times, which brought him closer to where Leona stood. "Sure was plenty warm today, jah?"

"Hot and humid," she agreed.

"How's your daed doin'? Any of his memory comin' back yet?"

"Not really. There are times when he says or does something that makes us believe he might remember some things from his adult life, but then he starts acting like a boy again."

Abner twisted the brim of his hat. "Sure is a shame to see him like that."

Leona's only reply was a quick nod. She didn't feel like discussing Papa's condition right now. All she wanted to do was go home and relax on the front porch with a glass of iced tea and her best friend, Cinnamon.

"It seems odd to go to church and not hear our own bishop preachin'," Abner continued. "He used to be such a fine man."

Leona bristled. "He still is a fine man. He's just lost in the past, that's all." She didn't know why she felt the need to defend her daed—especially since she, too, had been having such miserable thoughts about him.

Abner took another step toward her. "I meant no disrespect. And I sure didn't mean for you to get all riled."

"I'm not riled." As the words slipped off Leona's tongue, she knew they weren't true. She was riled. In fact, talking about Papa's predicament made her feel edgy and depressed. As time went on and they continued to see little or no improvement, she became more convinced that her daed would never remember he was Bishop Jacob Weaver and not a little boy.

Abner touched Leona's arm, and she jumped. "Sorry. Didn't mean to startle ya. You just look so sad, and I was wonderin' if there's anything I can do to help."

She shook her head. "There's not much anyone can do except God, and He seems to be looking the other way these days."

Abner's forehead wrinkled. "I can't believe I'm hearin' that kind of talk from the bishop's daughter."

Leona stared at the floor. She didn't feel close enough to Abner to bare her soul, and she didn't want him feeling sorry for her. "I—uh—should be getting home," she mumbled.

"Jah, me, too." Abner plopped his hat back on his head and pivoted toward the door.

When she heard the door click shut, she released a sigh. Did everyone in the community think like Abner did—that she wasn't a good bishop's daughter because she couldn't accept her daed's accident and had lost faith in God?

"Well, they can think whatever they want," she mumbled as tears pushed against her eyelids. "No one understands all that I'm going through right now."

"Are you sure you don't mind me leaving the store a little early today?" Naomi asked Caleb as she set her black bonnet in place over her white kapp.

He shook his head. "I know you're anxious to hear how the kinner did in school, and since Sarah and Susan are here to help, we'll get along fine."

She smiled, feeling grateful to be married to such a good man. "If I leave right now, I may be able to catch them before they get to your folks' place."

Caleb chuckled. "Knowing Josh and Nate, they're probably halfway there by now."

Naomi's smile turned upside down. "They'd better not have left Millie to walk alone."

"I'm sure they wouldn't do that." Caleb opened the back door and leaned down to kiss Naomi on the cheek. "See you at supper time."

"I'll make sure it's ready on time." Naomi hurried down the steps and out to the corral where they kept their horse and buggy. She was soon on her way. A short time later, she turned onto the road where the one-room schoolhouse was located. It was the same school she'd attended when she was a girl.

So much has occurred in my life since then, Naomi mused. *If I had known all that would happen once I became a woman, I might not have been in such a hurry to grow up.* She clucked to the horse to get him moving faster, determined not to dwell on the past. But then she thought about her daed and how he still acted cool toward her. *I've asked his forgiveness for hiding Zach's quilt. What more can I do?*

Naomi noticed several children walking along the shoulder of the road, but there was no sign of her three. She'd just reached the entrance to the school yard when she spotted Leona's buggy pulling out, so she tugged on the reins and guided her horse to the side of the road.

"If you came to pick up your kinner, they've already headed for home," Leona called as she drew near.

"I figured as much, but I thought I might catch 'em walking along the way."

"That's probably the case."

"How'd the first day of school go? Did my three behave themselves?"

Leona nodded. "No problems with discipline, although Millie didn't seem very interested in learning."

Naomi frowned. "What do you mean?"

"When I tried to get her to write the letters of the alphabet, she got several of them mixed up and acted as if she didn't want to try."

"Maybe she was too nervous to concentrate. During breakfast this morning, she expressed some concern about her first day of school."

"That's probably all it was," Leona agreed. "I'm sure in a couple of days she'll be fine."

Naomi opened her mouth to reply, but a noisy truck pulled alongside her rig. Jimmy Scott, wearing a straw hat like the Amish men wore this time of the year, leaned out the window and offered them a friendly wave.

If Jimmy had a different haircut and wore suspenders, he would almost look Amish, Naomi noted. *I wonder if he's wearing that hat to keep the sun out of his eyes, or if he's trying to fit in with the fellows he works with.*

"Are you on your way home or heading to a job?" Leona asked, nodding at Jimmy through his open window.

"I'm basically done for the day, but Arthur asked me to drop by your folks' place and see about painting their kitchen."

"I thought Arthur was planning to do the painting for us."

"He was, but he's been busy with other jobs and doesn't think he'll get around to it for several weeks, so I told him I'd be happy to do it."

Naomi couldn't help but notice the eager smile Jimmy offered Leona—or the one that Leona gave Jimmy in return. It made her wonder if her daed had been right when he'd mentioned to Caleb recently that he thought the Englisher had too much interest in Jacob's daughter. *Of course,* she reasoned, *Papa might be jealous because Jacob seems to enjoy Jimmy's company these days more than he does Papa's.*

"I'm heading home now, Jimmy," Leona said. "So if you'd like to meet me there, I can show you what needs to be done."

"That would be great." He gave the steering wheel a couple of taps. "If you want to go ahead of me, I'll drive slow and follow you."

"All right then. See you at the house." Leona got her horse moving and turned onto the main road. Jimmy pulled out behind her.

Naomi clucked her tongue. *I've not seen Leona smile at any fellow that way since Ezra died. Maybe Papa's right. Maybe there is cause for concern.*

Traffic was sparse on this sunny stretch of road, and through the undercarriage of Leona's buggy, Jimmy could see the horse's feet clopping briskly along. As he drove slowly behind Leona, he thought about how much he enjoyed being with her. Leona was pretty in a plain sort of way, and even though she wore glasses some of the time, it didn't detract from her natural beauty. *It's good to see her smiling today,* he thought. *She's been so sad since her dad's accident.*

Jimmy's cell phone rang, and he grabbed it off the seat. "Hello."

"Hi, son. How are you?"

"I'm a little bit sunburned and kind of thirsty right now, but other than that, I'm doing okay," he said with little enthusiasm. *I wish he would quit calling. It only adds to my frustration.*

"I—uh—had lunch with a friend of yours the other day."

"Oh? Who was that?"

"Holly Simmons, the lady who goes to your church. You know—the one who owns the health food store at the mall."

A ray of hope flickered in Jimmy's soul. If his dad was getting friendly with Holly, maybe he would see the light and start going to church, which was exactly where he needed to be if he was ever going to see his need for Christ.

"Jimmy, are you still there?"

"Yeah."

"Holly invited me to attend an AA meeting with her."

"What'd you tell her?"

"I said I wasn't an alcoholic and could quit drinking any time I wanted."

"You really believe that?"

"Well, I—"

Jimmy tapped the brake pedal a few times, realizing that he was getting too close to the back of Leona's buggy. "If you can quit drinking on your own, then why don't you?" he asked, feeling his irritation mount further.

"I will—when I'm ready." There was a long pause, and then Jim asked, "So, what's new with you? Any luck finding your Amish family?"

"No. I've struck out at every place I've looked, and I'm beginning to wonder if I should forget about trying to find them and concentrate only on helping the Weavers."

Jim grunted. "Maybe you should come home and forget about trying to rescue that family."

Jimmy tensed as his face grew hotter, and he knew it wasn't from the sunburn he'd gotten earlier today. He needed to get off the phone before he said something he might regret.

"I miss you, son, and it's awful lonely here without you."

It's not my fault you're alone or can't deal with your guilt. I didn't ask to be kidnapped, and I shouldn't have to pay for your trickery or lack of self-control where your drinking's concerned. "I've got to hang up now. Bye."

Jimmy followed Leona up her driveway, feeling a sense of relief to be off the phone. Maybe now he could concentrate on something more positive.

He turned off the ignition and hopped out of the truck the minute her horse stopped in front of the barn. "Want me to put him away for you?" he called to Leona.

"You wouldn't mind?"

"Not a bit. Eli's been teaching me how to handle his horse, and I've even driven his buggy a couple of times."

She smiled and nodded toward the house. "I'll go inside and fix us a glass of iced tea. Then, as soon as you get the horse put away, we can cool down with our drinks before you look at the kitchen to see what needs to be done."

"Sounds good to me."

The sun beat upon Leona's back, causing rivulets of sweat to trickle down her spine. She hurried for the house, anxious to get out of the intense heat.

She stepped into the kitchen a few minutes later and found it empty. By the time Jimmy came in, she had two glasses of cold tea and a plate of peanut butter cookies waiting on the table.

He removed his straw hat, placing it on the nearest wall peg. "I got a little too much sun today, so a cold drink will hit the spot."

Leona studied his face and realized that it was quite red. "Let me get something to put on that burn," she said, heading for the refrigerator.

"You keep sunburn medicine in there?"

"It's aloe vera, and it feels better going on if it's cold."

"Ah, I see." Jimmy took a seat at the table and gulped down half of his iced tea before she returned with the leaf from an aloe plant that had been sliced open.

"Would you like me to put it on for you?" Leona asked. "Or would you rather do it yourself?"

"You can see better where I need it the most, so if you don't mind, I'd be much obliged." Jimmy leaned his head back and closed his eyes as Leona gently slathered the gel on his face.

When her fingers made contact with his warm skin, it sent unexpected shivers all the way up her arm. *What's wrong with me? Why should being close to this man make me feel so giddy?* For an unguarded moment, she let herself imagine what it would be like to be courted by Jimmy.

Drawing in a deep breath, she ordered her runaway heart to be still. *I'm just attracted to him because he's been so kind and helpful since Papa's accident.*

"That feels better all ready. Danki," he said, pulling her thoughts aside.

She pulled her hand back and stared at him. "You said 'thank you' in Pennsylvania Dutch."

He grinned up at her. "Eli's been teaching me that, too."

"It's good," she said.

"Jah, is gut."

She nodded. "Yes, it's good."

Feeling the need to put some distance between them, Leona moved aside. She sat in the chair across from Jimmy and took a drink of her iced tea. It was hard to make sensible conversation or think straight with him looking at her in such a peculiar way. The only sound to break the silence was the steady *tick-tock* of the battery-operated clock on the wall and the persistent hum of the propane-operated refrigerator.

After Jimmy had eaten a few cookies and finished his tea, he pushed away from the table and stood. "Thanks for the refreshments and the sunburn remedy."

"You're welcome."

"Guess I'd better see what needs to be painted in here."

"I didn't realize you'd come home already," Mom said, stepping into the room. "Your daed's taking a nap, and I was resting on the sofa. Must have dozed off and didn't hear you come in."

The whites of Mom's eyes were red, and the skin around them was kind of puffy, making Leona wonder if things hadn't gone well with Papa today. She was about to voice her concerns when Mom squeezed Leona's arm and said, "I'm so sorry to be tellin' you this, daughter, but Cinnamon is dead."

CHAPTER 25

$\mathcal{L}$eona sat there several seconds as she let her mamm's words sink in. *My dog can't be dead. Cinnamon was alive this morning when I went to the barn to get the buggy horse. She hasn't even been sick.*

"I'm awful sorry," Mom said, shaking her head. "It was an accident, plain and simple."

"Wh–what happened?" Leona rasped.

"Your dog ran into the road and was hit by a car."

Leona's spine went rigid, and tears gathered in her eyes, wetting her lashes and threatening to spill over. "Cinnamon never goes into the road. I've trained her to stay on our property."

Mom pulled out the chair beside Leona and sat down. "Your daed was outside playing with his goat, and then Cinnamon came along and got in on the act. The goat chased the poor dog around the barn so many times I feared they would both get dizzy." She paused and drew in a quick breath. "I kept calling to the dog, and your daed chased after the goat. But the two of them ignored us and ran down the driveway and into the road. Then a car came whizzing past, and Cinnamon—"

Leona held her hands tightly against her ears, hoping to drown out her mother's next words.

"Cinnamon was killed instantly, and the goat ran into the cornfield with your daed right behind him."

Leona clenched her fists and tightened her features as she screamed, "This was Papa's fault!"

"I don't think you should put the blame on your dad's shoulders," Jimmy spoke up.

She looked at him, but tears clouded her vision. In the pain of hearing about Cinnamon's death, she'd almost forgotten Jimmy was in the room. "If Papa had been at work, the way he used to be, this would not have happened."

"Leona, please be reasonable," Mom said. "It's not your daed's fault he had an accident and lost his memory. And he's not to blame for the car hitting your dog, either."

Leona trembled as she fought for control. Mom didn't understand the way she felt. She never had. "Where is she? Where's Cinnamon now?"

"Your daed wanted to bury the poor dog, but I knew you'd want to see her first. So after he captured the goat, I had him move Cinnamon's body to the barn."

Leona stood, and with a convulsing sob, she rushed out the door.

Jimmy started after her, but Lydia reached out a hand to stop him. "I think it's best to let her go. She needs time to be alone and think things through."

"I can't believe she would blame Jacob for this. Doesn't she realize it wasn't his fault that the animals ran into the road?"

Lydia shrugged as a swirl of emotions spun around in her head. "Leona's been moody and depressed ever since her boyfriend died, and then, after Jacob's accident—well, I think she blames God for allowing it all to happen. I'm afraid if her daed's memory never returns, she might spend the rest of her life angry at God and leery of establishing any close relationships for fear of losing the one she loves."

Jimmy slowly shook his head, and Lydia wondered what he might be thinking, but before she could ask, the sound of heavy footsteps clomping outside the kitchen turned her attention to the door leading to the hallway. A few seconds later, Jacob entered the room with his arms stretched above his head. When he spotted Jimmy, he rushed over to the table and pulled out a chair. "I didn't know you was comin' here today. Did ya want to go fishin'? I'll bet Mama would fix us a picnic supper to take along."

"I can't go fishing this evening, Jacob," Jimmy said. "I came by to look at the kitchen."

"Mama's got a good kitchen. She makes wunderbaar peanut butter cookies in this kitchen." Jacob tapped Jimmy on the arm. "You hungry? I sure am." He looked over at Lydia and smiled. "Can me and Jimmy have some cookies and milk?"

She nodded and headed over to the ceramic cookie jar sitting on the cupboard. *If only Jacob would remember that I'm his wife and not his mother. I can understand why Leona gets so upset with him. Some days it's all I can do to keep a smile on my face.* She piled several peanut butter cookies onto a plate. *For Jacob's sake, I'll keep trying to have a positive attitude, and I can't give up hope that he will recover someday.*

"I've already eaten my share," Jimmy said when Lydia placed the cookies in front of him. "I need to see if the cupboards in here need to be painted as well as the ceiling and walls. Then I'll be on my way."

"You can't go now," Jacob mumbled, grabbing a cookie and popping the whole thing into his mouth. "I ain't seen ya yet today."

"As you probably know, my husband enjoys your company," Lydia said to Jimmy. "So if you have a few more minutes, maybe you could sit and visit awhile." She glanced toward the back door and frowned. "I think my daughter's had enough time alone, so I'm going to check on her now."

"I'll have a couple more cookies; then Jacob can help me look the kitchen over, and we'll see what all needs to be done," Jimmy said.

In Jacob's present condition, Lydia didn't see how he could be any help in deciding what part of the kitchen needed painting, but if it gave him something to do, then she had no problem with it. "There's a jug of milk in the refrigerator," she called on her way out the door.

"I think Mama's mad at me," Jacob said, leaning his elbows on the table. "She don't like my pet goat. I saw her kick at him once when she was hangin' clothes on the line and he kept trying to steal 'em from the basket."

"Maybe it would be best if you kept the goat locked in the pen with the other goats."

Jacob frowned. "That's what Ona says all the time."

Jimmy was pleased that Jacob had referred to Leona as Ona and not Mary. He'd either begun to remember that she was his daughter, or he'd simply come to accept the idea because his family had told him it was so. He'd obviously not figured out that Lydia was his wife, though, and that had to be hard on the poor woman.

Jacob scooted his chair back and ambled over to the refrigerator. He removed a gallon of milk and placed it on the table. Then he marched across the room and grabbed a glass from the cupboard. "You want some milk, Jimmy? It's plenty cold."

"No thanks." Jimmy pointed to his empty glass. "Leona and I had some iced tea awhile ago."

"Ona's gonna be real upset 'cause her dog is dead. Got hit by a car, she did."

"Yes, I heard about it from Lydia."

Jacob's face sobered. "Bad things happen to people, too. Mama keeps tellin' me that I fell and hit my head, but I don't remember fallin'." He gave his beard a couple of pulls. "Last thing I remember is walkin' home from school with my bruder, Dan. We stopped and picked some cherries that were growin' in the field along the way." He wrinkled his nose. "Guess they wasn't ripe yet 'cause they sure was sour. Dan took one bite and spit it right out. You never seen a person make such an ugly face."

Jimmy thought back to the time when his mother had made a cherry pie and hadn't put enough sugar in. She had cried when she realized that she'd ruined the pie.

Thinking about Mom made Jimmy feel sad, and he stared across the room at nothing in particular, fighting a wave of despair that gripped him as suddenly as a summer storm. Not only had the only mother he'd ever known been taken from him, but he'd also never had the opportunity to know his real mother or any of his Amish family. Life could be unfair, and it was hard to understand why God allowed so many tragedies. Then he glanced up at Jacob and reminded himself that the man who sat across from him couldn't remember anything past the first grade. It made his problems seem small by comparison.

Jacob tapped Jimmy on the arm. "How come you're lookin' so down-in-the-mouth? Are you sad about Ona's dog dyin', or is there somethin' funny up?"

Something funny up? Jimmy smiled. *That must be Jacob's way of asking if there's something amiss.* "I do feel bad about Leona's dog dying," he said with a nod, "but I was thinking about other things that make me feel sad."

Jacob leaned closer. "What makes ya sad? Did your dog die, too?"

"No. I never had a dog when I was growing up."

"How about a cat? Ever have one of them?"

Jimmy shook his head.

"Then why are ya sad?"

"You really want to know?"

"Jah."

"Well, for one thing, I recently learned that I was stolen when I was a baby."

"Really?"

Jimmy didn't know what had made him blurt that out, but now that he had, he felt like sharing more. He was sure the bishop wouldn't think he was making up the story or question his motives, and it might feel good to finally tell someone the reason he'd come to Pennsylvania.

"My real family is Amish," Jimmy said. "And I believe they live somewhere in Lancaster County."

Jacob's bushy eyebrows drew together, and he stared at Jimmy. "Ya don't look Amish to me. Your hair's not cut right, and ya ain't wearin' no suspenders."

"I'm not Amish now. The man who kidnapped me is English." Jimmy picked up his glass and rolled the remaining chunks of ice around, letting them *clink* against each other. "Until recently, I didn't know I'd been born Amish. That's why I'm here in Pennsylvania—to look for the family I lost."

Jacob brushed some cookie crumbs off the table. "I lost a kitten once. Somebody must have stole it 'cause it never came back."

Jimmy inwardly groaned. *I shouldn't have expected him to show much interest in my story.*

"You gonna look for your mamm and daed?" Jacob asked, taking another gulp of milk.

"I think my real mother is dead. At least that's what my dad—I mean, the man who took me—said."

"Dead, like Ona's dog?"

Jimmy nodded and drank the liquid from the melted ice in his glass. "I don't suppose you might know of anyone in these parts who sells homemade root beer or had a child taken from their yard?"

"Don't know nothin' about no baby bein' snatched away, but Mama bought me a bottle of root beer the other day. It came out of a machine in front of a store in town."

Jimmy blew out his breath and stood. This conversation was going nowhere, and it was time to do what he'd come here for. "Say, Jacob, how would you like to help me paint this kitchen next week?"

The bishop blinked a couple of times, clapped his hands together, and his deep laughter bounced off the kitchen walls. "I'd like that. Jah, I'd like that a lot!"

CHAPTER 26

$\mathcal{T}$he next few weeks were difficult as Leona mourned the loss of her dog and tried to stay away from Papa as much as possible. She still blamed him for Cinnamon's death, and rather than saying things she would regret later on, she'd decided it was best to keep some distance between them. She knew it wasn't right to hold a grudge, but her daed still did things to embarrass her, which only fueled her frustration.

During the last preaching service, Papa had stood up in the middle of one of the minister's sermons and quoted a Bible verse. Some said it was a sign that he was improving, but Leona thought it had been a childish thing to do, even if Papa had cited Luke 18:16 by memory. "But Jesus called them unto him, and said, 'Suffer little children to come unto me, and forbid them not: for of such is the kingdom of God.'"

Shrugging her thoughts aside, Leona moved to the window so she could watch her pupils playing in the school yard during recess. She'd sent her helper, Betty Zook, to oversee things while she looked over the afternoon reading assignment. *Maybe I should be the one outside with my students. Being in the fresh air and joining the kinner in a few games might do me some good. It would be better than standing here thinking about how mixed up my life has become.* She sighed. *If things could only be the same as they were when I was a girl. Papa and I aren't close like we once were, and things between Mom and me feel more strained than ever.*

"Papa is some better, though," she murmured, turning away from the window. Last Saturday, her daed had helped Jimmy work in their kitchen. Of course, Papa had only done some of the easier things like covering the floor with a drop cloth, stirring the can of paint, and sanding some of the cupboards before Jimmy painted them. At least it had kept him occupied, which had given Leona and her mother a chance to get something done without having to check up on him.

When the kitchen was finished, Jimmy had told Leona that he wanted to give her daed the chance to do more meaningful things, and he'd said he was planning to ask Arthur if they could find some chores for Papa to do on some of their paint jobs.

Leona appreciated the time Jimmy spent with her daed, but having the Englisher around so much made her feel rather unsettled. She'd been fighting a growing attraction to Jimmy, and that upset her almost as much as dealing with Papa's memory loss. It wasn't right that she should feel drawn to someone outside of her faith. It wasn't good for her to think so much about the Englisher, even daydreaming about what it would be like if they were married. Was this weakness in her spirit a product of her declining faith? *Maybe I'd better speak with someone about it. Maybe. . .*

A shrill scream halted Leona's thoughts, and she drew her attention back to the school yard. She noticed a group of children gathered in a circle, and thinking one of them might have been injured, she dashed out the front door.

"What happened?" she asked Emanuel Lapp, who came bounding up the steps as she was descending them.

"Some of the younger ones were playin', and Millie Hoffmeir fell," he said breathlessly. "Betty sent me to get you."

Leona rushed across the school yard and over to the group of children. Millie lay on the ground in the middle of the circle whimpering and holding her right arm. "What happened, Millie?"

The child looked up at Leona with tears in her eyes. "I—I fell off the teeter-totter. My arm hurts, Teacher."

"Can you wiggle your fingers?"

Millie nodded as she opened and closed them a few times.

"Are you able to move your arm?"

The child winced as she tried to lift her arm. It might only be a bad sprain, but Leona knew X-rays were needed to determine if it was broken. She decided to take the girl to the Hoffmeirs' store so her folks could get her to the doctor. She put a makeshift sling around the child's arm. Then, after instructing her helper to take charge of the class, she led Millie over to the buggy and carefully helped her climb in. As soon as Millie's older brother had the horse hitched up, Leona situated herself in the driver's seat, gathered up the reins, and headed out of the school yard.

"Here's a basket of fruit and some cookies," Fannie said to Abraham as he stashed two fishing poles into the back of his buggy. "There's also a thermos full of cold milk."

He smiled gratefully and took the wicker basket from her, placing it on the front seat of the buggy. "Danki. It's much appreciated."

"I think it will do both you and Jacob some good to spend a few hours together," she said.

"I hope you're right about that. Me and the boys have been so busy in the fields lately that I haven't had much time for socializing." Abraham leaned down to kiss his wife on the cheek. "I've been lookin' for an opportunity to be alone with Jacob, and I'm hoping during our time together he might remember something about the good times we used to have."

She nodded. "It would be wunderbaar if he did."

"That young English fellow from out West has been takin' up way too much of Jacob's time." Abraham frowned. "I probably shouldn't be sayin' this, but I don't trust Jimmy Scott any farther than I can toss a bale of hay. Maybe not even that far."

"He seems like a nice man to me." Fannie gave Abraham's arm a gentle squeeze. "Maybe you should get to know him better."

Abraham climbed into his buggy. "Not sure I want to get to know him." He grabbed up the reins and gave them a quick snap. The horse moved forward, and he turned to offer Fannie a wave. "I'll be home before supper."

By the time Abraham had picked up Jacob and headed his horse and buggy in the direction of the pond, the afternoon sun had reached its hottest point. He didn't care, for he knew they could find solace under the shade of a maple tree near the water. Besides, it would be good to spend time with his old friend again, and the heat of summer seemed like a small thing.

He glanced over at Jacob, who'd been leaning out the window and making remarks about the things he saw along the way. *Dear Lord,* Abraham prayed, *let me say or do something today that will stir some memories in my good friend's jumbled head.*

A short time later, Abraham lounged beside Jacob on the grassy banks near the water's edge, both of them holding a fishing pole.

"I like to fish," Jacob said with an eager expression, "and I'm hopin' to get me a couple today."

Abraham smiled. "Maybe you will."

Jacob gripped his pole and stared at Abraham. "Mama says you're my good friend."

"That's true. We've been friends since your folks moved to this area when you were twelve years old."

Jacob's forehead wrinkled, and he squinted as though he was trying to recall. "Sometimes my head hurts when I try to think about things I can't remember."

"That's all right." Abraham pointed to the water. "Let's just fish and enjoy our time together."

"Jah, okay."

They sat in companionable silence for the next half hour. Then, suddenly, Jacob leaned over to Abraham and said, "Jimmy's my friend, too, did ya know that?"

Abraham's only reply was a brief nod. The last person he wanted to talk about was Jimmy Scott. He didn't think Jacob needed to discuss the Englisher, either.

"Jimmy let me help him paint Mama's kitchen. That was fun."

Abraham clenched his teeth.

"Jimmy's sad 'cause someone stole his kitten and he don't know where to find it."

"I didn't know Jimmy had a kitten."

"Jah. Some man came along and snatched it away, so Jimmy came here to find it. I had a kitten stolen once, but now I've got me a pet goat named Billy."

Abraham groaned. All this talk about missing kittens and pet goats didn't give him much hope that Jacob's memory would ever return. He needed to find something they could talk about that might trigger some recent recollections.

"Ona don't like my goat," Jacob continued. "She thinks it's my fault her dog got killed 'cause the goat chased it into the street." He sniffed. "I don't like havin' her mad at me. I think she wishes it had been Billy who died 'stead of Cinnamon."

The dejected look on Jacob's face made Abraham's heart clench. For the first time since his friend's accident, Abraham found himself caring less about the man's memory returning and more about finding some way to offer comfort to one who was obviously hurting.

He pulled the wicker basket Fannie had given him between them and flipped open the lid. "How about some cookies and milk?"

Jacob nodded eagerly and smacked his lips. "Are they oatmeal cookies? Those are my favorite."

Abraham was glad Jacob's mood had improved so quickly. That was something to be grateful for, since they still hadn't caught any fish. "I think my wife made both chocolate chip and oatmeal cookies," he said with a smile.

As Leona drove home from Paradise later that day, she reflected on all that had happened since Millie's accident. When she'd taken the little girl to her folks' store and told them what happened, Naomi had been short with her, asking why she hadn't been outside with her students during recess and accusing her of not watching them closely enough. Leona had tried to explain that her helper had been with the kinner, but Naomi was too upset to listen.

When Caleb and Naomi took Millie to a nearby clinic, Leona waited to find out the extent of the child's injury and to help Naomi's two oldest girls, who had been left to run the store by themselves. Upon the Hoffmeirs' return, Leona was distressed to learn that Millie's arm was broken and she would miss school until she got used to her cast and the pain had lessened. With the problem she was having in learning to read and write, missing any time from school was not a good thing.

Before Leona left the store, she'd mentioned the trouble Millie was still having in school and suggested that she give the girl some extra lessons. Naomi had taken offense to that, and Leona left the store berating herself for being an incompetent teacher.

"If only there was a way to make things better," she murmured. "Ezra's dead, Papa's got amnesia, my dog is gone, and I can't do right by my students anymore. Maybe it would be best if I quit teaching. Maybe I should get away for a while—go off someplace where I can be alone to think things through." Leona tensed and tightened her grip on the reins.

"But where would I go, and what good would it do?" She remembered before Papa's amnesia, when he used to say that it didn't pay to run away from your problems. During the time when he'd actively been their bishop, he'd reminded the people to trust God in all things.

Blinking against stinging tears, she whispered a prayer for the first time in many weeks. "Lord, I need help. Please help me to believe again and to put my trust in You."

CHAPTER 27

*W*hile Jim waited for Holly, he stared out the window at a curious seagull that had landed on the deck railing outside the restaurant. Holly had agreed to meet him at noon, and though it was twelve fifteen, she still hadn't arrived. Could she have gotten caught up in heavy traffic or had trouble with her car?

He wrapped his fingers around the glass of iced tea the waitress had brought him. *Maybe Holly's not coming. Maybe she thinks I'm a lost cause because I won't go to church or AA meetings.* He took a drink and let the cool liquid trickle down his throat, wishing it were a bottle of beer. But he knew if Holly showed up and saw him with an alcoholic drink in his hand, she probably wouldn't agree to help him.

The young waitress with curly red hair approached the table a second time. "Would you like to order now, sir?"

"Uh—no, I'm waiting for someone." Jim glanced at his watch. It was now twelve thirty.

"I'll check back with you in a few minutes." The waitress smiled and moved away.

Jim tapped the edge of the table with his knuckles. *Why hasn't she called? Maybe I should call her.* He pulled his cell phone from the clip on his belt and punched in the cell number she'd given him when they'd agreed to meet for lunch. After several rings, he got her voice mail and hung up. He dialed the number at the health food store, and one of the employees answered. "This is Jim Scott. Is Holly there?"

"No, Mr. Scott. She's supposed to be having lunch with you."

"Well, she's not here, and I'm beginning to worry." Jim glanced out the window again. The seagull was gone, and so was Jim's appetite. He took another swallow of iced tea and tried to calm himself. *I'm not going to sit here all day waiting for that woman. If she's not here in the next five minutes, I'm leaving.*

When Jim heard footsteps approach, he mumbled, "Sorry, I'm still not ready to order."

"You may not be, but I am."

He looked up, and the sight of Holly standing in front of the table brought relief and a strange sense of excitement. She was wearing a jean skirt and a plain pink blouse, but he thought she looked like an angel. "I—I was worried that you wouldn't show," he said.

She smiled, and her matching dimples seemed to be winking at him. "Sorry I'm late, but I had to stop at a gas station because my oil light kept coming on. It was fine after I added a quart of oil. I was going to call, but I left my cell phone at home this morning."

Jim nodded. "I can't tell you how many times I've forgotten my phone." He stood and pulled out a chair for her.

Holly sat down and took a sip of water. "I hope you didn't think I'd stood you up."

Heat flooded his cheeks. "The thought had crossed my mind."

"I would never do something like that, Jim. If I couldn't make it or had changed my mind, I would have let you know."

"I appreciate that." He toyed with his napkin. *Should I tell her what's on my mind, or would it be better to wait until after we've eaten?*

"Have you heard anything from Jimmy lately?" Holly asked.

"Talked to him a few days ago." Jim was glad for the change of subject. He guessed he wasn't ready to put his feelings on the line or risk possible rejection by her saying no.

"How's he doing?"

He shrugged. "He's doesn't call much, but I guess he's okay."

"Do you have relatives living in Pennsylvania, or is Jimmy taking an extended vacation?"

He grimaced. *If I told her the truth, she'd be gone in a flash.* "He—uh—recently found out he was adopted, and he's gone on a quest to find his real family."

"Oh, I see."

"I'm worried he may like it in Pennsylvania and decide to stay."

"I think all parents wish their grown kids would stick close to home." Holly compressed her lips and stared out the window. "But since it doesn't always work out that way, it's best if parents allow their kids to make their own decisions about where they will live." Her voice had a soft quality about it, yet she spoke with assurance.

The waitress showed up then, and Jim ordered a French dip sandwich and fries. Holly asked for a shrimp salad and a cup of clam chowder. As soon as the waitress left, he looked over at Holly. "You're probably wondering why I invited you to lunch today, so I might as well get straight to the point."

She picked up her glass of water and took a drink. "Did you have an ulterior motive?"

"Well, I was hoping you might help me with something."

She leaned slightly forward, an expectant look on her face. "What do you need my help with?"

"I'm—uh—" He released a groan. "I've been really uptight lately, and the only way I can unwind or forget about my problems is to have a few drinks."

"A few drinks, or are you getting drunk?"

He flinched. "Well, I—sometimes."

"Drinking yourself into oblivion is not the answer, and I speak from experience." She stared at her placemat with furrowed brows. "I grew up in Puyallup. Soon after I graduated from high school, I met Frank Simmons, who was stationed at Fort Lewis."

"An army guy, huh?"

"Right. Frank and I had a whirlwind romance, and two months later, we were married and moved to Fort Polk, Louisiana." She sighed. "Frank really wanted kids, and after we discovered that I wasn't able to conceive, he became hostile toward me, and—" Her voice faltered. When she lifted her gaze to meet Jim's, he noticed tears in her eyes. "Frank died from a drug overdose ten years later, and though I'm not proud to say this, I was actually relieved when he was gone." She stared out the window. "The remorse I felt for feeling that way, coupled with the guilt I felt for not being able to give Frank any children was the excuse I used for drinking."

Jim swallowed around the lump in his throat. "People do unexpected things when they feel guilty."

"I wasn't a Christian back then, and I didn't have the support of family or friends. What started out as social drinking soon became a crutch." She smiled. "I'm grateful that a friend of mine introduced me to

Christ, because soon after I confessed my sins and became a Christian, my life began to change."

He grimaced. *Oh no, here it comes—the "you need to go to church" lecture.*

"I thought you mentioned before that you got help for your drinking at AA."

"I did. But help came in the form of my pastor and friends from church, too."

Jim stared at the table. "Would you be willing to help me?"

She reached across the table and touched his outstretched arm. "I'll do whatever I can, but you must be willing to cooperate—and that includes attending AA meetings."

He nodded, and the heavy weight that had rested on his shoulders for many years seemed to lift a little.

Jimmy opened his window as he headed down the road in the direction of the Weavers' place. The cool air, ushered in by the coming of fall, hit him full in the face. The longer he stayed in Lancaster County, the more he liked it. And the more he liked it, the more confused he became. He enjoyed the Amish people he'd come to know and was impressed with their gentle spirits and the way they helped others whenever there was a need—even those outside their faith. He was inspired by their plain lifestyle and enjoyed their simple, tasty food. There were times when he felt as if he truly belonged here. He'd even wondered about the possibility of joining the Amish faith, which would give him the right to court Leona Weaver. *But could I give up all the modern conveniences? And what if I told them what little I know about my Amish heritage? Would it make any difference in how they accept me? Or would they think I'd made up the story in order to win Leona's hand?*

Jimmy groaned. He hadn't seen Leona since last week when he'd given her and Lydia a ride to Lancaster so they could do some shopping at Wal-Mart. After he'd dropped them off at their home and Lydia had gone into the house, he'd been bold enough to invite Leona to go on a picnic with him. At first she seemed to consider it. Then she'd mumbled something about him being English and her not wanting to give anyone the wrong impression. She'd dashed into the house without another word.

"If I were to join the Amish faith, it would mean giving up my photography hobby. I'd have to exchange my truck for a horse and buggy, and adhere to the rules of the *Ordnung*." He gave the steering wheel a sharp rap with his knuckles. *If I hadn't been taken from my rightful family when I was a baby, none of this would even be a consideration. In fact, Leona and I might already be dating or even be married by now.*

As Jimmy continued down the road, his thoughts became more jumbled. He tapped the brakes and slowed for a horse and buggy up ahead. *Do I stay through the winter or return to Washington? And if I go back to the only home I've ever known, what's waiting for me there? I'm like a ship without a captain, and no one can help me get where I need to go.* He ground his teeth together. *If I even knew where that was. Jacob's the only person I've told the truth about why I came to Pennsylvania, and he was no help at all. Should I quit worrying about what will happen to Jim if I tell my kidnapping story to someone else?*

Leona sat in a wicker chair on the front porch with a bowl of strawberry ice cream in her lap. Her folks were in the kitchen eating their dessert, but she knew if she'd remained in the house, Papa would have bombarded her with a bunch of ridiculous questions, the way he'd done most of the day. Saturdays were difficult to get through, since Leona was usually at home and couldn't avoid her daed. She held up fairly well during the rest of the week—when she was at school or, on Sundays, when they were either in church or visiting others from their community on the off-weeks.

Leona reached down to rub the top of Cinnamon's head but stopped herself in time. *Cinnamon's dead, and she's not coming back. Ezra's dead and won't be back. The man I've known as my daed all these years is gone and won't be coming back, either.*

The rumble of a vehicle brought Leona's thoughts to a halt. She glanced up and was surprised to see Jimmy's truck pulling into the yard.

"What brings you by?" she asked when he joined her on the porch a minute later.

"I was out for a drive and thought I'd stop over and see how things are going with your daed." Jimmy grinned as if he was pleased for using one of their Pennsylvania Dutch words.

"Everything's pretty much the same around here," she said with a shake of her head. "No real change in Papa's memory, that's for sure."

Jimmy dropped into the wicker chair beside her. "Sorry to hear there's no change."

She lifted her bowl. "Would you like some strawberry ice cream?"

"Thanks anyway, but I had a huge slice of Esther Raber's apple-crumb pie not long ago." He patted his stomach. "That woman is one good cook, and if I'm not careful, she's gonna make me fat."

"As busy as you keep painting, I doubt you'll ever be fat."

"You could be right. My dad told me once that he's been painting since he was in his early twenties, and he's still fit and trim." He paused. "Of course he's not really my—"

Maa–aa! Maa–aa! Jimmy's words were cut off when Jacob's goat bounded onto the porch, leaped over the railing, and nearly knocked Leona out of her chair as it stuck its nose into her bowl of half-eaten ice cream.

"Get away from me!" she shouted, pushing the animal aside. "You're nothing but a *zwieschpalt*—!"

The goat let out another loud *maa-aa*; then it nosed into her dish again.

Before Leona had time to react, Jimmy jumped out of his chair and scooped the critter into his arms. "Want me to put your so-called troublemaker back in his pen?"

She nodded, inwardly pleased to realize Jimmy understood her rantings in Pennsylvania Dutch. "I'd appreciate it."

Jimmy bounded off the porch and headed to the goat pen, which was behind the barn. Several minutes later, he was back. "Someone must have left the gate open," he said. "I closed the gate and made sure it was secure."

"Danki." Leona set her bowl on the porch. "I have no appetite for this now. Not after that pesky goat stuck his nose full of germs into it."

"Your daed says you don't like his goat much," Jimmy commented as he sat back down.

Leona gripped the arms of her chair. "He's right about that. If it weren't for Billy, Cinnamon would still be alive."

"Jacob thinks you blame him for the goat chasing your dog into the road."

She released a quiet moan. "After he made a pet out of the goat, it started getting out of its pen and causing all kinds of havoc around here."

Jimmy stared at his hands, which were folded in his lap. "It's hard to forgive others sometimes, whether you know what they did was wrong or just an accident."

"That's true, and I'm having a hard time forgiving Papa for not keeping that dumb goat penned up." She hung her head as a feeling of anger and frustration threatened to choke her. "My faith was shaken when Ezra died, but this whole thing with Papa's memory loss has made it worse. I'm not sure I'll ever feel the same way about things as I used to."

Jimmy reached over and took her hand as a look of understanding swept over his face.

"I used to believe God was in control and wants the best for us," she murmured. "But after all the losses I've had to endure this past year, I've begun to wonder if God cares what happens to anyone."

"On some level, I think I understand how you feel. I've been hurt, too." Jimmy's dark eyes clouded over, and Leona could see the depth of his pain.

"Do you mind if I ask how you've been hurt?"

"I grew up thinking I was my parents' son—by blood, I mean. Then shortly after my twenty-first birthday, I learned that I'd been adopted."

"Oh, I see."

"After Mom died, I was sure God didn't care about me or my dad. Then, when I realized I'd been adopted, I felt rejected and wondered why my parents hadn't told me sooner." Jimmy winced. "One day, not long ago, I found out that I was—"

A horse and buggy rumbled into the yard, halting Jimmy's words. Leona turned as Abraham and Fannie climbed down from their buggy and started across the lawn toward the house.

"We came to visit your folks," Fannie called with a friendly wave.

Abraham stopped when he got to the porch and glared at Jimmy. "What are you doin' here?"

"I came by to see how Jacob's getting along."

"Then why aren't you in the house talkin' to the bishop instead of sittin' out here with his daughter?"

"I'm sure he'd planned to see Papa," Leona spoke up. "But we got to visiting and then—"

"Jah, I'll bet you did." Abraham continued to stare at Jimmy as though he'd done something wrong.

Jimmy shifted in his chair, and even though his face had turned red, he made no comment. Fannie tugged on her husband's arm, and he glanced over at her. "What?"

"Why don't we go inside, Abraham?"

He nodded and mumbled, "Sure, okay."

"Sorry about that," Leona said once the Fishers had gone into the house. "I don't know why Abraham is acting so ornery tonight."

Jimmy stood. "I'd better go."

"But I thought you wanted to see my daed."

"Some other time—when you don't have company." Jimmy sprinted off the porch without even saying good-bye.

CHAPTER 28

$\mathcal{B}$y the first of December, the thermometer hovered near the freezing point for several days. Rain fell, and the cool air turned it to a thick film of ice. Leona knew it wouldn't be much longer before the young people in their district could enjoy some good ice-skating.

"Do you think this cold weather means we're in for a bad winter?" Leona turned to her mamm, who stood in front of their wood-burning stove one Saturday morning making pancakes.

Mom shrugged and reached for her spatula. "Guess we'll have to wait and see how it goes."

"I may need to have another talk with Naomi about Millie," Leona said as she began setting the table.

"Oh? How come?"

"She's still not doing well in school, and I feel frustrated because nothing I've tried has made much difference."

"Have you brought the problem up at one of your teachers' meetings?" Mom asked. "I'm sure some of the other Amish teachers have dealt with learning problems similar to Millie's. Maybe one of 'em will suggest something you haven't tried yet."

"I'll mention it at the meeting that's scheduled for next week."

Mom glanced over at Leona and smiled. "It's good that you're so concerned about your students—just proves what a dedicated teacher you've become."

Leona made no reply but moved over to the cupboard to get a bottle of maple syrup. She was tempted to mention that if she were able to further her education, she might have more knowledge in dealing with children who had special needs, as Millie obviously had. But she decided to keep her thoughts to herself, knowing that the leaders of their church would never accept the idea of her furthering her education.

There were times, such as when Leona encountered a teaching problem she had no answers for, when she wished she hadn't been so hasty to join the Amish church as soon as she'd turned eighteen. If she had more education, she could probably do a better job of teaching, and she might not be having such a difficult time getting through to Millie.

"The pancakes are almost done. Would you mind callin' your daed in from the barn?" Mom's request forced Leona's thoughts to the back of her mind.

With a reluctant sigh, Leona grabbed her heavy shawl off the wall peg and hurried out the back door. She wasn't anxious to spend even a few minutes alone with Papa. Seeing him struggle with his loss of memory was always a reminder of all that she'd lost. She and Papa had been so close in days gone by. Now it was like there was a cavern between them.

When Leona entered the barn, she found her daed bent over a bucket of paint inside one of the horse's stalls, stirring it with a flat wooden stick. "That way and so. That way and so," he mumbled over and over.

"What are you doing, Papa?" She stepped into the stall and closed the door behind her.

He looked up and smiled. "Jimmy says I'm gettin' pretty good at paintin'. He thinks I need more practice. So I'm gonna paint all the horses' stalls today."

"I don't think this is the kind of practice Jimmy had in mind. It's probably not a good idea for you to do any painting when Arthur, Jimmy, or one of the other painters isn't around." Leona touched Papa's shoulder. "Mom sent me out to let you know that breakfast is ready."

He frowned. "I ain't no baby, and you shouldn't be tellin' me what to do. I'm a grown man, and I can paint this stall without anyone showin' me how."

Leona stepped back as a sense of hope lifted her shoulders. Had her daed's memory come back? Maybe God had finally answered her prayers. "Do—do you know who I am?"

He nodded. "Sure. You're my sister."

Leona shook her head. Maybe Papa just needed a little reminder. "I'm your daughter."

He blinked a couple of times and stared at her. "You sure about that?"

"Jah. I'm Leona."

Silence draped around them like the shawl covering her trembling shoulders, until Papa finally lifted his eyebrows and said, "Ona?"

"That's right. You made up that nickname when I was a little girl."

His eyes clouded over, but then he gave a quick nod. "Okay."

Leona felt a chill—one that left her feeling colder than the bitter weather outside. Would this nightmare with Papa living in the past one minute, then acting as if he knew something of the present the next minute ever come to an end? Visions of happier times they had spent together in the barn raced through her mind, and her shoulders drooped with a feeling of hopelessness. Those days were gone for good.

Trying to shake off the nagging thoughts, she turned and grasped the handle of the stall door, squeezing it so tightly that her fingers ached. "You'd better come inside for breakfast now. The pancakes Mom has made will be getting cold."

"Okay. Should I make out the lights?"

"Better let me do that."

Jimmy glanced at the cardboard box sitting on the front seat of his truck. "I sure hope she likes her gift. She needs something to get her mind off her troubles."

He felt a compelling need to offer Leona support, and he knew the reason for his concern went beyond his sense of Christian duty. What had begun as curiosity had quickly turned to attraction. His desire to spend time with Leona and shield her from pain had taken him down a road he'd least expected. Jimmy wasn't sure how or when it had happened, but he was well on his way to falling in love with the bishop's daughter. That thought didn't scare him nearly as much as his concern over what he was going to do about it. If he stayed in Lancaster County and joined the Amish faith, he would feel it necessary to reveal his past—despite the fact that he knew so little about it and had not found his real family. He still, for Mom's sake, wanted to keep Jim from going to jail. However, he knew it wouldn't be right to begin a relationship with secrets, so even if he decided to leave Pennsylvania and asked Leona to go with him, he would need to tell her about the kidnapping.

Jimmy reflected on the phone conversation he'd had with Allen a few days ago. Allen had asked Jimmy when he was coming home, and Jimmy had been evasive, saying he wasn't sure what he was going to do. He'd said he was needed here—that Arthur had come to rely on his help with the painting business. He'd also mentioned that he enjoyed spending time with Jacob while he taught him how to paint and do some of the chores he'd done before the accident. He had talked about Leona, too, saying he'd been looking for ways to ease some of the burden she and her folks had been faced with since Jacob's accident. And before he'd hung up the phone, he'd asked Allen to continue praying.

Jimmy's truck jerked, then slid to the right, reminding him that the roads were slippery. He pushed his musings aside, determined to concentrate on his driving. In the town of Puyallup, they didn't get much snow during the winter, but he'd been quick to realize that Lancaster County got more than its share of snow and ice. That meant if he planned to spend the winter here he would need to drive defensively and be prepared to handle his vehicle in all kinds of adverse conditions.

Soon Jimmy steered his truck up the Weavers' driveway and parked near the barn, where he discovered a horse and buggy tied to the hitching rail. "I hope Leona or her mother isn't planning to go anywhere today," he muttered. The roads were too icy, and even with his studded tires, he had slid in places.

He stepped out of the truck, hoisted the box into his arms, and headed for the back door, where most of the Weavers' friends and family entered whenever they came to visit. Shifting the box to one arm, he rapped his knuckles on the edge of the door. A few seconds later, Lydia answered, wearing a dark blue dress covered with a black apron sprinkled with a dusting of flour.

"I hope I'm not interrupting," he said, "but I was wondering if I could speak to Leona."

"Jah, sure." Lydia smiled. "Ever since we finished breakfast, we've been baking apple pies, so maybe you'd like to come in and try a piece." She held the door open, and that was when Jimmy caught sight of Leona standing in the kitchen holding a rolling pin. She, too, had streaks of flour on her dark apron.

The delicious smell of cinnamon teased Jimmy's senses and caused his stomach to rumble. "A hunk of pie does sound good," he said as he stared at Lydia's daughter. Leona stirred something in him, but he knew that as long as he remained English he could only admire her beauty and strength, never pursue it. *I wonder how it would be to come home to her every night. I wonder how it would feel to kiss—* Jimmy shook his uninvited thoughts aside and stepped forward. He could appreciate Leona's lips, which sometimes turned into a cute little smile, but it would be wrong for him to kiss them.

"I've brought you a gift, Leona," he said, nodding at the box he held. "Consider it an early Christmas present." He pulled out a chair and sat down, balancing the box on his knees.

Leona reached for a dish towel and wiped her hands before coming over to the table to join him. Lydia, obviously curious about what was in the box, also headed toward him.

Jimmy opened the flaps, reached inside, and lifted a very sleepy, very furry red puppy out of the box for Leona's inspection. "What do you think?"

"Such a cute dog," Lydia said excitedly before her daughter could respond. "She looks like Cinnamon when she was a pup. Don't you think so, Leona?"

Leona tilted her head and stared at the puppy in such an odd way that it made Jimmy wonder what she was thinking. "Do you like her?" He extended his arms, hoping she would take the animal from him.

The pup, now fully awake, began to squirm, but Leona sat there unmoving.

"She's yours," Jimmy said. He was beginning to think he'd made a mistake in buying the little Irish setter.

"She–she's not Cinnamon, and there isn't a dog on earth that could take her place." Leona's chin quivered, and tears glistened behind her glasses.

Jimmy was afraid she might run out of the room, so he put the puppy back in the box. "She needs a good home, and I was hoping you would like her," he mumbled as the little dog whimpered.

Lydia reached into the box and rubbed the pup's ears. "Sure is a cute one." She glanced over at her daughter, but Leona made no comment.

Lifting the box into his arms, Jimmy stood. "Guess I'd better head back to the pet store and return the puppy." He nodded at Leona. "I'm sorry for upsetting you. I should have realized it might be too soon."

"Jacob's out in the barn trying to paint one of the stalls, and I'm thinking maybe he would like to have that little critter," Lydia said. "He's made friends with nearly every animal on our farm, and I'm sure he'd be glad to have another pet."

Leona jumped up, planting both hands on her hips. "No! Papa's not responsible enough."

Lydia clucked her tongue. "Come now, Leona. Your daed's done real well carin' for the chickens, horses, and his goat."

"If Papa had kept that troublesome goat locked in the pen, he wouldn't have upset my dog and chased her into the street." Leona's voice caught on a sob. "I've said this before, and I'll say it again— Cinnamon would still be alive if it weren't for that goat!"

Lydia wrapped her arms around her daughter's trembling shoulders while Jimmy stood there, not knowing what to say or do. What he'd hoped would be a pleasant surprise for Leona had turned into a messy reminder of the dog she'd lost and her anger toward her dad.

Guess I'm no one to talk, he thought ruefully. *I haven't forgiven my dad for what he did, either.*

"I'll put the puppy in my truck and then stop by the barn to see how Jacob's doing." Jimmy offered Leona a quick smile and made a hasty exit. He'd only made it halfway across the yard when Leona called out to him.

"Jimmy, wait!"

He turned and saw her running through the carpet of frozen leaves on the lawn. "You shouldn't be out here with no coat," he admonished. "It's much too cold for that."

"I've changed my mind about the pup. It was nice of you to buy it for me, and I've decided to keep her, after all." Leona opened the flap on the cardboard box, and when she lifted the squirming puppy toward her face, it licked the end of her nose.

Jimmy smiled and took hold of her arm. "Let's get the two of you inside where it's warm, and then I think I would like to sample some of your mamm's apple pie."

She looked up at him, and a shadowy dimple quivered in one cheek. "Danki, Jimmy. Danki for being such a good friend."

CHAPTER 29

I appreciate your willingness to drive me to town," Leona said, glancing over at Jimmy. His wrinkled forehead let her know that his concentration was on the slippery road.

"Glad I could do it. I didn't think it was safe for you to drive your horse and buggy on these icy roads."

She released a tiny laugh. "I've handled the buggy in all kinds of weather, but it is much nicer to be taxied into town by such a capable driver."

He grunted. "I'm not sure how capable I am. We don't get much snow or ice during the winter in the town where I grew up. When we do, it usually only lasts a few days."

"I appreciate the care with which you're driving. It makes me nervous to travel too fast, whether it be in a car or a horse-pulled carriage."

Jimmy nodded. "You wouldn't care for my dad's driving then. He's one of those 'I don't want anyone ahead of me' kind of drivers."

Leona smiled and relaxed against the seat. "I haven't said much about the time you've spent helping my daed relearn to paint, but I want you to know that both Mom and I appreciate it."

"I'm hoping if Jacob works around the other painters awhile that it might spark some memories for him."

"That would be nice, but I'm not holding my breath."

"I'm sure the Lord has a plan for your daed's life, whether his memory returns or not."

"I wish I had your faith—Papa's, too, for that matter. He's got all kinds of faith in his ability to paint these days."

"Maybe that's because he thinks like a child. It's much easier for children to have faith than it is for adults, especially when things aren't going so well."

Leona made no comment, just stared out the window. The barren trees hanging over part of the road looked like bony fingers waiting to snatch away anyone's joy if they walked underneath. The truth was, it was easier to have faith and believe in miracles when you weren't the one going through the problem. Jimmy didn't understand everything she was going through right now. It was bad enough that she'd been trying to come to grips with Ezra's death, Papa's childish antics, and her failure as a teacher. Now she had to deal with the swirl of emotions that swept over her whenever she was near Jimmy. Until she'd met him, she'd convinced herself that she would never fall in love again. Now she was afraid she might be falling for the wrong man—an Englisher, no less.

"So, what are you going to name that new pup?" Jimmy asked, breaking into her disconcerting thoughts.

She puckered her lips. "Let's see. . . . The puppy's real soft and fluffy, so I could name her Fluffy."

Jimmy wrinkled his nose. "Not masculine enough."

"It's a girl pup," Leona said with a snicker.

"Oh yeah, that's right."

"She's also quite lively and determined."

"I'll say. I couldn't believe how the little stinker climbed out of that box when we put her in the barn. It was twice as tall as the one I brought her in, but it took a box three times as tall to keep her inside."

"That's how Cinnamon was, too. Always determined to get her own way."

Jimmy smacked the steering wheel with the palm of his hand. "Hey, since your last dog was named after a spice, why not call the pup Ginger or Nutmeg?"

Leona tipped her head as she contemplated his idea. "Ginger. . . I like that. Jah, I'll call her Ginger."

They drove in silence for the next few miles, but as they entered the town of Paradise, Jimmy spoke again. "Mind if I ask you a personal question?"

"What's that?"

"I've been wondering if you think you could be happy if you weren't Amish?"

Leona didn't know what had prompted such a question, but she responded honestly. "I–I'm not sure. I've wondered sometimes what it would be like if I were English and could get more education, but it would be hard to leave my folks—especially now, with Papa's condition to consider. It wouldn't be right to leave Mom alone to deal with him, either. Besides, if I were to leave, I would be shunned because I've already been baptized and joined the church."

"I see."

She glanced over at him. "What about you? Could you be happy if you weren't English?"

"I don't know. Maybe, but it would take some getting used to."

They were nearing the Hoffmeirs' store now, and Jimmy turned his pickup into the parking lot. "What time would you like me to come back for you?" he asked.

"I should be done in half an hour or so."

"I'll run a few errands of my own and try to be here by noon. Maybe we can stop somewhere for lunch before we head back to your place."

"That'd be nice." Leona climbed out of the truck, wondering if Jimmy enjoyed being with her as much as she enjoyed being with him. Despite her resolve not to become romantically involved with anyone, she had strong feelings for Jimmy. *Is it wrong to have lunch with him? Maybe not.* She'd seen many English drivers having lunch with the Amish people they taxied around.

"You girls can put those books we got in this morning on that empty lower shelf," Naomi instructed her teenage daughters.

Sarah reached into the cardboard box to grab a couple of books. "Okay, Mom. We'll see that it gets done."

"What if there isn't room for all of 'em?" Susan questioned.

"Then we'll find space on some other shelf." Naomi returned to the front counter where a letter she'd received this morning waited to be read. It was from Ginny Nelson, the English friend she'd run away with so many years ago. She hadn't heard from Ginny in over a year. Tearing the envelope open, Naomi silently read the short note.

Dear Naomi,
Sorry for not writing in such a long time, but Chad and I have

been busy trying to remodel the fitness center he bought a few years ago—after we moved from Puyallup to Bellevue.

How are things with you? I don't suppose you've had any word on Zach, or you probably would have written and said so. I still think of your little brother whenever I see a boy with wavy brown hair and eyes the color of dark chocolate. Of course, Zach wouldn't be a kid anymore, would he? I guess he'd be about twenty-one years old now.

Naomi set the letter aside and drew in a cleansing breath. Even now, after all these years, the mention of Zach's name reopened old wounds, making her feel guilty for leaving him on the picnic table. *If only we knew where he was. If we just had some assurance that he was alive and doing okay.*

The bell above the front door jingled to announce the arrival of a customer. Leona Weaver entered the store, and Naomi's husband, Caleb, walked in behind her. Apparently, he'd finished with the errand he had gone out to run awhile ago.

"Thanks for telling me about this, Leona," Caleb said. "It's important that we keep up on how our kinner are doing in school. If we can do anything to help, please let us know."

Naomi was about to ask what Caleb was talking about when Leona turned to her and said, "I came by to speak with you about Millie."

Naomi leaned forward, her elbows on the counter. "What about her?"

"She's still having trouble in school, and I've tried everything I can think of to teach her to read and write, but she doesn't seem to be getting it."

"Maybe we need to work with her more at home," Caleb suggested.

Naomi nodded. She'd planned to do that soon after Leona mentioned Millie was having a hard time, but things had been hectic at the store. Since fall had crept in, nearly everyone in her family had taken turns with the flu, which had kept her busier than ever. Then Millie had broken her arm, and Naomi had allowed her to slack off on everything, including homework. "I'll start reading to her tonight," she promised.

Leona shook her head. "Millie doesn't need to be read to. She needs to learn how to read."

Naomi's defenses rose. She didn't know why she felt so frustrated whenever Leona mentioned the difficulty Millie was having, but talking about it made her feel as if she had failed her daughter. "I'll work with her every night until she knows how to read."

"I was looking through a magazine while I waited in the dentist's office the other day, and I came across an article on learning disabilities." Leona paused and flicked her tongue across her bottom lip. "I think Millie may have dyslexia."

Caleb's forehead wrinkled. "What's that?"

"It involves not being able to read or write correctly," Leona explained. "For some people, the words seem to shake or move. The article said some might even see letters in reverse."

"So what can we do about this problem?" he questioned.

"I'm not sure yet. The article didn't give much information. I'm planning to discuss the problem at our next teachers' meeting and see if anyone has had experience in dealing with dyslexia or knows of anything I might try."

"Let us know what you find out. We'll do everything we can to help." Caleb looked over at Naomi and smiled. "Isn't that right?"

"Uh—of course. Danki for coming by, Leona." Naomi turned away. "I guess I'll check on the girls." As much as Naomi wanted Millie to do well in school, she couldn't accept the fact that the child might have a serious problem. And she couldn't help but wonder if she might have caused the problem by not giving Millie enough attention.

Since Leona had finished her business with the Hoffmeirs and knew she had a few minutes before Jimmy would be back, she decided to step into the quilt shop to say hello to Mary Ann. She found her and Abby sitting at the quilting table.

"How's business?" Leona asked, stepping between the two women.

"We're very busy, even with the cooler weather and not so many tourists as we had this summer." Abby smiled, then excused herself to wait on a customer who'd entered the store.

Leona glanced at Mary Ann, noticing how her fingers flew in and out of the quilting material like there was no tomorrow. "Sure wish I could sew like that," she said. "Even though Mom taught me all the basic skills when I was a girl, I've never been able to sew as well as some women my age."

"I'm not really an expert at sewing, but I do enjoy making quilts. And I think the more I make, the better I get." Mary Ann grinned up at her. "How are things with you?"

"Not so good." Leona glanced over her shoulder at the door to the adjoining store. "Millie's still having a hard time in school, and when I tried to talk to her mamm about it, she seemed kind of defensive."

"My big sister always has been sensitive about things. When it comes to one of her kinner not doing well in school, I'm guessing she feels as if she's failed as a mudder somehow."

Leona shook her head. "If anyone's failed Millie, it's me."

Mary Ann touched Leona's arm. "How can you say that? You're a good teacher, and from what I hear, all your scholars think you're the *bescht*."

"I don't feel as if I'm the best of anything these days."

"Of course you are. You'll figure out some way to deal with Millie's problem."

Leona was about to comment when Jimmy poked his head into the quilt shop and waved. "Oh, my ride's here, so I guess I'd better go."

Mary Ann nodded. "I'll be praying that God gives you the wisdom you need to help Millie."

"Danki," Leona said and then hurried from the room.

As Leona took a seat across from Jimmy in a booth at the Bird-in-Hand Family Restaurant, her muscles felt so tight she thought her bones might snap. She kept thinking about the response she'd gotten from Millie's parents concerning Millie having dyslexia, and she wondered why Naomi had seemed so defensive.

She scrunched her napkin into a tight little ball. *If I just had more knowledge about things like this, it might not be such a problem.*

"Would you like to choose something from the menu, or would you rather have the lunch buffet?" Jimmy asked.

"Uh—it doesn't really matter. I'll have whatever you're having."

He chuckled. "Now that's what I like—a woman who's easy to please."

"Not really. I get frustrated when things don't go as I'd hoped."

Leona studied the geometric design on her placemat, then looked up when she sensed he was staring at her. "You seem to take life as it comes, Jimmy. I mean, look how well you've adjusted to living here. It's almost as if you've been in Lancaster County all your life."

Jimmy's eyes brightened, and he leaned slightly forward. "You really think so?"

"I do. In fact, Arthur mentioned once that whenever you've worn a straw hat while you were working you looked like you could even be Amish."

"Well, maybe that's because—"

Jimmy's words were halted when the waitress came and asked if they were ready to order.

"I think I'll have the buffet. That way I can pick and choose all the things I like best." He smiled at the pretty English waitress, and she gave him a quick wink.

A pang of jealousy seared through Leona. "I—I'll have the same." She knew it was silly to feel this way. She had no claim on Jimmy. And never would.

Leona followed Jimmy to the salad bar, determined to shake off the sullen mood she'd been in since they'd left the Hoffmeirs' store.

They returned to the table a few minutes later, and Jimmy suggested they offer a silent prayer.

Leona looked up when she'd finished her prayer. Seeing that Jimmy was done praying, she picked up her salad fork.

"I sure like these pickled-beet eggs," he said, cutting one in half and forking it into his mouth. "I'd never heard of them 'til I came here."

"Do you miss Washington?" she asked.

"There are some things I miss about it."

"When do you think you'll go back?"

"I don't know. It all depends on how things go."

She tipped her head in question.

"You see, I came here on a mission, but I haven't found what I'm looking for yet."

"What mission?"

Jimmy leaned forward, resting his arms on the table. "I thought I was ready to share some things with you, but until I'm able to make a decision as to whether I should stay, it would probably be best if I don't talk about it."

Leona watched Jimmy fiddle with the end of his spoon, wondering if he had some sort of secret. If so, then why'd he bring up the subject if he wasn't planning to tell her what it was?

Jimmy crossed his arms and stared at her from across the table. She wished he wouldn't do that. It filled her with a strange mixture of longing and fear.

"I shared a few things with your daed not long ago, but I think I only confused the poor man," he said after a few seconds went by.

Like you're confusing me? Leona's tongue felt as if it was fastened to the roof of her mouth. *Why would Jimmy take Papa into his confidence and not me?*

"There is one thing I'd like to ask you, though."

"What's that?"

"I was wondering what the Amish would do if a person—an Englisher—hurt someone in their family."

Her forehead wrinkled. "I–I'm not sure what you mean."

"Would they prosecute the guy and send him to jail?"

She shook her head. "That's not the Amish way."

A look of relief spread over Jimmy's face as he leaned against his seat.

"Are you in some kind of trouble? Are you worried about going to jail?"

"Not me," he said in a near whisper. "It's someone I know, and I'm sure he'll be relieved to hear that he won't be prosecuted for what he did."

Leona was tempted to question Jimmy further, but she figured if he wanted her to know he would have shared the details. "I guess I'll go back to the buffet and see what else is there," she said, rising to her feet.

"You go ahead," he said. "I'm going to finish my salad first."

As Leona walked away, feelings of confusion and doubt swirled in her head. What kind of secret was Jimmy keeping from her, and why had she allowed herself to be swept away by a tide of emotions whenever she was with him?

CHAPTER 30

$\mathcal{W}$hen Leona answered a knock at the back door one Saturday morning, she was surprised to see Lettie Byler, the Amish schoolteacher Eli Raber had been courting, standing on the porch.

"Guder mariye, Lettie," Leona said. "What brings you by so early this morning?"

"After our last teachers' meeting, when you mentioned the problem one of your scholars was having, I decided to speak to my Mennonite friend, Katherine, who's a nurse. When I told her that you suspected Millie has dyslexia, she gave me this article on children with various learning disabilities." Lettie handed the piece of paper to Leona.

Hope welled up in Leona's soul. "Danki for sharing this with me."

"The article not only lists the symptoms of dyslexia, but it also offers some suggestions you might want to try."

"Jah, I'll surely do that." Leona opened the door wider. "It's too cold for us to be visiting on the porch. Won't you come inside and have a cup of tea with me and my mamm?"

"Maybe some other time," Lettie said sweetly. "I'm on my way to the Rabers' to see Eli. As I'm sure you've probably heard, he fell off a ladder last week while he was painting a supermarket. Thank the Lord he wasn't seriously hurt, but he did sprain his ankle real bad, so he hasn't been down to Strasburg to see me in a while."

The mention of Eli falling from a ladder made Leona shudder as memories of Papa's accident filled her mind with gloom. Even now, she could still see him falling to the ground and landing with a sickening thud.

"You're shivering, and I must let you get back inside where it's warm," Lettie said as she turned to go.

"Danki for coming by. I'll let you know how things go with Millie."

The following Monday, as Leona opened the door of the woodstove to stoke the fire before her pupils arrived, she thought about the article on dyslexia Lettie had given her. It had been full of helpful suggestions, listing various ideas, such as breaking words and information into smaller chunks and placing colored overlays over the top of the pages the child would be reading. It also mentioned the use of a tape recorder, computer CD, and videotapes, but Leona knew those wouldn't be acceptable tools in her Amish community.

She was, however, determined to try some of the suggestions on Millie today, and she'd even brought a sheet of blue cellophane to experiment with the color-changing idea.

Leona had just closed the door on the woodstove when she heard the sound of heavy footsteps clomping up the front steps. Glancing at the clock on the far wall and realizing it was only seven thirty, she figured the footsteps didn't belong to any of the students, since school wouldn't start for another hour.

She smoothed the sides of her dress to be sure there were no wrinkles, checked her head covering to make sure it was properly in place, and went to open the door. She was surprised to discover Abner standing on the porch with a box of firewood at his feet.

"It's my week to furnish wood for the schoolhouse," he said. "So I'm dropping it off now, before I head to work."

She glanced past him into the school yard. "Is Emanuel with you?"

Abner shook his head. "He didn't want to get here early, so he said he'd walk with some of the kinner who live near our place."

"That makes sense." Leona motioned to the box of firewood. "Danki for this, and if you wouldn't mind moving the box to the other end of the porch, it would be much appreciated."

"Sure, I can do that." Abner bent to pick up the box, and he carried it across the porch with little effort. Once he'd set it down, Leona figured he would be on his way. Instead, he shuffled over to where she waited and stood there as though he were waiting for something.

"Is there anything else I can help you with, Abner?"

"Jah, there is." He scuffed his boots against the wooden planks and stared at the porch.

"If it's about Emanuel, you'll be pleased to know that he's done real well here of late. I haven't had a bit of trouble with him misbehaving for many weeks."

"I'm glad to hear that, but it's not my little bruder I want to talk about. I—uh—wanted to ask you something about a—a friend of yours."

"Which friend are you referring to?"

"Mary Ann Fisher."

Leona folded her arms to ward off the cold, wishing she'd had the foresight to grab her jacket before opening the door. "Would you like to come inside where it's warmer?"

"Jah, sure. I guess that would be better than standin' here in this chilly weather." Abner tamped the snow off his boots and followed her into the schoolhouse.

"What did you want to ask me about Mary Ann?" Leona asked, once she'd shut the door and taken a seat behind her desk.

Abner removed his hat and leaned against one of the desks in the front row. "I—I was wonderin' if she's—uh—bein' courted by anyone."

Leona bit her lip to keep from smiling. Her concern that Abner might be interested in courting her had been put to rest. Apparently, he had an interest in Mary Ann and had been too shy to show it. "Why, no, Abner," she replied. "I don't believe Mary Ann's seeing anyone right now."

A look of relief flooded his face, and his cheeks turned pink. "That's good to hear." He stood there, twisting the end of his hat brim and staring at the floor. Finally, he lifted his gaze and said, "I don't suppose you'd be willing to put in a good word for me."

"You mean with Mary Ann?"

"Jah."

"I guess I could, but don't you think it would be better if you spoke to her on your own?"

"I'd kind of like to find out how she feels about me first. That way I won't be embarrassed if I ask to court her and she says no."

Leona nodded. "I'll speak with Mary Ann when I get a chance, and I'll let you know what she says."

"Danki. I'd appreciate that." Abner plopped his hat on his head, swung around, and headed for the door. "You're a good friend, Leona," he called over his shoulder.

"Seems I'm everyone's friend these days," she mumbled as he shut the door. "Everyone's friend but Papa's."

Jim glanced at the clock sitting on the small table beside his bed and was shocked to see that it was only 5:00 a.m., yet he felt fully awake, energetic, and ready to meet the day. It was the first time in many weeks that he'd felt so well, and he figured the reason was because he'd attended an AA meeting with Holly on Friday night. On Saturday, they'd gone to dinner so they could get better acquainted and discuss some of the things Jim had learned at the meeting. He'd come to realize during their meal that he was physically attracted to Holly, and he planned to take her on a real date soon.

Jim pondered a couple of things he'd learned at the AA meeting. *"Live and let live. Easy does it. Think, think, think. First things first,"* he quoted from four of the five slogans he'd seen posted on the meeting-room wall. Those all made good sense.

He burrowed into the pillows propped against his headboard, remembering how he'd chosen to ignore the last slogan because it didn't apply to him. "Slogan number five," he muttered. "*But for the grace of God.*"

"Where was God's grace when I learned that I couldn't father a child? Where was God's grace when Linda died from cancer?" Jim groaned. "Where was God's grace when my boy took off for Maryland without telling me he was going and ended up in Pennsylvania searching for his Amish family? And where is God's grace now, when Jimmy won't return any of my phone calls?"

As Jim crawled out of bed and ambled across the room, his initial exuberance melted away with each step. When he reached the window, he pulled the curtain aside and peered out. The predawn darkness greeted him.

He gritted his teeth and crushed the end of the curtain between his fingers. *I'm determined to get my life straightened around, and I don't need God or His grace to do it.*

"Good morning, boys and girls."

"Good morning, Teacher."

Leona scanned the room to see if any children were absent, then began the school day by reading James 1:5: " 'If any of you lack wisdom, let him ask of God, that giveth to all men liberally, and upbraideth not; and it shall be given him.' "

I need that verse as much as the scholars do today, Lord, she silently prayed. *Help me to know what to do in order to help Millie learn to read and write.*

When Leona had closed her Bible, the children rose, bowed their heads, and repeated the Lord's Prayer in unison. After the prayer, they filed to the front of the room and stood in their assigned places according to age and size so they could sing a few songs in German and English.

Then the students returned to their seats, and it was time for class to begin. Grades five to eight exchanged arithmetic papers and checked them before handing them to Leona. Grades three and four gave their papers to an older child to check; and grades three to eight began their lesson by doing the assignment Leona had posted on the blackboard before school.

The children in the first and second grades took turns reading by page, but Leona worked individually with Millie, asking her to read out of her primer by sentences. Since the article Lettie had given Leona said that breaking words into smaller chunks had helped some children with dyslexia, she decided to try that approach first. However, after a few tries, she soon realized it wasn't going to work for Millie.

"The letters are shakin', Teacher," the child complained. "And they're movin' around on the page."

Next, Leona tried substituting a rhyming word for another word on the page, to see if Millie was listening, but that didn't work, either.

Finally, she went to her desk and withdrew the piece of blue cellophane she'd brought from home and placed it over the top of the page Millie was trying to read. "What's this say?" she asked, pointing to the word *dog*.

"D-O-G." Millie smiled up at Leona. "Dog."

With a mounting sense of excitement, Leona pointed to another word.

"C-A-T. Cat."

"That's right." Leona patted the top of Millie's head. "Now keep reading."

Knowing she needed to work with some of the other pupils, Leona put her helper in charge of Millie and moved over to the other side of the room. She'd just reached Emanuel's desk and was about to ask him a question when the front door opened, and Naomi stepped in.

Most parents usually notified her when they planned to stop by. Once in a while, though, a parent would make a surprise visit. Apparently, that was what Naomi had in mind, for she stepped up to Leona and said, "I came to see how my kinner are doing—especially Millie."

Leona might have felt irritation because of the interruption, but under the circumstances, she thought Naomi's timing couldn't have been more perfect. "Come with me," she said. She couldn't keep the excitement from her voice. "I want to show you how well Millie's doing and explain what I believe is going to help her learn to read and write easier."

As Naomi stood beside the desk watching and listening to Millie read, Leona waited with anticipation to see how she would respond.

"What's the blue piece of cellophane doing on Millie's book?" Naomi asked, turning to Leona with a wrinkled forehead.

"A teacher friend of mine gave me an article on dyslexia," Leona explained. "It lists several things that have helped with the problem." She pointed to the cellophane. "Using a colored overlay has worked well for many children, but since I didn't have any, I decided to try the cellophane. I figured if it worked, I'd order some of the overlays from the company mentioned in the magazine."

Naomi pursed her lips. "I'm not sure I want Millie learning to read and write with fancy things you've read about. What's wrong with her learning the old-fashioned way, like my other kinner have done?"

Before Leona could respond, Millie looked up at her mother and said, "I'm learnin' to read, Mama." She pointed to the page before her and grinned. "See here. . . Dog. Cat. Stop. Go."

"Good, Millie." Naomi squeezed her daughter's arm; then she leaned close to Leona and whispered, "I'll see what Caleb has to say about this; then we'll let you know if we want you to order those fancy overlays or not."

Leona's only reply was a quick nod. As she moved back to Emanuel's desk, she lifted a silent prayer. *Open Naomi's heart to this new idea, Lord. And, please, since I can't get more education, fill me with wisdom in knowing the best ways to teach my students.*

CHAPTER 31

$\mathcal{T}$he walls in the one-room schoolhouse seemed to vibrate with excitement as the children prepared for this evening's Christmas program they were putting on for their parents. Even Leona felt a sense of exhilaration while she scurried about the room, making sure everyone knew their parts and setting all the props in place.

Besides the fact that Christmas was such a happy time of the year, Leona was pleased with how well Millie had been doing these last few weeks. The child's reading and writing skills had improved quite a bit, and she seemed more attentive and willing to learn. After speaking with Caleb and Naomi again, Leona had been given permission to order the colored plastic overlays. It seemed odd that such a simple thing as a change of color could make a difference in the words being read; but it had, and Leona was very pleased. She knew Millie's parents were happy, because Naomi had even thanked her.

Now, if something could only be done to help Papa's memory return, this would be the perfect Christmas. She scanned the room to see who had come to the program. Some of the parents were seated in their children's desks, many sat in chairs placed around the room, and a few stood against the back wall. Leona spotted her folks sitting in chairs beside her brother. Next to Arthur sat his wife, Doris, and their four youngest children, Mavis, Ephraim, Simeon, and Darion. Their other three children, Faith, Ruby, and Jolene, were all students in Leona's class, and they stood near the front of the room with everyone else who had a part in the Christmas play.

She noticed Jimmy sitting in one of the school desks and was glad she'd thought to invite him. Even though she knew they could never have a permanent relationship, it was nice to have Jimmy as a friend. From the looks of his smile, she knew he was glad he'd been invited.

Leona put a finger to her lips to quiet the excited scholars; then she smiled at the audience and stepped forward. "Thank you for coming to share this special evening with your kinner. We'd like to present the story of Jesus' birth and share several recitations and songs." Leona nodded at Josh Hoffmeir, who was dressed as an innkeeper. When he didn't respond, she motioned with her hand.

Josh's face turned crimson, but he quickly took his place behind the cardboard partition in front of Leona's desk. BETHLEHEM INN had been written in bold letters on the front of it. Emanuel Lapp, dressed as Joseph, walked up to the cardboard inn while Leona's niece Faith, who was dressed as Mary, stood off to one side.

Emanuel knocked on the edge of the cardboard, and Josh stepped out from behind the partition. "What can I do for you?"

"My wife and I have come to Bethlehem to pay our taxes, and we need a place to stay."

Josh shook his head. "I have no empty rooms."

"But Mary's due to have a baby soon, and she needs—"

"Sorry. There's nothin' here."

"Please, I implore you."

The innkeeper shook his head.

"She can have my room!" a booming voice shouted from the back of the schoolhouse.

All heads turned, several people snickered, and heat flooded Leona's face. With a look of determination, Papa shook his finger at Josh. "If Mary's gonna have a baby, it wouldn't be right to turn her away. You're not a nice man!"

Leona glanced at her mother and felt relief when Mom took hold of Papa's hand and whispered something in his ear. Papa hesitated but finally sat down.

Leona was glad her daed had come to see the program, but his childish outburst had been an embarrassment, not to mention another reminder that he wasn't really her daed anymore.

She forced her lips to form a smile and signaled the children to continue with the play. *Why, God? Why did You allow Papa to lose his memory? And why won't You make him well again?*

Jimmy could see by the horrified look on Leona's face that she'd been embarrassed when her dad shouted out his offer to give Mary his room. He wished he could shield Leona from further humiliation, but he knew that, like himself, Leona would have to come to grips with her pain. Besides, as much as he might wish it, she wasn't his girlfriend, so he had no right to try and shield her from anything.

As the play ended and the program continued with songs and recitations, Jimmy's thoughts switched gears. In a few more days, it would be Christmas, and he couldn't help but wonder what Jim would do to celebrate the holidays without him. *Probably get drunk on Christmas and stay that way until the New Year is rung in. Even when I was living at home, he used the holidays as an excuse to celebrate with alcohol, and now that we are at odds with each other, his drinking problem has probably gotten worse.* He stared at his clenched fists resting on his knees and grimaced. *I do feel sorry for him, but I can't reach him. My days of rescuing Jim Scott are over.*

"Are you sure you wouldn't like a hunk of gingerbread to go along with your tea?" Lydia asked Leona as they sat in the living room, drinking the chamomile tea Lydia had fixed soon after her husband had gone upstairs to bed.

"Just the tea is fine for me," Leona replied.

"There was a good turnout at the program tonight."

"Jah."

"It was a joy to watch the kinner act out the Nativity scene, sing Christmas carols, and recite their parts."

No response, just a deep sigh from her daughter.

Lydia reached over and touched Leona's hand. "Would it make you feel better if we talked about what happened with your daed during the innkeeper's scene?"

Leona shook her head. "There's not much point in talking about it. What's done is done."

"No harm came from it. . .not really."

Leona set her cup on the end table and turned to face her mother. "Weren't you embarrassed by Papa's outburst? Don't you get tired of him acting like a child?"

Lydia blinked. "Well, I—"

"Everyone was laughing at Papa tonight. Didn't that make you want to hide your face in shame?"

"I did feel bad for my Jacob because he didn't realize it was only a play." Lydia released a quiet moan. "My husband can't help what happened to him, and I think it's time you quit thinking of yourself and thank God that your daed is alive."

Leona waved her arms as if she were fighting off a swarm of bees. "I—I am glad for that, but—"

"But you think the Lord should heal him because it's what you want—because your daed does and says things that make you feel uncomfortable? You're not the only one who's suffered since your daed's accident. It's been hard on Arthur having to take over the painting business. It's been hard on our church allowing Jacob to hold his position as bishop when he can't fulfill any of his previous duties." Lydia drew in a deep breath, trying to gain control over her swirling emotions. "And it's been hard on me. When your daed fell off that ladder and suffered a brain injury, I lost my husband and was left with a little boy to raise."

Leona opened her mouth as if to say something, but Lydia rushed on. "Ever since this horrible tragedy, I've silently grieved—but not because I was embarrassed by my husband's actions. I'm worried about what will happen to him if I die before he does." Her throat constricted, and a tight sob escaped.

Leona turned sideways in her chair and clasped Lydia's hand. "Oh, Mom, I'm so sorry. I've been selfish and should have paid more attention to the way you were feeling. I don't want you to worry about Papa. If something should happen to you, I promise to see that he's cared for."

"You're a good daughter." Lydia squeezed Leona's hand. "I think we should go down on our knees and ask the heavenly Father to give us both more patience and a better understanding of your daed's needs. Faults are thin when love is thick, you know." She lifted herself from the chair and knelt on the floor. Leona did the same. This was one of the few times since her husband's accident that Lydia had felt this close to her daughter, and she thanked God for His goodness and tender mercies.

Abraham stood in front of his bedroom window and stared at the drifting snowflakes. Fannie was already asleep in bed, but he was stewing about his friend. Would Jacob's memory ever return? It had been several months since the accident, and there had been little change in the man's behavior.

A couple of times, Abraham had felt a ray of hope—like the day he'd heard Jacob call his wife by her real name, and another time when he and Jacob had been playing a game of checkers. After winning the game, Jacob had announced that he'd always been able to beat Abraham at checkers.

But then there are other times, he thought regrettably. *Like tonight at the schoolhouse when Jacob didn't realize he was a grown man and shouldn't be speaking out of turn.*

Abraham leaned against the window casing and closed his eyes. *Heavenly Father, please bring comfort to Lydia Weaver and her family during this Christmas season. Let Jacob know You're still with him, and if it's Your will, allow my friend to have his memory back.*

"Abraham, are you coming to bed?"

He whirled around at the sound of his wife's sleepy voice. "Jah, in a minute."

"What are you doing over there by the window?"

"Just thinkin'."

Fannie climbed out of bed and ambled over to his side. "Mind if I ask what you're thinking about?"

"Jacob's been on my mind ever since we got home from the Christmas program. I've been prayin' that God will give my friend his memory back."

"It's good you're concerned about Jacob." She slipped her arm around his waist. "I'm a little concerned about you, though."

"Why's that?"

"Things haven't been right with you and Naomi since you found Zach's quilt in her linen closet, and I'm wondering how much longer you're going to hold a grudge."

He frowned. "I ain't holdin' no grudge."

"Are you sure about that?"

He made no reply, just moved away from the window and toward the bed.

"Don't you think it's time you put the quilt out of your mind and forgave your daughter? It's kind of hard for our prayers to get through to God when there's bitterness in our hearts," she said, following him across the room.

"Jah, I know."

"In Matthew 6:14, Jesus said, 'For if ye forgive men their trespasses, your heavenly Father will also forgive you.' "

Abraham turned and pulled Fannie into his arms, resting his chin on top of her head. "You're right. I do need to forgive Naomi. I'll clear this up with her soon."

CHAPTER 32

$\mathcal{T}$he pond not far from Leona's home was frozen solid. So one Saturday in late January, Leona decided to take some of her older students ice-skating, along with a few of her former students.

Several of the girls were in the center of the pond making figure eights. Emanuel Lapp, Josh Hoffmeir, and the Fisher twins had gathered some wood and built a bonfire several feet away. Leona planned to have a hot dog roast after the young people had skated awhile; then she would let them toast marshmallows for dessert. She'd also brought two thermoses full of hot chocolate.

"Leona, come join us on the ice," Stella Fisher called.

"I'll be there as soon as I get my skates on!" Leona dropped to a seat on a fallen log, slipped off her shoes, and placed her feet inside the ice skates she'd received for Christmas a few years ago. This was her first time skating this winter, and it took a few minutes for her to get her balance. By the time she'd made it to the center of the frozen pond, she felt a bit more confident.

Leona had made only two trips around when she spotted Jimmy's truck pull into the area where the horses and buggies had been secured by some trees. She'd told him about her skating plans the other morning when he had stopped by their house to pick up her daed for a paint job, but she'd never expected him to show up here.

Jimmy climbed out of his truck and said a few words to the boys who stood by the fire; then he walked to the edge of the pond. "Looks like a fun way to spend the day!"

Leona glided across the ice and stopped in front of him. Had he come because of her? The thought sent a shiver tingling down her spine. "Would you like to join us?"

"I don't have any ice skates."

She glanced at his brown leather boots. His feet seemed small compared to most men his age. "I think Emanuel's foot is about the same size as yours, and since he seems to be more interested in poking sticks into the fire than skating, maybe he'd be willing to loan you his skates."

Jimmy looked kind of flustered. "I only came to watch. If I tried to take one step on that frozen pond, I'd probably fall on my face."

"No, you wouldn't. Not if you hang on to me." Leona shook her head. *Now, what made me say such a thing? That sounded so bold.*

"All right, you've talked me into it," he said with a chuckle.

Emanuel didn't mind giving up his skates. So once Jimmy had them laced up, Leona took his arm and helped him over to the pond.

"Don't let go," he said. "My legs feel like two sticks of rubber."

"All you have to do is put one foot in front of the other and glide," Leona instructed as she gave his hand a gentle tug.

They made their way slowly around the ice until Jimmy felt more confident. Then she let go of his hand. "Hey, this is fun." He tipped his head back and caught a few snowflakes on the tip of his tongue.

When Leona looked at Jimmy, she thought she saw a reflection of her own longing in his dark eyes, but maybe it was just wishful thinking. *If only we didn't come from two separate worlds. If only I wasn't so afraid...*

"Let's go to the middle and try a couple of turns." A mischievous twinkle danced in Jimmy's dark eyes.

"Are you sure you're ready for that?"

He leaned close to her ear and whispered, "With you by my side, I feel like I can do 'most anything."

"Okay." Leona could barely get the word out; her throat felt so tight. Did Jimmy have any idea how giddy she felt being this close to him?

Stella, Carolyn, and Ada moved aside as Leona and Jimmy stepped into the middle of the frozen pond. "Don't run off on our account," Jimmy said. "I won't knock you over—at least not on purpose."

The girls snickered, and Carolyn motioned toward the glow of the bonfire burning against the frosty air. "We're gettin' cold anyhow, so we'll go stand in front of the fire awhile."

Ada and Stella nodded in agreement, and the girls skated off.

"So how's that puppy of yours doing these days?" Jimmy asked as he and Leona continued to glide around the pond.

"Ginger's doin' great." She smiled. "In fact, I never know what she's going to do. There's not a dull moment around our place since she came to live with us, that's for certain sure."

"What's the little scamp done?"

"Let's see now. . . . Ginger's pretty aggressive, so instead of the goat chasing her the way he did Cinnamon, Ginger keeps him in his place. Then there's her little water-dish trick."

"Water-dish trick? What's that?"

"Whenever I fill Ginger's dish with fresh water, she takes a few drinks, grabs the edge of the dish between her teeth, and tips it over. I think she likes to see me go to the bother of filling it up again."

"I never had a dog when I was growing up, but I always wanted one," Jimmy said in a wistful tone.

"Maybe you should have kept Ginger instead of giving her to me."

He shook his head. "It wouldn't be practical for me to have a dog right now—not with me renting the Rabers' trailer."

"I'm sure they wouldn't mind if you had a pet."

"Maybe not, but since I'm not sure how long I'll be staying in Pennsylvania, it wouldn't be good to settle in with a dog I won't be able to keep if I do go back to Washington."

"Your daed doesn't like animals?"

Jimmy shook his head. "Not unless they're in the zoo behind bars. When I was growing up, I asked for a puppy every year at Christmas, but I never got one."

"Speaking of Christmas," Leona said, "I was surprised you didn't go home for the holiday."

"I feel that I'm needed here right now." Jimmy glanced over at her and smiled, but she saw a deep sadness in his eyes and wondered what he wasn't telling her. "The Rabers invited me to join their family, so it was a good Christmas," he quickly added.

"Ours was nice, too. My sisters and their families came from Kentucky, and our whole family was together on Christmas Day. Except for Papa acting like a kinner, it seemed almost like all the other Christmases we've shared."

"I'm glad." Jimmy skidded to a stop and held his hand out to Leona. "I think I'd be able to stay in better rhythm if I was holding someone's hand."

She hesitated a moment before slipping her hand into his. Immediately, she knew she'd made a mistake. Even through the thickness of their gloves, Leona was sure she could feel the heat of Jimmy's hand. *He's just a friend,* she reminded herself. *A friend who needs my help so he won't fall down.*

Jimmy pushed off quickly, and the wind picked up, lifting Leona's black bonnet right off her head. She reached up to grab it and had no more than let go of Jimmy's hand when down he went, landing hard on his back. A vision of Leona's daed toppling from the ladder flashed into her mind as she dropped to her knees beside Jimmy with a groan. At that moment, the slanting rays of sun went into hiding, and she closed her eyes, willing the menacing image of Papa's fall to disappear.

"Jimmy, are you okay? Can you hear me?"

Jimmy opened his eyes and blinked a couple of times as Leona's pretty face came into focus. "I think I just had the wind knocked out of me."

"Don't sit up! You may have something broken." The fear Jimmy saw in Leona's eyes and the panic edging her voice made him wonder if she might have strong feelings for him—the way he did for her.

"I'm fine, really." He rolled onto his side with a labored grunt and allowed her to help him to his feet. "Nothing's hurt except my pride."

Leona slipped her arm around his waist, and they made their way off the ice and over to the crackling fire.

Jimmy eased himself onto a log and gratefully accepted the cup of hot chocolate one of the girls offered him. He sniffed the sweet smell of marshmallows and smiled. "Thanks, this is exactly what I need."

"Are you sure you're all right?" Leona dropped down beside him and wrapped the edges of her long dress tightly around her legs. "You took a nasty spill on that ice."

"I'm fine. Just don't know how to ice-skate very well, that's all."

"It takes practice," Harley Fisher said.

Emanuel drew his dark eyebrows together. "Maybe you fell 'cause my skates were too tight."

Jimmy shook his head. "It wasn't your fault."

"My brother, Abner, likes to go ice fishing," Emanuel said. "That might be somethin' you could try instead."

"I'll give it some thought." Jimmy took a sip of hot chocolate and licked his lips.

"Before his accident, my daed used to go ice fishing with Abraham," Leona said. "Since Papa's not up to something like that right now, maybe you and Abraham could go together."

Jimmy stared at the frozen ground beneath his feet. "I doubt that will ever happen."

"How come?"

He looked up and nodded at the children, who seemed to be hanging on his every word—especially Abraham's twin boys.

"Stella, why don't you and the other girls go to my buggy and get the hot dogs and buns? The boys can look for some roasting sticks," Leona said, motioning with her hand.

The children scampered off, and Leona turned to face Jimmy. "What did you mean when you said going ice fishing with Abraham wasn't likely to happen?"

Jimmy grimaced. "I don't think he likes me."

Leona's forehead wrinkled. "What makes you say that?"

"He said something once about his need to protect you, and—"

"Protect me? Does Abraham think I need protecting from you?" Leona stared at Jimmy with wide eyes.

He nodded. "I think that is what he meant."

"Maybe he's leery of you because you're English."

"He doesn't like the English?"

"I wouldn't say that he doesn't like them." Leona leaned closer to Jimmy, and her voice lowered. "What I'm about to tell you happened when I was a little girl, so I don't actually remember it. But from what I've heard, an English man came to the Fishers' one day for some—"

"Here's the hot dogs," Stella announced as she and the other girls bounded into the clearing, interrupting Leona's story.

She shrugged. "Guess it's time to eat. Maybe we can finish this discussion some other time."

"I wish we didn't have to work so many Saturdays," Ed complained to

Jim as his crew set up the staging on the inside of the new discount store they'd recently been contracted to paint.

"Working on the weekends isn't my idea of fun, either, but this is a big job we need to get done by the end of next week."

Ed reached under his paint hat and scratched his head. "Is everything all right?"

"Sure. Why wouldn't it be?"

"You seem kind of moody today."

"I'm not moody."

Ed grunted. "You were irritable for several weeks after Jimmy headed back East, but after you went on a date with that health nut, you seemed to calm down some."

"Holly's not a health nut." Jim felt his defenses rise. "She runs a health food store and knows a lot about nutrition." He jabbed Ed's paunchy stomach with his finger. "That's something we all could benefit from, don't you think?"

Ed merely shrugged in reply.

Jim wasn't about to admit to Ed that since he'd finally worked up the courage and asked Holly for a date they had gone out several more times. Besides attending AA meetings together, they'd taken in a couple of movies and had gone to dinner twice more. Jim had managed to remain sober during that time, and he gave the credit to Holly, who seemed to be his only support right now. Jimmy sure wasn't there for him anymore. He'd only spoken to him twice in the last few months, and those had been times when Jim had initiated the call. Jimmy always seemed distant and managed to make up some excuse to get off the phone.

I think I've changed in many ways since I met Holly, Jim thought. *But am I ready to tell her that I kidnapped Jimmy? Would she understand the reason I took him, or would she condemn me—the way he has?*

He grabbed a gallon of paint and moved toward the staging that had been set in place. "We haven't got all day, fellows, so let's get to work!"

CHAPTER 33

$\mathcal{I}$ appreciate you bringing in a hot lunch for the scholars today." Leona ushered Naomi and Abby into the schoolhouse. They each carried a cardboard box.

"Since today's Valentine's Day, we thought it would be a nice treat for you and the kinner." Naomi set her box on one end of Leona's desk, and Abby placed hers on the other end. "Besides, I wanted the chance to tell you thanks for helping Millie. She's reading better these days, and it's because you took the time to learn about her problem and work with her."

Leona's cheeks warmed. She didn't need any thanks for what she'd done. It was part of her job as a teacher, and she was glad that, despite her lack of continued education, she'd been able to find a way to reach Millie.

"You looked for solutions even after I refused to accept the fact that my daughter might have a learning disability." Naomi's forehead wrinkled. "When I blamed myself for not taking enough time with Millie, Caleb reminded me that I tend to be too hard on myself, and I guess he's right. Ever since my brother was kidnapped, I've struggled with guilt and tried to do everything perfect, which is why I didn't deal well with Millie's problem. I felt that I had failed her somehow."

"Many parents feel that way when their kinner have any kind of trouble," Abby interjected. "We just need to remember that no one but God is perfect and do the best we can."

"Papa admitted to me the other day that he's not perfect, and he apologized for giving me the cold shoulder after he discovered Zach's quilt in my linen closet," Naomi said.

Abby smiled. "I'm so glad to hear that. I've been concerned because things weren't right between you and Abraham, and so has my mamm."

Leona nodded and squeezed Naomi's hand. Then she motioned to the front door. "I let the kinner go outside for a while, so when they come in, we can serve the hot meal."

"As we were pulling in, I noticed several of them building a snowman," Abby commented. "That brought back memories of when I was a girl growing up in Ohio. One of my favorite things to do during the wintertime was to make a huge snowman."

Naomi shook her head. "Not me. I always preferred to be inside where it was warm and I was safe from the icy snowballs being thrown around the school yard."

Leona leaned on her desk and visited with Naomi and Abby a few more minutes. Then she finally excused herself to ring the school bell. She had just stepped onto the porch when Nate Hoffmeir bounded up the steps. "Teacher, my cousin John couldn't make it to the outhouse in time, and he threw up in the bushes." He pointed across the yard.

Leona felt immediate concern. John had complained of a stomachache earlier this morning, but she hadn't thought much of it because he'd seemed well enough to go outside and play with the others. "Run inside and tell your mamm and Abby to set the lunch out for the others while I see about John," she said to Nate.

The boy raced into the building, and Leona, wishing she'd thought to put on a coat, tromped through the snow to check on the ailing child. She found John hunched over a clump of bushes, groaning and holding his stomach. "I've got a bellyache, and it hurts real bad," he said, looking up at her with tears in his eyes.

Leona patted him on the back "I'm sorry you aren't feeling well. It's probably the flu. Let's go inside, and I'll ask your aunt Naomi to take you home."

A short time later, they had John loaded into Naomi's buggy, and Abby, who had come in her own rig, agreed to stay and help Leona serve lunch to the children.

The rest of the afternoon passed swiftly, and Leona's pupils headed for home carrying the valentines they'd received, as well as the bag of candy Leona had given each of them.

"I should have thought to send John's candy and valentines with him," Leona said as Abby gathered her children together.

"I'll be going past Norman and Ruth's house on my way home, so

I'd be happy to drop John's things off to him." Abby grimaced. "I hope this isn't the beginning of another round of achy-bones flu. My kinner have already been out once with it this winter."

"I hope not, either." Leona closed the door behind Abby and her children. Then she set to work cleaning the sticky spots from spilled punch off the floor. She was nearly finished when she heard the nicker of a horse. She hurried to the window and looked out, wondering if one of the scholars had forgotten something.

As soon as the driver of the buggy stepped down from his rig, Leona realized it was Abner, so she opened the door to see what he wanted.

"I brought a valentine," he said as he started up the steps.

"What? Oh, I see." Gathering her wits about her, Leona motioned him into the schoolhouse.

Abner reached into his jacket pocket and handed her an envelope. She was about to open it when she noticed the words on the front. To: MARY ANN.

"Oh no," Leona moaned.

"What's wrong?" Abner asked with raised brows. "Did I spell her name wrong?"

She shook her head. "I feel terrible about this, Abner, but I've been so busy I forgot to speak with Mary Ann on your behalf."

His lips drooped as wrinkles appeared on his forehead. "Maybe I'd best take the card back then, since I don't know how Mary Ann will respond."

She contemplated his suggestion for a moment but then came up with one of her own. "How would it be if I delivered the card to Mary Ann? That will open the door for me to speak to her about you."

He nodded, but his frown remained in place. "What if she doesn't accept the valentine? What if she's not interested in me at all?"

Then you'll deal with it—same as I've had to deal with Ezra's untimely death, Leona thought. "It's better to know now, don't you think?"

His only reply was a hasty shrug.

Feeling the need to offer Abner a ray of hope, Leona quickly added, "Many Amish women Mary Ann's age are already married and starting their families, but I know for a fact that she's been waiting for the right man." She paused, searching for the right words. "I'm surprised Mary Ann hasn't realized you could be that man."

Abner averted his gaze to the floor. "Even though I've admired Mary Ann for some time, I've never had the nerve to say much to her, so there's no way she'd know what kind of man I am. Besides," he added with a grunt, "there ain't nothin' special about me."

"That's not true, Abner. You're kind, considerate, and a good provider for your mamm and little bruder. Those are fine qualities that a woman hoping to get married would look for in a husband."

Abner's ears turned pink as he started back across the room. "Well, guess I'd best be gettin' home. Emanuel's probably there already."

"Jah, the kinner left awhile ago." She followed him to the door. "I'll let you know what Mary Ann has to say about the valentine, and I promise to give it to her right away."

Abner gave Leona a backward wave and climbed into his buggy. He'd just pulled out of the school yard when Jimmy's truck pulled in.

Reaching up to make sure her covering was properly in place, she stepped forward to greet him. "Come inside. It's awfully cold."

"You can say that again." He offered her a smile so warm she thought it could have melted the snow covering the school yard.

As soon as they stepped into the schoolhouse, Leona motioned Jimmy over to the stove. "There's some treats left from our Valentine's Day party," she said, pointing to some cookies and a jug of punch on the table. "Would you care for something to eat or drink?"

"That'd be nice." Jimmy took a chocolate chip cookie and popped it into his mouth. "Umm. . . This is good." He washed it down with some punch and grinned at her like an eager child. "Did you make these?"

She shook her head. "Naomi Fisher baked 'em."

"Was that one of your students' parents I saw leaving in the buggy?" he asked, glancing toward the front window.

"It was Abner Lapp."

"Came to pick up his little brother, I'll bet."

"Actually, the kinner left some time ago. Abner dropped by to deliver this." She picked up the envelope from her desk. "It's a valentine card."

"I see." Jimmy's smile turned to a frown. "Guess you won't be wanting mine then."

Tears welled up in Leona's eyes, and she blinked to keep them from spilling over. "You—you brought me a valentine?"

He nodded soberly. "Should have known you probably had a

boyfriend and would be getting one from him. It's just that—well, I'd hoped—" His voice trailed off as he reached into his jacket pocket and pulled out an envelope. "Is it all right if I give it to you, anyway—from one friend to another?"

"Abner's not my boyfriend," she stammered. "The card he brought isn't for me."

"It's not?"

"No. He asked me to deliver it to Mary Ann Fisher. He was afraid to give it to her himself."

Jimmy's contagious smile was back in place, and he quickly handed her the envelope.

With trembling fingers, Leona tore open the flap and removed the card. It read: *In life's garden, friends are the flowers. Thanks for being my friend, Jimmy.*

"Danki. It's a very nice card, and I'm glad you're my friend, too." Her voice was barely above a whisper, and she had to blink several times to keep her tears from spilling over. *Oh, Jimmy, I wish we could be more than friends.*

Jimmy set down his empty cup, then took another cookie and stuffed it in his pocket. "I—uh—need to check on a paint job for Arthur before I head for the Rabers'. I probably should be on my way. Danki for the treat."

"You're welcome." Leona felt a sense of disappointment as she watched him leave the building. If she were willing to open her heart to love again, it would be to someone like Jimmy. But of course that was impossible since she was Amish and he was English. Besides, she was afraid of committing herself to a man, knowing he could be taken from her the way Ezra had been.

As Leona returned to cleaning the room, she released a sigh. *Life's full of disappointments, and losing a loved one is the worst kind. I've already suffered several injustices, and I'll do whatever I can to protect myself from more.*

Lydia reached for an orange from the fruit bowl on the kitchen counter and was shocked to discover that it wasn't a real orange at all. She turned to face Jacob, who sat at the table drinking a glass of milk. "Have you been playing tricks on me again?"

He grinned like a mischievous boy and bobbed his head up and down. "I wanted to see if you'd take notice."

"Oh, I noticed all right. Almost cut this up to put in the fruit salad I'm making for supper tonight." She held up the plastic orange. "Where'd you get this?"

"Found it in the one of the houses we was paintin' last week. The lady who lived there said I could have it."

Lydia grimaced. *What must that woman have thought when a grown man asked for a plastic orange?*

"What else are we havin' for supper?" Jacob asked.

"Chicken potpie, soft bread sticks, pickled beets, and fruit salad."

"How 'bout dessert?"

"I took a jar of applesauce from the root cellar this afternoon, and we'll probably have cookies if Leona brings some home from the Valentine's Day party she had for the scholars."

"Umm." Jacob smacked his lips. "Know what, Lydia?"

"What's that?"

"You look good in the face."

She smiled. In some ways, her husband hadn't changed so much since he'd lost his memory. He'd always had a sense of humor, and even some of his more boyish pranks seemed to fit with his jovial personality. He'd begun calling her "Lydia" again, but she knew it wasn't because he remembered her as his wife. It was simply a matter of her telling him over and over that she wasn't his mother and her name was Lydia.

"Danki, Jacob," she said. "I'm kind of partial to your face, too."

"Jimmy told a funny joke before he brought me home today," Jacob said.

"Do you want to share it with me?"

"Jah, sure." Jacob drank the last of his milk and wiped his mouth with the back of his hand. Lydia was tempted to say something about his manners but changed her mind. No point in ruining the camaraderie between them over something so small.

"Let's see now," Jacob began. "An Englisher stopped by an Amish man's house one day and said, 'I'm headin' to Blue Ball, so does it make any difference which road I take?' " He paused and rubbed the bridge of his nose. "The Amish man thought for a minute; then he answered,

'Nope. Don't make no difference to me.' "

Lydia chuckled. Thanks to Jimmy, Jacob was able to work half days, and he seemed much happier than he had before.

"Want to hear another joke? Richard told me a couple of good ones today."

"Sure, go ahead."

A knock sounded at the back door before Jacob could begin the next story. "Want me to get it?" he asked.

Lydia reached into the fruit bowl for an apple. "I'd appreciate that."

A rush of cold air whipped into the room when Jacob opened the door. Caleb Hoffmeir stomped his boots on the porch and stepped inside.

"It's good to see you, Caleb," Lydia said. "What brings you out our way on this cold afternoon?"

"Naomi wanted me to let Leona know that our nephew John is in the hospital."

Lydia crinkled her forehead. "I'm sorry to hear that. What's he there for?"

"He got sick at school today, and since Naomi had gone with Abby to serve the scholars a hot lunch, she volunteered to take him home. By the time they got halfway there, he'd thrown up several times. So Naomi took him to the clinic in town and got word to her brother and his wife, asking them to meet her there."

Jacob ambled across the room and plunked down in the chair. "I don't like doctors. You gotta watch out for 'em 'cause they poke around on you too much and ask a bunch of questions."

Lydia turned to Caleb. "What did the doctor at the clinic say about John?"

"They ran a couple of tests and sent him straightaway to the hospital in Lancaster." Caleb shook his head. "By the time they got him there, his appendix had burst open."

Lydia clucked her tongue. "That can be serious."

Caleb nodded. "They rushed him into surgery, and the last I heard, he's doin' as well as can be expected."

"We should pray for John," Jacob said in a serious tone. "God can heal the boy. I'm sure of it."

Caleb glanced at Lydia with a peculiar expression, and she wondered if his thoughts were the same as hers. Had her husband's comment come from Jacob the bishop, or was he merely repeating something he'd heard at one of their church services?

Before Lydia could voice the question, the back door swung open and Leona entered the kitchen. "Oh, it's you, Caleb," she said, removing her dark bonnet and brushing flakes of snow off the top. "I was wondering whose rig that was outside."

"He dropped by to give you news of John Fisher," Lydia said before Caleb could respond.

Leona nodded. "He got sick at school today, and Naomi took him home. I think he's got the flu."

"He ain't got no flu," Jacob spoke up.

"It's much worse than that," Caleb said. "John's appendix ruptured, and he's in the hospital recovering from surgery."

Leona's face turned chalky white. "All morning the boy complained of a stomachache. I should have realized how sick he was." She paced the length of the kitchen, her hands clasped in front of her as she slowly shook her head. "If he'd gotten to the hospital sooner, they might have caught it before his appendix ruptured."

"Now don't blame yourself," Lydia was quick to say. "You had no way of knowing it was more than a simple flu bug causing him to feel sick."

"Your mamm's right," Caleb agreed. "From what I understand, it's not easy to know when someone's having a problem with their appendix."

A look of doubt flashed onto Leona's face, and Lydia felt relief when her daughter finally nodded and said, "I'll have the class make John some get-well cards tomorrow. After school's out for the day, I'll see about getting a ride to Lancaster so I can visit him at the hospital."

Jacob folded his arms and shook his head. "Not me. I ain't goin' to no hospital. Never again!"

CHAPTER 34

The following afternoon, shortly after Leona's students went home, Jimmy showed up at the schoolhouse to drive her to the hospital. He promised to take her by Abby's quilt shop afterwards so she could deliver Abner's valentine to Mary Ann.

"I appreciate you doing this for me," Leona said as Jimmy opened the door on the passenger's side of his pickup.

"I'm willing to drive you wherever you need to go, so don't hesitate to ask." Jimmy smiled. "That goes for anyone else in your family who might ever need a ride."

"Danki." She said, sliding into her seat.

He closed the door and came around to the driver's side. "Have you been ice-skating lately?" he asked, once he was seated and had shut his own door.

Leona shook her head.

"Maybe we could go again this Saturday and then have lunch somewhere afterward."

"You—you mean, just the two of us?"

He nodded. "If that's all right with you?"

Leona knew it wouldn't look good if she went skating alone with Jimmy. If anyone saw them together, they might assume she and Jimmy were on a date.

She studied his handsome face. Was a date what he had in mind?

"You're awfully quiet," he said. "Are you afraid I might fall on the ice again?"

Leona's fingers trembled as she snapped her seat belt into place. "I–I'm concerned that someone might get the wrong idea if they see us alone together."

"We're alone now."

"This is different. You're driving me somewhere. Ice-skating by ourselves would be more like a—"

"Date?"

She nodded. "Some young Amish women do date English fellows when they're going through *rumschpringe*, but once a woman has been baptized and joined the church, she's expected to date only Amish men."

"Have you found a special Amish man yet?" he asked.

"No, and I'm not looking."

"If I were Amish or you were English, would you go out with me?"

Tears pricked the back of her eyes. "You're not Amish, and if we started courting, I would be shunned."

"Eli has explained some things about your way of life, and I realize how serious a shunning can be." He started to reach across the seat, but pulled his hand back. "Can we still be friends?"

She nodded slowly. A friendship with Jimmy was all she could ever have, even if he were Amish or she were English.

"What a surprise seeing you today," Mary Ann said when Leona walked into the quilt shop shortly before closing time. "I'll be leaving soon, and Abby's already gone for the day."

"I've been to the hospital to see John, and I asked Jimmy—he's my driver today—if he'd bring me here before taking me home."

"How's my nephew doing? Is he gonna be okay?"

"The doctor said it will take awhile for John to feel like his old self again, but he will live, and for that I'm very grateful."

"Me, too." Mary Ann took a seat on the stool behind the counter. "Whew, I'm tired, and my feet are hurtin' something awful. It's been a long day."

"I know how you feel." Leona opened her purse and reached inside. "I came by to give you this," she said, handing Abner's envelope to Mary Ann.

"What is it?"

"Why don't you open it and see?"

Mary Ann grabbed a pair of scissors and sliced the envelope open. When she pulled out the card, she smiled and said, "This is a surprise.

We haven't exchanged valentines since we were kinner."

"Oh, it's not from me."

"Who then?"

"Take a look inside."

Mary Ann's brows puckered as she read aloud what had been written inside the card. "A rainbow in the sky reminds us that God keeps His promises. A honeysuckle vine reminds me of you—pretty and sweet. Happy Valentine's Day—Abner Lapp."

"Well, what do you think?"

Mary Ann let the card slip from her fingers as she stared at Leona with obvious disbelief. "You're playing matchmaker?"

"Not really. I'm more the message deliverer."

"Are you trying to set me up with Abner?"

"It wasn't my idea. Abner asked me to give you the valentine, and he wants to know if you'd be willing to let him court you."

Mary Ann's mouth dropped open. "Why didn't he ask me himself?"

Leona leaned on the edge of the counter, wondering if she'd made a mistake by agreeing to act as Abner's go-between. "He's worried you might say no."

Mary Ann stared at the card for several seconds. Finally, she turned it over and reached for a pen.

"What are you doing?"

"Writing him a note in return. Since you're so good at playing messenger, I figured you'd be more than happy to deliver my response to him."

"What are you going to say?"

Mary Ann's lips slanted upward in a sly little smile. "Maybe I'll let him tell you that."

Leona clicked her tongue. It was typical of her good-natured friend to make her wait. Well, that was okay. She had made Abner wait when she'd promised to speak with Mary Ann on his behalf, so it was only fair that she'd have to wait to hear how Mary Ann responded to his question.

"Did you hear about Mark Stauffer's barn catching fire?" Mom asked Leona when she returned home shortly before supper.

"No, I hadn't heard a thing. Of course, Mark and Nancy's daughter wasn't in school today because she's been out all week with a cold." Leona hung her heavy jacket and dark bonnet on a wall peg and moved over to the counter where her mother was making a salad. "How bad was the fire?"

"It burned clear to the ground. I'm sure they'll have a barn raising as soon as the weather improves."

"What was the cause of the fire? Do you know?"

Mom shrugged. "We haven't had any thunder or lightning lately, just a lot of snow. I heard from Fannie that the firemen found no sign of foul play, so they're thinkin' it was probably the gases from the hay that ignited the fire."

"I'm sorry to hear this. No one ever likes to lose a barn."

"At least they were able to get the livestock out in time." Mom picked up a tomato and sliced it into the bowl. "During the winter months, I sure do miss our fresh produce. These store-bought vegetables don't taste nearly as good as what we grow in our garden."

"What can I do to help with supper?"

"You can check on the biscuits baking in the oven."

Leona slipped into her choring apron, opened the oven door, and peered inside. "They're not done yet."

"So, how's little John doing?" Mom asked. "Since you were late getting home, I figured you'd gone to the hospital to see him again."

"I did go, and he's doing okay."

Mom smiled. "I'm sure John's folks are happy about that."

"Jah." Leona lifted the lid on the Dutch oven near the back of their wood-burning stove and peeked at the fragrant, simmering stew.

"You seem kind of sullen this evening. Is there somethin' you're not telling me?"

Leona glanced at the door leading to the living room. "Where's Papa?"

"He's in the barn playing with your pup. Now that the goat's getting bigger, he seems to be losin' interest in it."

"I'm glad he's done with the goat, and it's good he's out in the barn."

"Why's that?"

"I don't want Papa to hear what I'm about to say. He might repeat it, and it would probably come out differently than the way I said it to you."

Mom nodded toward the table. "Let's have a seat, and you can tell me what's on your mind."

"What about supper?"

"The stew's done, and the salad's almost made, so we're just waiting on the biscuits." She ambled across the room and pulled out a chair. "I think we can rest our weary bones a few minutes, don't you?"

Leona took the seat opposite her mamm, grabbed a handful of napkins, and started folding them in half. She wasn't sure she should be sharing the things that weighed heavily on her mind, yet the burden of keeping it to herself was too much to bear.

Mom leaned across the table, pulled the napkins from Leona's hands, and set them off to one side. "Are you feeling naerfich about something?"

Leona bit her bottom lip so hard she tasted blood. "Jah, I am a little nervous."

"What is it, daughter? Are you feeling sick?"

"Not physically."

"What are you saying?"

"I feel sick right here." Leona placed her hand against her chest.

Mom's eyebrows furrowed.

"I'm in love with someone, but it's an impossible situation."

"Is that all?" Mom waved her hand. "With love, there's always a way."

Leona blinked rapidly in an attempt to hold off the tears that stung the back of her eyes. "Nee. There's not a way—not for me and Jimmy."

"What was that?" Mom's mouth dropped open, and her eyes grew round.

"I—I'm not sure when it happened, but I—I've fallen in love with Jimmy."

Mom clasped her hands in front of her and placed them on the table. "Oh, Leona, this is a serious thing."

"It would be, if either of us chose to pursue it, but—"

"You've got to stop seeing him right away."

"That's going to be hard, considering that Jimmy often comes over here to see Papa and he's sometimes our taxi driver."

"It will have to end—all of it!"

"But, Mom, what reason would we give for shutting Jimmy out of our lives? Papa's grown attached to him, and he'd be upset if Jimmy quit coming around."

Mom fiddled with the napkins she'd taken from Leona. "Does Jimmy know the way you feel?"

"I haven't told him, but I think he might suspect."

"Is he in love with you, as well?"

Leona drew in a shaky breath and released it slowly. "He hasn't actually said so, but I believe he might have feelings for me."

"Then we'll have to pray that he leaves Lancaster County—and the sooner the better."

"But Jimmy and I have agreed to be just friends, and even if we could be together, I would never open my heart up to another man and take the chance of losing him."

"That's *lecherich*, Leona," Mom said sharply. "We've had this discussion before, and you know how I feel about you closing off your heart to love because you're afraid of what the future might hold." She pursed her lips. "I want you to fall in love and get married someday—just not to an Englisher."

"You might think it's ridiculous for me to feel the way I do, but the man you love didn't die." Leona cringed, wishing she could take back her words and feeling awfully guilty for having said them. "I'm sorry, Mom. I didn't mean that." She sniffed. "I know how close Papa came to dying; truth be told, you really did lose him, because most of the time, he doesn't know who you are."

Mom dropped her gaze to the table and sat there breathing slowly in and out. Finally, she lifted her head. "Would you mind going out to the barn to tell your daed that supper's almost ready?"

"Sure, Mom." Leona pushed her chair aside, grabbed her heavy shawl from a wall peg, and opened the back door. *It was a mistake to tell Mom how I feel about Jimmy. I thought she and I had been drawing closer, but she doesn't understand how I feel about anything. I wish I had never confided in her!*

CHAPTER 35

$\mathcal{J}$immy was pleased that he'd been invited to help raise Mark Stauffer's new barn. It meant the Amish he'd been living near these last nine months had accepted him.

Have I really been here that long? he mused as he pulled into the open field where dozens of Amish buggies and several cars were parked. *I still don't know who my real family is or even if I could give up my modern way of life to join the Amish faith. Since I now know the Amish won't prosecute Jim for his crime, maybe I need to search harder for my family and start asking more questions. I could even run an ad in the paper or hang some signs around the county announcing that a man who had been kidnapped when he was a baby twenty years ago has returned to the area looking for his Amish family.*

His thoughts drifted back to the day he'd finally believed Jim's story about the kidnapping, and he moaned. *What a mess I'm in, all because of one man's sinful deed. I don't know who my real family is or even where I belong. I'm in love with an Amish woman, but I grew up English, so I don't know if I could ever leave that way of life. Even if I did join the Amish faith, there would be no guarantees that Leona and I could be together. She's been through a lot and is hiding from love to guard her heart from further pain.*

As Jimmy opened his truck door, the truth slammed into him with such force he nearly fell out of his truck. As he stood and regained his balance, a blast of chilly March air took his breath away.

I've been hiding, too, he thought. *By refusing to talk to Jim and unwilling to let go of my anger, I have pulled away from God.*

Jimmy gulped in some air. *Jim is the only dad I've ever known, and no matter how hard I try to forget him or how many times I call him Jim, he will always be Dad to me.*

He reached inside the truck for his cell phone, which he'd left lying on the seat. *I'd better call Dad right now and tell him I forgive him.*

"I'm glad you finally got here, Jimmy," Eli called as he bounded across the open field where several other cars had parked. Eli had ridden over to the Stauffers' place with his folks this morning, and they had left an hour sooner than Jimmy had.

"I'm glad I was invited," Jimmy responded as his friend drew near. He placed the phone back on the seat. *I've waited this long to call Dad; I guess a few more hours won't matter.*

Eli clasped Jimmy's shoulder. "Of course you'd be invited. After all, you work for our bishop's son, and you've shown yourself to be a good friend to many who are here today."

"Any idea what I can do to help?" Jimmy asked as he and Eli headed toward a group of men who stood near the foundation where the new barn would be.

Eli nodded toward the tall Amish man with a long, flowing beard who stood on the other side of the yard talking to some of the men. "That's Yost Zimmerman, and he's the one to ask. Yost has built more barns and been in charge of more barn raisings than anyone I know."

Jimmy hurried off to speak with Yost, but he'd only made it half-way there when he spotted Abraham Fisher and his two youngest boys. The twins were joking around, grabbing each other's hats and throwing them in the air, and Abraham had even gotten in on the act.

Jimmy felt a pang of jealousy as he thought about how he'd always wanted a brother or sister. *I wish my dad had paid me a little more attention instead of being too busy with his work so much of the time.* Jimmy thought about his mother and how she had been the one to see that he'd been able to do some fun things. She had taken him to the park when he was little, seen that he'd gone to church activities, and had been there to listen whenever he needed to talk. *If I ever have the opportunity to be a father, I'm going to be there for my kids, and I'll make sure they have good memories from their childhoods.*

Jimmy's thoughts went to Leona. She was the kind of woman he would like to marry, but she was out of his reach—unless he decided to join the Amish faith, and he didn't know if he could do that. *Give me some sense of direction, Lord,* he prayed. *Show me what I should do about this, and when I talk to Dad, give me the right words.*

"Where's your mamm today?" Naomi asked Leona as they entered Nancy Stauffer's kitchen to prepare the noon meal."

"She stayed home with Papa."

"Is your daed sick?"

"He's fine. Mom decided it wasn't a good idea for him to come here today."

"How come?"

"He'd have probably wanted to climb onto the roof with the others who are building your brother-in-law's barn." Leona shook her head. "The last thing we need is for Papa to fall again."

"I should say so. And we must pray that none of the men gets hurt today."

"That's for sure." Leona moved across the room to see where her help was needed, and Naomi did the same.

A short time later, Leona stood at the kitchen sink peeling carrots and watching the progress on the barn out the window. She spotted Jimmy among those on the ground handing pieces of wood up to the men on the roof. Since the day he'd driven her to the hospital to see John, he hadn't spoken more than a few words to her.

It's probably best that he's kept his distance, she thought with regret. *Every time we've been close, I've found myself wanting more than either of us can give.* She squeezed the carrot in her hand so hard she feared it might break, so she relaxed her grip. *It's best that Mom decided not to come with me today. Since she's so afraid Jimmy might lead me astray, she'd probably have watched my every move.*

Leona's thoughts wandered back to a conversation she'd overheard a few weeks ago between her mamm and Arthur. She'd gone to the barn to feed her puppy and had spotted the two of them standing inside one of the horse's stalls, speaking in hushed tones. . . .

"I tell you, son, that Englisher is getting too close to your sister," Mom said. *"I fear if something's not done about it soon, Leona will get hurt. I think you should let Jimmy go."*

"You mean fire him?"

"Jah."

"Aw, Mom, you can't ask me to do that. Jimmy's a good worker, and he has a lot of knowledge when it comes to painting. Besides, since Richard's on vacation right now and a couple of the fellows are down with the flu, I need Jimmy more than ever."

"What if he talks Leona into leaving the Amish faith?" Mom persisted. "Can't you see what that would do to our family?"

"Leona's strong in her beliefs. I'm sure she ain't goin' nowhere."

"If she does up and leave, then you'll be to blame." Mom turned on her heel and rushed out of the barn. Arthur just stood there scratching his head.

"Leona, did you hear what I said?"

Leona whirled around as her thoughts returned to the present. "Huh?"

"I wanted you to know that we've got everything ready, so when you're done with the vegetable platter, you can bring it outside to the serving table," Nancy said.

"Okay."

Nancy moved to Leona's side. "Are you all right? You seem kind of distracted today."

"I'm fine. Just caught up in my thoughts." Leona grabbed a cucumber and started peeling it real fast.

"All right. See you outside in a few minutes," Nancy said before hurrying away.

When Leona stepped out the back door a short time later, she found herself scanning the yard, searching for Jimmy. She knew it was wrong to pine for something she couldn't have, but even though the voice in her head said no, her heart said something different.

She gripped the vegetable platter a little tighter. *I have to do something to fight this attraction, and I need to do it soon before I lose my heart to him and do something that would hurt my family.*

Forcing her thoughts to the job at hand, Leona joined the other women who were serving the men their noon meal. There was plenty of food donated by the women in their community. While the men ate, they engaged in conversation, and some even told a few jokes.

"Did you hear the one about the Englisher who wasn't watching where he was going and ended up hitting the telephone pole?" Yost Zimmerman asked Matthew Fisher as he elbowed him in the ribs.

"Can't say that I have."

Leona smiled and picked up a pitcher of water. Moving down the line, she refilled each of the men's glasses, and that's when she noticed Jimmy sitting at a table to the left.

"Looks like things are going pretty well today," Naomi said, stepping up to her. "The men have Mark's barn nearly half done already."

"It's good the weather's decided to cooperate."

"And it's nice to see so many of our English neighbors and friends here today." Naomi nodded toward the table on their left. "Jimmy Scott's a hard worker. I saw him hauling boards up to the roof earlier, and he seemed to be working every bit as hard as any of the Amish men."

Leona's only reply was a slow nod.

"It amazes me the way he seems to fit in with our people. He's helped your daed in so many ways and has such a gentle spirit." Naomi continued to stare at Jimmy. "In some ways, he reminds me of my brother Samuel." She pointed to the table on their right. "See the way Samuel holds his head when he's talking?"

Leona craned her neck to get a better look.

"Jimmy does it the same way. I'll bet if he was dressed in Amish clothes and wore his hair like our men, he'd look like Amish. Don't you think?"

Leona could only offer a shrug in response, for if she'd said what was on her heart, she would have told Naomi that she wished Jimmy was Amish and she wished God would give her some guarantees that Jimmy wouldn't be taken from her the way Ezra had been.

"Guess I'll see if the coffeepot needs refilling," Naomi said as she moved away from the table.

Leona needed a few minutes alone, so she meandered around the side of the house and headed for the swing that hung from a huge maple tree. She seated herself and grasped the handles; then digging the toes of her sneakers into the ground, she pumped her legs to gain momentum. She'd only been swinging a few minutes when she spotted Jimmy coming around the house. He headed to the table where several washbasins had been set out and seemed to be looking at something in the palm of his right hand.

Leona cringed when she saw him reach into his pocket and pull out a small knife. She hopped off the swing and hurried over to him. "Are you having a problem?"

He held out his hand. "This is what I get for not wearing gloves today."

She grimaced when she saw the ugly splinter embedded in the palm of his hand. "Let's go inside, and I'll see about getting a needle and some tweezers so I can take out the sliver."

He shook his head. "That's okay. I'm sure I can get it with the tip of my pocketknife."

Just thinking about what could happen if the knife slipped and cut into Jimmy's flesh caused Leona to flinch.

"It'll be all right. I've done this before."

"If you're determined to use the knife, then at least let me help you."

He smiled and placed his hand in hers. "You're an angel of mercy."

When Jimmy's skin came in contact with Leona's, she shivered.

"Are you cold?"

"I'm fine. Just a little nervous."

"I have complete faith in your surgical abilities," he said with a chuckle.

Leona held the knife as steady as her trembling fingers would allow, and it took her several tries before she was able to pry the tip of the splinter loose. When she saw blood oozing from his hand and heard Jimmy groan, her knees nearly buckled.

"Easy now. You've almost got it."

She exhaled a sigh of relief as she pulled the knife aside and saw the splinter attached to the end. "It's out."

"Danki." Jimmy leaned so close that she could feel his warm breath tickle her nose.

"You're welcome."

"What's goin' on here?"

Leona jumped back.

Jimmy did the same.

Abraham Fisher planted his hands on his hips and stared at them.

"I—I was taking a splinter out of Jimmy's hand," Leona stammered.

She didn't know why she felt so flustered. They'd done nothing wrong.

Abraham glared at Jimmy. "I think you and me need to have a little talk—in private."

Leona didn't understand why Abraham wanted to speak with Jimmy alone, but she decided it would be best if she left. She gave Jimmy what she hoped was a reassuring smile and hurried away.

Jimmy pulled a handkerchief from the pocket of his blue jeans and wrapped it around his throbbing hand. "What did you want to talk to me about, Abraham?"

The man grunted. "As if you don't know."

"If it's about—"

"Lydia Weaver had a talk with me the other day," Abraham said, cutting Jimmy off. "It seems that Leona informed her mamm that she's in love with you."

Jimmy's mouth fell open. "She—she said that?"

Abraham gave a curt nod. "Lydia's worried that her daughter might do something foolish, like run away with you, and then she'd be shunned." He leveled Jimmy with a piercing gaze. "My daughter ran away from home once because she was influenced by a young English woman who didn't give a hoot about anyone but herself. I won't stand by now and watch the daughter of my good friend throw her life away on some English fellow who can't keep his hands to himself."

"Just a minute." Jimmy's voice raised a notch. "I've never touched Leona inappropriately. And you don't have to worry about her running off with me or being shunned."

Abraham opened his mouth as if to say more, but Jimmy sprinted off. "I'll never find what I'm looking for here, and staying in Lancaster County so long was a big mistake!"

CHAPTER 36

As Jim stepped onto the front porch of Holly's small, brick home, his heart began to pound and his hands grew sweaty. Today was Saturday, and she'd taken the day off, leaving her two employees in charge of the health food store. Jim wasn't working today, either, so he'd made plans for the two of them to tour the Museum of Glass as well as the Historical Museum in Tacoma. Holly had volunteered to fix Jim breakfast before they went, and even though he normally didn't eat much in the morning, he had accepted her invitation, wanting to have some time alone with her before their date. He'd gotten to know her fairly well during the last few months as they had talked frequently on the phone, attended AA meetings, and had gone on several informal dates. She'd invited him to church a couple of times, but after his continued refusals, she had finally quit asking.

Jim knew that if he was going to move beyond friendship with Holly, he would need to open up and tell her the truth about Jimmy, which was what he planned to do this morning during breakfast. He had already lost two important people in his life, and he hoped his confession wouldn't end his and Holly's relationship, because he didn't think he could endure another loss.

With a trembling hand, Jim drew in a deep breath and rang the doorbell. A few seconds later, Holly greeted him with a cheery smile.

"Good morning, Jim. I hope you like blueberry pancakes and sausage links, because that's what I've fixed for breakfast."

The sight of her standing there in a pair of blue jeans and a pink T-shirt put a lump in his throat. He thought Holly was beautiful, no matter what she wore. Physically, she reminded him of Linda in that she had blond hair and blue eyes, but Holly's personality was a lot different from that of his late wife's. Holly was self-assured and outgoing; Linda had been introverted and afraid of many things. At least she had been in the earlier part of their marriage. After she started hanging around Beth Walters and attending church, she'd changed in many ways, although she'd never become as emotionally secure as Holly seemed to be.

Pulling his thoughts aside, Jim returned Holly's smile and stepped into the house, hoping she couldn't tell how nervous he was.

"Come out to the kitchen, and you can keep me company while I put breakfast on the table," she said, motioning him to follow.

When they entered the cozy room a few minutes later, Jim took a seat at the table, and she poured him a cup of coffee.

"Thanks. My nerves are on edge this morning, and this might help."

Holly chuckled. "I always thought coffee was supposed to make a person more jittery, not calm you down."

"Guess you're right about that."

Holly brought a platter of sausage over to the table and placed it near Jim. "There's no reason for you to be nervous. I'm not such a bad cook, and I promise you won't die from food poisoning."

"It's not your cooking that has me worried." He took a sip of coffee but set the cup down when he realized the drink was too hot.

Holly went back to the stove, and this time she returned with a stack of pancakes. When she set it on the table, she took a seat next to Jim. "Let's get started eating, and then you can tell me what's got you worried."

"Yeah, okay," he mumbled.

"It won't embarrass you if I offer a prayer of thanks for our food, will it?"

He shook his head. He was used to Jimmy praying at the table, and Linda had done it, too, after she'd gotten religious.

Holly reached for Jim's hand and bowed her head.

Jim did the same; only he kept his eyes open, staring at the floral design on the plate before him.

"Father in heaven," Holly prayed, "thank You for this food and bless it to the nourishment of our bodies. Thank You for good friends and good company. Amen."

When she let go of Jim's hand, he reached for his coffee cup again, this time blowing on it to make sure it was cool enough to drink. As he lifted it to his lips, his hand began to shake, and some of the coffee spilled out. He set the cup down quickly and grabbed a napkin.

"Are you okay?" Holly asked with obvious concern. "Did you burn your hand?"

He shook his head. "I'll be fine. Just spilled some on the tablecloth."

She leaned closer and took his hand. "You're shaking, Jim. What's wrong?"

He squeezed her fingers, hoping the strength he found there would give him the courage to say what was on his mind. "I—I need to tell you something. Something that's been eating at me for twenty years."

"What is it, Jim?"

He started by explaining how he and Linda couldn't have children, and how several attempts to adopt had failed. Then he told her about the excitement they had felt when they'd made contact with a lawyer from Maryland and how they'd gone there to adopt a one-year-old boy.

"But the adoption never happened," he said, shaking his head. "The birth mother changed her mind, and I left the lawyer's office that day empty-handed and wondering how I was going to face Linda when I returned to our hotel and told her we had no baby to take home."

"That must have been awful. How soon afterward did you get Jimmy?" The compassion in Holly's eyes let Jim know he had her sympathy, and it gave him the courage to go on.

"A few hours," he replied.

"Huh?" Her eyebrows lifted. "How could your lawyer set up another adoption in such a short time?"

"He didn't."

"Then how—"

Jim quickly related the story of how he'd gone to an Amish farm for some root beer and ended up leaving with a child.

Holly's mouth dropped open. "You—you kidnapped a baby?"

He nodded slowly.

"Does—does Jimmy know about this?"

"Yeah. He found out when he went to Bel Air, Maryland, thinking he could get some information about his birth mother. After talking to the lawyer, it came out that there had been no adoption." Jim paused and swiped the napkin he'd used for the spilled coffee across his sweaty forehead. "When Jimmy confronted me about the failed adoption, I felt I had no choice but to tell him about the kidnapping." He groaned. "At first he didn't believe me, but he did go to Pennsylvania in search of his real family. Now he's not speaking to me."

Holly made no comment, just sat there, staring at her hands now clasped in front of her.

"The last time we talked, he hadn't gotten any leads, and I'm not much help because I can't remember where that Amish farm even was."

Holly lifted her gaze to meet his. "You're not the man I thought you were, Jim. You're not to be trusted, and I want you to leave—now." She pushed her chair back and dashed from the room.

Leona's hand shook as she sank into the wicker chair on the front porch and read the letter Eli Raber had given her when he'd stopped by the house on his way to town a few minutes ago.

> *Dear Leona:*
>
> *After my conversation with Abraham yesterday, I realized that I would be hurting you if I stayed here any longer. And it wouldn't be right for me to ask you to leave your Amish faith in order for us to be together. So I've decided to return to Washington and make peace with my dad and try to sort things out.*
>
> *I came to Lancaster County in search of something from my past, but since I didn't find what I was looking for, I guess the Lord said no to my request. As much as I've come to love you, I don't see any way for us to be together.*
>
> *I'm praying that God will heal your hurts and give you the desires of your heart. I'll never forget you or your family, and I'll continue to pray that your dad's memory will return. Even if that never happens, please remember these words from Romans 8:28: "And we know that all things work together for good to them that love God, to them who are the called according to his purpose."*
>
> *You must learn to forgive and trust God again, Leona. It's the only way you'll ever have any real joy or peace.*
>
> *Fondly,*
> *Jimmy*

Tears welled in Leona's eyes and blurred the words on the page. Jimmy was gone, and he wasn't coming back. He loved her, yet she knew that because he was English and she was Amish they could never have a life together.

Despite the fact that, for so many months, Leona had been afraid to fall in love again, it had happened, anyway. She'd fallen in love with Jimmy, and now he was gone.

She gripped the edge of the chair and squeezed her eyes shut. *There's something in Lancaster County that is linked to Jimmy's past, but I have no idea what it is. If Jimmy really loved me, why didn't he feel free to share it?*

Suddenly, a thought popped into Leona's head, and her eyes opened. "I need to speak with Abraham Fisher. I need to find out exactly what he said to Jimmy that made him decide to leave."

Abraham was on his way to the barn when he spotted a horse and buggy pulling into the yard. He waited to see who it was, and when the horse stopped in front of the hitching rail, Leona Weaver stepped down from her buggy.

He lifted his hand and waved. "It's a nice, warm Saturday morning, wouldn't ya say? A real pleasant change in the weather, which means spring is just over the hill."

"I need to speak with you," Leona said, making no reference to his comment about the weather.

Leona's furrowed brows and puckered lips let Abraham know something was amiss. "What is it? Are you here about your daed? Is Jacob okay?"

"Papa's the same. I came to speak with you about Jimmy Scott. I'd like to know what you said that made him decide to go back to Washington."

"He went home, huh?" *Now that's a relief.*

She nodded.

Abraham kicked a small stone with the toe of his boot. "There ain't much to say. I told him how things were, and that's all."

"What exactly did you say to him?" she persisted.

"Said I'd talked to your mamm and that she was worried you might do something foolish and get yourself shunned."

Leona shook her head. "Mom ought to know me better than that."

"Jah, well, I thought I knew my oldest daughter, too, yet she ran off with Virginia Meyers all those years ago because she couldn't face what she'd done. That hurt our whole family."

"I'm sure it did, but Naomi did come back home."

He gave another stone a swift kick. "I also told that young fellow that I couldn't stand by and watch my good friend's daughter throw her life away on some Englisher who can't keep his hands to himself."

"Jimmy's a decent man. I was only helping him get a splinter out of his hand, and I—I don't feel you had the right to chase him off."

"The Englisher does not belong here, plain and simple." Abraham headed for the barn, and a sense of irritation welled up in his soul when he realized Leona had followed. He stopped inside the barn door and whirled around. "Your daed's been my best friend for a good many years, and there's no way I could watch some fancy, young know-it-all wreck the lives of everyone in your family."

Leona's chin trembled as she stared at the ground. "Our lives were wrecked the day Papa fell from that ladder and lost his memory."

"That's not true. Jacob's learned to do many things since his accident. Arthur told me that your daed's painting skills are almost as good as they were before he fell."

"Who do you think taught Papa how to paint again?" Leona lifted her gaze, and Abraham saw tears shimmering in her eyes. "It was Jimmy, that's who."

He moved toward one of the mules' stalls, hoping she might take the hint and head for home. He felt sorry she was upset, but he couldn't deal with that right now.

Once more, she followed him. "I understand your concern for my daed, but Papa needs Jimmy's help. Can't you see that?"

"My concern isn't just for Jacob. I'm worried about you getting hurt or maybe shunned."

Leona sniffed and blotted the tears that had splattered onto her cheeks. "I would never do anything to bring shame to my family. There's no reason for you to be worried."

"Sorry I'm late, Papa," Jake said as he entered the barn. "I know you wanted to start plowin' the south field before noon, but Elsie's got the morning sickness real bad, and I didn't want to leave the house 'til her mamm showed up to help with the kinner."

Abraham shrugged. He was glad for the interruption. Maybe Leona would go home now and this discussion would end. "I haven't got the mules hitched up yet, anyhow," he said, looking at his son.

Jake glanced at Leona with a look of concern. "You okay?"

Her only reply was a quick nod.

"What brings you over here this morning?"

"I needed to speak with your daed about something."

Jake looked at Abraham as if he expected him to say something, but Abraham just stood there.

"How are my girls doing in school these days?" Jake asked, turning back to Leona.

"Just fine. They're both eager to learn."

"Won't be but a few months, and the kinner will be out of school for summer break," Jake commented.

"That's true."

Abraham cleared his throat. "You ready to help with the mules, son?"

"Sure, Papa, but if you and Leona aren't done talkin', I can bring the mules out on my own."

"I think we've said all that needs sayin'." Abraham looked at Leona. "Isn't that right?"

She nodded, turned, and rushed out of the barn.

CHAPTER 37

What time is it? How long have I been here? Jim rolled over to the edge of the couch and shielded his eyes from the ray of sun streaming through the living room window. "Holly," he moaned. "I miss you, Holly. Why'd you have to turn your back on me when I needed your love and understanding?" He thumped the small pillow lying half under his head. *I wonder if she's sorry for leaving what we'd begun. I wonder if she regrets sending me away.*

A car door slammed somewhere outside. At least he thought it was a car door. It could have been coming from the TV. No doubt he had left it on last night when he'd passed out on the couch after downing too many beers. He'd been drinking pretty hard for the last several days. Or had it been weeks since he'd told Holly about the kidnapping?

Jim's head felt fuzzy, and his body felt like someone had used him as a punching bag. His mouth was dry and tasted like he'd been chewing on a dirty sock, but he didn't care. Jim didn't care about anything anymore. Two days after he'd made his confession to Holly, Ed had walked off the job, saying he was tired of covering for Jim.

Jim wasn't sure how long it had been since he'd gone to work, but that didn't matter, either. He had lost his wife, his son, and now his girlfriend, so what difference did it make if he lost his business?

Clump, clump, clump—he heard heavy footsteps on the porch. *Who'd be comin' here so early in the morning?* At least he thought it was morning. It could be afternoon, for all he knew.

He heard the front door click open and tried to sit up, but a sharp pain sliced through his head, bringing him back to the couch. "Who–who's there?"

"It's me."

Jim squinted at the man who stood a few feet away holding a

suitcase in one hand. "Jimmy?"

"Yeah, it's me."

Certain that he must be dreaming, Jim squeezed his eyes shut.

"I've wasted enough time in Amish country, and I've come home, Dad."

Dad? Jim opened his eyes and blinked a couple of times. Either he was in the middle of the best dream he'd ever had, or Jimmy really had returned home. He grabbed the edge of the couch and managed to pull himself to a sitting position, but his stomach rolled, and his head spun like a top. "Oh, I—I feel sick," he moaned, letting his head slip back to the pillow.

Jimmy set his suitcase down and moved over to the couch. "Do you need me to get a bucket?"

"Beer. Get me a beer."

Anger boiled in Jimmy's chest like a raging sea. He'd given up on his mission to find his real family, said good-bye to the woman he loved, and driven over two thousand miles in four days to make things right with his dad. And for what? To find him like this?

"I'll get you some coffee, but no beer," he said, shaking his head in disgust.

"Beer. I need some beer."

"What you need is a swift kick in the pants."

His dad released a pathetic whimper. "You're right. I need to be punished. I'm a louse. The lowest of lows. . .the scum of the earth."

"You won't find any relief from your pain talking like that."

Dad gave no answer, just turned his face toward the back of the couch.

Jimmy grimaced. *What made me think I'd be able to make peace with this man who can't even make peace with himself?* "I'm going to the kitchen to make a pot of coffee. I'll be back as soon as it's ready," he muttered.

No answer, just a muffled snort.

Give me the wisdom and strength to deal with this, Lord, Jimmy prayed as he left the room. *And show my dad what he needs to do to make things right.*

As Leona helped her mamm hang their freshly washed clothes on the line, Ginger ran about nipping at the laundry basket and trying to steal the clothes that had yet to be hung.

"Get away now, you little rascal," she scolded, nudging the pup with the toe of her shoe.

One of the barn cats streaked past, and Ginger took off like a streak of lightning. Leona chuckled despite her dour mood, and her thoughts went immediately to Jimmy as they often did when she saw the puppy he had given her.

Ever since Leona had read Jimmy's note saying he was leaving Pennsylvania, she had grieved her losses and struggled with bitterness because of the things she and her family had been through in the last year. She'd thought she was coping better, but after Jimmy left, it seemed as though her wounds had been reopened and would never heal. She knew she couldn't continue to pine for a love she could never have, and she realized that she needed to get on with her life and try to strengthen her faith somehow. But that was easier said than done.

Leona also knew she had spoken out of turn when she'd questioned Abraham about what he'd said to Jimmy. When she'd seen him at the general store a few days ago, she had apologized for her sharp words. Abraham had accepted her apology but said he felt they were all better off now that Jimmy had returned to Washington.

Maybe Abraham's right, Leona thought as she reached for a pair of her daed's trousers. *If Jimmy had stayed in Lancaster County and continued to work for Arthur, I would have suffered every time I saw him, knowing we couldn't be together.*

The same day Leona had spoken with Abraham, she'd also visited with Mary Ann in Abby's quilt shop. When she'd told her friend how she felt about Jimmy leaving and mentioned that her faith had weakened to a point where she could hardly pray anymore, Mary Ann had reminded her that it wasn't good to let disruptions and disappointments control your emotions or keep you from worshipping God. Leona hadn't argued. She knew Mary Ann was right.

One of the hardest parts about Jimmy being gone was that almost every day Leona's daed asked for Jimmy, wondering why he didn't come around and worried that Jimmy might be mad at him. Mom had explained several times that Jimmy had gone home to Washington, but Papa still kept asking and sulking around like he'd lost his best friend.

Leona glanced over at her mamm, who'd been busy hanging sheets while she did the clothes. "I'm wondering what God has in mind for our family," she said.

" 'And we know that all things work together for good to them that love God, to them who are the called according to his purpose,' " Mom quoted from the book of Romans. It was the same verse Jimmy had mentioned in the letter he'd written Leona.

Leona clipped a shirt to the line. "That verse really confuses me, Mom. Everyone in our family loves God, and look how things have worked out for us. Papa still thinks he's a little boy, you've been having trouble with your blood sugar lately, and I'm en alt maedel schoolteacher pining for a love I can never have."

"You're not an old maid, and you shouldn't be pinin' for someone who doesn't share your faith," Mom said with a shake of her head.

"Jimmy may not be Amish, but he does have a strong faith in God."

"That may be, but since he's English and you're Amish, there can be no future for you together."

"I know. There's no future for me with any man."

Mom clicked her tongue. "I wish you wouldn't talk that way, Leona. Don't you think it's time you quit grieving for Ezra and get on with your life?"

Leona shook her head. "I'm just guarding my heart from getting hurt again."

"There are no guarantees in this life," her mamm said. "I think when the right man comes along you'll realize it's time to set your fears aside and trust God in all things."

"I'm finished with the clothes now," Leona said, feeling the need to change the subject. "So, I'd better head out to the barn and get my buggy horse. I want to get to the schoolhouse before any of the scholars show up."

"You're right. You wouldn't want to be late, and I'm about done here myself." Mom drew Leona into her arms and gave her a hug. "I love you, and I've been praying that God will give you many good things in the days ahead."

Leona blinked to keep her tears from spilling over. "Danki. I want that for you, as well."

"I–I've missed you, Jimmy." A tide of emotions welled up in Jim's chest as his son handed him a third cup of coffee.

"I've missed you, too, Dad."

"Why don't you have a seat and tell me why you've come home?"

Jimmy flopped into the rocking chair across from the couch with a groan. "I finally came to my senses."

"What's that supposed to mean?"

"It means I'm home where I belong. Going to Pennsylvania was a waste of time. I never should have left home in the first place, because I didn't find my Amish family and probably never would have even if I'd stayed and kept on searching." Jimmy looked around the room as though he was seeing it for the first time. "Guess I've been gone too long. Everything looks odd and almost surreal to me."

Jim could relate to that feeling. He'd spent most of his waking hours the last few days feeling as if he were in a dream. And when he hadn't been awake, he'd been in a drunken stupor. "I—I wish I could turn back the hands of time and put you back on the picnic table where I found you."

Jimmy stared at the unlit fireplace. "I came to the conclusion that I didn't belong there, and yet a part of me wanted to stay."

"Why didn't you then?"

"I left to protect her."

"Who?"

"Leona."

"The bishop's daughter?"

Jimmy nodded slowly. "I'm in love with her, Dad."

"How does she feel about you?"

"According to Abraham Fisher, Leona loves me, too."

Jim frowned. "Then what's the problem?"

"I'm the problem." Jimmy touched his chest. "I'm English. She's Amish."

"You're not really English. You were born Amish, and—"

"I know that, but I wasn't raised Amish; I don't know if I could ever convert." Jimmy released a deep sigh. "It wouldn't be right for Leona or me to give up the only way of life we've ever known in order to be together."

"Why wouldn't it be? I know plenty of people who've made huge sacrifices in the name of love." Jim didn't know why he was saying these things. He really didn't want Jimmy to live in Pennsylvania or join the Amish faith. He'd been hoping his son would come home, and now that he was here, he was saying things that might cause him to leave again. "I'm sorry things have turned out this way," he said. "If I just hadn't taken you from that Amish family when you were a baby, you would know where you belonged. You might even be married by now, or at least engaged to the woman you love."

"All the what-ifs won't change things between me and Leona." Jimmy leaned forward. "But there is one thing that can change, Dad."

"What's that?"

"Our relationship can change—and you can change if you want to."

"I tried that already." The taste of bile rose in Jim's throat. "I went to those stupid AA meetings, opened my heart to Holly, and look where it got me!" He squeezed his eyes shut in an effort to stop the pain. "She hates me now, Jimmy."

"I know Holly pretty well, Dad, and I doubt she's capable of hating you or anyone."

"You should have seen the look on her face when I told her I had kidnapped you. She said I wasn't the man she'd thought I was and that I couldn't be trusted. She was right, too, because I can't even trust myself." He grimaced. "I was so sure I could stay sober, but I'm weak and need a drink whenever things go sour."

"What you need is the Lord, Dad."

Jim waved his hand as though he were batting at a fly. "Don't give me any sermons."

Jimmy left his chair and knelt on the floor in front of the couch, then reached out and took Jim's hand. "The morning before I left Pennsylvania, I was going to call you and apologize for not returning any of your calls, and for speaking to you in such an unkind way after I finally realized you had kidnapped me."

"So why didn't you call me? Did you think it over, realize what a good-for-nothing I was, and then change your mind?"

Jimmy shook his head. "You're not a good-for-nothing, Dad. The reason I didn't call was because I got busy helping with a barn raising. And then, when I realized I needed to come home, I decided to surprise you by just showing up. Figured it would be better to apologize in person rather than on the phone." He paused. "And I wanted to let you know that I forgive you for what you did."

"I–I'm the one who needs to apologize," Jim blubbered. "And I don't deserve your forgiveness, either."

Jimmy looked like he was about to say something more, but the doorbell rang, interrupting their conversation. "Are you expecting company?"

Jim shook his head. "Didn't even expect you."

"I'll see who it is."

When Jimmy left the room, Jim sat up and reached for his coffee cup. He took a drink and was getting ready to swallow when Holly stepped into the room. He choked, sputtered, and spit the lukewarm coffee all over the front of his rumpled shirt. Holly was the last person he had expected to see today, and he didn't relish the idea of her seeing him like this.

CHAPTER 38

$\mathcal{L}$eona had no more than taken a seat on the porch swing when Ginger jumped up, wagging her tail and whimpering as if she were starved for attention.

"You little *daagdieb*," she said, allowing the dog to flop across her knees. "That's right. You're nothing but a scamp. You're getting too big for this, you know that?"

Ginger responded with a grunt; then she wet Leona's hand with her sloppy tongue.

Leona sat there, petting the dog's head and listening to a chorus of birds from a nearby tree until she heard a horse and buggy plod up the driveway. She turned her attention to the yard.

Mary Ann waved from her open buggy, and as soon as she had it stopped near the barn and had hitched the horse to the rail, she headed for the house. "I was hoping I'd find you here," she said, stepping onto the porch.

Leona nodded. "I got home from school awhile ago and decided to sit out here before I help Mom with supper."

Mary Ann took a seat in the wicker chair near the swing. "Looks like you're in good company."

"I barely sat down, and she was up in my lap. Silly critter thinks she's still a little pup."

"She reminds me of Cinnamon," Mary Ann said, reaching over to stroke the dog behind one ear. "It was nice of Jimmy to give Ginger to you."

"Jah, but I still miss Cinnamon." Tears welled up in Leona's eyes and threatened to spill over. As much as she missed Cinnamon, she missed Jimmy even more.

"It's never easy to lose someone you love," Mary Ann said. "But

God is always there to help us through the pain, and He often gives us someone to replace the one we've lost." Her lips formed a little smile. "For whatever reason, God chose not to return our missing brother to us, but He gave Papa and Fannie twin boys. I know that even though Titus and Timothy haven't taken Zach's place in Papa's heart he's found comfort and joy in being able to raise them."

Leona thought about her own situation and wondered whom God had brought into her life to replace the ones she had lost. Cinnamon had been replaced with Ginger, and Jimmy had come along to make her laugh and enjoy some things after Papa had been taken from her because of his memory loss. She guessed God might have had His hand in all of that. But what about Ezra? Who had taken his place in her heart? *Jimmy did,* a voice in her head taunted. *But you can't have him because he's English.*

"So what's the reason for your visit?" Leona asked her friend, needing to change the subject.

"I was on my way home from the quilt shop and decided to stop by and tell you thanks."

Leona tipped her head in question. "For what?"

"For paving the way for me and Abner."

"Oh, that. How are things going now that the two of you have begun courting?"

"Good. Real good." Mary Ann's face fairly glowed. "I'm thinkin' me and Fannie might need to plant a whole bunch of celery this year."

Leona's eyebrows lifted. "Has Abner asked you to marry him?" She couldn't imagine that the shy young fellow would move so quickly.

"Not yet, but I think it's only a matter of time. In fact, I wouldn't be surprised if we aren't one of the couples gettin' married this fall."

Leona clasped her friend's hand. "I'm glad things are working out for you." *Sure wish something would work out for me.*

"Wh—what are you doing here?" Jim sputtered as Holly took a seat on the couch beside him.

"I came to see you."

"I—I look a mess, and I'm sure I don't smell any better than I look," he said leaning away from her. "Besides, I've committed a terrible sin—I'm a kidnapper who deserves to be punished."

" 'If any one of you is without sin, let him be the first to throw a stone at her,' " Holly said, reaching over to wipe the dribble of coffee from his chin.

"What's that supposed to mean?"

"It's from the book of John, Dad." Jimmy plunked into the rocker across from them. "Jesus was admonishing the Pharisees who wanted to stone an adulterous woman. He reminded those men that they weren't without sin, and if any of them thought they were, then they should be the first to stone the woman."

"Guess that never happened," Jim said, "because no man or woman who's ever been born has been perfect or without sin." He groaned. "Of course, some of us have committed a lot more sins than others."

"No one except Christ is perfect," Holly corrected.

"Right."

"Last night as I was reading my Bible, I came across John 8:7, and it caught me up short, reminding me that I had done many despicable things while I was struggling with my alcoholic addiction. It wasn't right for me to judge you, Jim." Holly placed her hand on his arm. "I hope you will accept my apology."

"Your apology?" Jim's nose burned, and his eyes stung as he struggled not to break down. "It's me who needs forgiving. I've always liked to be in control, and when I found out I couldn't father a child, I was so determined to give Linda a baby that I did something no decent man would even consider." He paused and looked over at Jimmy. "After I stole you from your real family, keeping you and hiding my secret became an obsession. With every lie I told, I fell deeper into my own self-made pit of misery. After a while, I'd told so many lies that I even began to believe them."

"That's how sin entraps us, Jim," Holly said quietly. "Each sinful thing we do, then try to cover up is compounded by the next sin and the next."

"Kind of like trying to cover up poor siding on a house by putting on multiple coats of paint without scraping and priming," he said. "Immediately, the paint job will start deteriorating because it wasn't prepped properly."

"Good illustration," Jimmy chimed in.

Jim drew in a deep breath and expelled it quickly. "Any idea what this sin-sick man can do to free himself from the burden of sin and shame?"

"Yes!" Holly and Jimmy said in unison.

"I kind of figured you might."

Jimmy hurried across the room and pulled Linda's Bible off the bookshelf. "I'd like to read you something, Dad."

Holly slid over, and Jimmy took her place beside Jim. He opened the Bible, turned several pages, and pointed to a verse highlighted in yellow. "In Luke 5:31 and 32, Jesus said, " 'It is not the healthy who need a doctor, but the sick. I have not come to call the righteous, but sinners to repentance." He turned several pages. "And 1 John 1:9 says, " 'If we confess our sins, he is faithful and just and will forgive us our sins and purify us from all unrighteousness.' "

"All you need to do is call on God, Jim," Holly said. "Acknowledge that you're a sinner, ask His forgiveness, and accept Christ as your personal Savior."

"It's that simple?"

She nodded, and so did Jimmy.

"I—I don't how to pray—don't know the right words," Jim mumbled.

"There are no 'right' words." Jimmy reached for his dad's hand. "Just close your eyes and talk to God. Tell him what's on your heart and confess your sins."

With a catch in his throat and tears blinding his vision, Jim released his burdens to God. By the end of his prayer, he knew with a certainty that he had found forgiveness for his sins through Jesus Christ.

Jimmy yawned and stretched his arms over his head as he entered the kitchen the following morning. It was still dark outside, and it didn't feel right to be getting up so early to go to work. But he had agreed to act as his dad's foreman—at least until they could find someone to replace Ed. And since they had a paint job to do in Olympia, it meant they needed to get an early start. Jimmy had decided to make breakfast while his dad loaded their van with some supplies he kept in the garage.

He flicked on the light switch near the kitchen door and ambled across the room to turn on the coffeemaker. "Sure didn't have this little convenience in the trailer house I rented from the Rabers," he mumbled. "But then, I didn't miss having an electric coffeemaker so much, either."

During Jimmy's stay in Lancaster County, he'd become used to doing without a lot of modern conveniences. Living behind the Rabers' place had provided him with an opportunity to get better acquainted with Eli and his folks as well as learn many of the Amish ways.

While the coffee brewed, Jimmy went to the refrigerator and took out a carton of eggs. He removed six and cracked them into a bowl with the idea of making scrambled eggs. "These yolks are sure pale," he mumbled. "Nothing like the fresh ones Esther Raber used to fix for my breakfast."

The milk Jimmy added to the eggs was also store-bought, and he knew it wouldn't be nearly as good as the fresh goat's milk he'd become accustomed to drinking. With the exception of his camera, there weren't too many modern conveniences he couldn't do without. In fact, he hadn't even missed watching TV while he was away, and he wondered if he would even care to watch it now. Until he'd left Amish country, Jimmy hadn't realized how much he would miss the slower-paced, simple life.

"I told you not to bother with breakfast," Dad said as he entered the kitchen. "My stomach's not up for more than a cup of coffee and a donut this early in the morning."

Jimmy placed the frying pan on the stove and turned on the back burner. "You never have taken time to eat a healthy breakfast, Dad."

"Guess that's true."

"I figured after you and Holly started dating she might convert you into a health nut."

Dad removed two mugs from the cupboard and set them next to the coffeepot. "Holly has helped in many ways—getting me to go to AA meetings, listening to me gripe about complaining customers, and putting up with my sometimes gloomy moods." He grunted. "But I doubt she'll ever succeed in getting me to give up coffee and donuts."

Jimmy chuckled. "She has been good for you, and I'm glad she came by yesterday and had a part in leading you to the Lord."

"Yeah, me, too." Dad poured two cups of coffee, hauled them over to the table, and took a seat. "I think the two of you saved my life yesterday."

Jimmy dumped the egg mixture into the pan and stirred it with a spatula. "Actually, it was God who saved your life, by sending His Son to die for your sins."

"I know, and I feel as if that five-gallon bucket of paint I've been carrying on my shoulders for many years is finally gone."

"Oftentimes, when someone confesses their sins and accepts God's gift of eternal life, they feel that way—like they're free from the burden that had been pulling them down." Jimmy scooped the eggs onto two plates and joined his dad at the table. "Now that you've found forgiveness, in order to grow as a Christian, you'll need to get into God's Word and spend time in prayer. That will help you stay closer to Him."

Dad nodded. "I know that, too. I'm planning to go to church with you and Holly this coming Sunday."

"That's good news." Jimmy glanced at his dad. "Would you like me to ask the blessing?"

"I think I'd like to try my hand at that if you don't mind."

"Not at all." Jimmy closed his eyes, and his dad did the same.

"Dear God," Dad began in a hesitant voice. "I just want to say thanks for forgiving my sins—and for bringing my son home." There was a brief pause. "Oh, and thanks for this food I'm being forced to eat. Amen."

Jimmy chuckled and reached for the bottle of juice sitting in the middle of the table. "I'm glad things are back on track with you and Holly."

"Me, too," Dad said around a mouthful of egg.

"Are you getting serious about her?"

"Yeah—uh—well, sort of. Holly's a wonderful woman, but I'm not sure we could ever have a future together."

"Why not?"

Dad's eyebrows drew together. "As I'm sure you know, your mother and I had a lot of problems during our marriage."

Jimmy nodded. He remembered hearing his folks disagree about many things during his childhood. He had found Mom in tears more times than he cared to admit.

"Most of our problems were my fault because I frequently lost my temper and didn't treat your mother with the respect and love she deserved." Dad moaned. "I'm afraid if I were to get married again, I'd mess things up."

Jimmy touched his dad's arm. "Of course you would have your share of problems, but you're a Christian now; with the Lord as your guide, you will not only be able to deal better with your dependence on alcohol, but I think that marrying Holly, or any Christian woman, would be different for you this time around."

His dad stared at him a few seconds, and then his lips curved into a smile. "How'd you get to be so wise for one so young?"

"I'm not sure how wise I am, but I did learn a lot about love and marriage from Eli's folks. I've never met a more devoted couple than Philip and Esther Raber."

"You miss those people, don't you? I can see the look of longing on your face."

Jimmy nodded. He missed everyone he'd come to care about in Lancaster County—Leona Weaver, most of all.

"Do you miss the Amish way of life, too?"

"Yeah, I guess I do. Somewhere along the line, I learned to appreciate the simpler things. In fact, I was reading my Bible before I went to bed last night, and I came across a verse of scripture that made me stop and think."

"What'd it say?"

"It was from the book of Psalms, chapter 27, verse 11. 'Teach me thy way, O Lord, and lead me in a plain path.' "

Dad stared at him with a wrinkled forehead. "Do you think you belong here?"

"I–I'm not sure where I belong anymore."

"As much as I would hate to lose you, I want you to be happy, Jimmy."

"I want you to be happy, too." Jimmy's throat clogged with unshed tears. Feeling the need to change the subject, he said, "We'd better eat so we can get on the road, don't you think?"

"Yeah," his dad said with a nod. "This is the first day of my new life, and I want to start it off on the right foot."

CHAPTER 39

*Y*ou seem kind of distracted today. Is everything all right?" Holly asked Jim as they walked hand in hand along Owen Beach.

"I've had a lot on my mind lately," he admitted.

"Have you scheduled too many paint jobs?"

"Not really. Since we've had so much rain this spring, we haven't been able to do many outside jobs, but I'm sure the weather will cooperate soon."

As they continued down the rocky beach, Jim prayed for God's direction and the courage to say what was on his mind. Finally, he halted and dropped to one knee.

Holly squinted at the stones in front of him. "What's down there? Did you find another agate?"

Jim shook his head and stared up at her. His mouth felt dry, and he could barely breathe. He couldn't remember being this nervous since he was a teenager preparing to ask one of the high school cheerleaders for a date. "I'm—uh—in love with you, Holly, and I'm hoping that we can— Well—uh—when the time is right, would you consider marrying me?"

Nothing. No response. Holly just stood there with her lips pursed and her forehead wrinkled.

"If you don't say something soon, my knee's going to give out."

Holly's face relaxed, and she placed both hands against his cheeks. "I think we both need more time to get to know each other and allow our relationship to mature." She smiled. "But, yes, when the time is right, I will consider becoming your wife."

Jim stood, and drawing Holly into his arms, he kissed her gently on the mouth. When the kiss ended, he pulled back slightly. "How about the two of us going somewhere nice for lunch to celebrate my six-week sobriety and our future possible engagement?"

She nestled against his chest and murmured, "That sounds good to me."

When Leona stepped out of her buggy and headed for the schoolhouse early one morning in May, she was surprised to see Abner standing on the front porch. She glanced around thinking he might have brought his brother to school, but she saw no sign of Emanuel. "Guder mariye, Abner," she said as she reached the porch. "What brings you by here this morning?"

"Good mornin' to you, too." He stared down at his boots. "I—I wanted to tell ya something."

"Oh? What's that?"

Abner shifted his weight from one foot to the other and slowly raised his head to meet her gaze. "I—uh—wanted you to know how grateful I am that you put in a good word for me with Mary Ann."

Leona smiled. "I heard the two of you have been courting."

He nodded and leaned against the porch railing. "I've asked her to marry me in the fall, and she said she would."

Leona's smiled widened. "Congratulations! I'm happy for both of you."

"I'm glad you approve."

"Of course. Why wouldn't I? You're a nice man, and you'll be getting a wunderbaar woman."

"Jah, I agree." Abner turned to go, but he'd only taken a few steps when he turned back around. "Mary Ann's prayin' you'll fall in love with someone soon."

Before Leona could offer any kind of sensible reply, Abner sprinted across the lawn and hopped into his buggy.

" 'Mary Ann's prayin' you'll fall in love with someone soon,' " she mumbled. "Mary Ann must believe in miracles."

"What can we do to help?" Leona asked as she and her mother stepped into Naomi's kitchen two weeks later. Their entire family, including

Arthur and his brood, had been invited to the Hoffmeirs' for a picnic supper. Abraham and all of his family had also been included, and most of the men were in the backyard setting up tables.

"Ruth, Elsie, and Darlene are getting the meat ready to barbecue," Naomi said, nodding toward the counter where three of her sisters-in-law stood. She motioned to the table. "Abby, Mary Ann, and Nancy are making up the salads."

"My daughter and I can carry the plates and silverware outside if you'd like," Leona's mamm volunteered.

"Danki." Naomi smiled. "Many hands make light work."

"That's so true," Abby agreed.

"Lydia, if you don't mind taking over the job of flattening ground beef into patties, I'd like to help Leona set the table," Mary Ann spoke up. "It will give us a chance to visit before the meal is served."

"Don't mind a bit." Mom went over to the sink and washed her hands, and Leona opened the silverware drawer to take out what they would need.

"You're awful quiet this evening," Mary Ann said once she and Leona were outside on the porch. "Did you have a rough week at school?"

"Nothing out of the ordinary. I'm just feeling kind of down."

"Sorry to hear that. Maybe some time spent with family will cheer you up."

"Jah, maybe so." Leona draped her arm across Mary Ann's shoulder. "Abner dropped by the schoolhouse a few weeks ago and told me your good news. I'm real happy for you."

"Danki."

Leona sighed and stared at the porch.

"Are you sure you're okay? You look so down in the mouth."

"I'm feeling kind of frustrated over Papa."

"How come?"

"He hasn't been the same since Jimmy left, and he even seems to have regressed some."

"In what way?"

"He blabs everything he hears, teases my dog unmercifully, and bothers Mom to no end whenever she's trying to get things done. He won't even go on any paint jobs with Arthur now."

"I didn't realize that, and I'm sorry to hear it." Mary Ann placed a stack of paper plates on one of the picnic tables and turned to face Leona. "I hope I'm not speakin' out of turn here, but I don't think you've been the same since Jimmy left, either."

Leona sank to the wooden bench with a sigh. "I do miss him. The two of us had become friends, and—"

"And I have a hunch that you're in love with him." Mary Ann took a seat beside her. "Don't try to deny it, because it's written all over your face."

Leona stared at her hands, folded in her lap. "I know it was wrong to allow myself to have feelings for him, but it happened before I realized it."

"Then it's good that he left. If he'd stayed, you might have gone English and been shunned."

"Now you sound like your daed and my mamm." Leona bristled. "Don't you think I'm strong enough in the faith not to run off?"

"There are others who have done it," Mary Ann reminded. "And some families in our community have been torn apart because of the shunning that's followed."

"I would never do anything to hurt my family. They've been through enough already." Leona folded her arms. "Besides, even if Jimmy were Amish, I would never marry him."

"I read a verse of scripture in my Bible the other day," Mary Ann said, "and I'm thinkin' it's one you ought to hear."

"What was it?"

"It's found in 1 John 4:18, and it goes like this: " 'There is no fear in love; but perfect love casteth out fear: because fear hath torment. He that feareth is not made perfect in love.' You need to let go of your fears and open your heart to love again." Mary Ann squeezed Leona's fingers. "Just make sure it's with a nice Amish fella."

"I think we should get the table set like we came out here to do," Leona said. She'd heard enough talk about love and marriage and needed to think about something else. She quickly placed the silverware around the table. When she was done, she moved on to the next group of tables.

A few minutes later, a car rumbled into the yard and parked near the barn. When the driver stepped out, Leona's mouth fell open and she sank to the nearest bench. "*Was in der welt*—what in all the world?"

"Now what's that fellow doin' here?" Abraham grumbled to Fannie as he motioned to the car that had pulled into the Hoffmeirs' yard. "I thought Jimmy Scott had gone home for good."

"Guess you were wrong about that." Fannie gave Abraham a gentle nudge with her elbow. "Be nice, husband. Enough unkind words have already come from your mouth concerning that boy, and it's not your place to be judging him."

"I've only been trying to protect Jacob and his family."

"Jah, well, don't you think you ought to leave that job up to God?"

Abraham knew his wife was right. The Bible taught that only God had justification to judge. Even so, it gave him cause for concern when Jimmy walked up to Arthur and said, "After a lot of thought and prayer, I decided to return to Lancaster County to take care of some unfinished business. I'm hoping you might hire me again."

"Jah, sure, I'd be happy to." Arthur grinned at Jimmy and shook his hand. "You're a hard worker, and I've missed your helpful suggestions."

"Thanks. I appreciate that." Jimmy looked like he might be about to say something more, but before he could get a word out, Jacob sauntered up to him wearing a smile that stretched from ear to ear.

"Where have ya been?" the man asked, giving Jimmy a thump on the back. "I've sure missed ya."

"I've missed you, too." Jimmy shook Jacob's hand. Then he glanced over at Arthur. "I stopped by your place first but soon realized you weren't at home. Then when I arrived at Eli's house, he said you and your family were over here."

Leona stepped forward then, and Abraham held his breath, afraid of what she might say.

"It's nice to see you," she said, smiling at Jimmy in a way that made Abraham's stomach clench.

"It's good to see you, too, Leona." Jimmy's face turned as red as a tomato, and he glanced around the yard. "I didn't realize you were having a big gathering here. Sorry for interrupting."

"You ain't interruptin'." Jacob pointed to the barbecue that had recently been lit. "Why don't ya stay and eat supper with us?"

"That's a fine idea. We'd like you to join us," Arthur said with a nod.

"Are you sure you wouldn't mind?"

"Not a bit." Jacob thumped Jimmy on the back once more. "You can sit by me."

Abraham groaned and shook his head. *I think it would have been better if I'd stayed home today.*

Fannie reached for his hand and gave it a gentle squeeze.

When the meal was over, Leona took a seat in a chair she'd placed under a maple tree. She needed some time alone to sort out her feelings for Jimmy. She caught a glimpse of him playing a game of horseshoes with Jake, Norman, and Samuel Fisher. She was happy to see Jimmy but knew that having him living and working among her people again would be difficult. Still, it was wonderful to observe how happy her daed seemed to be. She hadn't seen him smile so much since Jimmy left Lancaster County a few months ago. *I'll simply have to deal with this. It wouldn't be fair to Papa for me to ask Jimmy to leave again.*

"Those four playing *hufeise*—horseshoes—seem to be having fun, don't they?" Fannie said to Abby as the two women walked past Leona.

"Jah," Abby replied. "If I didn't know better, I'd think Jimmy could be one of their brothers."

"What would make you say something like that?" Fannie asked her daughter.

"Jimmy's hair is almost the same shade of brown as Samuel's, and he has the same color eyes."

Leona squinted to get a better look. Abby was right. Jimmy did look similar to Samuel. If he'd been wearing Amish clothes, the two of them could have been mistaken for brothers. She leaned back in her chair and tried to relax. *It's just wishful thinking because I'd like for Jimmy to be Amish. Just because he's come back to Lancaster County doesn't give me the right to start hoping, wishing he were one of us.*

Leona's thoughts were halted when she heard a strange popping noise. She tipped her head and listened. There it was again. *Must be some birds or squirrels playing in the tree.* She glanced into the branches but didn't see anything out of the ordinary.

"Leona, get up! *Kumme! Schnell!*" Papa hollered from across the yard.

Why was her father calling for her to come quickly? Leona figured her daed had one of his silly jokes he wanted to share or had found some critter he thought she might like to see, so she was tempted to ignore his call. But out of respect, she stood and hurried over to the porch where he sat in a wicker chair. "What did you want, Papa?"

Before he could reply, an ear-piercing crack rent through the air. Leona whirled around in time to see a huge limb from the maple tree crash to the ground. It landed on the chair she had occupied moments ago, smashing it to bits.

She gasped and covered her mouth with the palm of her hand. "Oh, Papa, how did you know?"

Her daed looked bewildered at first, but then a slow smile spread across his face. "God put a voice in my head that told me to holler for you."

A feeling of gratitude swelled in Leona's soul, and she dropped to her knees beside her daed. All these months, she'd been sure God could no longer use Papa because he'd lost his memory and couldn't fulfill his role as their bishop, but now she realized that wasn't the case. She reflected on the last half of the verse she'd read the other day from Luke 18:16: "Suffer little children to come unto me, and forbid them not: for of such is the kingdom of God." Even though her daed thought and acted like a child, God had used him to warn her, which had saved her life.

At that moment, Leona also realized that, even though God had allowed some terrible things to happen in her life, He'd always been there, offering His love and tender mercies. *God doesn't want me to be afraid of living or loving. He wants me to put my trust in Him.*

"I'm sorry, Papa," she sobbed. "Please forgive me for ignoring you so many times, and for—for doubting your love."

He patted the top of her covering. "I forgive you, Ona."

When Jimmy heard Jacob's cry for Leona to get up, followed by a loud *crack*, he froze. The last time he had looked in Leona's direction, she'd been sitting in a chair under the maple tree. She was gone now, and her chair was lying flat on the ground with a huge limb covering it.

He glanced quickly across the yard, and when he spotted Leona kneeling in front of her father, he dropped his horseshoe on the ground and raced through the grass. "Leona, are you okay?" he panted, kneeling down beside her.

Her face was flushed, and her eyes shimmered with tears. "Thanks to Papa's warning, I'm fine."

Jimmy reached for Leona's hand, not even caring what the people who were watching might think about the gesture. "I haven't had the chance to tell you this yet, but the reason I came back to Pennsylvania wasn't just to work for Arthur."

"It wasn't?"

He shook his head. "You see, the truth is, I'm really—"

"Zach Fisher!" Jacob leaned forward and touched the back of Jimmy's right ear. "You've been gone such a long time. How old are you now, Zach?"

277

CHAPTER 40

$\mathcal{J}$immy sat next to Leona, trying to process what Jacob had said. *He must have me confused with someone else—someone from his childhood, maybe.*

Leona looked at Jimmy as though she were seeing him for the first time; then she looked back at her father and said, "Papa, what are you talking about? This is Jimmy Scott, not Zach Fisher."

"Jah, that's right," echoed several others who had gathered around Leona soon after her near mishap with the tree.

With a shake of his head, Jacob reached over and pulled Jimmy's ear partway back. "Abraham, you'd best take a good look at this."

Abraham, who had been standing behind Matthew, stepped forward. "What's wrong with you, Jacob? You're acting so *fremm*."

"Strange as it may seem, look here; he has a red, heart-shaped birthmark, just like Zach's."

Abraham hesitated but finally moved in for a closer look. Before he had a chance to say anything, Naomi pushed through the crowd and rushed over to Jimmy. "What birthmark? Let me see."

"My Zach did have a red blotch behind his ear that looked sort of like this," Abraham said as he leaned his head closer to Jimmy, squinted, then stepped back. "But you don't expect us to believe this is the same boy."

Naomi groaned. "Oh, but, Papa, what if it's true?"

It seemed as though everyone was staring at the mark behind Jimmy's ear, and it made him feel like a bug under a microscope. Who was this "Zach" they were talking about, and what did it have to do with him?

Pushing himself to his feet, Jimmy turned to face Jacob. "When you were a boy, did one of your friends have a birthmark like mine?"

278

Jacob shook his head. "You're Zach." He pointed to Abraham. "He's your daed."

A murmur went through the crowd; then everyone began talking at once. Jimmy felt as if his head might burst wide open, and he held up his hands to quiet them. "Would someone please tell me who Zach is, and what's all the fuss about my birthmark?"

"It's nothing." Abraham compressed his lips and folded his arms across his chest. "Jacob has you confused with my son who was kidnapped."

The shock of Abraham's words left Jimmy's mouth feeling so dry he could barely speak. Could the Fishers be the Amish family he had been searching for? Was it possible that Abraham, a man who obviously didn't care for him, was actually his father? Could he have been living and working among his own people all those months and not have known it? Jimmy swayed unsteadily as the possibility sank in.

"Are you all right? Maybe you'd better sit down." Leona reached up and took hold of Jimmy's arm, and he dropped to the ground beside her again.

"I—I have a story to tell—one I think you all need to hear," he rasped.

"We don't need any stories," Abraham grumbled. "We've already heard enough ridiculous talk."

Naomi took a seat on the other side of Leona. "What story, Jimmy? I'd like to hear what you have to say."

"Well, I don't want to hear it." Abraham folded his arms and scowled at Jimmy as if he'd done something horribly wrong.

Feeling more nervous by the minute, Jimmy moistened his lips with the tip of his tongue. He was determined to tell his story, even if Abraham didn't want to hear it. "The thing is, I grew up in Washington State, but I—uh—wasn't born there."

"What's this got to do with anything?" Abraham tone's was one of impatience, and he turned away with a huff.

He'd only taken a few steps when his son Samuel spoke up. "I think we should listen to what Jimmy's got to say, Papa. He might know something about my missing bruder."

"I agree with Samuel," Matthew put in. "We need to hear Jimmy out."

Abraham shook his head, but Fannie took hold of his arm. "Your boys are right about this, Abraham. We all need to listen to Jimmy's story."

Abraham only shrugged in response, but he did stop walking.

"I didn't know any of this until last spring, when Jim, my English dad, informed me that I wasn't born in Washington. He said I was born here, in Lancaster County." Jimmy paused and drew in a quick breath. "When I was a year old, my sister left me sitting on a picnic table while she went in the house to get some cold root beer for an English man."

"Oh!" Naomi covered her mouth with the palm of her hand and stared hard at Jimmy.

"*Puh!* That don't prove nothin'." Abraham grunted. "Lots of folks knew that story."

"I thought we were going to hear Jimmy out," Fannie said.

Abraham squinted at Jimmy again. "Tell us what else you know about that day."

"The name of the man who went there to buy root beer is Jim Scott. I grew up thinking he was my father. It wasn't until shortly after my twenty-first birthday that I learned I had been adopted and that my folks had gotten me through a lawyer in Bel Air, Maryland." Jimmy gulped in another breath of air. "So I went there to speak with the lawyer, but I was in for a big surprise."

"What surprise was that?" Matthew asked.

"I was told that there had been no adoption for Jim and Linda Scott through that office. The lawyer said my dad—Jim—never left his office with a baby because the birth mother had changed her mind and decided to keep the child."

Abraham gave Jimmy another one of his irritating scowls. "What's this got to do with my missing son?"

"I'm getting to that." Jimmy glanced at Leona, hoping she might say something that would give him a little encouragement, but she just sat there.

"Uh...anyway," he continued, "after I left the lawyer's office, I called Jim and demanded to know what had happened at the lawyer's office. He admitted that the adoption had fallen through, and then he told me some wild story, which I was sure he had made up, about him driving onto an Amish farm asking for root beer, and my Amish sister going into the house to get the root beer and leaving me on the table. He said I was wiggling around, and he was afraid I might fall off, so he picked me up." Jimmy paused again and swallowed a couple of times. "Then, with no thought of the consequences, Dad—I mean, Jim—dashed to his van and drove off."

Everyone who had gathered around Jimmy gaped at him without uttering a word. Jimmy wasn't sure if they thought he was some kind of a nut, or if they believed his wild story. He decided he'd better get the rest told while he still had a captive audience.

"So then, when we got to the hotel where Jim's wife was waiting, he told her that I was the child they'd come to adopt."

Naomi's sister Nancy let out a yelp. "Ach, my! You really are my little bruder!"

"I told you," Jacob said with a nod.

Abraham stood there with a stony face, but Naomi reached across Leona and grabbed hold of Jimmy's arm. "If what you've told us is true, then why haven't you said something to one of us before now?"

"And why'd you return to Washington and then come back again?" Jake asked.

Jimmy looked at Leona to gauge her reaction. Tears shimmered in her green eyes, but she was smiling. It bolstered his courage enough to say more. "I came here last summer with the hope of finding my real family, but every lead I had turned out to be a dead end. No one I spoke with knew anything about a kidnapping that had happened twenty years ago. And then I started working for Jacob and knew I needed to stick around to see what the Amish were all about."

"That doesn't explain why you never asked any of us if we knew anything about a kidnapped baby," Norman spoke up.

"I wanted to, but I was afraid if I blurted something like that out and nobody believed me I might be asked to leave." Jimmy groaned. "I was also concerned that if the truth came to light and I did actually find my family that my dad—Jim—might end up in jail."

"The Amish don't prosecute," Samuel said.

Jimmy nodded. "So I've been told."

"So what was your excuse for not saying anything then?" Norman asked.

"Jah," Jake agreed. "If you really had been kidnapped and wanted to find your real family, I would think you would have left no stone unturned."

"I did ask a couple of people, but they didn't know what I was talking about."

Abraham's frown deepened. "Who'd you ask?"

"I mentioned it to Jacob, but he didn't seem to understand much of what I had said. I also asked Eli, and he said he'd never heard anyone around here speak of losing a baby that way." Jimmy shrugged. "So I figured no one else in the area would know anything or believe my story."

"Eli's not been around long enough to know what happened back then," Jacob put in. "He and his folks moved here from Indiana four years ago. You should have asked someone who's been livin' here longer."

All eyes turned from Jimmy and focused on Jacob, and his wife grabbed him in a hug. "Oh, husband, you remember who you are!"

" 'Course I do. I'm Bishop Jacob Weaver, and you're my wife, Lydia."

Leona stood and leaned close to her daed. "Do you know me, Papa?"

"Said I did when I called you over here a few minutes ago, didn't I?"

She nodded and wrapped her arms around his neck. "We've had two miracles today. Your memory has returned, and Abraham's son has come home!"

Abraham stood there, slowly shaking his head as though in a daze. Jimmy, feeling much the same, struggled to his feet and moved over to stand beside Abraham. "Soon after I went back to Washington, I realized that while I'd been living and working here I had discovered a side of myself I didn't know existed." He paused and waited to see how Abraham would react.

"Go on."

"Then I read a verse of scripture found in Psalm 27:11 that made me stop and think about my life."

" 'Teach me thy way, O Lord, and lead me in a plain path,' " Abraham quoted.

Jimmy nodded. "I believe the Lord showed me through that verse that deep down inside I really am Amish, and I have decided that I want to follow the Plain path."

Abraham shifted from one foot to the other. Then he took one step forward.

Jimmy swallowed hard in an attempt to push down the lump that had lodged in his throat.

"I—I can't believe that after all these years God would finally answer my prayers." Abraham paused. "But I believe He has, and—" His voice broke, and he rocked back and forth on his heels. "And after I've treated you so badly, thinking you were out to destroy Leona's life—"

"It doesn't matter now. Nothing matters except trying to make up for the years we've lost." Jimmy opened his arms, and giving no thought as to whether he would be accepted, he embraced his father.

Abraham held his body rigid at first. Then he hugged Jimmy so hard he could barely catch his breath. "There's so much I want to tell you, son. So very much."

"And I want to hear it all."

Everyone shed a few tears as they took turns hugging Jimmy and welcoming him home.

"There are many things that each of us wants to hear." Naomi smiled at Jimmy. "We want to know the details of your life out there in Washington, too."

Jimmy nodded and reached for Leona's hand, pulling her gently to his side. "If there's no objections, I'd like to do whatever is required of me in order to join the Amish church." He looked over at Jacob, who winked at him, and then he smiled at Leona and said, "If this special woman will have me, I hope to make her my wife some day."

Leona looked a bit hesitant at first, but then her face relaxed and she looked at her father. "Well, Papa, what do you have to say about that?"

Jacob nodded and thumped Jimmy on the back. "I always knew I liked you—even when you weren't Zach Fisher."

After everyone's laughter died down, Jimmy sent up a silent prayer. *Thank You, God—for bringing me home.*

EPILOGUE

Eighteen months later

"Congratulations on your marriage." Jim hugged the newlyweds as they all stood in the Weavers' front yard, following the wedding ceremony. "Thanks for inviting Holly and me to witness your vows. I'm so proud of you, Jimmy—I mean, Zach." He swallowed hard. "I know Linda would be proud, too."

"Mom. She was my mom," Zach corrected. "And it's okay if you keep calling me Jimmy, because until I found my Amish family, it was the only name I'd ever known. To tell you the truth, even after living here over a year as Zach Fisher, I'm still trying to get used to my real name." He smiled at his bride, and the tender look she gave him spoke volumes. Jim was pleased with his son's choice for a wife. He knew from all he'd heard about the bishop's daughter that she was a special woman.

"Are you ready to meet Abraham now?" Zach asked.

Jim nodded, but he didn't move from the spot where he and his own new bride stood on the Weavers' front lawn.

"It's going to be all right, honey," Holly whispered in his ear. "The Lord will help you through this and give you the right words." She stepped away from Jim and took hold of Leona's arm. "Why don't we let our men tend to business while the two of us get better acquainted?"

"I think that's a fine idea." Leona gave her husband a hug. "I'll see you inside for the wedding supper."

Zach led the way, and Jim followed him across the yard to where a tall, bearded man stood talking with Bishop Weaver near the barn. When they approached, the bishop nodded and said, "I'd best go inside and see how things are going."

Zach stepped up to the other man and touched his shoulder.

"Abraham, this is my dad—I mean, Jim Scott."

As Jim reached his hand out to Abraham Fisher, his throat felt so clogged he wasn't sure he could speak. "For many years, I dreaded the thought of meeting you, but now I'm thankful God has given me this opportunity to tell you how sorry I am for taking your child."

Abraham nodded. "You already apologized in that letter you sent soon after Zach returned to Pennsylvania."

"Yes, but I—I needed to say it in person." Jim paused to regain his composure. "What I did was unthinkable, and I wouldn't blame you if you never forgave me for kidnapping Jimmy—I mean, Zach."

"In Matthew 6:14, Jesus said, 'For if ye forgive men their trespasses, your heavenly Father will also forgive you.'" Tears gathered in the corners of Abraham's eyes. "Many years ago, I forgave the one who had taken my son away, even though I didn't know if I'd ever see my boy again."

Zach squeezed Jim's arm, and he found comfort in the reassuring gesture. "I want you to know that, even though what I did was wrong, God used my horrible deed to bring about something good," Jim continued.

"What was that?" Abraham asked.

"If it hadn't been for your son's influence and the Christian example he set, I never would have come to know the Lord as my Savior."

Abraham gave his beard a couple of quick pulls. "I remember one time, soon after Zach's disappearance, my friend Jacob Weaver told me that God could take something bad like Zach being kidnapped and use it for good." He clasped Zach's shoulder with one hand and Jim's with the other. "I believe He has done just that."

Leona stood on the front porch talking to Holly and Fannie. Her gaze traveled across the yard to where her husband stood with the two men who both called him son. Leona marveled at the way God had brought Zach Fisher home to his real family, yet she couldn't help but feel some concern. She wanted to feel hopeful over the prospect of Abraham and Jim having this discussion, but a thread of caution wove its way into her soul. Would Abraham even speak to the man who had taken his son away? She knew Abraham had told Zach he'd forgiven Jim Scott, but now that the two of them stood face-to-face, would he still feel that way?

"My husband's done a lot of growing," Fannie said as though she could read Leona's thoughts.

Holly put her arm around Leona's waist and gave her a gentle squeeze. "Mine has, as well."

Leona nodded as tears clouded her vision. She had done a lot of growing in the last eighteen months, too. No longer was she bound by fear or consumed with bitterness. The day God saved her life through her daed's urgent call was the day she'd come to realize that, while there are no guarantees in life, God wanted her to trust Him completely. So, setting her fear of losing Zach aside, she had agreed that he could court her.

Zach joined the women a short time later. "I left my two daeds to talk things out. I think everything's going to be fine."

The screen door opened, and Naomi stepped onto the porch carrying a gift in her hands. "This is for you and Leona," she said, handing the package to Zach.

He balanced the box on the porch railing, and he and Leona opened it together. Inside was a small patchwork quilt. Zach stared at it several seconds; then a light dawned. "I—I think I've seen this before—or at least a quilt just like it. I found it in a bag of paint rags in my dad's garage when I was a kid."

Naomi nodded. "Abby Fisher gave it to me after she returned from a trip to Montana several years ago. She said an Amish woman she knew had found it at a thrift shop somewhere in the state of Washington." She smiled, and tears sprang to her eyes. "I recognized it right away and knew it had been your quilt when you were a baby. It was with you the day you were kidnapped."

"So that's why Jim seemed so upset when I showed it to him. He'd obviously been hiding it from my mom, afraid she might ask where he'd gotten it." Zach clutched the quilt tightly. "He must have gotten rid of it soon after that, because I never saw it again."

"And we know that in all things God works for the good of those who love him, who have been called according to his purpose," Holly quoted from Romans 8:28 as she touched Jimmy's shoulder.

He nodded. "I have to agree with that."

A gentle wind lapped the hem of Leona's blue wedding dress as the sun slipped from behind the clouds. At that moment, she knew for certain that God controlled everything in the universe. Her hand trailed along the edges of the narrow white ties of her kapp as she gazed at the pink, puffy clouds. "Thank You, Lord," she whispered. "You have given us all so much to be thankful for on this special day."

Jimmy took hold of her hand. "And I thank You for the love You've given me through all my family." He gently squeezed her fingers. "I especially thank You for allowing me to know, love, and finally marry the bishop's sweet daughter."

ACKNOWLEDGMENTS

The idea for this series was born several years ago when my husband and I visited an Amish farm for some root beer, and it is with great appreciation that I recognize those who have helped make the Daughters of Lancaster County series a reality: Rebecca Germany and Susan Downs, my patient, ever-helpful editors; Richard Brunstetter, my husband of forty-three years, who is always there to offer support and encouragement; Leeann Curtis and Birdie Etchison, for their critique help; Betty Yoder, Katherine Baar, Ruth Stoltzfus, Arie King, Sue Miller, and Monk and Marijane Troyer, for their research assistance. Most of all, I thank my heavenly Father, who gives me the inspiration and desire to write.

ABOUT THE AUTHOR

WANDA E. BRUNSTETTER enjoys writing about the Amish because they live a peaceful, simple life. Wanda's interest in the Amish and other Plain communities began when she married her husband, Richard, who grew up in a Mennonite church in Pennsylvania. Wanda has made numerous trips to Lancaster County and has several friends and family members living near that area. She and her husband have also traveled to other parts of the country, meeting various Amish families and getting to know them personally. She hopes her readers will learn to love the wonderful Amish people as much as she does.

Wanda and her husband, Richard, have been married forty-three years. They have two grown children and six grandchildren. In her spare time, Wanda enjoys reading, ventriloquism, gardening, stamping, and having fun with her family.

Wanda has written several novels, novellas, stories, articles, poems, and puppet scripts.

To learn more about Wanda, visit her Web site at www.wandabrunstetter.com and feel free to e-mail her at wanda@wandabrunstetter.com.